The Viking Portable Library

A partial list of other volumes in the Viking Portable Library appears at the end of the book.

The Portable
F. SCOTT FITZGERALD

Selected by Dorothy Parker

Introduction by John O'Hara

NEW YORK
THE VIKING PRESS
1949

PUBLISHED BY THE VIKING PRESS IN SEPTEMBER 1945

PUBLISHED ON THE SAME DAY IN THE DOMINION OF CANADA BY THE MACMILLAN COMPANY OF CANADA LIMITED

SECOND PRINTING OCTOBER 1945
THIRD PRINTING SEPTEMBER 1949

PRINTED IN U. S. A. BY THE COLONIAL PRESS INC.

CONTENTS

INTRODUCTION

BY

JOHN O'HARA

A little matter of twenty-five years ago I, along with half a million other men and women between fifteen and thirty, fell in love with a book. It was the real thing, that love. As one who tries to avoid the use of simile and metaphor, I cannot refrain here from comparing my first and countless subsequent meetings with that book to a first and subsequent meetings with The Girl. You meet a certain girl and you say to yourself, in the words of a 1928 song, "How long has this been going on?" The charm has to be there from the very beginning, but then you see that this time it is more than charm (although charm can be enough). The construction, of book or girl, has to be there from the very beginning, but then you see that this time it is more than the construction (although construction can be enough in the case of the girl). Well, not to hack away at the point too long or often, I took the book to bed with me, and I still do, which is more than I can say of any girl I knew in 1920.

After the appearance of that book I was excitedly interested in almost anything that was written by F. Scott Fitzgerald; his novels, short stories, and his non-fiction articles. He was born in September 1896 and I got here in January 1905, both of us just for the ride, but in spite of the at that time very important difference in our ages I regarded him as one of us. He knew what we were talking about and thinking about, if you could call it thinking, and what he knew was every bit as true of us who were of Earth '05 as of the '96 codgers.

The novel was *This Side of Paradise.* It is not included in this volume. Mrs. Parker did not consult me in making her selections for this volume, and it is only my job to write an introduction. I have no quarrel with her selections, either. Get that straight. Within the limitations of space she has brought together a truly representative collection, and please bear in mind not only that these words of mine are an introduction to this book, but that this book itself will turn out to be an introduction: an introduction to Scott Fitzgerald for the pleasure of those who haven't had the pleasure. This may not have been the publishers' or Mrs. Parker's intention, but I am fairly certain that it's going to work out that way.

Cantering along on that assumption, we can take first things first, and so, in book-jacket language, a word about the author. He would have been fifty next year, but if ever a man was not meant to be fifty, it was Fitzgerald. I don't mean that he tried as hard as Ernest Hemingway not to be fifty. Most of his life Ernest Hemingway has followed the big shooting as doggedly as Mr. Morgan used to go after the Scottish grouse, whereas Fitzgerald never heard a military shot fired in anger. Fitzgerald in his way, though, did go into battle, and when you read about the beating of Dick Diver by the Italian Fascist bums in *Tender Is the Night* you will see what I mean. Scott was ever one to like thinking of himself as a man of action and I commit no libel when I say he could be quarrelsome. The last time I talked to him he telephoned me—we were both in California—to ask me to serve as his second in a duel. A Hollywood trade paper had blasted a girl whom Fitzgerald admired. He wanted to fight a duel with the editor of the paper, and it seemed to me that if Scott won a duel with that editor he would be doing no disservice to the Hollywood community, but, stalling for time, I pointed out that under the code duello, as I understood it, the challenged and not the challenger had the choice of weapons. "I'm sure he's no better with foils or sabers than you are," I said, "but he may be a damn sight better shot."

"I didn't say anything about shooting," said Scott. "I'm just going in his office and beat the hell out of him, and I want you to come along so the rest of his bastards don't jump me."

I had a type-louse's-eye view of the two of us going to that print shop, pushing past the receptionist, and Scott taking the editor apart, which I honestly think he could have done. The two men were about the same weight and height, Scott was a bit younger than the editor, and he had Righteous Wrath and a Lady's Kerchief on his side. But I couldn't see the editor's goons standing idly by during this performance, and I couldn't see myself doing a William Farnum to a succession of Tom Santschis. Hot lead can be almost as effective coming from a linotype as from a firearm. I therefore attempted Reason. I told Scott that it was a laudable enterprise he had in mind, but pointed out to him that he would be doing the lady no good, that he was a married man with a daughter in college in the East, and that if he went storming into a "newspaper" office and we had a brawl in defense of a lady's honor we would just make the first pages of the early editions of practically every afternoon paper in the land—not to mention the Paris edition of the *New York Herald Tribune* and *Time* magazine. The notoriety would be notoriety and nothing else; if you kill a cop, all cops hate you; if you thrash a newspaper man all newspaper men except his immediate competitors hate you, and the stories that would appear would not be very understanding about his defense of the young lady in question.

"In other words, you're saying no," said Fitzgerald.

"If you insist on going, I'll go with you, but I don't want you to go and I don't want to go with you."

"That's all I wanted to know," he said. "I thought you were my one real friend in this town. I'll get Eddie —. He's diabetic and he doesn't get into fights, but he's a gentleman."

He hung up.

He was telephoning from a place where he had to call through the operator, so I immediately dialed Eddie, who was a friend of mine, and told him what to expect. The strange thing was that Scott did not telephone Eddie, who sat in his room all morning preparing arguments against Scott's project. Maybe Scott realized that what I said made sense; he surely knew instinctively without my telling him; and maybe he was actually counting on me as a friend to talk him out of the assault and battery (with intent to kill). Who knows? But I do know this much: although that was Spring and Scott didn't die until December, he never telephoned me again.

The above sad little anecdote could be matched or bettered by any of the men and women whom Scott knew and loved best: Dorothy Parker, Robert Benchley, Maxwell Perkins, Charles MacArthur, Hemingway, Gerald and Sara Murphy, Edith Wharton, Edmund Wilson, John Dos Passos, Ring Lardner, and Harold Ober; the Princeton pals whom he would suddenly remember after ten or twenty years and even boys who had gone to Newman, the lace-curtain Catholic prep school which he attended; the beauty and talent of Hollywood in the Twenties; the beauty and talent and corruption of the Riviera in the Twenties and Thirties; the favorite barkeeps everywhere; the Curb & Snaffle set in Maryland and Long Island; the casual pick-ups between Santa Barbara and St. Jean de Luz whom Scott would invest with something or other they didn't quite have, but who for a while would think they had it—whatever it may have been—all along, and which Scott would let them have whenever he thought of them. He never really lost track of anybody. The first man I ever met who knew Scott Fitzgerald was a trying snob who had been in Scott's class at Princeton, who came to my dinky home town for a Winter Assembly because the girl who asked him hadn't been able to sew up the captain of the Yale football team. Ten years later, when I was getting to know Fitzgerald pretty well, I mentioned the fellow. Scott hadn't seen him since my meeting, but Scott knew enough about his marital, social, and economic progress to make you think they were seeing each other all the time. Mind you, Scott didn't like him, never had, and hadn't known him well in college, but it was characteristic of Scott to be a sort of class secretary, except that the class included—at my guess—50,000 men and women. I have a pastime, which is to read *Who's Who,* and I am up on a large number of persons whom I haven't met, don't expect to meet, and don't particularly want to meet. With Scott it was something more; contributing an anecdote or a physical description or some scandal, success, or failure.

This predilection of Scott Fitzgerald's could easily have been confusing to him in his work. I imagine that part of the time he would find himself writing about people he knew, but frequently he must have had the sometimes doubtful pleasure of meeting a person whom he had once created for a story. The one was as real as the other. His work had that all the time: verisimilitude, reality, truth. This was true even when he took exercises in fantasy, a line of endeavor which usually bores me, because I haven't the patience and whatever other equipment is essential to the understanding of symbolism. He always knew what he was writing about, which is so, so untrue of so, so many so-so writers. It may not seem like much in 1945, when it is done all the time, but twenty-five years ago it was delightful to find a writer who would come right out and say Locomobile instead of high-powered motor car, Shanley's instead of gay cabaret, and George, instead of François, the *chasseur* at the Paris Ritz. These touches guaranteed that the writer knew what he was talking about and was not getting his information from Mr. Carnegie's local contribution to culture. The reader usually knew, without stopping to think much about it, that if a family owned a Franklin it was because they didn't feel they could afford a Pierce-Arrow. A prejudice persists among some eye-weary souls who are professional book critics that men's clothes, for instance, are not worthy of description. I can think of one fellow, for instance, who used to earn his living at book criticism but is now a sort of radio announcer, who used to suffer terribly when Brooks Brothers was mentioned. And yet if a writer were to put the fellow into Brooks Brothers clothes you would recognize him right away for a spy. If, as is most unlikely, the same critic knew about guns, I can imagine his shrieks at the luckless, careless writer who would confuse a Webley with a Savage, or if boats were being discussed, let the writer make a mistake about a suit of sail and the whole work would be suspect. And properly. This particular ex-reviewer doesn't, however, know much about clothes, and there are photographs to prove it. Scott Fitzgerald had the correct impressions because, quite apart from his gifts, the impressions were not those of a man who's never been there. As we used to say, he knew the forks.

It is a dangerous thing to bother about the rich. A

writer who does it in this country—at least during and since the times when barbers and bootblacks were piling up fabulous fortunes of from five to forty thousand dollars—will find himself regarded as a toy. The professional pipe-smokers—chiefly book critics and editorial writers—could understand *The Great Gatsby* because who couldn't? Too, Fitzgerald put one over in that book; he made the important rich man seem like an unimportant heel, and Gatsby, a man who happened to have a lot of money but was not a rich man, was made so pitiable that there were those who loved him. In the story frankly called "The Rich Boy" you get a four-reel motion picture of a rich man, in Technicolor, but the pipe-smokers never made much comment on that one, probably because it was a short story and they didn't have the name of O. Henry or Maupassant to identify it. But in two novels which dealt with the rich, Fitzgerald gave them, the rich, the business, yet the choice of those novels appearing in this volume was snooted by the conservative press no less than by the liberal and leftist. I was annoyed, but I don't recall having been surprised. In this country the rich don't write; there are really so few of them, and they can't write anyway. Americans who write, and those who write criticism, almost without exception are of middle-class origin no matter whom they write for or what they write, the *Wall Street Journal* or the *Daily Worker*. They have very little contact with the rich or none at all. The exceptions are the small number of men who get to know the rich at Yale, Harvard, or Princeton. Nowhere else. The rich don't go to other colleges. The rich I mean are the kind of people who can say, "If you have to ask how much a yacht will cost, you can't afford it." You give a thought to how few men get to know the rich in college, and how few of *them* become writers, and you will see why there is very little accurate writing about the rich, and you will see why there are no critical standards for dealing with the rich, and why the public will just as readily accept, oh, say, Louis Bromfield or Edna Ferber as it will Scott Fitzgerald. About the public I am not really complaining. An artist is his own fault. But a critic who passes judgment on a novel by Frederick Prokosch or the Shangri-La book—or for that matter, a novel about share-croppers—ought to be curious and careful and conscientious enough to be something besides casually contemptuous of a work of art. To wit: *Tender Is the Night.*

But Scott wasn't only a man who better than anyone else wrote about the rich. Actually most of his work was about the middle class, your family and mine. And in this book there is a short story called "Absolution" which shows he left the Plaza Hotel on occasion.

Yes, he had a place in American Literature. Scott Fitzgerald had a place in American Literature. Somewhere between Arthur Dwight Croveney and the Deep Blue Sea? All he was was our best novelist, one of our best novella-ists, and one of our finest writers of short stories. The dynamite money goes to other authors, one of whom I am sure was given her cheque for $46,000 and her Chinese visa with all the unlimited grace at Fitzgerald's command. To a now rather grumpy playwright went another 46 G's for his somewhat less than indigenous observation of the American scene. To a third American author, the same sum, complete with medal, for his capable christening of a character who culturally set us back a fast fifty years, because a lot of people were satisfied to be that character. Possibly it is not gracious of us Americans to refrain from establishing a ten-million-dollar fund to pass judgment on Swedish letters, Swedish being just as tough as American. And yet you look in an old *World Almanac* and re-examine the awards handed out by the trustees of Columbia University and it might strike you that Gothenburg—the one that is not in Nebraska—is at least as close to home as is Morningside Heights. Gothenburg and Morningside have in common no mention of F. Scott Fitzgerald.

The custom, which I intend to follow, is to compare the artist with his contemporaries. Hemingway was more of a contemporary of Fitzgerald's than Sinclair Lewis. Still, Lewis and Fitzgerald were writing about the same times, while Hemingway, good and influential as he was, wasn't using the same material. Fitzgerald and Lewis were covering the same ground at the important time, but it's funny to read the two men on the same subject. Lewis, then, and Lewis right this minute, is King of the Corn—and by way of being the Sweetheart of it. The names that Lewis dreams up are as improbable as those you will find in *The Chronicles of Clovis* or *The Unbearable Bassington.* Lewis now is accepted as a satirist when it can be devoutly doubted that he was trying to be anything but a commenter on the American scene. It always has seemed to me that one day Lewis woke up to find himself called a satirist, and became one by continuing to play straight. Fitzgerald was no satirist. Not even in *The Great Gatsby.* If he was being a satirist, as has been claimed, I don't get it, and I am no dope. He burlesqued—not too broadly, since it wasn't necessary—the squandering of money on Long Island in Prohibition days, it's a fact he did. That wasn't being satirical; that was only a slight heightening for the ultimate effect of showing for all time one very sad man who was, except for his love and death, an ass, and I wish I could go further and tell you what animal I am thinking of. (You put a saddle on the animal.) No, my friend, Fitzgerald had more than satire to offer. The satire was implicit for all to see, just as a writer's politics are there for anyone to see who has the curiosity and intelligence to wonder. Politically, Scott was an anarchist, as is anyone who is not a Fascist or a religious Communist. He never said he was cynical of all the governments and all the governing; it was just there to be seen. He never wore a badge saying, "Tee-hee, I'm a satirist."

I speak of Sinclair Lewis, who, of course, is Johnny One-Note. This fact remains a 33rd degree secret from the Nobel and Pulitzer judges, who patiently regard the American male as something between Will Rogers and the roles best played by Walter Huston. Come down heavy on your r's, don't dress Eastern, be a tall-size hypocrite, and your creator automatically wins half the heavyweight prize. Remember, too, if you are the author, that the female sex is to be handled in pasture, once over lightly. Any other treatment just shows how you stand on the question of virility. Fitzgerald didn't feel that way, act that way, or write that way. Fitzgerald could believe that an American man and woman were capable of married love, and that if a husband heard the call of the wild it wasn't inevitably toward the direction of a plump, inexperienced organist or a plump, bored woman in a hotel with a funny quasi-Indian name. For a man who has always been around and who periodically takes an austerely moral stand (curiously reminiscent of Rollin Kirby's Prohibition cartoons), Sinclair Lewis has some strange ideas about the sack-time of American men. On the subject of extra-legal love you will come across two sentences by Fitzgerald the like of which are not available in any Lewis that I recall. They read: "For a long time afterward Anson believed that a protective God sometimes interfered in human affairs. But Dolly Karger, lying awake and staring at the ceiling, never again believed in anything at all." Even without reading the story ("The Rich Boy") is there anything wrong or much lacking in that? Not to be too rough on Lewis, give him his due: he can write about bank buildings and receptacles for used razor blades and he can almost approximate the speech of an un-witty Abe Martin and he can make you remember that George F. Babbitt's middle initial stood for Follinsbee, but he hasn't put down a man or a woman who is the real thing. God knows I have encountered thousands of Babbitts, but I don't believe in Sinclair's particular George.

Who else is there who might be considered a professional contemporary of Fitzgerald's? Hemingway I will not discuss while there is a war on, for he writes best between wars and I think his best work already is familiar to many readers to whom this book really will be a Fitzgerald introduction. Who else? I honestly don't think of anyone else. The collegiate material was handled by Cyril Hume and Cornell Woolrich and Katharine Brush and Percy Marks and Stephen Vincent Benét and Lynn and Lois Montross, but who among the new Fitzgerald audience would know whether Benét wrote *The Wife of the Centaur* or *The Beginning of Wisdom*? There is even a strong possibility that only Benét's name among them would have a familiar sound. If I were to get on the squawk-box and say to Fighting 18: "Now hear this: Carl Van Vechten is aboard and will be pleased to answer any questions"—would the fighter pilots know what the hell to ask him? I hardly think so, but when you have read this book you might care to know that Van Vechten's slim volumes (*The Blind Bow Boy, The Tattooed Countess, Nigger Heaven*) had a little of the same screwy life that was caught by Fitzgerald in *The Great Gatsby*. A minor but sharp talent called Jack Thomas produced a pleasant little item called *Dry Martini,* but I myself haven't read that since Thomas died, which was almost fifteen years ago. Most certainly other writers were at their scrivening in the twenty years of Fitzgerald. The only trouble is I can't think of them without doing the kind of digging that I am postponing until I start bucking M.A., which must wait until I get my bachelor's, which must wait.

Notwithstanding his sure place as an American writer, it was a happy circumstance that Fitzgerald was not a lit'ry figure. He was not a literary-tea boy (none of the good ones are), and moreover his readers, the greater number of them, were people who could take a book or leave it alone. He was an artist and at the same time enough of an artisan to sell stories to *The Saturday Evening Post* and still say what he wanted to say. "Babylon Revisited" appeared in the *Post* while George Horace Lorimer, not exactly an *erotica* man, was boss. Except for a small part of the revelation of the incestuous relationship between Nicole and her father, *Tender Is the Night* was first serialized in the old *Scribner's.* He wrote a lot for the magazines without an ignominious amount of compromise. It goes without saying that all who read him in the *Post* did not buy his books, just as it goes without saying that all who bought his books did not take as gospel or even as ultimate entertainment every word he wrote. But he *was* a *popular* writer. He reached an astonishing number of people who spent not half as much money on books as they did on golf balls or lingerie clasps. Those who were old, and those already committed to being old, never got around to him as they did take to Louis Bromfield, say, who was around Fitzgerald's age and who also was around in Fitzgerald's era. What is to be hoped for with this collection is a new and enormous and appreciative audience not unlike in joy of discovery the Sherlock Holmes fans who came along many years after Doyle had put a stop to Holmes. In my generation (I am forty) and among men and women now in their fifties can right now be found a good-sized number who are able to compare notes on Fitzgerald's work without quite going so far as the Holmes' fans, who form clubs and go to their meetings by hansom cab and wear deerstalker caps. That is how real Fitzgerald character and incident have become to many of us. I go to the Plaza Hotel two or three times a week, not with any genuine expectation of running into Paula Legendre or Scott Fitzgerald. You will find a few pages on that Paula died in childbirth, and you already know that Scott is dead. And yet, last week, during those exhaustingly hot days, I saw Anson over and over again, sometimes in uniform and sometimes not. And last year I saw a pregnant girl who could have been Paula Legendre. And always, without fail, whether I'm going to the Plaza for a haircut or a drink (or even to talk over the arrangements covering this Introduction) I am half prepared to see Scott himself. He was elusive in life, God knows, and all through the writing of this piece he has refused to stay put, but the ectoplasm or the artist need not bother the reader or even me. For after all the *stuff* is here. The stuff is very much here, and it's mellow.

Long Island, July 23, 1945.

[illegible] and comforts and sympathies and [illegible] in my [illegible] who [illegible] [illegible] two pages on that [illegible] already knew that Scotland [illegible] [illegible] something in [illegible] And last year I gave a [illegible] [illegible] to the [illegible] over the arrangements [illegible] that I [illegible] prepared to see Scotland [illegible] the Lord [illegible] although the [illegible] [illegible] [illegible] follow.

[illegible] July 23, [illegible]

The Viking Portable Library

THE GREAT GATSBY

I

IN MY younger and more vulnerable years my father gave me some advice that I've been turning over in my mind ever since.

"Whenever you feel like criticizing any one," he told me, "just remember that all the people in this world haven't had the advantages that you've had."

He didn't say any more, but we've always been unusually communicative in a reserved way, and I understood that he meant a great deal more than that. In consequence, I'm inclined to reserve all judgments, a habit that has opened up many curious natures to me and also made me the victim of not a few veteran bores. The abnormal mind is quick to detect and attach itself to this quality when it appears in a normal person, and so it came about that in college I was unjustly accused of being a politician, because I was privy to the secret griefs of wild, unknown men. Most of the confidences were unsought—frequently I have feigned sleep, preoccupation, or a hostile levity when I realized by some unmistakable sign that an intimate revelation was quivering on the horizon; for the intimate revelations of young men, or at least the terms in which they express them, are usually plagiaristic and marred by obvious suppressions. Reserving judgments is a matter of infinite hope. I am still a little afraid of missing something if I forget that, as my father snobbishly suggested, and I snobbishly repeat, a sense of the fundamental decencies is parcelled out unequally at birth.

And, after boasting this way of my tolerance, I come to the admission that it has a limit. Conduct may be founded on the hard rock or the wet marshes, but after a certain point I don't care what it's founded on. When I came back from the East last autumn I felt that I wanted the world to be in uniform and at a sort of moral attention forever; I wanted no more riotous excursions with privileged glimpses into the human heart. Only Gatsby, the man who gives his name to this book, was exempt from my reaction—Gatsby, who represented everything for which I have an unaffected scorn. If personality is an unbroken series of successful gestures, then there was something gorgeous about him, some heightened sensitivity to the promises of life, as if he were related to one of those intricate machines that register earthquakes ten thousand miles away. This responsiveness had nothing to do with that flabby impressionability which is dignified under the name of the "creative temperament"—it was an extraordinary gift for hope, a romantic readiness such as I have never found in any other person and which it is not likely I shall ever find again. No—Gatsby turned out all right at the end; it is what preyed on Gatsby, what foul dust floated in the wake of his dreams that temporarily closed out my interest in the abortive sorrows and short-winded elations of men.

My family have been prominent, well-to-do people in this Middle Western city for three generations. The Carraways are something of a clan, and we have a tradition that we're descended from the Dukes of Buccleuch, but the actual founder of my line was my grandfather's brother, who came here in fifty-one, sent a substitute to the Civil War, and started the wholesale hardware business that my father carries on today.

I never saw this great-uncle, but I'm supposed to look like him—with special reference to the rather hard-boiled painting that hangs in father's office. I graduated from New Haven in 1915, just a quarter of a century after my father, and a little later I participated in that delayed Teutonic migration known as the Great War. I enjoyed the counter-raid so thoroughly that I came back restless. Instead of being the warm center of the world, the Middle West now seemed like the ragged edge of the universe—so I decided to go East and learn the bond business. Everybody I knew was in the bond business, so I supposed it could support one more single man. All my aunts and uncles talked it over as if they were choosing a prep school for me, and finally said, "Why—ye-es," with very grave, hesitant faces. Father agreed to finance me for a year, and after various delays I came East, permanently, I thought, in the spring of twenty-two.

The practical thing was to find rooms in the city, but it was a warm season, and I had just left a country of wide lawns and friendly trees, so when a young man at the office suggested that we take a house together in a commuting town, it sounded like a great idea. He found the house, a weather-beaten cardboard bungalow at eighty a month, but at the last minute the firm ordered him to Washington, and I went out to the country alone. I had a dog—at least I had him for a few days until he ran away—and an old Dodge and a Finnish woman, who made my bed and cooked breakfast and muttered Finnish wisdom to herself over the electric stove.

It was lonely for a day or so until one morning some man, more recently arrived than I, stopped me on the road.

"How do you get to West Egg village?" he asked helplessly.

I told him. And as I walked on I was lonely no longer. I was a guide, a pathfinder, an original settler. He had casually conferred on me the freedom of the neighborhood.

And so with the sunshine and the great bursts of leaves growing on the trees, just as things grow in fast movies, I had that familiar conviction that life was beginning over again with the summer.

There was so much to read, for one thing, and so much fine health to be pulled down out of the young breath-giving air. I bought a dozen volumes on banking and credit and investment securities, and they stood on my shelf in red and gold like new money from the mint, promising to unfold the shining secrets that only Midas and Morgan and Mæcenas knew. And I had the high intention of reading many other books besides. I was rather literary in college—one year I wrote a series of very solemn and obvious editorials for the *Yale News*—and now I was going to bring back all such things into my life and become again that most limited of all specialists, the "well-rounded man." This isn't just an epigram—life is much more successfully looked at from a single window, after all.

It was a matter of chance that I should have rented a house in one of the strangest communities in North America. It was on that slender riotous island which extends itself due east of New York—and where there are, among other natural curiosities, two unusual formations of land. Twenty miles from the city a pair of enormous eggs, identical in contour and separated only by a courtesy bay, jut out into the most domesticated body of salt water in the Western hemisphere, the great wet barnyard of Long Island Sound. They are not perfect ovals—like the egg in the Columbus story, they are both crushed flat at the contact end—but their physical resemblance must be a source of perpetual wonder to the gulls that fly overhead. To the wingless a more interesting phenomenon is their dissimilarity in every particular except shape and size.

I lived at West Egg, the—well, the less fashionable of the two, though this is a most superficial tag to express the bizarre and not a little sinister contrast between them. My house was at the very tip of the egg, only fifty yards from the Sound, and squeezed between two huge places that rented for twelve or fifteen thousand a season. The one on my right was a colossal affair by any standard—it was a factual imitation of some Hôtel de Ville in Normandy, with a tower on one side, spanking new under a thin beard of raw ivy, and a marble swimming pool, and more than forty acres of lawn and garden. It was Gatsby's mansion. Or, rather, as I didn't know Mr. Gatsby, it was a mansion, inhabited by a gentleman of that name. My own house was an eyesore, but it was a small eyesore, and it had been overlooked, so I had a view of the water, a partial view of my neighbor's lawn, and the consoling proximity of millionaires—all for eighty dollars a month.

Across the courtesy bay the white palaces of fashionable East Egg glittered along the water, and the history of the summer really begins on the evening I drove over there to have dinner with the Tom Buchanans. Daisy was my second cousin once removed, and I'd known Tom in college. And just after the war I spent two days with them in Chicago.

Her husband, among various physical accomplishments, had been one of the most powerful ends that ever played football at New Haven—a national figure in a way, one of those men who reach such an acute limited excellence at twenty-one that everything afterward savors of anticlimax. His family were enormously wealthy—even in college his freedom with money was a matter for reproach—but now he'd left Chicago and come East in a fashion that rather took your breath away; for instance, he'd brought down a string of polo ponies from Lake Forest. It was hard to realize that a man in my own generation was wealthy enough to do that.

Why they came East I don't know. They had spent a year in France for no particular reason, and then drifted here and there unrestfully wherever people played polo and were rich together. This was a permanent move, said Daisy over the telephone, but I didn't believe it—I had no sight into Daisy's heart, but I felt that Tom would drift on forever seeking, a little wistfully, for the dramatic turbulence of some irrecoverable football game.

And so it happened that on a warm windy evening I drove over to East Egg to see two old friends whom I scarcely knew at all. Their house was even more elaborate than I expected, a cheerful red-and-white Georgian Colonial mansion, overlooking the bay. The lawn started at the beach and ran toward the front door for a quarter of a mile, jumping over sun-dials and brick walks and burning gardens—finally when it reached the house drifting up the side in bright vines as though from the momentum of its run. The front was broken by a line of French windows, glowing now with reflected gold and wide open to the warm windy afternoon, and Tom Buchanan in riding clothes was standing with his legs apart on the front porch.

He had changed since his New Haven years. Now he was a sturdy straw-haired man of thirty with a rather hard mouth and a supercilious manner. Two shining arrogant eyes had established dominance over his face and gave him the appearance of always leaning aggressively forward. Not even the effeminate swank of his riding clothes could hide the enormous power of that body—he seemed to fill those glistening boots until he strained the top lacing, and you could see a great pack of muscle shifting when his shoulder moved under his thin coat. It was a body capable of enormous leverage—a cruel body.

His speaking voice, a gruff husky tenor, added to the impression of fractiousness he conveyed. There was a touch of paternal contempt in it, even toward people he liked—and there were men at New Haven who had hated his guts.

"Now, don't think my opinion on these matters is final," he seemed to say, "just because I'm stronger and more of a man than you are." We were in the same senior society, and while we were never intimate I always had the impression that he approved of me and wanted me to like him with some harsh, defiant wistfulness of his own.

We talked for a few minutes on the sunny porch.

"I've got a nice place here," he said, his eyes flashing about restlessly.

Turning me around by one arm, he moved a broad flat hand along the front vista, including in its sweep a sunken Italian garden, a half acre of deep, pungent roses, and a snub-nosed motor-boat that bumped the tide offshore.

"It belonged to Demaine, the oil man." He turned me around again, politely and abruptly. "We'll go inside."

We walked through a high hallway into a bright rosy-colored space, fragilely bound into the house by French windows at either end. The windows were ajar and gleaming white against the fresh grass outside that seemed to grow a little way into the house. A breeze blew through the room, blew curtains in at one end and out the other like pale flags, twisting them up toward the frosted wedding-cake of the ceiling, and then rippled over the wine-colored rug, making a shadow on it as wind does on the sea.

The only completely stationary object in the room was an enormous couch on which two young women were buoyed up as though upon an anchored balloon. They were both in white, and their dresses were rippling and fluttering as if they had just been blown back in after a short flight around the house. I must have stood for a few moments listening to the whip and snap of the curtains and the groan of a picture on the wall. Then there was a boom as Tom Buchanan shut the rear windows and the caught wind died out about the room, and the curtains and the rugs and the two young women ballooned slowly to the floor.

The younger of the two was a stranger to me. She was extended full length at her end of the divan, completely motionless, and with her chin raised a little, as if she were balancing something on it which was quite likely to fall. If she saw me out of the corner of her eyes she gave no hint of it—indeed, I was almost surprised into murmuring an apology for having disturbed her by coming in.

The other girl, Daisy, made an attempt to rise—she leaned slightly forward with a conscientious expression —then she laughed, an absurd, charming little laugh, and I laughed too and came forward into the room.

"I'm p-paralyzed with happiness."

She laughed again, as if she said something very witty, and held my hand for a moment, looking up into my face, promising that there was no one in the world she so much wanted to see. That was a way she had. She hinted in a murmur that the surname of the balancing girl was Baker. (I've heard it said that Daisy's murmur was only to make people lean toward her; an irrelevant criticism that made it no less charming.)

At any rate, Miss Baker's lips fluttered, she nodded at me almost imperceptibly, and then quickly tipped her head back again—the object she was balancing had obviously tottered a little and given her something of a fright. Again a sort of apology arose to my lips. Almost any exhibition of complete self-sufficiency draws a stunned tribute from me.

I looked back at my cousin, who began to ask me questions in her low, thrilling voice. It was the kind of voice that the ear follows up and down, as if each speech is an arrangement of notes that will never be played again. Her face was sad and lovely with bright things in it, bright eyes and a bright passionate mouth, but there was an excitement in her voice that men who had cared for her found difficult to forget: a singing compulsion, a whispered "Listen," a promise that she had done gay, exciting things just a while since and that there were gay, exciting things hovering in the next hour.

I told her how I had stopped off in Chicago for a day on my way East, and how a dozen people had sent their love through me.

"Do they miss me?" she cried ecstatically.

"The whole town is desolate. All the cars have the left rear wheel painted black as a mourning wreath, and there's a persistent wail all night along the north shore."

"How gorgeous! Let's go back, Tom. Tomorrow!" Then she added irrelevantly: "You ought to see the baby."

"I'd like to."

"She's asleep. She's three years old. Haven't you ever seen her?"

"Never."

"Well, you ought to see her. She's——"

Tom Buchanan, who had been hovering restlessly

about the room, stopped and rested his hand on my shoulder.

"What you doing, Nick?"

"I'm a bond man."

"Who with?"

I told him.

"Never heard of them," he remarked decisively.

This annoyed me.

"You will," I answered shortly. "You will if you stay in the East."

"Oh, I'll stay in the East, don't you worry," he said, glancing at Daisy and then back at me, as if he were alert for something more. "I'd be a God damned fool to live anywhere else."

At this point Miss Baker said: "Absolutely!" with such suddenness that I started—it was the first word she had uttered since I came into the room. Evidently it surprised her as much as it did me, for she yawned and with a series of rapid, deft movements stood up into the room.

"I'm stiff," she complained, "I've been lying on that sofa for as long as I can remember."

"Don't look at me," Daisy retorted, "I've been trying to get you to New York all afternoon."

"No, thanks," said Miss Baker to the four cocktails just in from the pantry, "I'm absolutely in training."

Her host looked at her incredulously.

"You are!" He took down his drink as if it were a drop in the bottom of a glass. "How you ever get anything done is beyond me."

I looked at Miss Baker, wondering what it was she "got done." I enjoyed looking at her. She was a slender, small-breasted girl, with an erect carriage, which she accentuated by throwing her body backward at the shoulders like a young cadet. Her gray sun-strained eyes looked back at me with polite reciprocal curiosity out of a wan, charming, discontented face. It occurred to me now that I had seen her, or a picture of her, somewhere before.

"You live in West Egg," she remarked contemptuously. "I know somebody there."

"I don't know a single——"

"You must know Gatsby."

"Gatsby?" demanded Daisy. "What Gatsby?"

Before I could reply that he was my neighbor dinner was announced; wedging his tense arm imperatively under mine, Tom Buchanan compelled me from the room as though he were moving a checker to another square.

Slenderly, languidly, their hands set lightly on their hips, the two young women preceded us out onto a rosy-colored porch, open toward the sunset, where four candles flickered on the table in the diminished wind.

"Why *candles?*" objected Daisy, frowning. She snapped them out with her fingers. "In two weeks it'll be the longest day in the year." She looked at us all radiantly. "Do you always watch for the longest day of the year and then miss it? I always watch for the longest day in the year and then miss it."

"We ought to plan something," yawned Miss Baker, sitting down at the table as if she were getting into bed.

"All right," said Daisy. "What'll we plan?" She turned to me helplessly: "What do people plan?"

Before I could answer her eyes fastened with an awed expression on her little finger.

"Look!" she complained; "I hurt it."

We all looked—the knuckle was black and blue.

"You did it, Tom," she said accusingly. "I know you

didn't mean to, but you *did* do it. That's what I get for marrying a brute of a man, a great, big, hulking physical specimen of a——"

"I hate that word hulking," objected Tom crossly, "even in kidding."

"Hulking," insisted Daisy.

Sometimes she and Miss Baker talked at once, unobtrusively and with a bantering inconsequence that was never quite chatter, that was as cool as their white dresses and their impersonal eyes in the absence of all desire. They were here, and they accepted Tom and me, making only a polite pleasant effort to entertain or to be entertained. They knew that presently dinner would be over and a little later the evening, too, would be over and casually put away. It was sharply different from the West, where an evening was hurried from phase to phase toward its close, in a continually disappointed anticipation or else in sheer nervous dread of the moment itself.

"You make me feel uncivilized, Daisy," I confessed on my second glass of corky but rather impressive claret. "Can't you talk about crops or something?"

I meant nothing in particular by this remark, but it was taken up in an unexpected way.

"Civilization's going to pieces," broke out Tom violently. "I've gotten to be a terrible pessimist about things. Have you read *The Rise of the Colored Empires* by this man Goddard?"

"Why, no," I answered, rather surprised by his tone.

"Well, it's a fine book, and everybody ought to read it. The idea is if we don't look out the white race will be—will be utterly submerged. It's all scientific stuff; it's been proved."

"Tom's getting very profound," said Daisy, with an expression of unthoughtful sadness. "He reads deep books with long words in them. What was that word we——"

"Well, these books are all scientific," insisted Tom, glancing at her impatiently. "This fellow has worked out the whole thing. It's up to us, who are the dominant race, to watch out or these other races will have control of things."

"We've got to beat them down," whispered Daisy, winking ferociously toward the fervent sun.

"You ought to live in California—" began Miss Baker, but Tom interrupted her by shifting heavily in his chair.

"This idea is that we're Nordics. I am, and you are, and you are, and—" After an infinitesimal hesitation he included Daisy with a slight nod, and she winked at me again. "—And we've produced all the things that go to make civilization—oh, science and art, and all that. Do you see?"

There was something pathetic in his concentration, as if his complacency, more acute than of old, was not enough to him any more. When, almost immediately, the telephone rang inside and the butler left the porch Daisy seized upon the momentary interruption and leaned toward me.

"I'll tell you a family secret," she whispered enthusiastically. "It's about the butler's nose. Do you want to hear about the butler's nose?"

"That's why I came over tonight."

"Well, he wasn't always a butler; he used to be the silver polisher for some people in New York that had a silver service for two hundred people. He had to polish it from morning till night, until finally it began to affect his nose——"

"Things went from bad to worse," suggested Miss Baker.

"Yes. Things went from bad to worse, until finally he had to give up his position."

For a moment the last sunshine fell with romantic affection upon her glowing face; her voice compelled me forward breathlessly as I listened—then the glow faded, each light deserting her with lingering regret, like children leaving a pleasant street at dusk.

The butler came back and murmured something close to Tom's ear, whereupon Tom frowned, pushed back his chair, and without a word went inside. As if his absence quickened something within her, Daisy leaned forward again, her voice glowing and singing.

"I love to see you at my table, Nick. You remind me of a—of a rose, an absolute rose. Doesn't he?" She turned to Miss Baker for confirmation: "An absolute rose?"

This was untrue. I am not even faintly like a rose. She was only extemporizing, but a stirring warmth flowed from her, as if her heart was trying to come out to you concealed in one of those breathless, thrilling words. Then suddenly she threw her napkin on the table and excused herself and went into the house.

Miss Baker and I exchanged a short glance consciously devoid of meaning. I was about to speak when she sat up alertly and said "Sh!" in a warning voice. A subdued impassioned murmur was audible in the room beyond, and Miss Baker leaned forward unashamed, trying to hear. The murmur trembled on the verge of coherence, sank down, mounted excitedly, and then ceased altogether.

"This Mr. Gatsby you spoke of is my neighbor—" I began.

"Don't talk. I want to hear what happens."

"Is something happening?" I inquired innocently.

"You mean to say you don't know?" said Miss Baker, honestly surprised. "I thought everybody knew."

"I don't."

"Why—" she said hesitantly, "Tom's got some woman in New York."

"Got some woman?" I repeated blankly.

Miss Baker nodded.

"She might have the decency not to telephone him at dinner time. Don't you think?"

Almost before I had grasped her meaning there was the flutter of a dress and the crunch of leather boots, and Tom and Daisy were back at the table.

"It couldn't be helped!" cried Daisy with tense gayety.

She sat down, glanced searchingly at Miss Baker and then at me, and continued: "I looked outdoors for a minute, and it's very romantic outdoors. There's a bird on the lawn that I think must be a nightingale come over on the Cunard or White Star Line. He's singing away—" Her voice sang: "It's romantic, isn't it, Tom?"

"Very romantic," he said, and then miserably to me: "If it's light enough after dinner, I want to take you down to the stables."

The telephone rang inside, startlingly, and as Daisy shook her head decisively at Tom the subject of the stables, in fact all subjects, vanished into air. Among the broken fragments of the last five minutes at table I remember the candles being lit again, pointlessly, and I was conscious of wanting to look squarely at every one, and yet to avoid all eyes. I couldn't guess what Daisy and Tom were thinking, but I doubt if even Miss Baker, who seemed to have mastered a certain hardy scepticism, was able utterly to put this fifth guest's shrill metallic urgency out of mind. To a certain temperament the situation might have seemed intriguing—my own instinct was to telephone immediately for the police.

The horses, needless to say, were not mentioned again. Tom and Miss Baker, with several feet of twilight between them, strolled back into the library, as if to a vigil beside a perfectly tangible body, while, trying to look pleasantly interested and a little deaf, I followed Daisy around a chain of connecting verandas to the porch in front. In its deep gloom we sat down side by side on a wicker settee.

Daisy took her face in her hands as if feeling its lovely shape, and her eyes moved gradually out into the velvet dusk. I saw that turbulent emotions possessed her, so I asked what I thought would be some sedative questions about her little girl.

"We don't know each other very well, Nick," she said suddenly. "Even if we are cousins. You didn't come to my wedding."

"I wasn't back from the war."

"That's true." She hesitated. "Well, I've had a very bad time, Nick, and I'm pretty cynical about everything."

Evidently she had reason to be. I waited but she didn't say any more, and after a moment I returned rather feebly to the subject of her daughter.

"I suppose she talks, and—eats, and everything."

"Oh, yes." She looked at me absently. "Listen, Nick; let me tell you what I said when she was born. Would you like to hear?"

"Very much."

"It'll show you how I've gotten to feel about—things. Well, she was less than an hour old and Tom was God knows where. I woke up out of the ether with an utterly abandoned feeling, and asked the nurse right away if it was a boy or a girl. She told me it was a girl, and so I turned my head away and wept. 'All right,' I said, 'I'm glad it's a girl. And I hope she'll be a fool—that's the best thing a girl can be in this world, a beautiful little fool.'

"You see I think everything's terrible anyhow," she went on in a convinced way. "Everybody thinks so—the most advanced people. And I *know*. I've been everywhere and seen everything and done everything." Her eyes flashed around her in a defiant way, rather like Tom's, and she laughed with thrilling scorn. "Sophisticated—God, I'm sophisticated!"

The instant her voice broke off, ceasing to compel my attention, my belief, I felt the basic insincerity of what she had said. It made me uneasy, as though the whole evening had been a trick of some sort to exact a contributary emotion from me. I waited, and sure enough, in a moment she looked at me with an absolute smirk on her lovely face, as if she had asserted her membership in a rather distinguished secret society to which she and Tom belonged.

Inside, the crimson room bloomed with light. Tom and Miss Baker sat at either end of the long couch and she read aloud to him from *The Saturday Evening Post*—the words, murmurous and uninfected, running together in a soothing tune. The lamp-light, bright on his boots and dull on the autumn-leaf yellow of her hair, glinted along the paper as she turned a page with a flutter of slender muscles in her arms.

When we came in she held us silent for a moment with a lifted hand.

"To be continued," she said, tossing the magazine on the table, "in our very next issue."

Her body asserted itself with a restless movement of her knee, and she stood up.

"Ten o'clock," she remarked, apparently finding the time on the ceiling. "Time for this good girl to go to bed."

"Jordan's going to play in the tournament tomorrow," explained Daisy, "over at Westchester."

"Oh—you're *Jor*dan Baker."

I knew now why her face was familiar—its pleasing contemptuous expression had looked out at me from many rotogravure pictures of the sporting life at Asheville and Hot Springs and Palm Beach. I had heard some story of her too, a critical, unpleasant story, but what it was I had forgotten long ago.

"Good night," she said softly. "Wake me at eight, won't you?"

"If you'll get up."

"I will. Good night Mr. Carraway. See you anon."

"Of course you will," confirmed Daisy. "In fact, I think I'll arrange a marriage. Come over often, Nick, and I'll sort of—oh—fling you together. You know—lock you up accidentally in linen closets and push you out to sea in a boat, and all that sort of thing——"

"Good night," called Miss Baker from the stairs. "I haven't heard a word."

"She's a nice girl," said Tom after a moment. "They oughtn't to let her run around the country this way."

"Who oughtn't to?" inquired Daisy coldly.

"Her family."

"Her family is one aunt about a thousand years old. Besides, Nick's going to look after her, aren't you, Nick? She's going to spend lots of week-ends out here this summer. I think the home influence will be very good for her."

Daisy and Tom looked at each other for a moment in silence.

"Is she from New York?" I asked quickly.

"From Louisville. Our white girlhood was passed together there. Our beautiful white——"

"Did you give Nick a little heart-to-heart talk on the veranda?" demanded Tom suddenly.

"Did I?" She looked at me. "I can't seem to remember, but I think we talked about the Nordic race. Yes, I'm sure we did. It sort of crept up on us and first thing you know——"

"Don't believe everything you hear, Nick," he advised me.

I said lightly that I had heard nothing at all, and a few minutes later I got up to go home. They came to the door with me and stood side by side in a cheerful square of light. As I started my motor Daisy peremptorily called: "Wait!

"I forgot to ask you something, and it's important. We heard you were engaged to a girl out West."

"That's right," corroborated Tom kindly. "We heard that you were engaged."

"It's a libel. I'm too poor."

"But we heard it," insisted Daisy, surprising me by opening up again in a flower-like way. "We heard it from three people, so it must be true."

Of course I knew what they were referring to, but I wasn't even vaguely engaged. The fact that gossip had published the banns was one of the reasons I had come East. You can't stop going with an old friend on account of rumors, and on the other hand I had no intention of being rumored into marriage.

Their interest rather touched me and made them less remotely rich—nevertheless, I was confused and a little disgusted as I drove away. It seemed to me that the thing for Daisy to do was to rush out of the house, child in arms—but apparently there were no such intentions in her head. As for Tom, the fact that he "had some woman in New York" was really less surprising than that he had been depressed by a book. Something was making him nibble at the edge of stale ideas as if his sturdy physical egotism no longer nourished his peremptory heart.

Already it was deep summer on roadhouse roofs and in front of wayside garages, where new red gas-pumps sat out in pools of light, and when I reached my estate at West Egg I ran the car under its shed and sat for a while on an abandoned grass roller in the yard. The wind had blown off, leaving a loud, bright night, with wings beating in the trees and a persistent organ sound as the full bellows of the earth blew the frogs full of life. The silhouette of a moving cat wavered across the moonlight, and turning my head to watch it, I saw that I was not alone—fifty feet away a figure had emerged from the shadow of my neighbor's mansion and was standing with his hands in his pockets regarding the silver pepper of the stars. Something in his leisurely movements and the secure position of his feet upon the lawn suggested that it was Mr. Gatsby himself, come out to determine what share was his of our local heavens.

I decided to call to him. Miss Baker had mentioned him at dinner, and that would do for an introduction. But I didn't call to him, for he gave a sudden intimation that he was content to be alone—he stretched out his arms toward the dark water in a curious way, and, far as I was from him, I could have sworn he was trembling. Involuntarily I glanced seaward—and distinguished nothing except a single green light, minute and far away, that might have been the end of a dock. When I looked once more for Gatsby he had vanished, and I was alone again in the unquiet darkness.

II

ABOUT half way between West Egg and New York the motor road hastily joins the railroad and runs beside it for a quarter of a mile, so as to shrink away from a certain desolate area of land. This is a valley of ashes—a fantastic farm where ashes grow like wheat into ridges and hills and grotesque gardens; where ashes take the forms of houses and chimneys and rising smoke and, finally, with a transcendent effort, of ash-gray men who move dimly and already crumbling through the powdery air. Occasionally a line of gray cars crawls along an invisible track, gives out a ghastly creak, and comes to rest, and immediately the ash-gray men swarm up with leaden spades and stir up an impenetrable cloud, which screens their obscure operations from your sight.

But above the gray land and the spasms of bleak dust which drift endlessly over it, you perceive, after a moment, the eyes of Doctor T. J. Eckleburg. The eyes of Doctor T. J. Eckleburg are blue and gigantic—their retinas are one yard high. They look out of no face, but, instead, from a pair of enormous yellow spectacles which pass over a non-existent nose. Evidently some wild wag of an oculist set them there to fatten his practice in the borough of Queens, and then sank down himself into eternal blindness, or forgot them and moved away. But his eyes, dimmed a little by many paintless days, under sun and rain, brood on over the solemn dumping ground.

The valley of ashes is bounded on one side by a small foul river, and, when the drawbridge is up to let barges through, the passengers on waiting trains can stare at the dismal scene for as long as half an hour. There is always a halt there of at least a minute, and it was because of this that I first met Tom Buchanan's mistress.

The fact that he had one was insisted upon wherever he was known. His acquaintances resented the fact that he turned up in popular cafés with her and, leaving her at a table, sauntered about, chatting with whomsoever he knew. Though I was curious to see her, I had no desire to meet her—but I did. I went up to New York with Tom on the train one afternoon, and when we stopped by the ashheaps he jumped to his feet and, taking hold of my elbow, literally forced me from the car.

"We're getting off," he insisted. "I want you to meet my girl."

I think he'd tanked up a good deal at luncheon, and his determination to have my company bordered on violence. The supercilious assumption was that on Sunday afternoon I had nothing better to do.

I followed him over a low whitewashed railroad fence, and we walked back a hundred yards along the road under Doctor Eckleburg's persistent stare. The only building in sight was a small block of yellow brick sitting on the edge of the waste land, a sort of compact Main Street ministering to it, and contiguous to absolutely nothing. One of the three shops it contained was for rent and another was an all-night restaurant, approached by a trail of ashes; the third was a garage—*Repairs.* GEORGE B. WILSON. *Cars bought and sold.*—and I followed Tom inside.

The interior was unprosperous and bare; the only car visible was the dust-covered wreck of a Ford which crouched in a dim corner. It had occurred to me that this shadow of a garage must be a blind, and that sumptuous and romantic apartments were concealed overhead, when the proprietor himself appeared in the door of an office, wiping his hands on a piece of waste. He was a blond, spiritless man, anæmic, and faintly handsome. When he saw us a damp gleam of hope sprang into his light blue eyes.

"Hello, Wilson, old man," said Tom, slapping him jovially on the shoulder. "How's business?"

"I can't complain," answered Wilson unconvincingly. "When are you going to sell me that car?"

"Next week; I've got my man working on it now."

"Works pretty slow, don't he?"

"No, he doesn't," said Tom coldly. "And if you feel that way about it, maybe I'd better sell it somewhere else after all."

"I don't mean that," explained Wilson quickly. "I just meant——"

His voice faded off and Tom glanced impatiently around the garage. Then I heard footsteps on a stairs, and in a moment the thickish figure of a woman blocked out the light from the office door. She was in the middle thirties, and faintly stout, but she carried her flesh sensuously as some women can. Her face, above a spotted dress of dark blue crêpe-de-chine, contained no facet or gleam of beauty, but there was an immediately perceptible vitality about her as if the nerves of her body were continually smouldering. She smiled slowly and, walking through her husband as if he were a ghost, shook hands with Tom, looking him flush in the eye. Then she wet her lips, and without turning around spoke to her husband in a soft, coarse voice:

"Get some chairs, why don't you, so somebody can sit down."

"Oh, sure," agreed Wilson hurriedly, and went toward the little office mingling immediately with the cement color of the walls. A white ashen dust veiled his dark suit and his pale hair as it veiled everything in the vicinity—except his wife, who moved close to Tom.

"I want to see you," said Tom intently. "Get on the next train."

"All right."

"I'll meet you by the news-stand on the lower level."

She nodded and moved away from him just as George Wilson emerged with two chairs from his office door.

We waited for her down the road and out of sight. It was a few days before the Fourth of July, and a gray, scrawny Italian child was setting torpedoes in a row along the railroad track.

"Terrible place, isn't it," said Tom, exchanging a frown with Doctor Eckleburg.

"Awful."

"It does her good to get away."

"Doesn't her husband object?"

"Wilson? He thinks she goes to see her sister in New York. He's so dumb he doesn't know he's alive."

So Tom Buchanan and his girl and I went up together to New York—or not quite together, for Mrs. Wilson sat discreetly in another car. Tom deferred that much to the sensibilities of those East Eggers who might be on the train.

She had changed her dress to a brown figured muslin, which stretched tight over her rather wide hips as Tom helped her to the platform in New York. At the news-stand she bought a copy of *Town Tattle* and a moving-picture magazine, and in the station drugstore some cold cream and a small flask of perfume. Upstairs, in the solemn echoing drive she let four taxicabs drive away before she selected a new one, lavender-colored with gray upholstery, and in this we slid out from the mass of the station into the glowing sunshine. But immediately she turned sharply from the window and, leaning forward, tapped on the front glass.

"I want to get one of those dogs," she said earnestly. "I want to get one for the apartment. They're nice to have—a dog."

We backed up to a gray old man who bore an absurd resemblance to John D. Rockefeller. In a basket swung from his neck cowered a dozen very recent puppies of an indeterminate breed.

"What kind are they?" asked Mrs. Wilson eagerly, as he came to the taxi-window.

"All kinds. What kind do you want, lady?"

"I'd like to get one of those police dogs; I don't suppose you got that kind?"

The man peered doubtfully into the basket, plunged in his hand and drew one up, wriggling, by the back of the neck.

"That's no police dog," said Tom.

"No, it's not exactly a pol*ice* dog," said the man with disappointment in his voice. "It's more of an Airedalc." He passed his hand over the brown washrag of a back. "Look at that coat. Some coat. That's a dog that'll never bother you with catching cold."

"I think it's cute," said Mrs. Wilson enthusiastically. "How much is it?"

"That dog?" He looked at it admiringly. "That dog will cost you ten dollars."

The Airedale—undoubtedly there was an Airedale concerned in it somewhere, though its feet were startlingly white—changed hands and settled down into Mrs. Wilson's lap, where she fondled the weatherproof coat with rapture.

"Is it a boy or a girl?" she asked delicately.

"That dog? That dog's a boy."

"It's a bitch," said Tom decisively. "Here's your money. Go and buy ten more dogs with it."

We drove over to Fifth Avenue, warm and soft, almost pastoral, on the summer Sunday afternoon. I wouldn't have been surprised to see a great flock of white sheep turn the corner.

"Hold on," I said, "I have to leave you here."

"No, you don't," interposed Tom quickly. "Myrtle'll be hurt if you don't come up to the apartment. Won't you, Myrtle?"

"Come on," she urged. "I'll telephone my sister Catherine. She's said to be very beautiful by people who ought to know."

"Well, I'd like to, but——"

We went on, cutting back again over the Park toward the West Hundreds. At 158th Street the cab stopped at one slice in a long white cake of apartment-houses. Throwing a regal homecoming glance around the neighborhood, Mrs. Wilson gathered up her dog and her other purchases, and went haughtily in.

"I'm going to have the McKees come up," she announced as we rose in the elevator. "And, of course, I got to call up my sister, too."

The apartment was on the top floor—a small living-room, a small dining-room, a small bedroom, and a bath. The living-room was crowded to the doors with a set of tapestried furniture entirely too large for it, so that to move about was to stumble continually over scenes of ladies swinging in the gardens of Versailles. The only picture was an over-enlarged photograph, apparently a hen sitting on a blurred rock. Looked at from a distance, however, the hen resolved itself into a bonnet, and the countenance of a stout old lady beamed down into the room. Several old copies of *Town Tattle* lay on the table together with a copy of *Simon Called Peter*, and some of the small scandal magazines of Broadway. Mrs. Wilson was first concerned with the dog. A reluctant elevator-boy went for a box full of straw and some milk, to which he added on his own initiative a tin of large, hard dog-biscuits—one of which decomposed apathetically in the saucer of milk all afternoon. Meanwhile Tom brought out a bottle of whiskey from a locked bureau door.

I have been drunk just twice in my life, and the second time was that afternoon; so everything that happened has a dim, hazy cast over it, although until after eight o'clock the apartment was full of cheerful sun. Sitting on Tom's lap Mrs. Wilson called up several people on the telephone; then there were no cigarettes, and I went out to buy some at the drugstore on the corner. When I came back they had both disappeared, so I sat down discreetly in the living-room and read a chapter of *Simon Called Peter*—either it was terrible stuff or the whiskey distorted things, because it didn't make any sense to me.

Just as Tom and Myrtle (after the first drink Mrs. Wilson and I called each other by our first names) reappeared, company commenced to arrive at the apartment door.

The sister, Catherine, was a slender, worldly girl of about thirty, with a solid, sticky bob of red hair, and a complexion powdered milky white. Her eyebrows had been plucked and then drawn on again at a more rakish angle but the efforts of nature toward the restoration of the old alignment gave a blurred air to her face. When she moved about there was an incessant clicking as innumerable pottery bracelets jingled up and down upon her arms. She came in with such a proprietary haste, and looked around so possessively at the furniture that I wondered if she lived here. But when I asked her she laughed immoderately, repeated my question aloud, and told me she lived with a girl friend at a hotel.

Mr. McKee was a pale, feminine man from the flat

below. He had just shaved, for there was a white spot of lather on his cheekbone, and he was most respectful in his greeting to every one in the room. He informed me that he was in the "artistic game," and I gathered later that he was a photographer and had made the dim enlargement of Mrs. Wilson's mother which hovered like an ectoplasm on the wall. His wife was shrill, languid, handsome, and horrible. She told me with pride that her husband had photographed her a hundred and twenty-seven times since they had been married.

Mrs. Wilson had changed her costume some time before, and was now attired in an elaborate afternoon dress of cream-colored chiffon, which gave out a continual rustle as she swept about the room. With the influence of the dress her personality had also undergone a change. The intense vitality that had been so remarkable in the garage was converted into impressive hauteur. Her laughter, her gestures, her assertions became more violently affected moment by moment, and as she expanded the room grew smaller around her, until she seemed to be revolving on a noisy, creaking pivot through the smoky air.

"My dear," she told her sister in a high, mincing shout, "most of these fellas will cheat you every time. All they think of is money. I had a woman up here last week to look at my feet, and when she gave me the bill you'd of thought she had my appendicitus out."

"What was the name of the woman?" asked Mrs. McKee.

"Mrs. Eberhardt. She goes around looking at people's feet in their own homes."

"I like your dress," remarked Mrs. McKee, "I think it's adorable."

Mrs. Wilson rejected the compliment by raising her eyebrow in disdain.

"It's just a crazy old thing," she said. "I just slip it on sometimes when I don't care what I look like."

"But it looks wonderful on you, if you know what I mean," pursued Mrs. McKee. "If Chester could only get you in that pose I think he could make something of it."

We all looked in silence at Mrs. Wilson, who removed a strand of hair from over her eyes and looked back at us with a brilliant smile. Mr. McKee regarded her intently with his head on one side, and then moved his hand back and forth slowly in front of his face.

"I should change the light," he said after a moment. "I'd like to bring out the modeling of the features. And I'd try to get hold of all the back hair."

"I wouldn't think of changing the light," cried Mrs. McKee. "I think it's——"

Her husband said "*Sh!*" and we all looked at the subject again, whereupon Tom Buchanan yawned audibly and got to his feet.

"You McKees have something to drink," he said. "Get some more ice and mineral water, Myrtle, before everybody goes to sleep."

"I told that boy about the ice." Myrtle raised her eyebrows in despair at the shiftlessness of the lower orders. "These people! You have to keep after them all the time."

She looked at me and laughed pointlessly. Then she flounced over to the dog, kissed it with ecstasy, and swept into the kitchen, implying that a dozen chefs awaited her orders there.

"I've done some nice things out on Long Island," asserted Mr. McKee.

Tom looked at him blankly.

"Two of them we have framed downstairs."

"Two what?" demanded Tom.

"Two studies. One of them I call *Montauk Point—The Gulls,* and the other I call *Montauk Point—The Sea.*"

The sister Catherine sat down beside me on the couch.

"Do you live down on Long Island, too?" she inquired.

"I live at West Egg."

"Really? I was down there at a party about a month ago. At a man named Gatsby's. Do you know him?"

"I live next door to him."

"Well, they say he's a nephew or a cousin of Kaiser Wilhelm's. That's where all his money comes from."

"Really?"

She nodded.

"I'm scared of him. I'd hate to have him get anything on me."

This absorbing information about my neighbor was interrupted by Mrs. McKee's pointing suddenly at Catherine:

"Chester, I think you could do something with *her,*" she broke out, but Mr. McKee only nodded in a bored way, and turned his attention to Tom.

"I'd like to do more work on Long Island, if I could get the entry. All I ask is that they should give me a start."

"Ask Myrtle," said Tom, breaking into a short shout of laughter as Mrs. Wilson entered with a tray. "She'll give you a letter of introduction, won't you, Myrtle?"

"Do what?" she asked, startled.

"You'll give McKee a letter of introduction to your husband, so he can do some studies of him." His lips moved silently for a moment as he invented. "*George B. Wilson at the Gasoline Pump,* or something like that."

Catherine leaned close to me and whispered in my ear:

"Neither of them can stand the person they're married to."

"Can't they?"

"Can't *stand* them." She looked at Myrtle and then at Tom. "What I say is, why go on living with them if they can't stand them? If I was them I'd get a divorce and get married to each other right away."

"Doesn't she like Wilson either?"

The answer to this was unexpected. It came from Myrtle, who had overheard the question, and it was violent and obscene.

"You see," cried Catherine triumphantly. She lowered her voice again. "It's really his wife that's keeping them apart. She's a Catholic, and they don't believe in divorce."

Daisy was not a Catholic, and I was a little shocked at the elaborateness of the lie.

"When they do get married," continued Catherine, "they're going West to live for a while until it blows over."

"It'd be more discreet to go to Europe."

"Oh, do you like Europe?" she exclaimed surprisingly. "I just got back from Monte Carlo."

"Really."

"Just last year. I went over there with another girl."

"Stay long?"

"No, we just went to Monte Carlo and back. We went by way of Marseilles. We had over twelve hundred dollars when we started, but we got gypped out of it all in two days in the private rooms. We had an awful time getting back, I can tell you. God, how I hated that town!"

The late afternoon sky bloomed in the window for a moment like the blue honey of the Mediterranean—then the shrill voice of Mrs. McKee called me back into the room.

"I almost made a mistake, too," she declared vigorously. "I almost married a little kike who'd been after me for years. I knew he was below me. Everybody kept saying to me: 'Lucille, that man's 'way below you!' But if I hadn't met Chester, he'd of got me sure."

"Yes, but listen," said Myrtle Wilson, nodding her head up and down, "at least you didn't marry him."

"I know I didn't."

"Well, I married him," said Myrtle, ambiguously. "And that's the difference between your case and mine."

"Why did you, Myrtle?" demanded Catherine. "Nobody forced you to."

Myrtle considered.

"I married him because I thought he was a gentleman," she said finally. "I thought he knew something about breeding, but he wasn't fit to lick my shoe."

"You were crazy about him for a while," said Catherine.

"Crazy about him!" cried Myrtle incredulously. "Who said I was crazy about him? I never was any more crazy about him than I was about that man there."

She pointed suddenly at me, and every one looked at me accusingly. I tried to show by my expression that I expected no affection.

"The only *crazy* I was was when I married him. I knew right away I made a mistake. He borrowed somebody's best suit to get married in, and never even told me about it, and the man came after it one day when he was out: 'Oh, is that your suit?' I said. 'This is the first I ever heard about it.' But I gave it to him and then

I lay down and cried to beat the band all afternoon."

"She really ought to get away from him," resumed Catherine to me. "They've been living over that garage for eleven years. And Tom's the first sweetie she ever had."

The bottle of whiskey—a second one—was now in constant demand by all present, excepting Catherine, who "felt just as good on nothing at all." Tom rang for the janitor and sent him for some celebrated sandwiches, which were a complete supper in themselves. I wanted to get out and walk eastward toward the park through the soft twilight, but each time I tried to go I became entangled in some wild, strident argument which pulled me back, as if with ropes, into my chair. Yet high over the city our line of yellow windows must have contributed their share of human secrecy to the casual watcher in the darkening streets, and I saw him too, looking up and wondering. I was within and without, simultaneously enchanted and repelled by the inexhaustible variety of life.

Myrtle pulled her chair close to mine, and suddenly her warm breath poured over me the story of her first meeting with Tom.

"It was on the two little seats facing each other that are always the last ones left on the train. I was going up to New York to see my sister and spend the night. He had on a dress suit and patent leather shoes, and I couldn't keep my eyes off him, but every time he looked at me I had to pretend to be looking at the advertisement over his head. When we came into the station he was next to me, and his white shirt-front pressed against my arm, and so I told him I'd have to call a policeman, but he knew I lied. I was so excited that when I got into a taxi with him I didn't hardly know I wasn't getting into a subway train. All I kept thinking about, over and over, was 'You can't live forever; you can't live forever.'"

She turned to Mrs. McKee and the room rang full of her artificial laughter.

"My dear," she cried, "I'm going to give you this dress as soon as I'm through with it. I've got to get another one tomorrow. I'm going to make a list of all the things I've got to get. A massage and a wave, and a collar for the dog, and one of those cute little ash-trays where you touch a spring, and a wreath with a black silk bow for mother's grave that'll last all summer. I got to write down a list so I won't forget all the things I got to do."

It was nine o'clock—almost immediately afterward I looked at my watch and found it was ten. Mr. McKee was asleep on a chair with his fists clenched in his lap, like a photograph of a man of action. Taking out my handkerchief I wiped from his cheek the spot of dried lather that had worried me all the afternoon.

The little dog was sitting on the table looking with blind eyes through the smoke, and from time to time groaning faintly. People disappeared, reappeared, made plans to go somewhere, and then lost each other, searched for each other, found each other a few feet away. Some time toward midnight Tom Buchanan and Mrs. Wilson stood face to face discussing in impassioned voices, whether Mrs. Wilson had any right to mention Daisy's name.

"Daisy! Daisy! Daisy!" shouted Mrs. Wilson. "I'll say it whenever I want to! Daisy! Dai——"

Making a short deft movement, Tom Buchanan broke her nose with his open hand.

Then there were bloody towels upon the bathroom floor, and women's voices scolding, and high over the confusion a long broken wail of pain. Mr. McKee awoke from his doze and started in a daze toward the door.

When he had gone halfway he turned around and stared at the scene—his wife and Catherine scolding and consoling as they stumbled here and there among the crowded furniture with articles of aid, and the despairing figure on the couch, bleeding fluently, and trying to spread a copy of *Town Tattle* over the tapestry scenes of Versailles. Then Mr. McKee turned and continued on out the door. Taking my hat from the chandelier, I followed.

"Come to lunch some day," he suggested, as we groaned down in the elevator.

"Where?"

"Anywhere."

"Keep your hands off the lever," snapped the elevator boy.

"I beg your pardon," said Mr. McKee with dignity, "I didn't know I was touching it."

"All right," I agreed, "I'll be glad to."

. . . I was standing beside his bed and he was sitting up between the sheets, clad in his underwear, with a great portfolio in his hands.

"Beauty and the Beast . . . Loneliness . . . Old Grocery Horse . . . Brook'n Bridge. . . ."

Then I was lying half asleep in the cold lower level of the Pennsylvania Station, staring at the morning *Tribune*, and waiting for the four o'clock train.

III

THERE was music from my neighbor's house through the summer nights. In his blue gardens men and girls came and went like moths among the whisperings and the champagne and the stars. At high tide in the afternoon I watched his guests diving from the tower of his raft, or taking the sun on the hot sand of his beach while his two motor-boats slit the waters of the Sound, drawing aquaplanes over cataracts of foam. On week-ends his Rolls-Royce became an omnibus, bearing parties to and from the city between nine in the morning and long past midnight, while his station wagon scampered like a brisk yellow bug to meet all trains. And on Mondays eight servants, including an extra gardener, toiled all day with mops and scrubbing-brushes and hammers and garden-shears, repairing the ravages of the night before.

Every Friday five crates of oranges and lemons arrived from a fruiterer in New York—every Monday these same oranges and lemons left his back door in a pyramid of pulpless halves. There was a machine in the kitchen which could extract the juice of two hundred oranges in half an hour if a little button was pressed two hundred times by a butler's thumb.

At least once a fortnight a corps of caterers came down with several hundred feet of canvas and enough colored lights to make a Christmas tree of Gatsby's enormous garden. On buffet tables, garnished with glistening hors-d'œuvre, spiced baked hams crowded against salads of harlequin designs and pastry pigs and turkeys bewitched to a dark gold. In the main hall a bar with a real brass rail was set up, and stocked with gins and liquors and with cordials so long forgotten that most of his female guests were too young to know one from another.

By seven o'clock the orchestra has arrived, no thin five-piece affair, but a whole pitful of oboes and trombones and saxophones and viols and cornets and piccolos, and low and high drums. The last swimmers have come in from the beach now and are dressing upstairs;

the cars from New York are parked five deep in the drive, and already the halls and salons and verandas are gaudy with primary colors, and hair bobbed in strange new ways, and shawls beyond the dreams of Castile. The bar is in full swing, and floating rounds of cocktails permeate the garden outside, until the air is alive with chatter and laughter, and casual innuendo and introductions forgotten on the spot, and enthusiastic meetings between women who never knew each other's names.

The lights grow brighter as the earth lurches away from the sun, and now the orchestra is playing yellow cocktail music, and the opera of voices pitches a key higher. Laughter is easier minute by minute, spilled with prodigality, tipped out at a cheerful word. The groups change more swiftly, swell with new arrivals, dissolve and form in the same breath; already there are wanderers, confident girls who weave here and there among the stouter and more stable, become for a sharp, joyous moment the center of a group, and then, excited with triumph, glide on through the sea-change of faces and voices and color under the constantly changing light.

Suddenly one of these gypsies, in trembling opal, seizes a cocktail out of the air, dumps it down for courage and, moving her hands like Frisco, dances out alone on the canvas platform. A momentary hush; the orchestra leader varies his rhythm obligingly for her, and there is a burst of chatter as the erroneous news goes around that she is Gilda Gray's understudy from the *Follies*. The party has begun.

I believe that on the first night I went to Gatsby's house I was one of the few guests who had actually been invited. People were not invited—they went there. They got into automobiles which bore them out to Long

Island, and somehow they ended up at Gatsby's door. Once there they were introduced by somebody who knew Gatsby, and after that they conducted themselves according to the rules of behavior associated with an amusement park. Sometimes they came and went without having met Gatsby at all, came for the party with a simplicity of heart that was its own ticket of admission.

I had been actually invited. A chauffeur in a uniform of robin's-egg blue crossed my lawn early that Saturday morning with a surprisingly formal note from his employer: the honor would be entirely Gatsby's, it said, if I would attend his "little party" that night. He had seen me several times, and had intended to call on me long before, but a peculiar combination of circumstances had prevented it—signed Jay Gatsby, in a majestic hand.

Dressed up in white flannels I went over to his lawn a little after seven, and wandered around rather ill at ease among swirls and eddies of people I didn't know—though here and there was a face I had noticed on the commuting train. I was immediately struck by the number of young Englishmen dotted about; all well dressed, all looking a little hungry, and all talking in low, earnest voices to solid and prosperous Americans. I was sure that they were selling something: bonds or insurance or automobiles. They were at least agonizingly aware of the easy money in the vicinity and convinced that it was theirs for a few words in the right key.

As soon as I arrived I made an attempt to find my host, but the two or three people of whom I asked his whereabouts stared at me in such an amazed way, and denied so vehemently any knowledge of his movements, that I slunk off in the direction of the cocktail table—the only place in the garden where a single man could linger without looking purposeless and alone.

I was on my way to get roaring drunk from sheer embarrassment when Jordan Baker came out of the house and stood at the head of the marble steps, leaning a little backward and looking with contemptuous interest down into the garden.

Welcome or not, I found it necessary to attach myself to some one before I should begin to address cordial remarks to the passers-by.

"Hello!" I roared, advancing toward her. My voice seemed unnaturally loud across the garden.

"I thought you might be here," she responded absently as I came up. "I remembered you lived next door to——"

She held my hand impersonally, as a promise that she'd take care of me in a minute, and gave ear to two girls in twin yellow dresses, who stopped at the foot of the steps.

"Hello!" they cried together. "Sorry you didn't win."

That was for the golf tournament. She had lost in the finals the week before.

"You don't know who we are," said one of the girls in yellow, "but we met you here about a month ago."

"You've dyed your hair since then," remarked Jordan, and I started, but the girls had moved casually on and her remark was addressed to the premature moon, produced like the supper, no doubt, out of a caterer's basket. With Jordan's slender golden arm resting in mine, we descended the steps and sauntered about the garden. A tray of cocktails floated at us through the twilight, and we sat down at a table with the two girls in yellow and three men, each one introduced to us as Mr. Mumble.

"Do you come to these parties often?" inquired Jordan of the girl beside her.

"The last one was the one I met you at," answered the

girl, in an alert confident voice. She turned to her companion: "Wasn't it for you, Lucille?"

It was for Lucille, too.

"I like to come," Lucille said. "I never care what I do, so I always have a good time. When I was here last I tore my gown on a chair, and he asked me my name and address—inside of a week I got a package from Croirier's with a new evening gown in it."

"Did you keep it?" asked Jordan.

"Sure I did. I was going to wear it tonight, but it was too big in the bust and had to be altered. It was gas blue with lavender beads. Two hundred and sixty-five dollars."

"There's something funny about a fellow that'll do a thing like that," said the other girl eagerly. "He doesn't want any trouble with *any*body."

"Who doesn't?" I inquired.

"Gatsby. Somebody told me——"

The two girls and Jordan leaned together confidentially.

"Somebody told me they thought he killed a man once."

A thrill passed over all of us. The three Mr. Mumbles bent forward and listened eagerly.

"I don't think it's so much *that*," argued Lucille sceptically; "it's more that he was a German spy during the war."

One of the men nodded in confirmation.

"I heard that from a man who knew all about him, grew up with him in Germany," he assured us positively.

"Oh, no," said the first girl, "it couldn't be that, because he was in the American army during the war." As our credulity switched back to her she leaned forward with enthusiasm. "You look at him sometimes when he thinks nobody's looking at him. I'll bet he killed a man."

She narrowed her eyes and shivered. Lucille shivered. We all turned and looked around for Gatsby. It was testimony to the romantic speculation he inspired that there were whispers about him from those who had found little that it was necessary to whisper about in this world.

The first supper—there would be another one after midnight—was now being served, and Jordan invited me to join her own party, who were spread around a table on the other side of the garden. There were three married couples and Jordan's escort, a persistent undergraduate given to violent innuendo, and obviously under the impression that sooner or later Jordan was going to yield him up her person to a greater or lesser degree. Instead of rambling, this party had preserved a dignified homogeneity, and assumed to itself the function of representing the staid nobility of the countryside—East Egg condescending to West Egg, and carefully on guard against its spectroscopic gayety.

"Let's get out," whispered Jordan, after a somehow wasteful and inappropriate half-hour; "this is much too polite for me."

We got up, and she explained that we were going to find the host: I had never met him, she said, and it was making me uneasy. The undergraduate nodded in a cynical, melancholy way.

The bar, where we glanced first, was crowded, but Gatsby was not there. She couldn't find him from the top of the steps, and he wasn't on the veranda. On a chance we tried an important-looking door, and walked into a high Gothic library, paneled with carved English oak, and probably transported complete from some ruin overseas.

A stout, middle-aged man, with enormous owl-eyed spectacles, was sitting somewhat drunk on the edge of a great table, staring with unsteady concentration at the shelves of books. As we entered he wheeled excitedly around and examined Jordan from head to foot.

"What do you think?" he demanded impetuously.

"About what?"

He waved his hand toward the book-shelves.

"About that. As a matter of fact you needn't bother to ascertain. I ascertained. They're real."

"The books?"

He nodded.

"Absolutely real—have pages and everything. I thought they'd be a nice durable cardboard. Matter of fact, they're absolutely real. Pages and— Here! Lemme show you."

Taking our scepticism for granted, he rushed to the bookcases and returned with Volume One of the Stoddard *Lectures*.

"See!" he cried triumphantly. "It's a bona-fide piece of printed matter. It fooled me. This fella's a regular Belasco. It's a triumph. What thoroughness! What realism! Knew when to stop, too—didn't cut the pages. But what do you want? What do you expect?"

He snatched the book from me and replaced it hastily on its shelf, muttering that if one brick was removed the whole library was liable to collapse.

"Who brought you?" he demanded. "Or did you just come? I was brought. Most people were brought."

Jordan looked at him alertly, cheerfully, without answering.

"I was brought by a woman named Roosevelt," he continued. "Mrs. Claude Roosevelt. Do you know her? I met her somewhere last night. I've been drunk for about a week now, and I thought it might sober me up to sit in a library."

"Has it?"

"A little bit, I think. I can't tell yet. I've only been here an hour. Did I tell you about the books? They're real. They're——"

"You told us."

We shook hands with him gravely and went back outdoors.

There was dancing now on the canvas in the garden; old men pushing young girls backward in eternal graceless circles, superior couples holding each other tortuously, fashionably, and keeping in the corners—and a great number of single girls dancing individualistically or relieving the orchestra for a moment of the burden of the banjo or the traps. By midnight the hilarity had increased. A celebrated tenor had sung in Italian, and a notorious contralto had sung in jazz, and between the numbers people were doing "stunts" all over the garden, while happy, vacuous bursts of laughter rose toward the summer sky. A pair of stage twins, who turned out to be the girls in yellow, did a baby act in costume, and champagne was served in glasses bigger than finger-bowls. The moon had risen higher, and floating in the Sound was a triangle of silver scales, trembling a little to the stiff, tinny drip of the banjoes on the lawn.

I was still with Jordan Baker. We were sitting at a table with a man of about my age and a rowdy little girl, who gave way upon the slightest provocation to uncontrollable laughter. I was enjoying myself now. I had taken two finger-bowls of champagne, and the scene had changed before my eyes into something significant, elemental, and profound.

At a lull in the entertainment the man looked at me and smiled.

"Your face is familiar," he said, politely. "Weren't you in the First Division during the war?"

"Why, yes. I was in the Twenty-eighth Infantry."

"I was in the Sixteenth until June nineteen-eighteen. I knew I'd seen you somewhere before."

We talked for a moment about some wet, gray little villages in France. Evidently he lived in this vicinity, for he told me that he had just bought a hydroplane, and was going to try it out in the morning.

"Want to go with me, old sport? Just near the shore along the Sound."

"What time?"

"Any time that suits you best."

It was on the tip of my tongue to ask his name when Jordan looked around and smiled.

"Having a gay time now?" she inquired.

"Much better." I turned again to my new acquaintance. "This is an unusual party for me. I haven't even seen the host. I live over there—" I waved my hand at the invisible hedge in the distance, "and this man Gatsby sent over his chauffeur with an invitation."

For a moment he looked at me as if he failed to understand.

"I'm Gatsby," he said suddenly.

"What!" I exclaimed. "Oh, I beg your pardon."

"I thought you knew, old sport. I'm afraid I'm not a very good host."

He smiled understandingly—much more than understandingly. It was one of those rare smiles with a quality of eternal reassurance in it, that you may come across four or five times in life. It faced—or seemed to face—the whole eternal world for an instant, and then concentrated on *you* with an irresistible prejudice in your favor. It understood you just as far as you wanted to be understood, believed in you as you would like to believe in yourself, and assured you that it had precisely the impression of you that, at your best, you hoped to convey. Precisely at that point it vanished—and I was looking at an elegant young roughneck, a year or two over thirty, whose elaborate formality of speech just missed being absurd. Some time before he introduced himself I'd got a strong impression that he was picking his words with care.

Almost at the moment when Mr. Gatsby identified himself, a butler hurried toward him with the information that Chicago was calling him on the wire. He excused himself with a small bow that included each of us in turn.

"If you want anything just ask for it, old sport," he urged me. "Excuse me. I will rejoin you later."

When he was gone I turned immediately to Jordan—constrained to assure her of my surprise. I had expected that Mr. Gatsby would be a florid and corpulent person in his middle years.

"Who is he?" I demanded. "Do you know?"

"He's just a man named Gatsby."

"Where is he from, I mean? And what does he do?"

"Now *you're* started on the subject," she answered with a wan smile. "Well, he told me once he was an Oxford man."

A dim background started to take shape behind him, but at her next remark it faded away.

"However, I don't believe it."

"Why not?"

"I don't know," she insisted, "I just don't think he went there."

Something in her tone reminded me of the other girl's "I think he killed a man," and had the effect of stimulating my curiosity. I would have accepted without question the information that Gatsby sprang from the swamps of Louisiana or from the lower East Side of New York. That was comprehensible. But young men didn't—at least in my provincial inexperience I believed they didn't—drift coolly out of nowhere and buy a palace on Long Island Sound.

"Anyhow, he gives large parties," said Jordan, changing the subject with an urban distaste for the concrete. "And I like large parties. They're so intimate. At small parties there isn't any privacy."

There was the boom of a bass drum, and the voice of the orchestra leader rang out suddenly above the echolalia of the garden.

"Ladies and gentlemen," he cried. "At the request of Mr. Gatsby we are going to play for you Mr. Vladimir Tostoff's latest work, which attracted so much attention at Carnegie Hall last May. If you read the papers, you know there was a big sensation." He smiled with jovial condescension, and added: "Some sensation!" Whereupon everybody laughed.

"The piece is known," he concluded lustily, "as Vladimir Tostoff's *Jazz History of the World*."

The nature of Mr. Tostoff's composition eluded me, because just as it began my eyes fell on Gatsby, standing alone on the marble steps and looking from one group to another with approving eyes. His tanned skin was drawn attractively tight on his face and his short hair looked as though it were trimmed every day. I could see nothing sinister about him. I wondered if the fact that he was not drinking helped to set him off from his guests, for it seemed to me that he grew more correct as the fraternal hilarity increased. When the *Jazz History of the World* was over, girls were putting their heads on men's shoulders in a puppyish, convivial way, girls were swooning backward playfully into men's arms, even into groups, knowing that some one would arrest their falls—but no one swooned backward on Gatsby, and no French bob touched Gatsby's shoulder, and no singing quartets were formed for Gatsby's head for one link.

"I beg your pardon."

Gatsby's butler was suddenly standing beside us.

"Miss Baker?" he inquired. "I beg your pardon, but Mr. Gatsby would like to speak to you alone."

"With me?" she exclaimed in surprise.

"Yes, madame."

She got up slowly, raising her eyebrows at me in astonishment, and followed the butler toward the house. I noticed that she wore her evening-dress, all her dresses, like sports clothes—there was a jauntiness about her movements as if she had first learned to walk upon golf courses on clean, crisp mornings.

I was alone and it was almost two. For some time confused and intriguing sounds had issued from a long, many-windowed room which overhung the terrace. Eluding Jordan's undergraduate, who was now engaged in an obstetrical conversation with two chorus girls, and who implored me to join him, I went inside.

The large room was full of people. One of the girls in yellow was playing the piano, and beside her stood a tall, red-haired young lady from a famous chorus, engaged in song. She had drunk a quantity of champagne, and during the course of her song she had decided, ineptly, that everything was very, very sad—she was not only singing, she was weeping too. Whenever there was a pause in the song she filled it with gasping, broken sobs, and then took up the lyric again in a quavering soprano. The tears coursed down her cheeks—not freely, however, for when they came into contact with her heavily beaded eyelashes they assumed an inky color, and pursued the rest of their way in slow black rivulets. A humorous suggestion was made that she sing the notes on her face, whereupon she threw up her hands, sank into a chair, and went off into a deep vinous sleep.

"She had a fight with a man who says he's her husband," explained a girl at my elbow.

I looked around. Most of the remaining women were now having fights with men said to be their husbands. Even Jordan's party, the quartet from East Egg, were rent asunder by dissension. One of the men was talking with curious intensity to a young actress, and his wife, after attempting to laugh at the situation in a dignified and indifferent way, broke down entirely and resorted to flank attacks—at intervals she appeared suddenly at his side like an angry diamond, and hissed: "You promised!" into his ear.

The reluctance to go home was not confined to wayward men. The hall was at present occupied by two deplorably sober men and their highly indignant wives. The wives were sympathizing with each other in slightly raised voices.

"Whenever he sees I'm having a good time he wants to go home."

"Never heard anything so selfish in my life."

"We're always the first ones to leave."

"So are we."

"Well, we're almost the last tonight," said one of the men sheepishly. "The orchestra left half an hour ago."

In spite of the wives' agreement that such malevolence was beyond credibility, the dispute ended in a short struggle, and both wives were lifted, kicking, into the night.

As I waited for my hat in the hall the door of the library opened and Jordan Baker and Gatsby came out together. He was saying some last word to her, but the eagerness in his manner tightened abruptly into formality as several people approached him to say good-by.

Jordan's party were calling impatiently to her from the porch, but she lingered for a moment to shake hands.

"I've just heard the most amazing thing," she whispered. "How long were we in there?"

"Why, about an hour."

"It was . . . simply amazing," she repeated abstractedly. "But I swore I wouldn't tell it and here I am tantalizing you." She yawned gracefully in my face. "Please come and see me. . . . Phone book. . . . Under the name of Mrs. Sigourney Howard. . . . My aunt. . . ." She was hurrying off as she talked—her brown hand waved a jaunty salute as she melted into her party at the door.

Rather ashamed that on my first appearance I had stayed so late, I joined the last of Gatsby's guests, who were clustered around him. I wanted to explain that I'd hunted for him early in the evening and to apologize for not having known him in the garden.

"Don't mention it," he enjoined me eagerly. "Don't give it another thought, old sport." The familiar expression held no more familiarity than the hand which reassuringly brushed my shoulder. "And don't forget we're going up in the hydroplane tomorrow morning, at nine o'clock."

Then the butler, behind his shoulder:

"Philadelphia wants you on the 'phone, sir."

"All right, in a minute. Tell them I'll be right there. . . . Good night."

"Good night."

"Good night." He smiled—and suddenly there seemed to be a pleasant significance in having been among the last to go, as if he had desired it all the time. "Good night, old sport. . . . Good night."

But as I walked down the steps I saw that the evening was not quite over. Fifty feet from the door a dozen headlights illuminated a bizarre and tumultuous scene. In the ditch beside the road, right side up, but violently shorn of one wheel, rested a new coupé which had left Gatsby's drive not two minutes before. The sharp jut of a wall accounted for the detachment of the wheel, which was now getting considerable attention from half a dozen curious chauffeurs. However, as they had left their cars blocking the road, a harsh, discordant din from those in the rear had been audible for some time, and added to the already violent confusion of the scene.

A man in a long duster had dismounted from the wreck and now stood in the middle of the road, looking from the car to the tire and from the tire to the observers in a pleasant, puzzled way.

"See!" he explained. "It went in the ditch."

The fact was infinitely astonishing to him, and I recognized first the unusual quality of wonder, and then the man—it was the late patron of Gatsby's library.

"How'd it happen?"

He shrugged his shoulders.

"I know nothing whatever about mechanics," he said decisively.

"But how did it happen? Did you run into the wall?"

"Don't ask me," said Owl Eyes, washing his hands of the whole matter. "I know very little about driving—next to nothing. It happened, and that's all I know."

"Well, if you're a poor driver you oughtn't to try driving at night."

"But I wasn't even trying," he explained indignantly, "I wasn't even trying."

An awed hush fell upon the bystanders.

"Do you want to commit suicide?"

"You're lucky it was just a wheel! A bad driver and not even *trying*!"

"You don't understand," explained the criminal. "I wasn't driving. There's another man in the car."

The shock that followed this declaration found voice in a sustained "Ah-h-h!" as the door of the coupé swung slowly open. The crowd—it was now a crowd—stepped back involuntarily, and when the door had opened wide there was a ghostly pause. Then, very gradually, part by part, a pale, dangling individual stepped out of the wreck, pawing tentatively at the ground with a large uncertain dancing shoe.

Blinded by the glare of the headlights and confused by the incessant groaning of the horns, the apparition stood swaying for a moment before he perceived the man in the duster.

"Wha's matter?" he inquired calmly. "Did we run outa gas?"

"Look!"

Half a dozen fingers pointed at the amputated wheel—he stared at it for a moment, and then looked upward as though he suspected that it had dropped from the sky.

"It came off," some one explained.

He nodded.

"At first I din' notice we'd stopped."

A pause. Then, taking a long breath and straightening his shoulders, he remarked in a determined voice:

"Wonder'ff tell me where there's a gas'line station?"

At least a dozen men, some of them a little better off than he was, explained to him that wheel and car were no longer joined by any physical bond.

"Back out," he suggested after a moment. "Put her in reverse."

"But the *wheel's* off!"

He hesitated.

"No harm in trying," he said.

The caterwauling horns had reached a crescendo and I turned away and cut across the lawn toward home. I glanced back once. A wafer of a moon was shining over Gatsby's house, making the night fine as before, and surviving the laughter and the sound of his still glowing garden. A sudden emptiness seemed to flow now from the windows and the great doors, endowing with complete isolation the figure of the host, who stood on the porch, his hand up in a formal gesture of farewell.

Reading over what I have written so far, I see I have given the impression that the events of three nights several weeks apart were all that absorbed me. On the contrary, they were merely casual events in a crowded summer, and, until much later, they absorbed me infinitely less than my personal affairs.

Most of the time I worked. In the early morning the sun threw my shadow westward as I hurried down the white chasms of lower New York to the Probity Trust. I knew the other clerks and young bond-salesmen by their first names, and lunched with them in dark, crowded restaurants on little pig sausages and mashed potatoes and coffee. I even had a short affair with a girl who lived in Jersey City and worked in the accounting department, but her brother began throwing mean looks in my direction, so when she went on her vacation in July I let it blow quietly away.

I took dinner usually at the Yale Club—for some reason it was the gloomiest event of my day—and then I went upstairs to the library and studied investments and securities for a conscientious hour. There were generally a few rioters around, but they never came into the library, so it was a good place to work. After that, if the night was mellow, I strolled down Madison Avenue past the old Murray Hill Hotel, and over 33rd Street to the Pennsylvania Station.

I began to like New York, the racy, adventurous feel of it at night, and the satisfaction that the constant flicker of men and women and machines gives to the restless eye. I liked to walk up Fifth Avenue and pick out romantic women from the crowd and imagine that in a few minutes I was going to enter into their lives, and no one would ever know or disapprove. Sometimes, in my mind, I followed them to their apartments on the corners of hidden streets, and they turned and smiled back at me before they faded through a door into warm darkness. At the enchanted metropolitan twilight I felt a haunting loneliness sometimes, and felt it in others—poor young clerks who loitered in front of windows waiting until it was time for a solitary restaurant dinner—young clerks in the dusk, wasting the most poignant moments of night and life.

Again at eight o'clock, when the dark lanes of the Forties were lined five deep with throbbing taxicabs, bound for the theater district, I felt a sinking in my heart. Forms leaned together in the taxis as they waited, and voices sang, and there was laughter from unheard jokes, and lighted cigarettes made unintelligible circles inside. Imagining that I, too, was hurrying toward gayety and sharing their intimate excitement, I wished them well.

For a while I lost sight of Jordan Baker, and then in midsummer I found her again. At first I was flattered to go places with her, because she was a golf champion, and everyone knew her name. Then it was something more. I wasn't actually in love, but I felt a sort of tender curiosity. The bored haughty face that she turned to the world concealed something—most affectations conceal something eventually, even though they don't in the beginning—and one day I found what it was. When we were on a house-party together up in Warwick, she left a borrowed car out in the rain with the top down, and then lied about it—and suddenly I remembered the story about her that had eluded me that night at Daisy's. At her first big golf tournament there was a row that nearly reached the newspapers—a suggestion that she had moved her ball from a bad lie in the semi-final round. The thing approached the proportions of a scandal—then died away. A caddy retracted his statement, and the only other witness admitted that he might have been mistaken. The incident and the name had remained together in my mind.

Jordan Baker instinctively avoided clever, shrewd men, and now I saw that this was because she felt safer on a plane where any divergence from a code would be thought impossible. She was incurably dishonest. She wasn't able to endure being at a disadvantage and, given this unwillingness, I suppose she had begun dealing in subterfuges when she was very young in order to keep that cool, insolent smile turned to the world and yet satisfy the demands of her hard, jaunty body.

It made no difference to me. Dishonesty in a woman is a thing you never blame deeply—I was casually sorry, and then I forgot. It was on that same house-party that we had a curious conversation about driving a car. It started because she passed so close to some workmen that our fender flicked a button on one man's coat.

"You're a rotten driver," I protested. "Either you

ought to be more careful, or you oughtn't to drive at all."

"I am careful."

"No, you're not."

"Well, other people are," she said lightly.

"What's that got to do with it?"

"They'll keep out of my way," she insisted. "It takes two to make an accident."

"Suppose you met somebody just as careless as yourself."

"I hope I never will," she answered. "I hate careless people. That's why I like you."

Her gray, sun-strained eyes stared straight ahead, but she had deliberately shifted our relations, and for a moment I thought I loved her. But I am slow-thinking and full of interior rules that act as brakes on my desires, and I knew that first I had to get myself definitely out of that tangle back home. I'd been writing letters once a week and signing them: "Love, Nick," and all I could think of was how, when that certain girl played tennis, a faint mustache of perspiration appeared on her upper lip. Nevertheless there was a vague understanding that had to be tactfully broken off before I was free.

Every one suspects himself of at least one of the cardinal virtues, and this is mine: I am one of the few honest people that I have ever known.

IV

ON SUNDAY morning while church bells rang in the villages alongshore, the world and its mistress returned to Gatsby's house and twinkled hilariously on his lawn.

"He's a bootlegger," said the young ladies, moving somewhere between his cocktails and his flowers. "One time he killed a man who had found out that he was nephew to Von Hindenburg and second cousin to the devil. Reach me a rose, honey, and pour me a last drop into that there crystal glass."

Once I wrote down on the empty spaces of a timetable the names of those who came to Gatsby's house that summer. It is an old timetable now, disintegrating at its folds, and headed "This schedule in effect July 5th, 1922." But I can still read the gray names, and they will give you a better impression than my generalities of those who accepted Gatsby's hospitality and paid him the subtle tribute of knowing nothing whatever about him.

From East Egg, then, came the Chester Beckers and the Leeches, and a man named Bunsen, whom I knew at Yale, and Doctor Webster Civet, who was drowned last summer up in Maine. And the Hornbeams and the Willie Voltaires, and a whole clan named Blackbuck, who always gathered in a corner and flipped up their noses like goats at whosoever came near. And the Ismays and the Chrysties (or rather Hubert Auerbach and Mr. Chrystie's wife), and Edgar Beaver, whose hair, they say, turned cotton-white one winter afternoon for no good reason at all.

Clarence Endive was from East Egg, as I remember. He came only once, in white knickerbockers, and had a fight with a bum named Etty in the garden. From farther out on the Island came the Cheadles and the O. R. P. Schraeders, and the Stonewall Jackson Abrams of Georgia, and the Fishguards and the Ripley Snells. Snell was there three days before he went to the penitentiary, so drunk out on the gravel drive that Mrs. Ulysses Swett's automobile ran over his right hand. The

Dancies came, too, and S. B. Whitebait, who was well over sixty, and Maurice A. Flink, and the Hammerheads, and Beluga the tobacco importer, and Beluga's girls.

From West Egg came the Poles and the Mulreadys and Cecil Roebuck and Cecil Schoen and Gulick the State senator and Newton Orchid, who controlled Films Par Excellence, and Eckhaust and Clyde Cohen and Don S. Schwartze (the son) and Arthur McCarty, all connected with the movies in one way or another. And the Catlips and the Bembergs and G. Earl Muldoon, brother to that Muldoon who afterward strangled his wife. Da Fontano the promoter came there, and Ed Legros and James B. ("Rot-Gut") Ferret and the De Jongs and Ernest Lilly—they came to gamble, and when Ferret wandered into the garden it meant he was cleaned out and Associated Traction would have to fluctuate profitably next day.

A man named Klipspringer was there so often and so long that he became known as "the boarder"—I doubt if he had any other home. Of theatrical people there were Gus Waize and Horace O'Donavan and Lester Myer and George Duckweed and Francis Bull. Also from New York were the Chromes and the Backhyssons and the Dennickers and Russell Betty and the Corrigans and the Kellehers and the Dewers and the Scullys and S. W. Belcher and the Smirkes and the young Quinns, divorced now, and Henry L. Palmetto, who killed himself by jumping in front of a subway train in Times Square.

Benny McClenahan arrived always with four girls. They were never quite the same ones in physical person, but they were so identical one with another that it inevitably seemed they had been there before. I have forgotten their names—Jaqueline, I think, or else Consuela, or Gloria or Judy or June, and their last names were either the melodious names of flowers and months or the sterner ones of the great American capitalists whose cousins, if pressed, they would confess themselves to be.

In addition to all these I can remember that Faustina O'Brien came there at least once and the Baedeker girls and young Brewer, who had his nose shot off in the war, and Mr. Albrucksburger and Miss Haag, his fiancée, and Ardita Fitz-Peters and Mr. P. Jewett, once head of the American Legion, and Miss Claudia Hip, with a man reputed to be her chauffeur, and a prince of something, whom we called Duke, and whose name, if I ever knew it, I have forgotten.

All these people came to Gatsby's house in the summer.

At nine o'clock, one morning late in July, Gatsby's gorgeous car lurched up the rocky drive to my door and gave out a burst of melody from its three-noted horn. It was the first time he had called on me, though I had gone to two of his parties, mounted in his hydroplane, and, at his urgent invitation, made frequent use of his beach.

"Good morning, old sport. You're having lunch with me today and I thought we'd ride up together."

He was balancing himself on the dashboard of his car with that resourcefulness of movement that is so peculiarly American—that comes, I suppose, with the absence of lifting work in youth and, even more, with the formless grace of our nervous, sporadic games. This quality was continually breaking through his punctilious manner in the shape of restlessness. He was never quite still; there was always a tapping foot somewhere or the impatient opening and closing of a hand.

He saw me looking with admiration at his car.

"It's pretty, isn't it, old sport?" He jumped off to give me a better view. "Haven't you ever seen it before?"

I'd seen it. Everybody had seen it. It was a rich cream color, bright with nickel, swollen here and there in its monstrous length with triumphant hat-boxes and supper-boxes and tool-boxes, and terraced with a labyrinth of wind-shields that mirrored a dozen suns. Sitting down behind many layers of glass in a sort of green leather conservatory, we started to town.

I had talked with him perhaps half a dozen times in the past month and found, to my disappointment, that he had little to say. So my first impression, that he was a person of some undefined consequence, had gradually faded and he had become simply the proprietor of an elaborate roadhouse next door.

And then came that disconcerting ride. We hadn't reached West Egg Village before Gatsby began leaving his elegant sentences unfinished and slapping himself indecisively on the knee of his caramel-colored suit.

"Look here, old sport," he broke out surprisingly, "what's your opinion of me, anyhow?"

A little overwhelmed, I began the generalized evasions which that question deserves.

"Well, I'm going to tell you something about my life," he interrupted. "I don't want you to get a wrong idea of me from all these stories you hear."

So he was aware of the bizarre accusations that flavored conversation in his halls.

"I'll tell you God's truth." His right hand suddenly ordered divine retribution to stand by. "I am the son of some wealthy people in the Middle West—all dead now. I was brought up in America but educated at Oxford, because all my ancestors have been educated there for many years. It is a family tradition."

He looked at me sideways—and I knew why Jordan Baker had believed he was lying. He hurried the phrase "educated at Oxford," or swallowed it, or choked on it, as though it had bothered him before. And with this doubt, his whole statement fell to pieces, and I wondered if there wasn't something a little sinister about him, after all.

"What part of the Middle West?" I inquired casually.

"San Francisco."

"I see."

"My family all died and I came into a good deal of money."

His voice was solemn, as if the memory of that sudden extinction of a clan still haunted him. For a moment I suspected that he was pulling my leg, but a glance at him convinced me otherwise.

"After that I lived like a young rajah in all the capitals of Europe—Paris, Venice, Rome—collecting jewels, chiefly rubies, hunting big game, painting a little, things for myself only, and trying to forget something very sad that had happened to me long ago."

With an effort I managed to restrain my incredulous laughter. The very phrases were worn so threadbare that they evoked no image except that of a turbaned "character" leaking sawdust at every pore as he pursued a tiger through the Bois de Boulogne.

"Then came the war, old sport. It was a great relief, and I tried very hard to die, but I seemed to bear an enchanted life. I accepted a commission as first lieutenant when it began. In the Argonne Forest I took the remains of my machine-gun battalion so far forward that there was a half mile gap on either side of us where the infantry couldn't advance. We stayed there two days and two nights, a hundred and thirty men with sixteen Lewis guns, and when the infantry came up at last they found the insignia of three German divisions among the piles of dead. I was promoted to be a major, and every Allied government gave me a decoration—even Montenegro, little Montenegro down on the Adriatic Sea!"

Little Montenegro! He lifted up the words and nodded at them—with his smile. The smile comprehended Montenegro's troubled history and sympathized with the brave struggles of the Montenegrin people. It appreciated fully the chain of national circumstances which had elicited this tribute from Montenegro's warm little heart. My incredulity was submerged in fascination now; it was like skimming hastily through a dozen magazines.

He reached in his pocket, and a piece of metal, slung on a ribbon, fell into my palm.

"That's the one from Montenegro."

To my astonishment, the thing had an authentic look. "Orderi de Danilo," ran the circular legend, "Montenegro, Nicolas Rex."

"Turn it."

"Major Jay Gatsby," I read, "For Valour Extraordinary."

"Here's another thing I always carry. A souvenir of Oxford days. It was taken in Trinity Quad—the man on my left is now the Earl of Doncaster."

It was a photograph of half a dozen young men in blazers loafing in an archway through which were visible a host of spires. There was Gatsby, looking a little, not much, younger—with a cricket bat in his hand.

Then it was all true. I saw the skins of tigers flaming in his palace on the Grand Canal; I saw him opening a chest of rubies to ease, with their crimson-lighted depths, the gnawings of his broken heart.

"I'm going to make a big request of you today," he

said, pocketing his souvenirs with satisfaction, "so I thought you ought to know something about me. I didn't want you to think I was just some nobody. You see, I usually find myself among strangers because I drift here and there trying to forget the sad thing that happened to me." He hesitated. "You'll hear about it this afternoon."

"At lunch?"

"No, this afternoon. I happened to find out that you're taking Miss Baker to tea."

"Do you mean you're in love with Miss Baker?"

"No, old sport, I'm not. But Miss Baker has kindly consented to speak to you about this matter."

I hadn't the faintest idea what "this matter" was, but I was more annoyed than interested. I hadn't asked Jordan to tea in order to discuss Mr. Jay Gatsby. I was sure the request would be something utterly fantastic, and for a moment I was sorry I'd ever set foot upon his overpopulated lawn.

He wouldn't say another word. His correctness grew on him as we neared the city. We passed Port Roosevelt, where there was a glimpse of red-belted oceangoing ships, and sped along a cobbled slum lined with the dark, undeserted saloons of the faded-gilt nineteen-hundreds. Then the valley of ashes opened out on both sides of us, and I had a glimpse of Mrs. Wilson straining at the garage pump with panting vitality as we went by.

With fenders spread like wings we scattered light through half Astoria—only half, for as we twisted among the pillars of the elevated I heard the familiar "jug-jug-*spat!*" of a motorcycle, and a frantic policeman rode alongside.

"All right, old sport," called Gatsby. We slowed

down. Taking a white card from his wallet, he waved it before the man's eyes.

"Right you are," agreed the policeman, tipping his cap. "Know you next time, Mr. Gatsby. Excuse *me!*"

"What was that?" I inquired. "The picture of Oxford?"

"I was able to do the commissioner a favor once, and he sends me a Christmas card every year."

Over the great bridge, with the sunlight through the girders making a constant flicker upon the moving cars, with the city rising up across the river in white heaps and sugar lumps all built with a wish out of non-olfactory money. The city seen from the Queensborough Bridge is always the city seen for the first time, in its first wild promise of all the mystery and the beauty in the world.

A dead man passed us in a hearse heaped with blooms, followed by two carriages with drawn blinds, and by more cheerful carriages for friends. The friends looked out at us with the tragic eyes and short upper lips of southeastern Europe, and I was glad that the sight of Gatsby's splendid car was included in their somber holiday. As we crossed Blackwell's Island a limousine passed us, driven by a white chauffeur, in which sat three modish Negroes, two bucks and a girl. I laughed aloud as the yolks of their eyeballs rolled toward us in haughty rivalry.

"Anything can happen now that we've slid over this bridge," I thought; "anything at all. . . ."

Even Gatsby could happen, without any particular wonder.

Roaring noon. In a well-fanned Forty-second Street cellar I met Gatsby for lunch. Blinking away the brightness of the street outside, my eyes picked him out obscurely in the anteroom, talking to another man.

"Mr. Carraway, this is my friend Mr. Wolfsheim."

A small, flat-nosed Jew raised his large head and regarded me with two fine growths of hair which luxuriated in either nostril. After a moment I discovered his tiny eyes in the half-darkness.

"—So I took one look at him," said Mr. Wolfsheim, shaking my hand earnestly, "and what do you think I did?"

"What?" I inquired politely.

But evidently he was not addressing me, for he dropped my hand and covered Gatsby with his expressive nose.

"I handed the money to Katspaugh and I said: 'All right, Katspaugh, don't pay him a penny till he shuts his mouth.' He shut it then and there."

Gatsby took an arm of each of us and moved forward into the restaurant, whereupon Mr. Wolfsheim swallowed a new sentence he was starting and lapsed into a somnambulatory abstraction.

"Highballs?" asked the head waiter.

"This is a nice restaurant here," said Mr. Wolfsheim, looking at the Presbyterian nymphs on the ceiling. "But I like across the street better!"

"Yes, highballs," agreed Gatsby, and then to Mr. Wolfsheim: "It's too hot over there."

"Hot and small—yes," said Mr. Wolfsheim, "but full of memories."

"What place is that?" I asked.

"The old Metropole."

"The old Metropole," brooded Mr. Wolfsheim gloomily. "Filled with faces dead and gone. Filled with friends gone now forever. I can't forget so long as I live the night they shot Rosy Rosenthal there. It was six of us at the table, and Rosy had eat and drunk a lot all evening. When it was almost morning the waiter came up to him with a funny look and says somebody wants to speak to him outside. 'All right,' says Rosy, and begins to get up, and I pulled him down in his chair.

"'Let the bastards come in here if they want you, Rosy, but don't you, so help me, move outside this room.'

"It was four o'clock in the morning then, and if we'd of raised the blinds we'd of seen daylight."

"Did he go?" I asked innocently.

"Sure he went." Mr. Wolfsheim's nose flashed at me indignantly. "He turned around in the door and says: 'Don't let that waiter take away my coffee!' Then he went out on the sidewalk, and they shot him three times in his full belly and drove away."

"Four of them were electrocuted," I said, remembering.

"Five, with Becker." His nostrils turned to me in an interested way. "I understand you're looking for a business gonnegtion."

The juxtaposition of these two remarks was startling. Gatsby answered for me:

"Oh, no," he exclaimed, "this isn't the man."

"No?" Mr. Wolfsheim seemed disappointed.

"This is just a friend. I told you we'd talk about that some other time."

"I beg your pardon," said Mr. Wolfsheim, "I had a wrong man."

A succulent hash arrived, and Mr. Wolfsheim, forgetting the more sentimental atmosphere of the old Metropole, began to eat with ferocious delicacy. His eyes, meanwhile, roved very slowly all around the room—he completed the arc by turning to inspect the people directly behind. I think that, except for my presence, he would have taken one short glance beneath our own table.

"Look here, old sport," said Gatsby leaning toward me, "I'm afraid I made you a little angry this morning in the car."

There was the smile again, but this time I held out against it.

"I don't like mysteries," I answered, "and I don't understand why you won't come out frankly and tell me what you want. Why has it all got to come through Miss Baker?"

"Oh, it's nothing underhand," he assured me. "Miss Baker's a great sportswoman, you know, and she'd never do anything that wasn't all right."

Suddenly he looked at his watch, jumped up, and hurried from the room, leaving me with Mr. Wolfsheim at the table.

"He has to telephone," said Mr. Wolfsheim, following him with his eyes. "Fine fellow, isn't he? Handsome to look at and a perfect gentleman."

"Yes."

"He's an Oggsford man."

"Oh!"

"He went to Oggsford College in England. You know Oggsford College?"

"I've heard of it."

"It's one of the most famous colleges in the world."

"Have you known Gatsby for a long time?" I inquired.

"Several years," he answered in a gratified way. "I made the pleasure of his acquaintance just after the war. But I knew I had discovered a man of fine breeding after I talked with him an hour. I said to myself: 'There's the kind of man you'd like to take home and introduce to your mother and sister.'" He paused "I see you're looking at my cuff buttons."

I hadn't been looking at them, but I did now. They were composed of oddly familiar pieces of ivory.

"Finest specimens of human molars," he informed me.

"Well!" I inspected them. "That's a very interesting idea."

"Yeah." He flipped his sleeves up under his coat. "Yeah, Gatsby's very careful about women. He would never so much as look at a friend's wife."

When the subject of this instinctive trust returned to the table and sat down Mr. Wolfsheim drank his coffee with a jerk and got to his feet.

"I have enjoyed my lunch," he said, "and I'm going to run off from you two young men before I outstay my welcome."

"Don't hurry, Meyer," said Gatsby, without enthusiasm. Mr. Wolfsheim raised his hand in a sort of benediction.

"You're very polite, but I belong to another generation," he announced solemnly. "You sit here and discuss your sports and your young ladies and your—" He supplied an imaginary noun with another wave of his hand. "As for me, I am fifty years old, and I won't impose myself on you any longer."

As he shook hands and turned away his tragic nose was trembling. I wondered if I had said anything to offend him.

"He becomes very sentimental sometimes," explained Gatsby. "This is one of his sentimental days. He's quite a character around New York—a denizen of Broadway."

"Who is he, anyhow, an actor?"

"No."

"A dentist?"

"Meyer Wolfsheim? No, he's a gambler." Gatsby hesitated, then added coolly: "He's the man who fixed the World's Series back in 1919."

"Fixed the World's Series?" I repeated.

The idea staggered me. I remembered, of course, that the World's Series had been fixed in 1919, but if I had thought of it at all I would have thought of it as a thing that merely *happened,* the end of some inevitable chain. It never occurred to me that one man could start to play with the faith of fifty million people—with the single-mindedness of a burglar blowing a safe.

"How did he happen to do that?" I asked after a minute.

"He just saw the opportunity."

"Why isn't he in jail?"

"They can't get him, old sport. He's a smart man."

I insisted on paying the check. As the waiter brought my change I caught sight of Tom Buchanan across the crowded room.

"Come along with me for a minute," I said; "I've got to say hello to some one."

When he saw us Tom jumped up and took half a dozen steps in our direction.

"Where've you been?" he demanded eagerly. "Daisy's furious because you haven't called up."

"This is Mr. Gatsby, Mr. Buchanan."

They shook hands briefly, and a strained, unfamiliar look of embarrassment came over Gatsby's face.

"How've you been, anyhow?" demanded Tom of me. "How'd you happen to come up this far to eat?"

"I've been having lunch with Mr. Gatsby."

I turned toward Mr. Gatsby, but he was no longer there.

One October day in nineteen-seventeen——

(said Jordan Baker that afternoon, sitting up very straight on a straight chair in the tea-garden at the Plaza Hotel)

—I was walking along from one place to another, half on the sidewalks and half on the lawns. I was happier on the lawns because I had on shoes from England with rubber nobs on the soles that bit into the soft ground. I had on a new plaid skirt also that blew a little in the wind, and whenever this happened the red, white, and blue banners in front of all the houses stretched out stiff and said *tut-tut-tut-tut*, in a disapproving way.

The largest of the banners and the largest of the lawns belonged to Daisy Fay's house. She was just eighteen, two years older than me, and by far the most popular of all the young girls in Louisville. She dressed in white, and had a little white roadster, and all day long the telephone rang in her house and excited young officers from Camp Taylor demanded the privilege of monopolizing her that night. "Anyways, for an hour!"

When I came opposite her house that morning her white roadster was beside the curb, and she was sitting in it with a lieutenant I had never seen before. They were so engrossed in each other that she didn't see me until I was five feet away.

"Hello, Jordan," she called unexpectedly. "Please come here."

I was flattered that she wanted to speak to me, because of all the older girls I admired her most. She asked me if I was going to the Red Cross and make bandages. I was. Well, then, would I tell them that she couldn't come that day? The officer looked at Daisy while she was speaking, in a way that every young girl wants to be looked at some time, and because it seemed romantic to me I have remembered the incident ever since. His name was Jay Gatsby, and I didn't lay eyes on him again for over four years—even after I'd met him on Long Island I didn't realize it was the same man.

That was nineteen-seventeen. By the next year I had a few beaux myself, and I began to play in tournaments, so I didn't see Daisy very often. She went with a slightly older crowd—when she went with anyone at all. Wild rumors were circulating about her—how her mother had found her packing her bag one winter night to go to New York and say good-by to a soldier who was going overseas. She was effectually prevented, but she wasn't on speaking terms with her family for several weeks. After that she didn't play around with the soldiers any more, but only with a few flat-footed, short-sighted young men in town, who couldn't get into the army at all.

By the next autumn she was gay again, gay as ever. She had a début after the Armistice, and in February she was presumably engaged to a man from New Orleans. In June she married Tom Buchanan of Chicago, with more pomp and circumstance than Louisville ever knew before. He came down with a hundred people in four private cars, and hired a whole floor of the Muhlbach Hotel, and the day before the wedding he gave her a string of pearls valued at three hundred and fifty thousand dollars.

I was a bridesmaid. I came into her room half an hour before the bridal dinner, and found her lying on her bed as lovely as the June night in her flowered dress—and as drunk as a monkey. She had a bottle of sauterne in one hand and a letter in the other.

"'Gratulate me," she muttered. "Never had a drink before, but oh how I do enjoy it."

"What's the matter, Daisy?"

I was scared, I can tell you; I'd never seen a girl like that before.

"Here, deares'." She groped around in a waste-basket she had with her on the bed and pulled out the string of pearls. "Take 'em downstairs and give 'em back to whoever they belong to. Tell 'em all Daisy's change' her mine. Say: 'Daisy's change' her mine!' "

She began to cry—she cried and cried. I rushed out and found her mother's maid, and we locked the door and got her into a cold bath. She wouldn't let go of the letter. She took it into the tub with her and squeezed it up into a wet ball, and only let me leave it in the soap-dish when she saw that it was coming to pieces like snow.

But she didn't say another word. We gave her spirits of ammonia and put ice on her forehead and hooked her back into her dress, and half an hour later, when we walked out of the room, the pearls were around her neck and the incident was over. Next day at five o'clock she married Tom Buchanan without so much as a shiver, and started off on a three months' trip to the South Seas.

I saw them in Santa Barbara when they came back, and I thought I'd never seen a girl so mad about her husband. If he left the room for a minute she'd look around uneasily, and say: "Where's Tom gone?" and wear the most abstracted expression until she saw him coming in the door. She used to sit on the sand with his head in her lap by the hour, rubbing her fingers over his eyes and looking at him with unfathomable delight. It was touching to see them together—it made you laugh in a hushed, fascinated way. That was in August. A week after I left Santa Barbara Tom ran into a wagon on the Ventura road one night, and ripped a front wheel off his car. The girl who was with him got into the papers, too, because her arm was broken—she was one of the chambermaids in the Santa Barbara Hotel.

The next April Daisy had her little girl, and they went to France for a year. I saw them one spring in Cannes, and later in Deauville, and then they came back to Chicago to settle down. Daisy was popular in Chicago, as you know. They moved with a fast crowd, all of them young and rich and wild, but she came out with an absolutely perfect reputation. Perhaps because she doesn't drink. It's a great advantage not to drink among hard-drinking people. You can hold your tongue, and, moreover, you can time any little irregularity of your own so that everybody else is so blind that they don't see or care. Perhaps Daisy never went in for amour at all—and yet there's something in that voice of hers. . . .

Well, about six weeks ago, she heard the name Gatsby for the first time in years. It was when I asked you—do you remember?—if you knew Gatsby in West Egg. After you had gone home she came into my room and woke me up, and said: "What Gatsby?" and when I described him—I was half asleep—she said in the strangest voice that it must be the man she used to know. It wasn't until then that I connected this Gatsby with the officer in her white car.

When Jordan Baker had finished telling all this we had left the Plaza for half an hour and were driving in a victoria through Central Park. The sun had gone down behind the tall apartments of the movie stars in the West Fifties, and the clear voices of children, already gathered like crickets on the grass, rose through the hot twilight:

"I'm the Sheik of Araby.
Your love belongs to me.
At night when you're asleep
Into your tent I'll creep——"

"It was a strange coincidence," I said.

"But it wasn't a coincidence at all."

"Why not?"

"Gatsby bought that house so that Daisy would be just across the bay."

Then it had not been merely the stars to which he had aspired on that June night. He came alive to me, delivered suddenly from the womb of his purposeless splendor.

"He wants to know," continued Jordan, "if you'll invite Daisy to your house some afternoon and then let him come over."

The modesty of the demand shook me. He had waited five years and bought a mansion where he dispensed starlight to casual moths—so that he could "come over" some afternoon to a stranger's garden.

"Did I have to know all this before he could ask such a little thing?"

"He's afraid, he's waited so long. He thought you might be offended. You see, he's regular tough underneath it all."

Something worried me.

"Why didn't he ask you to arrange a meeting?"

"He wants her to see his house," she explained. "And your house is right next door."

"Oh!"

"I think he half expected her to wander into one of his parties, some night," went on Jordan, "but she never did. Then he began asking people casually if they knew her, and I was the first one he found. It was that night he sent for me at his dance, and you should have heard the elaborate way he worked up to it. Of course, I immediately suggested a luncheon in New York—and I thought he'd go mad:

"'I don't want to do anything out of the way!' he kept saying. 'I want to see her right next door.'

"When I said you were a particular friend of Tom's, he started to abandon the whole idea. He doesn't know very much about Tom, though he says he's read a Chicago paper for years just on the chance of catching a glimpse of Daisy's name."

It was dark now, and as we dipped under a little bridge I put my arm around Jordan's golden shoulder and drew her toward me and asked her to dinner. Suddenly I wasn't thinking of Daisy and Gatsby any more, but of this clean, hard, limited person, who dealt in universal scepticism, and who leaned back jauntily just within the circle of my arm. A phrase began to beat in my ears with a sort of heady excitement: "There are only the pursued, the pursuing, the busy and the tired."

"And Daisy ought to have something in her life," murmured Jordan to me.

"Does she want to see Gatsby?"

"She's not to know about it. Gatsby doesn't want her to know. You're just supposed to invite her to tea."

We passed a barrier of dark trees, and then the façade of Fifty-ninth Street, a block of delicate pale light, beamed down into the park. Unlike Gatsby and Tom Buchanan, I had no girl whose disembodied face floated along the dark cornices and blinding signs, and so I drew up the girl beside me, tightening my arms. Her wan, scornful mouth smiled, and so I drew her up again closer, this time to my face.

V

WHEN I came home to West Egg that night I was afraid for a moment that my house was on fire. Two o'clock and the whole corner of the peninsula was blazing with light, which fell unreal on the shrubbery and made thin elongating glints upon the roadside wires. Turning a corner, I saw that it was Gatsby's house, lit from tower to cellar.

At first I thought it was another party, a wild rout that had resolved itself into "hide-and-go-seek" or "sardines-in-the-box" with all the house thrown open to the game. But there wasn't a sound. Only wind in the trees, which blew the wires and made the lights go off and on again as if the house had winked into the darkness. As my taxi groaned away I saw Gatsby walking toward me across his lawn.

"Your place looks like the World's Fair," I said.

"Does it?" He turned his eyes toward it absently. "I have been glancing into some of the rooms. Let's go to Coney Island, old sport. In my car."

"It's too late."

"Well, suppose we take a plunge in the swimming pool? I haven't made use of it all summer."

"I've got to go to bed."

"All right."

He waited, looking at me with suppressed eagerness.

"I talked with Miss Baker," I said after a moment. "I'm going to call up Daisy tomorrow and invite her over here to tea."

"Oh, that's all right," he said carelessly. "I don't want to put you to any trouble."

"What day would suit you?"

"What day would suit *you?*" he corrected me quickly. "I don't want to put you to any trouble, you see."

"How about the day after tomorrow?"

He considered for a moment. Then, with reluctance: "I want to get the grass cut," he said.

We both looked down at the grass—there was a sharp line where my ragged lawn ended and the darker, well-kept expanse of his began. I suspected that he meant my grass.

"There's another little thing," he said uncertainly, and hesitated.

"Would you rather put it off for a few days?" I asked.

"Oh, it isn't about that. At least—" He fumbled with a series of beginnings. "Why, I thought—why, look here, old sport, you don't make much money, do you?"

"Not very much."

This seemed to reassure him and he continued more confidently.

"I thought you didn't if you'll pardon my—you see, I carry on a little business on the side, a sort of side line, you understand. And I thought that if you don't make very much— You're selling bonds, aren't you, old sport?"

"Trying to."

"Well, this would interest you. It wouldn't take up much of your time and you might pick up a nice bit of money. It happens to be a rather confidential sort of thing."

I realize now that under different circumstances that conversation might have been one of the crises of my life. But, because the offer was obviously and tactlessly for a service to be rendered, I had no choice except to cut him off there.

"I've got my hands full," I said. "I'm much obliged but I couldn't take on any more work."

"You wouldn't have to do any business with Wolfsheim." Evidently he thought that I was shying away from the "gonnegtion" mentioned at lunch, but I assured him he was wrong. He waited a moment longer, hoping I'd begin a conversation, but I was too absorbed to be responsive, so he went unwillingly home.

The evening had made me light-headed and happy; I think I walked into a deep sleep as I entered my front door. So I don't know whether or not Gatsby went to

Coney Island, or for how many hours he "glanced into rooms" while his house blazed gaudily on. I called up Daisy from the office next morning, and invited her to come to tea.

"Don't bring Tom," I warned her.

"What?"

"Don't bring Tom."

"Who is 'Tom'?" she asked innocently.

The day agreed upon was pouring rain. At eleven o'clock a man in a raincoat, dragging a lawn mower, tapped at my front door and said that Mr. Gatsby had sent him over to cut my grass. This reminded me that I had forgotten to tell my Finn to come back, so I drove into West Egg Village to search for her among soggy whitewashed alleys and to buy some cups and lemons and flowers.

The flowers were unnecessary, for at two o'clock a green house arrived from Gatsby's, with innumerable receptacles to contain it. An hour later the front door opened nervously, and Gatsby, in a white flannel suit, silver shirt, and gold-colored tie, hurried in. He was pale, and there were dark signs of sleeplessness beneath his eyes.

"Is everything all right?" he asked immediately.

"The grass looks fine, if that's what you mean."

"What grass?" he inquired blankly. "Oh, the grass in the yard." He looked out the window at it, but, judging from his expression, I don't believe he saw a thing.

"Looks very good," he remarked vaguely. "One of the papers said they thought the rain would stop about four. I think it was *The Journal*. Have you got everything you need in the shape of—of tea?"

I took him into the pantry, where he looked a little reproachfully at the Finn. Together we scrutinized the twelve lemon cakes from the delicatessen shop.

"Will they do?" I asked.

"Of course, of course! They're fine!" and he added hollowly, ". . . old sport."

The rain cooled about half-past three to a damp mist, through which occasional thin drops swam like dew. Gatsby looked with vacant eyes through a copy of Clay's *Economics*, starting at the Finnish tread that shook the kitchen floor, and peering toward the bleared windows from time to time as if a series of invisible but alarming happenings were taking place outside. Finally he got up and informed me, in an uncertain voice, that he was going home.

"Why's that?"

"Nobody's coming to tea. It's too late!" He looked at his watch as if there was some pressing demand on his time elsewhere. "I can't wait all day."

"Don't be silly; it's just two minutes to four."

He sat down miserably, as if I had pushed him, and simultaneously there was the sound of a motor turning into my lane. We both jumped up, and, a little harrowed myself, I went out into the yard.

Under the dripping bare lilac-trees a large open car was coming up the drive. It stopped. Daisy's face, tipped sideways beneath a three-cornered lavender hat, looked out at me with a bright ecstatic smile.

"Is this absolutely where you live, my dearest one?"

The exhilarating ripple of her voice was a wild tonic in the rain. I had to follow the sound of it for a moment, up and down, with my ear alone, before any words came through. A damp streak of hair lay like a dash of blue paint across her cheek, and her hand was wet with glistening drops as I took it to help her from the car.

"Are you in love with me," she said low in my ear, "or why did I have to come alone?"

"That's the secret of Castle Rackrent. Tell your chauffeur to go far away and spend an hour."

"Come back in an hour, Ferdie." Then in a grave murmur: "His name is Ferdie."

"Does the gasoline affect his nose?"

"I don't think so," she said innocently. "Why?"

We went in. To my overwhelming surprise the living-room was deserted.

"Well, that's funny," I exclaimed.

"What's funny?"

She turned her head as there was a light dignified knocking at the front door. I went out and opened it. Gatsby, pale as death, with his hands plunged like weights in his coat pockets, was standing in a puddle of water glaring tragically into my eyes.

With his hands still in his coat pockets he stalked by me into the hall, turned sharply as if he were on a wire, and disappeared into the living-room. It wasn't a bit funny. Aware of the loud beating of my own heart I pulled the door to against the increasing rain.

For half a minute there wasn't a sound. Then from the living-room I heard a sort of choking murmur and part of a laugh, followed by Daisy's voice on a clear artificial note:

"I certainly am awfully glad to see you again."

A pause; it endured horribly. I had nothing to do in the hall, so I went into the room.

Gatsby, his hands still in his pockets, was reclining against the mantelpiece in a strained counterfeit of perfect ease, even of boredom. His head leaned back so far that it rested against the face of a defunct mantelpiece clock, and from this position his distraught eyes stared down at Daisy, who was sitting, frightened but graceful, on the edge of a stiff chair.

"We've met before," muttered Gatsby. His eyes glanced momentarily at me, and his lips parted with an abortive attempt at a laugh. Luckily the clock took this moment to tilt dangerously at the pressure of his head, whereupon he turned and caught it with trembling fingers and set it back in place. Then he sat down, rigidly, his elbow on the arm of the sofa and his chin in his hand.

"I'm sorry about the clock," he said.

My own face had now assumed a deep tropical burn. I couldn't muster up a single commonplace out of the thousand in my head.

"It's an old clock," I told them idiotically.

I think we all believed for a moment that it had smashed in pieces on the floor.

"We haven't met for many years," said Daisy, her voice as matter-of-fact as it could ever be.

"Five years next November."

The automatic quality of Gatsby's answer set us all back at least another minute. I had them both on their feet with the desperate suggestion that they help me make tea in the kitchen when the demoniac Finn brought it in on a tray.

Amid the welcome confusion of cups and cakes a certain physical decency established itself. Gatsby got himself into a shadow and, while Daisy and I talked, looked conscientiously from one to the other of us with tense, unhappy eyes. However, as calmness wasn't an end in itself, I made an excuse at the first possible moment, and got to my feet.

"Where are you going?" demanded Gatsby in immediate alarm.

"I'll be back."

"I've got to speak to you about something before you go."

He followed me wildly into the kitchen, closed the door, and whispered: "Oh, God!" in a miserable way.

"What's the matter?"

"This is a terrible mistake," he said, shaking his head from side to side, "a terrible, terrible mistake."

"You're just embarrassed, that's all," and luckily I added: "Daisy's embarrassed too."

"She's embarrassed?" he repeated incredulously.

"Just as much as you are."

"Don't talk so loud."

"You're acting like a little boy," I broke out impatiently. "Not only that, but you're rude. Daisy's sitting in there all alone."

He raised his hand to stop my words, looked at me with unforgettable reproach, and, opening the door cautiously, went back into the other room.

I walked out the back way—just as Gatsby had when he had made his nervous circuit of the house half an hour before—and ran for a huge black knotted tree, whose massed leaves made a fabric against the rain. Once more it was pouring, and my irregular lawn, well-shaved by Gatsby's gardener, abounded in small muddy swamps and prehistoric marshes. There was nothing to look at from under the tree except Gatsby's enormous house, so I stared at it, like Kant at his church steeple, for half an hour. A brewer had built it early in the "period" craze a decade before, and there was a story that he'd agreed to pay five years' taxes on all the neighboring cottages if the owners would have their roofs thatched with straw. Perhaps their refusal took the heart out of his plan to Found a Family—he went into an immediate decline. His children sold his house with the black wreath still on the door. Americans, while willing, even eager, to be serfs, have always been obstinate about being peasantry.

After half an hour, the sun shone again, and the grocer's automobile rounded Gatsby's drive with the raw material for his servants' dinner—I felt sure he wouldn't eat a spoonful. A maid began opening the upper windows of his house, appeared momentarily in each, and leaning from the large central bay, spat meditatively into the garden. It was time I went back. While the rain continued it had seemed like the murmur of their voices, rising and swelling a little now and then with gusts of emotion. But in the new silence I felt that silence had fallen within the house too.

I went in—after making every possible noise in the kitchen, short of pushing over the stove—but I don't believe they heard a sound. They were sitting at either end of the couch, looking at each other as if some question had been asked, or was in the air, and every vestige of embarrassment was gone. Daisy's face was smeared with tears, and when I came in she jumped up and began wiping at it with her handkerchief before a mirror. But there was a change in Gatsby that was simply confounding. He literally glowed; without a word or a gesture of exultation a new well-being radiated from him and filled the little room.

"Oh, hello old sport," he said, as if he hadn't seen me for years. I thought for a moment he was going to shake hands.

"It's stopped raining."

"Has it?" When he realized what I was talking about, that there were twinkle-bells of sunshine in the room, he smiled like a weather man, like an ecstatic patron of recurrent light, and repeated the news to Daisy. "What do you think of that? It's stopped raining."

"I'm glad, Jay." Her throat, full of aching, grieving beauty, told only of her unexpected joy.

"I want you and Daisy to come over to my house," he said, "I'd like to show her around."

"You're sure you want me to come?"

"Absolutely, old sport."

Daisy went upstairs to wash her face—too late I thought with humiliation of my towels—while Gatsby and I waited on the lawn.

"My house looks well, doesn't it?" he demanded. "See how the whole front of it catches the light."

I agreed that it was splendid.

"Yes." His eyes went over it, every arched door and square tower. "It took me just three years to earn the money that bought it."

"I thought you inherited your money."

"I did, old sport," he said automatically, "but I lost most of it in the big panic—the panic of the war."

I think he hardly knew what he was saying, for when I asked him what business he was in he answered: "That's my affair," before he realized that it wasn't an appropriate reply.

"Oh, I've been in several things," he corrected himself. "I was in the drug business and then I was in the oil business. But I'm not in either one now." He looked at me with more attention. "Do you mean you've been thinking over what I proposed the other night?"

Before I could answer, Daisy came out of the house and two rows of brass buttons on her dress gleamed in the sunlight.

"That huge place *there?*" she cried pointing.

"Do you like it?"

"I love it, but I don't see how you live there all alone."

"I keep it always full of interesting people, night and day. People who do interesting things. Celebrated people."

Instead of taking the short cut along the Sound we went down to the road and entered by the big postern. With enchanting murmurs Daisy admired this aspect or that of the feudal silhouette against the sky, admired the gardens, the sparkling odor of jonquils and the frothy odor of hawthorn and plum blossoms and the pale gold odor of kiss-me-at-the-gate. It was strange to reach the marble steps and find no stir of bright dresses in and out of the door, and hear no sound but bird voices in the trees.

And inside, as we wandered through Marie Antoinette music-rooms and Restoration Salons, I felt that there were guests concealed behind every couch and table, under orders to be breathlessly silent until we had passed through. As Gatsby closed the door of "the Merton College Library" I could have sworn I heard the owl-eyed man break into ghostly laughter.

We went upstairs, through period bedrooms swathed in rose and lavender silk and vivid with new flowers, through dressing-rooms and poolrooms, and bathrooms, with sunken baths—intruding into one chamber where a disheveled man in pajamas was doing liver exercises on the floor. It was Mr. Klipspringer, the "boarder." I had seen him wandering hungrily about the beach that morning. Finally we came to Gatsby's own apartment, a bedroom and a bath, and an Adam study, where we sat down and drank a glass of some chartreuse he took from a cupboard in the wall.

He hadn't once ceased looking at Daisy, and I think he revalued everything in his house according to the measure of response it drew from her well-loved eyes. Sometimes, too, he stared around at his possessions in a dazed way, as though in her actual and astounding presence none of it was any longer real. Once he nearly toppled down a flight of stairs.

His bedroom was the simplest room of all—except where the dresser was garnished with a toilet set of pure dull gold. Daisy took the brush with delight, and smoothed her hair, whereupon Gatsby sat down and shaded his eyes and began to laugh.

"It's the funniest thing, old sport," he said hilariously. "I can't— When I try to——"

He had passed visibly through two states and was entering upon a third. After his embarrassment and his unreasoning joy he was consumed with wonder at her presence. He had been full of the idea so long, dreamed it right through to the end, waited with his teeth set, so to speak, at an inconceivable pitch of intensity. Now, in the reaction, he was running down like an overwound clock.

Recovering himself in a minute he opened for us two hulking patent cabinets which held his massed suits and dressing-gowns and ties, and his shirts, piled like bricks in stacks a dozen high.

"I've got a man in England who buys me clothes. He sends over a selection of things at the beginning of each season, spring and fall."

He took out a pile of shirts and began throwing them, one by one, before us, shirts of sheer linen and thick silk and fine flannel, which lost their folds as they fell and covered the table in many-colored disarray. While we admired he brought more and the soft rich heap mounted higher—shirts with stripes and scrolls and plaids in coral and apple-green and lavender and faint orange, with monograms of Indian blue. Suddenly, with a strained sound, Daisy bent her head into the shirts and began to cry stormily.

"They're such beautiful shirts," she sobbed, her voice muffled in the thick folds. "It makes me sad because I've never seen such—such beautiful shirts before."

After the house, we were to see the grounds and the swimming pool, and the hydroplane and the midsummer flowers—but outside Gatsby's window it began to rain again, so we stood in a row looking at the corrugated surface of the Sound.

"If it wasn't for the mist we could see your home across the bay," said Gatsby. "You always have a green light that burns all night at the end of your dock."

Daisy put her arm through his abruptly, but he seemed absorbed in what he had just said. Possibly it had occurred to him that the colossal significance of that light had now vanished forever. Compared to the great distance that had separated him from Daisy it had seemed very near to her, almost touching her. It had seemed as close as a star to the moon. Now it was again a green light on a dock. His count of enchanted objects had diminished by one.

I began to walk about the room, examining various indefinite objects in the half darkness. A large photograph of an elderly man in yachting costume attracted me, hung on the wall over his desk.

"Who's this?"

"That? That's Mr. Dan Cody, old sport."

The name sounded faintly familiar.

"He's dead now. He used to be my best friend years ago."

There was a small picture of Gatsby, also in yachting costume, on the bureau—Gatsby with his head thrown back defiantly—taken apparently when he was about eighteen.

"I adore it," exclaimed Daisy. "The pompadour! You never told me you had a pompadour—or a yacht."

"Look at this," said Gatsby quickly. "Here's a lot of clippings—about you."

They stood side by side examining it. I was going to

ask to see the rubies when the phone rang, and Gatsby took up the receiver.

"Yes. . . . Well, I can't talk now. . . . I can't talk now, old sport. . . . I said a *small* town. . . . He must know what a small town is. . . . Well, he's no use to us if Detroit is his idea of a small town. . . ."

He rang off.

"Come here *quick!*" cried Daisy at the window.

The rain was still falling, but the darkness had parted in the west, and there was a pink and golden billow of foamy clouds above the sea.

"Look at that," she whispered, and then after a moment: "I'd like to just get one of those pink clouds and put you in it and push you around."

I tried to go then, but they wouldn't hear of it; perhaps my presence made them feel more satisfactorily alone.

"I know what we'll do," said Gatsby, "we'll have Klipspringer play the piano."

He went out of the room calling "Ewing!" and returned in a few minutes accompanied by an embarrassed, slightly worn young man, with shell-rimmed glasses and scanty blond hair. He was now decently clothed in a "sport shirt," open at the neck, sneakers, and duck trousers of a nebulous hue.

"Did we interrupt your exercises?" inquired Daisy politely.

"I was asleep," cried Mr. Klipspringer, in a spasm of embarrassment. "That is, I'd *been* asleep. Then I got up. . . ."

"Klipspringer plays the piano," said Gatsby, cutting him off. "Don't you, Ewing, old sport?"

"I don't play well. I don't—I hardly play at all. I'm all out of prac——"

"We'll go downstairs," interrupted Gatsby. He flipped

a switch. The gray windows disappeared as the house glowed full of light.

In the music-room Gatsby turned on a solitary lamp beside the piano. He lit Daisy's cigarette from a trembling match, and sat down with her on a couch far across the room, where there was no light save what the gleaming floor bounced in from the hall.

When Klipspringer had played *The Love Nest* he turned around on the bench and searched unhappily for Gatsby in the gloom.

"I'm all out of practice, you see. I told you I couldn't play. I'm all out of prac——"

"Don't talk so much, old sport," commanded Gatsby. "Play!"

"In the morning,
In the evening,
Ain't we got fun——"

Outside the wind was loud and there was a faint flow of thunder along the Sound. All the lights were going on in West Egg now; the electric trains, men-carrying, were plunging home through the rain from New York. It was the hour of a profound human change, and excitement was generating on the air.

"One thing's sure and nothing's surer
The rich get richer and the poor get—children.
In the meantime,
In between time——"

As I went over to say good-by I saw that the expression of bewilderment had come back into Gatsby's face, as though a faint doubt had occurred to him as to the quality of his present happiness. Almost five years! There must have been moments even that afternoon when Daisy tumbled short of his dreams—not through her own fault, but because of the colossal vitality of his illusion. It had gone beyond her, beyond everything.

He had thrown himself into it with a creative passion, adding to it all the time, decking it out with every bright feather that drifted his way. No amount of fire or freshness can challenge what a man can store up in his ghostly heart.

As I watched him he adjusted himself a little, visibly. His hand took hold of hers, and as she said something low in his ear he turned toward her with a rush of emotion. I think that voice held him most, with its fluctuating, feverish warmth, because it couldn't be overdreamed—that voice was a deathless song.

They had forgotten me, but Daisy glanced up and held out her hand; Gatsby didn't know me now at all. I looked once more at them and they looked back at me, remotely, possessed by intense life. Then I went out of the room and down the marble steps into the rain, leaving them there together.

VI

ABOUT this time an ambitious young reporter from New York arrived one morning at Gatsby's door and asked him if he had anything to say.

"Anything to say about what?" inquired Gatsby politely.

"Why—any statement to give out."

It transpired after a confused five minutes that the man had heard Gatsby's name around his office in a connection which he either wouldn't reveal or didn't fully understand. This was his day off and with laudable initiative he had hurried out "to see."

It was a random shot, and yet the reporter's instinct was right. Gatsby's notoriety, spread about by the hundreds who had accepted his hospitality and so become authorities upon his past, had increased all summer until he fell just short of being news. Contemporary legends such as the "underground pipe-line to Canada" attached themselves to him, and there was one persistent story that he didn't live in a house at all, but in a boat that looked like a house and was moved secretly up and down the Long Island shore. Just why these inventions were a source of satisfaction to James Gatz of North Dakota isn't easy to say.

James Gatz—that was really, or at least legally, his name. He had changed it at the age of seventeen and at the specific moment that witnessed the beginning of his career—when he saw Dan Cody's yacht drop anchor over the most insidious flat on Lake Superior. It was James Gatz who had been loafing along the beach that afternoon in a torn green jersey and a pair of canvas pants, but it was already Jay Gatsby who borrowed a rowboat, pulled out the *Tuolomee,* and informed Cody that a wind might catch him and break him up in half an hour.

I suppose he'd had the name ready for a long time, even then. His parents were shiftless and unsuccessful farm people—his imagination had never really accepted them as his parents at all. The truth was that Jay Gatsby of West Egg, Long Island, sprang from his Platonic conception of himself. He was a son of God—a phrase which, if it means anything, means just that—and he must be about His Father's business, the service of a vast, vulgar, and meretricious beauty. So he invented just the sort of Jay Gatsby that a seventeen-year-old boy would be likely to invent, and to this conception he was faithful to the end.

For over a year he had been beating his way along the south shore of Lake Superior as a clam-digger and a salmon-fisher or in any other capacity that brought him food and bed. His brown, hardening body lived naturally through the half-fierce, half-lazy work of the bracing days. He knew women early, and since they spoiled him he became contemptuous of them, of young virgins because they were ignorant, of the others because they were hysterical about things which in his overwhelming self-absorption he took for granted.

But his heart was in a constant, turbulent riot. The most grotesque and fantastic conceits haunted him in his bed at night. A universe of ineffable gaudiness spun itself out in his brain while the clock ticked on the wash-stand and the moon soaked with wet light his tangled clothes upon the floor. Each night he added to the pattern of his fancies until drowsiness closed down upon some vivid scene with an oblivious embrace. For a while these reveries provided an outlet for his imagination; they were a satisfactory hint of the unreality of reality, a promise that the rock of the world was founded securely on a fairy's wing.

An instinct toward his future glory had led him, some months before, to the small Lutheran College of St. Olaf's in southern Minnesota. He stayed there two weeks, dismayed at its ferocious indifference to the drums of his destiny, to destiny itself, and despising the janitor's work with which he was to pay his way through. Then he drifted back to Lake Superior, and he was still searching for something to do on the day that Dan Cody's yacht dropped anchor in the shallows alongshore.

Cody was fifty years old then, a product of the Nevada silver fields, of the Yukon, of every rush for metal since seventy-five. The transactions in Montana copper that made him many times a millionaire found him physically robust but on the verge of soft-mindedness, and, suspecting this, an infinite number of women tried to separate him from his money. The none too savory ramifications by which Ella Kaye, the newspaper woman, played Madame de Maintenon to his weakness and sent him to sea in a yacht, were common property of the turgid journalism of 1902. He had been coasting along all too hospitable shores for five years when he turned up as James Gatz's destiny in Little Girl Bay.

To young Gatz, resting on his oars and looking up at the railed deck, that yacht represented all the beauty and glamour in the world. I suppose he smiled at Cody —he had probably discovered that people liked him when he smiled. At any rate Cody asked him a few questions (one of them elicited the brand new name) and found that he was quick and extravagantly ambitious. A few days later he took him to Duluth and bought him a blue coat, six pairs of white duck trousers, and a yachting cap. And when the *Tuolomee* left for the West Indies and the Barbary Coast Gatsby left too.

He was employed in a vague personal capacity—while he remained with Cody he was in turn steward, mate, skipper, secretary, and even jailor, for Dan Cody sober knew what lavish doings Dan Cody drunk might soon be about, and he provided for such contingencies by reposing more and more trust in Gatsby. The arrangement lasted five years, during which the boat went three times around the Continent. It might have lasted indefinitely except for the fact that Ella Kaye came on board one night in Boston and a week later Dan Cody inhospitably died.

I remember the portrait of him up in Gatsby's bedroom, a gray, florid man with a hard, empty face—the pioneer debauchee, who during one phase of American life brought back to the Eastern seaboard the savage violence of the frontier brothel and saloon. It was indirectly due to Cody that Gatsby drank so little. Sometimes in the course of gay parties women used to rub champagne into his hair; for himself he formed the habit of letting liquor alone.

And it was from Cody that he inherited money—a legacy of twenty-five thousand dollars. He didn't get it. He never understood the legal device that was used against him, but what remained of the millions went intact to Ella Kaye. He was left with his singularly appropriate education; the vague contour of Jay Gatsby had filled out to the substantiality of a man.

He told me all this very much later, but I've put it down here with the idea of exploding those first wild rumors about his antecedents, which weren't even faintly true. Moreover he told it to me at a time of confusion, when I had reached the point of believing everything and nothing about him. So I take advantage of this short halt, while Gatsby, so to speak, caught his breath, to clear this set of misconceptions away.

It was a halt, too, in my association with his affairs. For several weeks I didn't see him or hear his voice on the phone—mostly I was in New York, trotting around with Jordan and trying to ingratiate myself with her senile aunt—but finally I went over to his house one Sunday afternoon. I hadn't been there two minutes when somebody brought Tom Buchanan in for a drink. I was startled, naturally, but the really surprising thing was that it hadn't happened before.

They were a party of three on horseback—Tom and a man named Sloane and a pretty woman in a brown riding-habit, who had been there previously.

"I'm delighted to see you," said Gatsby, standing on his porch. "I'm delighted that you dropped in."

As though they cared!

"Sit right down. Have a cigarette or a cigar." He

walked around the room quickly, ringing bells. "I'll have something to drink for you in just a minute."

He was profoundly affected by the fact that Tom was there. But he would be uneasy anyhow until he had given them something, realizing in a vague way that that was all they came for. Mr. Sloane wanted nothing. A lemonade? No, thanks. A little champagne? Nothing at all, thanks. . . . I'm sorry——

"Did you have a nice ride?"

"Very good roads around here."

"I suppose the automobiles——"

"Yeah."

Moved by an irresistible impulse, Gatsby turned to Tom, who had accepted the introduction as a stranger.

"I believe we've met somewhere before, Mr. Buchanan."

"Oh, yes," said Tom, gruffly polite, but obviously not remembering. "So we did. I remember very well."

"About two weeks ago."

"That's right. You were with Nick here."

"I know your wife," continued Gatsby, almost aggressively.

"That so?"

Tom turned to me.

"You live near here, Nick?"

"Next door."

"That so?"

Mr. Sloane didn't enter into the conversation, but lounged back haughtily in his chair; the woman said nothing either—until unexpectedly, after two highballs, she became cordial.

"We'll all come over to your next party, Mr. Gatsby," she suggested. "What do you say?"

"Certainly; I'd be delighted to have you."

"Be ver' nice," said Mr. Sloane, without gratitude. "Well—think ought to be starting home."

"Please don't hurry," Gatsby urged them. He had control of himself now, and he wanted to see more of Tom. "Why don't you—why don't you stay for supper? I wouldn't be surprised if some other people dropped in from New York."

"You come to supper with *me*," said the lady enthusiastically. "Both of you."

This included me. Mr. Sloane got to his feet.

"Come along," he said—but to her only.

"I mean it," she insisted. "I'd love to have you. Lots of room."

Gatsby looked at me questioningly. He wanted to go, and he didn't see that Mr. Sloane had determined he shouldn't.

"I'm afraid I won't be able to," I said.

"Well, you come," she urged, concentrating on Gatsby.

Mr. Sloane murmured something close to her ear.

"We won't be late if we start now," she insisted aloud.

"I haven't got a horse," said Gatsby. "I used to ride in the army, but I've never bought a horse. I'll have to follow you in my car. Excuse me for just a minute."

The rest of us walked out on the porch, where Sloane and the lady began an impassioned conversation aside.

"My God, I believe the man's coming," said Tom. "Doesn't he know she doesn't want him?"

"She says she does want him."

"She has a big dinner party and he won't know a soul there." He frowned. "I wonder where in the devil he met Daisy. By God, I may be old-fashioned in my ideas, but women run around too much these days to suit me. They meet all kinds of crazy fish."

Suddenly Mr. Sloane and the lady walked down the steps and mounted their horses.

"Come on," said Mr. Sloane to Tom, "we're late. We've got to go." And then to me: "Tell him we couldn't wait, will you?"

Tom and I shook hands, the rest of us exchanged a cool nod, and they trotted quickly down the drive, disappearing under the August foliage just as Gatsby, with hat and light overcoat in hand, came out the front door.

Tom was evidently perturbed at Daisy's running around alone, for on the following Saturday night he came with her to Gatsby's party. Perhaps his presence gave the evening its peculiar quality of oppressiveness —it stands out in my memory from Gatsby's other parties that summer. There were the same people, or at least the same sort of people, the same profusion of champagne, the same many-colored, many-keyed commotion, but I felt an unpleasantness in the air, a pervading harshness that hadn't been there before. Or perhaps I had merely grown used to it, grown to accept West Egg as a world complete in itself, with its own standards and its own great figures, second to nothing because it had no consciousness of being so, and now I was looking at it again, through Daisy's eyes. It is invariably saddening to look through new eyes at things upon which you have expended your own powers of adjustment.

They arrived at twilight, and, as we strolled out among the sparkling hundreds, Daisy's voice was playing murmurous tricks in her throat.

"These things excite me *so*," she whispered. "If you want to kiss me any time during the evening, Nick, just let me know and I'll be glad to arrange it for you. Just mention my name. Or present a green card. I'm giving out green——"

"Look around," suggested Gatsby.

"I'm looking around. I'm having a marvelous——"

"You must see the faces of many people you've heard about."

Tom's arrogant eyes roamed the crowd.

"We don't go around very much," he said; "in fact, I was just thinking I don't know a soul here."

"Perhaps you know that lady," Gatsby indicated a gorgeous, scarcely human orchid of a woman who sat in state under a white-plum tree. Tom and Daisy stared, with that particularly unreal feeling that accompanies the recognition of a hitherto ghostly celebrity of the movies.

"She's lovely," said Daisy.

"The man bending over her is her director."

He took them ceremoniously from group to group:

"Mrs. Buchanan . . . and Mr. Buchanan—" After an instant's hesitation he added: "the polo player."

"Oh, no," objected Tom quickly, "not me."

But evidently the sound of it pleased Gatsby, for Tom remained "the polo player" for the rest of the evening.

"I've never met so many celebrities," Daisy exclaimed. "I liked that man—what was his name?—with the sort of blue nose."

Gatsby identified him, adding that he was a small producer.

"Well, I liked him anyhow."

"I'd a little rather not be the polo player," said Tom pleasantly, "I'd rather look at all these famous people in—in oblivion."

Daisy and Gatsby danced. I remember being surprised by his graceful, conservative fox-trot—I had never seen him dance before. Then they sauntered over to my house and sat on the steps for half an hour, while at her request I remained watchfully in the garden. "In case there's a fire or a flood," she explained, "or any act of God."

Tom appeared from his oblivion as we were sitting down to supper together. "Do you mind if I eat with some people over here?" he said. "A fellow's getting off some funny stuff."

"Go ahead," answered Daisy genially, "and if you want to take down any addresses here's my little gold pencil." . . . She looked around after a moment and told me the girl was "common but pretty," and I knew that except for the half-hour she'd been alone with Gatsby she wasn't having a good time.

We were at a particularly tipsy table. That was my fault—Gatsby had been called to the phone, and I'd enjoyed these same people only two weeks before. But what had amused me then turned septic on the air now.

"How do you feel, Miss Baedeker?"

The girl addressed was trying, unsuccessfully, to slump against my shoulder. At this inquiry she sat up and opened her eyes.

"Wha'?"

A massive and lethargic woman, who had been urging Daisy to play golf with her at the local club tomorrow, spoke in Miss Baedeker's defense:

"Oh, she's all right now. When she's had five or six cocktails she always starts screaming like that. I tell her she ought to leave it alone."

"I do leave it alone," affirmed the accused hollowly.

"We heard you yelling, so I said to Doc Civet here: 'There's somebody that needs your help, Doc.' "

"She's much obliged, I'm sure," said another friend, without gratitude, "but you got her dress all wet when you stuck her head in the pool."

"Anything I hate is to get my head stuck in a pool,"

mumbled Miss Baedeker. "They almost drowned me once over in New Jersey."

"Then you ought to leave it alone," counted Doctor Civet.

"Speak for yourself!" cried Miss Baedeker violently. "Your hand shakes. I wouldn't let you operate on me!"

It was like that. Almost the last thing I remember was standing with Daisy and watching the moving-picture director and his Star. They were still under the white-plum tree and their faces were touching except for a pale, thin ray of moonlight between. It occurred to me that he had been very slowly bending toward her all evening to attain this proximity, and even while I watched I saw him stoop one ultimate degree and kiss at her cheek.

"I like her," said Daisy, "I think she's lovely."

But the rest offended her—and inarguably, because it wasn't a gesture but an emotion. She was appalled by West Egg, this unprecedented "place" that Broadway had begotten upon a Long Island fishing village—appalled by its raw vigor that chafed under the old euphemisms and by the too obtrusive fate that herded its inhabitants along a short-cut from nothing to nothing. She saw something awful in the very simplicity she failed to understand.

I sat on the front steps with them while they waited for their car. It was dark here in front; only the bright door sent ten square feet of light volleying out into the soft black morning. Sometimes a shadow moved against a dressing-room blind above, gave way to another shadow, an indefinite procession of shadows, that rouged and powdered in an invisible glass.

"Who is this Gatsby anyhow?" demanded Tom suddenly. "Some big bootlegger?"

"Where'd you hear that?" I inquired.

"I didn't hear it. I imagined it. A lot of these newly rich people are just big bootleggers, you know."

"Not Gatsby," I said shortly.

He was silent for a moment. The pebbles of the drive crunched under his feet.

"Well, he certainly must have strained himself to get this menagerie together."

A breeze stirred the gray haze of Daisy's fur collar.

"At least they are more interesting than the people we know," she said with an effort.

"You didn't look so interested."

"Well, I was."

Tom laughed and turned to me.

"Did you notice Daisy's face when that girl asked her to put her under a cold shower?"

Daisy began to sing with the music in a husky, rhythmic whisper, bringing out a meaning in each word that it had never had before and would never have again. When the melody rose, her voice broke up sweetly, following it, in a way contralto voices have, and each change tipped out a little of her warm human magic upon the air.

"Lots of people come who haven't been invited," she said suddenly. "That girl hadn't been invited. They simply force their way in and he's too polite to object."

"I'd like to know who he is and what he does," insisted Tom. "And I think I'll make a point of finding out."

"I can tell you right now," she answered. "He owned some drug-stores, a lot of drug-stores. He built them up himself."

The dilatory limousine came rolling up the drive.

"Good night, Nick," said Daisy.

Her glance left me and sought the lighted top of the

steps, where *Three O'Clock in the Morning,* a neat, sad little waltz of that year, was drifting out the open door. After all, in the very casualness of Gatsby's party there were romantic possibilities totally absent from her world. What was it up there in the song that seemed to be calling her back inside? What would happen now in the dim, incalculable hours? Perhaps some unbelievable guest would arrive, a person infinitely rare and to be marveled at, some authentically radiant young girl who with one fresh glance at Gatsby, one moment of magical encounter, would blot out those five years of unwavering devotion.

I stayed late that night, Gatsby asked me to wait until he was free, and I lingered in the garden until the inevitable swimming party had run up, chilled and exalted, from the black beach, until the lights were extinguished in the guest-rooms overhead. When he came down the steps at last the tanned skin was drawn unusually tight on his face, and his eyes were bright and tired.

"She didn't like it," he said immediately.

"Of course she did."

"She didn't like it," he insisted. "She didn't have a good time."

He was silent, and I guessed at his unutterable depression.

"I feel far away from her," he said. "It's hard to make her understand."

"You mean about the dance?"

"The dance?" He dismissed all the dances he had given with a snap of his fingers. "Old sport, the dance is unimportant."

He wanted nothing less of Daisy than that she should go to Tom and say: "I never loved you." After she had obliterated four years with that sentence they could decide upon the more practical measures to be taken. One of them was that, after she was free, they were to go back to Louisville and be married from her house—just as if it were five years ago.

"And she doesn't understand," he said. "She used to be able to understand. We'd sit for hours——"

He broke off and began to walk up and down a desolate path of fruit rinds and discarded favors and crushed flowers.

"I wouldn't ask too much of her," I ventured. "You can't repeat the past."

"Can't repeat the past?" he cried incredulously. "Why of course you can!"

He looked around him wildly, as if the past were lurking here in the shadow of his house, just out of reach of his hand.

"I'm going to fix everything just the way it was before," he said, nodding determinedly. "She'll see."

He talked a lot about the past, and I gathered that he wanted to recover something, some idea of himself perhaps, that had gone into loving Daisy. His life had been confused and disordered since then, but if he could once return to a certain starting place and go over it all slowly, he could find out what that thing was. . . .

. . . One autumn night, five years before, they had been walking down the street when the leaves were falling, and they came to a place where there were no trees and the sidewalk was white with moonlight. They stopped here and turned toward each other. Now it was a cool night with that mysterious excitement in it which comes at the two changes of the year. The quiet lights in the houses were humming out into the darkness and there was a stir and bustle among the stars. Out of the corner of his eye Gatsby saw that the blocks of the sidewalks really formed a ladder and mounted to a secret place above the trees—he could climb to it, if he climbed alone, and once there he could suck on the pap of life, gulp down the incomparable milk of wonder.

His heart beat faster and faster as Daisy's white face came up to his own. He knew that when he kissed this girl, and forever wed his unutterable visions to her perishable breath, his mind would never romp again like the mind of God. So he waited, listening for a moment longer to the tuning-fork that had been struck upon a star. Then he kissed her. At his lips' touch she blossomed for him like a flower and the incarnation was complete.

Through all he said, even through his appalling sentimentality, I was reminded of something—an elusive rhythm, a fragment of lost words, that I had heard somewhere a long time ago. For a moment a phrase tried to take shape in my mouth and my lips parted like a dumb man's, as though there was more struggling upon them than a wisp of startled air. But they made no sound, and what I had almost remembered was uncommunicable forever.

VII

IT WAS when curiosity about Gatsby was at its highest that the lights in his house failed to go on one Saturday night—and, as obscurely as it had begun, his career as Trimalchio was over. Only gradually did I become aware that the automobiles which turned expectantly into his drive stayed for just a minute and then drove sulkily away. Wondering if he were sick I went over to find out—an unfamiliar butler with a villainous face squinted at me suspiciously from the door-

"Is Mr. Gatsby sick?"

"Nope." After a pause he added "sir" in a dilatory, grudging way.

"I hadn't seen him around, and I was rather worried. Tell him Mr. Carraway came over."

"Who?" he demanded rudely.

"Carraway."

"Carraway. All right, I'll tell him."

Abruptly he slammed the door.

My Finn informed me that Gatsby had dismissed every servant in his house a week ago and replaced them with half a dozen others, who never went into West Egg Village to be bribed by the tradesmen, but ordered moderate supplies over the telephone. The grocery boy reported that the kitchen looked like a pigsty, and the general opinion in the village was that the new people weren't servants at all.

Next day Gatsby called me on the phone.

"Going away?" I inquired.

"No, old sport."

"I hear you fired all your servants."

"I wanted somebody who wouldn't gossip. Daisy comes over quite often—in the afternoons."

So the whole caravansary had fallen in like a card house at the disapproval in her eyes.

"They're some people Wolfsheim wanted to do something for. They're all brothers and sisters. They used to run a small hotel."

"I see."

He was calling up at Daisy's request—would I come to lunch at her house tomorrow? Miss Baker would be there. Half an hour later Daisy herself telephoned and seemed relieved to find that I was coming. Something was up. And yet I couldn't believe that they would choose this occasion for a scene—especially for the rather harrowing scene that Gatsby had outlined in the garden.

The next day was broiling, almost the last, certainly the warmest, of the summer. As my train emerged from the tunnel into sunlight, only the hot whistles of the National Biscuit Company broke the simmering hush at noon. The straw seats of the car hovered on the edge of combustion; the woman next to me perspired delicately for a while into her white shirtwaist, and then, as her newspaper dampened under her fingers, lapsed despairingly into deep heat with a desolate cry. Her pocketbook slapped to the floor.

"Oh, my!" she gasped.

I picked it up with a weary bend and handed it back to her, holding it at arm's length and by the extreme tip of the corners to indicate that I had no designs upon it—but every one near by, including the woman, suspected me just the same.

"Hot!" said the conductor to familiar faces. "Some weather! . . . Hot! . . . Hot! . . . Hot! . . . Is it hot enough for you? Is it hot? Is it . . . ?"

My commutation ticket came back to me with a dark stain from his hand. That any one should care in this heat whose flushed lips he kissed, whose head made damp the pajama pocket over his heart!

. . . Through the hall of the Buchanans' house blew a faint wind, carrying the sound of the telephone bell out to Gatsby and me as we waited at the door.

"The master's body!" roared the butler into the mouthpiece. "I'm sorry, madame, but we can't furnish it—it's far too hot to touch this noon!"

What he really said was: "Yes . . . Yes . . . I'll see."

He set down the receiver and came toward us, glistening slightly, to take our stiff straw hats.

"Madame expects you in the salon!" he cried, needlessly indicating the direction. In this heat every extra gesture was an affront to the common store of life.

The room, shadowed well with awnings, was dark and cool. Daisy and Jordan lay upon an enormous couch, like silver idols weighing down their own white dresses against the singing breeze of the fans.

"We can't move," they said together.

Jordan's fingers, powdered white over their tan, rested for a moment in mine.

"And Mr. Thomas Buchanan, the athlete?" I inquired.

Simultaneously I heard his voice, gruff, muffled, husky, at the hall telephone.

Gatsby stood in the center of the crimson carpet and gazed around with fascinated eyes. Daisy watched him and laughed, her sweet, exciting laugh; a tiny gust of powder rose from her bosom into the air.

"The rumor is," whispered Jordan, "that that's Tom's girl on the telephone."

We were silent. The voice in the hall rose high with annoyance: "Very well, then, I won't sell you the car at all. . . . I'm under no obligations to you at all . . . and as for your bothering me about it at lunch time, I won't stand that at all!"

"Holding down the receiver," said Daisy cynically.

"No, he's not," I assured her. "It's a bona-fide deal. I happen to know about it."

Tom flung open the door, blocked out its space for a moment with his thick body, and hurried into the room.

"Mr. Gatsby!" He put out his broad, flat hand with well-concealed dislike. "I'm glad to see you, sir. . . . Nick. . . ."

"Make us a cold drink," cried Daisy.

As he left the room again she got up and went over

to Gatsby and pulled his face down, kissing him on the mouth.

"You know I love you," she murmured.

"You forget there's a lady present," said Jordan.

Daisy looked around doubtfully.

"You kiss Nick too."

"What a low, vulgar girl!"

"I don't care!" cried Daisy, and began to clog on the brick fireplace. Then she remembered the heat and sat down guiltily on the couch just as a freshly laundered nurse leading a little girl came into the room.

"Bles-sed pre-cious," she crooned, holding out her arms. "Come to your own mother that loves you."

The child, relinquished by the nurse, rushed across the room and rooted shyly into her mother's dress.

"The bles-sed pre-cious! Did mother get powder on your old yellowy hair? Stand up now, and say—How-de-do."

Gatsby and I in turn leaned down and took the small reluctant hand. Afterward he kept looking at the child with surprise. I don't think he had ever really believed in its existence before.

"I got dressed before luncheon," said the child, turning eagerly to Daisy.

"That's because your mother wanted to show you off." Her face bent into the single wrinkle of the small white neck. "You dream, you. You absolute little dream."

"Yes," admitted the child calmly. "Aunt Jordan's got on a white dress too."

"How do you like mother's friends?" Daisy turned her around so that she faced Gatsby. "Do you think they're pretty?"

"Where's Daddy?"

"She doesn't look like her father," explained Daisy. "She looks like me. She's got my hair and shape of the face."

Daisy sat back upon the couch. The nurse took a step forward and held out her hand.

"Come, Pammy."

"Good-by, sweetheart!"

With a reluctant backward glance the well-disciplined child held to her nurse's hand and was pulled out the door, just as Tom came back, preceding four gin rickeys that clicked full of ice.

Gatsby took up his drink.

"They certainly look cool," he said, with visible tension.

We drank in long, greedy swallows.

"I read somewhere that the sun's getting hotter every year," said Tom genially. "It seems that pretty soon the earth's going to fall into the sun—or wait a minute—it's just the opposite—the sun's getting colder every year."

"Come outside," he suggested to Gatsby, "I'd like you to have a look at the place."

I went with them out to the veranda. On the green Sound, stagnant in the heat, one small sail crawled slowly toward the fresher sea. Gatsby's eyes followed it momentarily; he raised his hand and pointed across the bay.

"I'm right across from you."

"So you are."

Our eyes lifted over the rose-beds and the hot lawn and the weedy refuse of the dog-days alongshore. Slowly the white wings of the boat moved against the blue cool limit of the sky. Ahead lay the scalloped ocean and the abounding blessed isles.

"There's sport for you," said Tom, nodding. "I'd like to be out there with him for about an hour."

We had luncheon in the dining-room, darkened too against the heat, and drank down nervous gayety with the cold ale.

"What'll we do with ourselves this afternoon?" cried Daisy, "and the day after that, and the next thirty years?"

"Don't be morbid," Jordan said. "Life starts all over again when it gets crisp in the fall."

"But it's so hot," insisted Daisy, on the verge of tears, "and everything's so confused. Let's all go to town!"

Her voice struggled on through the heat, beating against it, molding its senselessness into forms.

"I've heard of making a garage out of a stable," Tom was saying to Gatsby, "but I'm the first man who ever made a stable out of a garage."

"Who wants to go to town?" demanded Daisy insistently. Gatsby's eyes floated toward her. "Ah," she cried, "you look so cool."

Their eyes met, and they stared together at each other, alone in space. With an effort she glanced down at the table.

"You always look so cool," she repeated.

She had told him that she loved him, and Tom Buchanan saw. He was astounded. His mouth opened a little, and he looked at Gatsby, and then back at Daisy as if he had just recognized her as some one he knew a long time ago.

"You resemble the advertisement of the man," she went on innocently. "You know the advertisement of the man——"

"All right," broke in Tom quickly, "I'm perfectly willing to go to town. Come on—we're all going to town."

He got up, his eyes still flashing between Gatsby and his wife. No one moved.

"Come on!" His temper cracked a little. "What's the matter, anyhow? If we're going to town, let's start."

His hand, trembling with his effort at self-control, bore to his lips the last of his glass of ale. Daisy's voice got us to our feet and out on to the blazing gravel drive.

"Are we just going to go?" she objected. "Like this? Aren't we going to let any one smoke a cigarette first?"

"Everybody smoked all through lunch."

"Oh, let's have fun," she begged him. "It's too hot to fuss."

He didn't answer.

"Have it your own way," she said. "Come on, Jordan."

They went upstairs to get ready while we three men stood there shuffling the hot pebbles with our feet. A silver curve of the moon hovered already in the western sky. Gatsby started to speak, changed his mind, but not before Tom wheeled and faced him expectantly.

"Have you got your stables here?" asked Gatsby with an effort.

"About a quarter of a mile down the road."

"Oh."

A pause.

"I don't see the idea of going to town," broke out Tom savagely. "Women get these notions in their heads——"

"Shall we take anything to drink?" called Daisy from an upper window.

"I'll get some whiskey," answered Tom. He went inside.

Gatsby turned to me rigidly:

"I can't say anything in his house, old sport."

"She's got an indiscreet voice," I remarked. "It's full of—" I hesitated.

"Her voice is full of money," he said suddenly.

That was it. I'd never understood before. It was full of money—that was the inexhaustible charm that rose and fell in it, the jingle of it, the cymbals' song of it. . . . High in a white palace the king's daughter, the golden girl. . . .

Tom came out of the house wrapping a quart bottle in a towel, followed by Daisy and Jordan wearing small tight hats of metallic cloth and carrying light capes over their arms.

"Shall we all go in my car?" suggested Gatsby. He felt the hot, green leather of the seat. "I ought to have left it in the shade."

"Is it standard shift?" demanded Tom.

"Yes."

"Well, you take my coupé and let me drive your car to town."

The suggestion was distasteful to Gatsby.

"I don't think there's much gas," he objected.

"Plenty of gas," said Tom boisterously. He looked at the gauge. "And if it runs out I can stop at a drug-store. You can buy anything at a drug-store nowadays."

A pause followed this apparently pointless remark. Daisy looked at Tom frowning, and an indefinable expression, at once definitely unfamiliar and vaguely recognizable, as if I had only heard it described in words, passed over Gatsby's face.

"Come on, Daisy," said Tom, pressing her with his hand toward Gatsby's car. "I'll take you in this circus wagon."

He opened the door, but she moved out from the circle of his arm.

"You take Nick and Jordan. We'll follow you in the coupé."

She walked close to Gatsby, touching his coat with her hand. Jordan and Tom and I got into the front seat of Gatsby's car, Tom pushed the unfamiliar gears tentatively, and we shot off into the oppressive heat, leaving them out of sight behind.

"Did you see that?" demanded Tom.

"See what?"

He looked at me keenly, realizing that Jordan and I must have known all along.

"You think I'm pretty dumb, don't you?" he suggested. "Perhaps I am, but I have a—almost a second sight, sometimes, that tells me what to do. Maybe you don't believe that, but science——"

He paused. The immediate contingency overtook him, pulled him back from the edge of the theoretical abyss.

"I've made a small investigation of this fellow," he continued. "I could have gone deeper if I'd known——"

"Do you mean you've been to a medium?" inquired Jordan humorously.

"What?" Confused, he stared at us as we laughed. "A medium?"

"About Gatsby."

"About Gatsby! No, I haven't. I said I'd been making a small investigation of his past."

"And you found he was an Oxford man," said Jordan helpfully.

"An Oxford man!" He was incredulous. "Like hell he is! He wears a pink suit."

"Nevertheless he's an Oxford man."

"Oxford, New Mexico," snorted Tom contemptuously, "or something like that."

"Listen, Tom. If you're such a snob, why did you invite him to lunch?" demanded Jordan crossly.

"Daisy invited him; she knew him before we were married—God knows where!"

We were all irritable now with the fading ale, and

aware of it we drove for a while in silence. Then as Doctor T. J. Eckleburg's faded eyes came into sight down the road, I remembered Gatsby's caution about gasoline.

"We've got enough to get us to town," said Tom.

"But there's a garage right here," objected Jordan. "I don't want to get stalled in this baking heat."

Tom threw on both brakes impatiently, and we slid to an abrupt dusty spot under Wilson's sign. After a moment the proprietor emerged from the interior of his establishment and gazed hollow-eyed at the car.

"Let's have some gas!" cried Tom roughly. "What do you think we stopped for—to admire the view?"

"I'm sick," said Wilson without moving. "Been sick all day."

"What's the matter?"

"I'm all run down."

"Well, shall I help myself?" Tom demanded. "You sounded well enough on the phone."

With an effort Wilson left the shade and support of the doorway and, breathing hard, unscrewed the cap of the tank. In the sunlight his face was green.

"I didn't mean to interrupt your lunch," he said. "But I need money pretty bad, and I was wondering what you were going to do with your old car."

"How do you like this one?" inquired Tom. "I bought it last week."

"It's a nice yellow one," said Wilson, as he strained at the handle.

"Like to buy it?"

"Big chance," Wilson smiled faintly. "No, but I could make some money on the other."

"What do you want money for, all of a sudden?"

"I've been here too long. I want to get away. My wife and I want to go West."

"Your wife does," exclaimed Tom, startled.

"She's been talking about it for ten years." He rested for a moment against the pump, shading his eyes. "And now she's going whether she wants to or not. I'm going to get her away."

The coupé flashed by us with a flurry of dust and the flash of a waving hand.

"What do I owe you?" demanded Tom harshly.

"I just got wised up to something funny the last two days," remarked Wilson. "That's why I want to get away. That's why I been bothering you about the car."

"What do I owe you?"

"Dollar twenty."

The relentless beating heat was beginning to confuse me and I had a bad moment there before I realized that so far his suspicions hadn't alighted on Tom. He had discovered that Myrtle had some sort of life apart from him in another world, and the shock had made him physically sick. I stared at him and then at Tom, who had made a parallel discovery less than an hour before—and it occurred to me that there was no difference between men, in intelligence or race, so profound as the difference between the sick and the well. Wilson was so sick that he looked guilty, unforgivably guilty—as if he had just got some poor girl with child.

"I'll let you have that car," said Tom. "I'll send it over tomorrow afternoon."

That locality was always vaguely disquieting, even in the broad glare of afternoon, and now I turned my head as though I had been warned of something behind. Over the ashheaps the giant eyes of Doctor T. J. Eckleburg kept their vigil, but I perceived, after a moment, that the other eyes were regarding us less than twenty feet away.

In one of the windows over the garage the curtains had been moved aside a little, and Myrtle Wilson was peering down at the car. So engrossed was she that she had no consciousness of being observed, and one emotion after another crept into her face like objects into a slowly developing picture. Her expression was curiously familiar—it was an expression I had often seen on women's faces, but on Myrtle Wilson's face it seemed purposeless and inexplicable until I realized that her eyes, wide with jealous terror, were fixed not on Tom, but on Jordan Baker, whom she took to be his wife.

There is no confusion like the confusion of a simple mind, and as we drove away Tom was feeling the hot whips of panic. His wife and his mistress, until an hour ago secure and inviolate, were slipping precipitately from his control. Instinct made him step on the accelerator with the double purpose of overtaking Daisy and leaving Wilson behind, and we sped along toward Astoria at fifty miles an hour, until, among the spidery girders of the elevated, we came in sight of the easygoing blue coupé.

"Those big movies around Fiftieth Street are cool," suggested Jordan. "I love New York on summer afternoons when everyone's away. There's something very sensuous about it—overripe, as if all sorts of funny fruits were going to fall into your hands."

The word "sensuous" had the effect of further disquieting Tom, but before he could invent a protest the coupé came to a stop, and Daisy signaled us to draw up alongside.

"Where are we going?" she cried.

"How about the movies?"

"It's so hot," she complained. "You go. We'll ride

around and meet you after." With an effort her wit rose faintly, "We'll meet you on some corner. I'll be the man smoking two cigarettes."

"We can't argue about it here," Tom said impatiently, as a truck gave out a cursing whistle behind us. "You follow me to the south side of Central Park, in front of the Plaza."

Several times he turned his head and looked back for their car, and if the traffic delayed them he slowed up until they came into sight. I think he was afraid they would dart down a side street and out of his life forever.

But they didn't. And we all took the less explicable step of engaging the parlor of a suite in the Plaza Hotel.

The prolonged and tumultuous argument that ended by herding us into that room eludes me, though I have a sharp physical memory that, in the course of it, my underwear kept climbing like a damp snake around my legs and intermittent beads of sweat raced cool across my back. The notion originated with Daisy's suggestion that we hire five bathrooms and take cold baths, and then assumed more tangible form as "a place to have a mint julep." Each of us said over and over that it was a "crazy idea"—we all talked at once to a baffled clerk and thought, or pretended to think, that we were being very funny . . .

The room was large and stifling, and, though it was already four o'clock, opening the windows admitted only a gust of hot shrubbery from the Park. Daisy went to the mirror and stood with her back to us, fixing her hair.

"It's a swell suite," whispered Jordan respectfully, and every one laughed.

"Open another window," commanded Daisy, without turning around.

"There aren't any more."

"Well, we'd better telephone for an axe——"

"The thing to do is to forget about the heat," said Tom impatiently. "You make it ten times worse by crabbing about it."

He unrolled the bottle of whiskey from the towel and put it on the table.

"Why not let her alone, old sport?" remarked Gatsby. "You're the one that wanted to come to town."

There was a moment of silence. The telephone book slipped from its nail and splashed to the floor, whereupon Jordan whispered, "Excuse me"—but this time no one laughed.

"I'll pick it up," I offered.

"I've got it." Gatsby examined the parted string, muttered "Hum!" in an interested way, and tossed the book on a chair.

"That's a great expression of yours, isn't it?" said Tom sharply.

"What is?"

"All this 'old sport' business. Where'd you pick that up?"

"Now see here, Tom," said Daisy, turning around from the mirror, "if you're going to make personal remarks I won't stay here a minute. Call up and order some ice for the mint julep."

As Tom took up the receiver the compressed heat exploded into sound and we were listening to the portentous chords of Mendelssohn's *Wedding March* from the ballroom below.

"Imagine marrying anybody in this heat!" cried Jordan dismally.

"Still—I was married in the middle of June," Daisy remembered, "Louisville in June! Somebody fainted. Who was it fainted, Tom?"

"Biloxi," he answered shortly.

"A man named Biloxi. 'Blocks' Biloxi, and he made boxes—that's a fact—and he was from Biloxi, Tennessee."

"They carried him into my house," appended Jordan, "because we lived just two doors from the church. And he stayed three weeks, until Daddy told him he had to get out. The day after he left Daddy died." After a moment she added. "There wasn't any connection."

"I used to know a Bill Biloxi from Memphis," I remarked.

"That was his cousin. I knew his whole family history before he left. He gave me an aluminum putter that I use today."

The music had died down as the ceremony began and now a long cheer floated in at the window, followed by intermittent cries of "Yea—ea—ea!" and finally by a burst of jazz as the dancing began.

"We're getting old," said Daisy. "If we were young we'd rise and dance."

"Remember Biloxi," Jordan warned her. "Where'd you know him, Tom?"

"Biloxi?" He concentrated with an effort. "I didn't know him. He was a friend of Daisy's."

"He was not," she denied. "I'd never seen him before. He came down in the private car."

"Well, he said he knew you. He said he was raised in Louisville. Asa Bird brought him around at the last minute and asked if we had room for him."

Jordan smiled.

"He was probably bumming his way home. He told me he was president of your class at Yale."

Tom and I looked at each other blankly.

"Bil*oxi*?"

"First place, we didn't have any president——"

Gatsby's foot beat a short, restless tattoo and Tom eyed him suddenly.

"By the way, Mr. Gatsby, I understand you're an Oxford man."

"Not exactly."

"Oh, yes, I understand you went to Oxford."

"Yes—I went there."

A pause. Then Tom's voice incredulous and insulting: "You must have gone there about the time Biloxi went to New Haven."

Another pause. A waiter knocked and came in with crushed mint and ice, but the silence was unbroken by his "thank you" and the soft closing of the door. This tremendous detail was to be cleared up at last.

"I told you I went there," said Gatsby.

"I heard you, but I'd like to know when."

"It was in nineteen-nineteen. I only stayed five months. That's why I can't really call myself an Oxford man."

Tom glanced around to see if we mirrored his unbelief. But we were all looking at Gatsby.

"It was an opportunity they gave to some of the officers after the Armistice," he continued. "We could go to any of the universities in England or France."

I wanted to get up and slap him on the back. I had one of those renewals of complete faith in him that I'd experienced before.

Daisy rose, smiling faintly, and went to the table.

"Open the whiskey, Tom," she ordered, "and I'll make you a mint julep. Then you won't seem so stupid to yourself. . . . Look at the mint!"

"Wait a minute," snapped Tom, "I want to ask Mr. Gatsby one more question."

"Go on," Gatsby said politely.

"What kind of a row are you trying to cause in my house anyhow?"

They were out in the open at last and Gatsby was content.

"He isn't causing a row," Daisy looked desperately from one to the other. "You're causing a row. Please have a little self-control."

"Self-control!" repeated Tom incredulously. "I suppose the latest thing is to sit back and let Mr. Nobody from Nowhere make love to your wife. Well, if that's the idea you can count me out. . . . Nowadays people begin by sneering at family life and family institutions, and next they'll throw everything overboard and have intermarriage between black and white."

Flushed with his impassioned gibberish, he saw himself standing alone on the last barrier of civilization.

"We're all white here," murmured Jordan.

"I know I'm not very popular. I don't give big parties. I suppose you've got to make your house into a pigsty in order to have any friends—in the modern world."

Angry as I was, as we all were, I was tempted to laugh whenever he opened his mouth. The transition from libertine to prig was so complete.

"I've got something to tell *you*, old sport—" began Gatsby. But Daisy guessed at his intention.

"Please don't!" she interrupted helplessly. "Please let's all go home. Why don't we all go home?"

"That's a good idea." I got up. "Come on, Tom. Nobody wants a drink."

"I want to know what Mr. Gatsby has to tell me."

"Your wife doesn't love you," said Gatsby. "She's never loved you. She loves me."

"You must be crazy!" exclaimed Tom automatically.

Gatsby sprang to his feet, vivid with excitement.

"She never loved you, do you hear?" he cried. "She only married you because I was poor and she was tired of waiting for me. It was a terrible mistake, but in her heart she never loved any one except me!"

At this point Jordan and I tried to go, but Tom and Gatsby insisted with competitive firmness that we remain—as though neither of them had anything to conceal and it would be a privilege to partake vicariously of their emotions.

"Sit down, Daisy," Tom's voice groped unsuccessfully for the paternal note. "What's been going on? I want to hear all about it."

"I told you what's been going on," said Gatsby. "Going on for five years—and you didn't know."

Tom turned to Daisy sharply.

"You've been seeing this fellow for five years?"

"Not seeing," said Gatsby. "No, we couldn't meet. But both of us loved each other all that time, old sport, and you didn't know. I used to laugh sometimes"—but there was no laughter in his eyes—"to think that you didn't know."

"Oh—that's all." Tom tapped his thick fingers together like a clergyman and leaned back in his chair.

"You're crazy!" he exploded. "I can't speak about what happened five years ago because I didn't know Daisy then—and I'll be damned if I see how you got within a mile of her unless you brought the groceries to the back door. But all the rest of that's a God damned lie. Daisy loved me when she married me and she loves me now."

"No," said Gatsby, shaking his head.

"She does, though. The trouble is that sometimes she gets foolish ideas in her head and doesn't know what she's doing." He nodded sagely. "And what's more I love

Daisy too. Once in a while I go off on a spree and make a fool of myself, but I always come back, and in my heart I love her all the time."

"You're revolting," said Daisy. She turned to me, and her voice, dropping an octave lower, filled the room with thrilling scorn: "Do you know why we left Chicago? I'm surprised that they didn't treat you to the story of that little spree."

Gatsby walked over and stood beside her.

"Daisy, that's all over now," he said earnestly. "It doesn't matter any more. Just tell him the truth—that you never loved him—and it's all wiped out forever."

She looked at him blindly. "Why—how could I love him—possibly?"

"You never loved him."

She hesitated. Her eyes fell on Jordan and me with a sort of appeal, as though she realized at last what she was doing—and as though she had never, all along, intended doing anything at all. But it was done now. It was too late.

"I never loved him," she said, with perceptible reluctance.

"Not at Kapiolani?" demanded Tom suddenly.

"No."

From the ballroom beneath, muffled and suffocating chords were drifting up on hot waves of air.

"Not that day I carried you down from the Punch Bowl to keep your shoes dry?" There was a husky tenderness in his tone. . . . "Daisy?"

"Please don't." Her voice was cold, but the rancor was gone from it. She looked at Gatsby. "There, Jay," she said—but her hand as she tried to light a cigarette was trembling. Suddenly she threw the cigarette and the burning match on the carpet.

"Oh, you want too much!" she cried to Gatsby. "I

love you now—isn't that enough? I can't help what's past." She began to sob helplessly. "I did love him once —but I loved you too."

Gatsby's eyes opened and closed.

"You loved me *too?*" he repeated.

"Even that's a lie," said Tom savagely. "She didn't know you were alive. Why—there're things between Daisy and me that you'll never know, things that neither of us can ever forget."

The words seemed to bite physically into Gatsby.

"I want to speak to Daisy alone," he insisted. "She's all excited now——"

"Even alone I can't say I never loved Tom," she admitted in a pitiful voice. "It wouldn't be true."

"Of course it wouldn't," agreed Tom.

She turned to her husband.

"As if it mattered to you," she said.

"Of course it matters. I'm going to take better care of you from now on."

"You don't understand," said Gatsby, with a touch of panic. "You're not going to take care of her any more."

"I'm not?" Tom opened his eyes wide and laughed. He could afford to control himself now. "Why's that?"

"Daisy's leaving you."

"Nonsense."

"I am, though," she said with a visible effort.

"She's not leaving me!" Tom's words suddenly leaned down over Gatsby. "Certainly not for a common swindler who'd have to steal the ring he put on her finger."

"I won't stand this!" cried Daisy. "Oh, please, let's get out."

"Who are you, anyhow?" broke out Tom. "You're one of that bunch that hangs around with Meyer Wolfsheim —that much I happen to know. I've made a little investigation into your affairs—and I'll carry it further tomorrow."

"You can suit yourself about that, old sport," said Gatsby steadily.

"I found out what your 'drug-stores' were." He turned to us and spoke rapidly. "He and this Wolfsheim bought up a lot of side-street drug-stores here and in Chicago and sold grain alcohol over the counter. That's one of his little stunts. I picked him for a bootlegger the first time I saw him, and I wasn't far wrong."

"What about it?" said Gatsby politely. "I guess your friend Walter Chase wasn't too proud to come in on it."

"And you left him in the lurch, didn't you? You let him go to jail for a month over in New Jersey. God! You ought to hear Walter on the subject of *you*."

"He came to us dead broke. He was very glad to pick up some money, old sport."

"Don't you call me 'old sport'!" cried Tom. Gatsby said nothing. "Walter could have you up on the betting laws too, but Wolfsheim scared him into shutting his mouth."

That unfamiliar yet recognizable look was back again in Gatsby's face.

"That drug-store business was just small change," continued Tom slowly, "but you've got something on now that Walter's afraid to tell me about."

I glanced at Daisy, who was staring terrified between Gatsby and her husband, and at Jordan, who had begun to balance an invisible but absorbing object on the tip of her chin. Then I turned back to Gatsby—and was startled at his expression. He looked—and this is said in all contempt for the babbled slander of his garden—as if he had "killed a man." For a moment the set of his face could be described in just that fantastic way.

It passed, and he began to talk excitedly to Daisy,

denying everything, defending his name against accusations that had not been made. But with every word she was drawing further and further into herself, so he gave that up, and only the dead dream fought on as the afternoon slipped away, trying to touch what was no longer tangible, struggling unhappily, undespairingly, toward that lost voice across the room.

The voice begged again to go.

"*Please*, Tom! I can't stand this any more."

Her frightened eyes told that whatever intentions, whatever courage she had had, were definitely gone.

"You two start on home, Daisy," said Tom. "In Mr. Gatsby's car."

She looked at Tom, alarmed now, but he insisted with magnanimous scorn.

"Go on. He won't annoy you. I think he realizes that his presumptuous little flirtation is over."

They were gone, without a word, snapped out, made accidental, isolated, like ghosts, even from our pity.

After a moment Tom got up and began wrapping the unopened bottle of whiskey in the towel.

"Want any of this stuff? Jordan? . . . Nick?"

I didn't answer.

"Nick?" He asked again.

"What?"

"Want any?"

"No . . . I just remembered that today's my birthday."

I was thirty. Before me stretched the portentous, menacing road of a new decade.

It was seven o'clock when we got into the coupé with him and started for Long Island. Tom talked incessantly, exulting and laughing, but his voice was as remote from Jordan and me as the foreign clamor on the sidewalk or the tumult of the elevated overhead.

Human sympathy has its limits, and we were content to let all their tragic arguments fade with the city lights behind. Thirty—the promise of a decade of loneliness, a thinning list of single men to know, a thinning brief-case of enthusiasm, thinning hair. But there was Jordan beside me, who, unlike Daisy, was too wise ever to carry well-forgotten dreams from age to age. As we passed over the dark bridge her wan face fell lazily against my coat's shoulder and the formidable stroke of thirty died away with the reassuring pressure of her hand.

So we drove on toward death through the cooling twilight.

The young Greek, Michaelis, who ran the coffee joint beside the ashheaps was the principal witness at the inquest. He had slept through the heat until after five, when he strolled over to the garage, and found George Wilson sick in his office—really sick, pale as his own pale hair and shaking all over. Michaelis advised him to go to bed, but Wilson refused, saying that he'd miss a lot of business if he did. While his neighbor was trying to persuade him a violent racket broke out overhead.

"I've got my wife locked in up there," explained Wilson calmly. "She's going to stay there till the day after tomorrow, and then we're going to move away."

Michaelis was astonished; they had been neighbors for four years, and Wilson had never seemed faintly capable of such a statement. Generally he was one of these worn-out men: when he wasn't working, he sat on a chair in the doorway and stared at the people and the cars that passed along the road. When any one spoke to him he invariably laughed in an agreeable, colorless way. He was his wife's man and not his own.

So naturally Michaelis tried to find out what had happened, but Wilson wouldn't say a word—instead he began to throw curious, suspicious glances at his visitor and ask him what he'd been doing at certain times on certain days. Just as the latter was getting uneasy, some workmen came past the door bound for his restaurant, and Michaelis took the opportunity to get away, intending to come back later. But he didn't. He supposed he forgot to, that's all. When he came outside again, a little after seven, he was reminded of the conversation because he heard Mrs. Wilson's voice, loud and scolding, downstairs in the garage.

"Beat me!" he heard her cry. "Throw me down and beat me, you dirty little coward!"

A moment later she rushed out into the dusk, waving her hands and shouting—before he could move from his door the business was over.

The "death car" as the newspapers called it, didn't stop; it came out of the gathering darkness, wavered tragically for a moment, and then disappeared around the next bend. Mavromichaelis wasn't even sure of its color—he told the first policeman that it was light green. The other car, the one going toward New York, came to rest a hundred yards beyond, and its driver hurried back to where Myrtle Wilson, her life violently extinguished, knelt in the road and mingled her thick dark blood with the dust.

Michaelis and this man reached her first, but when they had torn open her shirtwaist, still damp with perspiration, they saw that her left breast was swinging loose like a flap, and there was no need to listen for the heart beneath. The mouth was wide open and ripped a little at the corners, as though she had choked a little in giving up the tremendous vitality she had stored so long.

We saw the three or four automobiles and the crowd when we were still some distance away.

"Wreck!" said Tom. "That's good. Wilson'll have a little business at last."

He slowed down, but still without any intention of stopping, until, as we came nearer, the hushed, intent faces of the people at the garage door made him automatically put on the brakes.

"We'll take a look," he said doubtfully, "just a look."

I became aware now of a hollow, wailing sound which issued incessantly from the garage, a sound which as we got out of the coupé and walked toward the door resolved itself into the words "Oh, my God!" uttered over and over in a gasping moan.

"There's some bad trouble here," said Tom excitedly.

He reached up on tiptoes and peered over a circle of heads into the garage, which was lit only by a yellow light in a swinging metal basket overhead. Then he made a harsh sound in his throat, and with a violent thrusting movement of his powerful arms pushed his way through.

The circle closed up again with a running murmur of expostulation; it was a minute before I could see anything at all. Then new arrivals deranged the line, and Jordan and I were pushed suddenly inside.

Myrtle Wilson's body, wrapped in a blanket, and then in another blanket, as though she suffered from a chill in the hot night, lay on a work-table by the wall, and Tom, with his back to us, was bending over it, motionless. Next to him stood a motorcycle policeman taking down names with much sweat and correction in a little book. At first I couldn't find the source of the high, groaning words that echoed clamorously through the bare garage—then I saw Wilson standing on the raised threshold of his office, swaying back and forth and holding to the doorposts with both hands. Some man was talking to him in a low voice and attempting, from time to time, to lay a hand on his shoulder, but Wilson neither heard nor saw. His eyes would drop slowly from the swinging light to the laden table by the wall, and then jerk back to the light again, and he gave out incessantly his high, horrible call:

"Oh, my Ga-od! Oh, my Ga-od! Oh, Ga-od! Oh, my Ga-od!"

Presently Tom lifted his head with a jerk and, after staring around the garage with glazed eyes, addressed a mumbled incoherent remark to the policeman.

"M-a-y—" the policeman was saying, "—o——"

"No, r—" corrected the man, "M-a-v-r-o——"

"Listen to me!" muttered Tom fiercely.

"r" said the policeman, "o——"

"g——"

"g—" He looked up as Tom's broad hand fell sharply on his shoulder. "What you want, fella?"

"What happened?—that's what I want to know."

"Auto hit her. Ins'antly killed."

"Instantly killed," repeated Tom, staring.

"She ran out ina road. Son-of-a-bitch didn't even stopus car."

"There was two cars," said Michaelis, "one comin', one goin', see?"

"Going where?" asked the policeman keenly.

"One goin' each way. Well, she"—his hand rose toward the blankets but stopped half way and fell to his side—"she ran out there an' the one comin' from N'York knock right into her, goin' thirty or forty miles an hour."

"What's the name of this place here?" demanded the officer.

"Hasn't got any name."

A pale well-dressed Negro stepped near.

"It was a yellow car," he said, "big yellow car. New."

"See the accident?" asked the policeman.

"No, but the car passed me down the road, going faster'n forty. Going fifty, sixty."

"Come here and let's have your name. Look out now. I want to get his name."

Some words of this conversation must have reached Wilson, swaying in the office door, for suddenly a new theme found voice among his gasping cries:

"You don't have to tell me what kind of car it was! I know what kind of car it was!"

Watching Tom, I saw the wad of muscle back of his shoulder tighten under his coat. He walked quickly over to Wilson and, standing in front of him, seized him firmly by the upper arms.

"You've got to pull yourself together," he said with soothing gruffness.

Wilson's eyes fell upon Tom; he started up on his tiptoes and then would have collapsed to his knees had not Tom held him upright.

"Listen," said Tom, shaking him a little. "I just got here a minute ago, from New York. I was bringing you that coupé we've been talking about. That yellow car I was driving this afternoon wasn't mine—do you hear? I haven't seen it all afternoon."

Only the Negro and I were near enough to hear what he said, but the policeman caught something in the tone and looked over with truculent eyes.

"What's all that?" he demanded.

"I'm a friend of his." Tom turned his head but kept his hands firm on Wilson's body. "He says he knows the car that did it. . . . It was a yellow car."

Some dim impulse moved the policeman to look suspiciously at Tom.

"And what color's your car?"

"It's a blue car, a coupé."

"We've come straight from New York," I said.

Some one who had been driving a little behind us confirmed this, and the policeman turned away.

"Now, if you'll let me have that name again correct——"

Picking up Wilson like a doll, Tom carried him into the office, set him down in a chair, and came back.

"If somebody'll come here and sit with him," he snapped authoritatively. He watched while the two men standing closest glanced at each other and went unwillingly into the room. Then Tom shut the door on them and came down the single step, his eyes avoiding the table. As he passed close to me he whispered: "Let's get out."

Self-consciously, with his authoritative arms breaking the way, we pushed through the still gathering crowd, passing a hurried doctor, case in hand, who had been sent for in wild hope half an hour ago.

Tom drove slowly until we were beyond the bend—then his foot came down hard, and the coupé raced along through the night. In a little while I heard a low husky sob, and saw that the tears were overflowing down his face.

"The God damned coward!" he whimpered. "He didn't even stop his car."

The Buchanans' house floated suddenly toward us through the dark rustling trees. Tom stopped beside the porch and looked up at the second floor, where two windows bloomed with light among the vines.

"Daisy's home," he said. As we got out of the car he glanced at me and frowned slightly.

"I ought to have dropped you in West Egg, Nick. There's nothing we can do tonight."

A change had come over him, and he spoke gravely, and with decision. As we walked across the moonlight gravel to the porch he disposed of the situation in a few brisk phrases.

"I'll telephone for a taxi to take you home, and while you're waiting you and Jordan better go in the kitchen and have them get you some supper—if you want any." He opened the door. "Come in."

"No, thanks. But I'd be glad if you'd order me the taxi. I'll wait outside."

Jordan put her hand on my arm.

"Won't you come in, Nick?"

"No, thanks."

I was feeling a little sick and I wanted to be alone. But Jordan lingered for a moment more.

"It's only half-past nine," she said.

I'd be damned if I'd go in; I'd had enough of all of them for one day, and suddenly that included Jordan too. She must have seen something of this in my expression, for she turned abruptly away and ran up the porch steps into the house. I sat down for a few minutes with my head in my hands, until I heard the phone taken up inside and the butler's voice calling a taxi. Then I walked slowly down the drive away from the house, intending to wait by the gate.

I hadn't gone twenty yards when I heard my name and Gatsby stepped from between two bushes into the path. I must have felt pretty weird by that time, because I could think of nothing except the luminosity of his pink suit under the moon.

"What are you doing?" I inquired.

"Just standing here, old sport."

Somehow, that seemed a despicable occupation. For all I knew he was going to rob the house in a moment; I wouldn't have been surprised to see sinister faces, the faces of "Wolfsheim's people," behind him in the dark shrubbery.

"Did you see any trouble on the road?" he asked after a minute.

"Yes."

He hesitated.

"Was she killed?"

"Yes."

"I thought so; I told Daisy I thought so. It's better that the shock should all come at once. She stood it pretty well."

He spoke as if Daisy's reaction was the only thing that mattered.

"I got to West Egg by a side road," he went on, "and left the car in my garage. I don't think anybody saw us, but of course I can't be sure."

I disliked him so much by this time that I didn't find it necessary to tell him he was wrong.

"Who was the woman?" he inquired.

"Her name was Wilson. Her husband owns the garage. How the devil did it happen?"

"Well, I tried to swing the wheel—" He broke off, and suddenly I guessed at the truth.

"Was Daisy driving?"

"Yes," he said after a moment, "but of course I'll say I was. You see, when we left New York she was very nervous and she thought it would steady her to drive—and this woman rushed out at us just as we were passing a car coming the other way. It all happened in a minute, but it seemed to me that she wanted to speak to us, thought we were somebody she knew. Well, first Daisy turned away from the woman toward the other car, and then she lost her nerve and turned back. The second my hand reached the wheel I felt the shock—it must have killed her instantly."

"It ripped her open——"

"Don't tell me, old sport." He winced. "Anyhow—Daisy stepped on it. I tried to make her stop, but she couldn't, so I pulled on the emergency brake. Then she fell over into my lap and I drove on.

"She'll be all right tomorrow," he said presently. "I'm just going to wait here and see if he tries to bother her about that unpleasantness this afternoon. She's locked herself into her room, and if he tries any brutality she's going to turn the light out and on again."

"He won't touch her," I said. "He's not thinking about her."

"I don't trust him, old sport."

"How long are you going to wait?"

"All night, if necessary. Anyhow, till they all go to bed."

A new point of view occurred to me. Suppose Tom found out that Daisy had been driving. He might think he saw a connection in it—he might think anything. I looked at the house; there were two or three bright windows downstairs and the pink glow from Daisy's room on the second floor.

"You wait here," I said. "I'll see if there's any sign of a commotion."

I walked back along the border of the lawn, traversed the gravel softly, and tiptoed up the veranda steps. The drawing-room curtains were open, and I saw that the room was empty. Crossing the porch where we had dined that June night three months before, I came to a small rectangle of light which I guessed was the pantry window. The blind was drawn, but I found a rift at the sill.

Daisy and Tom were sitting opposite each other at the kitchen table, with a plate of cold fried chicken between them, and two bottles of ale. He was talking intently across the table at her, and in his earnestness his hand had fallen upon and covered her own. Once in a while she looked up at him and nodded in agreement.

They weren't happy, and neither of them had touched the chicken or the ale—and yet they weren't unhappy either. There was an unmistakable air of natural intimacy about the picture, and anybody would have said that they were conspiring together.

As I tiptoed from the porch I heard my taxi feeling its way along the dark road toward the house. Gatsby was waiting where I had left him in the drive.

"Is it all quiet up there?" he asked anxiously.

"Yes, it's all quiet." I hesitated. "You'd better come home and get some sleep."

He shook his head.

"I want to wait here till Daisy goes to bed. Good night, old sport."

He put his hands in his coat pockets and turned back eagerly to his scrutiny of the house, as though my presence marred the sacredness of the vigil. So I walked away and left him standing there in the moonlight—watching over nothing.

VIII

I COULDN'T sleep all night; a fog-horn was groaning incessantly on the Sound, and I tossed half-sick between grotesque reality and savage, frightening dreams. Toward dawn I heard a taxi go up Gatsby's drive, and immediately I jumped out of bed and began to dress—I felt that I had something to tell him, something to warn him about, and morning would be too late.

Crossing his lawn, I saw that his front door was still open and he was leaning against a table in the hall, heavy with dejection or sleep.

"Nothing happened," he said wanly. "I waited, and about four o'clock she came to the window and stood there for a minute and then turned out the light."

His house had never seemed so enormous to me as it did that night when we hunted through the great rooms for cigarettes. We pushed aside curtains that were like pavilions, and felt over innumerable feet of dark wall for electric light switches—once I tumbled with a sort of splash upon the keys of a ghostly piano. There was an inexplicable amount of dust everywhere, and the rooms were musty, as though they hadn't been aired for many days. I found the humidor on an unfamiliar table, with two stale, dry cigarettes inside. Throwing open the French windows of the drawing-room, we sat smoking out into the darkness.

"You ought to go away," I said. "It's pretty certain they'll trace your car."

"Go away *now*, old sport?"

"Go to Atlantic City for a week, or up to Montreal."

He wouldn't consider it. He couldn't possibly leave Daisy until he knew what she was going to do. He was clutching at some last hope and I couldn't bear to shake him free.

It was this night that he told me the strange story of his youth with Dan Cody—told it to me because "Jay Gatsby" had broken up like glass against Tom's hard malice, and the long secret extravaganza was played out. I think that he would have acknowledged anything now, without reserve, but he wanted to talk about Daisy.

She was the first "nice" girl he had ever known. In various unrevealed capacities he had come in contact with such people, but always with indiscernible barbed wire between. He found her excitingly desirable. He went to her house, at first with other officers from Camp Taylor, then alone. It amazed him—he had never been in such a beautiful house before. But what gave it an air of breathless intensity was that Daisy lived there—it was as casual a thing to her as his tent out at camp was to him. There was a ripe mystery about it, a hint of bedrooms upstairs more beautiful and cool than other bedrooms, of gay and radiant activities taking place through its corridors, and of romances that were not musty and laid away already in lavender, but fresh and breathing and redolent of this year's shining motor-cars and of dances whose flowers were scarcely withered. It excited him, too, that many men had already loved Daisy—it increased her value in his eyes. He felt their presence all about the house, pervading the air with the shades and echoes of still vibrant emotions.

But he knew that he was in Daisy's house by a colossal accident. However glorious might be his future as Jay Gatsby, he was at present a penniless young man without a past, and at any moment the invisible cloak of his uniform might slip from his shoulders. So he made the most of his time. He took what he could get, ravenously and unscrupulously—eventually he took Daisy one still October night, took her because he had no real right to touch her hand.

He might have despised himself, for he had certainly taken her under false pretenses. I don't mean that he had traded on his phantom millions, but he had deliberately given Daisy a sense of security; he let her believe that he was a person from much the same strata as herself—that he was fully able to take care of her. As a matter of fact, he had no such facilities—he had no comfortable family standing behind him, and he was liable at the whim of an impersonal government to be blown anywhere about the world.

But he didn't despise himself and it didn't turn out as he had imagined. He had intended, probably, to take what he could and go—but now he found that he had committed himself to the following of a grail. He knew that Daisy was extraordinary, but he didn't realize just how extraordinary a "nice" girl could be. She vanished into her rich house, into her rich, full life, leaving Gatsby—nothing. He felt married to her, that was all.

When they met again, two days later, it was Gatsby who was breathless, who was, somehow, betrayed. Her porch was bright with the bought luxury of star-shine; the wicker of the settee squeaked fashionably as she turned toward him and he kissed her curious and lovely mouth. She had caught a cold, and it made her voice huskier and more charming than ever, and Gatsby was overwhelmingly aware of the youth and mystery that wealth imprisons and preserves, of the freshness of many clothes, and of Daisy, gleaming like silver, safe and proud above the hot struggles of the poor.

"I can't describe to you how surprised I was to find out I loved her, old sport. I even hoped for a while that she'd throw me over, but she didn't, because she was in love with me too. She thought I knew a lot because I knew different things from her . . . Well, there I was, 'way off my ambitions, getting deeper in love every minute, and all of a sudden I didn't care. What was the use of doing great things if I could have a better time telling her what I was going to do?"

On the last afternoon before he went abroad, he sat with Daisy in his arms for a long, silent time. It was a cold fall day, with fire in the room and her cheeks flushed. Now and then she moved and he changed his arm a little, and once he kissed her dark shining hair. The afternoon had made them tranquil for a while, as if to give them a deep memory for the long parting the next day promised. They had never been closer in their month of love, nor communicated more profoundly one with another, than when she brushed silent lips against his coat's shoulder or when he touched the end of her fingers, gently, as though she were asleep.

He did extraordinarily well in the war. He was a captain before he went to the front, and following the Argonne battles he got his majority and the command of the divisional machine-guns. After the Armistice he tried frantically to get home, but some complication or misunderstanding sent him to Oxford instead. He was worried now—there was a quality of nervous despair in Daisy's letters. She didn't see why he couldn't come. She was feeling the pressure of the world outside, and she wanted to see him and feel his presence beside her and be reassured that she was doing the right thing after all.

For Daisy was young and her artificial world was redolent of orchids and pleasant, cheerful snobbery and orchestras which set the rhythm of the year, summing up the sadness and suggestiveness of life in new tunes. All night the saxophones wailed the hopeless comment of the *Beale Street Blues* while a hundred pairs of golden and silver slippers shuffled the shining dust. At the gray tea hour there were always rooms that throbbed incessantly with this low, sweet fever, while fresh faces drifted here and there like rose petals blown by the sad horns around the floor.

Through this twilight universe Daisy began to move again with the season; suddenly she was again keeping half a dozen dates a day with half a dozen men, and drowsing asleep at dawn with the beads and chiffon of an evening dress tangled among dying orchids on the floor beside her bed. And all the time something within her was crying for a decision. She wanted her life shaped now, immediately—and the decision must be made by some force—of love, of money, of unquestionable practicality—that was close at hand.

That force took shape in the middle of spring with the arrival of Tom Buchanan. There was a wholesome bulkiness about his person and his position, and Daisy was flattered. Doubtless there was a certain struggle and a certain relief. The letter reached Gatsby while he was still at Oxford.

It was dawn now on Long Island and we went about opening the rest of the windows downstairs, filling the house with gray-turning, gold-turning light. The shadow of a tree fell abruptly across the dew and ghostly birds began to sing among the blue leaves. There was a slow, pleasant movement in the air, scarcely a wind, promising a cool, lovely day.

"I don't think she ever loved him," Gatsby turned around from a window and looked at me challengingly. "You must remember, old sport, she was very excited this afternoon. He told her those things in a way that frightened her—that made it look as if I was some kind of cheap sharper. And the result was she hardly knew what she was saying."

He sat down gloomily.

"Of course she might have loved him just for a minute, when they were first married—and loved me more even then, do you see?"

Suddenly he came out with a curious remark.

"In any case," he said, "it was just personal."

What could you make of that, except to suspect some intensity in his conception of the affair that couldn't be measured?

He came back from France when Tom and Daisy were still on their wedding trip, and made a miserable but irresistible journey to Louisville on the last of his army pay. He stayed there a week, walking the streets where their footsteps had clicked together through the November night and revisiting the out-of-the-way places to which they had driven in her white car. Just as Daisy's house had always seemed to him more mysterious and gay than other houses, so his idea of the city itself, even though she was gone from it, was pervaded with a melancholy beauty.

He left, feeling that if he had searched harder, he might have found her—that he was leaving her behind. The day-coach—he was penniless now—was hot. He went out to the open vestibule and sat down on a folding-chair, and the station slid away and the backs of unfamiliar buildings moved by. Then out into the spring fields, where a yellow trolley raced them for a minute with people in it who might once have seen the pale magic of her face along the casual street.

The track curved and now it was going away from the sun, which, as it sank lower, seemed to spread itself in benediction over the vanishing city where she had drawn her breath. He stretched out his hand desperately as if to snatch only a wisp of air, to save a fragment of the spot that she had made lovely for him. But it was all going by too fast now for his blurred eyes and he knew that he had lost that part of it, the freshest and the best, forever.

It was nine o'clock when we finished breakfast and went out on the porch. The night had made a sharp difference in the weather and there was an autumn flavor in the air. The gardener, the last one of Gatsby's former servants, came to the foot of the steps.

"I'm going to drain the pool today, Mr. Gatsby. Leaves'll start falling pretty soon, and then there's always trouble with the pipes."

"Don't do it today," Gatsby answered. He turned to me apologetically. "You know, old sport, I've never used that pool all summer?"

I looked at my watch and stood up.

"Twelve minutes to my train."

I didn't want to go to the city. I wasn't worth a decent stroke of work, but it was more than that—I didn't want to leave Gatsby. I missed that train, and then another, before I could get myself away.

"I'll call you up," I said finally.

"Do, old sport."

"I'll call you about noon."

We walked slowly down the steps.

"I suppose Daisy'll call too." He looked at me anxiously, as if he hoped I'd corroborate this.

"I suppose so."

"Well, good-by."

We shook hands and I started away. Just before I reached the hedge I remembered something and turned around.

"They're a rotten crowd," I shouted across the lawn. "You're worth the whole damn bunch put together."

I've always been glad I said that. It was the only compliment I ever gave him, because I disapproved of him from beginning to end. First he nodded politely, and then his face broke into that radiant and understanding smile, as if we'd been in ecstatic cahoots on that fact all the time. His gorgeous pink rag of a suit made a bright spot of color against the white steps, and

I thought of the night when I first came to his ancestral home, three months before. The lawn and drive had been crowded with the faces of those who guessed at his corruption—and he had stood on those steps, concealing his incorruptible dream, as he waved them good-by.

I thanked him for his hospitality. We were always thanking him for that—I and the others.

"Good-by," I called. "I enjoyed breakfast, Gatsby."

Up in the city, I tried for a while to list the quotations on an interminable amount of stock, then I fell asleep in my swivel-chair. Just before noon the phone woke me, and I started up with sweat breaking out on my forehead. It was Jordan Baker; she often called me up at this hour because the uncertainty of her own movements between hotels and clubs and private houses made her hard to find in any other way. Usually her voice came over the wire as something fresh and cool, as if a divot from a green golf-links had come sailing in at the office window, but this morning it seemed harsh and dry.

"I've left Daisy's house," she said. "I'm at Hempstead, and I'm going down to Southampton this afternoon."

Probably it had been tactful to leave Daisy's house, but the act annoyed me, and her next remark made me rigid.

"You weren't so nice to me last night."

"How could it have mattered then?"

Silence for a moment. Then:

"However—I want to see you."

"I want to see you, too."

"Suppose I don't go to Southampton, and come into town this afternoon?"

"No—I don't think this afternoon."

"Very well."

"It's impossible this afternoon. Various——"

We talked like that for a while, and then abruptly we weren't talking any longer. I don't know which of us hung up with a sharp click, but I know I didn't care. I couldn't have talked to her across a tea-table that day if I never talked to her again in this world.

I called Gatsby's house a few minutes later, but the line was busy. I tried four times; finally an exasperated central told me the wire was being kept open for long distance from Detroit. Taking out my timetable, I drew a small circle around the three-fifty train. Then I leaned back in my chair and tried to think. It was just noon.

When I passed the ashheaps on the train that morning I had crossed deliberately to the other side of the car. I supposed there'd be a curious crowd around there all day with little boys searching for dark spots in the dust, and some garrulous man telling over and over what had happened, until it became less and less real even to him and he could tell it no longer, and Myrtle Wilson's tragic achievement was forgotten. Now I want to go back a little and tell what happened at the garage after we left there the night before.

They had difficulty in locating the sister, Catherine. She must have broken her rule against drinking that night, for when she arrived she was stupid with liquor and unable to understand that the ambulance had already gone to Flushing. When they convinced her of this, she immediately fainted, as if that was the intolerable part of the affair. Some one, kind or curious, took her in his car and drove her in the wake of her sister's body.

Until long after midnight a changing crowd lapped

up against the front of the garage, while George Wilson rocked himself back and forth on the couch inside. For a while the door of the office was open, and every one who came into the garage glanced irresistibly through it. Finally some one said it was a shame, and closed the door. Michaelis and several other men were with him; first, four or five men, later two or three men. Still later Michaelis had to ask the last stranger to wait there fifteen minutes longer, while he went back to his own place and made a pot of coffee. After that, he stayed there alone with Wilson until dawn.

About three o'clock the quality of Wilson's incoherent muttering changed—he grew quieter and began to talk about the yellow car. He announced that he had a way of finding out whom the yellow car belonged to, and then he blurted out that a couple of months ago his wife had come from the city with her face bruised and her nose swollen.

But when he heard himself say this, he flinched and began to cry "Oh, my God!" again in his groaning voice. Michaelis made a clumsy attempt to distract him.

"How long have you been married, George? Come on there, try and sit still a minute and answer my question. How long have you been married?"

"Twelve years."

"Ever had any children? Come on, George, sit still—I asked you a question. Did you ever have any children?"

The hard brown beetles kept thudding against the dull light, and whenever Michaelis heard a car go tearing along the road outside it sounded to him like the car that hadn't stopped a few hours before. He didn't like to go into the garage, because the work bench was stained where the body had been lying, so he moved uncomfortably around the office—he knew every object in it before morning—and from time to time sat down beside Wilson trying to keep him more quiet.

"Have you got a church you go to sometimes, George? Maybe even if you haven't been there for a long time? Maybe I could call up the church and get a priest to come over and he could talk to you, see?"

"Don't belong to any."

"You ought to have a church, George, for times like this. You must have gone to church once. Didn't you get married in a church? Listen, George, listen to me. Didn't you get married in a church?"

"That was a long time ago."

The effort of answering broke the rhythm of his rocking—for a moment he was silent. Then the same half-knowing, half-bewildered look came back into his faded eyes.

"Look in the drawer there," he said, pointing at the desk.

"Which drawer?"

"That drawer—that one."

Michaelis opened the drawer nearest his hand. There was nothing in it but a small, expensive dog-leash, made of leather and braided silver. It was apparently new.

"This?" he inquired, holding it up.

Wilson stared and nodded.

"I found it yesterday afternoon. She tried to tell me about it, but I knew it was something funny."

"You mean your wife bought it?"

"She had it wrapped in tissue paper on her bureau."

Michaelis didn't see anything odd in that, and he gave Wilson a dozen reasons why his wife might have bought the dog-leash. But conceivably Wilson had heard some of these same explanations before, from Myrtle, because he began saying "Oh, my God!" again in a whisper—his comforter left several explanations in the air.

"Then he killed her," said Wilson. His mouth dropped open suddenly.

"Who did?"

"I have a way of finding out."

"You're morbid, George," said his friend. "This has been a strain to you and you don't know what you're saying. You'd better try and sit quiet till morning."

"He murdered her."

"It was an accident, George."

Wilson shook his head. His eyes narrowed and his mouth widened slightly with the ghost of a superior "Hm!"

"I know," he said definitely, "I'm one of these trusting fellas and I don't think any harm to *no*body, but when I get to know a thing I know it. It was the man in that car. She ran out to speak to him and he wouldn't stop."

Michaelis had seen this too, but it hadn't occurred to him that there was any special significance in it. He believed that Mrs. Wilson had been running away from her husband, rather than trying to stop any particular car.

"How could she of been like that?"

"She's a deep one," said Wilson, as if that answered the question. "Ah-h-h——"

He began to rock again, and Michaelis stood twisting the leash in his hand.

"Maybe you got some friend that I could telephone for, George?"

This was a forlorn hope—he was almost sure that Wilson had no friend: there was not enough of him for his wife. He was glad a little later when he noticed a change in the room, a blue quickening by the window, and realized that dawn wasn't far off. About five o'clock it was blue enough outside to snap off the light.

Wilson's glazed eyes turned out to the ashheaps, where small gray clouds took on fantastic shapes and scurried here and there in the faint dawn wind.

"I spoke to her," he muttered, after a long silence. "I told her she might fool me but she couldn't fool God. I took her to the window"—with an effort he got up and walked to the rear window and leaned with his face pressed against it—"and I said 'God knows what you've been doing, everything you've been doing. You may fool me, but you can't fool God!' "

Standing behind him, Michaelis saw with a shock that he was looking at the eyes of Doctor T. J. Eckleburg, which had just emerged, pale and enormous, from the dissolving night.

"God sees everything," repeated Wilson.

"That's an advertisement," Michaelis assured him. Something made him turn away from the window and look back into the room. But Wilson stood there a long time, his face close to the windowpane, nodding into the twilight.

By six o'clock Michaelis was worn out, and grateful for the sound of a car stopping outside. It was one of the watchers of the night before who had promised to come back, so he cooked breakfast for three, which he and the other man ate together. Wilson was quieter now, and Michaelis went home to sleep; when he awoke four hours later and hurried back to the garage, Wilson was gone.

His movements—he was on foot all the time—were afterward traced to Port Roosevelt and then to Gad's Hill, where he bought a sandwich that he didn't eat, and a cup of coffee. He must have been tired and walking slowly, for he didn't reach Gad's Hill until noon. Thus far there was no difficulty in accounting for his time—there were boys who had seen a man "acting sort of crazy," and motorists at whom he stared oddly from the side of the road. Then for three hours he disappeared from view. The police, on the strength of what he said to Michaelis, that he "had a way of finding out," supposed that he spent that time going from garage to garage thereabout, inquiring for a yellow car. On the other hand, no garage man who had seen him ever came forward, and perhaps he had an easier, surer way of finding out what he wanted to know. By half-past two he was in West Egg, where he asked some one the way to Gatsby's house. So by that time he knew Gatsby's name.

At two o'clock Gatsby put on his bathing suit and left word with the butler that if any one phoned word was to be brought to him at the pool. He stopped at the garage for a pneumatic mattress that had amused his guests during the summer, and the chauffeur helped him pump it up. Then he gave instructions that the open car wasn't to be taken out under any circumstances—and this was strange, because the front right fender needed repair.

Gatsby shouldered the mattress and started for the pool. Once he stopped and shifted it a little, and the chauffeur asked him if he needed help, but he shook his head and in a moment disappeared among the yellowing trees.

No telephone message arrived, but the butler went without his sleep and waited for it until four o'clock—until long after there was any one to give it to if it came. I have an idea that Gatsby himself didn't believe it would come, and perhaps he no longer cared. If that was true he must have felt that he had lost the old warm world, paid a high price for living too long with a single dream. He must have looked up at an unfamiliar sky through frightening leaves and shivered as he found what a grotesque thing a rose is and how raw the sunlight was upon the scarcely created grass. A new world, material without being real, where poor ghosts, breathing dreams like air, drifted fortuitously about . . . like that ashen, fantastic figure gliding toward him through the amorphous trees.

The chauffeur—he was one of Wolfsheim's proteges—heard the shots—afterward he could only say that he hadn't thought anything much about them. I drove from the station directly to Gatsby's house and my rushing anxiously up the front steps was the first thing that alarmed any one. But they knew then, I firmly believe. With scarcely a word said, four of us, the chauffeur, butler, gardener, and I, hurried down to the pool.

There was a faint, barely perceptible movement of the water as the fresh flow from one end urged its way toward the drain at the other. With little ripples that were hardly the shadows of waves, the laden mattress moved irregularly down the pool. A small gust of wind that scarcely corrugated the surface was enough to disturb its accidental course with its accidental burden. The touch of a cluster of leaves revolved it slowly, tracing, like the leg of transit, a thin red circle in the water.

It was after we started with Gatsby toward the house that the gardener saw Wilson's body a little way off in the grass, and the holocaust was complete.

IX

AFTER two years I remember the rest of that day, and that night and the next day, only as an endless drill of police and photographers and newspaper men in and out of Gatsby's front door. A rope stretched across the main gate and a policeman by it kept out the curious, but little boys soon discovered that they could enter through my yard, and there were always a few of them clustered open-mouthed about the pool. Someone with a positive manner, perhaps a detective, used the expression "madman" as he bent over Wilson's body that afternoon, and the adventitious authority of his voice set the key for the newspaper reports next morning.

Most of those reports were a nightmare—grotesque, circumstantial, eager, and untrue. When Michaelis's testimony at the inquest brought to light Wilson's suspicions of his wife I thought the whole tale would shortly be served up in racy pasquinade—but Catherine, who might have said anything, didn't say a word. She showed a surprising amount of character about it too—looked at the coroner with determined eyes under that corrected brow of hers, and swore that her sister had never seen Gatsby, that her sister was completely happy with her husband, that her sister had been into no mischief whatever. She convinced herself of it, and cried into her handkerchief, as if the very suggestion was more than she could endure. So Wilson was reduced to a man "deranged by grief" in order that the case might remain in its simplest form. And it rested there.

But all this part of it seemed remote and unessential. I found myself on Gatsby's side, and alone. From the moment I telephoned news of the catastrophe to West Egg village, every surmise about him, and every practical question, was referred to me. At first I was surprised and confused; then, as he lay in his house and didn't move or breathe or speak, hour upon hour, it grew upon me that I was responsible, because no one else was interested—interested, I mean, with that intense personal interest to which every one has some vague right at the end.

I called up Daisy half an hour after we found him, called her instinctively and without hesitation. But she and Tom had gone away early that afternoon, and taken baggage with them.

"Left no address?"

"No."

"Say when they'd be back?"

"No."

"Any idea where they are? How I could reach them?"

"I don't know. Can't say."

I wanted to get somebody for him. I wanted to go into the room where he lay and reassure him: "I'll get somebody for you, Gatsby. Don't worry. Just trust me and I'll get somebody for you——"

Meyer Wolfsheim's name wasn't in the phone book. The butler gave me his office address on Broadway, and I called Information, but by the time I had the number it was long after five, and no one answered the phone.

"Will you ring again?"

"I've rung them three times."

"It's very important."

"Sorry. I'm afraid no one's there."

I went back to the drawing-room and thought for an instant that they were chance visitors, all these official people who suddenly filled it. But, though they drew back the sheet and looked at Gatsby with shocked eyes, his protest continued in my brain:

"Look here, old sport, you've got to get somebody for me. You've got to try hard. I can't go through this alone."

Someone started to ask me questions, but I broke away and going upstairs looked hastily through the unlocked parts of his desk—he'd never told me definitely that his parents were dead. But there was nothing—only the picture of Dan Cody, a token of forgotten violence, staring down from the wall.

Next morning I sent the butler to New York with a letter to Wolfsheim, which asked for information and urged him to come out on the next train. That request seemed superfluous when I wrote it. I was sure he'd start when he saw the newspapers, just as I was sure there'd be a wire from Daisy before noon—but neither a wire nor Mr. Wolfsheim arrived; no one arrived except more police and photographers and newspaper men. When the butler brought back Wolfsheim's answer I began to have a feeling of defiance, of scornful solidarity between Gatsby and me against them all.

Dear Mr. Carraway. This has been one of the most terrible shocks of my life to me I hardly can believe it that it is true at all. Such a mad act as that man did should make us all think. I cannot come down now as I am tied up in some very important business and cannot get mixed up in this thing now. If there is anything I can do a little later let me know in a letter by Edgar. I hardly know where I am when I hear about a thing like this and am completely knocked down and out.

Yours truly

MEYER WOLFSHEIM

and then hasty addenda beneath:

Let me know about the funeral etc do not know his family at all.

When the phone rang that afternoon and Long Distance said Chicago was calling I thought this would be Daisy at last. But the connection came through as a man's voice, very thin and far away.

"This is Slagle speaking. . . ."

"Yes?" The name was unfamiliar.

"Hell of a note, isn't it? Get my wire?"

"There haven't been any wires."

"Young Parke's in trouble," he said rapidly. "They picked him up when he handed the bonds over the counter. They got a circular from New York giving 'em the numbers just five minutes before. What d'you know about that, hey? You never can tell in these hick towns——"

"Hello!" I interrupted breathlessly. "Look here—this isn't Mr. Gatsby. Mr. Gatsby's dead."

There was a long silence on the other end of the wire, followed by an exclamation . . . then a quick squawk as the connection was broken.

I think it was on the third day that a telegram signed Henry C. Gatz arrived from a town in Minnesota. It said only that the sender was leaving immediately and to postpone the funeral until he came.

It was Gatsby's father, a solemn old man, very helpless and dismayed, bundled up in a long cheap ulster against the warm September day. His eyes leaked continuously with excitement, and when I took the bag and umbrella from his hands he began to pull so incessantly at his sparse gray beard that I had difficulty in getting off his coat. He was on the point of collapse, so I took him into the music-room and made him sit down while I sent for something to eat. But he wouldn't eat, and the glass of milk spilled from his trembling hand.

"I saw it in the Chicago newspaper," he said. "It was all in the Chicago newspaper. I started right away."

"I didn't know how to reach you."

His eyes, seeing nothing, moved ceaselessly about the room.

"It was a madman," he said. "He must have been mad."

"Wouldn't you like some coffee?" I urged him.

"I don't want anything. I'm all right now, Mr.——"

"Carraway."

"Well, I'm all right now. Where have they got Jimmy?"

I took him into the drawing-room, where his son lay, and left him there. Some little boys had come up on the steps and were looking into the hall; when I told them who had arrived, they went reluctantly away.

After a little while Mr. Gatz opened the door and came out, his mouth ajar, his face flushed slightly, his eyes leaking isolated and unpunctual tears. He had reached an age where death no longer has the quality of ghastly surprise, and when he looked around him now for the first time and saw the height and splendor of the hall and the great rooms opening out from it into other rooms, his grief began to be mixed with an awed pride. I helped him to a bedroom upstairs; while he took off his coat and vest I told him that all arrangements had been deferred until he came.

"I didn't know what you'd want, Mr. Gatsby——"

"Gatz is my name."

"—Mr. Gatz. I thought you might want to take the body West."

He shook his head.

"Jimmy always liked it better down East. He rose up to his position in the East. Were you a friend of my boy's, Mr. ——?"

"We were close friends."

"He had a big future before him, you know. He was only a young man, but he had a lot of brain power here."

He touched his head impressively, and I nodded.

"If he'd of lived, he'd of been a great man. A man

like James J. Hill. He'd of helped build up the country."

"That's true," I said, uncomfortably.

He fumbled at the embroidered coverlet, trying to take it from the bed, and lay down stiffly—was instantly asleep.

That night an obviously frightened person called up, and demanded to know who I was before he would give his name.

"This is Mr. Carraway," I said.

"Oh!" He sounded relieved. "This is Klipspringer."

I was relieved too, for that seemed to promise another friend at Gatsby's grave. I didn't want it to be in the papers and draw a sight-seeing crowd, so I'd been calling up a few people myself. They were hard to find.

"The funeral's tomorrow," I said. "Three o'clock, here at the house. I wish you'd tell anybody who'd be interested."

"Oh, I will," he broke out hastily. "Of course I'm not likely to see anybody, but if I do."

His tone made me suspicious.

"Of course you'll be there yourself."

"Well, I'll certainly try. What I called up about is——"

"Wait a minute," I interrupted. "How about saying you'll come?"

"Well, the fact is—the truth of the matter is that I'm staying with some people up here in Greenwich, and they rather expect me to be with them tomorrow. In fact, there's a sort of picnic or something. Of course I'll do my very best to get away."

I ejaculated an unrestrained "Huh!" and he must have heard me, for he went on nervously:

"What I called up about was a pair of shoes I left there. I wonder if it'd be too much trouble to have the butler send them on. You see, they're tennis shoes, and I'm sort of helpless without them. My address is care of B. F.——"

I didn't hear the rest of the name, because I hung up the receiver.

After that I felt a certain shame for Gatsby—one gentleman to whom I telephoned implied that he had got what he deserved. However, that was my fault, for he was one of those who used to sneer most bitterly at Gatsby on the courage of Gatsby's liquor, and I should have known better than to call him.

The morning of the funeral I went up to New York to see Meyer Wolfsheim; I couldn't seem to reach him any other way. The door that I pushed open, on the advice of an elevator boy, was marked "The Swastika Holding Company," and at first there didn't seem to be anyone inside. But when I'd shouted "hello" several times in vain, an argument broke out behind a partition, and presently a lovely Jewess appeared at an interior door and scrutinized me with black hostile eyes.

"Nobody's in," she said. "Mr. Wolfsheim's gone to Chicago."

The first part of this was obviously untrue, for someone had begun to whistle *The Rosary,* tunelessly, inside.

"Please say that Mr. Carraway wants to see him."

"I can't get him back from Chicago, can I?"

At this moment a voice, unmistakably Wolfsheim's, called "Stella!" from the other side of the door.

"Leave your name on the desk," she said quickly. "I'll give it to him when he gets back."

"But I know he's there."

She took a step toward me and began to slide her hands indignantly up and down her hips.

"You young men think you can force your way in

here any time," she scolded. "We're getting sickantired of it. When I say he's in Chicago, he's in Chi*cago*."

I mentioned Gatsby.

"Oh-h!" She looked at me over again. "Will you just— What was your name?"

She vanished. In a moment Meyer Wolfsheim stood solemnly in the doorway, holding out both hands. He drew me into his office, remarking in a reverent voice that it was a sad time for all of us, and offered me a cigar.

"My memory goes back to when first I met him," he said. "A young major just out of the army and covered over with medals he got in the war. He was so hard up he had to keep on wearing his uniform because he couldn't buy some regular clothes. First time I saw him was when he come into Winebrenner's poolroom at Forty-third Street and asked for a job. He hadn't eat anything for a couple of days. 'Come on have some lunch with me,' I said. He ate more than four dollars' worth of food in half an hour."

"Did you start him in business?" I inquired.

"Start him! I made him."

"Oh."

"I raised him up out of nothing, right out of the gutter. I saw right away he was a fine-appearing, gentlemanly young man, and when he told me he was an Oggsford I knew I could use him good. I got him to join up in the American Legion and he used to stand high there. Right off he did some work for a client of mine up to Albany. We were so thick like that in everything" —he held up two bulbous fingers—"always together."

I wondered if this partnership had included the World's Series transaction in 1919.

"Now he's dead," I said after a moment. "You were

his closest friend, so I know you'll want to come to his funeral this afternoon."

"I'd like to come."

"Well, come then."

The hair in his nostrils quivered slightly, and as he shook his head his eyes filled with tears.

"I can't do it—I can't get mixed up in it," he said.

"There's nothing to get mixed up in. It's all over now."

"When a man gets killed I never like to get mixed up in it in any way. I keep out. When I was a young man it was different—if a friend of mine died, no matter how, I stuck with them to the end. You may think that's sentimental, but I mean it—to the bitter end."

I saw that for some reason of his own he was determined not to come, so I stood up.

"Are you a college man?" he inquired suddenly.

For a moment I thought he was going to suggest a "gonnegtion," but he only nodded and shook my hand.

"Let us learn to show our friendship for a man when he is alive and not after he is dead," he suggested. "After that, my own rule is to let everything alone."

When I left his office the sky had turned dark and I got back to West Egg in a drizzle. After changing my clothes I went next door and found Mr. Gatz walking up and down excitedly in the hall. His pride in his son and in his son's possessions was continually increasing and now he had something to show me.

"Jimmy sent me this picture." He took out his wallet with trembling fingers. "Look there."

It was a photograph of the house, cracked in the corners and dirty with many hands. He pointed out every detail to me eagerly. "Look there!" and then sought admiration from my eyes. He had shown it so often that

I think it was more real to him now than the house itself.

"Jimmy sent it to me. I think it's a very pretty picture. It shows up well."

"Very well. Had you seen him lately?"

"He come out to see me two years ago and bought me the house I live in now. Of course we was broke up when he run off from home, but I see now there was a reason for it. He knew he had a big future in front of him. And ever since he made a success he was very generous with me."

He seemed reluctant to put away the picture, held it for another minute, lingeringly, before my eyes. Then he returned the wallet and pulled from his pocket a ragged old copy of a book called *Hopalong Cassidy*.

"Look here, this is a book he had when he was a boy. It just shows you."

He opened it at the back cover and turned it around for me to see. On the last fly-leaf was printed the word SCHEDULE, and the date September 12, 1906. And underneath:

Rise from bed	6.00	A.M.
Dumbbell exercise and wall-scaling	6.15–6.30	"
Study electricity, etc.	7.15–8.15	"
Work	8.30–4.30	P.M.
Baseball and sports	4.30–5.00	"
Practice elocution, poise and how to attain it	5.00–6.00	"
Study needed inventions	7.00–9.00	"

GENERAL RESOLVES

No wasting time at Shafters or [a name, indecipherable]
No more smokeing or chewing.
Bath every other day
Read one improving book or magazine per week
Save $5.00 [crossed out] $3.00 per week
Be better to parents

"I come across this book by accident," said the old man. "It just shows you, don't it?

"Jimmy was bound to get ahead. He always had some resolves like this or something. Do you notice what he's got about improving his mind? He was always great for that. He told me I et like a hog once, and I beat him for it."

He was reluctant to close the book, reading each item aloud and then looking eagerly at me. I think he rather expected me to copy down the list for my own use.

A little before three the Lutheran minister arrived from Flushing, and I began to look involuntarily out the windows for other cars. So did Gatsby's father. And as the time passed and the servants came in and stood waiting in the hall, his eyes began to blink anxiously, and he spoke of the rain in a worried, uncertain way. The minister glanced several times at his watch, so I took him aside and asked him to wait for half an hour. But it wasn't any use. Nobody came.

About five o'clock our procession of three cars reached the cemetery and stopped in a thick drizzle beside the gate—first a motor hearse, horribly black and wet, then Mr. Gatz and the minister and I in the limousine, and a little later four or five servants and the postman from West Egg, in Gatsby's station wagon, all wet to the skin. As we started through the gate into the cemetery I heard a car stop and then the sound of someone splashing after us over the soggy ground. I looked around. It was the man with owl-eyed glasses whom I had found marveling over Gatsby's books in the library one night three months before.

I'd never seen him since then. I don't know how he knew about the funeral, or even his name. The rain poured down his thick glasses, and he took them off and wiped them to see the protecting canvas unrolled from Gatsby's grave.

I tried to think about Gatsby then for a moment, but he was already too far away, and I could only remember, without resentment, that Daisy hadn't sent a message or a flower. Dimly I heard someone murmur "Blessed are the dead that the rain falls on," and then the owl-eyed man said "Amen to that," in a brave voice.

We straggled down quickly through the rain to the cars. Owl Eyes spoke to me by the gate.

"I couldn't get to the house," he remarked.

"Neither could anybody else."

"Go on!" He started. "Why, my God! they used to go there by the hundreds."

He took off his glasses and wiped them again, outside and in.

"The poor son-of-a-bitch," he said.

One of my most vivid memories is of coming back West from prep school and later from college at Christmas time. Those who went farther than Chicago would gather in the old dim Union Station at six o'clock of a December evening, with a few Chicago friends, already caught up into their own holiday gayeties, to bid them a hasty good-by. I remember the fur coats of the girls returning from Miss This-or-That's and the chatter of frozen breath and the hands waving overhead as we caught sight of old acquaintances, and the matchings of invitations: "Are you going to the Ordways'? the Herseys'? the Schultzes'?" and the long green tickets clasped tight in our gloved hands. And last the murky yellow cars of the Chicago, Milwaukee & St. Paul railroad looking cheerful as Christmas itself on the tracks beside the gate.

When we pulled out into the winter night and the real snow, our snow, began to stretch out beside us and twinkle against the windows, and the dim lights of small Wisconsin stations moved by, a sharp wild brace came suddenly into the air. We drew in deep breaths of it as we walked back from dinner through the cold vestibules, unutterably aware of our identity with this country for one strange hour, before we melted indistinguishably into it again.

That's my Middle West—not the wheat or the prairies or the lost Swede towns, but the thrilling returning trains of my youth, and the street lamps and sleigh bells in the frosty dark and the shadows of holly wreaths thrown by lighted windows on the snow. I am part of that, a little solemn with the feel of those long winters, a little complacent from growing up in the Carraway house in a city where dwellings are still called through decades by a family's name. I see now that this has been a story of the West, after all—Tom and Gatsby, Daisy and Jordan and I, were all Westerners, and perhaps we possessed some deficiency in common which made us subtly unadaptable to Eastern life.

Even when the East excited me most, even when I was most keenly aware of its superiority to the bored, sprawling, swollen towns beyond the Ohio, with their interminable inquisitions which spared only the children and the very old—even then it had always for me a quality of distortion. West Egg, especially, still figures in my more fantastic dreams. I see it as a night scene by El Greco: a hundred houses, at once conventional and grotesque, crouching under a sullen, overhanging sky and a lustreless moon. In the foreground four solemn men in dress suits are walking along the sidewalk with a stretcher on which lies a drunken woman in a white evening dress. Her hand, which dangles over the side, sparkles cold with jewels. Gravely the men turn in at a house—the wrong house. But no one knows the woman's name, and no one cares.

After Gatsby's death the East was haunted for me like that, distorted beyond my eyes' power of correction. So when the blue smoke of brittle leaves was in the air and the wind blew the wet laundry stiff on the line I decided to come back home.

There was one thing to be done before I left, an awkward, unpleasant thing that perhaps had better have been let alone. But I wanted to leave things in order and not just trust that obliging and indifferent sea to sweep my refuse away. I saw Jordan Baker and talked over and around what had happened to us together, and what had happened afterward to me, and she lay perfectly still, listening, in a big chair.

She was dressed to play golf, and I remember thinking she looked like a good illustration, her chin raised a little jauntily, her hair the color of an autumn leaf, her face the same brown tint as the fingerless glove on her knee. When I had finished she told me without comment that she was engaged to another man. I doubted that, though there were several she could have married at a nod of her head, but I pretended to be surprised. For just a minute I wondered if I wasn't making a mistake, then I thought it all over again quickly and got up to say good-by.

"Nevertheless you did throw me over," said Jordan suddenly. "You threw me over on the telephone. I don't give a damn about you now, but it was a new experience for me, and I felt a little dizzy for a while."

We shook hands.

"Oh, and do you remember"—she added—"a conversation we had once about driving a car?"

"Why—not exactly."

"You said a bad driver was only safe until she met another bad driver? Well, I met another bad driver, didn't I? I mean it was careless of me to make such a wrong guess. I thought you were rather an honest, straightforward person. I thought it was your secret pride."

"I'm thirty," I said. "I'm five years too old to lie to myself and call it honor."

She didn't answer. Angry, and half in love with her, and tremendously sorry, I turned away.

One afternoon late in October I saw Tom Buchanan. He was walking ahead of me along Fifth Avenue in his alert, aggressive way, his hands out a little from his body as if to fight off interference, his head moving sharply here and there, adapting itself to his restless eyes. Just as I slowed up to avoid overtaking him he stopped and began frowning into the windows of a jewelry store. Suddenly he saw me and walked back, holding out his hand.

"What's the matter, Nick? Do you object to shaking hands with me?"

"Yes. You know what I think of you."

"You're crazy, Nick," he said quickly. "Crazy as hell. I don't know what's the matter with you."

"Tom," I inquired, "what did you say to Wilson that afternoon?"

He stared at me without a word, and I knew I had guessed right about those missing hours. I started to turn away, but he took a step after me and grabbed my arm.

"I told him the truth," he said. "He came to the door while we were getting ready to leave, and when I sent down word that we weren't in he tried to force his way upstairs. He was crazy enough to kill me if I hadn't told him who owned the car. His hand was on a revolver in his pocket every minute he was in the house—" He broke off defiantly. "What if I did tell him? That fellow had it coming to him. He threw dust into your eyes just like he did in Daisy's, but he was a tough one. He ran over Myrtle like you'd run over a dog and never even stopped his car."

There was nothing I could say, except the one unutterable fact that it wasn't true.

"And if you think I didn't have my share of suffering—look here, when I went to give up that flat and saw that damn box of dog biscuits sitting there on the sideboard, I sat down and cried like a baby. By God, it was awful——"

I couldn't forgive him or like him, but I saw that what he had done was, to him, entirely justified. It was all very careless and confused. They were careless people, Tom and Daisy—they smashed up things and creatures and then retreated back into their money or their vast carelessness, or whatever it was that kept them together, and let other people clean up the mess they had made. . . .

I shook hands with him; it seemed silly not to, for I felt suddenly as though I were talking to a child. Then he went into the jewelry store to buy a pearl necklace—or perhaps only a pair of cuff buttons—rid of my provincial squeamishness forever.

Gatsby's house was still empty when I left—the grass on his lawn had grown as long as mine. One of the taxi drivers in the village never took a fare past the entrance gate without stopping for a minute and pointing inside; perhaps it was he who drove Daisy and Gatsby over to East Egg the night of the accident, and perhaps he had made a story about it all his own. I didn't want to hear it and I avoided him when I got off the train.

I spent my Saturday nights in New York, because those gleaming, dazzling parties of his were with me so vividly that I could still hear the music and the laughter, faint and incessant, from his garden, and the cars going up and down his drive. One night I did hear a material car there, and saw its lights stop at his front steps. But I didn't investigate. Probably it was some final guest who had been away at the ends of the earth and didn't know that the party was over.

On the last night, with my trunk packed and my car sold to the grocer, I went over and looked at that huge incoherent failure of a house once more. On the white steps an obscene word, scrawled by some boy with a piece of brick, stood out clearly in the moonlight, and I erased it, drawing my shoe raspingly along the stone. Then I wandered down to the beach and sprawled out on the sand.

Most of the big shore places were closed now and there were hardly any lights except the shadowy, moving glow of a ferryboat across the Sound. And as the moon rose higher the inessential houses began to melt away until gradually I became aware of the old island here that flowered once for Dutch sailors' eyes—a fresh, green breast of the new world. Its vanished trees, the trees that had made way for Gatsby's house, had once pandered in whispers to the last and greatest of all human dreams; for a transitory enchanted moment man must have held his breath in the presence of this continent, compelled into an æsthetic contemplation he neither understood nor desired, face to face for the last time in history with something commensurate to his capacity for wonder.

And as I sat there brooding on the old, unknown world, I thought of Gatsby's wonder when he first picked out the green light at the end of Daisy's dock.

He had come a long way to this blue lawn, and his dream must have seemed so close that he could hardly fail to grasp it. He did not know that it was already behind him, somewhere back in that vast obscurity beyond the city, where the dark fields of the republic rolled on under the night.

Gatsby believed in the green light, the orgiastic future that year by year recedes before us. It eluded us then, but that's no matter—tomorrow we will run faster, stretch out our arms farther. . . . And one fine morning——

So we beat on, boats against the current, borne back ceaselessly into the past.

TENDER IS THE NIGHT

BOOK ONE

I

ON the pleasant shore of the French Riviera, about half way between Marseilles and the Italian border, stands a large, proud, rose-colored hotel. Deferential palms cool its flushed façade, and before it stretches a short dazzling beach. Lately it has become a summer resort of notable and fashionable people; a decade ago it was almost deserted after its English clientele went north in April. Now, many bungalows cluster near it, but when this story begins only the cupolas of a dozen old villas rotted like water lilies among the massed pines between Gausse's Hôtel des Étrangers and Cannes, five miles away.

The hotel and its bright tan prayer rug of a beach were one. In the early morning the distant image of Cannes, the pink and cream of old fortifications, the purple Alps that bounded Italy, were cast across the water and lay quavering in the ripples and rings sent up by sea-plants through the clear shallows. Before eight a man came down to the beach in a blue bathrobe and with much preliminary application to his person of the chilly water, and much grunting and loud breathing, floundered a minute in the sea. When he had gone, beach and bay were quiet for an hour. Merchantmen crawled westward on the horizon; bus boys shouted in the hotel court; the dew dried upon the pines. In another hour the horns of motors began to blow down from the winding road along the low range of the

Maures, which separates the littoral from true Provençal France.

A mile from the sea, where pines give way to dusty poplars, is an isolated railroad stop, whence one June morning in 1925 a victoria brought a woman and her daughter down to Gausse's Hotel. The mother's face was of a fading prettiness that would soon be patted with broken veins; her expression was both tranquil and aware in a pleasant way. However, one's eyes moved on quickly to her daughter, who had magic in her pink palms and her cheeks lit to a lovely flame, like the thrilling flush of children after their cold baths in the evening. Her fine high forehead sloped gently up to where her hair, bordering it like an armorial shield, burst into lovelocks and waves and curlicues of ash blonde and gold. Her eyes were bright, big, clear, wet, and shining, the color of her cheeks was real, breaking close to the surface from the strong young pump of her heart. Her body hovered delicately on the last edge of childhood—she was almost eighteen, nearly complete, but the dew was still on her.

As sea and sky appeared below them in a thin, hot line the mother said:

"Something tells me we're not going to like this place."

"I want to go home anyhow," the girl answered.

They both spoke cheerfully but were obviously without direction and bored by the fact—moreover, just any direction would not do. They wanted high excitement, not from the necessity of stimulating jaded nerves but with the avidity of prize-winning schoolchildren who deserved their vacations.

"We'll stay three days and then go home. I'll wire right away for steamer tickets."

At the hotel the girl made the reservation in idiomatic

but rather flat French, like something remembered. When they were installed on the ground floor she walked into the glare of the French windows and out a few steps onto the stone veranda that ran the length of the hotel. When she walked she carried herself like a ballet-dancer, not slumped down on her hips but held up in the small of her back. Out there the hot light clipped close her shadow and she retreated—it was too bright to see. Fifty yards away the Mediterranean yielded up its pigments, moment by moment, to the brutal sunshine; below the balustrade a faded Buick cooked on the hotel drive.

Indeed, of all the region only the beach stirred with activity. Three British nannies sat knitting the slow pattern of Victorian England, the pattern of the forties, the sixties, and the eighties, into sweaters and socks, to the tune of gossip as formalized as incantation; closer to the sea a dozen persons kept house under striped umbrellas, while their dozen children pursued unintimidated fish through the shallows or lay naked and glistening with cocoanut oil out in the sun.

As Rosemary came onto the beach a boy of twelve ran past her and dashed into the sea with exultant cries. Feeling the impactive scrutiny of strange faces, she took off her bathrobe and followed. She floated face down for a few yards and finding it shallow staggered to her feet and plodded forward, dragging slim legs like weights against the resistance of the water. When it was about breast high, she glanced back toward shore: a bald man in a monocle and a pair of tights, his tufted chest thrown out, his brash navel sucked in, was regarding her attentively. As Rosemary returned the gaze the man dislodged the monocle, which went into hiding amid the facetious whiskers of his chest, and poured himself a glass of something from a bottle in his hand.

Rosemary laid her face on the water and swam a choppy little four-beat crawl out to the raft. The water reached up for her, pulled her down tenderly out of the heat, seeped in her hair and ran into the corners of her body. She turned round and round in it, embracing it, wallowing in it. Reaching the raft she was out of breath, but a tanned woman with very white teeth looked down at her, and Rosemary, suddenly conscious of the raw whiteness of her own body, turned on her back and drifted toward shore. The hairy man holding the bottle, spoke to her as she came out.

"I say—they have sharks out behind the raft." He was of indeterminate nationality, but spoke English with a slow Oxford drawl. "Yesterday they devoured two British sailors from the *flotte* at Golfe Juan."

"Heavens!" exclaimed Rosemary.

"They come in for the refuse from the *flotte*."

Glazing his eyes to indicate that he had only spoken in order to warn her, he minced off two steps and poured himself another drink.

Not unpleasantly self-conscious, since there had been a slight sway of attention toward her during this conversation, Rosemary looked for a place to sit. Obviously each family possessed the strip of sand immediately in front of its umbrella; besides there was much visiting and talking back and forth—the atmosphere of a community upon which it would be presumptuous to intrude. Farther up, where the beach was strewn with pebbles and dead sea-weed, sat a group with flesh as white as her own. They lay under small hand-parasols instead of beach umbrellas and were obviously less indigenous to the place. Between the dark people and the light, Rosemary found room and spread out her peignoir on the sand.

Lying so, she first heard their voices and felt their

feet skirt her body and their shapes pass between the sun and herself. The breath of an inquisitive dog blew warm and nervous on her neck; she could feel her skin broiling a little in the heat and hear the small exhausted wa-*waa* of the expiring waves. Presently her ear distinguished individual voices and she became aware that someone referred to scornfully as "that North guy" had kidnaped a waiter from a café in Cannes last night in order to saw him in two. The sponsor of the story was a white-haired woman in full evening dress, obviously a relic of the previous evening, for a tiara still clung to her head and a discouraged orchid expired from her shoulder. Rosemary, forming a vague antipathy to her and her companions, turned away.

Nearest her, on the other side, a young woman lay under a roof of umbrellas making out a list of things from a book open on the sand. Her bathing suit was pulled off her shoulders and her back, a ruddy, orange brown, set off by a string of creamy pearls, shone in the sun. Her face was hard and lovely and pitiful. Her eyes met Rosemary's but did not see her. Beyond her was a fine man in a jockey cap and red-striped tights; then the woman Rosemary had seen on the raft, and who looked back at her, seeing her; then a man with a long face and a golden, leonine head, with blue tights and no hat, talking very seriously to an unmistakably Latin young man in black tights, both of them picking at little pieces of sea-weed in the sand. She thought they were mostly Americans, but something made them unlike the Americans she had known of late.

After a while she realized that the man in the jockey cap was giving a quiet little performance for this group; he moved gravely about with a rake, ostensibly removing gravel and meanwhile developing some esoteric burlesque held in suspension by his grave face. Its faintest ramification had become hilarious, until whatever he said released a burst of laughter. Even those who, like herself, were too far away to hear, sent out antennæ of attention until the only person on the beach not caught up in it was the young woman with the string of pearls. Perhaps from modesty of possession she responded to each salvo of amusement by bending closer over her list.

The man of the monocle and bottle spoke suddenly out of the sky above Rosemary.

"You are a ripping swimmer."

She demurred.

"Jolly good. My name is Campion. Here is a lady who says she saw you in Sorrento last week and knows who you are and would so like to meet you."

Glancing around with concealed annoyance Rosemary saw the untanned people were waiting. Reluctantly she got up and went over to them.

"Mrs. Abrams—Mrs. McKisco—Mr. McKisco—Mr. Dumphry——"

"We know who you are," spoke up the woman in evening dress. "You're Rosemary Hoyt and I recognized you in Sorrento and asked the hotel clerk and we all think you're perfectly marvelous and we want to know why you're not back in America making another marvelous moving picture."

They made a superfluous gesture of moving over for her. The woman who had recognized her was not a Jewess, despite her name. She was one of those elderly "good sports" preserved by an imperviousness to experience and a good digestion into another generation.

"We wanted to warn you about getting burned the first day," she continued cheerily, "because *your* skin is important, but there seems to be so darn much formality on this beach that we didn't know whether you'd mind."

II

"WE thought maybe you were in the plot," said Mrs. McKisco. She was a shabby-eyed, pretty young woman with a disheartening intensity. "We don't know who's in the plot and who isn't. One man my husband had been particularly nice to turned out to be a chief character—practically the assistant hero."

"The plot?" inquired Rosemary, half understanding. "Is there a plot?"

"My dear, we don't *know*," said Mrs. Abrams, with a convulsive, stout woman's chuckle. "We're not in it. We're the gallery."

Mr. Dumphry, a tow-headed, effeminate young man, remarked: "Mama Abrams is a plot in herself," and Campion shook his monocle at him, saying: "Now, Royal, don't be too ghastly for words." Rosemary looked at them all uncomfortably, wishing her mother had come down here with her. She did not like these people, especially in her immediate comparison of them with those who had interested her at the other end of the beach. Her mother's modest but compact social gift got them out of unwelcome situations swiftly and firmly. But Rosemary had been a celebrity for only six months, and sometimes the French manners of her early adolescence and the democratic manners of America, these latter superimposed, made a certain confusion and let her in for just such things.

Mr. McKisco, a scrawny, freckle-and-red man of thirty, did not find the topic of the "plot" amusing. He had been staring at the sea—now after a swift glance at his wife he turned to Rosemary and demanded aggressively:

"Been here long?"

"Only a day."

"Oh."

Evidently feeling that the subject had been thoroughly changed, he looked in turn at the others.

"Going to stay all summer?" asked Mrs. McKisco, innocently. "If you do you can watch the plot unfold."

"Gor God's sake, Violet, drop the subject!" exploded her husband. "Get a new joke, for God's sake!"

Mrs. McKisco swayed toward Mrs. Abrams and breathed audibly:

"He's nervous."

"I'm not nervous," disagreed McKisco. "It just happens I'm not nervous at all."

He was burning visibly—a grayish flush had spread over his face, dissolving all his expressions into a vast ineffectuality. Suddenly remotely conscious of his condition he got up to go in the water, followed by his wife, and seizing the opportunity Rosemary followed.

Mr. McKisco drew a long breath, flung himself into the shallows and began a stiff-armed batting of the Mediterranean, obviously intended to suggest a crawl—his breath exhausted he arose and looked around with an expression of surprise that he was still in sight of shore.

"I haven't learned to breathe yet. I never quite understood how they breathed." He looked at Rosemary inquiringly.

"I think you breathe out under water," she explained. "And every fourth beat you roll your head over for air."

"The breathing's the hardest part for me. Shall we go to the raft?"

The man with the leonine head lay stretched out upon the raft, which tipped back and forth with the motion of the water. As Mrs. McKisco reached for it a sudden tilt struck her arm up roughly, whereupon the man started up and pulled her on board.

"I was afraid it hit you." His voice was slow and shy; he had one of the saddest faces Rosemary had ever seen, the high cheek-bones of an Indian, a long upper lip, and enormous deep-set dark golden eyes. He had spoken out of the side of his mouth, as if he hoped his words would reach Mrs. McKisco by a circuitous and unobtrusive route; in a minute he had shoved off into the water and his long body lay motionless toward shore.

Rosemary and Mrs. McKisco watched him. When he had exhausted his momentum he abruptly bent double, his thin thighs rose above the surface, and he disappeared totally, leaving scarcely a fleck of foam behind.

"He's a good swimmer," Rosemary said.

Mrs. McKisco's answer came with surprising violence.

"Well, he's a rotten musician." She turned to her husband, who after two unsuccessful attempts had managed to climb on the raft, and having attained his balance was trying to make some kind of compensatory flourish, achieving only an extra stagger. "I was just saying that Abe North may be a good swimmer but he's a rotten musician."

"Yes," agreed McKisco, grudgingly. Obviously he had created his wife's world, and allowed her few liberties in it.

"Antheil's my man." Mrs. McKisco turned challengingly to Rosemary, "Antheil and Joyce. I don't suppose you ever hear much about those sort of people in Hollywood, but my husband wrote the first criticism of *Ulysses* that ever appeared in America."

"I wish I had a cigarette," said McKisco calmly. "That's more important to me just now."

"He's got insides—don't you think so, Albert?"

Her voice faded off suddenly. The woman of the pearls had joined her two children in the water, and now Abe North came up under one of them like a volcanic island, raising him on his shoulders. The child yelled with fear and delight and the woman watched with a lovely peace, without a smile.

"Is that his wife?" Rosemary asked.

"No, that's Mrs. Diver. They're not at the hotel." Her eyes, photographic, did not move from the woman's face. After a moment she turned vehemently to Rosemary.

"Have you been abroad before?"

"Yes—I went to school in Paris."

"Oh! Well then you probably know that if you want to enjoy yourself here the thing is to get to know some real French families. What do these people get out of it?" She pointed her left shoulder toward shore. "They just stick around with each other in little cliques. Of course, we had letters of introduction and met all the best French artists and writers in Paris. That made it very nice."

"I should think so."

"My husband is finishing his first novel, you see."

Rosemary said: "Oh, he is?" She was not thinking anything special, except wondering whether her mother had got to sleep in this heat.

"It's on the idea of *Ulysses*," continued Mrs. McKisco. "Only instead of taking twenty-four hours my husband takes a hundred years. He takes a decayed old French aristocrat and puts him in contrast with the mechanical age——"

"Oh, for God's sake, Violet, don't go telling everybody the idea," protested McKisco. "I don't want it to get all around before the book's published."

Rosemary swam back to the shore, where she threw her peignoir over her already sore shoulders and lay down again in the sun. The man with the jockey cap was now going from umbrella to umbrella carrying a bottle and little glasses in his hands; presently he and his friends grew livelier and closer together and now they were all under a single assemblage of umbrellas—she gathered that someone was leaving and that this was a last drink on the beach. Even the children knew that excitement was generating under that umbrella and turned toward it—and it seemed to Rosemary that it all came from the man in the jockey cap.

Noon dominated sea and sky—even the white line of Cannes, five miles off, had faded to a mirage of what was fresh and cool; a robin-breasted sailing boat pulled in behind it a strand from the outer, darker sea. It seemed that there was no life anywhere in all this expanse of coast except under the filtered sunlight of those umbrellas, where something went on amid the color and the murmur.

Campion walked near her, stood a few feet away and Rosemary closed her eyes, pretending to be asleep; then she half-opened them and watched two dim, blurred pillars that were legs. The man tried to edge his way into a sand-colored cloud, but the cloud floated off into the vast hot sky. Rosemary fell really asleep.

She awoke drenched with sweat to find the beach deserted save for the man in the jockey cap, who was folding a last umbrella. As Rosemary lay blinking, he walked nearer and said:

"I was going to wake you before I left. It's not good to get too burned right away."

"Thank you." Rosemary looked down at her crimson legs. "Heavens!"

She laughed cheerfully, inviting him to talk, but Dick

Diver was already carrying a tent and a beach umbrella up to a waiting car, so she went into the water to wash off the sweat. He came back and gathering up a rake, a shovel, and a sieve, stowed them in a crevice of a rock. He glanced up and down the beach to see if he had left anything.

"Do you know what time it is?" Rosemary asked.

"It's about half-past one."

They faced the seascape together momentarily.

"It's not a bad time," said Dick Diver. "It's not one of the worst times of the day."

He looked at her and for a moment she lived in the bright blue worlds of his eyes, eagerly and confidently. Then he shouldered his last piece of junk and went up to his car, and Rosemary came out of the water, shook out her peignoir and walked up to the hotel.

III

IT was almost two when they went into the dining-room. Back and forth over the deserted tables a heavy pattern of beams and shadows swayed with the motion of the pines outside. Two waiters, piling plates and talking loud Italian, fell silent when they came in and brought them a tired version of the table d'hôte luncheon.

"I fell in love on the beach," said Rosemary.

"Who with?"

"First with a whole lot of people who looked nice. Then with one man."

"Did you talk to him?"

"Just a little. Very handsome. With reddish hair." She was eating, ravenously. "He's married though—it's usually the way."

Her mother was her best friend and had put every last possibility into the guiding of her, not so rare a thing in the theatrical profession, but rather special in that Mrs. Elsie Speers was not recompensing herself for a defeat of her own. She had no personal bitterness or resentments about life—twice satisfactorily married and twice widowed, her cheerful stoicism had each time deepened. One of her husbands had been a cavalry officer and one an army doctor, and they both left something to her that she tried to present intact to Rosemary. By not sparing Rosemary she had made her hard—by not sparing her own labor and devotion she had cultivated an idealism in Rosemary, which at present was directed toward herself and saw the world through her eyes. So that while Rosemary was a "simple" child she was protected by a double sheath of her mother's armor and her own—she had a mature distrust of the trivial, the facile and the vulgar. However, with Rosemary's sudden success in pictures Mrs. Speers felt that it was time she were spiritually weaned; it would please rather than pain her if this somewhat bouncing, breathless and exigent idealism would focus on something except herself.

"Then you like it here?" she asked.

"It might be fun if we knew those people. There were some other people, but they weren't nice. They recognized me—no matter where we go everybody's seen 'Daddy's Girl.'"

Mrs. Speers waited for the glow of egotism to subside; then she said in a matter-of-fact way: "That reminds me, when are you going to see Earl Brady?"

"I thought we might go this afternoon—if you're rested."

"You go—I'm not going."

"We'll wait till to-morrow then."

"I want you to go alone. It's only a short way—it isn't as if you didn't speak French."

"Mother—aren't there some things I don't have to do?"

"Oh, well, then go later—but some day before we leave."

"All right, Mother."

After lunch they were both overwhelmed by the sudden flatness that comes over American travelers in quiet foreign places. No stimuli worked upon them, no voices called them from without, no fragments of their own thoughts came suddenly from the minds of others, and missing the clamor of Empire they felt that life was not continuing here.

"Let's only stay three days, Mother," Rosemary said when they were back in their rooms. Outside a light wind blew the heat around, straining it through the trees and sending little hot gusts through the shutters.

"How about the man you fell in love with on the beach?"

"I don't love anybody but you, Mother, darling."

Rosemary stopped in the lobby and spoke to Gausse *père* about trains. The concierge, lounging in light-brown khaki by the desk, stared at her rigidly, then suddenly remembered the manners of his métier. She took the bus and rode with a pair of obsequious waiters to the station, embarrassed by their deferential silence, wanting to urge them: "Go on, talk, enjoy yourselves. It doesn't bother me."

The first-class compartment was stifling; the vivid advertising cards of the railroad companies—the Pont du Gard at Arles, the Amphitheatre at Orange, winter sports at Chamonix—were fresher than the long motionless sea outside. Unlike American trains that were absorbed in an intense destiny of their own, and scornful of people on another world less swift and breathless, this train was part of the country through which it passed. Its breath stirred the dust from the palm leaves, the cinders mingled with the dry dung in the gardens. Rosemary was sure she could lean from the window and pull flowers with her hand.

A dozen cabbies slept in their hacks outside the Cannes station. Over on the promenade the Casino, the smart shops, and the great hotels turned blank iron masks to the summer sea. It was unbelievable that there could ever have been a "season," and Rosemary, half in the grip of fashion, became a little self-conscious, as though she were displaying an unhealthy taste for the moribund; as though people were wondering why she was here in the lull between the gaiety of last winter and next winter, while up north the true world thundered by.

As she came out of a drug store with a bottle of coconut oil, a woman, whom she recognized as Mrs. Diver, crossed her path with arms full of sofa cushions, and went to a car parked down the street. A long, low black dog barked at her, a dozing chauffeur woke with a start. She sat in the car, her lovely face set, controlled, her eyes brave and watchful, looking straight ahead toward nothing. Her dress was bright red and her brown legs were bare. She had thick, dark, gold hair like a chow's.

With half an hour to wait for her train Rosemary sat down in the Café des Alliés on the Croisette, where the trees made a green twilight over the tables and an orchestra wooed an imaginary public of cosmopolites with the Nice Carnival Song and last year's American tune. She had bought *Le Temps* and *The Saturday Evening Post* for her mother, and as she drank her citronade she opened the latter at the memoirs of a Russian princess, finding the dim conventions of the nineties realer and nearer than the headlines of the French paper. It was the same feeling that had oppressed her at the hotel—accustomed to seeing the starkest grotesqueries of a continent heavily underlined as comedy or tragedy, untrained to the task of separating out the essential for herself, she now began to feel that French life was empty and stale. This feeling was surcharged by listening to the sad tunes of the orchestra, reminiscent of the melancholy music played for acrobats in vaudeville. She was glad to go back to Gausse's Hotel.

Her shoulders were too burned to swim with the next day, so she and her mother hired a car—after much haggling, for Rosemary had formed her valuations of money in France—and drove along the Riviera, the delta of many rivers. The chauffeur, a Russian Czar of the period of Ivan the Terrible, was a self-appointed guide, and the resplendent names—Cannes, Nice, Monte Carlo—began to glow through their torpid camouflage, whispering of old kings come here to dine or die, of rajahs tossing Buddha's eyes to English ballerinas, of Russian princes turning the weeks into Baltic twilights in the lost caviare days. Most of all, there was the scent of the Russians along the coast—their closed book shops and grocery stores. Ten years ago, when the season ended in April, the doors of the Orthodox Church were locked, and the sweet champagnes they favored were put away until their return. "We'll be back next season," they said, but this was premature, for they were never coming back any more.

It was pleasant to drive back to the hotel in the late afternoon, above a sea as mysteriously colored as the agates and cornelians of childhood, green as green milk, blue as laundry water, wine dark. It was pleasant to pass people eating outside their doors, and to hear the fierce mechanical pianos behind the vines of country estaminets. When they turned off the Corniche d'Or and down to Gausse's Hotel through the darkening banks of trees, set one behind another in many greens, the moon already hovered over the ruins of the aqueducts. . . .

Somewhere in the hills behind the hotel there was a dance, and Rosemary listened to the music through the ghostly moonshine of her mosquito net, realizing that there was gaiety too somewhere about, and she thought of the nice people on the beach. She thought she might meet them in the morning, but they obviously formed a self-sufficient little group, and once their umbrellas, bamboo rugs, dogs, and children were set out in place the part of the plage was literally fenced in. She resolved in any case not to spend her last two mornings with the other ones.

IV

THE matter was solved for her. The McKiscos were not yet there and she had scarcely spread her peignoir when two men—the man with the jockey cap and the tall blonde man, given to sawing waiters in two—left the group and came down toward her.

"Good morning," said Dick Diver. He broke down. "Look—sunburn or no sunburn, why did you stay away yesterday? We worried about you."

She sat up and her happy little laugh welcomed their intrusion.

"We wondered," Dick Diver said, "if you wouldn't come over this morning. We go in, we take food and drink, so it's a substantial invitation."

He seemed kind and charming—his voice promised that he would take care of her, and that a little later he would open up whole new worlds for her, unroll an endless succession of magnificent possibilities. He managed the introduction so that her name wasn't mentioned and then let her know easily that everyone knew who she was but were respecting the completeness of her private life—a courtesy that Rosemary had not met with save from professional people since her success.

Nicole Diver, her brown back hanging from her pearls, was looking through a recipe book for chicken Maryland. She was about twenty-four, Rosemary guessed—her face could have been described in terms of conventional prettiness, but the effect was that it had been made first on the heroic scale with strong structure and marking, as if the features and vividness of brow and coloring, everything we associate with temperament and character had been molded with a Rodinesque intention, and then chiselled away in the direction of prettiness to a point where a single slip would have irreparably diminished its force and quality. With the mouth the sculptor had taken desperate chances—it was the cupid's bow of a magazine cover, yet it shared the distinction of the rest.

"Are you here for a long time?" Nicole asked. Her voice was low, almost harsh.

Suddenly Rosemary let the possibility enter her mind that they might stay another week.

"Not very long," she answered vaguely. "We've been abroad a long time—we landed in Sicily in March and we've been slowly working our way north. I got pneumonia making a picture last January and I've been recuperating."

"Mercy! How did that happen?"

"Well, it was from swimming," Rosemary was rather reluctant at embarking upon personal revelations. "One day I happened to have the grippe and didn't know it, and they were taking a scene where I dove into a canal in Venice. It was a very expensive set, so I had to dive and dive and dive all morning. Mother had a doctor right there, but it was no use—I got pneumonia." She changed the subject determinedly before they could speak. "Do you like it here—this place?"

"They have to like it," said Abe North slowly. "They invented it." He turned his noble head slowly so that his eyes rested with tenderness and affection on the two Divers.

"Oh, did you?"

"This is only the second season that the hotel's been open in summer," Nicole explained. "We persuaded Gausse to keep on a cook and a *garçon* and a *chasseur*—it paid its way and this year it's doing even better."

"But you're not in the hotel."

"We built a house, up at Tarmes."

"The theory is," said Dick, arranging an umbrella to clip a square of sunlight off Rosemary's shoulder, "that all the northern places, like Deauville, were picked out by Russians and English who don't mind the cold, while half of us Americans come from tropical climates—that's why we're beginning to come here."

The young man of Latin aspect had been turning the pages of the *New York Herald*.

"Well, what nationality are these people?" he demanded, suddenly, and read with a slight French intonation, "'Registered at the Hotel Palace at Vevey are Mr. Pandely Vlasco, Mme. Bonneasse'—I don't exaggerate—'Corinna Medonca, Mme. Pasche, Seraphim Tullio, Maria Amalia Roto Mais, Moises Teubel, Mme. Paragoris, Apostle Alexandre, Yolanda Yosfuglu and Geneveva de Momus!' She attracts me most—Geneveva de Momus. Almost worth running up to Vevey to take a look at Geneveva de Momus."

He stood up with sudden restlessness, stretching himself with one sharp movement. He was a few years younger than Diver or North. He was tall and his body was hard but overspare save for the bunched force gathered in his shoulders and upper arms. At first glance he seemed conventionally handsome—but there was a faint disgust always in his face which marred the full fierce luster of his brown eyes. Yet one remembered them afterward, when one had forgotten the inability of the mouth to endure boredom and the young forehead with its furrows of fretful and unprofitable pain.

"We found some fine ones in the news of Americans last week," said Nicole. "Mrs. Evelyn Oyster and—what were the others?"

"There was Mr. S. Flesh," said Diver, getting up also. He took his rake and began to work seriously at getting small stones out of the sand.

"Oh, yes—S. Flesh—doesn't he give you the creeps?"

It was quiet alone with Nicole—Rosemary found it even quieter than with her mother. Abe North and Barban, the Frenchman, were talking about Morocco, and Nicole having copied her recipe picked up a piece of sewing. Rosemary examined their appurtenances—four large parasols that made a canopy of shade, a portable bath house for dressing, a pneumatic rubber horse, new things that Rosemary had never seen, from the first burst of luxury manufacturing after the War, and probably in the hands of the first of purchasers. She had gathered that they were fashionable people, but though her mother had brought her up to beware such people as drones, she did not feel that way here. Even in their absolute immobility, complete as that of the morning, she felt a purpose, a working over something, a direction, an act of creation different from any she had known. Her immature mind made no speculations upon the nature of their relation to each other, she was only concerned with their attitude toward herself—but she perceived the web of some pleasant interrelation, which she expressed with the thought that they seemed to have a very good time.

She looked in turn at the three men, temporarily expropriating them. All three were personable in different ways; all were of a special gentleness that she felt was part of their lives, past and future, not circumstanced by events, not at all like the company manners of actors, and she detected also a far-reaching delicacy that was different from the rough and ready good fellowship of directors, who represented the intellectuals in her life. Actors and directors—those were the only men she had ever known, those and the heterogeneous, indistinguishable mass of college boys, interested only in love at first sight, whom she had met at the Yale prom last fall.

These three were different. Barban was less civilized, more skeptical and scoffing, his manners were formal, even perfunctory. Abe North had, under his shyness, a desperate humor that amused but puzzled her. Her serious nature distrusted its ability to make a supreme impression on him.

But Dick Diver—he was all complete there. Silently she admired him. His complexion was reddish and weather-burned, so was his short hair—a light growth of it rolled down his arms and hands. His eyes were of a bright, hard blue. His nose was somewhat pointed and there was never any doubt at whom he was looking or talking—and this is a flattering attention, for who looks at us?—glances fall upon us, curious or disinterested, nothing more. His voice, with some faint Irish melody running through it, wooed the world, yet she felt the layer of hardness in him, of self-control and of self-discipline, her own virtues. Oh, she chose him, and Nicole, lifting her head saw her choose him, heard the little sigh at the fact that he was already possessed.

Toward noon the McKiscos, Mrs. Abrams, Mr. Dumphry, and Signor Campion came on the beach. They had brought a new umbrella that they set up with side glances toward the Divers, and crept under with satisfied expressions—all save Mr. McKisco, who remained derisively without. In his raking Dick had passed near them and now he returned to the umbrellas.

"The two young men are reading the Book of Etiquette together," he said in a low voice.

"Planning to mix wit' de quality," said Abe.

Mary North, the very tanned young woman whom Rosemary had encountered the first day on the raft, came in from swimming and said with a smile that was a rakish gleam:

"So Mr. and Mrs. Neverquiver have arrived."

"They're this man's friends," Nicole reminded her, indicating Abe. "Why doesn't he go and speak to them? Don't you think they're attractive?"

"I think they're very attractive," Abe agreed. "I just don't think they're attractive, that's all."

"Well, I *have* felt there were too many people on the beach this summer," Nicole admitted. "*Our* beach that Dick made out of a pebble pile." She considered, and then lowering her voice out of the range of the trio of nannies who sat back under another umbrella. "Still they're preferable to those British last summer who kept shouting about: 'Isn't the sea blue? Isn't the sky white? Isn't little Nellie's nose red?' "

Rosemary thought she would not like to have Nicole for an enemy.

"But you didn't see the fight," Nicole continued. "The day before you came, the married man, the one with the name that sounds like a substitute for gasoline or butter——"

"McKisco?"

"Yes—well they were having words and she tossed some sand in his face. So naturally he sat on top of her and rubbed her face in the sand. We were—electrified. I wanted Dick to interfere."

"I think," said Dick Diver, staring down abstractedly at the straw mat, "that I'll go over and invite them to dinner."

"No, you won't," Nicole told him quickly.

"I think it would be a very good thing. They're here —let's adjust ourselves."

"We're very well adjusted," she insisted, laughing. "I'm not going to have *my* nose rubbed in the sand. I'm a mean, hard woman," she explained to Rosemary, and then raising her voice: "Children, put on your bathing suits!"

Rosemary felt that this swim would become the typical one of her life, the one that would always pop up in her memory at the mention of swimming. Simultaneously the whole party moved toward the water, super-ready from the long, forced inaction, passing from the heat to the cool with the *gourmandise* of a tingling curry eaten with chilled white wine. The Divers' day was spaced like the day of the older civilizations to yield the utmost from the materials at hand, and to give all the transitions their full value, and she did not know that there would be another transition presently from the utter absorption of the swim to the garrulity of the Provençal lunch hour. But again she had the sense that Dick was taking care of her, and she delighted in responding to the eventual movement as if it had been an order.

Nicole handed her husband the curious garment on

which she had been working. He went into the dressing tent and inspired a commotion by appearing in a moment clad in transparent black lace drawers. Close inspection revealed that actually they were lined with flesh-colored cloth.

"Well, if that isn't a pansy's trick!" exclaimed Mr. McKisco contemptuously—then turning quickly to Mr. Dumphry and Mr. Campion, he added, "Oh, I beg your pardon."

Rosemary bubbled with delight at the trunks. Her naïveté responded whole-heartedly to the expensive simplicity of the Divers, unaware of its complexity and its lack of innocence, unaware that it was all a selection of quality rather than quantity from the run of the world's bazaar; and that the simplicity of behavior also, the nursery-like peace and good will, the emphasis on the simpler virtues, was part of a desperate bargain with the gods and had been attained through struggles she could not have guessed at. At that moment the Divers represented externally the exact furthermost evolution of a class, so that most people seemed awkward beside them—in reality a qualitative change had already set in that was not at all apparent to Rosemary.

She stood with them as they took sherry and ate crackers. Dick Diver looked at her with cold blue eyes; his kind, strong mouth said thoughtfully and deliberately:

"You're the only girl I've seen for a long time that actually did look like something blooming."

In her mother's lap afterward Rosemary cried and cried.

"I love him, Mother. I'm desperately in love with him—I never knew I could feel that way about anybody.

And he's married and I like her too—it's just hopeless. Oh, I love him so!"

"I'm curious to meet him."

"She invited us to dinner Friday."

"If you're in love it ought to make you happy. You ought to laugh."

Rosemary looked up and gave a beautiful little shiver of her face and laughed. Her mother always had a great influence on her.

V

ROSEMARY went to Monte Carlo nearly as sulkily as it was possible for her to be. She rode up the rugged hill to La Turbie, to an old Gaumont lot in process of reconstruction, and as she stood by the grilled entrance waiting for an answer to the message on her card, she might have been looking into Hollywood. The bizarre débris of some recent picture, a decayed street scene in India, a great cardboard whale, a monstrous tree bearing cherries large as basketballs, bloomed there by exotic dispensation, autochthonous as the pale amaranth, mimosa, cork oak or dwarfed pine. There were a quick-lunch shack and two barnlike stages and everywhere about the lot, groups of waiting, hopeful, painted faces.

After ten minutes a young man with hair the color of canary feathers hurried down to the gate.

"Come in, Miss Hoyt. Mr. Brady's on the set, but he's very anxious to see you. I'm sorry you were kept waiting, but you know some of these French dames are worse about pushing themselves in——"

The studio manager opened a small door in the blank wall of stage building and with sudden glad familiarity Rosemary followed him into half darkness. Here and there figures spotted the twilight, turning up ashen faces to her like souls in purgatory watching the passage of a mortal through. There were whispers and soft voices and, apparently from afar, the gentle tremolo of a small organ. Turning the corner made by some flats, they came upon the white crackling glow of a stage, where a French actor—his shirt front, collar, and cuffs tinted a brilliant pink—and an American actress stood motionless face to face. They stared at each other with dogged eyes, as though they had been in the same position for hours; and still for a long time nothing happened, no one moved. A bank of lights went off with a savage hiss, went on again; the plaintive tap of a hammer begged admission to nowhere in the distance; a blue face appeared among the blinding lights above, called something unintelligible into the upper blackness. Then the silence was broken by a voice in front of Rosemary.

"Baby, you don't take off the stockings, you can spoil ten more pairs. That dress is fifteen pounds."

Stepping backward the speaker ran against Rosemary, whereupon the studio manager said, "Hey, Earl—Miss Hoyt."

They were meeting for the first time. Brady was quick and strenuous. As he took her hand she saw him look her over from head to foot, a gesture she recognized and that made her feel at home, but gave her always a faint feeling of superiority to whoever made it. If her person was property she could exercise whatever advantage was inherent in its ownership.

"I thought you'd be along any day now," Brady said, in a voice that was just a little too compelling for private life, and that trailed with it a faintly defiant cockney accent. "Have a good trip?"

"Yes, but we're glad to be going home."

"No-o-o!" he protested. "Stay awhile—I want to talk to you. Let me tell you that was some picture of yours—

that 'Daddy's Girl.' I saw it in Paris. I wired the coast right away to see if you were signed."

"I just had—I'm sorry."

"God, what a picture!"

Not wanting to smile in silly agreement Rosemary frowned.

"Nobody wants to be thought of forever for just one picture," she said.

"Sure—that's right. What're your plans?"

"Mother thought I needed a rest. When I get back we'll probably either sign up with First National or keep on with Famous."

"Who's we?"

"My mother. She decides business matters. I couldn't do without her."

Again he looked her over completely, and, as he did, something in Rosemary went out to him. It was not liking, not at all the spontaneous admiration she had felt for the man on the beach this morning. It was a click. He desired her and, so far as her virginal emotions went, she contemplated a surrender with equanimity. Yet she knew she would forget him half an hour after she left him—like an actor kissed in a picture.

"Where are you staying?" Brady asked. "Oh, yes, at Gausse's. Well, my plans are made for this year, too, but that letter I wrote you still stands. Rather make a picture with you than any girl since Connie Talmadge was a kid."

"I feel the same way. Why don't you come back to Hollywood?"

"I can't stand the damn place. I'm fine here. Wait till after this shot and I'll show you around."

Walking onto the set he began to talk to the French actor in a low, quiet voice.

Five minutes passed—Brady talked on, while from

time to time the Frenchman shifted his feet and nodded. Abruptly, Brady broke off, calling something to the lights that startled them into a humming glare. Los Angeles was loud about Rosemary now. Unappalled she moved once more through the city of thin partitions, wanting to be back there. But she did not want to see Brady in the mood she sensed he would be in after he had finished and she left the lot with a spell still upon her. The Mediterranean world was less silent now that she knew the studio was there. She liked the people on the streets and bought herself a pair of *espadrilles* on the way to the train.

Her mother was pleased that she had done so accurately what she was told to do, but she still wanted to launch her out and away. Mrs. Speers was fresh in appearance but she was tired; death beds make people tired indeed and she had watched beside a couple.

VI

FEELING good from the rosy wine at lunch, Nicole Diver folded her arms high enough for the artificial camellia on her shoulder to touch her cheek, and went out into her lovely grassless garden. The garden was bounded on one side by the house, from which it flowed and into which it ran, on two sides by the old village, and on the last by the cliff falling by ledges to the sea.

Along the walls on the village side all was dusty, the wriggling vines, the lemon and eucalyptus trees, the casual wheel-barrow, left only a moment since, but already grown into the path, atrophied and faintly rotten. Nicole was invariably somewhat surprised that by turning in the other direction past a bed of peonies she walked into an area so green and cool that the leaves and petals were curled with tender damp.

Knotted at her throat she wore a lilac scarf that even in the achromatic sunshine cast its color up to her face and down around her moving feet in a lilac shadow. Her face was hard, almost stern, save for the soft gleam of piteous doubt that looked from her green eyes. Her once fair hair had darkened, but she was lovelier now at twenty-four than she had been at eighteen, when her hair was brighter than she.

Following a walk marked by an intangible mist of bloom that followed the white border stones she came to a space overlooking the sea where there were lanterns asleep in the fig trees and a big table and wicker chairs and a great market umbrella from Sienna, all gathered about an enormous pine, the biggest tree in the garden. She paused there a moment, looking absently at a growth of nasturtiums and iris tangled at its foot, as though sprung from a careless handful of seeds, listening to the plaints and accusations of some nursery squabble in the house. When this died away on the summer air, she walked on, between kaleidoscopic peonies massed in pink clouds, black and brown tulips and fragile mauve-stemmed roses, transparent like sugar flowers in a confectioner's window—until, as if the scherzo of color could reach no further intensity, it broke off suddenly in mid-air, and moist steps went down to a level five feet below.

Here there was a well with the boarding around it dank and slippery even on the brightest days. She went up the stairs on the other side and into the vegetable garden; she walked rather quickly; she liked to be active, though at times she gave an impression of repose that was at once static and evocative. This was because she knew few words and believed in none, and in the world she was rather silent, contributing just her share of urbane humor with a precision that approached meagerness. But at the moment when strangers tended to grow uncomfortable in the presence of this economy she would seize the topic and rush off with it, feverishly surprised with herself—then bring it back and relinquish it abruptly, almost timidly, like an obedient retriever, having been adequate and something more.

As she stood in the fuzzy green light of the vegetable garden, Dick crossed the path ahead of her going to his work house. Nicole waited silently till he had passed; then she went on through lines of prospective salads to a little menagerie where pigeons and rabbits and a parrot made a medley of insolent noises at her. Descending to another ledge she reached a low, curved wall and looked down seven hundred feet to the Mediterranean Sea.

She stood in the ancient hill village of Tarmes. The villa and its grounds were made out of a row of peasant dwellings that abutted on the cliff—five small houses had been combined to make the house and four destroyed to make the garden. The exterior walls were untouched so that from the road far below it was indistinguishable from the violet gray mass of the town.

For a moment Nicole stood looking down at the Mediterranean but there was nothing to do with that, even with her tireless hands. Presently Dick came out of his one-room house carrying a telescope and looked east toward Cannes. In a moment Nicole swam into his field of vision, whereupon he disappeared into his house and came out with a megaphone. He had many light mechanical devices.

"Nicole," he shouted, "I forgot to tell you that as a final apostolic gesture I invited Mrs. Abrams, the woman with the white hair."

"I suspected it. It's an outrage."

The ease with which her reply reached him seemed to belittle his megaphone, so she raised her voice and called, "Can you hear me?"

"Yes." He lowered the megaphone and then raised it stubbornly. "I'm going to invite some more people too. I'm going to invite the two young men."

"All right," she agreed placidly.

"I want to give a really *bad* party. I mean it. I want to give a party where there's a brawl and seductions and people going home with their feelings hurt and women passed out in the *cabinet de toilette*. You wait and see."

He went back into his house and Nicole saw that one of his most characteristic moods was upon him, the excitement that swept everyone up into it and was inevitably followed by his own form of melancholy, which he never displayed but at which she guessed. This excitement about things reached an intensity out of proportion to their importance, generating a really extraordinary virtuosity with people. Save among a few of the tough-minded and perennially suspicious, he had the power of arousing a fascinated and uncritical love. The reaction came when he realized the waste and extravagance involved. He sometimes looked back with awe at the carnivals of affection he had given, as a general might gaze upon a massacre he had ordered to satisfy an impersonal blood lust.

But to be included in Dick Diver's world for a while was a remarkable experience: people believed he made special reservations about them, recognizing the proud uniqueness of their destinies, buried under the compromises of how many years. He won everyone quickly with an exquisite consideration and a politeness that moved so fast and intuitively that it could be examined only in its effect. Then, without caution, lest the first bloom of the relation wither, he opened the gate to his amusing world. So long as they subscribed to it completely, their happiness was his preoccupation, but at the first flicker of doubt as to its all-inclusiveness he evaporated before their eyes, leaving little communicable memory of what he had said or done.

At eight-thirty that evening he came out to meet his first guests, his coat carried rather ceremoniously, rather promisingly, in his hand, like a toreador's cape. It was characteristic that after greeting Rosemary and her mother he waited for them to speak first, as if to allow them the reassurance of their own voices in new surroundings.

To resume Rosemary's point of view it should be said that, under the spell of the climb to Tarmes and the fresher air, she and her mother looked about appreciatively. Just as the personal qualities of extraordinary people can make themselves plain in an unaccustomed change of expression, so the intensely calculated perfection of Villa Diana transpired all at once through such minute failures as the chance apparition of a maid in the background or the perversity of a cook. While the first guests arrived bringing with them the excitement of the night, the domestic activity of the day receded past them gently, symbolized by the Diver children and their governess still at supper on the terrace.

"What a beautiful garden!" Mrs. Speers exclaimed.

"Nicole's garden," said Dick. "She won't let it alone—she nags it all the time, worries about its diseases. Any day now I expect to have her come down with Powdery Mildew or Fly Speck, or Late Blight." He pointed his forefinger decisively at Rosemary, saying with a lightness seeming to conceal a paternal interest, "I'm going to save your reason—I'm going to give you a hat to wear on the beach."

He turned them from the garden to the terrace, where he poured a cocktail. Earl Brady arrived, discovering Rosemary with surprise. His manner was softer than at the studio, as if his differentness had been put on at the gate, and Rosemary, comparing him instantly with Dick Diver, swung sharply toward the latter. In comparison Earl Brady seemed faintly gross, faintly ill-bred; once more, though, she felt an electric response to his person.

He spoke familiarly to the children who were getting up from their outdoor supper.

"Hello, Lanier, how about a song? Will you and Topsy sing me a song?"

"What shall we sing?" agreed the little boy, with the odd chanting accent of American children brought up in France.

"That song about '*mon ami Pierrot.*' "

Brother and sister stood side by side without self-consciousness and their voices soared sweet and shrill upon the evening air.

"Au clair de la lune
    Mon ami Pierrot
Prête-moi ta plume
    Pour écrire un mot
Ma chandelle est morte
    Je n'ai plus de feu
Ouvre-moi ta porte
    Pour l'amour de Dieu."

The singing ceased and the children, their faces aglow with the late sunshine, stood smiling calmly at their success. Rosemary was thinking that the Villa Diana was the center of the world. On such a stage some memorable thing was sure to happen. She lighted up higher as the gate tinkled open and the rest of the guests arrived in a body—the McKiscos, Mrs. Abrams, Mr. Dumphry, and Mr. Campion came up to the terrace.

Rosemary had a sharp feeling of disappointment—she looked quickly at Dick, as though to ask an explanation of this incongruous mingling. But there was nothing unusual in his expression. He greeted his new guests with a proud bearing and an obvious deference to their infinite and unknown possibilities. She believed in him so much that presently she accepted the rightness of the McKiscos' presence as if she had expected to meet them all along.

"I've met you in Paris," McKisco said to Abe North, who with his wife had arrived on their heels, "in fact I've met you twice."

"Yes, I remember," Abe said.

"Then where was it?" demanded McKisco, not content to let well enough alone.

"Why, I think—" Abe got tired of the game, "I can't remember."

The interchange filled a pause and Rosemary's instinct was that something tactful should be said by somebody, but Dick made no attempt to break up the grouping formed by these late arrivals, not even to disarm Mrs. McKisco of her air of supercilious amusement. He did not solve this social problem because he knew it was not of importance at the moment and would solve itself. He was saving his newness for a larger effort, waiting a more significant moment for his guests to be conscious of a good time.

Rosemary stood beside Tommy Barban—he was in a particularly scornful mood and there seemed to be some special stimulus working upon him. He was leaving in the morning.

"Going home?"

"Home? I have no home. I am going to a war."

"What war?"

"What war? Any war. I haven't seen a paper lately but I suppose there's a war—there always is."

"Don't you care what you fight for?"

"Not at all—so long as I'm well treated. When I'm in a rut I come to see the Divers, because then I know that in a few weeks I'll want to go to war."

Rosemary stiffened.

"You like the Divers," she reminded him.

"Of course—especially her—but they make me want to go to war."

She considered this, to no avail. The Divers made her want to stay near them forever.

"You're half American," she said, as if that should solve the problem.

"Also I'm half French, and I was educated in England and since I was eighteen I've worn the uniforms of eight countries. But I hope I did not give you the impression that I am not fond of the Divers—I am, especially of Nicole."

"How could any one help it?" she said simply.

She felt far from him. The undertone of his words repelled her and she withdrew her adoration for the Divers from the profanity of his bitterness. She was glad he was not next to her at dinner and she was still thinking of his words "especially her" as they moved toward the table in the garden.

For a moment now she was beside Dick Diver on the path. Alongside his hard, neat brightness everything faded into the surety that he knew everything. For a year, which was forever, she had had money and a certain celebrity and contact with the celebrated, and these latter had presented themselves merely as powerful enlargements of the people with whom the doctor's widow and her daughter had associated in a hôtel-pension in Paris. Rosemary was a romantic and her career had not provided many satisfactory opportunities on that score. Her mother, with the idea of a career for Rosemary, would not tolerate any such spurious substitutes as the excitations available on all sides, and indeed Rosemary was already beyond that—she was In the movies but not at all At them. So when she had seen approval of Dick Diver in her mother's face it meant that he was "the real thing"; it meant permission to go as far as she could.

"I was watching you," he said, and she knew he meant it. "We've grown very fond of you."

"I fell in love with you the first time I saw you," she said quietly.

He pretended not to have heard, as if the compliment were purely formal.

"New friends," he said, as if it were an important point, "can often have a better time together than old friends."

With that remark, which she did not understand precisely, she found herself at the table, picked out by slowly emerging lights against the dark dusk. A chord of delight struck inside her when she saw that Dick had taken her mother on his right hand; for herself she was between Luis Campion and Brady.

Surcharged with her emotion she turned to Brady with the intention of confiding in him, but at her first mention of Dick a hard-boiled sparkle in his eyes gave her to understand that he refused the fatherly office. In turn she was equally firm when he tried to monopolize her hand, so they talked shop or rather she listened while he talked shop, her polite eyes never leaving his face, but her mind was so definitely elsewhere that she felt he must guess the fact. Intermittently she caught the gist of his sentences and supplied the rest from her subconscious, as one picks up the striking of a clock in the middle with only the rhythm of the first uncounted strokes lingering in the mind.

VII

IN a pause Rosemary looked away and up the table where Nicole sat between Tommy Barban and Abe North, her chow's hair foaming and frothing in the candlelight. Rosemary listened, caught sharply by the rich clipped voice in infrequent speech:

"The poor man," Nicole exclaimed. "Why did you want to saw him in two?"

"*Na*turally I wanted to see what was inside a waiter. Wouldn't you like to know what was inside a waiter?"

"Old menus," suggested Nicole with a short laugh. "Pieces of broken china and tips and pencil stubs."

"Exactly—but the thing was to prove it scientifically. And of course doing it with that musical saw would have eliminated any sordidness."

"Did you intend to play the saw while you performed the operation?" Tommy inquired.

"We didn't get quite that far. We were alarmed by the screams. We thought he might rupture something."

"All sounds very peculiar to me," said Nicole. "Any musician that'll use another musician's saw to——"

They had been at table half an hour and a perceptible change had set in—person by person had given up something, a preoccupation, an anxiety, a suspicion, and now they were only their best selves and the Divers' guests. Not to have been friendly and interested would have seemed to reflect on the Divers, so now they were all trying, and seeing this, Rosemary liked everyone—except McKisco, who had contrived to be the unassimilated member of the party. This was less from ill will than from his determination to sustain with wine the good spirits he had enjoyed on his arrival. Lying back in his place between Earl Brady, to whom he had addressed several withering remarks about the movies, and Mrs. Abrams, to whom he said nothing, he stared at Dick Diver with an expression of devastating irony, the effect being occasionally interrupted by his attempts to engage Dick in a cater-cornered conversation across the table.

"Aren't you a friend of Van Buren Denby?" he would say.

"I don't believe I know him."

"I thought you were a friend of his," he persisted irritably.

When the subject of Mr. Denby fell of its own weight, he essayed other equally irrelative themes, but each time the very deference of Dick's attention seemed to paralyze him, and after a moment's stark pause the conversation that he had interrupted would go on without him. He tried breaking into other dialogues, but it was like continually shaking hands with a glove from which the hand had been withdrawn—so finally, with a resigned air of being among children, he devoted his attention entirely to the champagne.

Rosemary's glance moved at intervals around the table, eager for the others' enjoyment, as if they were her future stepchildren. A gracious table light, emanating from a bowl of spicy pinks, fell upon Mrs. Abrams' face, cooked to a turn in Veuve Cliquot, full of vigor, tolerance, adolescent good will; next to her sat Mr. Royal Dumphry, his girl's comeliness less startling in the pleasure world of evening. Then Violet McKisco, whose prettiness had been piped to the surface of her, so that she ceased her struggle to make tangible to herself her shadowy position as the wife of an arriviste who had not arrived.

Then came Dick, with his arms full of the slack he had taken up from others, deeply merged in his own party.

Then her mother, forever perfect.

Then Barban talking to her mother with an urbane fluency that made Rosemary like him again. Then Nicole. Rosemary saw her suddenly in a new way and found her one of the most beautiful people she had ever known. Her face, the face of a saint, a viking Madonna, shone through the faint motes that snowed across the candlelight, drew down its flush from the wine-colored lanterns in the pine. She was still as still.

Abe North was talking to her about his moral code: "Of course I've got one," he insisted, "—a man can't live without a moral code. Mine is that I'm against the burning of witches. Whenever they burn a witch I get all hot under the collar." Rosemary knew from Brady that he was a musician who after a brilliant and precocious start had composed nothing for seven years.

Next was Campion, managing somehow to restrain his most blatant effeminacy, and even to visit upon those near him a certain disinterested motherliness. Then Mary North with a face so merry that it was impossible not to smile back into the white mirrors of her teeth—the whole area around her parted lips was a lovely little circle of delight.

Finally Brady, whose heartiness became, moment by moment, a social thing instead of a crude assertion and reassertion of his own mental health, and his preservation of it by a detachment from the frailties of others.

Rosemary, as dewy with belief as a child from one of Mrs. Burnett's vicious tracts, had a conviction of homecoming, of a return from the derisive and salacious improvisations of the frontier. There were fireflies riding on the dark air and a dog baying on some low and faraway ledge of the cliff. The table seemed to have risen a little toward the sky like a mechanical dancing platform, giving the people around it a sense of being alone with each other in the dark universe, nourished by its only food, warmed by its only lights. And, as if a curious hushed laugh from Mrs. McKisco were a signal that such a detachment from the world had been attained, the two Divers began suddenly to warm and glow and expand, as if to make up to their guests, already so subtly assured of their importance, so flattered with politeness, for anything they might still miss from that country well left behind. Just for a moment they seemed to speak to every one at the table, singly and together, assuring them of their friendliness, their affection. And for a moment the faces turned up toward them were like the faces of poor children at a Christmas tree. Then abruptly the table broke up—the moment when the guests had been daringly lifted above conviviality into the rarer atmosphere of sentiment, was over before it could be irreverently breathed, before they had half realized it was there.

But the diffused magic of the hot sweet South had withdrawn into them—the soft-pawed night and the ghostly wash of the Mediterranean far below—the magic left these things and melted into the two Divers and became part of them. Rosemary watched Nicole pressing upon her mother a yellow evening bag she had admired, saying, "I think things ought to belong to the people that like them"—and then sweeping into it all the yellow articles she could find, a pencil, a lipstick, a little note book, "because they all go together."

Nicole disappeared and presently Rosemary noticed that Dick was no longer there; the guests distributed themselves in the garden or drifted in toward the terrace.

"Do you want," Violet McKisco asked Rosemary, "to go to the bathroom?"

Not at that precise moment.

"I want," insisted Mrs. McKisco, "to go to the bathroom." As a frank outspoken woman she walked toward the house, dragging her secret after her, while Rosemary looked after with reprobation. Earl Brady proposed that they walk down to the sea wall but she felt that this was her time to have a share of Dick Diver when he reappeared, so she stalled, listening to McKisco quarrel with Barban.

"Why do you want to fight the Soviets?" McKisco said. "The greatest experiment ever made by humanity? And the Riff? It seems to me it would be more heroic to fight on the just side."

"How do you find out which it is?" asked Barban dryly.

"Why—usually everybody intelligent knows."

"Are you a Communist?"

"I'm a Socialist," said McKisco, "I sympathize with Russia."

"Well, I'm a soldier," Barban answered pleasantly. "My business is to kill people. I fought against the Riff because I am a European, and I have fought the Communists because they want to take my property from me."

"Of all the narrow-minded excuses," McKisco looked around to establish a derisive liaison with someone else, but without success. He had no idea what he was up against in Barban, neither of the simplicity of the other man's bag of ideas nor of the complexity of his training. McKisco knew what ideas were, and as his mind grew he was able to recognize and sort an increasing number of them—but faced by a man whom he considered "dumb," one in whom he found no ideas he could recognize as such, and yet to whom he could not feel personally superior, he jumped at the conclusion that Barban was the end product of an archaic world, and as such, worthless. McKisco's contacts with the princely classes in America had impressed upon him their uncertain and fumbling snobbery, their delight in ignorance and their deliberate rudeness, all lifted from the English with no regard paid to factors that make English philistinism and rudeness purposeful, and applied in a land where a little knowledge and civility buy more than they do anywhere else—an attitude which reached its apogee in the "Harvard manner" of about 1900. He thought that this Barban was of that type, and being drunk rashly forgot that he was in awe of him—this led up to the trouble in which he presently found himself.

Feeling vaguely ashamed for McKisco, Rosemary waited, placid but inwardly on fire, for Dick Diver's return. From her chair at the deserted table with Barban, McKisco, and Abe she looked up along the path edged with shadowy myrtle and fern to the stone terrace, and falling in love with her mother's profile against a lighted door, was about to go there when Mrs. McKisco came hurrying down from the house.

She exuded excitement. In the very silence with which she pulled out a chair and sat down, her eyes staring, her mouth working a little, they all recognized a person crop-full of news, and her husband's "What's the matter, Vi?" came naturally, as all eyes turned toward her.

"My dear—" she said at large, and then addressed Rosemary, "my dear—it's nothing. I really can't say a word."

"You're among friends," said Abe.

"Well, upstairs I came upon a scene, my dears——"

Shaking her head cryptically she broke off just in

time, for Tommy arose and addressed her politely but sharply:

"It's inadvisable to comment on what goes on in this house."

VIII

VIOLET breathed loud and hard once and with an effort brought another expression into her face. Dick came finally and with a sure instinct he separated Barban and the McKiscos and became excessively ignorant and inquisitive about literature with McKisco —thus giving the latter the moment of superiority which he required. The others helped him carry lamps up—who would not be pleased at carrying lamps helpfully through the darkness? Rosemary helped, meanwhile responding patiently to Royal Dumphry's inexhaustible curiosity about Hollywood.

Now—she was thinking—I've earned a time alone with him. He must know that because his laws are like the laws Mother taught me.

Rosemary was right—presently he detached her from the company on the terrace, and they were alone together, borne away from the house toward the seaside wall with what were less steps than irregularly spaced intervals through some of which she was pulled, through others blown.

They looked out over the Mediterranean. Far below, the last excursion boat from the Isles des Lerins floated across the bay like a Fourth-of-July balloon foot-loose in the heavens. Between the black isles it floated, softly parting the dark tide.

"I understand why you speak as you do of your mother," he said. "Her attitude toward you is very fine, I think. She has a sort of wisdom that's rare in America."

"Mother is perfect," she prayed.

"I was talking to her about a plan I have—she told me that how long you both stayed in France depended on you."

On *you*, Rosemary all but said aloud.

"So since things are over down here——"

"Over?" she inquired.

"Well, this is over—this part of the summer is over. Last week Nicole's sister left, to-morrow Tommy Barban leaves, Monday Abe and Mary North are leaving. Maybe we'll have more fun this summer but this particular fun is over. I want it to die violently instead of fading out sentimentally—that's why I gave this party. What I'm coming to is—Nicole and I are going up to Paris to see Abe North off for America—I wonder if you'd like to go with us."

"What did Mother say?"

"She seemed to think it would be fine. She doesn't want to go herself. She wants you to go alone."

"I haven't seen Paris since I've been grown," said Rosemary. "I'd love to see it with you."

"That's nice of you." Did she imagine that his voice was suddenly metallic? "Of course we've been excited about you from the moment you came on the beach. That vitality, we were sure it was professional—especially Nicole was. It'd never use itself up on any one person or group."

Her instinct cried out to her that he was passing her along slowly toward Nicole and she put her own brakes on, saying with an equal hardness:

"I wanted to know all of you too—especially you. I told you I fell in love with you the first time I saw you."

She was right going at it that way. But the space between heaven and earth had cooled his mind, destroyed the impulsiveness that had led him to bring her here, and made him aware of the too obvious appeal, the struggle with an unrehearsed scene and unfamiliar words.

He tried now to make her want to go back to the house and it was difficult, and he did not quite want to lose her. She felt only the draft blowing as he joked with her good-humoredly.

"You don't know what you want. You go and ask your mother what you want."

She was stricken. She touched him, feeling the smooth cloth of his dark coat like a chasuble. She seemed about to fall to her knees—from that position she delivered her last shot.

"I think you're the most wonderful person I ever met —except my mother."

"You have romantic eyes."

His laughter swept them on up toward the terrace where he delivered her to Nicole. . . .

Too soon it had become time to go and the Divers helped them all to go quickly. In the Divers' big Isotta there would be Tommy Barban and his baggage—he was spending the night at the hotel to catch an early train—with Mrs. Abrams, the McKiscos and Campion. Earl Brady was going to drop Rosemary and her mother on his way to Monte Carlo, and Royal Dumphry rode with them because the Divers' car was crowded. Down in the garden lanterns still glowed over the table where they had dined, as the Divers stood side by side in the gate, Nicole blooming away and filling the night with graciousness, and Dick bidding good-by to everyone by name. To Rosemary it seemed very poignant to drive away and leave them in their house. Again she wondered what Mrs. McKisco had seen in the bathroom.

IX

IT was a limpid black night, hung as in a basket from a single dull star. The horn of the car ahead was muffled by the resistance of the thick air. Brady's chauffeur drove slowly; the tail-light of the other car appeared from time to time at turnings—then not at all. But after ten minutes it came into sight again, drawn up at the side of the road. Brady's chauffeur slowed up behind but immediately it began to roll forward slowly and they passed it. In the instant they passed it they heard a blur of voices from behind the reticence of the limousine and saw that the Divers' chauffeur was grinning. Then they went on, going fast through the alternating banks of darkness and thin night, descending at last in a series of roller-coaster swoops, to the great bulk of Gausse's Hotel.

Rosemary dozed for three hours and then lay awake, suspended in the moonshine. Cloaked by the erotic darkness she exhausted the future quickly, with all the eventualities that might lead up to a kiss, but with the kiss itself as blurred as a kiss in pictures. She changed position in bed deliberately, the first sign of insomnia she had ever had, and tried to think with her mother's mind about the question. In this process she was often acute beyond her experience, with remembered things from old conversations that had gone into her half-heard.

Rosemary had been brought up with the idea of work. Mrs. Speers had spent the slim leavings of the men who had widowed her on her daughter's education, and when she blossomed out at sixteen with that extraordinary hair, rushed her to Aix-les-Bains and marched her unannounced into the suite of an American producer who was recuperating there. When the producer went to New York they went too. Thus Rosemary had passed her entrance examinations. With the ensuing success and the promise of comparative stability that followed, Mrs. Speers had felt free to tacitly imply to-night:

"You were brought up to work—not especially to marry. Now you've found your first nut to crack and it's a good nut—go ahead and put whatever happens down to experience. Wound yourself or him—whatever happens it can't spoil you because economically you're a boy, not a girl."

Rosemary had never done much thinking, save about the illimitability of her mother's perfections, so this final severance of the umbilical cord disturbed her sleep. A false dawn sent the sky passing through the tall French windows, and getting up she walked out on the terrace, warm to her bare feet. There were secret noises in the air, an insistent bird achieved an ill-natured triumph with regularity in the trees above the tennis court; foot-falls followed a round drive in the rear of the hotel, taking their tone in turn from the dust road, the crushed-stone walk, the cement steps, and then revers-ing the process in going away. Beyond the inky sea and far up that high, black shadow of a hill lived the Divers. She thought of them both together, heard them still singing faintly a song like rising smoke, like a hymn, very remote in time and far away. Their children slept, their gate was shut for the night.

She went inside and dressing in a light gown and es-padrilles went out her window again and along the con-tinuous terrace toward the front door, going fast since she found that other private rooms, exuding sleep, gave upon it. She stopped at the sight of a figure seated on the wide white stairway of the formal entrance—then she saw that it was Luis Campion and that he was weeping.

He was weeping hard and quietly and shaking in the same parts as a weeping woman. A scene in a rôle she had played last year swept over her irresistibly and advancing she touched him on the shoulder. He gave a little yelp before he recognized her.

"What is it?" Her eyes were level and kind and not slanted into him with hard curiosity. "Can I help you?"

"Nobody can help me. I knew it. I have only myself to blame. It's always the same."

"What is it—do you want to tell me?"

He looked at her to see.

"No," he decided. "When you're older you'll know what people who love suffer. The agony. It's better to be cold and young than to love. It's happened to me before but never like this—so accidental—just when everything was going well."

His face was repulsive in the quickening light. Not by a flicker of her personality, a movement of the smallest muscle, did she betray her sudden disgust with whatever it was. But Campion's sensitivity realized it and he changed the subject rather suddenly.

"Abe North is around here somewhere."

"Why, he's staying at the Divers'!"

"Yes, but he's up—don't you know what happened?"

A shutter opened suddenly in a room two stories above and an English voice spat distinctly:

"Will you kaindlay stup tucking!"

Rosemary and Luis Campion went humbly down the steps and to a bench beside the road to the beach.

"Then you have no idea what's happened? My dear, the most extraordinary thing—" He was warming up now, hanging on to his revelation. "I've never seen a thing come so suddenly—I have always avoided violent people—they upset me so I sometimes have to go to bed for days."

He looked at her triumphantly. She had no idea what he was talking about.

"My dear," he burst forth, leaning toward her with his whole body as he touched her on the upper leg, to show it was no mere irresponsible venture of his hand—he was so sure of himself. "There's going to be a duel."

"Wh-at?"

"A duel with—we don't know what yet."

"Who's going to duel?"

"I'll tell you from the beginning." He drew a long breath and then said, as if it were rather to her discredit but he wouldn't hold it against her. "Of course, you were in the other automobile. Well, in a way you were lucky—I lost at least two years of my life, it came so suddenly."

"What came?" she demanded.

"I don't know what began it. First she began to talk——"

"Who?"

"Violet McKisco." He lowered his voice as if there were people under the bench. "But don't mention the Divers because he made threats against anybody who mentioned it."

"Who did?"

"Tommy Barban, so don't you say I so much as mentioned them. None of us ever found out anyhow what it was Violet had to say because he kept interrupting her, and then her husband got into it and now, my dear, we have the duel. This morning—at five o'clock—in an hour." He sighed suddenly thinking of his own griefs. "I almost wish it were I. I might as well be killed now

I have nothing to live for." He broke off and rocked to and fro with sorrow.

Again the iron shutter parted above and the same British voice said:

"Rilly, this must stup immejetely."

Simultaneously Abe North, looking somewhat distracted, came out of the hotel, perceived them against the sky, white over the sea. Rosemary shook her head warningly before he could speak and they moved to another bench further down the road. Rosemary saw that Abe was a little tight.

"What are *you* doing up?" he demanded.

"I just got up." She started to laugh, but remembering the voice above, she restrained herself.

"Plagued by the nightingale," Abe suggested, and repeated, "probably plagued by the nightingale. Has this sewing-circle member told you what happened?"

Campion said with dignity:

"I only know what I heard with my own ears."

He got up and walked swiftly away; Abe sat down beside Rosemary.

"Why did you treat him so badly?"

"Did I?" he asked surprised. "He's been weeping around here all morning."

"Well, maybe he's sad about something."

"Maybe he is."

"What about a duel? Who's going to duel? I thought there was something strange in that car. Is it true?"

"It certainly is coo-coo but it seems to be true."

X

THE trouble began at the time Earl Brady's car passed the Divers' car stopped on the road—Abe's account melted impersonally into the thronged night—Violet McKisco was telling Mrs. Abrams something she had found out about the Divers—she had gone upstairs in their house and she had come upon something there which had made a great impression on her. But Tommy is a watch-dog about the Divers. As a matter of fact she is inspiring and formidable—but it's a mutual thing, and the fact of The Divers together is more important to their friends than many of them realize. Of course it's done at a certain sacrifice—sometimes they seem just rather charming figures in a ballet, and worth just the attention you give a ballet, but it's more than that—you'd have to know the story. Anyhow Tommy is one of those men that Dick's passed along to Nicole and when Mrs. McKisco kept hinting at her story, he called them on it. He said:

"Mrs. McKisco, please don't talk further about Mrs. Diver."

"I wasn't talking to you," she objected.

"I think it's better to leave them out."

"Are they so sacred?"

"Leave them out. Talk about something else."

He was sitting on one of the two little seats beside Campion. Campion told me the story.

"Well, you're pretty high-handed," Violet came back.

You know how conversations are in cars late at night, some people murmuring and some not caring, giving up after the party, or bored or asleep. Well, none of them knew just what happened until the car stopped and Barban cried in a voice that shook everybody, a voice for cavalry.

"Do you want to step out here—we're only a mile from the hotel and you can walk it or I'll drag you there. *You've got to shut up and shut your wife up!*"

"You're a bully," said McKisco. "You know you're stronger muscularly than I am. But I'm not afraid of you—what they ought to have is the code duello——"

There's where he made his mistake because Tommy, being French, leaned over and clapped him one, and then the chauffeur drove on. That was where you passed them. Then the women began. That was still the state of things when the car got to the hotel.

Tommy telephoned some man in Cannes to act as second and McKisco said he wasn't going to be seconded by Campion, who wasn't crazy for the job anyhow, so he telephoned me not to say anything but to come right down. Violet McKisco collapsed and Mrs. Abrams took her to her room and gave her a bromide whereupon she fell comfortably asleep on the bed. When I got there I tried to argue with Tommy but the latter wouldn't accept anything short of an apology and McKisco rather spunkily wouldn't give it.

When Abe had finished Rosemary asked thoughtfully:

"Do the Divers know it was about them?"

"No—and they're not ever going to know they had anything to do with it. That damn Campion had no business talking to you about it, but since he did—I told the chauffeur I'd get out the old musical saw if he opened his mouth about it. This fight's between two men—what Tommy needs is a good war."

"I hope the Divers don't find out," Rosemary said.

Abe peered at his watch.

"I've got to go up and see McKisco—do you want to come?—he feels sort of friendless—I bet he hasn't slept."

Rosemary had a vision of the desperate vigil that high-strung, badly organized man had probably kept. After a moment balanced between pity and repugnance she agreed, and full of morning energy, bounced upstairs beside Abe.

McKisco was sitting on his bed with his alcoholic combativeness vanished, in spite of the glass of champagne in his hand. He seemed very puny and cross and white. Evidently he had been writing and drinking all night. He stared confusedly at Abe and Rosemary and asked:

"Is it time?"

"No, not for half an hour."

The table was covered with papers which he assembled with some difficulty into a long letter; the writing on the last pages was very large and illegible. In the delicate light of electric lamps fading, he scrawled his name at the bottom, crammed it into an envelope and handed it to Abe. "For my wife."

"You better souse your head in cold water," Abe suggested.

"You think I'd better?" inquired McKisco doubtfully. "I don't want to get too sober."

"Well, you look terrible now."

Obediently McKisco went into the bathroom.

"I'm leaving everything in an awful mess," he called. "I don't know how Violet will get back to America. I don't carry any insurance. I never got around to it."

"Don't talk nonsense, you'll be right here eating breakfast in an hour."

"Sure, I know." He came back with his hair wet and looked at Rosemary as if he saw her for the first time. Suddenly tears stood in his eyes. "I never have finished my novel. That's what makes me so sore. You don't like me," he said to Rosemary, "but that can't be helped. I'm primarily a literary man." He made a vague discouraged sound and shook his head helplessly. "I've made lots of mistakes in my life—many of them. But I've been one of the most prominent—in some ways——"

He gave this up and puffed at a dead cigarette.

"I do like you," said Rosemary, "but I don't think you ought to fight a duel."

"Yeah, I should have tried to beat him up, but it's done now. I've let myself be drawn into something that I had no right to be. I have a very violent temper—" He looked closely at Abe as if he expected the statement to be challenged. Then with an aghast laugh he raised the cold cigarette butt toward his mouth. His breathing quickened.

"The trouble was I suggested the duel—if Violet had only kept her mouth shut I could have fixed it. Of course even now I can just leave, or sit back and laugh at the whole thing—but I don't think Violet would ever respect me again."

"Yes, she would," said Rosemary. "She'd respect you more."

"No—you don't know Violet. She's very hard when she gets an advantage over you. We've been married twelve years, we had a little girl seven years old and she died and after that you know how it is. We both played around on the side a little, nothing serious but drifting apart—she called me a coward out there tonight."

Troubled, Rosemary didn't answer.

"Well, we'll see there's as little damage done as possible," said Abe. He opened the leather case. "These are Barban's duelling pistols—I borrowed them so you could get familiar with them. He carries them in his suitcase." He weighed one of the archaic weapons in his hand. Rosemary gave an exclamation of uneasiness and McKisco looked at the pistols anxiously.

"Well—it isn't as if we were going to stand up and pot each other with forty-fives," he said.

"I don't know," said Abe cruelly; "the idea is you can sight better along a long barrel."

"How about distance?" asked McKisco.

"I've inquired about that. If one or the other parties has to be definitely eliminated they make it eight paces, if they're just good and sore it's twenty paces, and if it's only to vindicate their honor it's forty paces. His second agreed with me to make it forty."

"That's good."

"There's a wonderful duel in a novel of Pushkin's," recollected Abe. "Each man stood on the edge of a precipice, so if he was hit at all he was done for."

This seemed very remote and academic to McKisco, who stared at him and said, "What?"

"Do you want to take a quick dip and freshen up?"

"No—no, I couldn't swim." He sighed. "I don't see what it's all about," he said helplessly. "I don't see why I'm doing it."

It was the first thing he had ever done in his life. Actually he was one of those for whom the sensual world does not exist, and faced with a concrete fact he brought to it a vast surprise.

"We might as well be going," said Abe, seeing him fail a little.

"All right." He drank off a stiff drink of brandy, put the flask in his pocket, and said with almost a savage air: "What'll happen if I kill him—will they throw me in jail?"

"I'll run you over the Italian border."

He glanced at Rosemary—and then said apologetically to Abe:

"Before we start there's one thing I'd like to see you about alone."

"I hope neither of you gets hurt," Rosemary said. "I think it's very foolish and you ought to try to stop it."

XI

SHE found Campion downstairs in the deserted lobby.

"I saw you go upstairs," he said excitedly. "Is he all right? When is the duel going to be?"

"I don't know." She resented his speaking of it as a circus, with McKisco as the tragic clown.

"Will you go with me?" he demanded, with the air of having seats. "I've hired the hotel car."

"I don't want to go."

"Why not? I imagine it'll take years off my life but I wouldn't miss it for words. We could watch it from quite far away."

"Why don't you get Mr. Dumphry to go with you?"

His monocle fell out, with no whiskers to hide in—he drew himself up.

"I never want to see him again."

"Well, I'm afraid I can't go. Mother wouldn't like it."

As Rosemary entered her room Mrs. Speers stirred sleepily and called to her:

"Where've you been?"

"I just couldn't sleep. You go back to sleep, Mother."

"Come in my room." Hearing her sit up in bed, Rosemary went in and told her what had happened.

"Why don't you go and see it?" Mrs. Speers suggested. "You needn't go up close and you might be able to help afterwards."

Rosemary did not like the picture of herself looking on and she demurred, but Mrs. Speer's consciousness was still clogged with sleep and she was reminded of night calls to death and calamity when she was the wife of a doctor. "I like you to go places and do things on your own initiative without me—you did much harder things for Rainy's publicity stunts."

Still Rosemary did not see why she should go, but she obeyed the sure, clear voice that had sent her into the stage entrance of the Odéon in Paris when she was twelve and greeted her when she came out again.

She thought she was reprieved when from the steps she saw Abe and McKisco drive away—but after a moment the hotel car came around the corner. Squealing delightedly Luis Campion pulled her in beside him.

"I hid there because they might not let us come. I've got my movie camera, you see."

She laughed helplessly. He was so terrible that he was no longer terrible, only dehumanized.

"I wonder why Mrs. McKisco didn't like the Divers?" she said. "They were very nice to her."

"Oh, it wasn't that. It was something she saw. We never did find exactly what it was because of Barban."

"Then that wasn't what made you so sad."

"Oh, no," he said, his voice breaking, "that was something else that happened when we got back to the hotel. But now I don't care—I wash my hands of it completely."

They followed the other car east along the shore past Juan les Pins, where the skeleton of the new Casino was rising. It was past four and under a blue-gray sky the first fishing boats were creaking out into a glaucous sea. Then they turned off the main road and into the back country.

"It's the golf course," cried Campion. "I'm sure that's where it's going to be."

He was right. When Abe's car pulled up ahead of them the east was crayoned red and yellow, promising a sultry day. Ordering the hotel car into a grove of pines Rosemary and Campion kept in the shadow of a wood and skirted the bleached fairway where Abe and McKisco were walking up and down, the latter raising his head at intervals like a rabbit scenting. Presently there were moving figures over by a farther tee and the watchers made out Barban and his French second—the latter carried the box of pistols under his arm.

Somewhat appalled, McKisco slipped behind Abe and took a long swallow of brandy. He walked on choking and would have marched directly up into the other party, but Abe stopped him and went forward to talk to the Frenchman. The sun was over the horizon.

Campion grabbed Rosemary's arm.

"I can't stand it," he squeaked, almost voiceless. "It's too much. This will cost me——"

"Let go," Rosemary said peremptorily. She breathed a frantic prayer in French.

The principals faced each other, Barban with the sleeve rolled up from his arm. His eyes gleamed restlessly in the sun, but his motion was deliberate as he wiped his palm on the seam of his trousers. McKisco, reckless with brandy, pursed his lips in a whistle and pointed his long nose about nonchalantly, until Abe stepped forward with a handkerchief in his hand. The French second stood with his face turned away. Rosemary caught her breath in terrible pity and gritted her teeth with hatred for Barban; then:

"One—two—three!" Abe counted in a strained voice.

They fired at the same moment. McKisco swayed but recovered himself. Both shots had missed.

"Now, that's enough!" cried Abe.

The duellists walked in, and everyone looked at Barban inquiringly.

"I declare myself unsatisfied."

"What? Sure you're satisfied," said Abe impatiently. "You just don't know it."

"Your man refuses another shot?"

"You're damn right, Tommy. You insisted on this and my client went through with it."

Tommy laughed scornfully.

"The distance was ridiculous," he said. "I'm not accustomed to such farces—your man must remember he's not now in America."

"No use cracking at America," said Abe rather sharply. And then, in a more conciliatory tone, "This has gone far enough, Tommy." They parleyed briskly for a moment—then Barban nodded and bowed coldly to his late antagonist.

"No shake hand?" suggested the French doctor.

"They already know each other," said Abe.

He turned to McKisco.

"Come on, let's get out."

As they strode off, McKisco, in exultation, gripped his arm.

"Wait a minute!" Abe said. "Tommy wants his pistol back. He might need it again."

McKisco handed it over.

"To hell with him," he said in a tough voice. "Tell him he can——"

"Shall I tell him you want another shot?"

"Well, I did it," cried McKisco, as they went along. "And I did it pretty well, didn't I? I wasn't yellow."

"You were pretty drunk," said Abe bluntly.

"No, I wasn't."

"All right, then, you weren't."

"Why would it make any difference if I had a drink or so?"

As his confidence mounted he looked resentfully at Abe.

"What difference does that make?" he repeated.

"If you can't see it, there's no use going into it."

"Don't you know everybody was drunk all the time during the war?"

"Well, let's forget it."

But the episode was not quite over. There were urgent footsteps in the heather behind them and the doctor drew up alongside.

"Pardon, Messieurs," he panted. *"Voulez-vous régler mes honoraires? Naturellement c'est pour soins médicaux seulement. M. Barban n'a qu'un billet de mille et ne peut pas les régler et l'autre a laissé son portemonnaie chez lui."*

"Trust a Frenchman to think of that," said Abe, and then to the doctor. *"Combien?"*

"Let me pay this," said McKisco.

"No, I've got it. We were all in about the same danger."

Abe paid the doctor while McKisco suddenly turned into the bushes and was sick there. Then paler than before he strutted on with Abe toward the car through the now rosy morning.

Campion lay gasping on his back in the shrubbery, the only casualty of the duel, while Rosemary suddenly hysterical with laughter kept kicking at him with her *espadrille.* She did this persistently until she roused him—the only matter of importance to her now was that in a few hours she would see the person whom she still referred to in her mind as "the Divers" on the beach.

XII

THEY were at Voisins waiting for Nicole, six of them, Rosemary, the Norths, Dick Diver and two young French musicians. They were looking over the other patrons of the restaurant to see if they had repose —Dick said no American men had any repose, except himself, and they were seeking an example to confront him with. Things looked black for them—not a man had come into the restaurant for ten minutes without raising his hand to his face.

"We ought never to have given up waxed mustaches," said Abe. "Nevertheless Dick isn't the *only* man with repose——"

"Oh, yes, I am."

"—but he may be the only sober man with repose."

A well-dressed American had come in with two women who swooped and fluttered unself-consciously around a table. Suddenly, he perceived that he was being watched—whereupon his hand rose spasmodically and arranged a phantom bulge in his necktie. In another unseated party a man endlessly patted his shaven cheek with his palm, and his companion mechanically raised and lowered the stub of a cold cigar. The luckier ones fingered eyeglasses and facial hair, the unequipped stroked blank mouths, or even pulled desperately at the lobes of their ears.

A well-known general came in, and Abe, counting on the man's first year at West Point—that year during which no cadet can resign and from which none ever recovers—made a bet with Dick of five dollars.

His hands hanging naturally at his sides, the general waited to be seated. Once his arms swung suddenly backward like a jumper's and Dick said, "Ah!" supposing he had lost control, but the general recovered and they breathed again—the agony was nearly over, the *garçon* was pulling out his chair. . . .

With a touch of fury the conqueror shot up his hand and scratched his gray immaculate head.

"You see," said Dick smugly, "I'm the only one."

Rosemary was quite sure of it and Dick, realizing that he never had a better audience, made the group into so bright a unit that Rosemary felt an impatient disregard for all who were not at their table. They had been two days in Paris but actually they were still under the beach umbrella. When, as at the ball of the Corps des Pages the night before, the surroundings seemed formidable to Rosemary, who had yet to attend a Mayfair party in Hollywood, Dick would bring the scene within range by greeting a few people, a sort of selection—the Divers seemed to have a large acquaintance, but it was always as if the person had not seen them for a long, long time, and was utterly bowled over, "Why, where do you *keep* yourselves?"—and then re-create the unity of his own party by destroying the outsiders softly but permanently with an ironic *coup de grâce.* Presently Rosemary seemed to have known those people herself in some deplorable past, and then got on to them, rejected them, discarded them.

Their own party was overwhelmingly American and sometimes scarcely American at all. It was themselves he gave back to them, blurred by the compromises of how many years.

Into the dark, smoky restaurant, smelling of the rich raw foods on the buffet, slid Nicole's sky-blue suit like a stray segment of the weather outside. Seeing from their eyes how beautiful she was, she thanked them with a smile of radiant appreciation. They were all very nice people for a while, very courteous and all that. Then they grew tired of it and they were funny and bitter, and finally they made a lot of plans. They laughed at things that they would not remember clearly afterward—laughed a lot and the men drank three bottles of wine. The trio of women at the table were representative of the enormous flux of American life. Nicole was the granddaughter of a self-made American capitalist and the granddaughter of a Count of the House of

Lippe Weissenfeld. Mary North was the daughter of a journeyman paper-hanger and a descendant of President Tyler. Rosemary was from the middle of the middle class, catapulted by her mother onto the uncharted heights of Hollywood. Their point of resemblance to each other and their difference from so many American women, lay in the fact that they were all happy to exist in a man's world—they preserved their individuality through men and not by opposition to them. They would all three have made alternatively good courtesans or good wives not by the accident of birth but through the greater accident of finding their man or not finding him.

So Rosemary found it a pleasant party, that luncheon, nicer in that there were only seven people, about the limit of a good party. Perhaps, too, the fact that she was new to their world acted as a sort of catalytic agent to precipitate out all their old reservations about one another. After the table broke up, a waiter directed Rosemary back into the dark hinterland of all French restaurants, where she looked up a phone number by a dim orange bulb, and called Franco-American Films. Sure, they had a print of "Daddy's Girl"—it was out for the moment, but they would run it off later in the week for her at 341 Rue des Saintes Anges—ask for Mr. Crowder.

The semi-booth gave on the *vestiaire* and as Rosemary hung up the receiver she heard two low voices not five feet from her on the other side of a row of coats.

"—So you love me?"

"Oh, *do* I!"

It was Nicole—Rosemary hesitated in the door of the booth—then she heard Dick say:

"I want you terribly—let's go to the hotel now." Nicole gave a little gasping sigh. For a moment the words conveyed nothing at all to Rosemary—but the tone did. The vast secretiveness of it vibrated to herself.

"I want you."

"I'll be at the hotel at four."

Rosemary stood breathless as the voices moved away. She was at first even astonished—she had seen them in their relation to each other as people without personal exigencies—as something cooler. Now a strong current of emotion flowed through her, profound and unidentified. She did not know whether she was attracted or repelled, but only that she was deeply moved. It made her feel very alone as she went back into the restaurant, but it was touching to look in upon, and the passionate gratitude of Nicole's "Oh *do* I!" echoed in her mind. The particular mood of the passage she had witnessed lay ahead of her; but however far she was from it her stomach told her it was all right—she had none of the aversion she had felt in the playing of certain love scenes in pictures.

Being far away from it she nevertheless irrevocably participated in it now, and shopping with Nicole she was much more conscious of the assignation than Nicole herself. She looked at Nicole in a new way, estimating her attractions. Certainly she was the most attractive woman Rosemary had ever met—with her hardness, her devotions and loyalties, and a certain elusiveness, which Rosemary, thinking now through her mother's middle-class mind, associated with her attitude about money. Rosemary spent money she had earned—she was here in Europe due to the fact that she had gone in the pool six times that January day with her temperature roving from 99° in the early morning to 103°, when her mother stopped it.

With Nicole's help Rosemary bought two dresses and

two hats and four pairs of shoes with her money. Nicole bought from a great list that ran two pages, and bought the things in the windows besides. Everything she liked that she couldn't possibly use herself, she bought as a present for a friend. She bought colored beads, folding beach cushions, artificial flowers, honey, a guest bed, bags, scarfs, love birds, miniatures for a doll's house and three yards of some new cloth the color of prawns. She bought a dozen bathing suits, a rubber alligator, a traveling chess set of gold and ivory, big linen handkerchiefs for Abe, two chamois leather jackets of kingfisher blue and burning bush from Hermes—bought all these things not a bit like a high-class courtesan buying underwear and jewels, which were after all professional equipment and insurance—but with an entirely different point of view. Nicole was the product of much ingenuity and toil. For her sake trains began their run at Chicago and traversed the round belly of the continent to California; chicle factories fumed and link belts grew link by link in factories; men mixed toothpaste in vats and drew mouthwash out of copper hogsheads; girls canned tomatoes quickly in August or worked rudely at the Five-and-Tens on Christmas Eve; half-breed Indians toiled on Brazilian coffee plantations and dreamers were muscled out of patent rights in new tractors—these were some of the people who gave a tithe to Nicole, and as the whole system swayed and thundered onward it lent a feverish bloom to such processes of hers as wholesale buying, like the flush of a fireman's face holding his post before a spreading blaze. She illustrated very simple principles, containing in herself her own doom, but illustrated them so accurately that there was grace in the procedure, and presently Rosemary would try to imitate it.

It was almost four. Nicole stood in a shop with a love bird on her shoulder, and had one of her infrequent outbursts of speech.

"Well, what if you hadn't gone in that pool that day—I sometimes wonder about such things. Just before the war we were in Berlin—I was thirteen, it was just before Mother died. My sister was going to a court ball and she had three of the royal princes on her dance card, all arranged by a chamberlain and everything. Half an hour before she was going to start she had a side ache and a high fever. The doctor said it was appendicitis and she ought to be operated on. But Mother had her plans made, so Baby went to the ball and danced till two with an ice pack strapped on under her evening dress. She was operated on at seven o'clock next morning."

It was good to be hard, then; all nice people were hard on themselves. But it was four o'clock and Rosemary kept thinking of Dick waiting for Nicole now at the hotel. She must go there, she must not make him wait for her. She kept thinking, "Why don't you go?" and then suddenly, "Or let me go if you don't want to." But Nicole went to one more place to buy corsages for them both and sent one to Mary North. Only then she seemed to remember and with sudden abstraction she signalled for a taxi.

"Good-by," said Nicole. "We had fun, didn't we?"

"Loads of fun," said Rosemary. It was more difficult than she thought and her whole self protested as Nicole drove away.

XIII

DICK turned the corner of the traverse and continued along the trench walking on the duckboard. He came to a periscope, looked through it a moment, then he got up on the step and peered over the parapet. In front of him beneath a dingy sky was Beaumont Hamel; to his left the tragic hill of Thiepval. Dick stared at them through his field glasses, his throat straining with sadness.

He went on along the trench, and found the others waiting for him in the next traverse. He was full of excitement and he wanted to communicate it to them, to make them understand about this, though actually Abe North had seen battle service and he had not.

"This land here cost twenty lives a foot that summer," he said to Rosemary. She looked out obediently at the rather bare green plain with its low trees of six years' growth. If Dick had added that they were now being shelled she would have believed him that afternoon. Her love had reached a point where now at last she was beginning to be unhappy, to be desperate. She didn't know what to do—she wanted to talk to her mother.

"There are lots of people dead since and we'll all be dead soon," said Abe consolingly.

Rosemary waited tensely for Dick to continue.

"See that little stream—we could walk to it in two minutes. It took the British a month to walk to it—a whole empire walking very slowly, dying in front and pushing forward behind. And another empire walked very slowly backward a few inches a day, leaving the dead like a million bloody rugs. No Europeans will ever do that again in this generation."

"Why, they've only just quit over in Turkey," said Abe. "And in Morocco——"

"That's different. This western-front business couldn't be done again, not for a long time. The young men think they could do it but they couldn't. They could fight the first Marne again but not this. This took religion and years of plenty and tremendous sureties and the exact relation that existed between the classes. The Russians and Italians weren't any good on this front. You had to have a whole-souled sentimental equipment going back further than you could remember. You had to remember Christmas, and postcards of the Crown Prince and his fiancée, and little cafés in Valence and beer gardens in Unter den Linden and weddings at the *mairie*, and going to the Derby, and your grandfather's whiskers."

"General Grant invented this kind of battle at Petersburg in sixty-five."

"No, he didn't—he just invented mass butchery. This kind of battle was invented by Lewis Carroll and Jules Verne and whoever wrote *Undine*, and country deacons bowling and *marraines* in Marseilles and girls seduced in the back lanes of Würtemberg and Westphalia. Why, this was a love battle—there was a century of middle-class love spent here. This was the last love battle."

"You want to hand over this battle to D. H. Lawrence," said Abe.

"All my beautiful lovely safe world blew itself up here with a great gust of high explosive love," Dick mourned persistently. "Isn't that true, Rosemary?"

"I don't know," she answered with a grave face. "You know everything."

They dropped behind the others. Suddenly a shower of earth gobs and pebbles came down on them and Abe yelled from the next traverse:

"The war spirit's getting into me again. I have a hundred years of Ohio love behind me and I'm going to bomb out this trench." His head popped up over the embankment. "You're dead—don't you know the rules? That was a grenade."

Rosemary laughed and Dick picked up a retaliatory handful of stones and then put them down.

"I couldn't kid here," he said rather apologetically. "The silver cord is cut and the golden bowl is broken and all that, but an old romantic like me can't do anything about it."

"I'm romantic too."

They came out of the neat restored trench, and faced a memorial to the Newfoundland dead. Reading the inscription Rosemary burst into sudden tears. Like most women she liked to be told how she should feel, and she liked Dick's telling her which things were ludicrous and which things were sad. But most of all she wanted him to know how she loved him, now that the fact was upsetting everything, now that she was walking over the battle-field in a thrilling dream.

After that they got in their car and started back toward Amiens. A thin warm rain was falling on the new scrubby woods and underbrush and they passed great funeral pyres of sorted duds, shells, bombs, grenades, and equipment, helmets, bayonets, gun stocks and rotten leather, abandoned six years in the ground. And suddenly around a bend the white caps of a great sea of graves. Dick asked the chauffeur to stop.

"There's that girl—and she still has her wreath."

They watched as he got out and went over to the girl, who stood uncertainly by the gate with a wreath in her hand. Her taxi waited. She was a red-haired girl from Tennessee whom they had met on the train this morning, come from Knoxville to lay a memorial on her brother's grave. There were tears of vexation on her face.

"The War Department must have given me the wrong number," she whimpered. "It had another name on it. I been lookin' for it since two o'clock, and there's so many graves."

"Then if I were you I'd just lay it on any grave without looking at the name," Dick advised her.

"You reckon that's what I ought to do?"

"I think that's what he'd have wanted you to do."

It was growing dark and the rain was coming down harder. She left the wreath on the first grave inside the gate, and accepted Dick's suggestion that she dismiss her taxi-cab and ride back to Amiens with them.

Rosemary shed tears again when she heard of the mishap—altogether it had been a watery day, but she felt that she had learned something, though exactly what it was she did not know. Later she remembered all the hours of the afternoon as happy—one of those uneventful times that seem at the moment only a link between past and future pleasure but turn out to have been the pleasure itself.

Amiens was an echoing purple town, still sad with the war, as some railroad stations were:—the Gare du Nord and Waterloo station in London. In the daytime one is deflated by such towns, with their little trolley cars of twenty years ago crossing the great gray cobblestoned squares in front of the cathedral, and the very weather seems to have a quality of the past, faded weather like that of old photographs. But after dark all that is most satisfactory in French life swims back into the picture—the sprightly tarts, the men arguing with a hundred *voilàs* in the cafés, the couples drifting, head to head, toward the satisfactory inexpensiveness of nowhere. Waiting for the train they sat in a big arcade, tall enough to release the smoke and chatter and music upward and obligingly the orchestra launched into "Yes, We Have No Bananas,"—they clapped, because the leader looked so pleased with himself. The Tennessee girl forgot her sorrow and enjoyed herself, even began flirtations of tropical eye-rollings and pawings, with Dick and Abe. They teased her gently.

Then, leaving infinitesimal sections of Wurtemburgers, Prussian Guards, Chasseurs Alpins, Manchester mill hands and old Etonians to pursue their eternal dissolution under the warm rain, they took the train for Paris. They ate sandwiches of mortadel sausage and bel paese cheese made up in the station restaurant, and drank Beaujolais. Nicole was abstracted, biting her lip restlessly and reading over the guide-books to the battle-field that Dick had brought along—indeed, he had made a quick study of the whole affair, simplifying it always until it bore a faint resemblance to one of his own parties.

XIV

WHEN they reached Paris Nicole was too tired to go on to the grand illumination at the Decorative Arts Exposition as they had planned. They left her at the Hôtel Roi George, and as she disappeared between the intersecting planes made by lobby lights of the glass doors, Rosemary's oppression lifted. Nicole was a force—not necessarily well disposed or predictable like her mother—an incalculable force. Rosemary was somewhat afraid of her.

At eleven she sat with Dick and the Norths at a houseboat café just opened on the Seine. The river shimmered with lights from the bridges and cradled many cold moons. On Sundays sometimes when Rosemary and her mother had lived in Paris they had taken the little steamer up to Suresnes and talked about plans for the future. They had little money but Mrs. Speers was so sure of Rosemary's beauty and had implanted in her so much ambition, that she was willing to gamble the money on "advantages"; Rosemary in turn was to repay her mother when she got her start. . . .

Since reaching Paris Abe North had had a thin vinous fur over him; his eyes were bloodshot from sun and wine. Rosemary realized for the first time that he was always stopping in places to get a drink, and she wondered how Mary North liked it. Mary was quiet, so quiet save for her frequent laughter that Rosemary had learned little about her. She liked the straight dark hair brushed back until it met some sort of natural cascade that took care of it—from time to time it eased with a jaunty slant over the corner of her temple, until it was almost in her eye when she tossed her head and caused it to fall sleek into place once more.

"We'll turn in early to-night, Abe, after this drink." Mary's voice was light but it held a little flicker of anxiety. "You don't want to be poured on the boat."

"It's pretty late now," Dick said. "We'd all better go."

The noble dignity of Abe's face took on a certain stubbornness, and he remarked with determination:

"Oh, no." He paused gravely. "Oh, no, not yet. We'll have another bottle of champagne."

"No more for me," said Dick.

"It's Rosemary I'm thinking of. She's a natural alcoholic—keeps a bottle of gin in the bathroom and all that —her mother told me."

He emptied what was left of the first bottle into Rosemary's glass. She had made herself quite sick the first day in Paris with quarts of lemonade; after that she had taken nothing with them, but now she raised the champagne and drank at it.

"But what's this?" exclaimed Dick. "You told me you didn't drink."

"I didn't say I was never going to."

"What about your mother?"

"I'm just going to drink this one glass." She felt some necessity for it. Dick drank, not too much, but he drank, and perhaps it would bring her closer to him, be a part of the equipment for what she had to do. She drank it quickly, choked and then said, "Besides, yesterday was my birthday—I was eighteen."

"Why didn't you tell us?" they said indignantly.

"I knew you'd make a fuss over it and go to a lot of trouble." She finished the champagne. "So this is the celebration."

"It most certainly is not," Dick assured her. "The dinner tomorrow night is your birthday party and don't forget it. Eighteen—why that's a terribly important age."

"I used to think until you're eighteen nothing matters," said Mary.

"That's right," Abe agreed. "And afterward it's the same way."

"Abe feels that nothing matters till he gets on the boat," said Mary. "This time he really has got everything planned out when he gets to New York." She spoke as though she were tired of saying things that no longer had a meaning for her, as if in reality the course that she and her husband followed, or failed to follow, had become merely an intention.

"He'll be writing music in America and I'll be working at singing in Munich, so when we get together again there'll be nothing we can't do."

"That's wonderful," agreed Rosemary, feeling the champagne.

"Meanwhile, another touch of champagne for Rosemary. Then she'll be more able to rationalize the acts of her lymphatic glands. They only begin to function at eighteen."

Dick laughed indulgently at Abe, whom he loved, and

in whom he had long lost hope: "That's medically incorrect and we're going." Catching the faint patronage Abe said lightly:

"Something tells me I'll have a new score on Broadway long before you've finished your scientific treatise."

"I hope so," said Dick evenly. "I hope so. I may even abandon what you call my 'scientific treatise.'"

"Oh, Dick!" Mary's voice was startled, was shocked. Rosemary had never before seen Dick's face utterly expressionless; she felt that this announcement was something momentous and she was inclined to exclaim with Mary, "Oh, Dick!"

But suddenly Dick laughed again, added to his remark "—abandon it for another one," and got up from the table.

"But Dick, sit down. I want to know——"

"I'll tell you some time. Good night, Abe. Good night, Mary."

"Good night, dear Dick." Mary smiled as if she were going to be perfectly happy sitting there on the almost deserted boat. She was a brave, hopeful woman and she was following her husband somewhere, changing herself to this kind of person or that, without being able to lead him a step out of his path, and sometimes realizing with discouragement how deep in him the guarded secret of her direction lay. And yet an air of luck clung about her, as if she were a sort of token. . . .

XV

"WHAT is it you are giving up?" demanded Rosemary, facing Dick earnestly in the taxi.

"Nothing of importance."

"Are you a scientist?"

"I'm a doctor of medicine."

"Oh-h!" She smiled delightedly. "My father was a doctor too. Then why don't you—" she stopped.

"There's no mystery. I didn't disgrace myself at the height of my career, and hide away on the Riviera. I'm just not practising. You can't tell, I'll probably practise again some day."

Rosemary put up her face quietly to be kissed. He looked at her for a moment as if he didn't understand. Then holding her in the hollow of his arm he rubbed his cheek against her cheek's softness, and then looked down at her for another long moment.

"Such a lovely child," he said gravely.

She smiled up at him; her hands playing conventionally with the lapels of his coat. "I'm in love with you and Nicole. Actually that's my secret—I can't even talk about you to anybody because I don't want any more people to know how wonderful you are. Honestly—I love you and Nicole—I do."

—So many times he had heard this—even the formula was the same.

Suddenly she came toward him, her youth vanishing as she passed inside the focus of his eyes and he had kissed her breathlessly as if she were any age at all. Then she lay back against his arm and sighed.

"I've decided to give you up," she said.

Dick started—had he said anything to imply that she possessed any part of him?

"But that's very mean," he managed to say lightly, "just when I was getting interested."

"I've loved you so—" As if it had been for years. She was weeping a little now. "I've loved you so-o-o."

Then he should have laughed, but he heard himself saying, "Not only are you beautiful but you are somehow on the grand scale. Everything you do, like pretending to be in love or pretending to be shy gets across."

In the dark cave of the taxi, fragrant with the perfume Rosemary had bought with Nicole, she came close again, clinging to him. He kissed her without enjoying it. He knew that there was passion there, but there was no shadow of it in her eyes or on her mouth; there was a faint spray of champagne on her breath. She clung nearer desperately and once more he kissed her and was chilled by the innocence of her kiss, by the glance that at the moment of contact looked beyond him out into the darkness of the night, the darkness of the world. She did not know yet that splendor is something in the heart; at the moment when she realized that and melted into the passion of the universe he could take her without question or regret.

Her room in the hotel was diagonally across from theirs and nearer the elevator. When they reached the door she said suddenly:

"I know you don't love me—I don't expect it. But you said I should have told you about my birthday. Well, I did, and now for my birthday present I want you to come into my room a minute while I tell you something. Just one minute."

They went in and he closed the door, and Rosemary stood close to him, not touching him. The night had drawn the color from her face—she was pale as pale now, she was a white carnation left after a dance.

"When you smile—" he had recovered his paternal attitude, perhaps because of Nicole's silent proximity—"I always think I'll see a gap where you've lost some baby teeth."

But he was too late—she came close up against him with a forlorn whisper.

"Take me."

"Take you where?"

Astonishment froze him rigid.

"Go on," she whispered. "Oh, please go on, whatever they do. I don't care if I don't like it—I never expected to—I've always hated to think about it but now I don't. I want you to."

She was astonished at herself—she had never imagined she could talk like that. She was calling on things she had read, seen, dreamed through a decade of convent hours. Suddenly she knew too that it was one of her greatest rôles and she flung herself into it more passionately.

"This is not as it should be," Dick deliberated. "Isn't it just the champagne? Let's more or less forget it."

"Oh, no, *now.* I want you to do it now, take me, show me, I'm absolutely yours and I want to be."

"For one thing, have you thought how much it would hurt Nicole?"

"She won't know—this won't have anything to do with her."

He continued kindly.

"Then there's the fact that I love Nicole."

"But you can love more than just one person, can't you? Like I love Mother and I love you—more. I love you more now."

"—the fourth place you're not in love with me but you might be afterwards, and that would begin your life with a terrible mess."

"No, I promise I'll never see you again. I'll get Mother and go to America right away."

He dismissed this. He was remembering too vividly the youth and freshness of her lips. He took another tone.

"You're just in that mood."

"Oh, please, I don't care even if I had a baby. I could

go into Mexico like a girl at the studio. Oh, this is so different from anything I ever thought—I used to hate it when they kissed me seriously." He saw she was still under the impression that it must happen. "Some of them had great big teeth, but you're all different and beautiful. I want you to do it."

"I believe you think people just kiss some way and you want me to kiss you."

"Oh, don't tease me—I'm not a baby. I know you're not in love with me." She was suddenly humble and quiet. "I didn't expect that much. I know I must seem just nothing to you."

"Nonsense. But you seem young to me." His thoughts added, "—there'd be so much to teach you."

Rosemary waited, breathing eagerly till Dick said: "And lastly things aren't arranged so that this could be as you want."

Her face drooped with dismay and disappointment and Dick said automatically, "We'll have to simply—" He stopped himself, followed her to the bed, sat down beside her while she wept. He was suddenly confused, not about the ethics of the matter, for the impossibility of it was sheerly indicated from all angles, but simply confused, and for a moment his usual grace, the tensile strength of his balance, was absent.

"I knew you wouldn't," she sobbed. "It was just a forlorn hope."

He stood up.

"Good night, child. This is a damn shame. Let's drop it out of the picture." He gave her two lines of hospital patter to go to sleep on. "So many people are going to love you and it might be nice to meet your first love all intact, emotionally too. That's an old-fashioned idea, isn't it?" She looked up at him as he took a step toward the door; she looked at him without the slightest idea as to what was in his head, she saw him take another step in slow motion, turn and look at her again, and she wanted for a moment to hold him and devour him, wanted his mouth, his ears, his coat collar, wanted to surround him and engulf him; she saw his hand fall on the doorknob. Then she gave up and sank back on the bed. When the door closed she got up and went to the mirror, where she began brushing her hair, sniffling a little. One hundred and fifty strokes Rosemary gave it, as usual, then a hundred and fifty more. She brushed it until her arm ached, then she changed arms and went on brushing. . . .

XVI

SHE woke up cooled and shamed. The sight of her beauty in the mirror did not reassure her but only awakened the ache of yesterday and a letter, forwarded by her mother, from the boy who had taken her to the Yale prom last fall, which announced his presence in Paris was no help—all that seemed far away. She emerged from her room for the ordeal of meeting the Divers weighted with a double trouble. But it was hidden by a sheath as impermeable as Nicole's when they met and went together to a series of fittings. It was consoling, though, when Nicole remarked, apropos of a distraught saleswoman: "Most people think everybody feels about them much more violently than they actually do—they think other people's opinions of them swing through great arcs of approval or disapproval." Yesterday in her expansiveness Rosemary would have resented that remark—today in her desire to minimize what had happened she welcomed it eagerly. She admired Nicole for her beauty and her wisdom, and also for the first time in her life she was jealous. Just before leaving Gausse's hotel her mother had said in that casual tone, which Rosemary knew concealed her most significant opinions, that Nicole was a great beauty, with the frank implication that Rosemary was not. This did not bother Rosemary, who had only recently been allowed to learn that she was even personable; so that her prettiness never seemed exactly her own but rather an acquirement, like her French. Nevertheless, in the taxi she looked at Nicole, matching herself against her. There were all the potentialities for romantic love in that lovely body and in the delicate mouth, sometimes tight, sometimes expectantly half open to the world. Nicole had been a beauty as a young girl and she would be a beauty later when her skin stretched tight over her high cheek-bones—the essential structure was there. She had been white-Saxon-blonde but she was more beautiful now that her hair had darkened than when it had been like a cloud and more beautiful than she.

"We lived there," Rosemary suddenly pointed to a building in the Rue des Saints-Pères.

"That's strange. Because when I was twelve Mother and Baby and I once spent a winter there," and she pointed to a hotel directly across the street. The two dingy fronts stared at them, gray echoes of girlhood.

"We'd just built our Lake Forest house and we were economizing," Nicole continued. "At least Baby and I and the governess economized and Mother traveled."

"We were economizing too," said Rosemary, realizing that the word meant different things to them.

"Mother always spoke of it very carefully as a small hotel—" Nicole gave her quick magnetic little laugh "—I mean instead of saying a 'cheap' hotel. If any swanky friends asked us our address we'd never say, 'We're in a dingy little hole over in the apache quarter where we're glad of running water,'—we'd say 'We're in a small hotel.' As if all the big ones were too noisy and vulgar for us. Of course the friends always saw through us and told everyone about it, but Mother always said it showed we knew our way around Europe. She did, of course: she was born a German citizen. But her mother was American, and she was brought up in Chicago, and she was more American than European."

They were meeting the others in two minutes, and Rosemary reconstructed herself once more as they got out of the taxi in the Rue Guynemer, across from the Luxembourg Gardens. They were lunching in the Norths' already dismantled apartment high above the green mass of leaves. The day seemed different to Rosemary from the day before— When she saw him face to face their eyes met and brushed like birds' wings. After that everything was all right, everything was wonderful, she knew that he was beginning to fall in love with her. She felt wildly happy, felt the warm sap of emotion being pumped through her body. A cool, clear confidence deepened and sang in her. She scarcely looked at Dick but she knew everything was all right.

After luncheon the Divers and the Norths and Rosemary went to the Franco-American Films, to be joined by Collis Clay, her young man from New Haven, to whom she had telephoned. He was a Georgian, with the peculiarly regular, even stenciled ideas of Southerners who are educated in the North. Last winter she had thought him attractive—once they held hands in an automobile going from New Haven to New York; now he no longer existed for her.

In the projection room she sat between Collis Clay and Dick while the mechanic mounted the reels of "Daddy's Girl" and a French executive fluttered about her trying to talk American slang. "Yes, boy," he said when there was trouble with the projector, "I have not any benenas." Then the lights went out, there was the sudden click and a flickering noise and she was alone with Dick at last. They looked at each other in the half darkness.

"Dear Rosemary," he murmured. Their shoulders touched. Nicole stirred restlessly at the end of the row and Abe coughed convulsively and blew his nose; then they all settled down and the picture ran.

There she was—the school girl of a year ago, hair down her back and rippling out stiffly like the solid hair of a tanagra figure; there she was—*so* young and innocent—the product of her mother's loving care; there she was—embodying all the immaturity of the race, cutting a new cardboard paper doll to pass before its empty harlot's mind. She remembered how she had felt in that dress, especially fresh and new under the fresh young silk.

Daddy's girl. Was it a 'itty-bitty bravekins and did it suffer? Ooo-ooo-tweet, de tweetest thing, wasn't she dest too tweet? Before her tiny fist the forces of lust and corruption rolled away; nay, the very march of destiny stopped; inevitably became evitable, syllogism, dialectic, all rationality fell away. Women would forget the dirty dishes at home and weep, even within the picture one woman wept so long that she almost stole the film away from Rosemary. She wept all over a set that cost a fortune, in a Duncan Phyfe dining-room, in an aviation port, and during a yacht race that was only used in two flashes, in a subway and finally in a bathroom. But Rosemary triumphed. Her fineness of character, her courage and steadfastness intruded upon by the vulgarity of the world, and Rosemary showing what it took with a face that had not yet become mask-like—yet it was actually so moving that the emotions of the whole row of people went out to her at intervals during the picture.

There was a break once and the light went on and after the chatter of applause Dick said to her sincerely: "I'm simply astounded. You're going to be one of the best actresses on the stage."

Then back to "Daddy's Girl": happier days now, and a lovely shot of Rosemary and her parent united at the last in a father complex so apparent that Dick winced for all psychologists at the vicious sentimentality. The screen vanished, the lights went on, the moment had come.

"I've arranged one other thing," announced Rosemary to the company at large, "I've arranged a test for Dick."

"A what?"

"A screen test, they'll take one now."

There was an awful silence—then an irrepressible chortle from the Norths. Rosemary watched Dick comprehend what she meant, his face moving first in an Irish way; simultaneously she realized that she had made some mistake in the playing of her trump and still she did not suspect that the card was at fault.

"I don't want a test," said Dick firmly; then, seeing the situation as a whole, he continued lightly, "Rosemary, I'm disappointed. The pictures make a fine career for a woman—but my God, they can't photograph me. I'm an old scientist all wrapped up in his private life."

Nicole and Mary urged him ironically to seize the opportunity; they teased him, both faintly annoyed at not having been asked for a sitting. But Dick closed the subject with a somewhat tart discussion of actors: "The strongest guard is placed at the gateway to nothing," he said. "Maybe because the condition of emptiness is too shameful to be divulged."

In the taxi with Dick and Collis Clay—they were dropping Collis, and Dick was taking Rosemary to a tea from which Nicole and the Norths had resigned in order to do the things Abe had left undone till the last—in the taxi Rosemary reproached him.

"I thought if the test turned out to be good I could take it to California with me. And then maybe if they liked it you'd come out and be my leading man in a picture."

He was overwhelmed. "It was a darn sweet thought, but I'd rather look at *you*. You were about the nicest sight I ever looked at."

"That's a great picture," said Collis. "I've seen it four times. I know one boy at New Haven who's seen it a dozen times—he went all the way to Hartford to see it one time. And when I brought Rosemary up to New Haven he was so shy he wouldn't meet her. Can you beat that? This girl knocks them cold."

Dick and Rosemary looked at each other, wanting to be alone, but Collis failed to understand.

"I'll drop you where you're going," he suggested. "I'm staying at the Lutetia."

"We'll drop you," said Dick.

"It'll be easier for me to drop you. No trouble at all."

"I think it will be better if we drop you."

"But—" began Collis; he grasped the situation at last and began discussing with Rosemary when he would see her again.

Finally, he was gone, with the shadowy unimportance but the offensive bulk of the third party. The car stopped unexpectedly, unsatisfactorily, at the address Dick had given. He drew a long breath.

"Shall we go in?"

"I don't care," Rosemary said. "I'll do anything you want."

He considered.

"I almost have to go in—she wants to buy some pictures from a friend of mine who needs the money."

Rosemary smoothed the brief expressive disarray of her hair.

"We'll stay just five minutes," he decided. "You're not going to like these people."

She assumed that they were dull and stereotyped people, or gross and drunken people, or tiresome, insistent people, or any of the sorts of people that the Divers avoided. She was entirely unprepared for the impression that the scene made on her.

XVII

IT WAS a house hewn from the frame of Cardinal de Retz's palace in the Rue Monsieur, but once inside the door there was nothing of the past, nor of any present that Rosemary knew. The outer shell, the masonry, seemed rather to enclose the future so that it was an electric-like shock, a definite nervous experience, perverted as a breakfast of oatmeal and hashish, to cross that threshold, if it could be so called, into the long hall of blue steel, silver-gilt, and the myriad facets of many oddly beveled mirrors. The effect was unlike that of any part of the Decorative Arts Exhibition—for there were people *in* it, not in front of it. Rosemary had the detached false-and-exalted feeling of being on a set and she guessed that everyone else present had that feeling too.

There were about thirty people, mostly women, and all fashioned by Louisa M. Alcott or Madame de Ségur; and they functioned on this set as cautiously, as precisely, as does a human hand picking up jagged broken glass. Neither individually nor as a crowd could they be said to dominate the environment, as one comes to dominate a work of art he may possess, no matter how esoteric, no one knew what this room meant because it was evolving into something else, becoming everything a room was not; to exist in it was as difficult as walking on a highly polished moving stairway, and no one could succeed at all save with the aforementioned qualities of a hand moving among broken glass—which qualities limited and defined the majority of those present.

These were of two sorts. There were the Americans and English who had been dissipating all spring and summer, so that now everything they did had a purely nervous inspiration. They were very quiet and lethargic at certain hours and then they exploded into sudden quarrels and breakdowns and seductions. The other class, who might be called the exploiters, was formed by the sponges, who were sober, serious people by comparison, with a purpose in life and no time for fooling. These kept their balance best in that environment, and what tone there was, beyond the apartment's novel organization of light values, came from them.

The Frankenstein took down Dick and Rosemary at a gulp—it separated them immediately and Rosemary suddenly discovered herself to be an insincere little person, living all in the upper registers of her throat and wishing the director would come. There was however such a wild beating of wings in the room that she did not feel her position was more incongruous than anyone else's. In addition, her training told and after a series of semi-military turns, shifts, and marches she found herself presumably talking to a neat, slick girl with a lovely boy's face, but actually absorbed by a conversation taking place on a sort of gun-metal ladder diagonally opposite her and four feet away.

There was a trio of young women sitting on the bench. They were all tall and slender with small heads groomed like manikins' heads, and as they talked the heads waved gracefully about above their dark tailored suits, rather like long-stemmed flowers and rather like cobras' hoods.

"Oh, they give a good show," said one of them, in a deep rich voice. "Practically the best show in Paris—I'd be the last one to deny that. But after all—" She sighed. "Those phrases he uses over and over—'Oldest inhabitant gnawed by rodents.' You laugh once."

"I prefer people whose lives have more corrugated surfaces," said the second, "and I don't like her."

"I've never really been able to get very excited about them, or their entourage either. Why, for example the entirely liquid Mr. North?"

"He's out," said the first girl. "But you must admit that the party in question can be one of the most charming human beings you have ever met."

It was the first hint Rosemary had had that they were talking about the Divers, and her body grew tense with indignation. But the girl talking to her, in the starched blue shirt with the bright blue eyes and the red cheeks and the very gray suit, a poster of a girl, had begun to play up. Desperately she kept sweeping things from between them, afraid that Rosemary couldn't see her, sweeping them away until presently there was not so much as a veil of brittle humor hiding the girl, and with distaste Rosemary saw her plain.

"Couldn't you have lunch, or maybe dinner, or lunch the day after?" begged the girl. Rosemary looked about for Dick, finding him with the hostess, to whom he had been talking since they came in. Their eyes met and he nodded slightly, and simultaneously the three cobra women noticed her; their long necks darted toward her and they fixed finely critical glances upon her. She looked back at them defiantly, acknowledging that she had heard what they said. Then she threw off her exigent vis-à-vis with a polite but clipped parting that she had just learned from Dick, and went over to join him. The hostess—she was another tall rich American girl, promenading insouciantly upon the national prosperity—was asking Dick innumerable questions about Gausse's Hôtel, whither she evidently wanted to come, and battering persistently against his reluctance. Rosemary's presence reminded her that she had been recalcitrant as a hostess and glancing about she said: "Have you met any one amusing, have you met Mr.—" Her eyes groped for a male who might interest Rosemary, but Dick said they must go. They left immediately, moving over the brief threshold of the future to the sudden past of the stone façade without.

"Wasn't it terrible?" he said.

"Terrible," she echoed obediently.

"Rosemary?"

She murmured, "What?" in an awed voice.

"I feel terribly about this."

She was shaken with audibly painful sobs. "Have you got a handkerchief?" she faltered. But there was little time to cry, and lovers now they fell ravenously on the quick seconds while outside the taxi windows the green and cream twilight faded, and the fire-red, gas-blue, ghost-green signs began to shine smokily through the tranquil rain. It was nearly six, the streets were in movement, the *bistros* gleamed, the Place de la Concorde moved by in pink majesty as the cab turned north.

They looked at each other at last, murmuring names that were a spell. Softly the two names lingered on the air, died away more slowly than other words, other names, slower than music in the mind.

"I don't know what came over me last night," Rosemary said. "That glass of champagne? I've never done anything like that before."

"You simply said you loved me."

"I do love you—I can't change that." It was time for Rosemary to cry, so she cried a little in her handkerchief.

"I'm afraid I'm in love with you," said Dick, "and that's not the best thing that could happen."

Again the names—then they lurched together as if the taxi had swung them. Her breasts crushed flat against him, her mouth was all new and warm, owned in common. They stopped thinking with an almost painful relief, stopped seeing; they only breathed and sought each other. They were both in the gray gentle world of a mild hangover of fatigue when the nerves relax in bunches like piano strings, and crackle suddenly like wicker chairs. Nerves so raw and tender must surely join other nerves, lips to lips, breast to breast. . . .

They were still in the happier stage of love. They were full of brave illusions about each other, tremendous illusions, so that the communion of self with self seemed to be on a plane where no other human relations mattered. They both seemed to have arrived there with an extraordinary innocence as though a series of pure accidents had driven them together, so many accidents that at last they were forced to conclude that they were for each other. They had arrived with clean hands, or so it seemed, after no traffic with the merely curious and clandestine.

But for Dick that portion of the road was short; the turning came before they reached the hotel.

"There's nothing to do about it," he said, with a feeling of panic. "I'm in love with you but it doesn't change what I said last night."

"That doesn't matter now. I just wanted to make you love me—if you love me everything's all right."

"Unfortunately I do. But Nicole mustn't know—she mustn't suspect even faintly. Nicole and I have got to go on together. In a way that's more important than just wanting to go on."

"Kiss me once more."

He kissed her, but momentarily he had left her.

"Nicole mustn't suffer—she loves me and I love her—you understand that."

She did understand—it was the sort of thing she understood well, not hurting people. She knew the Divers loved each other because it had been her primary assumption. She had thought however that it was a rather cooled relation, and actually rather like the love of herself and her mother. When people have so much for outsiders didn't it indicate a lack of inner intensity?

"And I mean love," he said, guessing her thoughts. "Active love—it's more complicated than I can tell you. It was responsible for that crazy duel."

"How did you know about the duel? I thought we were to keep it from you."

"Do you think Abe can keep a secret?" He spoke with incisive irony. "Tell a secret over the radio, publish it in a tabloid, but never tell it to a man who drinks more than three or four a day."

She laughed in agreement, staying close to him.

"So you understand my relations with Nicole are complicated. She's not very strong—she looks strong but she isn't. And this makes rather a mess."

"Oh, say that later! But kiss me now—love me now. I'll love you and never let Nicole see."

"You darling."

They reached the hotel and Rosemary walked a little behind him, to admire him, to adore him. His step was alert as if he had just come from some great doings and was hurrying on toward others. Organizer of private gaiety, curator of a richly incrusted happiness. His hat was a perfect hat and he carried a heavy stick and yellow gloves. She thought what a good time they would all have being with him tonight.

They walked upstairs—five flights. At the first landing they stopped and kissed; she was careful on the next landing, on the third more careful still. On the next—there were two more—she stopped half way and kissed him fleetingly good-by. At his urgency she walked down with him to the one below for a minute—and then up and up. Finally it was good-by with their hands stretching to touch along the diagonal of the banister and then the fingers slipping apart. Dick went back downstairs to make some arrangements for the evening—Rosemary ran to her room and wrote a letter to her mother; she was conscience-stricken because she did not miss her mother at all.

XVIII

ALTHOUGH the Divers were honestly apathetic to organized fashion, they were nevertheless too acute to abandon its contemporaneous rhythm and beat—Dick's parties were all concerned with excitement, and a chance breath of fresh night air was the more precious for being experienced in the intervals of the excitement.

The party that night moved with the speed of a slapstick comedy. They were twelve, they were sixteen, they were quartets in separate motors bound on a quick Odyssey over Paris. Everything had been foreseen. People joined them as if by magic, accompanied them as specialists, almost guides, through a phase of the evening, dropped out and were succeeded by other people, so that it appeared as if the freshness of each one had been husbanded for them all day. Rosemary appreciated how different it was from any party in Hollywood, no matter how splendid in scale. There was, among many diversions, the car of the Shah of Persia. Where Dick had commandeered this vehicle, what bribery was employed, these were facts of irrelevance. Rosemary accepted it as merely a new facet of the fabulous, which for two years had filled her life. The car had been built on a special chassis in America. Its wheels were of silver, so was the radiator. The inside of the body was inlaid with innumerable brilliants which would be replaced with true gems by the court jeweller when the car arrived in Teheran the following week. There was only one real seat in back, because the Shah must ride alone, so they took turns riding in it and sitting on the marten fur that covered the floor.

But always there was Dick. Rosemary assured the image of her mother, ever carried with her, that never, never had she known anyone so nice, so thoroughly nice as Dick was that night. She compared him with the two Englishmen, whom Abe addressed conscientiously as "Major Hengest and Mr. Horsa," and with the heir to a Scandinavian throne and the novelist just back from Russia, and with Abe, who was desperate and witty, and with Collis Clay, who joined them somewhere and stayed along—and felt there was no comparison. The enthusiasm, the selflessness behind the whole performance ravished her, the technic of moving many varied types, each as immobile, as dependent on supplies of attention as an infantry battalion is dependent on rations, appeared so effortless that he still had pieces of his own most personal self for everyone.

—Afterward she remembered the times when she had felt the happiest. The first time was when she and Dick danced together and she felt her beauty sparkling bright against his tall, strong form as they floated, hovering like people in an amusing dream—he turned her here and there with such a delicacy of suggestion that she was like a bright bouquet, a piece of precious cloth being displayed before fifty eyes. There was a moment when they were not dancing at all, simply clinging together. Sometime in the early morning they were alone, and her damp powdery young body came up close to him in a crush of tired cloth, and stayed there, crushed against a background of other people's hats and wraps. . . .

The time she laughed most was later, when six of them, the best of them, noblest relics of the evening, stood in the dusky front lobby of the Ritz telling the night concierge that General Pershing was outside and wanted caviare and champagne. "He brooks no delay. Every man, every gun is at his service." Frantic waiters emerged from nowhere, a table was set in the lobby, and Abe came in representing General Pershing while they stood up and mumbled remembered fragments of war songs at him. In the waiters' injured reaction to this anti-climax they found themselves neglected, so they built a waiter trap—a huge and fantastic device constructed of all the furniture in the lobby and functioning like one of the bizarre machines of a Goldberg cartoon. Abe shook his head doubtfully at it.

"Perhaps it would be better to steal a musical saw and——"

"That's enough," Mary interrupted. "When Abe begins bringing up that it's time to go home." Anxiously she confided to Rosemary:

"I've got to get Abe home. His boat train leaves at eleven. It's so important—I feel the whole future depends on his catching it, but whenever I argue with him he does the exact opposite."

"I'll try and persuade him," offered Rosemary.

"Would you?" Mary said doubtfully. "Maybe you could."

Then Dick came up to Rosemary:

"Nicole and I are going home and we thought you'd want to go with us."

Her face was pale with fatigue in the false dawn. Two wan dark spots in her cheek marked where the color was by day.

"I can't," she said. "I promised Mary North to stay along with them—or Abe'll never go to bed. Maybe you could do something."

"Don't you know you can't do anything about people?" he advised her. "If Abe was my room-mate in college, tight for the first time, it'd be different. Now there's nothing to do."

"Well, I've got to stay. He says he'll go to bed if we only come to the Halles with him," she said, almost defiantly.

He kissed the inside of her elbow quickly.

"Don't let Rosemary go home alone," Nicole called to Mary as they left. "We feel responsible to her mother."

—Later Rosemary and the Norths and a manufacturer of dolls' voices from Newark and ubiquitous Collis and a big splendidly dressed oil Indian named George T. Horseprotection were riding along on top of thousands of carrots in a market wagon. The earth in the carrot beards was fragrant and sweet in the darkness, and Rosemary was so high up in the load that she could hardly see the others in the long shadow between infrequent street lamps. Their voices came from far off, as if they were having experiences different from hers, different and far away, for she was with Dick in her heart, sorry she had come with the Norths, wishing she was at the hotel and him asleep across the hall, or that he was here beside her with the warm darkness streaming down.

"Don't come up," she called to Collis, "the carrots will all roll." She threw one at Abe who was sitting beside the driver, stiffly like an old man. . . .

Later she was homeward bound at last in broad daylight, with the pigeons already breaking over Saint-Sulpice. All of them began to laugh spontaneously because they knew it was still last night while the people in the streets had the delusion that it was bright hot morning.

"At last I've been on a wild party," thought Rosemary, "but it's no fun when Dick isn't there."

She felt a little betrayed and sad, but presently a moving object came into sight. It was a huge horse-chestnut tree in full bloom bound for the Champs Élysées, strapped now into a long truck and simply shaking with laughter—like a lovely person in an undignified position yet confident none the less of being lovely. Looking at it with fascination Rosemary identified herself with it, and laughed cheerfully with it, and everything all at once seemed gorgeous.

XIX

ABE left from the Gare Saint Lazare at eleven—he stood alone under the fouled glass dome, relic of the seventies, era of the Crystal Palace; his hands, of that vague gray color that only twenty-four hours can produce, were in his coat pockets to conceal the trembling fingers. With his hat removed it was plain that only the top layer of his hair was brushed back—the lower levels were pointed resolutely sidewise. He was scarcely recognizable as the man who had swum upon Gausse's beach a fortnight ago.

He was early; he looked from left to right with his eyes only; it would have taken nervous forces out of his control to use any other part of his body. New-looking baggage went past him; presently prospective passengers, with dark little bodies, were calling: "Jew-uls-*Hoo-oo!*" in dark piercing voices.

At the minute when he wondered whether or not he had time for a drink at the buffet, and began clutching at the soggy wad of thousand-franc notes in his pocket, one end of his pendulous glance came to rest upon the apparition of Nicole at the stairhead. He watched her—she was self-revelatory in her little expressions as people seem to someone waiting for them, who as yet is himself unobserved. She was frowning, thinking of her children, less gloating over them than merely animally counting them—a cat checking her cubs with a paw.

When she saw Abe, the mood passed out of her face; the glow of the morning skylight was sad, and Abe made a gloomy figure with dark circles that showed through the crimson tan under his eyes. They sat down on a bench.

"I came because you asked me," said Nicole defensively. Abe seemed to have forgotten why he asked her and Nicole was quite content to look at the travelers passing by.

"That's going to be the belle of your boat—that one with all the men to say good-by—you see why she bought that dress?" Nicole talked faster and faster. "You see why nobody else would buy it except the belle of the world cruise? See? No? Wake up! That's a story dress—that extra material tells a story and somebody on world cruise would be lonesome enough to want to hear it."

She bit close her last words; she had talked too much for her; and Abe found it difficult to gather from her serious set face that she had spoken at all. With an effort he drew himself up to a posture that looked as if he were standing up while he was sitting down.

"The afternoon you took me to that funny ball—you know, St. Genevieve's—" he began.

"I remember. It was fun, wasn't it?"

"No fun for me. I haven't had fun seeing you this time. I'm tired of you both, but it doesn't show because you're even more tired of me—you know what I mean. If I had any enthusiasm, I'd go on to new people."

There was a rough nap on Nicole's velvet gloves as she slapped him back:

"Seems rather foolish to be unpleasant, Abe. Anyhow you don't mean that. I can't see why you've given up about everything."

Abe considered, trying hard not to cough or blow his nose.

"I suppose I got bored; and then it was such a long way to go back in order to get anywhere."

Often a man can play the helpless child in front of a woman, but he can almost never bring it off when he feels most like a helpless child.

"No excuse for it," Nicole said crisply.

Abe was feeling worse every minute—he could think of nothing but disagreeable and sheerly nervous remarks. Nicole thought that the correct attitude for her was to sit staring straight ahead, hands in her lap. For a while there was no communication between them—each was racing away from the other, breathing only insofar as there was blue space ahead, a sky not seen by the other. Unlike lovers they possessed no past; unlike man and wife, they possessed no future; yet up to this morning Nicole had liked Abe better than any one except Dick—and he had been heavy, belly-frightened, with love for her for years.

"Tired of women's worlds," he spoke up suddenly.

"Then why don't you make a world of your own?"

"Tired of friends. The thing is to have sycophants."

Nicole tried to force the minute hand around on the station clock, but, "You agree?" he demanded.

"I am a woman and my business is to hold things together."

"My business is to tear them apart."

"When you get drunk you don't tear anything apart except yourself," she said, cold now, and frightened and unconfident. The station was filling but no one she knew came. After a moment her eyes fell gratefully on a tall girl with straw hair like a helmet, who was dropping letters in the mail slot.

"A girl I have to speak to, Abe. Abe, wake up! You fool!"

Patiently Abe followed her with his eyes. The woman turned in a startled way to greet Nicole, and Abe recognized her as some one he had seen around Paris. He took advantage of Nicole's absence to cough hard and retchingly into his handkerchief, and to blow his nose loud. The morning was warmer and his underwear was soaked with sweat. His fingers trembled so violently that it took four matches to light a cigarette; it seemed absolutely necessary to make his way into the buffet for a drink, but immediately Nicole returned.

"That was a mistake," she said with frosty humor. "After begging me to come and see her, she gave me a good snubbing. She looked at me as if I were rotted." Excited, she did a little laugh, as with two fingers high in the scales. "Let people come to you."

Abe recovered from a cigarette cough and remarked:

"Trouble is when you're sober you don't want to see anybody, and when you're tight nobody wants to see you."

"Who, me?" Nicole laughed again; for some reason the late encounter had cheered her.

"No—me."

"Speak for yourself. I like people, a lot of people—I like——"

Rosemary and Mary North came in sight, walking slowly and searching for Abe, and Nicole burst forth grossly with "Hey! Hi! Hey!" and laughed and waved the package of handkerchiefs she had bought for Abe.

They stood in an uncomfortable little group weighted down by Abe's gigantic presence: he lay athwart them like the wreck of a galleon, dominating with his presence his own weakness and self-indulgence, his narrowness and bitterness. All of them were conscious of the solemn dignity that flowed from him, of his achievement, fragmentary, suggestive and surpassed. But they were frightened at his survivant will, once a will to live, now become a will to die.

Dick Diver came and brought with him a fine glowing surface on which the three women sprang like monkeys with cries of relief, perching on his shoulders, on the beautiful crown of his hat or the gold head of his cane. Now, for a moment, they could disregard the spectacle of Abe's gigantic obscenity. Dick saw the situation quickly and grasped it quietly. He pulled them out of themselves into the station, making plain its wonders. Nearby, some Americans were saying good-by in voices that mimicked the cadence of water running into a large old bathtub. Standing in the station, with Paris in back of them, it seemed as if they were vicariously leaning a little over the ocean, already undergoing a sea-change, a shifting about of atoms to form the essential molecule of a new people.

So the well-to-do Americans poured through the station onto the platforms with frank new faces, intelligent, considerate, thoughtless, thought-for. An occasional English face among them seemed sharp and emergent. When there were enough Americans on the platform the first impression of their immaculacy and their money began to fade into a vague racial dusk that hindered and blinded both them and their observers.

Nicole seized Dick's arm crying, "Look!" Dick turned in time to see what took place in half a minute. At a Pullman entrance two cars off, a vivid scene detached itself from the tenor of many farewells. The young woman with the helmet-like hair to whom Nicole had spoken made an odd dodging little run away from the man to whom she was talking and plunged a frantic hand into her purse; then the sound of two revolver shots cracked the narrow air of the platform. Simultaneously the engine whistled sharply and the train began to move, momentarily dwarfing the shots in significance. Abe waved again from his window, oblivious to what had happened. But before the crowd closed in, the others had seen the shots take effect, seen the target sit down upon the platform.

Only after a hundred years did the train stop; Nicole, Mary, and Rosemary waited on the outskirts while Dick fought his way through. It was five minutes before he found them again—by this time the crowd had split into two sections, following, respectively, the man on a stretcher and the girl walking pale and firm between distraught gendarmes.

"It was Maria Wallis," Dick said hurriedly. "The man she shot was an Englishman—they had an awful time finding out who, because she shot him through his identification card." They were walking quickly from the train, swayed along with the crowd. "I found out what *poste de police* they're taking her to so I'll go there——"

"But her sister lives in Paris," Nicole objected. "Why not phone her? Seems very peculiar nobody thought of that. She's married to a Frenchman, and he can do more than we can."

Dick hesitated, shook his head and started off.

"Wait!" Nicole cried after him. "That's foolish—how can you do any good—with your French?"

"At least I'll see they don't do anything outrageous to her."

"They're certainly going to hold on to her," Nicole assured him briskly. "She *did* shoot the man. The best thing is to phone right away to Laura—she can do more than we can."

Dick was unconvinced—also he was showing off for Rosemary.

"You wait," said Nicole firmly, and hurried off to a telephone booth.

"When Nicole takes things into her hands," he said with affectionate irony, "there is nothing more to be done."

He saw Rosemary for the first time that morning. They exchanged glances, trying to recognize the emotions of the day before. For a moment each seemed unreal to the other—then the slow warm hum of love began again.

"You like to help everybody, don't you?" Rosemary said.

"I only pretend to."

"Mother likes to help everybody—of course she can't help as many people as you do." She sighed. "Sometimes I think I'm the most selfish person in the world."

For the first time the mention of her mother annoyed rather than amused Dick. He wanted to sweep away her mother, remove the whole affair from the nursery footing upon which Rosemary persistently established it.

But he realized that this impulse was a loss of control—what would become of Rosemary's urge toward him if, for even a moment, he relaxed. He saw, not without panic, that the affair was sliding to rest; it could not stand still, it must go on or go back; for the first time it occurred to him that Rosemary had her hand on the lever more authoritatively than he.

Before he had thought out a course of procedure, Nicole returned.

"I found Laura. It was the first news she had and her voice kept fading away and then getting loud again—as if she was fainting and then pulling herself together. She said she knew something was going to happen this morning."

"Maria ought to be with Diaghileff," said Dick in a gentle tone, in order to bring them back to quietude. "She has a nice sense of *décor*—not to say rhythm. Will any of us ever see a train pulling out without hearing a few shots?"

They bumped down the wide steel steps. "I'm sorry for the poor man," Nicole said. "Course that's why she talked so strange to me—she was getting ready to open fire."

She laughed, Rosemary laughed too, but they were both horrified, and both of them deeply wanted Dick to make a moral comment on the matter and not leave it to them. This wish was not entirely conscious, especially on the part of Rosemary, who was accustomed to having shell fragments of such events shriek past her head. But a totality of shock had piled up in her too. For the moment, Dick was too shaken by the impetus of his newly recognized emotion to resolve things into the pattern of the holiday, so the women, missing something, lapsed into a vague unhappiness.

Then, as if nothing had happened, the lives of the Divers and their friends flowed out into the street.

However, everything had happened—Abe's departure and Mary's impending departure for Salzburg this afternoon had ended the time in Paris. Or perhaps the shots, the concussions that had finished God knew what dark matter, had terminated it. The shots had entered into all their lives: echoes of violence followed them out onto the pavement where two porters held a post-mortem beside them as they waited for a taxi.

"Tu as vu le revolver? Il était très petit, vrai perle—un jouet."

"Mais, assez puissant!" said the other porter sagely. *"Tu as vu sa chemise? Assez de sang pour se croire à la guerre."*

XX

IN THE square, as they came out, a suspended mass of gasoline exhaust cooked slowly in the July sun. It was a terrible thing—unlike pure heat it held no promise of rural escape but suggested only roads choked with the same foul asthma. During their luncheon, outdoors, across from the Luxembourg Gardens, Rosemary had cramps and felt fretful and full of impatient lassitude—it was the foretaste of this that had inspired her self-accusation of selfishness in the station.

Dick had no suspicion of the sharpness of the change; he was profoundly unhappy and the subsequent increase of egotism tended momentarily to blind him to what was going on round about him, and deprive him of the long ground-swell of imagination that he counted on for his judgments.

After Mary North left them, accompanied by the Italian singing teacher who had joined them for coffee and was taking her to her train, Rosemary, too, stood up, bound for an engagement at her studio: "meet some officials."

"And oh—" she proposed "—if Collis Clay, that Southern boy—if he comes while you are still sitting here, just tell him I couldn't wait; tell him to call me tomorrow."

Too insouciant, in reaction from the late disturbance, she had assumed the privileges of a child—the result being to remind the Divers of their exclusive love for their own children; Rosemary was sharply rebuked in a short passage between the women: "You'd better leave the message with a waiter," Nicole's voice was stern and unmodulated, "we're leaving immediately."

Rosemary got it, took it without resentment.

"I'll let it go then. Good-by, you darlings."

Dick asked for the check; the Divers relaxed, chewing tentatively on toothpicks.

"Well—" they said together.

He saw a flash of unhappiness on her mouth, so brief that only he would have noticed, and he could pretend not to have seen. What did Nicole think? Rosemary was one of a dozen people he had "worked over" in the past years: these had included a French circus clown, Abe and Mary North, a pair of dancers, a writer, a painter, a comedienne from the Grand Guignol, a half-crazy pederast from the Russian Ballet, a promising tenor they had staked to a year in Milan. Nicole well knew how seriously these people interpreted his interest and enthusiasm; but she realized also that, except while their children were being born, Dick had not spent a night apart from her since their marriage. On the other hand, there was a pleasingness about him that simply had to be used—those who possessed that pleasingness had to keep their hands in, and go along attaching people that they had no use to make of.

Now Dick hardened himself and let minutes pass without making any gesture of confidence, any representation of constantly renewed surprise that they were one together.

Collis Clay out of the South edged a passage between the closely packed tables and greeted the Divers cavalierly. Such salutations always astonished Dick—acquaintances saying "Hi!" to them, or speaking only to one of them. He felt so intensely about people that in moments of apathy he preferred to remain concealed; that one could parade a casualness into his presence was a challenge to the key on which he lived.

Collis, unaware that he was without a wedding garment, heralded his arrival with: "I reckon I'm late—the beyed has flown." Dick had to wrench something out of himself before he could forgive him for not having first complimented Nicole.

She left almost immediately and he sat with Collis, finishing the last of his wine. He rather liked Collis—he was "post-war"; less difficult than most of the Southerners he had known at New Haven a decade previously. Dick listened with amusement to the conversation that accompanied the slow, profound stuffing of a pipe. In the early afternoon children and nurses were trekking into the Luxembourg Gardens; it was the first time in months that Dick had let this part of the day out of his hands.

Suddenly his blood ran cold as he realized the content of Collis's confidential monologue.

"—she's not so cold as you'd probably think. I admit I thought she was cold for a long time. But she got into a jam with a friend of mine going from New York to

Chicago at Easter—a boy named Hillis she thought was pretty nutsey at New Haven—she had a compartment with a cousin of mine but she and Hillis wanted to be alone, so in the afternoon my cousin came and played cards in our compartment. Well, after about two hours we went back and there was Rosemary and Bill Hillis standing in the vestibule arguing with the conductor—Rosemary white as a sheet. Seems they locked the door and pulled down the blinds and I guess there was some heavy stuff going on when the conductor came for the tickets and knocked on the door. They thought it was us kidding them and wouldn't let him in at first, and when they did, he was plenty sore. He asked Hillis if that was his compartment and whether he and Rosemary were married that they locked the door, and Hillis lost his temper trying to explain there was nothing wrong He said the conductor had insulted Rosemary and he wanted him to fight, but that conductor could have made trouble—and believe me I had an awful time smoothing it over."

With every detail imagined, with even envy for the pair's community of misfortune in the vestibule, Dick felt a change taking place within him. Only the image of a third person, even a vanished one, entering into his relation with Rosemary was needed to throw him off his balance and send through him waves of pain, misery, desire, desperation. The vividly pictured hand on Rosemary's cheek, the quicker breath, the white excitement of the event viewed from outside, the inviolable secret warmth within.

—Do you mind if I pull down the curtain?

—Please do. It's too light in here.

Collis Clay was now speaking about fraternity politics at New Haven, in the same tone, with the same emphasis. Dick had gathered that he was in love with

Rosemary in some curious way Dick could not have understood. The affair with Hillis seemed to have made no emotional impression on Collis save to give him the joyful conviction that Rosemary was "human."

"Bones got a wonderful crowd," he said. "We all did, as a matter of fact. New Haven's so big now the sad thing is the men we have to leave out."

—Do you mind if I pull down the curtain?

—Please do. It's too light in here.

. . . Dick went over Paris to his bank—writing a check, he looked along the row of men at the desks deciding to which one he would present it for an O.K. As he wrote he engrossed himself in the material act, examining meticulously the pen, writing laboriously upon the high glass-topped desk. Once he raised glazed eyes to look toward the mail department, then glazed his spirit again by concentration upon the objects he dealt with.

Still he failed to decide to whom the check should be presented, which man in the line would guess least of the unhappy predicament in which he found himself and, also, which one would be least likely to talk. There was Perrin, the suave New Yorker, who had asked him to luncheons at the American Club, there was Casasus, the Spaniard, with whom he usually discussed a mutual friend in spite of the fact that the friends had passed out of his life a dozen years before; there was Muchhause, who always asked him whether he wanted to draw upon his wife's money or his own.

As he entered the amount on the stub, and drew two lines under it, he decided to go to Pierce, who was young and for whom he would have to put on only a small show. It was often easier to give a show than to watch one.

He went to the mail desk first—as the woman who

served him pushed up with her bosom a piece of paper that had nearly escaped the desk, he thought how differently women use their bodies from men. He took his letters aside to open: There was a bill for seventeen psychiatric books from a German concern, a bill from Brentano's, a letter from Buffalo from his father, in a handwriting that year by year became more indecipherable; there was a card from Tommy Barban postmarked Fez and bearing a facetious communication; there were letters from doctors in Zurich, both in German; a disputed bill from a plasterer in Cannes; a bill from a furniture maker; a letter from the publisher of a medical journal in Baltimore, miscellaneous announcements and an invitation to a showing of pictures by an incipient artist; also there were three letters for Nicole, and a letter for Rosemary sent in his care.

—Do you mind if I pull down the curtain?

He went toward Pierce but he was engaged with a woman, and Dick saw with his heels that he would have to present his check to Casasus at the next desk, who was free.

"How are you, Diver?" Casasus was genial. He stood up, his mustache spreading with his smile. "We were talking about Featherstone the other day and I thought of you—he's out in California now."

Dick widened his eyes and bent forward a little.

"In Cali*for*nia?"

"That's what I heard."

Dick held the check poised; to focus the attention of Casasus upon it he looked toward Pierce's desk, holding the latter for a moment in a friendly eye-play conditioned by an old joke of three years before when Pierce had been involved with a Lithuanian countess. Pierce played up with a grin until Casasus had authorized the check and had no further recourse to detain Dick, whom he liked, than to stand up holding his pince-nez and repeat, "Yes, he's in California."

Meanwhile Dick had seen that Perrin, at the head of the line of desks, was in conversation with the heavyweight champion of the world; from a sidesweep of Perrin's eye Dick saw that he was considering calling him over and introducing him, but that he finally decided against it.

Cutting across the social mood of Casasus with the intensity he had accumulated at the glass desk—which is to say he looked hard at the check, studying it, and then fixed his eyes on grave problems beyond the first marble pillar to the right of the banker's head and made a business of shifting the cane, hat, and letters he carried—he said good-by and went out. He had long ago purchased the doorman; his taxi sprang to the curb.

"I want to go to the Films Par Excellence Studio—it's on a little street in Passy. Go to the Muette. I'll direct you from there."

He was rendered so uncertain by the events of the last forty-eight hours that he was not even sure of what he wanted to do; he paid off the taxi at the Muette and walked in the direction of the studio, crossing to the opposite side of the street before he came to the building. Dignified in his fine clothes, with their fine accessories, he was yet swayed and driven as an animal. Dignity could come only with an overthrowing of his past, of the effort of the last six years. He went briskly around the block with the fatuousness of one of Tarkington's adolescents, hurrying at the blind places lest he miss Rosemary's coming out of the studio. It was a melancholy neighborhood. Next door to the place he saw a sign: "*1000 chemises.*" The shirts filled the window, piled, cravated, stuffed, or draped with shoddy grace on the showcase floor: "*1000 chemises*"—count them! On either side he read: *"Papeterie," "Pâtisserie," "Solde," "Réclame"*—and Constance Talmadge in *"Déjeuner de Soleil,"* and farther away there were more somber announcements: *"Vêtements Ecclésiastiques," "Déclaration de Décès"* and *"Pompes Funèbres."* Life and death.

He knew that what he was now doing marked a turning point in his life—it was out of line with everything that had preceded it—even out of line with what effect he might hope to produce upon Rosemary. Rosemary saw him always as a model of correctness—his presence walking around this block was an intrusion. But Dick's necessity of behaving as he did was a projection of some submerged reality: he was compelled to walk there, or stand there, his shirt-sleeve fitting his wrist and his coat sleeve encasing his shirt-sleeve like a sleeve valve, his collar molded plastically to his neck, his red hair cut exactly, his hand holding his small brief-case like a dandy—just as another man once found it necessary to stand in front of a church in Ferrara, in sackcloth and ashes. Dick was paying some tribute to things unforgotten, unshriven, unexpurgated.

XXI

AFTER three-quarters of an hour of standing around, he became suddenly involved in a human contact. It was just the sort of thing that was likely to happen to him when he was in the mood of not wanting to see anyone. So rigidly did he sometimes guard his exposed self-consciousness that frequently he defeated his own purposes; as an actor who underplays a part sets up a craning forward, a stimulated emotional attention in an audience, and seems to create in others an ability to bridge the gap he has left open. Similarly we are seldom sorry for those who need and crave our pity—we reserve this for those who, by other means, make us exercise the abstract function of pity.

So Dick might, himself, have analyzed the incident that ensued. As he paced the Rue des Saints-Anges he was spoken to by a thin-faced American, perhaps thirty, with an air of being scarred and a slight but sinister smile. As Dick gave him the light he requested, he placed him as one of a type of which he had been conscious since early youth—a type that loafed about tobacco stores with one elbow on the counter and watched, through heaven knew what small chink of the mind, the people who came in and out. Intimate to garages, where he had vague business conducted in undertones, to barber shops, to the lobbies of theatres—in such places, at any rate, Dick placed him. Sometimes the face bobbed up in one of Tad's more savage cartoons—in boyhood Dick had often thrown an uneasy glance at the dim borderland of crime on which he stood.

"How do you like Paris, Buddy?"

Not waiting for an answer the man tried to fit in his footsteps with Dick's: "Where you from?" he asked encouragingly.

"From Buffalo."

"I'm from San Antone—but I been over here since the war."

"You in the army?"

"*I'll* say I was. Eighty-fourth Division—ever heard of that outfit?"

The man walked a little ahead of him and fixed him with eyes that were practically menacing.

"Staying in Paris awhile, Buddy? Or just passing through."

"Passing through."

"What hotel you staying at?"

Dick had begun laughing to himself—the party had the intention of rifling his room that night. His thoughts were read apparently without self-consciousness.

"With a build like yours you oughtn't to be afraid of me, Buddy. There's a lot of bums around just laying for American tourists, but you needn't be afraid of me."

Becoming bored, Dick stopped walking: "I just wonder why you've got so much time to waste."

"I'm in business here in Paris."

"In what line?"

"Selling papers."

The contrast between the formidable manner and the mild profession was absurd—but the man amended it with:

"Don't worry; I made plenty money last year—ten or twenty francs for a Sunny *Times* that cost six."

He produced a newspaper clipping from a rusty wallet and passed it over to one who had become a fellow stroller—the cartoon showed a stream of Americans pouring from the gangplank of a liner freighted with gold.

"Two hundred thousand—spending ten million a summer."

"What you doing out here in Passy?"

His companion looked around cautiously. "Movies," he said darkly. "They got an American studio over there. And they need guys can speak English. I'm waiting for a break."

Dick shook him off quickly and firmly.

It had become apparent that Rosemary either had escaped on one of his early circuits of the block or else had left before he came into the neighborhood; he went into the bistro on the corner, bought a lead disk and, squeezed in an alcove between the kitchen and the foul toilet, he called the Roi George. He recognized Cheyne-Stokes tendencies in his respiration—but like everything the symptom served only to turn him in toward his emotion. He gave the number of the hotel; then stood holding the phone and staring into the café; after a long while a strange little voice said hello.

"This is Dick—I had to call you."

A pause from her—then bravely, and in key with his emotion: "I'm glad you did."

"I came to meet you at your studio—I'm out in Passy across the way from it. I thought maybe we'd ride around through the Bois."

"Oh, I only stayed there a minute! I'm so sorry." A silence.

"Rosemary."

"Yes, Dick."

"Look, I'm in an extraordinary condition about you. When a child can disturb a middle-aged gent—things get difficult."

"You're not middle-aged, Dick—you're the youngest person in the world."

"Rosemary?" Silence while he stared at a shelf that held the humbler poisons of France—bottles of Otard, Rhum St. James, Marie Brizzard, Punch Orangeade, André Fernet Blanco, Cherry Rochet, and Armagnac.

"Are you alone?"

—Do you mind if I pull down the curtain?

"Who do you think I'd be with?"

"That's the state I'm in. I'd like to be with you now."

Silence, then a sigh and an answer. "I wish you were with me now."

There was the hotel room where she lay behind a telephone number, and little gusts of music wailed around her—

"And two—for tea.
And me for you,
And you for me
Alow-own."

There was the remembered dust of powder over her tan—when he kissed her face it was damp around the corners of her hair; there was the flash of a white face under his own, the arc of a shoulder.

"It's impossible," he said to himself. In a minute he was out in the street marching along toward the Muette, or away from it, his small brief-case still in his hand, his gold-headed stick held at a sword-like angle.

Rosemary returned to her desk and finished a letter to her mother.

"—I only saw him for a little while but I thought he was wonderful looking. I fell in love with him (Of course I Do Love Dick Best but you know what I mean). He really is going to direct the picture and is leaving immediately for Hollywood, and I think we ought to leave, too. Collis Clay has been here. I like him all right but have not seen much of him because of the Divers, who really are divine, about the Nicest People I ever Knew. I am feeling not very well today and am taking the Medicine, though see No need for it. I'm not even Going to Try to tell you All that's Happened until I see *You!!!* So when you get this letter *wire, wire, wire!* Are you coming north or shall I come south with the Divers?"

At six Dick called Nicole.

"Have you any special plans?" he asked. "Would you like to do something quiet—dinner at the hotel and then a play?"

"Would you? I'll do whatever you want. I phoned

Rosemary a while ago and she's having dinner in her room. I think this upset all of us, don't you?"

"It didn't upset me," he objected. "Darling, unless you're physically tired let's do something. Otherwise we'll get south and spend a week wondering why we didn't see Boucher. It's better than brooding——"

This was a blunder and Nicole took him up sharply.

"Brooding about what?"

"About Maria Wallis."

She agreed to go to a play. It was a tradition between them that they should never be too tired for anything, and they found it made the days better on the whole and put the evenings more in order. When, inevitably, their spirits flagged they shifted the blame to the weariness and fatigue of others. Before they went out, as fine-looking a couple as could be found in Paris, they knocked softly at Rosemary's door. There was no answer; judging that she was asleep they walked into a warm strident Paris night, snatching a vermouth and bitters in the shadow by Fouquet's bar.

XXII

NICOLE awoke late, murmuring something back into her dream before she parted her long lashes tangled with sleep. Dick's bed was empty—only after a minute did she realize that she had awakened by a knock at their salon door.

"*Entrez!*" she called, but there was no answer, and after a moment she slipped on a dressing-gown and went to open it. A *sergent de ville* confronted her courteously and stepped inside the door.

"Mr. Afghan North—he is here?"

"What? No—he's gone to America."

"When did he leave, Madame?"

"Yesterday morning."

He shook his head and waved his forefinger at her in a quicker rhythm.

"He was in Paris last night. He is registered here but his room is not occupied. They told me I had better ask at this room."

"Sounds very peculiar to me—we saw him off yesterday morning on the boat train."

"Be that as it may, he has been seen here this morning. Even his *carte d'identité* has been seen. And there you are."

"We know nothing about it," she proclaimed in amazement.

He considered. He was an ill-smelling, handsome man.

"You were not with him at all last night?"

"But no."

"We have arrested a Negro. We are convinced we have at last arrested the correct Negro."

"I assure you that I haven't an idea what you're talking about. If it's the Mr. Abraham North, the one we know, well, if he was in Paris last night we weren't aware of it."

The man nodded, sucked his upper lip, convinced but disappointed.

"What happened?" Nicole demanded.

He showed his palms, puffing out his closed mouth. He had begun to find her attractive and his eyes flickered at her.

"What do you wish, Madame? A summer affair. Mr. Afghan North was robbed and he made a complaint. We have arrested the miscreant. Mr. Afghan should come to identify him and make the proper charges."

Nicole pulled her dressing-gown closer around her

and dismissed him briskly. Mystified she took a bath and dressed. By this time it was after ten and she called Rosemary but got no answer—then she phoned the hotel office and found that Abe had indeed registered, at six-thirty this morning. His room, however, was still unoccupied. Hoping for a word from Dick she waited in the parlor of the suite; just as she had given up and decided to go out, the office called and announced:

"Meestaire Crawshow, *un nègre*."

"On what business?" she demanded.

"He says he knows you and the doctaire. He says there is a Meestaire Freeman into prison that is a friend of all the world. He says there is injustice and he wishes to see Meestaire North before he himself is arrested."

"We know nothing about it." Nicole disclaimed the whole business with a vehement clap of the receiver. Abe's bizarre reappearance made it plain to her how fatigued she was with his dissipation. Dismissing him from her mind she went out, ran into Rosemary at the dressmaker's, and shopped with her for artificial flowers and all-colored strings of colored beads on the Rue de Rivoli. She helped Rosemary choose a diamond for her mother, and some scarfs and novel cigarette cases to take home to business associates in California. For her son she bought Greek and Roman soldiers, a whole army of them, costing over a thousand francs. Once again they spent their money in different ways, and again Rosemary admired Nicole's method of spending. Nicole was sure that the money she spent was hers—Rosemary still thought her money was miraculously lent to her and she must consequently be very careful of it.

It was fun spending money in the sunlight of the foreign city, with healthy bodies under them that sent streams of color up to their faces; with arms and hands, legs and ankles that they stretched out confidently, reaching or stepping with the confidence of women lovely to men.

When they got back to the hotel and found Dick, all bright and new in the morning, both of them had a moment of complete childish joy.

He had just received a garbled telephone call from Abe who, so it appeared, had spent the forenoon in hiding.

"It was one of the most extraordinary telephone conversations I've ever held."

Dick had talked not only to Abe but to a dozen others. On the phone these supernumeraries had been typically introduced as: "—man wants to talk to you is in the teput dome, well he says he was in it—what is it?

"Hey, somebody, shut-up—anyhow, he was in some shandel-scandal and he kaa *pos*sibly go home. My own *per*sonal is that—my personal is he's had a—" Gulps sounded and thereafter what the party had, rested with the unknown.

The phone yielded up a supplementary offer:

"I thought it would appeal to you anyhow as a psychologist." The vague personality who corresponded to this statement was eventually hung onto the phone; in the sequence he failed to appeal to Dick, as a psychologist, or indeed as anything else. Abe's conversation flowed on as follows:

"Hello."

"Well?"

"Well, hello."

"Who are you?"

"Well." There were interpolated snorts of laughter. "Well, I'll put somebody else on the line."

Sometimes Dick could hear Abe's voice, accompanied by scufflings, droppings of the receiver, far-away fragments such as, "No, I don't, Mr. North. . . ." Then a pert decided voice had said: "If you are a friend of Mr. North you will come down and take him away."

Abe cut in, solemn and ponderous, beating it all down with an overtone of earth-bound determination.

"Dick, I've launched a race riot in Montmartre. I'm going over and get Freeman out of jail. If a Negro from Copenhagen that makes shoe polish—hello, can you hear me—well, look, if anybody comes there—" Once again the receiver was a chorus of innumerable melodies.

"Why you back in Paris?" Dick demanded.

"I got as far as Evreux, and I decided to take a plane back so I could compare it with St. Sulpice. I mean I don't intend to bring St. Sulpice back to Paris. I don't even mean Baroque! I meant St. Germain. For God's sake, wait a minute and I'll put the *chasseur* on the wire."

"For God's sake, don't."

"Listen—did Mary get off all right?"

"Yes."

"Dick, I want you to talk with a man I met here this morning, the son of a naval officer that's been to every doctor in Europe. Let me tell you about him——"

Dick had rung off at this point—perhaps that was a piece of ingratitude for he needed grist for the grinding activity of his mind.

"Abe used to be so nice," Nicole told Rosemary. "So nice. Long ago—when Dick and I were first married. If you had known him then. He'd come to stay with us for weeks and weeks and we scarcely knew he was in the house. Sometimes he'd play—sometimes he'd be in the library with a muted piano, making love to it by the hour—Dick, do you remember that maid? She thought he was a ghost and sometimes Abe used to meet her in the hall and moo at her, and it cost us a whole tea service once—but we didn't care."

So much fun—so long ago. Rosemary envied them their fun, imagining a life of leisure unlike her own. She knew little of leisure but she had the respect for it of those who have never had it. She thought of it as a resting, without realizing that the Divers were as far from relaxing as she was herself.

"What did this to him?" she asked. "Why does he have to drink?"

Nicole shook her head right and left, disclaiming responsibility for the matter: "So many smart men go to pieces nowadays."

"And when haven't they?" Dick asked. "Smart men play close to the line because they have to—some of them can't stand it, so they quit."

"It must lie deeper than that." Nicole clung to her conversation; also she was irritated that Dick should contradict her before Rosemary. "Artists like—well, like Fernand don't seem to have to wallow in alcohol. Why is it just Americans who dissipate?"

There were so many answers to this question that Dick decided to leave it in the air, to buzz victoriously in Nicole's ears. He had become intensely critical of her. Though he thought she was the most attractive human creature he had even seen, though he got from her everything he needed, he scented battle from afar, and subconsciously he had been hardening and arming himself, hour by hour. He was not given to self-indulgence and he felt comparatively graceless at this moment of indulging himself, blinding his eyes with the hope that Nicole guessed at only an emotional excitement about Rosemary. He was not sure—last night at the theatre she had referred pointedly to Rosemary as a child.

The trio lunched downstairs in an atmosphere of carpets and padded waiters, who did not march at the stomping quick-step of those men who brought good food to the tables whereon they had recently dined. Here there were families of Americans staring around at families of Americans, and trying to make conversation with one another.

There was a party at the next table that they could not account for. It consisted of an expansive, somewhat secretarial, would-you-mind-repeating young man, and a score of women. The women were neither young nor old nor of any particular social class; yet the party gave the impression of a unit, held more closely together for example than a group of wives stalling through a professional congress of their husbands. Certainly it was more of a unit than any conceivable tourist party.

An instinct made Dick suck back the grave derision that formed on his tongue; he asked the waiter to find out who they were.

"Those are the gold-star muzzers," explained the waiter.

Aloud and in low voices they exclaimed. Rosemary's eyes filled with tears.

"Probably the young ones are the wives," said Nicole.

Over his wine Dick looked at them again; in their happy faces, the dignity that surrounded and pervaded the party, he perceived all the maturity of an older America. For a while the sobered women who had come to mourn for their dead, for something they could not repair, made the room beautiful. Momentarily, he sat again on his father's knee, riding with Moseby while the old loyalties and devotions fought on around him. Almost with an effort he turned back to his two women at the table and faced the whole new world in which he believed.

—Do you mind if I pull down the curtain?

XXIII

ABE NORTH was still in the Ritz bar, where he had been since nine in the morning. When he arrived seeking sanctuary the windows were open and great beams were busy at pulling up the dust from smoky carpets and cushions. *Chasseurs* tore through the corridors, liberated and disembodied, moving for the moment in pure space. The sit-down bar for women, across from the bar proper, seemed very small—it was hard to imagine what throngs it could accommodate in the afternoon.

The famous Paul, the concessionaire, had not arrived, but Claude, who was checking stock, broke off his work with no improper surprise to make Abe a pick-me-up. Abe sat on a bench against a wall. After two drinks he began to feel better—so much better that he mounted to the barber's shop and was shaved. When he returned to the bar Paul had arrived—in his custom-built motor, from which he had disembarked correctly at the Boulevard des Capucines. Paul liked Abe and came over to talk.

"I was supposed to ship home this morning," Abe said. "I mean yesterday morning, or whatever this is."

"Why din you?" asked Paul.

Abe considered, and happened finally to a reason: "I was reading a serial in *Liberty* and the next installment was due here in Paris—so if I'd sailed I'd have missed it—then I never would have read it."

"It must be a very good story."

"It's a terr-r-rible story."

Paul arose chuckling and paused, leaning on the back of a chair:

"If you really want to get off, Mr. North, there are friends of yours going tomorrow on the *France*—Mister what is this name—and Slim Pearson. Mister—I'll think of it—tall with a new beard."

"Yardly," Abe supplied.

"Mr. Yardly. They're both going on the *France*."

He was on his way to his duties but Abe tried to detain him: "If I didn't have to go by way of Cherbourg. The baggage went that way."

"Get your baggage in New York," said Paul, receding.

The logic of the suggestion fitted gradually into Abe's pitch—he grew rather enthusiastic about being cared for, or rather of prolonging his state of irresponsibility.

Other clients had meanwhile drifted into the bar: first came a huge Dane whom Abe had somewhere encountered. The Dane took a seat across the room, and Abe guessed he would be there all the day, drinking, lunching, talking or reading newspapers. He felt a desire to out-stay him. At eleven the college boys began to step in, stepping gingerly lest they tear one another bag from bag. It was about then he had the *chasseur* telephone to the Divers; by the time he was in touch with them he was in touch also with other friends—and his hunch was to put them all on different phones at once—the result was somewhat general. From time to time his mind reverted to the fact that he ought to go over and get Freeman out of jail, but he shook off all facts as parts of the nightmare.

By one o'clock the bar was jammed; amidst the consequent mixture of voices the staff of waiters functioned, pinning down their clients to the facts of drink and money.

"That makes two stingers . . . and one more . . . two martinis and one . . . nothing for you, Mr. Quarterly . . . that makes three rounds. That makes seventy-five francs, Mr. Quarterly. Mr. Schaeffer said he had this—you had the last . . . I can only do what you say . . . thanks vera-much."

In the confusion Abe had lost his seat; now he stood gently swaying and talking to some of the people with whom he had involved himself. A terrier ran a leash around his legs but Abe managed to extricate himself without upsetting and became the recipient of profuse apologies. Presently he was invited to lunch, but declined. It was almost Briglith, he explained, and there was something he had to do at Briglith. A little later, with the exquisite manners of the alcoholic that are like the manners of a prisoner or a family servant, he said good-by to an acquaintance, and turning around discovered that the bar's great moment was over as precipitately as it had begun.

Across from him the Dane and his companions had ordered luncheon. Abe did likewise but scarcely touched it. Afterward, he just sat, happy to live in the past. The drink made past happy things contemporary with the present, as if they were still going on, contemporary even with the future as if they were about to happen again.

At four the *chasseur* approached him:

"You wish to see a colored fellow of the name Jules Peterson?"

"God! How did he find me?"

"I didn't tell him you were present."

"Who did?" Abe fell over his glasses but recovered himself.

"Says he's already been around to all the American bars and hotels."

"Tell him I'm not here—" As the *chasseur* turned away Abe asked: "Can he come in here?"

"I'll find out."

Receiving the question Paul glanced over his shoulder; he shook his head, then seeing Abe he came over.

"I'm sorry; I can't allow it."

Abe got himself up with an effort and went out to the Rue Cambon.

XXIV

WITH his miniature leather brief-case in his hand Richard Diver walked from the seventh *arrondissement*—where he left a note for Maria Wallis signed "Dicole," the word with which he and Nicole had signed communications in the first days of love—to his shirt-makers where the clerks made a fuss over him out of proportion to the money he spent. Ashamed at promising so much to these poor Englishmen, with his fine manners, his air of having the key to security, ashamed of making a tailor shift an inch of silk on his arm. Afterward he went to the bar of the Crillon and drank a small coffee and two fingers of gin.

As he entered the hotel the halls had seemed unnaturally bright; when he left he realized that it was because it had already turned dark outside. It was a windy four-o'clock night with the leaves on the Champs Élysées singing and failing, thin and wild. Dick turned down the Rue de Rivoli, walking two squares under the arcades to his bank where there was mail. Then he took a taxi and started up the Champs Élysées through the first patter of rain, sitting alone with his love.

Back at two o'clock in the Roi George corridor the beauty of Nicole had been to the beauty of Rosemary as the beauty of Leonardo's girl was to that of the girl of an illustrator. Dick moved on through the rain, demoniac and frightened, the passions of many men inside him and nothing simple that he could see.

Rosemary opened her door full of emotions no one else knew of. She was now what is sometimes called a "little wild thing"—by twenty-four full hours she was not yet unified and she was absorbed in playing around with chaos; as if her destiny were a picture puzzle—counting benefits, counting hopes, telling off Dick, Nicole, her mother, the director she met yesterday, like stops on a string of beads.

When Dick knocked she had just dressed and been watching the rain, thinking of some poem, and of full gutters in Beverly Hills. When she opened the door she saw him as something fixed and God-like as he had always been, as older people are to younger, rigid and unmalleable. Dick saw her with an inevitable sense of disappointment. It took him a moment to respond to the unguarded sweetness of her smile, her body calculated to a millimeter to suggest a bud yet guarantee a flower. He was conscious of the print of her wet foot on a rug through the bathroom door.

"Miss Television," he said with a lightness he did not feel. He put his gloves, his brief-case on the dressing-table, his stick against the wall. His chin dominated the lines of pain around his mouth, forcing them up into his forehead and the corner of his eyes, like fear that cannot be shown in public.

"Come and sit on my lap close to me," he said softly, "and let me see about your lovely mouth."

She came over and sat there and while the dripping slowed down outside—drip—dri-i-ip, she laid her lips to the beautiful cold image she had created.

Presently she kissed him several times in the mouth, her face getting big as it came up to him; he had never seen anything so dazzling as the quality of her skin, and since sometimes beauty gives back the images of one's best thoughts he thought of his responsibility about Nicole, and of the responsibility of her being two doors down across the corridor.

"The rain's over," he said. "Do you see the sun on the slate?"

Rosemary stood up and leaned down and said her most sincere thing to him:

"Oh, we're such *actors*—you and I."

She went to her dresser and the moment that she laid her comb flat against her hair there was a slow persistent knocking at the door.

They were shocked motionless; the knock was repeated insistently, and in the sudden realization that the door was not locked Rosemary finished her hair with one stroke, nodded at Dick who had quickly jerked the wrinkles out of the bed where they had been sitting, and started for the door. Dick said in quite a natural voice, not too loud:

"—so if you don't feel up to going out, I'll tell Nicole and we'll have a very quiet last evening."

The precautions were needless for the situation of the parties outside the door was so harassed as to preclude any but the most fleeting judgments on matters not pertinent to themselves. Standing there was Abe, aged by several months in the last twenty-four hours, and a very frightened, concerned colored man whom Abe introduced as Mr. Peterson of Stockholm.

"He's in a terrible situation and it's my fault," said Abe. "We need some good advice."

"Come in our rooms," said Dick.

Abe insisted that Rosemary come too and they crossed the hall to the Divers' suite. Jules Peterson, a small, respectable Negro, on the suave model that heels the Republican party in the border States, followed.

It appeared that the latter had been a legal witness to the early morning dispute in Montparnasse; he had accompanied Abe to the police station and supported his assertion that a thousand-franc note had been seized out of his hand by a Negro, whose identification was one of the points of the case. Abe and Jules Peterson, accompanied by an agent of police, returned to the bistro and too hastily identified as the criminal a Negro, who, so it was established after an hour, had only entered the place after Abe left. The police had further complicated the situation by arresting the prominent Negro restaurateur, Freeman, who had only drifted through the alcoholic fog at a very early stage and then vanished. The true culprit, whose case, as reported by his friends, was that he had merely commandeered a fifty-franc note to pay for drinks that Abe had ordered, had only recently and in a somewhat sinister rôle, reappeared upon the scene.

In brief, Abe had succeeded in the space of an hour in entangling himself with the personal lives, consciences, and emotions of one Afro-European and three Afro-Americans inhabiting the French Latin quarter. The disentanglement was not even faintly in sight and the day had passed in an atmosphere of unfamiliar Negro faces bobbing up in unexpected places and around unexpected corners, and insistent Negro voices on the phone.

In person, Abe had succeeded in evading all of them, save Jules Peterson. Peterson was rather in the position of the friendly Indian who had helped a white. The Negroes who suffered from the betrayal were not so much after Abe as after Peterson, and Peterson was very much after what protection he might get from Abe.

Up in Stockholm Peterson had failed as a small manufacturer of shoe polish and now possessed only his formula and sufficient trade tools to fill a small box; however, his new protector had promised in the early hours to set him up in business in Versailles. Abe's former chauffeur was a shoemaker there and Abe had handed Peterson two hundred francs on account.

Rosemary listened with distaste to this rigmarole; to appreciate its grotesquerie required a more robust sense of humor than hers. The little man with his portable manufactory, his insincere eyes that, from time to time, rolled white semicircles of panic into view; the figure of Abe, his face as blurred as the gaunt fine lines of it would permit—all this was as remote from her as sickness.

"I ask only a chance in life," said Peterson with the sort of precise yet distorted intonation peculiar to colonial countries. "My methods are simple, my formula is so good that I was drove away from Stockholm, ruined, because I did not care to dispose of it."

Dick regarded him politely—interest formed, dissolved, he turned to Abe:

"You go to some hotel and go to bed. After you're all straight Mr. Peterson will come and see you."

"But don't you appreciate the mess that Peterson's in?" Abe protested.

"I shall wait in the hall," said Mr. Peterson with delicacy. "It is perhaps hard to discuss my problems in front of me."

He withdrew after a short travesty of a French bow; Abe pulled himself to his feet with the deliberation of a locomotive.

"I don't seem highly popular today."

"Popular but not probable," Dick advised him. "My advice is to leave this hotel—by way of the bar, if you want. Go to the Chambord, or if you'll need a lot of service, go over to the Majestic."

"Could I annoy you for a drink?"

"There's not a thing up here," Dick lied.

Resignedly Abe shook hands with Rosemary; he composed his face slowly, holding her hand a long time and forming sentences that did not emerge.

"You are the most—one of the most——"

She was sorry, and rather revolted at his dirty hands, but she laughed in a well-bred way, as though it were nothing unusual to her to watch man walking in a slow dream. Often people display a curious respect for a man drunk, rather like the respect of simple races for the insane. Respect rather than fear. There is something awe-inspiring in one who has lost all inhibitions, who will do anything. Of course we make him pay afterward for his moment of superiority, his moment of impressiveness. Abe turned to Dick with a last appeal.

"If I go to a hotel and get all steamed and curry-combed, and sleep awhile, and fight off these Senegalese—could I come and spend the evening by the fireside?"

Dick nodded at him, less in agreement than in mockery and said: "You have a high opinion of your current capacities."

"I bet if Nicole was here she'd let me come back."

"All right." Dick went to a trunk tray and brought a box to the central table; inside were innumerable cardboard letters.

"You can come if you want to play anagrams."

Abe eyed the contents of the box with physical revulsion, as though he had been asked to eat them like oats.

"What are anagrams? Haven't I had enough strange——"

"It's a quiet game. You spell words with them—any word except alcohol."

"I bet you can spell alcohol," Abe plunged his hand among the counters. "Can I come back if I can spell alcohol?"

"You can come back if you want to play anagrams."

Abe shook his head resignedly.

"If you're in that frame of mind there's no use—I'd just be in the way." He waved his finger reproachfully at Dick. "But remember what George the Third said, that if Grant was drunk he wished he would bite the other generals."

With a last desperate glance at Rosemary from the golden corners of his eyes, he went out. To his relief Peterson was no longer in the corridor. Feeling lost and homeless he went back to ask Paul the name of that boat.

XXV

WHEN he had tottered out, Dick and Rosemary embraced fleetingly. There was a dust of Paris over both of them through which they scented each other: the rubber guard on Dick's fountain pen, the faintest odor of warmth from Rosemary's neck and shoulders. For another half-minute Dick clung to the situation; Rosemary was first to return to reality.

"I must go, youngster," she said.

They blinked at each other across a widening space, and Rosemary made an exit that she had learned young, and on which no director had ever tried to improve.

She opened the door of her room and went directly to her desk where she had suddenly remembered leaving her wristwatch. It was there; slipping it on she glanced down at the daily letter to her mother, finishing the last sentence in her mind. Then, rather gradually, she realized without turning about that she was not alone in the room.

In an inhabited room there are refracting objects only half noticed: varnished wood, more or less polished brass, silver and ivory, and beyond these a thousand conveyers of light and shadow so mild that one scarcely thinks of them as that, the tops of picture-frames, the edges of pencils or ash-trays, of crystal or china ornaments; the totality of this refraction—appealing to equally subtle reflexes of the vision as well as to those associational fragments in the subconscious that we seem to hang on to, as a glass-fitter keeps the irregularly shaped pieces that may do some time—this fact might account for what Rosemary afterward mystically described as "realizing" that there was some one in the room, before she could determine it. But when she did realize it she turned swift in a sort of ballet step and saw that a dead Negro was stretched upon her bed.

As she cried "Aaouu!" and her still unfastened wrist-watch banged against the desk she had the preposterous idea that it was Abe North. Then she dashed for the door and across the hall.

Dick was straightening up; he had examined the gloves worn that day and thrown them into a pile of soiled gloves in a corner of a trunk. He had hung up coat and vest and spread his shirt on another hanger—a trick of his own. "You'll wear a shirt that's a little dirty where you won't wear a mussed shirt." Nicole had come in and was dumping one of Abe's extraordinary ash-trays into the waste-basket when Rosemary tore into the room.

"*Dick! Dick!* Come and see!"

Dick jogged across the hall into her room. He knelt to Peterson's heart, and felt the pulse—the body was warm, the face, harassed and indirect in life, was gross and bitter in death; the box of materials was held under one arm but the shoe that dangled over the bedside was bare of polish and its sole was worn through. By French law Dick had no right to touch the body but he moved the arm a little to see something—there was a stain on the green coverlet, there would be faint blood on the blanket beneath.

Dick closed the door and stood thinking; he heard cautious steps in the corridor and then Nicole calling him by name. Opening the door he whispered: "Bring the *couverture* and top blanket from one of our beds—don't let anyone see you." Then, noticing the strained look on her face, he added quickly, "Look here, you mustn't get upset over this—it's only some nigger scrap."

"I want it to be over."

The body, as Dick lifted it, was light and ill-nourished. He held it so that further hemorrhages from the wound would flow into the man's clothes. Laying it beside the bed he stripped off the coverlet and top blanket and then opening the door an inch, listened—there was a clank of dishes down the hall followed by a loud patronizing "*Merci, Madame,*" but the waiter went in the other direction, toward the service stairway. Quickly Dick and Nicole exchanged bundles across the corridor; after spreading this covering on Rosemary's bed, Dick stood sweating in the warm twilight, considering. Certain points had become apparent to him in the moment following his examination of the body; first, that Abe's first hostile Indian had tracked the friendly Indian and discovered him in the corridor, and when the latter had taken desperate refuge in Rosemary's room, had hunted down and slain him; second, that if the situation were allowed to develop naturally, no power on earth could keep the smear off Rosemary—the paint was scarcely dry on the Arbuckle case. Her contract was contingent upon an obligation to continue rigidly and unexceptionally as "Daddy's Girl."

Automatically Dick made the old motion of turning up his sleeves though he wore a sleeveless undershirt, and bent over the body. Getting a purchase on the shoulders of the coat he kicked open the door with his heel, and dragged the body quickly into a plausible position in the corridor. He came back into Rosemary's room and smoothed back the grain of the plush floor rug. Then he went to the phone in his suite and called the manager-owner of the hotel.

"McBeth?—it's Doctor Diver speaking—something very important. Are we on a more or less private line?"

It was good that he had made the extra effort which had firmly entrenched him with Mr. McBeth. Here was one use for all the pleasingness that Dick had expended over a large area he would never retrace. . . .

"Going out of the suite we came on a dead Negro . . . in the hall . . . no, no, he's a civilian. Wait a minute now—I knew you didn't want any guests to blunder on the body so I'm phoning you. Of course I must ask you to keep my name out of it. I don't want any French red tape just because I discovered the man."

What exquisite consideration for the hotel! Only because Mr. McBeth, with his own eyes, had seen these traits in Doctor Diver two nights before, could he credit the story without question.

In a minute Mr. McBeth arrived and in another minute he was joined by a gendarme. In the interval he found time to whisper to Dick, "You can be sure the name of any guest will be protected. I'm only too grateful to you for your pains."

Mr. McBeth took an immediate step that may only be imagined, but that influenced the gendarme so as to make him pull his mustaches in a frenzy of uneasiness and greed. He made perfunctory notes and sent a telephone call to his post. Meanwhile with a celerity that Jules Peterson, as a business man, would have quite understood, the remains were carried into another apartment of one of the most fashionable hotels in the world.

Dick went back to his *salon.*

"What *happ*ened?" cried Rosemary. "Do all the Americans in Paris just shoot at each other all the time?"

"This seems to be the open season," he answered. "Where's Nicole?"

"I think she's in the bathroom."

She adored him for saving her—disasters that could have attended upon the event had passed in prophecy through her mind; and she had listened in wild worship to his strong, sure, polite voice making it all right. But before she reached him in a sway of soul and body his attention focused on something else: he went into the bedroom and toward the bathroom. And now Rosemary, too, could hear, louder and louder, a verbal inhumanity that penetrated the keyholes and the cracks in the doors, swept into the suite and in the shape of horror took form again.

With the idea that Nicole had fallen in the bathroom and hurt herself, Rosemary followed Dick. That was not the condition of affairs at which she stared before Dick shouldered her back and brusquely blocked her view.

Nicole knelt beside the tub swaying sidewise and sidewise. "It's you!" she cried, "—it's you come to intrude on the only privacy I have in the world—with your spread with red blood on it. I'll wear it for you—I'm not ashamed, though it was such a pity. On All Fools' Day we had a party on the Zurichsee, and all the fools were there, and I wanted to come dressed in a spread but they wouldn't let me——"

"Control yourself!"

"—so I sat in the bathroom and they brought me a domino and said wear that. I did. What else could I do?"

"Control yourself, Nicole!"

"I never expected you to love me—it was too late—only don't come in the bathroom, the only place I can go for privacy, dragging spreads with red blood on them and asking me to fix them."

"Control yourself. Get up——"

Rosemary, back to the *salon,* heard the bathroom door bang, and stood trembling: now she knew what Violet McKisco had seen in the bathroom at Villa Diana. She answered the ringing phone and almost cried with relief when she found it was Collis Clay, who had traced her to the Divers' apartment. She asked him to come up while she got her hat, because she was afraid to go into her room alone.

BOOK II

I

IN THE spring of 1917, when Doctor Richard Diver first arrived in Zurich, he was twenty-six years old, a fine age for a man, indeed the very acme of bachelorhood. Even in war-time days, it was a fine age for Dick, who was already too valuable, too much of a capital investment to be shot off in a gun. Years later it seemed to him that even in this sanctuary he did not escape lightly, but about that he never fully made up his mind—in 1917 he laughed at the idea, saying apologetically that the war didn't touch him at all. Instructions from his local board were that he was to complete his studies in Zurich and take a degree as he had planned.

Switzerland was an island, washed on one side by the waves of thunder around Gorizia and on another by the cataracts along the Somme and the Aisne. For once there seemed more intriguing strangers than sick ones in the cantons, but that had to be guessed at—the men who whispered in the little cafés of Berne and Geneva were as likely to be diamond salesmen or commercial travelers. However, no one had missed the long trains of blinded or one-legged men, or dying trunks, that crossed each other between the bright lakes of Constance and Neuchâtel. In the beer-halls and shop-windows were bright posters presenting the Swiss defending their frontiers in 1914—with inspiring ferocity young men and old men glared down from the mountains at phantom French and Germans; the purpose was to assure the Swiss heart that it had shared the contagious glory of those days. As the massacre continued the posters withered away, and no country was more surprised than its sister republic when the United States bungled its way into the war.

Doctor Diver had seen around the edges of the war by that time: he was an Oxford Rhodes Scholar from Connecticut in 1914. He returned home for a final year at Johns Hopkins, and took his degree. In 1916 he managed to get to Vienna under the impression that, if he did not make haste, the great Freud would eventually succumb to an airplane bomb. Even then Vienna was old with death but Dick managed to get enough coal and oil to sit in his room in the Damenstiff Strasse and write the pamphlets that he later destroyed, but that, rewritten, were the backbone of the book he published in Zurich in 1920.

Most of us have a favorite, a heroic period, in our lives and that was Dick Diver's. For one thing he had no idea that he was charming, that the affection he gave and inspired was anything unusual among healthy people. In his last year at New Haven some one referred to him as "lucky Dick"—the name lingered in his head.

"Lucky Dick, you big stiff," he would whisper to himself, walking around the last sticks of flame in his room. "You hit it, my boy. Nobody knew it was there before you came along."

At the beginning of 1917, when it was becoming difficult to find coal, Dick burned for fuel almost a hundred textbooks that he had accumulated; but only, as he laid each one on the fire, with an assurance chuckling inside him that he was himself a digest of what was within the book, that he could brief it five years from now, if it deserved to be briefed. This went on at any odd hour, if necessary, with a floor rug over his shoulders, with the fine quiet of the scholar which is nearest of all things to heavenly peace—but which, as will presently be told, had to end.

For its temporary continuance he thanked his body that had done the flying rings at New Haven, and now swam in the winter Danube. With Elkins, second secretary at the Embassy, he shared an apartment, and there were two nice girl visitors—which was that and not too much of it, nor too much of the Embassy either. His contact with Ed Elkins aroused in him a first faint doubt as to the quality of his mental processes; he could not feel that they were profoundly different from the thinking of Elkins—Elkins, who would name you all the quarterbacks in New Haven for thirty years.

"—And Lucky Dick can't be one of these clever men; he must be less intact, even faintly destroyed. If life won't do it for him it's not a substitute to get a disease, or a broken heart, or an inferiority complex, though it'd be nice to build out some broken side till it was better than the original structure."

He mocked at his reasoning, calling it specious and "American"—his criteria of uncerebral phrase-making was that it was American. He knew, though, that the price of his intactness was incompleteness.

"The best I can wish you, my child," so said the Fairy Blackstick in Thackeray's *The Rose and the Ring,* "is a little misfortune."

In some moods he griped at his own reasoning: Could I help it that Pete Livingstone sat in the locker-room Tap Day when everybody looked all over hell for him? And I got an election when otherwise I wouldn't have got Elihu, knowing so few men. He was good and right and I ought to have sat in the locker-room instead. Maybe I would, if I'd thought I had a chance at an election. But Mercer kept coming to my room all those weeks. I guess I knew I had a chance all right, all right. But it would have served me right if I'd swallowed my pin in the shower and set up a conflict.

After the lectures at the university he used to argue this point with a young Rumanian intellectual who reassured him: "There's no evidence that Goethe ever had a 'conflict' in the modern sense, or a man like Jung, for instance. You're not a romantic philosopher—you're a scientist. Memory, force, character—especially good sense. That's going to be your trouble—judgment about yourself—once I knew a man who worked two years on the brain of an armadillo, with the idea that he would sooner or later know more about the brain of an armadillo than any one. I kept arguing with him that he was not really pushing out the extension of the human range—it was too arbitrary. And sure enough, when he sent his work to the medical journal they refused it—they had just accepted a thesis by another man on the same subject."

Dick got up to Zurich on less Achilles' heels than would be required to equip a centipede, but with plenty—the illusions of eternal strength and health, and of the essential goodness of people; illusions of a nation, the lies of generations of frontier mothers who had to croon falsely that there were no wolves outside the cabin door. After he took his degree, he received his orders to join a neurological unit forming in Bar-sur-Aube.

In France, to his disgust, the work was executive rather than practical. In compensation he found time to complete the short textbook and assemble the material for his next venture. He returned to Zurich in the spring of 1919 discharged.

The foregoing has the ring of a biography, without the satisfaction of knowing that the hero, like Grant, lolling in his general store in Galena, is ready to be called to an intricate destiny. Moreover it is confusing to come across a youthful photograph of some one known in a rounded maturity and gaze with a shock upon a fiery, wiry, eagle-eyed stranger. Best to be reassuring—Dick Diver's moment now began.

II

IT WAS a damp April day, with long diagonal clouds over the Albishorn and water inert in the low places. Zurich is not unlike an American city. Missing something ever since his arrival two days before, Dick perceived that it was the sense he had had in finite French lanes that there was nothing more. In Zurich there was a lot besides Zurich—the roofs upled the eyes to tinkling cow pastures, which in turn modified hilltops further up—so life was a perpendicular starting off to a postcard heaven. The Alpine lands, home of the toy and the funicular, the merry-go-round and the thin chime, were not a being *here*, as in France, with French vines growing over one's feet on the ground.

In Salzburg once Dick had felt the superimposed

quality of a bought and borrowed century of music; once in the laboratories of the university in Zurich, delicately poking at the cervical of a brain, he had felt like a toy-maker rather than like the tornado who had hurried through the old red buildings of Hopkins, two years before, unstayed by the irony of the gigantic Christ in the entrance hall.

Yet he had decided to remain another two years in Zurich, for he did not underestimate the value of toy-making, of infinite precision, of infinite patience.

Today he went out to see Franz Gregorovious at Dohmler's clinic on the Zurichsee. Franz, resident pathologist at the clinic, a Vaudois by birth, a few years older than Dick, met him at the tram stop. He had a dark and magnificent aspect of Cagliostro about him, contrasted with holy eyes; he was the third of the Gregoroviouses—his grandfather had instructed Krapaelin when psychiatry was just emerging from the darkness of all time. In personality he was proud, fiery, and sheep-like—he fancied himself as a hypnotist. If the original genius of the family had grown a little tired, Franz would without doubt become a fine clinician.

On the way to the clinic he said: "Tell me of your experiences in the war. Are you changed like the rest? You have the same stupid and unaging American face, except I know you're not stupid, Dick."

"I didn't see any of the war—you must have gathered that from my letters, Franz."

"That doesn't matter—we have some shell-shocks who merely heard an air raid from a distance. We have a few who merely read newspapers."

"It sounds like nonsense to me."

"Maybe it is, Dick. But, we're a rich person's clinic—we don't use the word nonsense. Frankly, did you come down to see me or to see that girl?"

They looked sideways at each other; Franz smiled enigmatically.

"Naturally I saw all the first letters," he said in his official basso. "When the change began, delicacy prevented me from opening any more. Really it had become your case."

"Then she's well?" Dick demanded.

"Perfectly well, I have charge of her, in fact I have charge of the majority of the English and American patients. They call me Doctor Gregory."

"Let me explain about that girl," Dick said. "I only saw her one time, that's a fact. When I came out to say good-by to you just before I went over to France. It was the first time I put on my uniform and I felt very bogus in it—went around saluting private soldiers and all that."

"Why didn't you wear it today?"

"Hey! I've been discharged three weeks. Here's the way I happened to see that girl. When I left you I walked down toward that building of yours on the lake to get my bicycle."

"—toward the 'Cedars'?"

"—a wonderful night, you know—moon over that mountain——"

"The Krenzegg."

"—I caught up with a nurse and a young girl. I didn't think the girl was a patient; I asked the nurse about tram times and we walked along. The girl was about the prettiest thing I ever saw."

"She still is."

"She'd never seen an American uniform and we talked, and I didn't think anything about it." He broke off, recognizing a familiar perspective, and then resumed: "—except, Franz, I'm not as hard-boiled as you are yet; when I see a beautiful shell like that I can't help feeling a regret about what's inside it. That was absolutely all—till the letters began to come."

"It was the best thing that could have happened to her," said Franz dramatically, "a transference of the most fortuitous kind. That's why I came down to meet you on a very busy day. I want you to come into my office and talk a long time before you see her. In fact, I sent her into Zurich to do errands." His voice was tense with enthusiasm. "In fact, I sent her without a nurse, with a less stable patient. I'm intensely proud of this case, which I handled, with your accidental assistance."

The car had followed the shore of the Zurichsee into a fertile region of pasture farms and low hills, steepled with châlets. The sun swam out into a blue sea of sky and suddenly it was a Swiss valley at its best—pleasant sounds and murmurs and a good fresh smell of health and cheer.

Professor Dohmler's plant consisted of three old buildings and a pair of new ones, between a slight eminence and the shore of the lake. At its founding, ten years before, it had been the first modern clinic for mental illness; at a casual glance no layman would recognize it as a refuge for the broken, the incomplete, the menacing, of this world, though two buildings were surrounded with vine-softened walls of a deceptive height. Some men raked straw in the sunshine; here and there, as they rode into the grounds, the car passed the white flag of a nurse waving beside a patient on a path.

After conducting Dick to his office, Franz excused himself for half an hour. Left alone Dick wandered about the room and tried to reconstruct Franz from the litter of his desk, from his books and the books of and by his father and grandfather; from the Swiss piety of a huge claret-colored photo of the former on the wall. There was smoke in the room; pushing open a French window, Dick let in a cone of sunshine. Suddenly his thoughts swung to the patient, the girl.

He had received about fifty letters from her written over a period of eight months. The first one was apologetic, explaining that she had heard from America how girls wrote to soldiers whom they did not know. She had obtained the name and address from Doctor Gregory and she hoped he would not mind if she sometimes sent word to wish him well, etc., etc.

So far it was easy to recognize the tone—from *Daddy-Long-Legs* and *Molly-Make-Believe*, sprightly and sentimental epistolary collections enjoying a vogue in the States. But there the resemblance ended.

The letters were divided into two classes, of which the first class, up to about the time of the armistice, was of marked pathological turn, and of which the second class, running from thence up to the present, was entirely normal, and displayed a richly maturing nature. For these latter letters Dick had come to wait eagerly in the last dull months at Bar-sur-Aube—yet even from the first letters he had pieced together more than Franz would have guessed of the story.

MON CAPITAINE:

I thought when I saw you in your uniform you were so handsome. Then I thought Je m'en fiche French too and German. You thought I was pretty too but I've had that before and a long time I've stood it. If you come here again with that attitude base and criminal and not even faintly what I had been taught to associate with the rôle of gentleman then heaven help you. However, you seem quieter than the others, all soft like a big cat. I have only gotten to like

(2)

boys who are rather sissies. Are you a sissy? There were some somewhere.

Excuse all this, it is the third letter I have written you and will send immediately or will never send. I've thought a lot about moonlight too, and there are many witnesses I could find if I could only be out of here.

(3)

They said you were a doctor, but so long as you are a cat it is different. My head aches so, so excuse this walking there like an ordinary with a white cat will explain, I think. I can speak three languages, four with English, and am sure I could be useful interpreting if you arrange such thing in France I'm sure I could control everything with the belts all bound around everybody like it was Wednesday. It is

(4)

now Saturday and you are far away, perhaps killed.

Come back to me some day, for I will be here always on this green hill. Unless they will let me write my father, whom I loved dearly.

Excuse this. I am not myself today. I will write when I feel better.

Cherio

NICOLE WARREN.

Excuse all this.

CAPTAIN DIVER:

I know introspection is not good for a highly nervous state like mine, but I would like you to know where I stand. Last year or whenever it was in Chicago when I got so I couldn't speak to servants or walk in the street I kept waiting for some one to tell me. It was the duty of some one who understood. The blind must be led. Only no one would tell me everything—they would just tell me half and I was already too muddled to put two and two together. One man was nice—he was a French officer and he understood. He gave me a flower and said it was "plus petite et moins entendue." We were friends. Then he took it away. I grew

(2)

sicker and there was no one to explain to me. They had a song about Joan of Arc that they used to sing at me but that was just mean—it would just make me cry, for there was nothing the matter with my head then. They kept making reference to sports, too, but I didn't care by that time.

So there was that day I went walking on Michigan Boulevard on and on for miles and finally they followed me in an

(3)

automobile, but I wouldn't get in. Finally they pulled me in and there were nurses. After that time I began to realize it all, because I could feel what was happening in others. So you see how I stand. And what good can it be for me to stay here with the doctors harping constantly in the things I was here to get over. So today I have written my father to come and take me away. I am glad you are so interested

(4)

in examining people and sending them back. It must be so much fun.

And again, from another letter:

You might pass up your next examination and write me a letter. They just sent me some phonograph records in case I should forget my lesson and I broke them all so the nurse won't speak to me. They were in English, so that the nurses would not understand. One doctor in Chicago said I was bluffing, but what he really meant was that I was a twin six and he had never seen one before. But I was very busy being mad then, so I didn't care what he said, when I am very busy being mad I don't usually care what they say, not if I were a million girls.

You told me that night you'd teach me to play. Well, I

(2)

think love is all there is or should be. Anyhow I am glad your interest in examinations keeps you busy.

Tout à vous,

NICOLE WARREN.

There were other letters among whose helpless cæsuras lurked darker rhythms.

DEAR CAPTAIN DIVER:

I write to you because there is no one else to whom I can turn and it seems to me if this farcicle situation is apparent to one as sick as me it should be apparent to you. The mental trouble is all over and besides that I am completely broken and humiliated, if that was what they wanted. My family have shamefully neglected me, there's no use asking them for help or pity. I have had enough and it is simply ruining my health and wasting my time pretending that

(2)

what is the matter with my head is curable.

Here I am in what appears to be a semi-insane-asylum, all because nobody saw fit to tell me the truth about anything. If I had only known what was going on like I know now I could have stood it I guess for I am pretty strong, but those who should have, did not see fit to enlighten me.

(3)

And now, when I know and have paid such a price for knowing, they sit there with their dogs lives and say I should believe what I did believe. Especially one does but I know now.

I am lonesome all the time far away from friends and family across the Atlantic I roam all over the place in a half daze. If you could get me a position as interpreter (I know French and German like a native, fair Italian and a

(4)

little Spanish) or in the Red Cross Ambulance or as a train nurse, though I would have to train you would prove a great blessing.

And again:

Since you will not accept my explanation of what is the matter you could at least explain to me what you think, because you have a kind cat's face, and not that funny look that seems to be so fashionable here. Dr. Gregory gave me a snapshot of you, not as handsome as you are in your uniform, but younger looking.

MON CAPITAINE:

It was fine to have your postcard. I am so glad you take such interest in disqualifying nurses—oh, I understood your note very well indeed. Only I thought from the moment I met you that you were different.

DEAR CAPITAINE:

I think one thing today and another tomorrow. That is really all that's the matter with me, except a crazy defiance and a lack of proportion. I would gladly welcome any alienist you might suggest. Here they lie in their bath tubs and sing Play in Your Own Backyard as if I had my backyard to play in or any hope which I can find by looking either

(2)

backward or forward. They tried it again in the candy store again and I almost hit the man with the weight, but they held me.

I am not going to write you any more. I am too unstable.

And then a month with no letters. And then suddenly the change.

—I am slowly coming back to life . . .

—Today the flowers and the clouds . . .

—The war is over and I scarcely knew there was a war . . .

—How kind you have been! You must be very wise behind your face like a white cat, except you don't look like that in the picture Dr. Gregory gave me . . .

—Today I went to Zurich, how strange a feeling to see a city again.

—Today we went to Berne, it was so nice with the clocks.

—Today we climbed high enough to find asphodel and edelweiss . . .

After that the letters were fewer, but he answered them all. There was one:

I wish someone were in love with me like boys were ages ago before I was sick. I suppose it will be years, though, before I could think of anything like that.

But when Dick's answer was delayed for any reason, there was a fluttering burst of worry—like a worry of a lover: "Perhaps I have bored you," and: "Afraid I have presumed," and: "I keep thinking at night you have been sick."

In actuality Dick was sick with the flu. When he recovered, all except the formal part of his correspondence was sacrificed to the consequent fatigue, and shortly afterward the memory of her became overlaid by the vivid presence of a Wisconsin telephone girl at headquarters in Bar-sur-Aube. She was red-lipped like a poster, and known obscenely in the messes as "The Switchboard."

Franz came back into his office feeling self-important. Dick thought he would probably be a fine clinician, for the sonorous or staccato cadences by which he disciplined nurse or patient came not from his nervous system but from a tremendous and harmless vanity. His true emotions were more ordered and kept to himself.

"Now about the girl, Dick," he said. "Of course, I want to find out about you and tell you about myself, but first about the girl, because I have been waiting to tell you about it so long."

He searched for and found a sheaf of papers in a filing cabinet but after shuffling through them he found they were in his way and put them on his desk. Instead he told Dick the story.

III

ABOUT a year and a half before, Doctor Dohmler had some vague correspondence with an American gentleman living in Lausanne, a Mr. Devereux Warren, of the Warren family of Chicago. A meeting was arranged and one day Mr. Warren arrived at the clinic with his daughter Nicole, a girl of sixteen. She was obviously not well and the nurse who was with her took her to walk about the grounds while Mr. Warren had his consultation.

Warren was a strikingly handsome man looking less than forty. He was a fine American type in every way, tall, broad, well-made—*"un homme très chic,"* as Doctor Dohmler described him to Franz. His large gray eyes were sun-veined from rowing on Lake Geneva, and he had that special air about him of having known the best of this world. The conversation was in German, for it developed that he had been educated at Göttingen. He was nervous and obviously very moved by his errand.

"Doctor Dohmler, my daughter isn't right in the head. I've had lots of specialists and nurses for her and she's taken a couple of rest cures but the thing has grown too big for me and I've been strongly recommended to come to you."

"Very well," said Doctor Dohmler. "Suppose you start at the beginning and tell me everything."

"There isn't any beginning, at least there isn't any insanity in the family that I know of, on either side. Nicole's mother died when she was eleven and I've sort of been father and mother both to her, with the help of governesses—father and mother both to her."

He was very moved as he said this. Doctor Dohmler saw that there were tears in the corners of his eyes and noticed for the first time that there was whiskey on his breath.

"As a child she was a darling thing—everybody was crazy about her, everybody that came in contact with her. She was smart as a whip and happy as the day is long. She liked to read or draw or dance or play the piano—anything. I used to hear my wife say she was the only one of our children who never cried at night. I've got an older girl, too, and there was a boy that died, but Nicole was—Nicole was—Nicole——"

He broke off and Doctor Dohmler helped him.

"She was a perfectly normal, bright, happy child."

"Perfectly."

Doctor Dohmler waited. Mr. Warren shook his head, blew a long sigh, glanced quickly at Doctor Dohmler and then at the floor again.

"About eight months ago, or maybe it was six months ago or maybe ten—I try to figure but I can't remember exactly where we were when she began to do funny things—crazy things. Her sister was the first one to say anything to me about it—because Nicole was always the same to me," he added rather hastily, as if someone had accused him of being to blame, "—the same loving little girl. The first thing was about a valet."

"Oh, yes," said Doctor Dohmler, nodding his venerable head, as if, like Sherlock Holmes, he had expected a valet and only a valet to be introduced at this point.

"I had a valet—been with me for years—Swiss, by the way." He looked up for Doctor Dohmler's patriotic approval. "And she got some crazy idea about him. She thought he was making up to her—of course, at the time I believed her and I let him go, but I know now it was all nonsense."

"What did she claim he had done?"

"That was the first thing—the doctors couldn't pin her down. She just looked at them as if they ought to know what he'd done. But she certainly meant he'd made some kind of indecent advances to her—she didn't leave us in any doubt of that."

"I see."

"Of course, I've read about women getting lonesome and thinking there's a man under the bed and all that, but why should Nicole get such an idea? She could have all the young men she wanted. We were in Lake Forest—that's a summer place near Chicago where we have a place—and she was out all day playing golf or tennis with boys. And some of them pretty gone on her at that."

All the time Warren was talking to the dried old package of Doctor Dohmler, one section of the latter's mind kept thinking intermittently of Chicago. Once in his youth he could have gone to Chicago as fellow and docent at the university, and perhaps become rich there and owned his own clinic instead of being only a minor shareholder in a clinic. But when he had thought of what he considered his own thin knowledge spread over that whole area, over all those wheat fields, those endless prairies, he had decided against it. But he had read about Chicago in those days, about the great feudal families of Armour, Palmer, Field, Crane, Warren, Swift, and McCormick and many others, and since that time not a few patients had come to him from that stratum of Chicago and New York.

"She got worse," continued Warren. "She had a fit or something—the things she said got crazier and crazier. Her sister wrote some of them down—" He handed a much-folded piece of paper to the doctor. "Almost always about men going to attack her, men she knew or men on the street—anybody——"

He told of their alarm and distress, of the horrors families go through under such circumstances, of the ineffectual efforts they had made in America, finally of the faith in a change of scene that had made him run the submarine blockade and bring his daughter to Switzerland.

"—on a United States cruiser," he specified with a touch of hauteur. "It was possible for me to arrange that, by a stroke of luck. And, may I add," he smiled apologetically, "that as they say: money is no object."

"Certainly not," agreed Dohmler dryly.

He was wondering why and about what the man was lying to him. Or, if he was wrong about that, what was the falsity that pervaded the whole room, the handsome figure in tweeds sprawling in his chair with a sportsman's ease? That was a tragedy out there, in the February day, the young bird with wings crushed somehow, and inside here it was all too thin, thin and wrong.

"I would like—to talk to her—a few minutes now," said Doctor Dohmler, going into English as if it would bring him closer to Warren.

Afterward when Warren had left his daughter and returned to Lausanne, and several days had passed, the doctor and Franz entered upon Nicole's card:

*Diagnostic: Schizophrénie. Phase aiguë en décroissance. La peur des hommes est un symptôme de la maladie, et n'est point constitutionelle. . . . Le pronostic doit rester réservé.**

And then they waited with increasing interest as the days passed for Mr. Warren's promised second visit.

It was slow in coming. After a fortnight Doctor Dohmler wrote. Confronted with further silence he committed what was for those days *"une folie,"* and telephoned to the Grand Hotel at Vevey. He learned from Mr. Warren's valet that he was at the moment packing to sail for America. But reminded that the forty francs Swiss for the call would show up on the clinic books, the blood of the Tuileries Guard rose to Doctor Dohmler's aid and Mr. Warren was got to the phone.

"It is—absolutely necessary—that you come. Your daughter's health—all depends. I can take no responsibility."

"But look here, Doctor, that's just what you're for. I have a hurry call to go home!"

Doctor Dohmler had never yet spoken to anyone so far away but he dispatched his ultimatum so firmly into

* Diagnosis: Divided Personality, Acute and down-hill phase of the illness. The fear of men is a symptom of the illness and is not at all constitutional. . . . The prognosis must be reserved.

the phone that the agonized American at the other end yielded. Half an hour after this second arrival on the Zurichsee, Warren had broken down, his fine shoulders shaking with awful sobs inside his easy-fitting coat, his eyes redder than the very sun on Lake Geneva, and they had the awful story.

"It just happened," he said hoarsely. "I don't know—I don't know.

"After her mother died when she was little she used to come into my bed every morning, sometimes she'd sleep in my bed. I was sorry for the little thing. Oh, after that, whenever we went places in an automobile or a train we used to hold hands. She used to sing to me. We used to say, 'Now let's not pay any attention to anybody else this afternoon—let's just have each other—for this morning you're mine.'" A broken sarcasm came into his voice. "People used to say what a wonderful father and daughter we were—they used to wipe their eyes. We were just like lovers—and then all at once we were lovers—and ten minutes after it happened I could have shot myself—except I guess I'm such a God-damned degenerate I didn't have the nerve to do it."

"Then what?" said Doctor Dohmler, thinking again of Chicago and of a mild pale gentleman with a pince-nez who had looked him over in Zurich thirty years before. "Did this thing go on?"

"Oh, no! She almost—she seemed to freeze up right away. She'd just say, 'Never mind, never mind, Daddy. It doesn't matter. Never mind.'"

"There were no consequences?"

"No." He gave one short convulsive sob and blew his nose several times. "Except now there're plenty of consequences."

As the story concluded Dohmler sat back in the focal

armchair of the middle class and said to himself sharply, "Peasant!"—it was one of the few absolute worldly judgments that he had permitted himself for twenty years. Then he said:

"I would like for you to go to a hotel in Zurich and spend the night and come see me in the morning."

"And then what?"

Doctor Dohmler spread his hands wide enough to carry a young pig.

"Chicago," he suggested.

IV

"THEN we knew where we stood," said Franz. "Dohmler told Warren we would take the case if he would agree to keep away from his daughter indefinitely, with an absolute minimum of five years. After Warren's first collapse, he seemed chiefly concerned as to whether the story would ever leak back to America.

"We mapped out a routine for her and waited. The prognosis was bad—as you know, the percentage of cures, even so-called social cures, is very low at that age."

"These first letters looked bad," agreed Dick.

"Very bad—very typical. I hesitated about letting the first one get out of the clinic. Then I thought it will be good for Dick to know we're carrying on here. It was generous of you to answer them."

Dick sighed. "She was such a pretty thing—she enclosed a lot of snapshots of herself. And for a month there I didn't have anything to do. All I said in my letters was 'Be a good girl and mind the doctors.' "

"That was enough—it gave her somebody to think of outside. For a while she didn't have anybody—only one sister that she doesn't seem very close to. Besides, reading her letters helped us here—they were a measure of her condition."

"I'm glad."

"You see now what happened? She felt complicity—that's neither here nor there, except as we want to re-value her ultimate stability and strength of character. First came this shock. Then she went off to a boarding-school and heard the girls talking—so from sheer self-protection she developed the idea that she had had no complicity—and from there it was easy to slide into a phantom world where all men, the more you liked them and trusted them, the more evil——"

"Did she ever go into the—horror directly?"

"No, and as a matter of fact when she began to seem normal, about October, we were in a predicament. If she had been thirty years old we would have let her make her own adjustment, but she was so young we were afraid she might harden with it all twisted inside her. So Doctor Dohmler said to her frankly, 'Your duty now is to yourself. This doesn't by any account mean the end of anything for you—your life is just at its beginning," and so forth and so forth. She really has an excellent mind, so he gave her a little Freud to read, not too much, and she was very interested. In fact, we've made rather a pet of her around here. But she is reticent," he added; he hesitated: "We have wondered if in her recent letters to you which she mailed herself from Zurich, she has said anything that would be illuminating about her state of mind and her plans for the future."

Dick considered.

"Yes and no—I'll bring the letters out here if you want. She seems hopeful and normally hungry for life—even rather romantic. Sometimes she speaks of 'the past' as people speak who have been in prison. But you never know whether they refer to the crime or the imprisonment or the whole experience. After all I'm only a sort of stuffed figure in her life."

"Of course, I understand your position exactly, and I express our gratitude once again. That was why I wanted to see you before you see her."

Dick laughed.

"You think she's going to make a flying leap at my person?"

"No, not that. But I want to ask you to go very gently. You are attractive to women, Dick."

"Then God help me! Well, I'll be gentle and repulsive —I'll chew garlic whenever I'm going to see her and wear a stubble beard. I'll drive her to cover."

"Not garlic!" said Franz, taking him seriously. "You don't want to compromise your career. But you're partly joking."

"—and I can limp a little. And there's no real bathtub where I'm living, anyhow."

"You're entirely joking," Franz relaxed—or rather assumed the posture of one relaxed. "Now tell me about yourself and your plans?"

"I've only got one, Franz, and that's to be a good psychologist—maybe to be the greatest one that ever lived."

Franz laughed pleasantly, but he saw that this time Dick wasn't joking.

"That's very good—and very American," he said. "It's more difficult for us." He got up and went to the French window. "I stand here and I see Zurich—there is the steeple of the Gross-Münster. In its vault my grandfather is buried. Across the bridge from it lies my ancestor Lavater, who would not be buried in any church. Nearby is the statue of another ancestor, Heinrich Pestalozzi, and one of Doctor Alfred Escher. And over everything there is always Zwingli—I am continually confronted with a pantheon of heroes."

"Yes, I see." Dick got up. "I was only talking big. Everything's just starting over. Most of the Americans in France are frantic to get home, but not me—I draw military pay all the rest of the year if I only attend lectures at the university. How's that for a government on the grand scale that knows its future great men? Then I'm going home for a month and see my father. Then I'm coming back—I've been offered a job."

"Where?"

"Your rivals—Gisler's Clinic on Interlacken."

"Don't touch it," Franz advised him. "They've had a dozen young men there in a year. Gisler's a manic-depressive himself, his wife and her lover run the clinic—of course, you understand that's confidential."

"How about your old scheme for America?" asked Dick lightly. "We were going to New York and start an up-to-date establishment for billionaires."

"That was students' talk."

Dick dined with Franz and his bride and a small dog with a smell of burning rubber, in their cottage on the edge of the grounds. He felt vaguely oppressed, not by the atmosphere of modest retrenchment, nor by Frau Gregorovious, who might have been prophesied, but by the sudden contracting of horizons to which Franz seemed so reconciled. For him the boundaries of asceticism were differently marked—he could see it as a means to an end, even as a carrying on with a glory it would itself supply, but it was hard to think of deliberately cutting life down to the scale of an inherited suit. The domestic gestures of Franz and his wife as they turned in a cramped space lacked grace and adventure. The post-war months in France, and the lavish liquidations taking place under the ægis of American splendor, had affected Dick's outlook. Also, men and women had made much of him, and perhaps what had brought him back to the center of the great Swiss watch, was an intuition that this was not too good for a serious man.

He made Kaethe Gregorovious feel charming, meanwhile becoming increasingly restless at the all-pervading cauliflower—simultaneously hating himself too for this incipience of he knew not what superficiality.

"God, am I like the rest after all?"—So he used to think starting awake at night—"Am I like the rest?"

This was poor material for a socialist but good material for those who do much of the world's rarest work. The truth was that for some months he had been going through that partitioning of the things of youth wherein it is decided whether or not to die for what one no longer believes. In the dead white hours in Zurich staring into a stranger's pantry across the upshine of a street-lamp, he used to think that he wanted to be good, he wanted to be kind, he wanted to be brave and wise, but it was all pretty difficult. He wanted to be loved, too, if he could fit it in.

V

THE veranda of the central building was illuminated from open French windows, save where the black shadows of stripling walls and the fantastic shadows of iron chairs slithered down into a gladiola bed. From the figures that shuffled between the rooms Miss Warren emerged first in glimpses and then sharply when she saw him; as she crossed the threshold her face caught the room's last light and brought it outside with her. She walked to a rhythm—all that week there had been singing in her ears, summer songs of ardent skies and wild shade, and with his arrival the singing had become so loud she could have joined in with it.

"How do you do, Captain," she said, unfastening her eyes from his with difficulty, as though they had become entangled. "Shall we sit out here?" She stood still, her glance moving about for a moment. "It's summer practically."

A woman had followed her out, a dumpy woman in a shawl, and Nicole presented Dick: "Señora——"

Franz excused himself and Dick grouped three chairs together.

"The lovely night," the Señora said.

"*Muy bella,*" agreed Nicole; then to Dick, "Are you here for a long time?"

"I'm in Zurich for a long time, if that's what you mean."

"This is really the first night of real spring," the Señora suggested.

"To stay?"

"At least till July."

"I'm leaving in June."

"June is a lovely month here," the Señora commented. "You should stay for June and then leave in July when it gets really too hot."

"You're going where?" Dick asked Nicole.

"Somewhere with my sister—somewhere exciting, I hope, because I've lost so much time. But perhaps they'll think I ought to go to a quiet place at first—perhaps Como. Why don't you come to Como?"

"Ah, Como—" began the Señora.

Within the building a trio broke into Suppe's "Light Cavalry." Nicole took advantage of this to stand up and the impression of her youth and beauty grew on Dick until it welled up inside him in a compact paroxysm of emotion. She smiled, a moving childish smile that was like all the lost youth in the world.

"The music's too loud to talk against—suppose we walk around. *Buenas noches, Señora.*"

"G't night—g't night."

They went down two steps to the path—where in a moment a shadow cut across it. She took his arm.

"I have some phonograph records my sister sent me from America," she said. "Next time you come here I'll play them for you—I know a place to put the phonograph where no one can hear."

"That'll be nice."

"Do you know 'Hindustan'?" she asked wistfully. "I'd never heard it before, but I like it. And I've got 'Why Do They Call Them Babies?' and 'I'm Glad I Can Make You Cry.' I suppose you've danced to all those tunes in Paris?"

"I haven't been to Paris."

Her cream-colored dress, alternately blue or gray as they walked, and her very blonde hair, dazzled Dick—whenever he turned toward her she was smiling a little, her face lighting up like an angel's when they came into the range of a roadside arc. She thanked him for everything, rather as if he had taken her to some party, and as Dick became less and less certain of his relation to her, her confidence increased—there was that excitement about her that seemed to reflect all the excitement of the world.

"I'm not under any restraint at all," she said. "I'll play you two good tunes called 'Wait Till the Cows Come Home' and 'Good-by, Alexander.' "

He was late the next time, a week later, and Nicole was waiting for him at a point in the path which he would pass walking from Franz's house. Her hair drawn back of her ears brushed her shoulders in such a way that the face seemed to have just emerged from it, as if this were the exact moment when she was coming from a wood into clear moonlight. The unknown yielded her up; Dick wished she had no background, that she was just a girl lost with no address save the night from which she had come. They went to the cache where she had left the phonograph, turned a corner by the workshop, climbed a rock, and sat down behind a low wall, facing miles and miles of rolling night.

They were in America now, even Franz with his conception of Dick as an irresistible Lothario would never have guessed that they had gone so far away. They were so sorry, dear; they went down to meet each other in a taxi, honey; they had preferences in smiles and had met in Hindustan, and shortly afterward they must have quarrelled, for nobody knew and nobody seemed to care—yet finally one of them had gone and left the other crying, only to feel blue, to feel sad.

The thin tunes, holding lost times and future hopes in liaison, twisted upon the Valais night. In the lulls of the phonograph a cricket held the scene together with a single note. By and by Nicole stopped playing the machine and sang to him.

"Lay a silver dollar
On the ground
And watch it roll
Because it's round—"

On the pure parting of her lips no breath hovered. Dick stood up suddenly.

"What's the matter, you don't like it?"

"Of course I do."

"Our cook at home taught it to me:

"A woman never knows
What a good man she's got
Till after she turns him down. . . ."

"You like it?"

She smiled at him, making sure that the smile gathered up everything inside her and directed it toward him, making him a profound promise of herself for so little, for the beat of a response, the assurance of a complimentary vibration in him. Minute by minute the sweetness drained down into her out of the willow trees, out of the dark world.

She stood up too, and stumbling over the phonograph, was momentarily against him, leaning into the hollow of his rounded shoulder.

"I've got one more record," she said. "—Have you heard 'So Long, Letty'? I suppose you have."

"Honestly, you don't understand—I haven't heard a thing."

Nor known, nor smelt, nor tasted, he might have added; only hot-cheeked girls in hot secret rooms. The young maidens he had known at New Haven in 1914 kissed men, saying "There!" hands at the man's chest to push him away. Now there was this scarcely saved waif of disaster bringing him the essence of a continent. . . .

VI

IT WAS May when he next found her. The luncheon in Zurich was a council of caution; obviously the logic of his life tended away from the girl; yet when a stranger stared at her from a near-by table, eyes burning disturbingly like an uncharted light, he turned to the man with an urbane version of intimidation and broke the regard.

"He was just a peeper," he explained cheerfully. "He was just looking at your clothes. Why do you have so many different clothes?"

"Sister says we're very rich," she offered humbly. "Since Grandmother is dead."

"I forgive you."

He was enough older than Nicole to take pleasure in her youthful vanities and delights, the way she paused fractionally in front of the hall mirror on leaving the restaurant, so that the incorruptible quicksilver could give her back to herself. He delighted in her stretching out her hands to new octaves now that she found herself beautiful and rich. He tried honestly to divorce her from any obsession that he had stitched her together—glad to see her build up happiness and confidence apart from him; the difficulty was that, eventually, Nicole brought everything to his feet, gifts of sacrificial ambrosia, of worshipping myrtle.

The first week of summer found Dick re-established in Zurich. He had arranged his pamphlets and what work he had done in the Service into a pattern from which he intended to make his revise of *A Psychology for Psychiatrists*. He thought he had a publisher; he had established contact with a poor student who would iron out his errors in German. Franz considered it a rash business, but Dick pointed out the disarming modesty of the theme.

"This is stuff I'll never know so well again," he insisted. "I have a hunch it's a thing that only fails to be basic because it's never had material recognition. The weakness of this profession is its attraction for the man a little crippled and broken. Within the walls of the profession he compensates by tending toward the clinical, the 'practical'—he has won his battle without a struggle.

"On the contrary, you are a good man, Franz, because fate selected you for your profession before you were born. You better thank God you had no 'bent'—I got to be a psychiatrist because there was a girl at St. Hilda's in Oxford that went to the same lectures. Maybe I'm getting trite but I don't want to let my current ideas slide away with a few dozen glasses of beer."

"All right," Franz answered. "You are an American. You can do this without professional harm. I do not like these generalities. Soon you will be writing little books called 'Deep Thoughts for the Layman,' so simplified that they are positively guaranteed not to cause thinking. If my father were alive he would look at you and grunt, Dick. He would take his napkin and fold it so, and hold his napkin ring, this very one—" he held it up, a boar's head was carved in the brown wood—"and he would say, 'Well my impression is—' then he would look at you and think suddenly 'What is the use?' then he would stop and grunt again; then we would be at the end of dinner."

"I am alone today," said Dick testily. "But I may not be alone tomorrow. After that I'll fold up my napkin like your father and grunt."

Franz waited a moment.

"How about our patient?" he asked.

"I don't know."

"Well, you should know about her by now."

"I like her. She's attractive. What do you want me to do—take her up in the edelweiss?"

"No, I thought since you go in for scientific books you might have an idea."

"—devote my life to her?"

Franz called his wife in the kitchen: "*Du lieber Gott! Bitte, bringe Dick noch ein Glas-Bier.*"

"I don't want any more if I've got to see Dohmler."

"We think it's best to have a program. Four weeks have passed away—apparently the girl is in love with you. That's not our business if we were in the world, but here in the clinic we have a stake in the matter."

"I'll do whatever Doctor Dohmler says," Dick agreed.

But he had little faith that Dohmler would throw much light on the matter; he himself was the incalculable element involved. By no conscious volition of his own, the thing had drifted into his hands. It reminded him of a scene in his childhood when everyone in the house was looking for the lost key to the silver closet, Dick knowing he had hid it under the handkerchiefs in his mother's top drawer; at that time he had experienced a philosophical detachment, and this was repeated now when he and Franz went together to Professor Dohmler's office.

The professor, his face beautiful under straight whiskers, like a vine-overgrown veranda of some fine old house, disarmed him. Dick knew some individuals with more talent, but no person of a class qualitatively superior to Dohmler.

—Six months later he thought the same way when he saw Dohmler dead, the light out on the veranda, the vines of his whiskers tickling his stiff white collar, the many battles that had swayed before the chink-like eyes stilled forever under the frail delicate lids——

". . . Good morning, sir." He stood formally, thrown back to the army.

Professor Dohmler interlaced his tranquil fingers. Franz spoke in terms half of liaison officer, half of secretary, till his senior cut through him in mid-sentence.

"We have gone a certain way," he said mildly. "It's you, Doctor Diver, who can best help us now."

Routed out, Dick confessed: "I'm not so straight on it myself."

"I have nothing to do with your personal reactions," said Dohmler. "But I have much to do with the fact that this so-called 'transference,'" he darted a short ironic look at Franz which the latter returned in kind, "must be terminated. Miss Nicole does well indeed, but she is in no condition to survive what she might interpret as a tragedy."

Again Franz began to speak, but Doctor Dohmler motioned him silent.

"I realize that your position has been difficult."

"Yes, it has."

Now the professor sat back and laughed, saying on the last syllable of his laughter, with his sharp little gray eyes shining through: "Perhaps you have got sentimentally involved yourself."

Aware that he was being drawn on, Dick, too, laughed.

"She's a pretty girl—anybody responds to that to a certain extent. I have no intention——"

Again Franz tried to speak—again Dohmler stopped him with a question directed pointedly at Dick. "Have you thought of going away?"

"I can't go away."

Doctor Dohmler turned to Franz: "Then we can send Miss Warren away."

"As you think best, Professor Dohmler," Dick conceded. "It's certainly a situation."

Professor Dohmler raised himself like a legless man mounting a pair of crutches.

"But it is a professional situation," he cried quietly.

He sighed himself back into his chair, waiting for the reverberating thunder to die out about the room. Dick saw that Dohmler had reached his climax, and he was not sure that he himself had survived it. When the thunder had diminished Franz managed to get his word in.

"Doctor Diver is a man of fine character," he said. "I feel he only has to appreciate the situation in order to deal correctly with it. In my opinion Dick can co-operate right here, without any one going away."

"How do you feel about that?" Professor Dohmler asked Dick.

Dick felt churlish in the face of the situation; at the same time he realized in the silence after Dohmler's pronouncement that the state of inanimation could not be indefinitely prolonged; suddenly he spilled everything.

"I'm half in love with her—the question of marrying her has passed through my mind."

"Tch! Tch!" uttered Franz.

"Wait." Dohmler warned him. Franz refused to wait: "What! And devote half your life to being doctor and nurse and all—never! I know what these cases are. One time in twenty it's finished in the first push—better never see her again!"

"What do you think?" Dohmler asked Dick.

"Of course Franz is right."

VII

IT WAS late afternoon when they wound up the discussion as to what Dick should do, he must be most kind and yet eliminate himself. When the doctors stood up at last, Dick's eyes fell outside the window to where a light rain was falling—Nicole was waiting, expectant, somewhere in that rain. When, presently, he went out buttoning his oil-skin at the throat, pulling down the brim of his hat, he came upon her immediately under the roof of the main entrance.

"I know a new place we can go," she said. "When I was ill I didn't mind sitting inside with the others in the evening—what they said seemed like everything else. Naturally now I see them as ill and it's—it's——"

"You'll be leaving soon."

"Oh, soon. My sister, Beth, but she's always been called Baby, she's coming in a few weeks to take me somewhere; after that I'll be back here for a last month."

"The older sister?"

"Oh, quite a bit older. She's twenty-four—she's very English. She lives in London with my father's sister. She was engaged to an Englishman but he was killed—I never saw him."

Her face, ivory gold against the blurred sunset that strove through the rain, had a promise Dick had never seen before: the high cheek-bones, the faintly wan quality, cool rather than feverish, was reminiscent of the frame of a promising colt—a creature whose life did not promise to be only a projection of youth upon a grayer screen, but instead, a true growing; the face would be handsome in middle life; it would be handsome in old age: the essential structure and the economy were there.

"What are you looking at?"

"I was just thinking that you're going to be rather happy."

Nicole was frightened: "Am I? All right—things couldn't be worse than they have been."

In the covered woodshed to which she had led him, she sat cross-legged upon her golf shoes, her burberry wound about her and her cheeks stung alive by the damp air. Gravely she returned his gaze, taking in his somewhat proud carriage that never quite yielded to the wooden post against which he leaned; she looked into his face that always tried to discipline itself into molds of attentive seriousness, after excursions into joys and mockeries of its own. That part of him which seemed to fit his reddish Irish coloring she knew least; she was afraid of it, yet more anxious to explore—this was his more masculine side: the other part, the trained part, the consideration in the polite eyes, she expropriated without question, as most women did.

"At least this institution has been good for languages," said Nicole. "I've spoken French with two doctors, and

German with the nurses, and Italian, or something like it, with a couple of scrub-women and one of the patients, and I've picked up a lot of Spanish from another."

"That's fine."

He tried to arrange an attitude but no logic seemed forthcoming.

"—Music too. Hope you didn't think I was only interested in ragtime. I practise every day—the last few months I've been taking a course in Zurich on the history of music. In fact it was all that kept me going at times—music and the drawing." She leaned suddenly and twisted a loose strip from the sole of her shoe, and then looked up. "I'd like to draw you just the way you are now."

It made him sad when she brought out her accomplishments for his approval.

"I envy you. At present I don't seem to be interested in anything except my work."

"Oh, I think that's fine for a man," she said quickly. "But for a girl I think she ought to have lots of minor accomplishments and pass them on to her children."

"I suppose so," said Dick with deliberated indifference.

Nicole sat quiet. Dick wished she would speak so that he could play the easy rôle of wet blanket, but now she sat quiet.

"You're all well," he said. "Try to forget the past; don't overdo things for a year or so. Go back to America and be a débutante and fall in love—and be happy."

"I couldn't fall in love." Her injured shoe scraped a cocoon of must from the log on which she sat.

"Sure you can," Dick insisted. "Not for a year maybe, but sooner or later." Then he added brutally: "You can have a perfectly normal life with a houseful of beautiful descendants. The very fact that you could make a complete comeback at your age proves that the precipitating factors were pretty near everything. Young woman, you'll be pulling your weight long after your friends are carried off screaming."

—But there was a look of pain in her eyes as she took the rough dose, the harsh reminder.

"I know I wouldn't be fit to marry any one for a long time," she said humbly.

Dick was too upset to say any more. He looked out into the grain field trying to recover his hard brassy attitude.

"You'll be all right—everybody here believes in you. Why, Doctor Gregory is so proud of you that he'll probably——"

"I hate Doctor Gregory."

"Well, you shouldn't."

Nicole's world had fallen to pieces, but it was only a flimsy and scarcely created world; beneath it her emotions and instincts fought on. Was it an hour ago she had waited by the entrance, wearing her hope like a corsage at her belt?

. . . Dress stay crisp for him, button stay put, bloom narcissus—air stay still and sweet.

"It will be nice to have fun again," she fumbled on. For a moment she entertained a desperate idea of telling him how rich she was, what big houses she lived in, that really she was a valuable property—for a moment she made herself into her grandfather, Sid Warren, the horse-trader. But she survivied the temptation to confuse all values and shut these matters into their Victorian side-chambers—even though there was no home left to her, save emptiness and pain.

"I have to go back to the clinic. It's not raining now."

Dick walked beside her, feeling her unhappiness, and wanting to drink the rain that touched her cheek.

"I have some new records," she said. "I can hardly wait to play them. Do you know——"

After supper that evening, Dick thought, he would finish the break; also he wanted to kick Franz's bottom for having partially introduced him to such a sordid business. He waited in the hall. His eyes followed a beret, not wet with waiting like Nicole's beret, but covering a skull recently operated on. Beneath it human eyes peered, found him and came over:

"Bonjour, Docteur."

"Bonjour, Monsieur."

"Il fait beau temps."

"Oui, merveilleux."

"Vous êtes ici maintenant?"

"Non, pour la journée seulement."

"Ah, bon. Alors—au revoir, Monsieur."

Glad at having survived another contact, the wretch in the beret moved away. Dick waited. Presently a nurse came downstairs and delivered him a message.

"Miss Warren asks to be excused, Doctor. She wants to lie down. She wants to have dinner upstairs tonight."

The nurse hung on his response, half expecting him to imply that Miss Warren's attitude was pathological.

"Oh, I see. Well—" He rearranged the flow of his own saliva, the pulse of his heart. "I hope she feels better. Thanks."

He was puzzled and discontent. At any rate it freed him.

Leaving a note for Franz begging off from supper, he walked through the countryside to the tram station. As he reached the platform, with spring twilight gilding the rails and the glass in the slot machines, he began to feel that the station, the hospital, was hovering between being centripetal and centrifugal. He felt frightened. He was glad when the substantial cobble-stones of Zurich clicked once more under his shoes.

He expected to hear from Nicole next day but there was no word. Wondering if she was ill, he called the clinic and talked to Franz.

"She came downstairs to luncheon yesterday and today," said Franz. "She seemed a little abstracted and in the clouds. How did it go off?"

Dick tried to plunge over the Alpine crevasse between the sexes.

"We didn't get to it—at least I didn't think we did. I tried to be distant, but I didn't think enough happened to change her attitude if it ever went deep."

Perhaps his vanity had been hurt that there was no coup de grâce to administer.

"From some things she said to her nurse I'm inclined to think she understood."

"All right."

"It was the best thing that could have happened. She doesn't seem over-agitated—only a little in the clouds."

"All right, then."

"Dick, come soon and see me."

VIII

DURING the next weeks Dick experienced a vast dissatisfaction. The pathological origin and mechanistic defeat of the affair left a flat and metallic taste. Nicole's emotions had been used unfairly—what if they turned out to have been his own? Necessarily he must absent himself from felicity a while—in dreams he saw her walking on the clinic path swinging her wide straw hat. . . .

One time he saw her in person; as he walked past the Palace Hotel, a magnificent Rolls curved into the half-moon entrance. Small within its gigantic proportions, and buoyed up by the power of a hundred superfluous horses, sat Nicole and a young woman whom he assumed was her sister. Nicole saw him and momentarily her lips parted in an expression of fright. Dick shifted his hat and passed, yet for a moment the air around him was loud with the circlings of all the goblins on the Gross-Münster. He tried to write the matter out of his mind in a memorandum that went into detail as to the solemn régime before her; the possibilities of another "push" of the malady under the stresses which the world would inevitably supply—in all a memorandum that would have been convincing to any one save to him who had written it.

The total value of this effort was to make him realize once more how far his emotions were involved; thenceforth he resolutely provided antidotes. One was the telephone girl from Bar-sur-Aube, now touring Europe from Nice to Coblenz, in a desperate roundup of the men she had known in her never-to-be-equalled holiday; another was the making of arrangements to get home on a government transport in August; a third was a consequent intensification of work on his proofs for the book that this autumn was to be presented to the German-speaking world of psychiatry.

Dick had outgrown the book; he wanted now to do more spade work; if he got an exchange fellowship he could count on plenty of routine.

Meanwhile he had projected a new work: *An Attempt at a Uniform and Pragmatic Classification of the Neuroses and Psychoses, Based on an Examination of Fifteen Hundred Pre-Krapaelin and Post-Krapaelin Cases as They Would Be Diagnosed in the Terminology of the Different Contemporary Schools*—and another sonorous paragraph—*Together with a Chronology of Such*

Subdivisions of Opinion as Have Arisen Independently.

This title would look monumental in German.*

Going into Montreux Dick pedalled slowly, gaping at the Jugenhorn whenever possible, and blinded by glimpses of the lake through the alleys of the shore hotels. He was conscious of the groups of English, emergent after four years and walking with detective-story suspicion in their eyes, as though they were about to be assaulted in this questionable country by German trained-bands. There were building and awakening everywhere on this mound of débris formed by a mountain torrent. At Berne and at Lausanne on the way south, Dick had been eagerly asked if there would be Americans this year. "By August, if not in June?"

He wore leather shorts, an army shirt, mountain shoes. In his knapsack were a cotton suit and a change of underwear. At the Glion funicular he checked his bicycle and took a small beer on the terrace of the station buffet, meanwhile watching the little bug crawl down the eighty-degree slope of the hill. His ear was full of dried blood from La Tour de Pelz, where he had sprinted under the impression that he was a spoiled athlete. He asked for alcohol and cleared up the exterior while the funicular slid down port. He saw his bicycle embarked, slung his knapsack into the lower compartment of the car, and followed it in.

Mountain-climbing cars are built on a slant similar to the angle of a hat-brim of a man who doesn't want to be recognized. As water gushed from the chamber under the car, Dick was impressed with the ingenuity of the

---

* *Ein Versuch die Neurosen und Psychosen gleichmassig und pragmatisch zu klassifizieren auf Grund der Untersuchung von funfzehn hundert pre-Krapaelin und post-Krapaelin Fallen wie sie diagnostiziert sein wurden in der Terminologie von den verschiedenen Schulen der Gegenwart, zusammen mit einer Chronologie solcher Subdivisionen der Meinung welche unabhangig entstanden sind.*

whole idea—a complementary car was now taking on mountain water at the top and would pull the lightened car up by gravity, as soon as the brakes were released. It must have been a great inspiration. In the seat across, a couple of British were discussing the cable itself.

"The ones made in England always last five or six years. Two years ago the Germans underbid us, and how long do you think their cable lasted?"

"How long?"

"A year and ten months. Then the Swiss sold it to the Italians. They don't have rigid inspections of cables."

"I can see it would be a terrible thing for Switzerland if a cable broke."

The conductor shut a door; he telephoned his confrere among the undulati, and with a jerk the car was pulled upward, heading for a pinpoint on an emerald hill above. After it cleared the low roofs, the skies of Vaud, Valais, Swiss Savoy, and Geneva spread around the passengers in cyclorama. On the centre of the lake, cooled by the piercing current of the Rhône, lay the true center of the Western World. Upon it floated swans like boats and boats like swans, both lost in the nothingness of the heartless beauty. It was a bright day, with sun glittering on the grass beach below and the white courts of the Kursal. The figures on the courts threw no shadows.

When Chillon and the island palace of Salagnon came into view Dick turned his eyes inward. The funicular was above the highest houses of the shore; on both sides a tangle of foliage and flowers culminated at intervals in masses of color. It was a rail-side garden, and in the car was a sign: *"Défense de cueillir les fleurs."*

Though one must not pick flowers on the way up, the blossoms trailed in as they passed—Dorothy Perkins roses dragged patiently through each compartment slowly waggling with the motion of the funicular, letting go at the last to swing back to their rosy cluster. Again and again these branches went through the car.

In the compartment above and in front of Dick's, a group of English were standing up and exclaiming upon the backdrop of sky, when suddenly there was a confusion among them—they parted to give passage to a couple of young people who made apologies and scrambled over into the rear compartment of the funicular—Dick's compartment. The young man was a Latin with the eyes of a stuffed deer; the girl was Nicole.

The two climbers gasped momentarily from their efforts; as they settled into seats, laughing and crowding the English to the corners, Nicole said, "Hel*lo*." She was lovely to look at; immediately Dick saw that something was different; in a second he realized it was her fine-spun hair, bobbed like Irene Castle's and fluffed into curls. She wore a sweater of powder blue and a white tennis skirt—she was the first morning in May and every taint of the clinic was departed.

"Plunk!" she gasped. "Whoo-oo that guard. They'll arrest us at the next shop. Doctor Diver, the Conte de Marmora."

"Gee-imminy!" She felt her new hair, panting. "Sister bought first-class tickets—it's a matter of principle with her." She and Marmora exchanged glances and shouted: "Then we found that first-class is the hearse part behind the chauffeur—shut in with curtains for a rainy day, so you can't see anything. But Sister's very dignified—" Again Nicole and Marmora laughed with young intimacy.

"Where you bound?" asked Dick.

"Caux. You, too?" Nicole looked at his costume. "That your bicycle they got up in front?"

"Yes. I'm going to coast down Monday."

"With me on your handle-bars? I mean, really—will you? I can't think of more fun."

"But I will carry you down in my arms," Marmora protested intensely. "I will roller-skate you—or I will throw you and you will fall slowly like a feather."

The delight in Nicole's face—to be a feather again instead of a plummet, to float and not to drag. She was a carnival to watch—at times primly coy, posing, grimacing and gesturing—sometimes the shadow fell and the dignity of old suffering flowed down into her finger tips. Dick wished himself away from her, fearing that he was a reminder of a world well left behind. He resolved to go to the other hotel.

When the funicular came to rest those new to it stirred in suspension between the blues of two heavens. It was merely for a mysterious exchange between the conductor of the car going up and the conductor of the car coming down. Then up and up over a forest path and a gorge—then again up a hill that became solid with narcissus, from passengers to sky. The people in Montreux playing tennis in the lakeside courts were pinpoints now. Something new was in the air; freshness—freshness embodying itself in music as the car slid into Glion and they heard the orchestra in the hotel garden.

When they changed to the mountain train the music was drowned by the rushing water released from the hydraulic chamber. Almost overhead was Caux, where the thousand windows of a hotel burned in the late sun.

But the approach was different—a leather-lunged engine pushed the passengers round and round in a corkscrew, mounting, rising; they chugged through low-level clouds and for a moment Dick lost Nicole's face in the spray of the slanting donkey-engine; they skirted a lost streak of wind with the hotel growing in size at each spiral, until with a vast surprise they were there, on top of the sunshine.

In the confusion of arrival, as Dick slung his knapsack and started forward on the platform to get his bicycle, Nicole was beside him.

"Aren't you at our hotel?" she asked.

"I'm economizing."

"Will you come down and have dinner?" Some confusion with baggage ensued. "This is my sister—Doctor Diver from Zurich."

Dick bowed to a young woman of twenty-five, tall and confident. She was both formidable and vulnerable, he decided, remembering other women with flower-like mouths grooved for bits.

"I'll drop in after dinner," Dick promised. "First I must get acclimated."

He wheeled off his bicycle, feeling Nicole's eyes following him, feeling her helpless first love, feeling it twist around inside him. He went three hundred yards up the slope to the other hotel, he engaged a room and found himself washing without a memory of the intervening ten minutes, only a sort of drunken flush pierced with voices, unimportant voices that did not know how much he was loved.

IX

THEY were waiting for him and incomplete without him. He was still the incalculable element; Miss Warren and the young Italian wore their anticipation as obviously as Nicole. The salon of the hotel, a room of fabled acoustics, was stripped for dancing but there was a small gallery of Englishwomen of a certain age, with neckbands, dyed hair, and faces powdered pinkish gray; and of American women of a certain age, with snowy-white transformations, black dresses, and lips of cherry red. Miss Warren and Marmora were at a corner table—Nicole was diagonally across from them forty yards away, and as Dick arrived he heard her voice:

"Can you hear me? I'm speaking naturally."

"Perfectly."

"Hello, Doctor Diver."

"What's this?"

"You realize the people in the center of the floor can't hear what I say, but you can?"

"A waiter told us about it," said Miss Warren. "Corner to corner—it's like wireless."

It was exciting up on the mountain, like a ship at sea. Presently Marmora's parents joined them. They treated the Warrens with respect—Dick gathered that their fortunes had something to do with a bank in Milan that had something to do with the Warren fortunes. But Baby Warren wanted to talk to Dick, wanted to talk to him with the impetus that sent her out vagrantly toward all new men, as though she were on an inelastic tether and considered that she might as well get to the end of it as soon as possible. She crossed and recrossed her knees frequently in the manner of tall restless virgins.

"—Nicole told me that you took part care of her, and had a lot to do with her getting well. What I can't understand is what *we're* supposed to do—they were so indefinite at the sanatorium; they only told me she ought to be natural and gay. I knew the Marmoras were up here so I asked Tino to meet us at the funicular. And you see what happens—the very first thing Nicole has him crawling over the sides of the car as if they were both insane——"

"That was absolutely normal," Dick laughed. "I'd call it a good sign. They were showing off for each other."

"But how can *I* tell? Before I knew it, almost in front of my eyes, she had her hair cut off, in Zurich, because of a picture in *Vanity Fair.*"

"That's all right. She's a schizzoid—a permanent eccentric. You can't change that."

"What is it?"

"Just what I said—an eccentric."

"Well, how can any one tell what's eccentric and what's crazy?"

"Nothing is going to be crazy—Nicole is all fresh and happy, you needn't be afraid."

Baby shifted her knees about—she was a compendium of all the discontented women who had loved Byron a hundred years before, yet, in spite of the tragic affair with the guards' officer there was something wooden and onanistic about her.

"I don't mind the responsibility," she declared, "but I'm in the air. We've never had anything like this in the family before—we know Nicole had some shock and my opinion is it was about a boy, but we don't really know. Father says he would have shot him if he could have found out."

The orchestra was playing "Poor Butterfly"; young Marmora was dancing with his mother. It was a tune new enough to them all. Listening, and watching Nicole's shoulders as she chattered to the elder Marmora, whose hair was dashed with white like a piano keyboard, Dick thought of the shoulders of a violin, and then he thought of the dishonor, the secret. Oh, butterfly—the moments pass into hours——

"Actually *I* have a plan," Baby continued with apologetic hardness. "It may seem absolutely impractical to you but they say Nicole will need to be looked after for a few years. I don't know whether you know Chicago or not——"

"I don't."

"Well, there's a North Side and a South Side and they're very much separated. The North Side is chic and all that, and we've always lived over there, at least for many years, but lots of old families, old Chicago families, if you know what I mean, still live on the South Side. The University is there. I mean it's stuffy to some people, but anyhow it's different from the North Side. I don't know whether you understand."

He nodded. With some concentration he had been able to follow her.

"Now of course we have lots of connections there—Father controls certain chairs and fellowships and so forth at the University, and I thought if we took Nicole home and threw her with that crowd—you see she's quite musical and speaks all these languages—what could be better in her condition than if she fell in love with some good doctor——"

A burst of hilarity surged up in Dick, the Warrens were going to buy Nicole a doctor— You got a nice doctor you can let us use? There was no use worrying about Nicole when they were in the position of being able to buy her a nice young doctor, the paint scarcely dry on him.

"But how about the doctor?" he said automatically.

"There must be many who'd jump at the chance."

The dancers were back, but Baby whispered quickly: "This is the sort of thing I mean. Now where is Nicole—she's gone off somewhere. Is she upstairs in her room? What am *I* supposed to do? I never know whether it's something innocent or whether I ought to go find her."

"Perhaps she just wants to be by herself—people living alone get used to loneliness." Seeing that Miss Warren was not listening he stopped. "I'll take a look around."

For a moment all the outdoors shut in with mist was like spring with the curtains drawn. Life was gathered near the hotel. Dick passed some cellar windows where bus boys sat on bunks and played cards over a liter of Spanish wine. As he approached the promenade, the stars began to come through the white crests of the high Alps. On the horseshoe walk overlooking the lake Nicole was the figure motionless between two lamp stands, and he approached silently across the grass. She turned to him with an expression of: "Here *you* are," and for a moment he was sorry he had come.

"Your sister wondered."

"Oh!" She was accustomed to being watched. With an effort she explained herself: "Sometimes I get a little—it gets a little too much. I've lived so quietly. Tonight that music was too much. It made me want to cry——"

"I understand."

"This has been an awfully exciting day."

"I know."

"I don't want to do anything anti-social—I've caused everybody enough trouble. But tonight I wanted to get away."

It occurred to Dick suddenly, as it might occur to a dying man that he had forgotten to tell where his will was, that Nicole had been "re-educated" by Dohmler and the ghostly generations behind him; it occurred to him also that there would be so much she would have to be told. But having recorded this wisdom within himself, he yielded to the insistent face-value of the situation and said:

"You're a nice person—just keep using your own judgment about yourself."

"You like me?"

"Of course."

"Would you—" They were strolling along toward the

dim end of the horseshoe, two hundred yards ahead. "If I hadn't been sick would you—I mean, would I have been the sort of girl you might have—oh, slush, you know what I mean."

He was in for it now, possessed by a vast irrationality. She was so near that he felt his breathing change but again his training came to his aid in a boy's laugh and a trite remark.

"You're teasing yourself, my dear. Once I knew a man who fell in love with his nurse—" The anecdote rambled on, punctuated by their footsteps. Suddenly Nicole interrupted in succinct Chicagoese: "Bull!"

"That's a very vulgar expression."

"What about it?" she flared up. "You don't think I've got any common sense—before I was sick I didn't have any, but I have now. And if I don't know you're the most attractive man I ever met you must think I'm still crazy. It's my hard luck, all right—but don't pretend I don't *know*—I know everything about you and me."

Dick was at an additional disadvantage. He remembered the statement of the elder Miss Warren as to the young doctors that could be purchased in the intellectual stockyards of the South Side of Chicago, and he hardened for a moment. "You're a fetching kid, but I couldn't fall in love."

"You won't give me a chance."

"*What!*"

The impertinence, the right to invade implied, astounded him. Short of anarchy he could not think of any chance that Nicole Warren deserved.

"Give me a chance now."

The voice fell low, sank into her breast and stretched the tight bodice over her heart as she came up close. He felt the young lips, her body sighing in relief against the arm growing stronger to hold her. There were now no more plans than if Dick had arbitrarily made some indissoluble mixture, with atoms joined and inseparable; you could throw it all out but never again could they fit back into atomic scale. As he held her and tasted her, and as she curved in further and further toward him, with her own lips, new to herself, drowned and engulfed in love, yet solaced and triumphant, he was thankful to have an existence at all, if only as a reflection in her wet eyes.

"My God," he gasped, "you're fun to kiss."

That was talk, but Nicole had a better hold on him now and she held it; she turned coquette and walked away, leaving him as suspended as in the funicular of the afternoon. She felt: There, that'll show him, how conceited; how he could do with me; oh, wasn't it wonderful! I've got him, he's mine. Now in the sequence came flight, but it was all so sweet and new that she dawdled, wanting to draw all of it in.

She shivered suddenly. Two thousand feet below she saw the necklace and bracelet of lights that were Montreux and Vevey, beyond them a dim pendant of Lausanne. From down there somewhere ascended a faint sound of dance music. Nicole was up in her head now, cool as cool, trying to collate the sentimentalities of her childhood, as deliberate as a man getting drunk after battle. But she was still afraid of Dick, who stood near her, leaning, characteristically, against the iron fence that rimmed the horseshoe; and this prompted her to say: "I can remember how I stood waiting for you in the garden—holding all my self in my arms like a basket of flowers. It was that to me anyhow—I thought I was sweet—waiting to hand that basket to you."

He breathed over her shoulder and turned her insistently about; she kissed him several times, her face getting big every time she came close, her hands holding him by the shoulders.

"It's raining hard."

Suddenly there was a booming from the wine slopes across the lake; cannons were shooting at hail-bearing clouds in order to break them. The lights of the promenade went off, went on again. Then the storm came swiftly, first falling from the heavens, then doubly falling in torrents from the mountains and washing loud down the roads and stone ditches; with it came a dark, frightening sky and savage filaments of lightning and world-splitting thunder, while ragged, destroying clouds fled along past the hotel. Mountains and lake disappeared—the hotel crouched amid tumult, chaos and darkness.

By this time Dick and Nicole had reached the vestibule, where Baby Warren and the three Marmoras were anxiously awaiting them. It was exciting coming out of the wet fog—with the doors banging, to stand and laugh and quiver with emotion, wind in their ears and rain on their clothes. Now in the ballroom the orchestra was playing a Strauss waltz, high and confusing.

. . . For Doctor Diver to marry a mental patient? How did it happen? Where did it begin?

"Won't you come back after you've changed?" Baby Warren asked after a close scrutiny.

"I haven't got any change, except some shorts."

As he trudged up to his hotel in a borrowed raincoat he kept laughing derisively in his throat.

"*Big* chance—oh, yes. My God!—they decided to buy a doctor? Well, they better stick to whoever they've got in Chicago." Revolted by his harshness he made amends to Nicole, remembering that nothing had ever felt so young as her lips, remembering rain like tears shed for him that lay upon her softly shining porcelain cheeks . . . the silence of the storm ceasing woke him about three o'clock and he went to the window. Her beauty climbed the rolling slope, it came into the room, rustling ghost-like through the curtains. . . .

. . . He climbed two thousand meters to Rochers de Naye the following morning, amused by the fact that his conductor of the day before was using his day off to climb also.

Then Dick descended all the way to Montreux for a swim, got back to his hotel in time for dinner. Two notes awaited him.

I'm not ashamed about last night—it was the nicest thing that ever happened to me and even if I never saw you again, Mon Capitaine, I would be glad it happened.

That was disarming enough—the heavy shade of Dohmler retreated as Dick opened the second envelope:

Dear Doctor Diver: I phoned but you were out. I wonder if I may ask you a great big favor. Unforeseen circumstances call me back to Paris, and I find I can make better time by way of Lausanne. Can you let Nicole ride as far as Zurich with you, since you are going back Monday? and drop her at the sanitarium? Is this too much to ask?

Sincerely,

Beth Evan Warren.

Dick was furious—Miss Warren had known he had a bicycle with him; yet she had so phrased her note that it was impossible to refuse. Throw us together! Sweet propinquity and the Warren money!

He was wrong; Baby Warren had no such intentions. She had looked Dick over with worldly eyes; she had measured him with the warped rule of an Anglophile and found him wanting—in spite of the fact that she found him toothsome. But for her he was too "intellectual" and she pigeonholed him with a shabby-snobby crowd she had once known in London—he put himself out too much to be really of the correct stuff. She could not see how he could be made into her idea of an aristocrat.

In addition to that he was stubborn—she had seen him leave her conversation and get down behind his eyes in that odd way that people did, half a dozen times. She had not liked Nicole's free and easy manner as a child and now she was sensibly habituated to thinking of her as a "gone coon"; and anyhow Doctor Diver was not the sort of medical man she could envisage in the family.

She only wanted to use him innocently as a convenience.

But her request had the effect that Dick assumed she desired. A ride in a train can be a terrible, heavy-hearted or comic thing; it can be a trial flight; it can be a prefiguration of another journey just as a given day with a friend can be long, from the taste of hurry in the morning up to the realization of both being hungry and taking food together. Then comes the afternoon with the journey fading and dying, but quickening again at the end. Dick was sad to see Nicole's meager joy; yet it was a relief for her, going back to the only home she knew. They made no love that day, but when he left her outside the sad door on the Zurichsee and she turned and looked at him he knew her problem was one they had together for good now.

X

IN ZURICH in September Doctor Diver had tea with Baby Warren.

"I think it's ill advised," she said, "I'm not sure I truly understand your motives."

"Don't let's be unpleasant."

"After all I'm Nicole's sister."

"That doesn't give you the right to be unpleasant." It irritated Dick that he knew so much that he could not tell her. "Nicole's rich, but that doesn't make me an adventurer."

"That's just it," complained Baby stubbornly. "Nicole's rich."

"Just how much money has she got?" he asked.

She started; and with a silent laugh he continued, "You see how silly this is? I'd rather talk to some man in your family——"

"Everything's been left to me," she persisted. "It isn't we think you're an adventurer. We don't know who you are."

"I'm a doctor of medicine," he said. "My father is a clergyman, now retired. We lived in Buffalo and my past is open to investigation. I went to New Haven; afterward I was a Rhodes scholar. My great-grandfather was Governor of North Carolina and I'm a direct descendant of Mad Anthony Wayne."

"Who was Mad Anthony Wayne?" Baby asked suspiciously.

"Mad Anthony Wayne?"

"I think there's enough madness in this affair."

He shook his head hopelessly, just as Nicole came out on the hotel terrace and looked around for them.

"He was too mad to leave as much money as Marshall Field," he said.

"That's all very well——"

Baby was right and she knew it. Face to face, her father would have it on almost any clergyman. They were an American ducal family without a title—the very name written in a hotel register, signed to an introduction, used in a difficult situation, caused a psychological metamorphosis in people, and in return this change had crystallized her own sense of position. She knew these facts from the English, who had known them for over two hundred years. But she did not know that twice Dick had come close to flinging the marriage in her face. All that saved it this time was Nicole finding their table and glowing away, white and fresh and new in the September afternoon.

How do you do, lawyer. We're going to Como tomorrow for a week and then back to Zurich. That's why I wanted you and sister to settle this, because it doesn't matter to us how much I'm allowed. We're going to live very quietly in Zurich for two years and Dick has enough to take care of us. No, Baby, I'm more practical than you think— It's only for clothes and things I'll need it. . . . Why, that's more than—can the estate really afford to give me all that? I know I'll never manage to spend it. Do you have that much? Why do you have more—is it because I'm supposed to be incompetent? All right, let my share pile up then. . . . No, Dick refuses to have anything whatever to do with it. I'll have to feel bloated for us both. . . . Baby, you have no more idea of what Dick is like than, than— Now where do I sign? Oh, I'm sorry.

. . . Isn't it funny and lonely being together, Dick? No place to go except close. Shall we just love and love? Ah, but I love the most, and I can tell when you're away from me, even a little. I think it's wonderful to be just like everybody else, to reach out and find you all warm beside me in the bed.

. . . If you will kindly call my husband at the hospital. Yes, the little book is selling everywhere—they want it published in six languages. I was to do the French translation but I'm tired these days—I'm afraid of falling, I'm so heavy and clumsy—like a broken roly-poly that can't stand up straight. The cold stethoscope against my heart and my strongest feeling *"Je m'en fiche de tout."*—Oh, that poor woman in the hospital with the blue baby, much better dead. Isn't it fine there are three of us now?

. . . That seems unreasonable, Dick—we have every reason for taking the bigger apartment. Why should we penalize ourselves just because there's more Warren money than Diver money. Oh, thank you, *cameriere*, but we've changed our minds. This English clergyman tells us that your wine here in Orvieto is excellent. It doesn't travel? That must be why we have never heard of it, because we love wine.

The lakes are sunk in the brown clay and the slopes have all the creases of a belly. The photographer gave us the picture of me, my hair limp over the rail on the boat to Capri. "Good-bye, Blue Grotte," sang the boatman, "come again soo-oon." And afterward tracing down the hot sinister shin of the Italian boot with the wind soughing around those eerie castles, the dead watching from up on those hills.

. . . This ship is nice, with our heels hitting the deck together. This is the blowy corner and each time we turn it I slant forward against the wind and pull my coat together without losing step with Dick. We are chanting nonsense:

"Oh—oh—oh—oh
Other flamingoes than me,
Oh—oh—oh—oh
Other flamingoes than me——"

Life is fun with Dick—the people in deck chairs look at us, and a woman is trying to hear what we are singing. Dick is tired of singing it, so go on alone, Dick. You will walk differently alone, dear, through a thicker atmosphere, forcing your way through the shadows of chairs, through the dripping smoke of the funnels. You will feel your own reflection sliding along the eyes of those who look at you. You are no longer insulated; but I suppose you must touch life in order to spring from it.

Sitting on the stanchion of this lifeboat I look seaward and let my hair blow and shine. I am motionless against the sky and the boat is made to carry my form onward into the blue obscurity of the future, I am Pallas Athene carved reverently on the front of a galley. The waters are lapping in the public toilets and the agate green foliage of spray changes and complains about the stern.

. . . We traveled a lot that year—from Woolloomooloo Bay to Biskra. On the edge of the Sahara we ran into a plague of locusts and the chauffeur explained kindly that they were bumble-bees. The sky was low at night, full of the presence of a strange and watchful God. Oh, the poor little naked Ouled Naïl; the night was noisy with drums from Senegal and flutes and whining camels, and the natives pattering about in shoes made of old automobile tires.

But I was gone again by that time—trains and beaches they were all one. That was why he took me traveling, but after my second child, my little girl, Topsy, was born everything got dark again.

. . . If I could get word to my husband who has seen fit to desert me here, to leave me in the hands of incompetents. You tell me my baby is black—that's farcical, that's very cheap. We went to Africa merely to see Timgad, since my principal interest in life is archeology. I am tired of knowing nothing and being reminded of it all the time.

. . . When I get well I want to be a fine person like you, Dick—I would study medicine except it's too late. We must spend my money and have a house—I'm tired of apartments and waiting for you. You're bored with Zurich and you can't find time for writing here and you say that it's a confession of weakness for a scientist not to write. And I'll look over the whole field of knowledge and pick out something and really know about it, so I'll have it to hang on to if I go to pieces again. You'll help me, Dick, so I won't feel so guilty. We'll live near a warm beach where we can be brown and young together.

. . . This is going to be Dick's work house. Oh, the idea came to us both at the same moment. We had passed Tarmes a dozen times and we rode up here and found the houses empty, except two stables. When we bought we acted through a Frenchman, but the navy sent spies up here in no time when they found that Americans had bought part of a hill village. They looked for cannons all through the building material, and finally Baby had to twitch wires for us at the Affaires Étrangères in Paris.

No one comes to the Riviera in summer, so we expect to have a few guests and to work. There are some French people here—Mistinguette last week, surprised to find the hotel open, and Picasso and the man who wrote *Pas sur la Bouche*.

. . . Dick, why did you register Mr. and Mrs. Diver instead of Doctor and Mrs. Diver? I just wondered—it just floated through my mind.—You've taught me that work is everything and I believe you. You used to say a man knows things and when he stops knowing things he's like anybody else, and the thing is to get power before he stops knowing things. If you want to turn things topsy-turvy, all right, but must your Nicole follow you walking on her hands, darling?

. . . Tommy says I am silent. Since I was well the first time I talked a lot to Dick late at night, both of us sitting up in bed and lighting cigarettes, then diving down afterward out of the blue dawn and into the pillows, to keep the light from our eyes. Sometimes I sing, and play with the animals, and I have a few friends too—Mary, for instance. When Mary and I talk neither of us listens to the other. Talk is men. When I talk I say to myself that I am probably Dick. Already I have even been my son, remembering how wise and slow he is. Sometimes I am Doctor Dohmler and one time I may even be an aspect of you, Tommy Barban. Tommy is in love with me, I think, but gently, reassuringly. Enough, though, so that he and Dick have begun to disapprove of each other. All in all, everything has never gone better. I am among friends who like me. I am here on this tranquil beach with my husband and two children. Everything is all right—if I can finish translating this damn recipe for chicken à la Maryland into French. My toes feel warm in the sand.

"Yes, I'll look. More new people—oh, that girl—yes. Who did you say she looked like. . . . No, I haven't, we don't get much chance to see the new American pictures over here. Rosemary who? Well, we're getting very fashionable for July—seems very peculiar to me. Yes, she's lovely, but there can be too many people."

XI

DOCTOR Richard Diver and Mrs. Elsie Speers sat in the Café des Alliés in August, under cool and dusty trees. The sparkle of the mica was dulled by the baked ground, and a few gusts of mistral from down the coast seeped through the Esterel and rocked the fishing boats in the harbor, pointing the masts here and there at a featureless sky.

"I had a letter this morning," said Mrs. Speers. "What a terrible time you all must have had with those Negroes! But Rosemary said you were perfectly wonderful to her."

"Rosemary ought to have a service stripe. It was pretty harrowing—the only person it didn't disturb was Abe North—he flew off to Havre—he probably doesn't know about it yet."

"I'm sorry Mrs. Diver was upset," she said carefully.

Rosemary had written:

Nicole seemed Out of her Mind. I didn't want to come South with them because I felt Dick had enough on his hands.

"She's all right now." He spoke almost impatiently. "So you're leaving tomorrow. When will you sail?"

"Right away."

"My God, it's awful to have you go."

"We're glad we came here. We've had a good time, thanks to you. You're the first man Rosemary ever cared for."

Another gust of wind strained around the porphyry hills of La Napoule. There was a hint in the air that the earth was hurrying on toward other weather; the lush midsummer moment outside of time was already over.

"Rosemary's had crushes, but sooner or later she always turned the man over to me—" Mrs. Speers laughed, "—for dissection."

"So I was spared."

"There was nothing I could have done. She was in love with you before I ever saw you. I told her to go ahead."

He saw that no provision had been made for him, or for Nicole, in Mrs. Speers' plans—and he saw that her amorality sprang from the conditions of her own withdrawal. It was her right, the pension on which her own emotions had retired. Women are necessarily capable of almost anything in their struggle for survival and can scarcely be convicted of such man-made crimes as "cruelty." So long as the shuffle of love and pain went on within proper walls Mrs. Speers could view it with as much detachment and humor as a eunuch. She had not even allowed for the possibility of Rosemary's being damaged—or was she certain that she couldn't be?

"If what you say is true I don't think it did her any harm." He was keeping up to the end the pretense that he could still think objectively about Rosemary. "She's over it already. Still—so many of the important times in life begin by seeming incidental."

"This wasn't incidental," Mrs. Speers insisted. "You were the first man—you're an ideal to her. In every letter she says that."

"She's so polite."

"You and Rosemary are the politest people I've ever known, but she means this."

"My politeness is a trick of the heart."

This was partly true. From his father Dick had learned the somewhat conscious good manners of the young Southerner coming north after the Civil War. Often he used them and just as often he despised them because they were not a protest against how unpleasant selfishness was but against how unpleasant it looked.

"I'm in love with Rosemary," he told her suddenly. "It's a kind of self-indulgence saying that to you."

It seemed very strange and official to him, as if the very tables and chairs in the Café des Alliés would remember it forever. Already he felt her absence from these skies: on the beach he could only remember the sun-torn flesh of her shoulder; at Tarmes he crushed out her footprints as he crossed the garden; and now the orchestra launching into the Nice Carnival Song, an echo of last year's vanished gaieties, started the little dance that went on all about her. In a hundred hours she had come to possess all the world's dark magic; the blinding belladonna, the caffein converting physical into nervous energy, the mandragora that imposes harmony.

With an effort he once more accepted the fiction that he shared Mrs. Speers' detachment.

"You and Rosemary aren't really alike," he said. "The wisdom she got from you is all molded up into her persona, into the mask she faces the world with. She doesn't think; her real depths are Irish and romantic and illogical."

Mrs. Speers knew too that Rosemary, for all her delicate surface, was a young mustang, perceptibly by Captain Doctor Hoyt, U.S.A. Cross-sectioned, Rosemary would have displayed an enormous heart, liver and soul, all crammed close together under the lovely shell.

Saying good-by, Dick was aware of Elsie Speers' full charm, aware that she meant rather more to him than merely a last unwillingly relinquished fragment of Rosemary. He could possibly have made up Rosemary—he could never have made up her mother. If the cloak, spurs, and brilliants in which Rosemary had walked off were things with which he had endowed her, it was nice in contrast to watch her mother's grace knowing it was surely something he had not evoked. She had an air of seeming to wait, as if for a man to get through with something more important than herself, a battle or an operation, during which he must not be hurried or interfered with. When the man had finished she would be waiting, without fret or impatience, somewhere on a high stool, turning the pages of a newspaper.

"Good-by—and I want you both to remember always how fond of you Nicole and I have grown."

Back at the Villa Diana, he went to his work-room, and opened the shutters, closed against the mid-day glare. On his two long tables, in ordered confusion, lay the materials of his book. Volume I, concerned with Classification, had achieved some success in a small subsidized edition. He was negotiating for its reissue. Volume II was to be a great amplification of his first little book, *A Psychology for Psychiatrists.* Like so many men he had found that he had only one or two ideas—that his little collection of pamphlets now in its fiftieth German edition contained the germ of all he would ever think or know.

But he was currently uneasy about the whole thing. He resented the wasted years at New Haven, but mostly he felt a discrepancy between the growing luxury in which the Divers lived, and the need for display which apparently went along with it. Remembering his Rumanian friend's story, about the man who had worked for years on the brain of an armadillo, he suspected that patient Germans were sitting close to the libraries of Berlin and Vienna callously anticipating him. He had about decided to brief the work in its present condition and publish it in an undocumented volume of a hundred thousand words as an introduction to more scholarly volumes to follow.

He confirmed this decision walking around the rays of late afternoon in his work-room. With the new plan he could be through by spring. It seemed to him that when a man with his energy was pursued for a year by increasing doubts, it indicated some fault in the plan.

He laid the bars of gilded metal that he used as paperweights along the sheaves of notes. He swept up, for no servant was allowed in here, treated his washroom sketchily with Bon Ami, repaired a screen and sent off an order to a publishing house in Zurich. Then he drank an ounce of gin with twice as much water.

He saw Nicole in the garden. Presently he must encounter her and the prospect gave him a leaden feeling. Before her he must keep up a perfect front, now and tomorrow, next week and next year. All night in Paris he had held her in his arms while she slept light under the luminal; in the early morning he broke in upon her confusion before it could form, with words of tenderness and protection, and she slept again with his face against the warm scent of her hair. Before she woke he had arranged everything at the phone in the next room. Rosemary was to move to another hotel. She was to be "Daddy's Girl" and even to give up saying good-by to them. The proprietor of the hotel, Mr. MacBeth, was to be the three Chinese monkeys. Packing amid the piled boxes and tissue paper of many purchases, Dick and Nicole left for the Riviera at noon.

Then there was a reaction. As they settled down in the wagon-lit Dick saw that Nicole was waiting for it, and it came quickly and desperately, before the train was out of the ceinture—his only instinct was to step off while the train was still going slow, rush back and see where Rosemary was, what she was doing. He opened a book and bent his pince-nez upon it, aware that Nicole was watching him from her pillow across the compartment. Unable to read, he pretended to be tired and shut his eyes but she was still watching him, and though still she was half asleep from the hangover of the drug, she was relieved and almost happy that he was hers again.

It was worse with his eyes shut for it gave a rhythm of finding and losing, finding and losing; but so as not to appear restless he lay like that until noon. At luncheon things were better—it was always a fine meal;

a thousand lunches in inns and restaurants, wagon-lits, buffets, and airplanes were a mighty collation to have taken together. The familiar hurry of the train waiters, the little bottles of wine and mineral water, the excellent food of the Paris-Lyons-Méditerranée gave them the illusion that everything was the same as before, but it was almost the first trip he had ever taken with Nicole that was a going away rather than a going toward. He drank a whole bottle of wine save for Nicole's single glass; they talked about the house and the children. But once back in the compartment a silence fell over them like the silence in the restaurant across from the Luxembourg. Receding from a grief, it seems necessary to retrace the same steps that brought us there. An unfamiliar impatience settled on Dick; suddenly Nicole said:

"It seemed too bad to leave Rosemary like that—do you suppose she'll be all right?"

"Of course. She could take care of herself anywhere—" Lest this belittle Nicole's ability to do likewise, he added, "After all, she's an actress, and even though her mother's in the background she *has* to look out for herself."

"She's very attractive."

"She's an infant."

"She's attractive though."

They talked aimlessly back and forth, each speaking for the other.

"She's not as intelligent as I thought," Dick offered.

"She's quite smart."

"Not very, though—there's a persistent aroma of the nursery."

"She's very—very pretty," Nicole said in a detached, emphatic way, "and I thought she was very good in the picture."

"She was well directed. Thinking it over, it wasn't very individual."

"I thought it was. I can see how she'd be very attractive to men."

His heart twisted. To what men? How many men?

—Do you mind if I pull down the curtain?

—Please do, it's too light in here.

Where now? And with whom?

"In a few years she'll look ten years older than you."

"On the contrary. I sketched her one night on a theater program, I think she'll last."

They were both restless in the night. In a day or two Dick would try to banish the ghost of Rosemary before it became walled up with them, but for the moment he had no force to do it. Sometimes it is harder to deprive oneself of a pain than of a pleasure and the memory so possessed him that for the moment there was nothing to do but to pretend. This was more difficult because he was currently annoyed with Nicole, who, after all these years, should recognize symptoms of strain in herself and guard against them. Twice within a fortnight she had broken up: there had been the night of the dinner at Tarmes when he had found her in her bedroom dissolved in crazy laughter telling Mrs. McKisco she could not go in the bathroom because the key was thrown down the well. Mrs. McKisco was astonished and resentful, baffled and yet in a way comprehending. Dick had not been particularly alarmed then, for afterward Nicole was repentant. She called at Gausse's Hotel but the McKiscos were gone.

The collapse in Paris was another matter, adding significance to the first one. It prophesied possibly a new cycle, a new *pousse* of the malady. Having gone through unprofessional agonies during her long relapse following Topsy's birth, he had, perforce, hardened himself about her, making a cleavage between Nicole sick and Nicole well. This made it difficult now to distinguish between his self-protective professional detachment and some new coldness in his heart. As an indifference cherished, or left to atrophy, becomes an emptiness, to this extent he had learned to become empty of Nicole, serving her against his will with negations and emotional neglect. One writes of scars healed, a loose parallel to the pathology of the skin, but there is no such thing in the life of an individual. There are open wounds, shrunk sometimes to the size of a pin-prick but wounds still. The marks of suffering are more comparable to the loss of a finger, or of the sight of an eye. We may not miss them, either, for one minute in a year, but if we should there is nothing to be done about it.

XII

HE found Nicole in the garden with her arms folded high on her shoulders. She looked at him with straight gray eyes, with a child's searching wonder.

"I went to Cannes," he said. "I ran into Mrs. Speers. She's leaving tomorrow. She wanted to come up and say good-by to you, but I slew the idea."

"I'm sorry. I'd like to have seen her. I like her."

"Who else do you think I saw—Bartholomew Tailor."

"You didn't."

"I couldn't have missed that face of his, the old experienced weasel. He was looking over the ground for Ciro's Menagerie—they'll all be down next year. I suspected Mrs. Abrams was a sort of outpost."

"And Baby was outraged the first summer we came here."

"They don't really give a damn where they are, so I don't see why they don't stay and freeze in Deauville."

"Can't we start rumors about cholera or something?"

"I told Bartholomew that some categories died off like flies here—I told him the life of a suck was as short as the life of a machine-gunner in the war."

"You didn't."

"No, I didn't," he admitted. "He was very pleasant. It was a beautiful sight, he and I shaking hands there on the boulevard. The meeting of Sigmund Freud and Ward McAllister."

Dick didn't want to talk—he wanted to be alone so that his thoughts about work and the future would overpower his thoughts of love and today. Nicole knew about it but only darkly and tragically, hating him a little in an animal way, yet wanting to rub against his shoulder.

"The darling," Dick said lightly.

He went into the house, forgetting something he wanted to do there, and then remembering it was the piano. He sat down whistling and played by ear:

> "Just picture you upon my knee
> With tea for two and two for tea
> And me for you and you for me——"

Through the melody flowed a sudden realization that Nicole, hearing it, would guess quickly at a nostalgia for the past fortnight. He broke off with a casual chord and left the piano.

It was hard to know where to go. He glanced about the house that Nicole had made, that Nicole's grandfather had paid for. He owned only his work house and the ground on which it stood. Out of three thousand a year and what dribbled in from his publications he paid for his clothes and personal expenses, for cellar charges, and for Lanier's education, so far confined to a nurse's wage. Never had a move been contemplated without Dick's figuring his share. Living rather ascetically, traveling third-class when he was alone, with the cheapest wine, and good care of his clothes, and penalizing himself for any extravagances, he maintained a qualified financial independence. After a certain point, though, it was difficult—again and again it was necessary to decide together as to the uses to which Nicole's money should be put. Naturally Nicole, wanting to own him, wanting him to stand still forever, encouraged any slackness on his part, and in multiplying ways he was constantly inundated by a trickling of goods and money. The inception of the idea of the cliff villa which they had elaborated as a fantasy one day was a typical example of the forces divorcing them from the first simple arrangements in Zurich.

"Wouldn't it be fun if—" it had been; and then, "Won't it be fun when——"

It was not so much fun. His work became confused with Nicole's problems; in addition, her income had increased so fast of late that it seemed to belittle his work. Also, for the purpose of her cure, he had for many years pretended to a rigid domesticity from which he was drifting away, and this pretense became more arduous in this effortless immobility, in which he was inevitably subjected to microscopic examination. When Dick could no longer play what he wanted to play on the piano, it was an indication that life was being refined down to a point. He stayed in the big room a long time listening to the buzz of the electric clock, listening to time.

In November the waves grew black and dashed over the sea wall onto the shore road—such summer life as had survived disappeared and the beaches were melancholy and desolate under the mistral and rain. Gausse's Hotel was closed for repairs and enlargement and the scaffolding of the summer Casino at Juan les Pins grew larger and more formidable. Going into Cannes or Nice, Dick and Nicole met new people—members of orchestras, restaurateurs, horticultural enthusiasts, ship builders—for Dick had bought an old dinghy—and members of the Syndicat d'Initiative. They knew their servants well and gave thought to the children's education. In December, Nicole seemed well-knit again; when a month had passed without tension, without the tight mouth, the unmotivated smile, the unfathomable remark, they went to the Swiss Alps for the Christmas holidays.

XIII

WITH his cap, Dick slapped the snow from his dark blue ski-suit before going inside. The great hall, its floor pockmarked by two decades of hobnails, was cleared for the tea dance, and four-score young Americans, domiciled in schools near Gstaad, bounced about to the frolic of "Don't Bring Lulu," or exploded violently with the first percussions of the Charleston. It was a colony of the young, simple, and expensive—the *Sturmtruppen* of the rich were at St. Moritz. Baby Warren felt that she had made a gesture of renunciation in joining the Divers here.

Dick picked out the two sisters easily across the delicately haunted, soft-swaying room—they were posterlike, formidable in their snow costumes, Nicole's of cerulean blue, Baby's of brick red. The young Englishman was talking to them; but they were paying no attention, lulled to the staring point by the adolescent dance.

Nicole's snow-warm face lighted up further as she saw Dick. "Where is he?"

"He missed the train—I'm meeting him later." Dick

sat down, swinging a heavy boot over his knee. "You two look very striking together. Every once in a while I forget we're in the same party and get a big shock at seeing you."

Baby was a tall, fine-looking woman, deeply engaged in being almost thirty. Symptomatically she had pulled two men with her from London, one scarcely down from Cambridge, one old and hard with Victorian lecheries. Baby had certain spinsters' characteristics—she was alien from touch, she started if she was touched suddenly, and such lingering touches as kisses and embraces slipped directly through the flesh into the forefront of her consciousness. She made few gestures with her trunk, her body proper—instead, she stamped her foot and tossed her head in almost an old-fashioned way. She relished the foretaste of death, prefigured by the catastrophes of friends—persistently she clung to the idea of Nicole's tragic destiny.

Baby's younger Englishman had been chaperoning the women down appropriate inclines and harrowing them on the bob-run. Dick, having turned an ankle in a too ambitious telemark, loafed gratefully about the "nursery slope" with the children or drank kvass with a Russian doctor at the hotel.

"Please be happy, Dick," Nicole urged him. "Why don't you meet some of these ickle durls and dance with them in the afternoon?"

"What would I say to them?"

Her low almost harsh voice rose a few notes, simulating a plaintive coquetry: "Say: 'Ickle durl, oo is de pwettiest sing.' What do you think you say?"

"I don't like ickle durls. They smell of castile soap and peppermint. When I dance with them, I feel as if I'm pushing a baby carriage."

It was a dangerous subject—he was careful, to the point of self-consciousness, to stare far over the heads of young maidens.

"There's a lot of business," said Baby. "First place, there's news from home—the property we used to call the station property. The railroads only bought the center of it at first. Now they've bought the rest, and it belonged to Mother. It's a question of investing the money."

Pretending to be repelled by this gross turn in the conversation, the Englishman made for a girl on the floor. Following him for an instant with the uncertain eyes of an American girl in the grip of a life-long Anglophilia, Baby continued defiantly:

"It's a lot of money. It's three hundred thousand apiece. I keep an eye on my own investments but Nicole doesn't know anything about securities, and I don't suppose you do either."

"I've got to meet the train," Dick said evasively.

Outside he inhaled damp snowflakes that he could no longer see against the darkening sky. Three children sledding past shouted a warning in some strange language; he heard them yell at the next bend and a little farther on he heard sleighbells coming up the hill in the dark. The holiday station glittered with expectancy, boys and girls waiting for new boys and girls, and by the time the train arrived, Dick had caught the rhythm, and pretended to Franz Gregorovious that he was clipping off a half-hour from an endless roll of pleasures. But Franz had some intensity of purpose at the moment that fought through any superimposition of mood on Dick's part. "I may get up to Zurich for a day," Dick had written, "or you can manage to come to Lausanne." Franz had managed to come all the way to Gstaad.

He was forty. Upon his healthy maturity reposed a set of pleasant official manners, but he was most at home in a somewhat stuffy safety from which he could despise the broken rich whom he re-educated. His scientific heredity might have bequeathed him a wider world but he seemed to have deliberately chosen the standpoint of an humbler class, a choice typified by his selection of a wife. At the hotel Baby Warren made a quick examination of him, and failing to find any of the hallmarks she respected, the subtler virtues or courtesies by which the privileged classes recognized one another, treated him thereafter with her second manner. Nicole was always a little afraid of him. Dick liked him, as he liked his friends, without reservations.

For the evening they were sliding down the hill into the village, on those little sleds which serve the same purpose as gondolas do in Venice. Their destination was a hotel with an old-fashioned Swiss tap-room, wooden and resounding, a room of clocks, kegs, steins, and antlers. Many parties at long tables blurred into one great party and ate fondue—a peculiarly indigestible form of Welsh rarebit, mitigated by hot spiced wine.

It was jolly in the big room; the younger Englishman remarked it and Dick conceded that there was no other word. With the pert heady wine he relaxed and pretended that the world was all put together again by the gray-haired men of the golden nineties who shouted old glees at the piano, by the young voices and the bright costumes toned into the room by the swirling smoke. For a moment he felt that they were in a ship with landfall just ahead; in the faces of all the girls was the same innocent expectation of the possibilities inherent in the situation and the night. He looked to see if that special girl was there and got an impression that she was at the table behind them—then he forgot her and invented a rigmarole and tried to make his party have a good time.

"I must talk to you," said Franz in English. "I have only twenty-four hours to spend here."

"I suspected you had something on your mind."

"I have a plan that is—so marvelous." His hand fell upon Dick's knee. "I have a plan that will be the making of us two."

"Well?"

"Dick—there is a clinic we could have together—the old clinic of Braun on the Zugersee. The plant is all modern except for a few points. He is sick—he wants to go up in Austria, to die probably. It is a chance that is just insuperable. You and me—what a pair! Now don't say anything yet until I finish."

From the yellow glint in Baby's eyes, Dick saw she was listening.

"We must undertake it together. It would not bind you too tight—it would give you a base, a laboratory, a center. You could stay in residence say no more than half the year, when the weather is fine. In winter you could go to France or America and write your texts fresh from clinical experience." He lowered his voice. "And for the convalescence in your family, there are the atmosphere and regularity of the clinic at hand." Dick's expression did not encourage this note so Franz dropped it with the punctuation of his tongue leaving his lip quickly. "We could be partners. I the executive manager, you the theoretician, the brilliant consultant and all that. I know myself—I know I have no genius and you have. But, in my way, I am thought very capable; I am utterly competent at the most modern clinical methods. Sometimes for months I have served as the practical head of the old clinic. The professor says this plan is excellent, he advises me to go ahead. He says he is going to live forever, and work up to the last minute."

Dick formed imaginary pictures of the prospect as a preliminary to any exercise of judgment.

"What's the financial angle?" he asked.

Franz threw up his chin, his eyebrows, the transient wrinkles of his forehead, his hands, his elbows, his shoulders; he strained up the muscles of his legs, so that the cloth of his trousers bulged, pushed up his heart into his throat and his voice into the roof of his mouth.

"There we have it! Money!" he bewailed. "I have little money. The price in American money is two hundred thousand dollars. The innovation—ary—" he tasted the coinage doubtfully, "—steps, that you will agree are necessary, will cost twenty thousand dollars American. But the clinic is a gold mine—I tell you, I haven't seen the books. For an investment of two hundred and twenty thousand dollars we have an assured income of——"

Baby's curiosity was such that Dick brought her into the conversation.

"In your experience, Baby," he demanded, "have you found that when a European wants to see an American *very* pressingly it is invariably something concerned with money?"

"What is it?" she said innocently.

"This young *Privatdocent* thinks that he and I ought to launch into big business and try to attract nervous breakdowns from America."

Worried, Franz stared at Baby as Dick continued:

"But who are we, Franz? You bear a big name and I've written two textbooks. Is that enough to attract anybody? And I haven't got that much money—I haven't got a tenth of it." Franz smiled cynically. "Honestly I haven't. Nicole and Baby are rich as Crœsus but I haven't managed to get my hands on any of it yet."

They were all listening now—Dick wondered if the girl at the table behind was listening too. The idea attracted him. He decided to let Baby speak for him, as one often lets women raise their voices over issues that are not in their hands. Baby became suddenly her grandfather, cool and experimental.

"I think it's a suggestion you ought to consider, Dick. I don't know what Doctor Gregory was saying—but it seems to me——"

Behind him the girl had leaned forward into a smoke ring and was picking up something from the floor. Nicole's face, fitted into his own across the table—her beauty, tentatively nesting and posing, flowed into his love, ever braced to protect it.

"Consider it, Dick," Franz urged excitedly. "When one writes on psychiatry, one should have actual clinical contacts. Jung writes, Bleuler writes, Freud writes, Forel writes, Adler writes—also they are in constant contact with mental disorder."

"Dick has me," laughed Nicole. "I should think that'd be enough mental disorder for one man."

"That's different," said Franz cautiously.

Baby was thinking that if Nicole lived beside a clinic she would always feel quite safe about her.

"We must think it over carefully," she said.

Though amused at her insolence, Dick did not encourage it.

"The decision concerns me, Baby," he said gently. "It's nice of you to want to buy me a clinic."

Realizing she had meddled, Baby withdrew hurriedly:

"Of course, it's entirely your affair."

"A thing as important as this will take weeks to decide. I wonder how I like the picture of Nicole and me anchored to Zurich—" He turned to Franz, anticipating: "—I know. Zurich has a gashouse and running water and electric light—I lived there three years."

"I will leave you to think it over," said Franz. "I am confident——"

One hundred pair of five-pound boots had begun to clump toward the door, and they joined the press. Outside in the crisp moonlight, Dick saw the girl tying her sled to one of the sleighs ahead. They piled into their own sleigh and at the crisp-cracking whips the horses strained, breasting the dark air. Past them figures ran and scrambled, the younger ones shoving each other from sleds and runners, landing in the soft snow, then panting after the horses to drop exhausted on a sled or wail that they were abandoned. On either side the fields were beneficently tranquil; the space through which the cavalcade moved was high and limitless. In the country there was less noise as though they were all listening atavistically for wolves in the wide snow.

In Saanen, they poured into the municipal dance, crowded with cow herders, hotel servants, shop-keepers, ski teachers, guides, tourists, peasants. To come into the warm enclosed place after the pantheistic animal feeling without, was to reassume some absurd and impressive knightly name, as thunderous as spurred boots in war, as football cleats on the cement of a locker-room floor. There was conventional yodeling, and the familiar rhythm of it separated Dick from what he had first found romantic in the scene. At first he thought it was because he had hounded the girl out of his consciousness; then it came to him under the form of what Baby had said: "We must think it over carefully—" and the unsaid lines back of that: "We own you, and you'll admit it sooner or later. It is absurd to keep up the pretense of independence."

It had been years since Dick had bottled up malice against a creature—since freshman year at New Haven when he had come upon a popular essay about "mental hygiene." Now he lost his temper at Baby and simultaneously tried to coop it up within him, resenting her cold rich insolence. It would be hundreds of years before any emergent Amazons would ever grasp the fact that a man is vulnerable only in his pride, but delicate as Humpty-Dumpty once that is meddled with—though some of them paid the fact a cautious lip-service. Doctor Diver's profession of sorting the broken shells of another sort of egg had given him a dread of breakage. But:

"There's too much good manners," he said on the way back to Gstaad in the smooth sleigh.

"Well, I think that's nice," said Baby.

"No, it isn't," he insisted to the anonymous bundle of fur. "Good manners are an admission that everybody is so tender that they have to be handled with gloves. Now, human respect—you don't call a man a coward or a liar lightly, but if you spend your life sparing people's feelings and feeding their vanity, you get so you can't distinguish what *should* be respected in them."

"I think Americans take their manners rather seriously," said the elder Englishman.

"I guess so," said Dick. "My father had the kind of manners he inherited from the days when you shot first and apologized afterward. Men armed—why, you Europeans haven't carried arms in civil life since the beginning of the eighteenth century——"

"Not actually, perhaps——"

"Not *act*ually. Not really."

"Dick, you've always had such beautiful manners," said Baby conciliatingly.

The women were regarding him across the zoo of robes with some alarm. The younger Englishman did not understand—he was one of the kind who were always jumping around cornices and balconies, as if they thought they were in the rigging of a ship—and filled the ride to the hotel with a preposterous story about a boxing match with his best friend in which they loved and bruised each other for an hour, always with great reserve. Dick became facetious.

"So every time he hit you you considered him an even better friend?"

"I respected him more."

"It's the premise I don't understand. You and your best friend scrap about a trivial matter——"

"If you don't understand, I can't explain it to you," said the young Englishman coldly.

—This is what I'll get if I begin saying what I think, Dick said to himself.

He was ashamed at baiting the man, realizing that the absurdity of the story rested in the immaturity of the attitude combined with the sophisticated method of its narration.

The carnival spirit was strong and they went with the crowd into the grill, where a Tunisian barman manipulated the illumination in a counterpoint, whose other melody was the moon off the ice rink staring in the big windows. In that light, Dick found the girl devitalized, and uninteresting—he turned from her to enjoy the darkness, the cigarette points going green and silver when the lights shone red, the band of white that fell across the dancers as the door to the bar was opened and closed.

"Now tell me, Franz," he demanded, "do you think

after sitting up all night drinking beer, you can go back and convince your patients that you have any character? Don't you think they'll see you're a gastropath?"

"I'm going to bed," Nicole announced. Dick accompanied her to the door of the elevator.

"I'd come with you but I must show Franz that I'm not intended for a clinician."

Nicole walked into the elevator.

"Baby has lots of common sense," she said meditatively.

"Baby is one of——"

The door slashed shut—facing a mechanical hum, Dick finished the sentence in his mind, "—Baby is a trivial, selfish woman."

But two days later, sleighing to the station with Franz, Dick admitted that he thought favorably upon the matter.

"We're beginning to turn in a circle," he admitted. "Living on this scale, there's an unavoidable series of strains, and Nicole doesn't survive them. The pastoral quality down on the summer Riviera is all changing anyhow—next year they'll have a Season."

They passed the crisp green rinks where Wiener waltzes blared and the colors of many mountain schools flashed against the pale-blue skies.

"—I hope we'll be able to do it, Franz. There's nobody I'd rather try it with than you——"

Good-by, Gstaad! Good-by, fresh faces, cold sweet flowers, flakes in the darkness. Good-by, Gstaad, good-by!

XIV

DICK awoke at five after a long dream of war, walked to the window and stared out it at the Zugersee. His dream had begun in somber majesty;

navy blue uniforms crossed a dark plaza behind bands playing the second movement of Prokofieff's "Love of Three Oranges." Presently there were fire engines, symbols of disaster, and a ghastly uprising of the mutilated in a dressing station. He turned on his bed-lamp light and made a thorough note of it ending with the half-ironic phrase: "Non-combatant's shell-shock."

As he sat on the side of his bed, he felt the room, the house and the night as empty. In the next room Nicole muttered something desolate and he felt sorry for whatever loneliness she was feeling in her sleep. For him time stood still and then every few years accelerated in a rush, like the quick re-wind of a film, but for Nicole the years slipped away by clock and calendar and birthday, with the added poignance of her perishable beauty.

Even this past year and a half on the Zugersee seemed wasted time for her, the seasons marked only by the workmen on the road turning pink in May, brown in July, black in September, white again in Spring. She had come out of her first illness alive with new hopes, expecting so much, yet deprived of any subsistence except Dick, bringing up children she could only pretend gently to love, guided orphans. The people she liked, rebels mostly, disturbed her and were bad for her—she sought in them the vitality that had made them independent or creative or rugged, sought in vain—for their secrets were buried deep in childhood struggles they had forgotten. They were more interested in Nicole's exterior harmony and charm, the other face of her illness. She led a lonely life owning Dick who did not want to be owned.

Many times he had tried unsuccessfully to let go his hold on her. They had many fine times together, fine talks between the loves of the white nights, but always when he turned away from her into himself he left her holding Nothing in her hands and staring at it, calling it many names, but knowing it was only the hope that he would come back soon.

He scrunched his pillow hard, lay down, and put the back of his neck against it as a Japanese does to slow the circulation, and slept again for a time. Later, while he shaved, Nicole awoke and marched around, giving abrupt, succinct orders to children and servants. Lanier came in to watch his father shave—living beside a psychiatric clinic he had developed an extraordinary confidence in and admiration for his father, together with an exaggerated indifference toward most other adults; the patients appeared to him either in their odd aspects, or else as devitalized, over-correct creatures without personality. He was a handsome, promising boy and Dick devoted much time to him, in the relationship of a sympathetic but exacting officer and a respectful enlisted man.

"Why," Lanier asked, "do you always leave a little lather on the top of your hair when you shave?"

Cautiously Dick parted soapy lips: "I have never been able to find out. I've often wondered. I think it's because I get the first finger soapy when I make the line of my side-burn, but how it gets up on top of my head I don't know."

"I'm going to watch it all tomorrow."

"That's your only question before breakfast."

"I don't really call it a question."

"That's one on you."

Half an hour later Dick started up to the administration building. He was thirty-eight—still declining a beard he yet had a more medical aura about him than he had worn upon the Riviera. For eighteen months now he had lived at the clinic—certainly one of the best-appointed in Europe. Like Dohmler's it was of the modern type—no longer a single dark and sinister building but a small, scattered, yet deceitfully integrated village—Dick and Nicole had added much in the domain of taste, so that the plant was a thing of beauty, visited by every psychologist passing through Zurich. With the addition of a caddy house it might very well have been a country club. The Eglantine and the Beeches, houses for those sunk into eternal darkness, were screened by little copses from the main building, camouflaged strong-points. Behind was a large truck farm, worked partly by the patients. The workshops for ergo-therapy were three, placed under a single roof, and there Doctor Diver began his morning's inspection. The carpentry shop, full of sunlight, exuded the sweetness of sawdust, of a lost age of wood; always half a dozen men were there, hammering, planing, buzzing—silent men, who lifted solemn eyes from their work as he passed through. Himself a good carpenter, he discussed with them the efficiency of some tools for a moment in a quiet, personal, interested voice. Adjoining was the book-bindery, adapted to the most mobile of patients who were not always, however, those who had the greatest chance for recovery. The last chamber was devoted to bead-work, weaving, and work in brass. The faces of the patients here wore the expression of one who has just sighed profoundly, dismissing something insoluble—but their sighs only marked the beginning of another ceaseless round of ratiocination, not in a line as with normal people but in the same circle. Round, round, and round. Around forever. But the bright colors of the stuffs they worked with gave strangers a momentary illusion that all was well, as in a kindergarten. These patients brightened as Doctor Diver came in. Most of them liked him better than they liked Doctor Gregorovious. Those who had once lived in the great world invariably liked him better. There were a few who thought he neglected them, or that he was not simple, or that he posed. Their responses were not dissimilar to those that Dick evoked in non-professional life, but here they were warped and distorted.

One Englishwoman spoke to him always about a subject which she considered her own.

"Have we got music tonight?"

"I don't know," he answered. "I haven't seen Doctor Lladislau. How did you enjoy the music that Mrs. Sachs and Mr. Longstreet gave us last night?"

"It was so-so."

"I thought it was fine—especially the Chopin."

"I thought it was so-so."

"When are you going to play for us yourself?"

She shrugged her shoulders, as pleased at this question as she had been for several years.

"Some time. But I only play so-so."

They knew that she did not play at all—she had had two sisters who were brilliant musicians, but she had never been able to learn the notes when they had been young together.

From the workshop Dick went to visit the Eglantine and the Beeches. Exteriorly these houses were as cheerful as the others; Nicole had designed the decoration and the furniture on a necessary base of concealed grills and bars and immovable furniture. She had worked with so much imagination—the inventive quality, which she lacked, being supplied by the problem itself—that no instructed visitor would have dreamed that the light, graceful filigree work at a window was a strong, unyielding end of a tether, that the pieces reflecting modern tubular tendencies were stancher than the massive creations of the Edwardians—even the flowers lay in iron fingers and every casual ornament and fixture was as necessary as a girder in a skyscraper. Her tireless eyes had made each room yield up its greatest usefulness. Complimented, she referred to herself brusquely as a master plumber.

For those whose compasses were not depolarized there seemed many odd things in these houses. Doctor Diver was often amused in the Eglantine, the men's building—here there was a strange little exhibitionist who thought that if he could walk unclothed and unmolested from the Étoile to the Place de la Concorde he would solve many things—and, perhaps, Dick thought, he was quite right.

His most interesting case was in the main building. The patient was a woman of thirty who had been in the clinic six months; she was an American painter who had lived long in Paris. They had no very satisfactory history of her. A cousin had happened upon her all mad and gone and after an unsatisfactory interlude at one of the whoopee cures that fringed the city, dedicated largely to tourist victims of drug and drink, he had managed to get her to Switzerland. On her admittance she had been exceptionally pretty—now she was a living agonizing sore. All blood tests had failed to give a positive reaction and the trouble was unsatisfactorily catalogued as nervous eczema. For two months she had lain under it, as imprisoned in the Iron Maiden. She was coherent, even brilliant, within the limits of her special hallucinations.

She was particularly his patient. During spells of overexcitement he was the only doctor who could "do anything with her." Several weeks ago, on one of many nights that she had passed in sleepless torture Franz had succeeded in hypnotizing her into a few hours of needed rest, but he had never again succeeded. Hypnosis was a tool that Dick distrusted and seldom used, for he knew that he could not always summon up the mood in himself—he had once tried it on Nicole and she had scornfully laughed at him.

The woman in room twenty could not see him when he came in—the area about her eyes was too tightly swollen. She spoke in a strong, rich, deep, thrilling voice.

"How long will this last? Is it going to be forever?"

"It's not going to be very long now. Doctor Lladislau tells me there are whole areas cleared up."

"If I knew what I had done to deserve this I could accept it with equanimity."

"It isn't wise to be mystical about it—we recognize it as a nervous phenomenon. It's related to the blush—when you were a girl, did you blush easily?"

She lay with her face turned to the ceiling.

"I have found nothing to blush for since I cut my wisdom teeth."

"Haven't you committed your share of petty sins and mistakes?"

"I have nothing to reproach myself with."

"You're very fortunate."

The woman thought a moment; her voice came up through her bandaged face afflicted with subterranean melodies:

"I'm sharing the fate of the women of my time who challenged men to battle."

"To your vast surprise it was just like all battles," he answered, adopting her formal diction.

"Just like all battles." She thought this over. "You pick a set-up, or else win a Pyrrhic victory, or you're wrecked and ruined—you're a ghostly echo from a broken wall."

"You are neither wrecked nor ruined," he told her. "Are you quite sure you've been in a real battle?"

"Look at me!" she cried furiously.

"You've suffered, but many women suffered before they mistook themselves for men." It was becoming an argument and he retreated. "In any case you mustn't confuse a single failure with a final defeat."

She sneered. "Beautiful words," and the phrase transpiring up through the crust of pain humbled him.

"We would like to go into the true reasons that brought you here—" he began but she interrupted.

"I am here as a symbol of something. I thought perhaps you would know what it was."

"You are sick," he said mechanically.

"Then what was it I had almost found?"

"A greater sickness."

"That's all?"

"That's all." With disgust he heard himself lying, but here and now the vastness of the subject could only be compressed into a lie. "Outside of that there's only confusion and chaos. I won't lecture to you—we have too acute a realization of your physical suffering. But it's only by meeting the problems of every day, no matter how trifling and boring they seem, that you can make things drop back into place again. After that—perhaps you'll be able again to examine——"

He had slowed up to avoid the inevitable end of his thought: "—the frontiers of consciousness." The frontiers that artists must explore were not for her, ever. She was fine-spun, inbred—eventually she might find rest in some quiet mysticism. Exploration was for those with a measure of peasant blood, those with big thighs and thick ankles who could take punishment as they took bread and salt, on every inch of flesh and spirit.

—Not for you, he almost said. It's too tough a game for you.

Yet in the awful majesty of her pain he went out to

her unreservedly, almost sexually. He wanted to gather her up in his arms, as he so often had Nicole, and cherish even her mistakes, so deeply were they part of her. The orange light through the drawn blind, the sarcophagus of her figure on the bed, the spot of face, the voice searching the vacuity of her illness and finding only remote abstractions.

As he arose the tears fled lava-like into her bandages.

"That is for something," she whispered. "Something must come out of it."

He stooped and kissed her forehead.

"We must all try to be good," he said.

Leaving her room he sent the nurse in to her. There were other patients to see: an American girl of fifteen who had been brought up on the basis that childhood was intended to be all fun—his visit was provoked by the fact that she had just hacked off all her hair with a nail scissors. There was nothing much to be done for her—a family history of neurosis and nothing stable in her past to build on. The father, normal and conscientious himself, had tried to protect a nervous brood from life's troubles and had succeeded merely in preventing them from developing powers of adjustment to life's inevitable surprises. There was little that Dick could say: "Helen, when you're in doubt you must ask a nurse, you must learn to take advice. Promise me you will."

What was a promise with the head sick? He looked in upon a frail exile from the Caucasus buckled securely in a sort of hammock which in turn was submerged in a warm medical bath, and upon the three daughters of a Portuguese general who slid almost imperceptibly toward paresis. He went into the room next to them and told a collapsed psychiatrist that he was better, always better, and the man tried to read his face for conviction, since he hung on the real world only through such reassurance as he could find in the resonance, or lack of it, in Doctor Diver's voice. After that Dick discharged a shiftless orderly and by then it was the lunch hour.

XV

MEALS with the patients were a chore he approached with apathy. The gathering, which of course did not include residents at the Eglantine or the Beeches, was conventional enough at first sight, but over it brooded always a heavy melancholy. Such doctors as were present kept up a conversation but most of the patients, as if exhausted by their morning's endeavor, or depressed by the company, spoke little, and ate looking into their plates.

Luncheon over, Dick returned to his villa. Nicole was in the salon wearing a strange expression.

"Read that," she said.

He opened the letter. It was from a woman recently discharged, though with skepticism on the part of the faculty. It accused him in no uncertain terms of having seduced her daughter, who had been at her mother's side during the crucial stage of the illness. It presumed that Mrs. Diver would be glad to have this information and learn what her husband was "really like."

Dick read the letter again. Couched in clear and concise English he yet recognized it as the letter of a maniac. Upon a single occasion he had let the girl, a flirtatious little brunette, ride into Zurich with him, upon her request, and in the evening had brought her back to the clinic. In an idle, almost indulgent way, he kissed her. Later, she tried to carry the affair further, but he was not interested and subsequently, probably consequently, the girl had come to dislike him, and taken her mother away.

"This letter is deranged," he said. "I had no relations of any kind with that girl. I didn't even like her."

"Yes, I've tried thinking that," said Nicole.

"Surely you don't believe it?"

"I've been sitting here."

He sank his voice to a reproachful note and sat beside her.

"This is absurd. This is a letter from a mental patient."

"I was a mental patient."

He stood up and spoke more authoritatively.

"Suppose we don't have any nonsense, Nicole. Go and round up the children and we'll start."

In the car, with Dick driving, they followed the little promontories of the lake, catching the burn of light and water in the windshield, tunneling through cascades of evergreen. It was Dick's car, a Renault so dwarfish that they all stuck out of it except the children, between whom Mademoiselle towered mast-like in the rear seat. They knew every kilometer of the road—where they would smell the pine needles and the black stove smoke. A high sun with a face traced on it beat fierce on the straw hats of the children.

Nicole was silent; Dick was uneasy at her straight hard gaze. Often he felt lonely with her, and frequently she tired him with the short floods of personal revelations that she reserved exclusively for him, "I'm like this—I'm more like that," but this afternoon he would have been glad had she rattled on in staccato for a while and given him glimpses of her thoughts. The situation was always most threatening when she backed up into herself and closed the doors behind her.

At Zug Mademoiselle got out and left them. The Divers approached the Agiri Fair through a menagerie of mammoth steam-rollers that made way for them. Dick parked the car, and as Nicole looked at him without moving, he said: "Come on, darl." Her lips drew apart into a sudden awful smile, and his belly quailed, but as if he hadn't seen it he repeated: "Come on. So the children can get out."

"Oh, I'll come all right," she answered, tearing the words from some story spinning itself out inside her, too fast for him to grasp. "Don't worry about that. I'll come——"

"Then come."

She turned from him as he walked beside her but the smile still flickered across her face, derisive and remote. Only when Lanier spoke to her several times did she manage to fix her attention upon an object, a Punch-and-Judy show, and to orient herself by anchoring to it.

Dick tried to think what to do. The dualism in his views of her—that of the husband, that of the psychiatrist—was increasingly paralyzing his faculties. In these six years she had several times carried him over the line with her, disarming him by exciting emotional pity or by a flow of wit, fantastic and disassociated, so that only after the episode did he realize with the consciousness of his own relaxation from tension, that she had succeeded in getting a point against his better judgment.

A discussion with Topsy about the guignol—as to whether the Punch was the same Punch they had seen last year in Cannes—having been settled, the family walked along again between the booths under the open sky. The women's bonnets, perching over velvet vests, the bright, spreading skirts of many cantons, seemed demure against the blue and orange paint of the wagons and displays. There was the sound of a whining, tinkling hootchy-kootchy show.

Nicole began to run very suddenly, so suddenly that for a moment Dick did not miss her. Far ahead he saw her yellow dress twisting through the crowd, an ochre stitch along the edge of reality and unreality, and started after her. Secretly she ran and secretly he followed. As the hot afternoon went shrill and terrible with her flight he had forgotten the children; then he wheeled and ran back to them, drawing them this way and that by their arms, his eyes jumping from booth to booth.

"*Madame*," he cried to a young woman behind a white lottery wheel, "*Est-ce que je peux laisser ces petits avec vous deux minutes? C'est très urgent—je vous donnerai dix francs.*"

"*Mais oui.*"

He headed the children into the booth. "*Alors—restez avec cette gentille dame.*"

"*Oui, Dick.*"

He darted off again but he had lost her; he circled the merry-go-round keeping up with it till he realized he was running beside it, staring always at the same horse. He elbowed through the crowd in the *buvette;* then remembering a predilection of Nicole's he snatched up an edge of a fortune-teller's tent and peered within. A droning voice greeted him: "*La septième fille d'une septième fille née sur les rives du Nil—entrez, Monsieur——*"

Dropping the flap he ran along toward where the *plaisance* terminated at the lake and a small ferris wheel revolved slowly against the sky. There he found her.

She was alone in what was momentarily the top boat of the wheel, and as it descended he saw that she was laughing hilariously; he slunk back in the crowd, a crowd which, at the wheel's next revolution, spotted the intensity of Nicole's hysteria.

"*Regardez-moi ça!*"

"*Regarde donc cette Anglaise!*"

Down she dropped again—this time the wheel and its music were slowing and a dozen people were around her car, all of them impelled by the quality of her laughter to smile in sympathetic idiocy. But when Nicole saw Dick her laughter died—she made a gesture of slipping by and away from him but he caught her arm and held it as they walked away.

"Why did you lose control of yourself like that?"

"You know very well why."

"No, I don't."

"That's just preposterous—let me loose—that's an insult to my intelligence. Don't you think I saw that girl look at you—that little dark girl. Oh, this is farcical—a child, not more than fifteen. Don't you think I saw?"

"Stop here a minute and quiet down."

They sat at a table, her eyes in a profundity of suspicion, her hand moving across her line of sight as if it were obstructed. "I want a drink—I want a brandy."

"You can't have brandy—you can have a bock if you want it."

"Why can't I have a brandy?"

"We won't go into that. Listen to me—this business about a girl is a delusion, do you understand that word?"

"It's always a delusion when I see what you don't want me to see."

He had a sense of guilt as in one of those nightmares where we are accused of a crime which we recognize as something undeniably experienced, but which upon waking we realize we have not committed. His eyes wavered from hers.

"I left the children with a gypsy woman in a booth. We ought to get them."

"Who do you think you are?" she demanded. "Svengali?"

Fifteen minutes ago they had been a family. Now as she was crushed into a corner by his unwilling shoulder, he saw them all, child and man, as a perilous accident.

"We're going home."

"Home!" she roared in a voice so abandoned that its louder tones wavered and cracked. "And sit and think that we're all rotting and the children's ashes are rotting in every box I open? That filth!"

Almost with relief he saw that her words sterilized her, and Nicole, sensitized down to the corium of the skin, saw the withdrawal in his face. Her own face softened and she begged, "Help me, help me, Dick!"

A wave of agony went over him. It was awful that such a fine tower should not be erected, only suspended, suspended from him. Up to a point that was right: men were for that, beam and idea, girder and logarithm; but somehow Dick and Nicole had become one and equal, not apposite and complementary; she was Dick too, the drought in the marrow of his bones. He could not watch her disintegrations without participating in them. His intuition rilled out of him as tenderness and compassion—he could only take the characteristically modern course, to interpose—he would get a nurse from Zurich, to take her over tonight.

"You *can* help me."

Her sweet bullying pulled him forward off his feet. "You've helped me before—you can help me now."

"I can only help you the same old way."

"Some one can help me."

"Maybe so. You can help yourself most. Let's find the children."

There were numerous lottery booths with white wheels—Dick was startled when he inquired at the first and encountered blank disavowals. Evil-eyed, Nicole stood apart, denying the children, resenting them as part of a downright world she sought to make amorphous. Presently Dick found them, surrounded by women who were examining them with delight like fine goods, and by peasant children staring.

"Merci, Monsieur, ah Monsieur est trop généreux. C'était un plaisir, M'sieur, Madame. Au revoir, mes petits."

They started back with a hot sorrow streaming down upon them; the car was weighted with their mutual apprehension and anguish, and the children's mouths were grave with disappointment. Grief presented itself in its terrible, dark unfamiliar color. Somewhere around Zug, Nicole, with a convulsive effort, reiterated a remark she had made before about a misty yellow house set back from the road that looked like a painting not yet dry, but it was just an attempt to catch at a rope that was playing out too swiftly.

Dick tried to rest—the struggle would come presently at home and he might have to sit a long time, restating the universe for her. A "schizophrene" is well named as a split personality—Nicole was alternately a person to whom nothing need be explained and one to whom nothing *could* be explained. It was necessary to treat her with active and affirmative insistence, keeping the road to reality always open, making the road to escape harder going. But the brilliance, the versatility of madness is akin to the resourcefulness of water seeping through, over and around a dike. It requires the united front of many people to work against it. He felt it necessary that this time Nicole cure herself; he wanted to wait until she remembered the other times, and revolted from them. In a tired way, he planned that they would again resume the régime relaxed a year before.

He had turned up a hill that made a short cut to the clinic, and now as he stepped on the accelerator for a short straightaway run parallel to the hillside the car swerved violently left, swerved right, tipped on two wheels and, as Dick, with Nicole's voice screaming in his ear, crushed down the mad hand clutching the steering wheel, righted itself, swerved once more and shot off the road; it tore through low underbrush, tipped again and settled slowly at an angle of ninety degrees against a tree.

The children were screaming and Nicole was screaming and cursing and trying to tear at Dick's face. Thinking first of the list of the car and unable to estimate it Dick bent away Nicole's arm, climbed over the top side and lifted out the children; then he saw the car was in a stable position. Before doing anything else he stood there shaking and panting.

"You—!" he cried.

She was laughing hilariously, unashamed, unafraid, unconcerned. No one coming on the scene would have imagined that she had caused it; she laughed as after some mild escape of childhood.

"You were scared, weren't you?" she accused him. "You wanted to live!"

She spoke with such force that in his shocked state Dick wondered if he had been frightened for himself—but the strained faces of the children, looking from parent to parent, made him want to grind her grinning mask into jelly.

Directly above them, half a kilometer by the winding road but only a hundred yards climbing, was an inn; one of its wings showed through the wooded hill.

"Take Topsy's hand," he said to Lanier, "like that,

tight, and climb up that hill—see the little path? When you get to the inn tell them *'La voiture Divare est cassée.'* Some one must come right down."

Lanier, not sure what had happened, but suspecting the dark and unprecedented, asked:

"What will you do, Dick?"

"We'll stay here with the car."

Neither of them looked at their mother as they started off. "Be careful crossing the road up there! Look both ways!" Dick shouted after them.

He and Nicole looked at each other directly, their eyes like blazing windows across a court of the same house. Then she took out a compact, looked in its mirror, and smoothed back the temple hair. Dick watched the children climbing for a moment until they disappeared among the pines half way up; then he walked around the car to see the damage and plan how to get it back on the road. In the dirt he could trace the rocking course they had pursued for over a hundred feet; he was filled with a violent disgust that was not like anger.

In a few minutes the proprietor of the inn came running down.

"My God!" he exclaimed. "How did it happen, were you going fast? What luck! Except for that tree you'd have rolled down hill!"

Taking advantage of Emile's reality, the wide black apron, the sweat upon the rolls of his face, Dick signaled to Nicole in a matter-of-fact way to let him help her from the car; whereupon she jumped over the lower side, lost her balance on the slope, feel to her knees and got up again. As she watched the men trying to move the car her expression became defiant. Welcoming even that mood Dick said:

"Go and wait with the children, Nicole."

Only after she had gone did he remember that she had wanted cognac, and that there was cognac available up there—he told Emile never mind about the car; they would wait for the chauffeur and the big car to pull it up onto the road. Together they hurried up to the inn.

XVI

"I WANT to go away," he told Franz. "For a month or so, for as long as I can."

"Why not, Dick? That was our original arrangement—it was you who insisted on staying. If you and Nicole——"

"I don't want to go away with Nicole. I want to go away alone. This last thing knocked me sideways—if I get two hours' sleep in twenty-four, it's one of Zwingli's miracles."

"You wish a real leave of abstinence."

"The word is 'absence.' Look here: if I go to Berlin to the Psychiatric Congress could you manage to keep the peace? For three months she's been all right and she likes her nurse. My God, you're the only human being in this world I can ask this of."

Franz grunted, considering whether or not he could be trusted to think always of his partner's interest.

In Zurich the next week Dick drove to the airport and took the big plane for Munich. Soaring and roaring into the blue he felt numb, realizing how tired he was. A vast persuasive quiet stole over him, and he abandoned sickness to the sick, sound to the motors, direction to the pilot. He had no intention of attending so much as a single session of the congress—he could imagine it well enough, new pamphlets by Bleuler and the elder Forel that he could much better digest at home, the paper by the American who cured dementia præcox by pulling out his patient's teeth or cauterizing their tonsils, the half-derisive respect with which this idea would be greeted, for no more reason than that America was such a rich and powerful country. The other delegates from America—red-headed Schwartz with his saint's face and his infinite patience in straddling two worlds, as well as dozens of commercial alienists with hang-dog faces, who would be present partly to increase their standing, and hence their reach for the big plums of the criminal practice, partly to master novel sophistries that they could weave into their stock in trade, to the infinite confusion of all values. There would be cynical Latins, and some man of Freud's from Vienna. Articulate among them would be the great Jung, bland, super-vigorous, on his rounds between the forests of anthropology and the neuroses of school-boys. At first there would be an American cast to the congress, almost Rotarian in its forms and ceremonies, then the closer-knit European vitality would fight through, and finally the Americans would play their trump card, the announcement of colossal gifts and endowments, of great new plants and training schools, and in the presence of the figures the Europeans would blanch and walk timidly. But he would not be there to see.

They skirted the Vorarlberg Alps, and Dick felt a pastoral delight in watching the villages. There were always four or five in sight, each one gathered around a church. It was simple looking at the earth from far off, simple as playing grim games with dolls and soldiers. This was the way statesmen and commanders and all retired people looked at things. Anyhow, it was a good draft of relief.

An Englishman spoke to him from across the aisle

but he found something antipathetic in the English lately. England was like a rich man after a disastrous orgy who makes up to the household by chatting with them individually, when it is obvious to them that he is only trying to get back his self-respect in order to usurp his former power.

Dick had with him what magazines were available on the station quays: *The Century, The Motion Picture, L'Illustration,* and the *Fliegende Blätter,* but it was more fun to descend in his imagination into the villages and shake hands with the rural characters. He sat in the churches as he sat in his father's church in Buffalo, amid the starchy must of Sunday clothes. He listened to the wisdom of the Near East, was Crucified, Died, and was Buried in the cheerful church, and once more worried between five or ten cents for the collection plate, because of the girl who sat in the pew behind.

The Englishman suddenly borrowed his magazines with a little small change of conversation, and Dick, glad to see them go, thought of the voyage ahead of him. Wolf-like under his sheep's clothing of long-staple Australian wool, he considered the world of pleasure—the incorruptible Mediterranean with sweet old dirt caked in the olive trees, the peasant girl near Savona with a face as green and rose as the color of an illuminated missal. He would take her in his hands and snatch her across the border. . . .

. . . But there he deserted her—he must press on toward the Isles of Greece, the cloudy waters of unfamiliar ports, the lost girl on shore, the moon of popular songs. A part of Dick's mind was made up of the tawdry souvenirs of his boyhood. Yet in that somewhat littered Five-and-Ten, he had managed to keep alive the low painful fire of intelligence.

XVII

TOMMY BARBAN was a ruler, Tommy was a hero—Dick happened upon him in the Marienplatz in Munich, in one of those cafés where small gamblers diced on "tapestry" mats. The air was full of politics, and the slap of cards.

Tommy was at a table laughing his martial laugh: "Um-buh—ha-ha! Um-buh—ha-ha!" As a rule, he drank little; courage was his game and his companions were always a little afraid of him. Recently an eighth of the area of his skull had been removed by a Warsaw surgeon and was knitting under his hair, and the weakest person in the café could have killed him with a flip of a knotted napkin.

"—This is Prince Chillicheff—" A battered, powder-gray Russian of fifty "—and Mr. McKibben—and Mr. Hannan—" the latter was a lively ball of black eyes and hair, a clown; and he said immediately to Dick:

"The first thing before we shake hands—what do you mean by fooling around with my aunt?"

"Why, I——"

"You heard me. What are you doing here in Munich anyhow?"

"Um-bah—ha-ha!" laughed Tommy.

"Haven't you got aunts of your own? Why don't you fool with them?"

Dick laughed, whereupon the man shifted his attack:

"Now let's not have any more talk about aunts. How do I know you didn't make up the whole thing? Here you are a complete stranger with an acquaintance of less than half an hour, and you come up to me with a cock-and-bull story about your aunts. How do I know what you have concealed about you?"

Tommy laughed again, then he said good-naturedly, but firmly, "That's enough, Carly. Sit down, Dick—how're you? How's Nicole?"

He did not like any man very much nor feel their presence with much intensity—he was all relaxed for combat; as a fine athlete playing secondary defense in any sport is really resting much of the time, while a lesser man only pretends to rest and is at a continual and self-destroying nervous tension.

Hannan, not entirely suppressed, moved to an adjoining piano, and with recurring resentment on his face whenever he looked at Dick, played chords, from time to time muttering, "Your aunts," and, in a dying cadence, "I didn't say aunts anyhow. I said pants."

"Well, how're you?" repeated Tommy. "You don't look so—" he fought for a word "—so jaunty as you used to, so spruce, you know what I mean."

The remark sounded too much like one of those irritating accusations of waning vitality and Dick was about to retort by commenting on the extraordinary suits worn by Tommy and Prince Chillicheff, suits of a cut and pattern fantastic enough to have sauntered down Beale Street on a Sunday—when an explanation was forthcoming.

"I see you are regarding our clothes," said the Prince. "We have just come out of Russia."

"These were made in Poland by the court tailor," said Tommy. "That's a fact—Pilsudski's own tailor."

"You've been touring?" Dick asked.

They laughed, the Prince inordinately meanwhile clapping Tommy on the back.

"Yes, we have been touring. That's it, touring. We have made the Grand Tour of all the Russias. In state."

Dick waited for an explanation. It came from Mr. McKibben in two words.

"They escaped."

"Have you been prisoners in Russia?"

"It was I," explained Prince Chillicheff, his dead yellow eyes staring at Dick. "Not a prisoner but in hiding."

"Did you have much trouble getting out?"

"Some trouble. We left three Red Guards dead at the border. Tommy left two—" He held up two fingers like a Frenchman—"I left one."

"That's the part I don't understand," said Mr. McKibben. "Why they should have objected to your leaving."

Hannan turned from the piano and said, winking at the others: "Mac thinks a Marxian is somebody who went to St. Mark's school."

It was an escape story in the best tradition—an aristocrat hiding nine years with a former servant and working in a government bakery; the eighteen-year-old daughter in Paris who knew Tommy Barban. . . . During the narrative Dick decided that this parched papier mâché relic of the past was scarcely worth the lives of three young men. The question arose as to whether Tommy and Chillicheff had been frightened.

"When I was cold," Tommy said. "I always get scared when I'm cold. During the war I was always frightened when I was cold."

McKibben stood up.

"I must leave. Tomorrow morning I'm going to Innsbruck by car with my wife and children—and the governess."

"I'm going there tomorrow, too," said Dick.

"Oh, are you?" exclaimed McKibben. "Why not come with us? It's a big Packard and there's only my wife and my children and myself—and the governess——"

"I can't possibly——"

"Of course she's not really a governess," McKibben concluded, looking rather pathetically at Dick. "As a matter of fact my wife knows your sister-in-law, Baby Warren."

But Dick was not to be drawn in a blind contract.

"I've promised to travel with two men."

"Oh," McKibben's face fell. "Well, I'll say good-by." He unscrewed two blooded wire-hairs from a near-by table and departed; Dick pictured the jammed Packard pounding toward Innsbruck with the McKibbens and their children and their baggage and yapping dogs—and the governess.

"The paper says they know the man who killed him," said Tommy. "But his cousins did not want it in the papers, because it happened in a speakeasy. What do you think of that?"

"It's what's known as family pride."

Hannan played a loud chord on the piano to attract attention to himself.

"I don't believe his first stuff holds up," he said. "Even barring the Europeans there are a dozen Americans can do what North did."

It was the first indication Dick had had that they were talking about Abe North.

"The only difference is that Abe did it first," said Tommy.

"I don't agree," persisted Hannan. "He got the reputation for being a good musician because he drank so much that his friends had to explain him away somehow——"

"What's this about Abe North? What about him? Is he in a jam?"

"Didn't you read the *Herald* this morning?"

"No."

"He's dead. He was beaten to death in a speakeasy

in New York. He just managed to crawl home to the Racquet Club to die——"

"*Abe North?*"

"Yes, sure, they——"

"*Abe North?*" Dick stood up. "Are you sure he's dead?"

Hannan turned around to McKibben: "It wasn't the Racquet Club he crawled to—it was the Harvard Club. I'm sure he didn't belong to the Racquet."

"The paper said so," McKibben insisted.

"It must have been a mistake. I'm quite sure."

"*Beaten to death in a speakeasy.*"

"But I happen to know most of the members of the Racquet Club," said Hannan. "It *must* have been the Harvard Club."

Dick got up, Tommy too. Prince Chillicheff started out of a wan study of nothing, perhaps of his chances of ever getting out of Russia, a study that had occupied him so long that it was doubtful if he could give it up immediately, and joined them in leaving.

"*Abe North beaten to death.*"

On the way to the hotel, a journey of which Dick was scarcely aware, Tommy said:

"We're waiting for a tailor to finish some suits so we can get to Paris. I'm going into stock-broking and they wouldn't take me if I showed up like this. Everybody in your country is making millions. Are you really leaving tomorrow? We can't even have dinner with you. It seems the Prince had an old girl in Munich. He called her up but she'd been dead five years and we're having dinner with the two daughters."

The Prince nodded.

"Perhaps I could have arranged for Doctor Diver."

"No, no," said Dick hastily.

He slept deep and awoke to a slow mournful march

passing his window. It was a long column of men in uniform, wearing the familiar helmet of 1914, thick men in frock coats and silk hats, burghers, aristocrats, plain men. It was a society of veterans going to lay wreaths on the tombs of the dead. The column marched slowly with a sort of swagger for a lost magnificence, a past effort, a forgotten sorrow. The faces were only formally sad but Dick's lungs burst for a moment with regret for Abe's death, and his own youth of ten years ago.

XVIII

HE REACHED Innsbruck at dusk, sent his bags up to a hotel and walked into town. In the sunset the Emperor Maximilian knelt in prayer above his bronze mourners; a quartet of Jesuit novices paced and read in the university garden. The marble souvenirs of old sieges, marriages, anniversaries, faded quickly when the sun was down, and he had *Erbsen-suppe* with *Würstchen* cut up in it, drank four *Helles* of Pilsener and refused a formidable dessert known as "*Kaiser-schmarren.*"

Despite the overhanging mountains Switzerland was far away, Nicole was far away. Walking in the garden later when it was quite dark he thought about her with detachment, loving her for her best self. He remembered once when the grass was damp and she came to him on hurried feet, her thin slippers drenched with dew. She stood upon his shoes nestling close and held up her face, showing it as a book open at a page.

"Think how you love me," she whispered. "I don't ask you to love me always like this, but I ask you to remember. Somewhere inside me there'll always be the person I am tonight."

But Dick had come away for his soul's sake, and he began thinking about that. He had lost himself—he could not tell the hour when, or the day or the week, the month or the year. Once he had cut through things, solving the most complicated equations as the simplest problems of his simplest patients. Between the time he found Nicole flowering under a stone on the Zurichsee and the moment of his meeting with Rosemary the spear had been blunted.

Watching his father's struggles in poor parishes had wedded a desire for money to an essentially unacquisitive nature. It was not a healthy necessity for security —he had never felt more sure of himself, more thoroughly his own man, than at the time of his marriage to Nicole. Yet he had been swallowed up like a gigolo, and somehow permitted his arsenal to be locked up in the Warren safety-deposit vaults.

"There should have been a settlement in the Continental style; but it isn't over yet. I've wasted eight years teaching the rich the ABC's of human decency, but I'm not done. I've got too many unplayed trumps in my hand."

He loitered among the fallow rose bushes and the beds of damp sweet indistinguishable fern. It was warm for October but cool enough to wear a heavy tweed coat buttoned by a little elastic tape at the neck. A figure detached itself from the black shape of a tree and he knew it was the woman whom he had passed in the lobby coming out. He was in love with every pretty woman he saw now, their forms at a distance, their shadows on a wall.

Her back was toward him as she faced the lights of the town. He scratched a match that she must have heard, but she remained motionless.

—Was it an invitation? Or an indication of obliviousness? He had long been outside of the world of simple desires and their fulfillments, and he was inept and uncertain. For all he knew there might be some code among the wanderers of obscure spas by which they found each other quickly.

—Perhaps the next gesture was his. Strange children should smile at each other and say, "Let's play."

He moved closer, the shadow moved sideways. Possibly he would be snubbed like the scapegrace drummers he had heard of in youth. His heart beat loud in contact with the unprobed, undissected, unanalyzed, unaccounted for. Suddenly he turned away, and, as he did, the girl, too, broke the black frieze she made with the foliage, rounded a bench at a moderate but determined pace and took the path back to the hotel.

With a guide and two other men, Dick started up the Birkkarspitze next morning. It was a fine feeling once they were above the cowbells of the highest pastures—Dick looked forward to the night in the shack, enjoying his own fatigue, enjoying the captaincy of the guide, feeling a delight in his own anonymity. But at mid-day the weather changed to black sleet and hail and mountain thunder. Dick and one of the other climbers wanted to go on but the guide refused. Regretfully they struggled back to Innsbruck to start again tomorrow.

After dinner and a bottle of heavy local wine in the deserted dining-room, he felt excited, without knowing why, until he began thinking of the garden. He had passed the girl in the lobby before supper and this time she had looked at him and approved of him, but it kept worrying him: Why? When I could have had a good share of the pretty women of my time for the asking, why start that now? With a wraith, with a fragment of my desire? Why?

His imagination pushed ahead—the old asceticism, the actual unfamiliarity, triumphed: God, I might as well go back to the Riviera and sleep with Janice Caricamento or the Wilburhazy girl. To belittle all these years with something cheap and easy?

He was still excited, though, and he turned from the veranda and went up to his room to think. Being alone in body and spirit begets loneliness, and loneliness begets more loneliness.

Upstairs he walked around thinking of the matter and laying out his climbing clothes advantageously on the faint heater; he again encountered Nicole's telegram, still unopened, with which diurnally she accompanied his itinerary. He had delayed opening it before supper—perhaps because of the garden. It was a cablegram from Buffalo, forwarded through Zurich.

"Your father died peacefully tonight. HOLMES."

He felt a sharp wince at the shock, a gathering of the forces of resistance; then it rolled up through his loins and stomach and throat.

He read the message again. He sat down on the bed, breathing and staring; thinking first the old selfish child's thought that comes with the death of a parent, how will it affect me now that this earliest and strongest of protections is gone?

The atavism passed and he walked the room still, stopping from time to time to look at the telegram. Holmes was formally his father's curate but actually, and for a decade, rector of the church. How did he die? Of old age—he was seventy-five. He had lived a long time.

Dick felt sad that he had died alone—he had survived his wife, and his brothers and sisters; there were cousins in Virginia but they were poor and not able to come North, and Holmes had had to sign the telegram.

Dick loved his father—again and again he referred judgments to what his father would probably have thought or done. Dick was born several months after the death of two young sisters and his father, guessing what would be the effect on Dick's mother, had saved him from a spoiling by becoming his moral guide. He was of tired stock yet he raised himself to that effort.

In the summer father and son walked downtown together to have their shoes shined—Dick in his starched duck sailor suit, his father always in beautifully cut clerical clothes—and the father was very proud of his handsome little boy. He told Dick all he knew about life, not much but most of it true, simple things, matters of behavior that came within his clergyman's range. "Once in a strange town when I was first ordained, I went into a crowded room and was confused as to who was my hostess. Several people I knew came toward me, but I disregarded them because I had seen a gray-haired woman sitting by a window far across the room. I went over to her and introduced myself. After that I made many friends in that town."

His father had done that from a good heart—his father had been sure of what he was, with a deep pride of the two proud widows who had raised him to believe that nothing could be superior to "good instincts," honor, courtesy, and courage.

The father always considered that his wife's small fortune belonged to his son, and in college and in medical school sent him a check for all of it four times a year. He was one of those about whom it was said with smug finality in the gilded age: "Very much the gentleman, but not much get-up-and-go about him."

. . . Dick sent down for a newspaper. Still pacing to and from the telegram open on his bureau, he chose a ship to go to America. Then he put in a call for Nicole in Zurich, remembering so many things as he waited, and wishing he had always been as good as he had intended to be.

XIX

FOR an hour, tied up with his profound reaction to his father's death, the magnificent façade of the homeland, the harbor of New York, seemed all sad and glorious to Dick, but once ashore the feeling vanished, nor did he find it again in the streets or the hotels or the trains that bore him first to Buffalo, and then south to Virginia with his father's body. Only as the local train shambled into the low-forested clayland of Westmoreland County, did he feel once more identified with his surroundings; at the station he saw a star he knew, and a cold moon bright over Chesapeake Bay; he heard the rasping wheels of buckboards turning, the lovely fatuous voices, the sound of sluggish primeval rivers flowing softly under soft Indian names.

Next day at the churchyard his father was laid among a hundred Divers, Dorseys, and Hunters. It was very friendly leaving him there with all his relations around him. Flowers were scattered on the brown unsettled earth. Dick had no more ties here now and did not believe he would come back. He knelt on the hard soil. These dead, he knew them all, their weather-beaten faces with blue flashing eyes, the spare violent bodies, the souls made of new earth in the forest-heavy darkness of the seventeenth century.

"Good-by, my father—good-by, all my fathers."

On the long-roofed steamship piers one is in a country that is no longer here and not yet there. The hazy yellow vault is full of echoing shouts. There are the rumble of trucks and the clump of trunks, the strident chatter of cranes, the first salt smell of the sea. One hurries through, even though there's time; the past, the continent, is behind; the future is the glowing mouth in the side of the ship; the dim, turbulent alley is too confusedly the present.

Up the gangplank and the vision of the world adjusts itself, narrows. One is a citizen of a commonwealth smaller than Andorra, no longer sure of anything. The men at the purser's desk are as oddly shaped as the cabins; disdainful are the eyes of voyagers and their friends. Next the loud mournful whistles, the portentous vibration, and the boat, the human idea—is in motion. The pier and its faces slide by and for a moment the boat is a piece accidentally split off from them; the faces become remote, voiceless, the pier is one of many blurs along the water front. The harbor flows swiftly toward the sea.

With it flowed Albert McKisco, labeled by the newspapers as its most precious cargo. McKisco was having a vogue. His novels were pastiches of the work of the best people of his time, a feat not to be disparaged, and in addition he possessed a gift for softening and debasing what he borrowed, so that many readers were charmed by the ease with which they could follow him. Success had improved him and humbled him. He was no fool about his capacities—he realized that he possessed more vitality than many men of superior talent, and he was resolved to enjoy the success he had earned. "I've done nothing yet," he would say. "I don't think I've got any real genius. But if I keep trying I may write a good book." Fine dives have been made from flimsier spring-boards. The innumerable snubs of the past were forgotten. Indeed, his success was founded psychologically upon his duel with Tommy Barban, upon the basis of which, as it withered in his memory, he had created, afresh, a new self-respect.

Spotting Dick Diver the second day out, he eyed him tentatively, then introduced himself in a friendly way and sat down. Dick laid aside his reading and, after the few minutes that it took to realize the change in McKisco, the disappearance of the man's annoying sense of inferiority, found himself pleased to talk to him. McKisco was "well-informed" on a range of subjects wider than Goethe's—it was interesting to listen to the innumerable facile combinations that he referred to as his opinions. They struck up an acquaintance, and Dick had several meals with them. The McKiscos had been invited to sit at the captain's table but with nascent snobbery they told Dick that they "couldn't stand that bunch."

Violet was very grand now, decked out by the grand *couturières*, charmed about the little discoveries that well-bred girls make in their teens. She could, indeed, have learned them from her mother in Boise but her soul was born dismally in the small movie houses of Idaho, and she had had no time for her mother. Now she "belonged"—together with several million other people—and she was happy, though her husband still shushed her when she grew violently naïve.

The McKiscos got off at Gibraltar. Next evening in Naples Dick picked up a lost and miserable family of two girls and their mother in the bus from the hotel to the station. He had seen them on the ship. An overwhelming desire to help, or to be admired, came over him: he showed them fragments of gaiety; tentatively he bought them wine, with pleasure saw them begin to regain their proper egotism. He pretended they were this and that, and falling in with his own plot, and drinking too much to sustain the illusion, and all this time the women thought only that this was a windfall from heaven. He withdrew from them as the night waned and the train rocked and snorted at Cassino and Frosinone. After weird American partings in the station at Rome, Dick went to the Hotel Quirinal, somewhat exhausted.

At the desk he suddenly stared and upped his head. As if a drink were acting on him, warming the lining of his stomach, throwing a flush up into his brain, he saw the person he had come to see, the person for whom he had made the Mediterranean crossing.

Simultaneously Rosemary saw him, acknowledging him before placing him; she looked back startled, and, leaving the girl she was with, she hurried over. Holding himself erect, holding his breath, Dick turned to her. As she came across the lobby, her beauty all groomed, like a young horse dosed with Black-seed oil, and hoops varnished, shocked him awake; but it all came too quick for him to do anything except conceal his fatigue as best he could. To meet her starry-eyed confidence he mustered an insincere pantomime implying, "You *would* turn up here—of all the people in the world."

Her gloved hands closed over his on the desk; "Dick—we're making 'The Grandeur that was Rome'—at least we think we are; we may quit any day."

He looked at her hard, trying to make her a little self-conscious, so that she would observe less closely his unshaven face, his crumpled and slept-in collar. Fortunately, she was in a hurry.

"We begin early because the mists rise at eleven—phone me at two."

In his room Dick collected his faculties. He left a call for noon, stripped off his clothes and dove literally into a heavy sleep.

He slept over the phone call but awoke at two, refreshed. Unpacking his bag, he sent out suits and laundry. He shaved, lay for half an hour in a warm bath and had breakfast. The sun had dipped into the Via Nazionale and he let it through the portières with a jingling of old brass rings. Waiting for a suit to be pressed, he discovered from the *Corriere della Sera* that "*una novella di Sainclair Lewis* Wall Street *nella quale autore analizza la vita sociale di una piccola citta Americana.*" Then he tried to think about Rosemary.

At first he thought nothing. She was young and magnetic, but so was Topsy. He guessed that she had had lovers and had loved them in the last four years. Well, you never knew exactly how much space you occupied in people's lives. Yet from this fog his affection emerged—the best contacts are when one knows the obstacles and still wants to preserve a relation. The past drifted back and he wanted to hold her eloquent giving-of-herself in its precious shell, till he enclosed it, till it no longer existed outside him. He tried to collect all that might attract her—it was less than it had been four years ago. Eighteen might look at thirty-four through a rising mist of adolescence; but twenty-two would see thirty-eight with discerning clarity. Moreover, Dick had been at an emotional peak at the time of the previous encounter; since then there had been a lesion of enthusiasm.

When the valet returned he put on a white shirt and collar and a black tie with a pearl; the cords of his reading-glasses passed through another pearl of the same size that swung a casual inch below. After sleep, his face had resumed the ruddy brown of many Riviera summers, and to limber himself up he stood on his hands on a chair until his fountain pen and coins fell out. At three he called Rosemary and was bidden to come up.

Momentarily dizzy from his acrobatics, he stopped in the bar for a gin-and-tonic.

"Hi, Doctor Diver!"

Only because of Rosemary's presence in the hotel did Dick place the man immediately as Collis Clay. He had his old confidence and an air of prosperity and big sudden jowls.

"Do you know Rosemary's here?" Collis asked.

"I ran into her."

"I was in Florence and I heard she was here so I came down last week. You'd never know mama's little girl." He modified the remark, "I mean she was so carefully brought up and now she's a woman of the world—if you know what I mean. Believe me, has she got some of these Roman boys tied up in bags! And how!"

"You studying in Florence?"

"Me? Sure, I'm studying architecture there. I go back Sunday—I'm staying for the races."

With difficulty Dick restrained him from adding the drink to the account he carried in the bar, like a stock-market report.

XX

WHEN Dick got out of the elevator he followed a tortuous corridor and turned at length toward a distant voice outside a lighted door. Rosemary was in black pajamas; a luncheon table was still in the room; she was having coffee.

"You're still beautiful," he said. "A little more beautiful than ever."

"Do you want coffee, youngster?"

"I'm sorry I was so unpresentable this morning."

"You didn't look well—you all right now? Want coffee?"

"No, thanks."

"You're fine again, I was scared this morning. Mother's coming over next month, if the company stays. She always asks me if I've seen you over here, as if she thought we were living next door. Mother always liked you—she always felt you were some one I ought to know."

"Well, I'm glad she still thinks of me."

"Oh, she does," Rosemary reassured him. "A very great deal."

"I've seen you here and there in pictures," said Dick. "Once I had 'Daddy's Girl' run off just for myself!"

"I have a good part in this one if it isn't cut."

She crossed behind him, touching his shoulder as she passed. She phoned for the table to be taken away and settled in a big chair.

"I was just a little girl when I met you, Dick. Now I'm a woman."

"I want to hear everything about you."

"How is Nicole—and Lanier and Topsy?"

"They're fine. They often speak of you——"

The phone rang. While she answered it Dick examined two novels—one by Edna Ferber, one by Albert McKisco. The waiter came for the table; bereft of its presence Rosemary seemed more alone in her black pajamas.

". . . I have a caller. . . . No, not very well. I've got to go to the costumer's for a long fitting. . . . No, not now. . . ."

As though with the disappearance of the table she felt released, Rosemary smiled at Dick—that smile as if they two together had managed to get rid of all the trouble in the world and were now at peace in their own heaven. . . .

"That's done," she said. "Do you realize I've spent the last hour getting ready for you?"

But again the phone called her. Dick got up to change his hat from the bed to the luggage stand, and in alarm Rosemary put her hand over the mouthpiece of the phone. "You're not going!"

"No."

When the communication was over he tried to drag the afternoon together saying: "I expect some nourishment from people now."

"Me too," Rosemary agreed. "The man that just phoned me once knew a second cousin of mine. Imagine calling anybody up for a reason like that!"

Now she lowered the lights for love. Why else should she want to shut off his view of her? He sent his words to her like letters, as though they left him some time before they reached her.

"Hard to sit here and be close to you, and not kiss you." Then they kissed passionately in the center of the floor. She pressed against him, and went back to her chair.

It could not go on being merely pleasant in the room. Forward or backward; when the phone rang once more he strolled into the bedchamber and lay down on her bed, opening Albert McKisco's novel. Presently Rosemary came in and sat beside him.

"You have the longest eyelashes," she remarked.

"We are now back at the Junior Prom. Among those present are Miss Rosemary Hoyt, the eyelash fancier——"

She kissed him and he pulled her down so that they lay side by side, and then they kissed till they were both breathless. Her breathing was young and eager and exciting. Her lips were faintly chapped but soft in the corners.

When they were still limbs and feet and clothes, struggles of his arms and back, and her throat and breasts, she whispered, "No, not now—those things are rhythmic."

Disciplined he crushed his passion into a corner of his mind, but bearing up her fragility on his arm until she was poised half a foot above him, he said lightly:

"Darling—that doesn't matter."

Her face had changed with his looking up at it; there was the eternal moonlight in it.

"That would be poetic justice if it should be you," she said. She twisted away from him, walked to the mirror, and boxed her disarranged hair with her hands. Presently she drew a chair close to the bed and stroked his cheek.

"Tell me the truth about you," he demanded.

"I always have."

"In a way—but nothing hangs together."

They both laughed but he pursued.

"Are you actually a virgin?"

"No-o-o!" she sang. "I've slept with six hundred and forty men—if that's the answer you want."

"It's none of my business."

"Do you want me for a case in psychology?"

"Looking at you as a perfectly normal girl of twenty-two, living in the year nineteen twenty-eight, I guess you've taken a few shots at love."

"It's all been—abortive," she said.

Dick couldn't believe her. He could not decide whether she was deliberately building a barrier between them or whether this was intended to make an eventual surrender more significant.

"Let's go walk in the Pincio," he suggested.

He shook himself straight in his clothes and smoothed

his hair. A moment had come and somehow passed. For three years Dick had been the ideal by which Rosemary measured other men and inevitably his stature had increased to heroic size. She did not want him to be like other men, yet here were the same exigent demands, as if he wanted to take some of herself away, carry it off in his pocket.

Walking on the greensward between cherubs and philosophers, fauns and falling water, she took his arm snugly, settling into it with a series of little readjustments, as if she wanted it to be right because it was going to be there forever. She plucked a twig and broke it, but she found no spring in it. Suddenly seeing what she wanted in Dick's face she took his gloved hand and kissed it. Then she cavorted childishly for him until he smiled and she laughed and they began having a good time.

"I can't go out with you tonight, darling, because I promised some people a long time ago. But if you'll get up early I'll take you out to the set tomorrow."

He dined alone at the hotel, went to bed early, and met Rosemary in the lobby at half-past six. Beside him in the car she glowed away fresh and new in the morning sunshine. They went out through the Porta San Sebastiano and along the Appian Way until they came to the huge set of the forum, larger than the forum itself. Rosemary turned him over to a man who led him about the great props; the arches and tiers of seats and the sanded arena. She was working on a stage which represented a guard-room for Christian prisoners, and presently they went there and watched Nicotera, one of many hopeful Valentinos, strut and pose before a dozen female "captives," their eyes melancholy and startling with mascara.

Rosemary appeared in a knee-length tunic.

"Watch this," she whispered to Dick. "I want your opinion. Everybody that's seen the rushes says——"

"What are the rushes?"

"When they run off what they took the day before. They say it's the first thing I've had sex appeal in."

"I don't notice it."

"You wouldn't! But I have."

Nicotera in his leopard skin talked attentively to Rosemary while the electrician discussed something with the director, meanwhile leaning on him. Finally the director pushed his hand off roughly and wiped a sweating forehead, and Dick's guide remarked: "He's on the hop again, and how!"

"Who?" asked Dick, but before the man could answer the director walked swiftly over to them.

"Who's on the hop—you're on the hop yourself." He spoke vehemently to Dick, as if to a jury. "When he's on the hop he always thinks everybody else is, and how!" He glared at the guide a moment longer, then he clapped his hands: "All right—everybody on the set."

It was like visiting a great turbulent family. An actress approached Dick and talked to him for five minutes under the impression that he was an actor recently arrived from London. Discovering her mistake she scuttled away in panic. The majority of the company felt either sharply superior or sharply inferior to the world outside, but the former feeling prevailed. They were people of bravery and industry; they were risen to a position of prominence in a nation that for a decade had wanted only to be entertained.

The session ended as the light grew misty—a fine light for painters, but, for the camera, not to be compared with the clear California air. Nicotera followed Rosemary to the car and whispered something to her—

she looked at him without smiling as she said good-by.

Dick and Rosemary had luncheon at the Castelli dei Cæsari, a splendid restaurant in a high-terraced villa overlooking the ruined forum of an undetermined period of the decadence. Rosemary took a cocktail and a little wine, and Dick took enough so that his feeling of dissatisfaction left him. Afterward they drove back to the hotel, all flushed and happy, in a sort of exalted quiet. She wanted to be taken and she was, and what had begun with a childish infatuation on a beach was accomplished at last.

XXI

ROSEMARY had another dinner date, a birthday party for a member of the company. Dick ran into Collis Clay in the lobby, but he wanted to dine alone, and pretended an engagement at the Excelsior. He drank a cocktail with Collis and his vague dissatisfaction crystallized as impatience—he no longer had an excuse for playing truant to the clinic. This was less an infatuation than a romantic memory. Nicole was his girl —too often he was sick at heart about her, yet she was his girl. Time with Rosemary was self-indulgence—time with Collis was nothing plus nothing.

In the doorway of the Excelsior he ran into Baby Warren. Her large beautiful eyes, looking precisely like marbles, stared at him with surprise and curiosity. "I thought you were in America, Dick! Is Nicole with you?"

"I came back by way of Naples."

The black band on his arm reminded her to say: "I'm so sorry to hear of your trouble."

Inevitably they dined together.

"Tell me about everything," she demanded.

Dick gave her a version of the facts, and Baby

frowned. She found it necessary to blame someone for the catastrophe in her sister's life.

"Do you think Doctor Dohmler took the right course with her from the first?"

"There's not much variety in treatment any more—of course you try to find the right personality to handle a particular case."

"Dick, I don't pretend to advise you or to know much about it but don't you think a change might be good for her—to get out of that atmosphere of sickness and live in the world like other people?"

"But you were keen for the clinic," he reminded her. "You told me you'd never feel really safe about her——"

"That was when you were leading that hermit's life on the Riviera, up on a hill way off from anybody. I didn't mean to go back to that life. I meant, for instance, London. The English are the best-balanced race in the world."

"They are not," he disagreed.

"They are. I know them, you see. I meant it might be nice for you to take a house in London for the spring season—I know a dove of a house in Talbot Square you could get, furnished. I mean, living with sane, well-balanced English people."

She would have gone on to tell him all the old propaganda stories of 1914 if he had not laughed and said:

"I've been reading a book by Michael Arlen and if that's——"

She ruined Michael Arlen with a wave of her salad spoon.

"He only writes about degenerates. I mean the worth-while English."

As she thus dismissed her friends they were replaced in Dick's mind only by a picture of the alien, unresponsive faces that peopled the small hotels of Europe.

"Of course it's none of my business," Baby repeated, as a preliminary to a further plunge, "but to leave her alone in an atmosphere like that——"

"I went to America because my father died."

"I understand that, I told you how sorry I was." She fiddled with the glass grapes on her necklace. "But there's so *much* money now. Plenty for everything, and it ought to be used to get Nicole well."

"For one thing I can't see myself in London."

"Why not? I should think you could work there as well as anywhere else."

He sat back and looked at her. If she had ever suspected the rotted old truth, the real reason for Nicole's illness, she had certainly determined to deny it to herself, shoving it back in a dusty closet like one of the paintings she bought by mistake.

They continued the conversation in the Ulpia, where Collis Clay came over to their table and sat down, and a gifted guitar player thrummed and rumbled "Suona Fanfara Mia" in the cellar piled with wine casks.

"It's possible that I was the wrong person for Nicole," Dick said. "Still she would probably have married someone of my type, someone she thought she could rely on —indefinitely."

"You think she'd be happier with somebody else?" Baby thought aloud suddenly. "Of course it could be arranged."

Only as she saw Dick bend forward with helpless laughter did she realize the preposterousness of her remark.

"Oh, you understand," she assured him. "Don't think for a moment that we're not grateful for all you've done. And we know you've had a hard time——"

"For God's sake," he protested. "If I didn't love Nicole it might be different."

"But you do love Nicole?" she demanded in alarm.

Collis was catching up with the conversation now and Dick switched it quickly: "Suppose we talk about something else—about you, for instance. Why don't you get married? We heard you were engaged to Lord Paley, the cousin of the——"

"Oh, no." She became coy and elusive. "That was last year."

"Why don't you marry?" Dick insisted stubbornly.

"I don't know. One of the men I loved was killed in the war, and the other one threw me over."

"Tell me about it. Tell me about your private life, Baby, and your opinions. You never do—we always talk about Nicole."

"Both of them were Englishmen. I don't think there's any higher type in the world than a first-rate Englishman, do you? If there is I haven't met him. This man—oh, it's a long story. I hate long stories, don't you?"

"And how!" said Collis.

"Why, no—I like them if they're good."

"That's something you do so well, Dick. You can keep a party moving by just a little sentence or a saying here and there. I think that's a wonderful talent."

"It's a trick," he said gently. That made three of her opinions he disagreed with.

"Of course I like formality—I like things to be just so, and on the grand scale. I know you probably don't but you must admit it's a sign of solidity in me."

Dick did not even bother to dissent from this.

"Of course I know people say Baby Warren is racing around over Europe, chasing one novelty after another, and missing the best things in life, but I think on the contrary that I'm one of the few people who really go after the best things. I've known the most interesting people of my time." Her voice blurred with the tinny drumming of another guitar number, but she called over it, "I've made very few big mistakes——"

"—Only the very big ones, Baby."

She had caught something facetious in his eye and she changed the subject. It seemed impossible for them to hold anything in common. But he admired something in her, and he deposited her at the Excelsior with a series of compliments that left her shimmering.

Rosemary insisted on treating Dick to lunch next day. They went to a little *trattoria* kept by an Italian who had worked in America, and ate ham and eggs and waffles. Afterward, they went to the hotel. Dick's discovery that he was not in love with her, nor she with him, had added to rather than diminished his passion for her. Now that he knew he would not enter further into her life, she became the strange woman for him. He supposed many men meant no more than that when they said they were in love—not a wild submergence of soul, a dipping of all colors into an obscuring dye, such as his love for Nicole had been. Certain thoughts about Nicole, that she should die, sink into mental darkness, love another man, made him physically sick.

Nicotera was in Rosemary's sitting-room, chattering about a professional matter. When Rosemary gave him his cue to go, he left with humorous protests and a rather insolent wink at Dick. As usual the phone clamored and Rosemary was engaged at it for ten minutes, to Dick's increasing impatience.

"Let's go up to my room," he suggested, and she agreed.

She lay across his knees on a big sofa; he ran his fingers through the lovely forelocks of her hair.

"Let me be curious about you again?" he asked.

"What do you want to know?"

"About men. I'm curious, not to say prurient."

"You mean how long after I met you?"

"Or before."

"Oh, no." She was shocked. "There was nothing before. You were the first man I cared about. You're still the only man I really care about." She considered. "It was about a year, I think."

"Who was it?"

"Oh, a man."

He closed in on her evasion.

"I'll bet I can tell you about it: the first affair was unsatisfactory and after that there was a long gap. The second was better, but you hadn't been in love with the man in the first place. The third was all right——"

Torturing himself he ran on. "Then you had one real affair that fell of its own weight, and by that time you were getting afraid that you wouldn't have anything to give to the man you finally loved." He felt increasingly Victorian. "Afterwards there were half a dozen just episodic affairs, right up to the present. Is that close?"

She laughed between amusement and tears.

"It's about as wrong as it could be," she said, to Dick's relief. "But some day I'm going to find somebody and love him and love him and never let him go."

Now his phone rang and Dick recognized Nicotera's voice, asking for Rosemary. He put his palm over the transmitter.

"Do you want to talk to him?"

She went to the phone and jabbered in a rapid Italian Dick could not understand.

"This telephoning takes time," he said. "It's after four and I have an engagement at five. You better go play with Signor Nicotera."

"Don't be silly."

"Then I think that while I'm here you ought to count him out."

"It's difficult." She was suddenly crying. "Dick, I do love you, never anybody like you. But what have you got for me?"

"What has Nicotera got for anybody?"

"That's different."

—Because youth called to youth.

"He's a spic!" he said. He was frantic with jealousy, he didn't want to be hurt again.

"He's only a baby," she said, sniffling. "You know I'm yours first."

In reaction he put his arms about her but she relaxed wearily backward; he held her like that for a moment as in the end of an adagio, her eyes closed, her hair falling straight back like that of a girl drowned.

"Dick, let me go. I never felt so mixed up in my life."

He was a gruff red bird and instinctively she drew away from him as his unjustified jealousy began to snow over the qualities of consideration and understanding with which she felt at home.

"I want to know the truth," he said.

"Yes, then. We're a lot together, he wants to marry me, but I don't want to. What of it? What do you expect me to do? You never asked me to marry you. Do you want me to play around forever with half-wits like Collis Clay?"

"You were with Nicotera last night?"

"That's none of your business," she sobbed. "Excuse me, Dick, it is your business. You and Mother are the only two people in the world I care about."

"How about Nicotera?"

"How do I know?"

She had achieved the elusiveness that gives hidden significance to the least significant remarks.

"Is it like you felt toward me in Paris?"

"I feel comfortable and happy when I'm with you. In Paris it was different. But you never know how you once felt. Do you?"

He got up and began collecting his evening clothes—if he had to bring all the bitterness and hatred of the world into his heart, he was not going to be in love with her again.

"I don't care about Nicotera!" she declared. "But I've got to go to Livorno with the company tomorrow. Oh, why did this have to happen?" There was a new flood of tears. "It's such a shame. Why did you come here? Why couldn't we just have the memory anyhow? I feel as if I'd quarreled with Mother."

As he began to dress, she got up and went to the door.

"I won't go to the party tonight." It was her last effort. "I'll stay with you. I don't want to go anyhow."

The tide began to flow again, but he retreated from it.

"I'll be in my room," she said. "Good-by, Dick."

"Good-by."

"Oh, such a shame, such a shame. Oh, such a shame. What's it all about anyhow?"

"I've wondered for a long time."

"But why bring it to me?"

"I guess I'm the Black Death," he said slowly. "I don't seem to bring people happiness any more."

XXII

THERE were five people in the Quirinal bar after dinner, a high-class Italian frail who sat on a stool making persistent conversation against the bartender's bored: "*Si . . . Si . . . Si,*" a light, snobbish Egyptian who was lonely but chary of the woman, and the two Americans.

Dick was always vividly conscious of his surroundings, while Collis Clay lived vaguely, the sharpest impressions dissolving upon a recording apparatus that had early atrophied, so the former talked and the latter listened, like a man sitting in a breeze.

Dick, worn away by the events of the afternoon, was taking it out on the inhabitants of Italy. He looked around the bar as if he hoped an Italian had heard him and would resent his words.

"This afternoon I had tea with my sister-in-law at the Excelsior. We got the last table and two men came up and looked around for a table and couldn't find one. So one of them came up to us and said, 'Isn't this table reserved for the Princess Orsini?' and I said: 'There was no sign on it,' and he said: 'But I think it's reserved for the Princess Orsini.' I couldn't even answer him."

"What'd he do?"

"He retired." Dick switched around in his chair. "I don't like these people. The other day I left Rosemary for two minutes in front of a store and an officer started walking up and down in front of her, tipping his hat."

"I don't know," said Collis after a moment. "I'd rather be here than up in Paris with somebody picking your pocket every minute."

He had been enjoying himself, and he held out against anything that threatened to dull his pleasure.

"I don't know," he persisted. "I don't mind it here."

Dick evoked the picture that the few days had imprinted on his mind, and stared at it. The walk toward the American Express past the odorous confectioneries of the Via Nationale, through the foul tunnel up to the Spanish Steps, where his spirit soared before the flower stalls and the house where Keats had died. He cared only about people; he was scarcely conscious of places except for their weather, until they had been invested with color by tangible events. Rome was the end of his dream of Rosemary.

A bell-boy came in and gave him a note.

"I did not go to the party," it said. *"I am in my room. We leave for Livorno early in the morning."*

Dick handed the note and a tip to the boy.

"Tell Miss Hoyt you couldn't find me." Turning to Collis he suggested the Bonbonieri.

They inspected the tart at the bar, granting her the minimum of interest exacted by her profession, and she stared back with bright boldness; they went through the deserted lobby oppressed by draperies holding Victorian dust in stuffy folds, and they nodded at the night concierge who returned the gesture with the bitter servility peculiar to night servants. Then in a taxi they rode along cheerless streets through a dank November night. There were no women in the streets, only pale men with dark coats buttoned to the neck, who stood in groups beside shoulders of cold stone.

"My God!" Dick sighed.

"What's a matter?"

"I was thinking of that man this afternoon: 'This table is reserved for the Princess Orsini.' Do you know what these old Roman families are? They're bandits, they're the ones who got possession of the temples and palaces after Rome went to pieces and preyed on the people."

"I like Rome," insisted Collis. "Why won't you try the races?"

"I don't like races."

"But all the women turn out——"

"I know I wouldn't like anything here. I like France, where everybody thinks he's Napoleon—down here everybody thinks he's Christ."

At the Bonbonieri they descended to a paneled cabaret, hopelessly impermanent amid the cold stone. A listless band played a tango and a dozen couples covered the wide floor with those elaborate and dainty steps so offensive to the American eye. A surplus of waiters precluded the stir and bustle that even a few busy men can create; over the scene as its form of animation brooded an air of waiting for something, for the dance, the night, the balance of forces which kept it stable, to cease. It assured the impressionable guest that whatever he was seeking he would not find it here.

This was plain as plain to Dick. He looked around, hoping his eye would catch on something, so that spirit instead of imagination could carry on for an hour. But there was nothing and after a moment he turned back to Collis. He had told Collis some of his current notions, and he was bored with his audience's short memory and lack of response. After half an hour of Collis he felt a distinct lesion of his own vitality.

They drank a bottle of Italian mousseaux, and Dick became pale and somewhat noisy. He called the orchestra leader over to their table; this was a Bahama Negro, conceited and unpleasant, and in a few minutes there was a row.

"You asked me to sit down."

"All right. And I gave you fifty lire, didn't I?"

"All right. All right. All right."

"All right, I gave you fifty lire, didn't I? Then you come up and asked me to put some more in the horn!"

"You asked me to sit down, didn't you? Didn't you?"

"I asked you to sit down but I gave you fifty lire, didn't I?"

"All right. All right."

The Negro got up sourly and went away, leaving Dick in a still more evil humor. But he saw a girl smiling at him from across the room and immediately the pale Roman shapes around him receded into decent, humble perspective. She was a young English girl, with blonde hair and a healthy, pretty English face and she smiled at him again with an invitation he understood, that denied the flesh even in the act of tendering it.

"There's a quick trick or else I don't know bridge," said Collis.

Dick got up and walked to her across the room.

"Won't you dance?"

The middle-aged Englishman with whom she was sitting said, almost apologetically: "I'm going out soon."

Sobered by excitement Dick danced. He found in the girl a suggestion of all the pleasanter English things; the story of safe gardens ringed around by the sea was implicit in her bright voice and as he leaned back to look at her, he meant what he said to her so sincerely that his voice trembled. When her current escort should leave, she promised to come and sit with them. The Englishman accepted her return with repeated apologies and smiles.

Back at his table Dick ordered another bottle of spumante.

"She looks like somebody in the movies," he said. "I can't think who." He glanced impatiently over his shoulder. "Wonder what's keeping her?"

"I'd like to get in the movies," said Collis thoughtfully. "I'm supposed to go into my father's business but it doesn't appeal to me much. Sit in an office in Birmingham for twenty years——"

His voice resisted the pressure of materialistic civilization.

"Too good for it?" suggested Dick.

"No, I don't mean that."

"Yes, you do."

"How do you know what I mean? Why don't you practice as a doctor, if you like to work so much?"

Dick had made them both wretched by this time, but simultaneously they had become vague with drink and in a moment they forgot; Collis left, and they shook hands warmly.

"Think it over," said Dick sagely.

"Think what over?"

"You know." It had been something about Collis going into his father's business—good sound advice.

Clay walked off into space. Dick finished his bottle and then danced with the English girl again, conquering his unwilling body with bold revolutions and stern determined marches down the floor. The most remarkable thing suddenly happened. He was dancing with the girl, the music stopped—and she had disappeared.

"Have you seen her?"

"Seen who?"

"The girl I was dancing with. Su'nly disappeared. Must be in the building."

"No! No! That's the ladies' room."

He stood up by the bar. There were two other men there, but he could think of no way of starting a conversation. He could have told them all about Rome and the violent origins of the Colonna and Gaetani families but he realized that as a beginning that would be somewhat abrupt. A row of Yenci dolls on the cigar counter fell suddenly to the floor; there was a subsequent confusion and he had a sense of having been the cause of it, so he went back to the cabaret and drank a cup of black coffee. Collis was gone and the English girl was gone and there seemed nothing to do but go back to the hotel and lie down with his black heart. He paid his check and got his hat and coat.

There was dirty water in the gutters and between the rough cobblestones; a marshy vapor from the Campagna, a sweat of exhausted cultures tainted the morning air. A quartet of taxi-drivers, their little eyes bobbing in dark pouches, surrounded him. One who leaned insistently in his face he pushed harshly away.

"*Quanto a Hotel Quirinal?*"

"*Cento lire.*"

Six dollars. He shook his head and offered thirty lire which was twice the day-time fare, but they shrugged their shoulders as one pair, and moved off.

"*Trente-cinque lire e mancie,*" he said firmly.

"*Cento lire.*"

He broke into English.

"To go half a mile? You'll take me for forty lire."

"Oh, no."

He was very tired. He pulled open the door of a cab and got in.

"Hotel Quirinal!" he said to the driver who stood obstinately outside the window. "Wipe that sneer off your face and take me to the Quirinal."

"Ah, no."

Dick got out. By the door of the Bonbonieri some one was arguing with the taxi-drivers, some one who now tried to explain their attitude to Dick; again one of the men pressed close, insisting and gesticulating and Dick shoved him away.

"I want to go the Quirinal Hotel."

"He says wan huner lire," explained the interpreter.

"I understand. I'll give him fif'y lire. Go on away." This last to the insistent man who had edged up once more. The man looked at him and spat contemptuously.

The passionate impatience of the week leaped up in Dick and clothed itself like a flash in violence, the honorable, the traditional resource of his land; he stepped forward and clapped the man's face.

They surged about him, threatening, waving their arms, trying ineffectually to close in on him—with his back against the wall Dick hit out clumsily, laughing a little and for a few minutes the mock fight, an affair of foiled rushes and padded, glancing blows, swayed back and forth in front of the door. Then Dick tripped and fell; he was hurt somewhere but he struggled up again wrestling in arms that suddenly broke apart. There was a new voice and a new argument but he leaned against the wall, panting and furious at the indignity of his position. He saw there was no sympathy for him but he was unable to believe that he was wrong.

They were going to the police station and settle it there. His hat was retrieved and handed to him, and with someone holding his arm lightly he strode around the corner with the taxi-men and entered a bare barrack where *carabinieri* lounged under a single dim light.

At a desk sat a captain, to whom the officious individual who had stopped the battle spoke at length in Italian, at times pointing at Dick, and letting himself be interrupted by the taxi-men who delivered short bursts of invective and denunciation. The captain began to nod impatiently. He held up his hand and the hydra-headed address, with a few parting exclamations, died away. Then he turned to Dick.

"*Spick Italiano?*" he asked.

"No."

"*Spick Français?*"

"*Oui,*" said Dick, glowering.

"*Alors. Écoute. Va au Quirinal. Espèce d'endormi. Écoutes: vous êtes saoûl. Payez ce que le chauffeur demande. Comprenez-vous?*"

Diver shook his head.

"Non, je ne veux pas."

"Come?"

"Je paierai quarante lires. C'est bien assez."

The captain stood up.

"Écoute!" he cried portentously, *"Vous êtes saoûl. Vous avez battu le chauffeur. Comme ci, comme ça."* He struck the air excitedly with right hand and left, *"C'est bon que je vous donne la liberté. Payez ce qu'il a dit–cento lire. Va au Quirinal."*

Raging with humiliation, Dick stared back at him.

"All right." He turned blindly to the door—before him, leering and nodding, was the man who had brought him to the police station. "I'll go home," he shouted, "but first I'll fix this baby."

He walked past the staring *carabinieri* and up to the grinning face, hit it with a smashing left beside the jaw. The man dropped to the floor.

For a moment he stood over him in savage triumph—but even as a first pang of doubt shot through him the world reeled; he was clubbed down, and fists and boots beat on him in a savage tattoo. He felt his nose break like a shingle and his eyes jerk as if they had snapped back on a rubber band into his head. A rib splintered under a stamping heel. Momentarily he lost consciousness, regained it as he was raised to a sitting position and his wrists jerked together with handcuffs. He struggled automatically. The plainclothes lieutenant whom he had knocked down, stood dabbing his jaw with a handkerchief and looking into it for blood; he came over to Dick, poised himself, drew back his arm and smashed him to the floor.

When Doctor Diver lay quite still a pail of water was sloshed over him. One of his eyes opened dimly as he was being dragged along by the wrists through a bloody haze, and he made out the human and ghastly face of one of the taxi-drivers.

"Go to the Excelsior hotel," he cried faintly. "Tell Miss Warren. Two hundred lire! Miss Warren. *Due centi lire!* Oh, you dirty—you God——"

Still he was dragged along through the bloody haze, choking and sobbing, over vague irregular surfaces into some small place where he was dropped upon a stone floor. The men went out, a door clanged, he was alone.

XXIII

UNTIL one o'clock Baby Warren lay in bed, reading one of Marion Crawford's curiously inanimate Roman stories; then she went to a window and looked down into the street. Across from the hotel two *carabinieri,* grotesque in swaddling capes and harlequin hats, swung voluminously from this side and that, like mains'ls coming about, and watching them she thought of the guards' officer who had stared at her so intensely at lunch. He had possessed the arrogance of a tall member of a short race, with no obligation save to be tall. Had he come up to her and said: "Let's go along, you and I," she would have answered: "Why not?"—at least it seemed so now, for she was still disembodied by an unfamiliar background.

Her thoughts drifted back slowly through the guardsman to the two *carabinieri,* to Dick—she got into bed and turned out the light.

A little before four she was awakened by a brusque knocking.

"Yes—what is it?"

"It's the concierge, Madame."

She pulled on her kimono and faced him sleepily.

"Your friend named Deever he's in a trouble. He had trouble with the police, and they have him in the jail.

He sent a taxi up to tell, the driver says that he promised him two hundred lire." He paused cautiously for this to be approved. "The driver says Mr. Deever in the bad trouble. He had a fight with the police and is terribly bad hurt."

"I'll be right down."

She dressed to an accompaniment of anxious heartbeats and ten minutes later stepped out of the elevator into the dark lobby. The chauffeur who brought the message was gone; the concierge hailed another one and told him the location of the jail. As they rode, the darkness lifted and thinned outside and Baby's nerves, scarcely awake, cringed faintly at the unstable balance between night and day. She began to race against the day; sometimes on the broad avenues she gained but whenever the thing that was pushing up paused for a moment, gusts of wind blew here and there impatiently and the slow creep of light began once more. The cab went past a loud fountain splashing in a voluminous shadow, turned into an alley so curved that the buildings were warped and strained following it, bumped and rattled over cobblestones, and stopped with a jerk where two sentry boxes were bright against a wall of green damp. Suddenly from the violet darkness of an archway came Dick's voice, shouting and screaming.

"Are there any English? Are there any Americans? Are there any English? Are there any—oh, my God! You dirty Wops!"

His voice died away and she heard a dull sound of beating on the door. Then the voice began again.

"Are there any Americans? Are there any English?"

Following the voice she ran through the arch into a court, whirled about in momentary confusion and located the small guard-room whence the cries came. Two *carabinieri* started to their feet, but Baby brushed past them to the door of the cell.

"Dick!" she called. "What's the trouble?"

"They've put out my eye," he cried. "They handcuffed me and then they beat me, the goddamn—the——"

Flashing around Baby took a step toward the two *carabinieri*.

"What have you done to him?" she whispered so fiercely that they flinched before her gathering fury.

"Non capisco inglese."

In French she execrated them; her wild, confident rage filled the room, enveloped them until they shrank and wriggled from the garments of blame with which she invested them. "Do something! Do something!"

"We can do nothing until we are ordered."

"*Bene*. Bay-nay! Bene!"

Once more Baby let her passion scorch around them until they sweated out apologies for their impotence, looking at each other with the sense that something had after all gone terribly wrong. Baby went to the cell door, leaned against it, almost caressing it, as if that could make Dick feel her presence and power, and cried: "I'm going to the Embassy, I'll be back." Throwing a last glance of infinite menace at the *carabinieri* she ran out.

She drove to the American Embassy where she paid off the taxi-driver upon his insistence. It was still dark when she ran up the steps and pressed the bell. She had pressed it three times before a sleepy English porter opened the door to her.

"I want to see someone," she said. "Anyone—but right away."

"No one's awake, Madame. We don't open until nine o'clock."

Impatiently she waved the hour away.

"This is important. A man—an American has been terribly beaten. He's in an Italian jail."

"No one's awake now. At nine o'clock——"

"I can't wait. They've put out a man's eye—my brother-in-law, and they won't let him out of jail. I must talk to someone—can't you see? Are you crazy? Are you an idiot, you stand there with that look in your face?"

"Hime unable to do anything, Madame."

"You've got to wake someone up!" She seized him by the shoulders and jerked him violently. "It's a matter of life and death. If you won't wake someone a terrible thing will happen to you——"

"Kindly don't lay hands on me, Madame."

From above and behind the porter floated down a weary Groton voice.

"What is it there?"

The porter answered with relief.

"It's a lady, sir, and she has shook me." He had stepped back to speak and Baby pushed forward into the hall. On an upper landing, just aroused from sleep and wrapped in a white embroidered Persian robe, stood a singular young man. His face was of a monstrous and unnatural pink, vivid yet dead, and over his mouth was fastened what appeared to be a gag. When he saw Baby he moved his head back into a shadow.

"What is it?" he repeated.

Baby told him, in her agitation edging forward to the stairs. In the course of her story she realized that the gag was in reality a mustache bandage and that the man's face was covered with pink cold cream, but the fact fitted quietly into the nightmare. The thing to do, she cried passionately, was for him to come to the jail with her at once and get Dick out.

"It's a bad business," he said.

"Yes," she agreed conciliatingly. "Yes?"

"This trying to fight the police." A note of personal affront crept into his voice. "I'm afraid there's nothing to be done until nine o'clock."

"Till nine o'clock," she repeated aghast. "But you can do something, certainly! You can come to the jail with me and see that they don't hurt him any more."

"We aren't permitted to do anything like that. The Consulate handles these things. The Consulate will be open at nine."

His face, constrained to impassivity by the binding strap, infuriated Baby.

"I can't wait until nine. My brother-in-law says they've put his eye out—he's seriously hurt! I have to get to him. I have to find a doctor." She let herself go and began to cry angrily as she talked, for she knew that he would respond to her agitation rather than her words. "You've got to do something about this. It's your business to protect American citizens in trouble."

But he was of the Eastern seaboard and too hard for her. Shaking his head patiently at her failure to understand his position he drew the Persian robe closer about him and came down a few steps.

"Write down the address of the Consulate for this lady," he said to the porter, "and look up Doctor Colazzo's address and telephone number and write that down too." He turned to Baby, with the expression of an exasperated Christ. "My dear lady, the diplomatic corps represents the Government of the United States to the Government of Italy. It has nothing to do with the protection of citizens, except under specific instructions from the State Department. Your brother-in-law has broken the laws of this country and been put in jail, just as an Italian might be put in jail in New York. The only people who can let him go are the Italian courts and if your brother-in-law has a case you can get aid and advice from the Consulate, which protects the rights of American citizens. The Consulate does not open until nine o'clock. Even if it were my brother I couldn't do anything——"

"Can you phone the Consulate?" she broke in.

"We can't interfere with the Consulate. When the Consul gets there at nine——"

"Can you give me his home address?"

After a fractional pause the man shook his head. He took the memorandum from the porter and gave it to her.

"Now I'll ask you to excuse me."

He had manœuvred her to the door: for an instant the violet dawn fell shrilly upon his pink mask and upon the linen sack that supported his mustache; then Baby was standing on the front steps alone. She had been in the embassy ten minutes.

The piazza whereon it faced was empty save for an old man gathering cigarette butts with a spiked stick. Baby caught a taxi presently and went to the Consulate but there was no one there save a trio of wretched women scrubbing the stairs. She could not make them understand that she wanted the Consul's home address —in a sudden resurgence of anxiety she rushed out and told the chauffeur to take her to the jail. He did not know where it was, but by the use of the words *semper dritte*, *dextra* and *sinestra* she manœuvred him to its approximate locality, where she dismounted and explored a labyrinth of familiar alleys. But the buildings and the alleys all looked alike. Emerging from one trail into the Piazza d'Espagna she saw the American Express Company and her heart lifted at the word "American" on the sign. There was a light in the window and hurrying across the square she tried the door, but it was locked, and inside the clock stood at seven. Then she thought of Collis Clay.

She remembered the name of his hotel, a stuffy villa sealed in red plush across from the Excelsior. The woman on duty at the office was not disposed to help her—she had no authority to disturb Mr. Clay, and refused to let Miss Warren go up to his room alone; convinced finally that this was not an affair of passion she accompanied her.

Collis lay naked upon his bed. He had come in tight and, awakening, it took him some moments to realize his nudity. He atoned for it by an excess of modesty. Taking his clothes into the bathroom he dressed in haste, muttering to himself "Gosh. She certainly musta got a good look at me." After some telephoning, he and Baby found the jail and went to it.

The cell door was open and Dick was slumped on a chair in the guard-room. The *carabinière* had washed some of the blood from his face, brushed him and set his hat concealingly upon his head. Baby stood in the doorway trembling.

"Mr. Clay will stay with you," she said. "I want to get the Consul and a doctor."

"All right."

"Just stay quiet."

"All right."

"I'll be back."

She drove to the Consulate; it was after eight now, and she was permitted to sit in the ante-room. Toward nine the Consul came in and Baby, hysterical with impotence and exhaustion, repeated her story. The Consul was disturbed. He warned her against getting into brawls in strange cities, but he was chiefly concerned that she should wait outside—with despair she read in his elderly eye that he wanted to be mixed up as little as possible in this catastrophe. Waiting on his action, she passed the minutes by phoning a doctor to go to Dick. There were other people in the ante-room and several were admitted to the Consul's office. After half an hour she chose the moment of someone's coming out and pushed past the secretary into the room.

"This is outrageous! An American has been beaten half to death and thrown into prison and you make no move to help."

"Just a minute, Mrs.——"

"I've waited long enough. You come right down to the jail and get him out!"

"Mrs.——"

"We're people of considerable standing in America—" Her mouth hardened as she continued. "If it wasn't for the scandal we can—I shall see that your indifference to this matter is reported in the proper quarter. If my brother-in-law were a British citizen he'd have been free hours ago, but you're more concerned with what the police will think than about what you're here for."

"Mrs.——"

"You put on your hat and come with me right away."

The mention of his hat alarmed the Consul who began to clean his spectacles hurriedly and to ruffle his papers. This proved of no avail: the American Woman, aroused, stood over him; the clean-sweeping irrational temper that had broken the moral back of a race and made a nursery out of a continent, was too much for him. He rang for the vice-consul—Baby had won.

Dick sat in the sunshine that fell profusely through the guard-room window. Collis was with him and two *carabinieri,* and they were waiting for something to happen. With the narrowed vision of his one eye Dick could see the *carabinieri;* they were Tuscan peasants with short upper lips and he found it difficult to associate them with the brutality of last night. He sent one of them to fetch him a glass of beer.

The beer made him light-headed and the episode was momentarily illumined by a ray of sardonic humor. Collis was under the impression that the English girl had something to do with the catastrophe, but Dick was sure she had disappeared long before it happened. Collis was still absorbed by the fact that Miss Warren had found him naked on his bed.

Dick's rage had retreated into him a little and he felt a vast criminal irresponsibility. What had happened to him was so awful that nothing could make any difference unless he could choke it to death, and, as this was unlikely, he was hopeless. He would be a different person henceforward, and in his raw state he had bizarre feelings of what the new self would be. The matter had about it the impersonal quality of an act of God. No mature Aryan is able to profit by a humiliation; when he forgives it has become part of his life, he has identified himself with the thing which has humiliated him—an upshot that in this case was impossible.

When Collis spoke of retribution, Dick shook his head and was silent. A lieutenant of *carabinieri,* pressed burnished, vital, came into the room like three men and the guards jumped to attention. He seized the empty beer bottle and directed a stream of scolding at his men. The new spirit was in him, and the first thing was to get the beer bottle out of the guard-room. Dick looked at Collis and laughed.

The vice-consul, an over-worked young man named Swanson, arrived, and they started to the court; Collis and Swanson on either side of Dick and the two *cara-*

binieri close behind. It was a yellow, hazy morning; the squares and arcades were crowded and Dick, pulling his hat low over his head, walked fast, setting the pace, until one of the short-legged *carabinieri* ran alongside and protested. Swanson arranged matters.

"I've disgraced you, haven't I?" said Dick jovially.

"You're liable to get killed fighting Italians," replied Swanson sheepishly. "They'll probably let you go this time but if you were an Italian you'd get a couple of months in prison. And how!"

"Have you ever been in prison?"

Swanson laughed.

"I like him," announced Dick to Clay. "He's a very likeable young man and he gives people excellent advice, but I'll bet he's been to jail himself. Probably spent weeks at a time in jail."

Swanson laughed.

"I mean you want to be careful. You don't know how these people are."

"Oh, I know how they are," broke out Dick, irritably. "They're god-damn stinkers." He turned around to the *carabinieri:* "Did you get that?"

"I'm leaving you here," Swanson said quickly. "I told your sister-in-law I would—our lawyer will meet you upstairs in the court-room. You want to be careful."

"Good-by." Dick shook hands politely. "Thank you very much. I feel you have a future——"

With another smile Swanson hurried away, resuming his official expression of disapproval.

Now they came into a courtyard on all four sides of which outer stairways mounted to the chambers above. As they crossed the flags a groaning, hissing, booing sound went up from the loiterers in the courtyard, voices full of fury and scorn. Dick stared about.

"What's that?" he demanded, aghast.

One of the *carabinieri* spoke to a group of men and the sound died away.

They came into the court-room. A shabby Italian lawyer from the Consulate spoke at length to the judge while Dick and Collis waited aside. Someone who knew English turned from the window that gave on the yard and explained the sound that had accompanied their passage through. A native of Frascati had raped and slain a five-year-old child and was to be brought in that morning—the crowd had assumed it was Dick.

In a few minutes the lawyer told Dick that he was freed—the court considered him punished enough.

"Enough!" Dick cried. "Punished for what?"

"Come along," said Collis. "You can't do anything now."

"But what did I do, except get into a fight with some taxi-men?"

"They claim you went up to a detective as if you were going to shake hands with him and hit him——"

"That's not true! I told him I was going to hit him—I didn't know he was a detective."

"You better go along," urged the lawyer.

"Come along." Collis took his arm and they descended the steps.

"I want to make a speech," Dick cried. "I want to explain to these people how I raped a five-year-old girl. Maybe I did——"

"Come along."

Baby was waiting with a doctor in a taxi-cab. Dick did not want to look at her and he disliked the doctor, whose stern manner revealed him as one of that least palpable of European types, the Latin moralist. Dick summed up his conception of the disaster, but no one had much to say. In his room in the Quirinal the doctor washed off the rest of the blood and the oily sweat, set his nose, his fractured ribs and fingers, disinfected the smaller wounds and put a hopeful dressing on the eye. Dick asked for a quarter of a grain of morphine, for he was still wide awake and full of nervous energy. With the morphine he fell asleep; the doctor and Collis left and Baby waited with him until a woman could arrive from the English nursing home. It had been a hard night but she had the satisfaction of feeling that, whatever Dick's previous record was, they now possessed a moral superiority over him for as long as he proved of any use.

BOOK III

I

FRAU KAETHE GREGOROVIOUS overtook her husband on the path of their villa.

"How was Nicole?" she asked mildly; but she spoke out of breath, giving away the fact that she had held the question in her mind during her run.

Franz looked at her in surprise.

"Nicole's not sick. What makes you ask, dearest one?"

"You see her so much—I thought she must be sick."

"We will talk of this in the house."

Kaethe agreed meekly. His study was over in the administration building and the children were with their tutor in the living-room; they went up to the bedroom.

"Excuse me, Franz," said Kaethe before he could speak. "Excuse me, dear, I had no right to say that. I know my obligations and I am proud of them. But there is a bad feeling between Nicole and me."

"Birds in their little nests agree," Franz thundered. Finding the tone inappropriate to the sentiment he repeated his command in the spaced and considered rhythm with which his old master, Doctor Dohmler, could cast significance on the tritest platitude. "Birds—in—their—nests—*agree!*"

"I realize that. You haven't seen me fail in courtesy toward Nicole."

"I see you failing in common sense. Nicole is half a patient—she will possibly remain something of a patient all her life. In the absence of Dick I am responsible." He hesitated; sometimes as a quiet joke he tried to keep news from Kaethe. "There was a cable from Rome this morning. Dick has had grippe and is starting home tomorrow."

Relieved, Kaethe pursued her course in a less personal tone:

"I think Nicole is less sick than any one thinks—she only cherishes her illness as an instrument of power. She ought to be in the cinema, like your Norma Talmadge—that's where all American women would be happy."

"Are you jealous of Norma Talmadge, on a film?"

"I don't like Americans. They're selfish, *sel*fish!"

"You like Dick?"

"I like him," she admitted. "He's different, he thinks of others."

—And so does Norma Talmadge, Franz said to himself. Norma Talmadge must be a fine, noble woman beyond her loveliness. They must compel her to play foolish rôles; Norma Talmadge must be a woman whom it would be a great privilege to know.

Kaethe had forgotten about Norma Talmadge, a vivid shadow that she had fretted bitterly upon one night as they were driving home from the movies in Zurich.

"—Dick married Nicole for her money," she said.

"That was his weakness—you hinted as much yourself one night."

"You're being malicious."

"I shouldn't have said that," she retracted. "We must all live together like birds, as you say. But it's difficult when Nicole acts as—when Nicole pulls herself back a little, as if she were holding her breath—as if I *smelt* bad!"

Kaethe had touched a material truth. She did most of her work herself, and, frugal, she bought few clothes. An American shop-girl, laundering two changes of underwear every night, would have noticed a hint of yesterday's reawakened sweat about Kaethe's person, less a smell than an ammoniacal reminder of the eternity of toil and decay. To Franz this was as natural as the thick dark scent of Kaethe's hair, and he would have missed it equally; but to Nicole, born hating the smell of a nurse's fingers dressing her, it was an offense only to be endured.

"And the children," Kaethe continued. "She doesn't like them to play with our children—" but Franz had heard enough:

"Hold your tongue—that kind of talk can hurt me professionally, since we owe this clinic to Nicole's money. Let us have lunch."

Kaethe realized that her outburst had been ill-advised, but Franz's last remark reminded her that other Americans had money, and a week later she put her dislike of Nicole into new words.

The occasion was the dinner they tendered the Divers upon Dick's return. Hardly had their footfalls ceased on the path when she shut the door and said to Franz:

"Did you see around his eyes? He's been on a debauch!"

"Go gently," Franz requested. "Dick told me about

that as soon as he came home. He was boxing on the trans-Atlantic ship. The American passengers box a lot on these trans-Atlantic ships."

"I believe that?" she scoffed. "It hurts him to move one of his arms and he has an unhealed scar on his temple—you can see where the hair's been cut away."

Franz had not noticed these details.

"But what?" Kaethe demanded. "Do you think that sort of thing does the clinic any good? The liquor I smelt on him tonight, and several other times since he's been back."

She slowed her voice to fit the gravity of what she was about to say: "Dick is no longer a serious man."

Franz rocked his shoulders up the stairs, shaking off her persistence. In their bedroom he turned on her.

"He is most certainly a serious man and a brilliant man. Of all the men who have recently taken their degrees in neuro-pathology in Zurich, Dick has been regarded as the most brilliant—more brilliant than I could ever be."

"For shame!"

"It's the truth—the shame would be not to admit it. I turn to Dick when cases are highly involved. His publications are still standard in their line—go into any medical library and ask. Most students think he's an Englishman—they don't believe that such thoroughness could come out of America." He groaned domestically, taking his pajamas from under the pillow, "I can't understand why you talk this way, Kaethe—I thought you liked him."

"For shame!" Kaethe said. "You're the solid one, you do the work. It's a case of hare and tortoise—and in my opinion the hare's race is almost done."

"Tch! Tch!"

"Very well, then. It's true."

With his open hand he pushed down air briskly.

"Stop!"

The upshot was that they had exchanged viewpoints like debaters. Kaethe admitted to herself that she had been too hard on Dick, whom she admired and of whom she stood in awe, who had been so appreciative and understanding of herself. As for Franz, once Kaethe's idea had had time to sink in, he never after believed that Dick was a serious person. And as time went on he convinced himself that he had never thought so.

II

DICK told Nicole an expurgated version of the catastrophe in Rome—in his version he had gone philanthropically to the rescue of a drunken friend. He could trust Baby Warren to hold her tongue, since he had painted the disastrous effect of the truth upon Nicole. All this, however, was a low hurdle compared to the lingering effect of the episode upon him.

In reaction he took himself for an intensified beating in his work, so that Franz, trying to break with him, could find no basis on which to begin a disagreement. No friendship worth the name was ever destroyed in an hour without some painful flesh being torn—so Franz let himself believe with ever-increasing conviction that Dick traveled intellectually and emotionally at such a rate of speed that the vibrations jarred him—this was a contrast that had previously been considered a virtue in their relation. So, for the shoddiness of needs, are shoes made out of last year's hide.

Yet it was May before Franz found an opportunity to insert the first wedge. Dick came into his office white and tired one noon and sat down, saying:

"Well, she's gone."

"She's dead?"

"The heart quit."

Dick sat exhausted in the chair nearest the door. During three nights he had remained with the scabbed anonymous woman-artist he had come to love, formally to portion out the adrenalin, but really to throw as much wan light as he could into the darkness ahead.

Half appreciating his feeling, Franz traveled quickly over an opinion:

"It was neuro-syphilis. All the Wassermans we took won't tell me differently. The spinal fluid——"

"Never mind," said Dick. "Oh, God, never mind! If she cared enough about her secret to take it away with her, let it go at that."

"You better lay off for a day."

"Don't worry, I'm going to."

Franz had his wedge; looking up from the telegram that he was writing to the woman's brother he inquired: "Or do you want to take a little trip?"

"Not now."

"I don't mean a vacation. There's a case in Lausanne. I've been on the phone with a Chilian all morning——"

"She was so damn brave," said Dick. "And it took her so long." Franz shook his head sympathetically and Dick got himself together. "Excuse me for interrupting you."

"This is just a change—the situation is a father's problem with his son—the father can't get the son up here. He wants somebody to come down there."

"What is it? Alcoholism? Homosexuality? When you say Lausanne——"

"A little of everything."

"I'll go down. Is there any money in it?"

"Quite a lot, I'd say. Count on staying two or three

days, and get the boy up here if he needs to be watched. In any case take your time, take your ease; combine business with pleasure."

After two hours' train sleep Dick felt renewed, and he approached the interview with Señor Pardo y Cuidad Real in good spirits.

These interviews were much of a type. Often the sheer hysteria of the family representative was as interesting psychologically as the condition of the patient. This one was no exception: Señor Pardo y Cuidad Real, a handsome iron-gray Spaniard, noble of carriage, with all the appurtenances of wealth and power, raged up and down his suite in the Hôtel des Trois Mondes and told the story of his son with no more self-control than a drunken woman.

"I am at the end of my invention. My son is corrupt. He was corrupt at Harrow, he was corrupt at King's College, Cambridge. He's incorrigibly corrupt. Now that there is this drinking it is more and more obvious how he is, and there is continual scandal. I have tried everything—I worked out a plan with a doctor friend of mine, sent them together for a tour of Spain. Every evening Francisco had an injection of cantharides and then the two went together to a reputable bordello—for a week or so it seemed to work but the result was nothing. Finally last week in this very room, rather in that bathroom—" he pointed at it, "—I made Francisco strip to the waist and lashed him with a whip——"

Exhausted with his emotion he sat down and Dick spoke:

"That was foolish—the trip to Spain was futile also—" He struggled against an upsurging hilarity—that any reputable medical man should have lent himself to such an amateurish experiment! "—Señor, I must tell you that in these cases we can promise nothing. In the case of the drinking we can often accomplish something—with proper co-operation. The first thing is to see the boy and get enough of his confidence to find whether he has any insight into the matter."

—The boy, with whom he sat on the terrace, was about twenty, handsome and alert.

"I'd like to know your attitude," Dick said. "Do you feel that the situation is getting worse? And do you want to do anything about it?"

"I suppose I do," said Francisco, "I am very unhappy."

"Do you think it's from the drinking or from the abnormality?"

"I think the drinking is caused by the other." He was serious for a while—suddenly an irrepressible facetiousness broke through and he laughed, saying, "It's hopeless. At King's I was known as the Queen of Chili. That trip to Spain—all it did was to make me nauseated by the sight of a woman."

Dick caught him up sharply.

"If you're happy in this mess, then I can't help you and I'm wasting my time."

"No, let's talk—I despise most of the others so." There was some manliness in the boy, perverted now into an active resistance to his father. But he had that typically roguish look in his eyes that homosexuals assume in discussing the subject.

"It's a hole-and-corner business at best," Dick told him. "You'll spend your life on it, and its consequences, and you won't have time or energy for any other decent or social act. If you want to face the world you'll have to begin by controlling your sensuality—and, first of all, the drinking that provokes it——"

He talked automatically, having abandoned the case ten minutes before. They talked pleasantly through another hour about the boy's home in Chili and about his ambitions. It was as close as Dick had ever come to comprehending such a character from any but the pathological angle—he gathered that this very charm made it possible for Francisco to perpetrate his outrages, and, for Dick, charm always had an independent existence, whether it was the mad gallantry of the wretch who had died in the clinic this morning, or the courageous grace which this lost young man brought to a drab old story. Dick tried to dissect it into pieces small enough to store away—realizing that the totality of a life may be different in quality from its segments, and also that life during the forties seemed capable of being observed only in segments. His love for Nicole and Rosemary, his friendship with Abe North, with Tommy Barban in the broken universe of the war's ending—in such contacts the personalities had seemed to press up so close to him that he became the personality itself—there seemed some necessity of taking all or nothing; it was as if for the remainder of his life he was condemned to carry with him the egos of certain people, early met and early loved, and to be only as complete as they were complete themselves. There was some element of loneliness involved—so easy to be loved—so hard to love.

As he sat on the veranda with young Francisco, a ghost of the past swam into his ken. A tall, singularly swaying male detached himself from the shrubbery and approached Dick and Francisco with feeble resolution. For a moment he formed such an apologetic part of the vibrant landscape that Dick scarcely remarked him—then Dick was on his feet, shaking hands with an abstracted air, thinking, "My God, I've stirred up a nest!" and trying to collect the man's name.

"This is Doctor Diver, isn't it?"

"Well, well—Mr. Dumphry, isn't it?"

"Royal Dumphry. I had the pleasure of having dinner one night in that lovely garden of yours."

"Of course." Trying to dampen Mr. Dumphry's enthusiasm, Dick went into impersonal chronology. "It was in nineteen—twenty-four—or twenty-five——"

He had remained standing, but Royal Dumphry, shy as he had seemed at first, was no laggard with his pick and spade; he spoke to Francisco in a flip, intimate manner, but the latter, ashamed of him, joined Dick in trying to freeze him away.

"Doctor Diver—one thing I want to say before you go. I've never forgotten that evening in your garden—how nice you and your wife were. To me it's one of the finest memories in my life, one of the happiest ones. I've always thought of it as the most civilized gathering of people that I have ever known."

Dick continued a crab-like retreat toward the nearest door of the hotel.

"I'm glad you remembered it so pleasantly. Now I've got to see——"

"I understand," Royal Dumphry pursued sympathetically. "I hear he's dying."

"Who's dying?"

"Perhaps I shouldn't have said that—but we have the same physician."

Dick paused, regarding him in astonishment. "Who're you talking about?"

"Why, your wife's father—perhaps I——"

"My *what?*"

"I suppose—you mean I'm the first person——"

"You mean my wife's father is here, in Lausanne?"

"Why, I thought you knew—I thought that was why you were here."

"What doctor is taking care of him?"

Dick scrawled the name in a notebook, excused himself, and hurried to a telephone booth.

It was convenient for Doctor Dangeu to see Doctor Diver at his house immediately.

Doctor Dangeu was a young Génevois; for a moment he was afraid that he was going to lose a profitable patient, but, when Dick reassured him, he divulged the fact that Mr. Warren was indeed dying.

"He is only fifty but the liver has stopped restoring itself; the precipitating factor is alcoholism."

"Doesn't respond?"

"The man can take nothing except liquids—I give him three days, or at most, a week."

"Does his elder daughter, Miss Warren, know his condition?"

"By his own wish no one knows except the manservant. It was only this morning I felt I had to tell him—he took it excitedly, although he has been in a very religious and resigned mood from the beginning of his illness."

Dick considered: "Well—" he decided slowly, "in any case I'll take care of the family angle. But I imagine they would want a consultation."

"As you like."

"I know I speak for them when I ask you to call in one of the best-known medicine men around the lake—Herbrugge, from Geneva."

"I was thinking of Herbrugge."

"Meanwhile I'm here for a day at least and I'll keep in touch with you."

That evening Dick went to Señor Pardo y Cuidad Real and they talked.

"We have large estates in Chili—" said the old man. "My son could well be taking care of them. Or I can get him in any one of a dozen enterprises in Paris—"

He shook his head and paced across the windows against a spring rain so cheerful that it didn't even drive the swans to cover. "My only son! Can't you take him with you?"

The Spaniard knelt suddenly at Dick's feet.

"Can't you cure my only son? I believe in you—you can take him with you, cure him."

"It's impossible to commit a person on such grounds. I wouldn't if I could."

The Spaniard got up from his knees.

"I have been hasty—I have been driven——"

Descending to the lobby Dick met Doctor Dangeu in the elevator.

"I was about to call your room," the latter said. "Can we speak out on the terrace?"

"Is Mr. Warren dead?" Dick demanded.

"He is the same—the consultation is in the morning. Meanwhile he wants to see his daughter—your wife—with the greatest fervor. It seems there was some quarrel——"

"I know all about that."

The doctors looked at each other, thinking.

"Why don't you talk to him before you make up your mind?" Dangeu suggested. "His death will be graceful—merely a weakening and sinking."

With an effort Dick consented.

"All right."

The suite in which Charles Warren was gracefully weakening and sinking was of the same size as that of the Señor Pardo y Cuidad Real—throughout this hotel there were many chambers wherein rich ruins, fugitives from justice, claimants to the thrones of mediatized principalities, lived on the derivatives of opium or barbitol listening eternally as to an inescapable radio, to the coarse melodies of old sins. This corner of Europe does not so much draw people as accept them without inconvenient questions. Routes cross here—people bound for private sanitoriums or tuberculosis resorts in the mountains, people who are no longer *persona grata* in France or Italy.

The suite was darkened. A nun with a holy face was nursing the man whose emaciated fingers stirred a rosary on the white sheet. He was still handsome and his voice summoned up a thick burr of individuality as he spoke to Dick, after Dangeu had left them together.

"We get a lot of understanding at the end of life. Only now, Doctor Diver, do I realize what it was all about."

Dick waited.

"I've been a bad man. You must know how little right I have to see Nicole again, yet a Bigger Man than either of us says to forgive and to pity." The rosary slipped from his weak hands and slid off the smooth bed covers. Dick picked it up for him. "If I could see Nicole for ten minutes I would go happy out of the world."

"It's not a decision I can make for myself," said Dick. "Nicole is not strong." He made his decision but pretended to hesitate. "I can put it up to my professional associate."

"What your associate says goes with me—very well, Doctor. Let me tell you my debt to you is so large——"

Dick stood up quickly.

"I'll let you know the result through Doctor Dangeu."

In his room he called the clinic on the Zugersee. After a long time Kaethe answered from her own house.

"I want to get in touch with Franz."

"Franz is up on the mountain. I'm going up myself—is it something I can tell him, Dick?"

"It's about Nicole—her father is dying here in Lausanne. Tell Franz that, to show him it's important; and ask him to phone me from up there."

"I will."

"Tell him I'll be in my room here at the hotel from three to five, and again from seven to eight, and after that to page me in the dining-room."

In plotting these hours he forgot to add that Nicole was not to be told; when he remembered it he was talking into a dead telephone. Certainly Kaethe should realize.

. . . Kaethe had no exact intention of telling Nicole about the call when she rode up the deserted hill of mountain wild-flowers and secret winds, where the patients were taken to ski in winter and to climb in spring. Getting off the train she saw Nicole shepherding the children through some organized romp. Approaching, she drew her arm gently along Nicole's shoulder, saying: "You are clever with children—you must teach them more about swimming in the summer."

In the play they had grown hot, and Nicole's reflex in drawing away from Kaethe's arm was automatic to the point of rudeness. Kaethe's hand fell awkwardly into space, and then she too reacted, verbally, and deplorably.

"Did you think I was going to embrace you?" she demanded sharply. "It was only about Dick, I talked on the phone to him and I was sorry——"

"Is anything the matter with Dick?"

Kaethe suddenly realized her error, but she had taken a tactless course and there was no choice but to answer as Nicole pursued her with reiterated questions: ". . . then *why* were you sorry?"

"Nothing about Dick. I must talk to Franz."

"It *is* about Dick."

There was terror in her face and collaborating alarm in the faces of the Diver children, near at hand. Kaethe collapsed with: "Your father is ill in Lausanne—Dick wants to talk to Franz about it."

"Is he very sick?" Nicole demanded—just as Franz came up with his hearty hospital manner. Gratefully Kaethe passed the remnant of the buck to him—but the damage was done.

"I'm going to Lausanne," announced Nicole.

"One minute," said Franz. "I'm not sure it's advisable. I must first talk on the phone to Dick."

"Then I'll miss the train down," Nicole protested, "and then I'll miss the three o'clock from Zurich! If my father is dying I must—" She left this in the air, afraid to formulate it. "I *must* go. I'll have to run for the train." She was running even as she spoke toward the sequence of flat cars that crowned the bare hill with bursting steam and sound. Over her shoulder she called back, "If you phone Dick tell him I'm coming, Franz!" . . .

. . . Dick was in his own room in the hotel reading the *New York Herald* when the swallow-like nun rushed in—simultaneously the phone rang.

"Is he dead?" Dick demanded of the nun, hopefully.

"*Monsieur, il est parti*—he has gone away."

"*Comment?*"

"*Il est parti*—his man and his baggage have gone away too!"

It was incredible. A man in that condition to arise and depart.

Dick answered the phone-call from Franz. "You shouldn't have told Nicole," he protested.

"Kaethe told her, very unwisely."

"I suppose it was my fault. Never tell a thing to a

woman till it's done. However, I'll meet Nicole . . . say, Franz, the craziest thing has happened down here —the old boy took up his bed and walked. . . ."

"At what? What did you say?"

"I say he walked, old Warren—he walked!"

"But why not?"

"He was supposed to be dying of general collapse . . . He got up and walked away, back to Chicago, I guess. . . . I don't know, the nurse is here now. . . . I don't know, Franz—I've just heard about it. . . . Call me later."

He spent the better part of two hours tracing Warren's movements. The patient had found an opportunity between the change of day and night nurses to resort to the bar where he had gulped down four whiskeys; he paid his hotel bill with a thousand-dollar note, instructing the desk that the change should be sent after him, and departed, presumably for America. A last-minute dash by Dick and Dangeu to overtake him at the station resulted only in Dick's failing to meet Nicole; when they did meet in the lobby of the hotel she seemed suddenly tired, and there was a tight purse to her lips that disquieted him.

"How's father?" she demanded.

"He's much better. He seemed to have a good deal of reserve energy after all." He hesitated, breaking it to her easy. "In fact he got up and went away."

Wanting a drink, for the chase had occupied the dinner hour, he led her, puzzled, toward the grill, and continued as they occupied two leather easy-chairs and ordered a highball and a glass of beer: "The man who was taking care of him made a wrong prognosis or something—wait a minute, I've hardly had time to think the thing out myself."

"He's *gone?*"

"He got the evening train for Paris."

They sat silent. From Nicole flowed a vast tragic apathy.

"It was instinct," Dick said, finally. "He was really dying, but he tried to get a resumption of rhythm—he's not the first person that ever walked off his death-bed—like an old clock—you know, you shake it and somehow from sheer habit it gets going again. Now your father——"

"Oh, don't tell me," she said.

"His principal fuel was fear," he continued. "He got afraid, and off he went. He'll probably live till ninety——"

"Please don't tell me any more," she said. "Please don't—I couldn't stand any more."

"All right. The little devil I came down to see is hopeless. We may as well go back tomorrow."

"I don't see why you have to—come in contact with all this," she burst forth.

"Oh, don't you? Sometimes I don't either."

She put her hand on his.

"Oh, I'm sorry I said that, Dick."

Some one had brought a phonograph into the bar and they sat listening to "The Wedding of the Painted Doll."

III

ONE morning a week later, stopping at the desk for his mail, Dick became aware of some extra commotion outside: Patient Von Cohn Morris was going away. His parents, Australians, were putting his baggage vehemently into a large limousine, and beside them stood Doctor Lladislau protesting with ineffectual attitudes against the violent gesturings of Morris, senior.

The young man was regarding his embarkation with aloof cynicism as Doctor Diver approached.

"Isn't this a little sudden, Mr. Morris?"

Mr. Morris started as he saw Dick—his florid face and the large checks on his suit seemed to turn off and on like electric lights. He approached Dick as though to strike him.

"High time we left, we and those who have come with us," he began, and paused for breath. "It is high time, Doctor Diver. High time."

"Will you come in my office?" Dick suggested.

"Not I! I'll talk to you, but I'm washing my hands of you and your place."

"I'm sorry about that."

He shook his finger at Dick. "I was just telling this doctor here. We've wasted our time and our money."

Doctor Lladislau stirred in a feeble negative, signaling up a vague Slavic evasiveness. Dick had never liked Lladislau. He managed to walk the excited Australian along the path in the direction of his office, trying to persuade him to enter; but the man shook his head.

"It's *you,* Doctor Diver, *you,* the very man. I went to Doctor Lladislau because you were not to be found, Doctor Diver, and because Doctor Gregorovious is not expected until the nightfall, and I would not wait. No, sir! I would not wait a minute after my son told me the truth."

He came up menacingly to Dick, who kept his hands loose enough to drop him if it seemed necessary. "My son is here for alcoholism, and he told us he smelt liquor on your breath. Yes, sir!" He made a quick, apparently unsuccessful sniff. "Not once, but twice Von Cohn says he has smelt liquor on your breath. I and my lady have never touched a drop of it in our lives. We hand Von

Cohn to you to be cured, and within a month he twice smells liquor on your breath! What kind of cure is that there?"

Dick hesitated; Mr. Morris was quite capable of making a scene on the clinic drive.

"After all, Mr. Morris, some people are not going to give up what they regard as food because of your son——"

"But you're a doctor, man!" cried Morris furiously. "When the workmen drink their beer that's bad 'cess to them—but you're here supposing to cure——"

"This has gone too far. Your son came to us because of kleptomania."

"What was behind it?" The man was almost shrieking. "Drink—black drink. Do you know what color black is? It's black! My own uncle was hung by the neck because of it, you hear! My son comes to a sanitorium, and a doctor reeks of it!"

"I must ask you to leave."

"You *ask* me! We *are* leaving!"

"If you could be a little temperate we could tell you the results of the treatment to date. Naturally, since you feel as you do, we would not want your son as a patient——"

"You dare to use the word temperate to me?"

Dick called to Doctor Lladislau and as he approached, said: "Will you represent us in saying good-by to the patient and to his family?"

He bowed slightly to Morris and went into his office, and stood rigid for a moment just inside the door. He watched until they drove away, the gross parents, the bland, degenerate offspring: it was easy to prophesy the family's swing around Europe, bullying their betters with hard ignorance and hard money. But what absorbed Dick after the disappearance of the caravan was the question as to what extent he had provoked this. He drank claret with each meal, took a nightcap, generally in the form of hot rum, and sometimes he tippled with gin in the afternoons—gin was the most difficult to detect on the breath. He was averaging a half-pint of alcohol a day, too much for his system to burn up.

Dismissing a tendency to justify himself, he sat down at his desk and wrote out, like a prescription, a régime that would cut his liquor in half. Doctors, chauffeurs, and Protestant clergymen could never smell of liquor, as could painters, brokers, cavalry leaders; Dick blamed himself only for indiscretion. But the matter was by no means clarified half an hour later when Franz, revivified by an Alpine fortnight, rolled up the drive, so eager to resume work that he was plunged in it before he reached his office. Dick met him there.

"How was Mount Everest?"

"We could very well have done Mount Everest the rate we were doing. We thought of it. How goes it all? How is my Kaethe, how is your Nicole?"

"All goes smooth domestically. But my God, Franz, we had a rotten scene this morning."

"How? What was it?"

Dick walked around the room while Franz got in touch with his villa by telephone. After the family exchange was over, Dick said: "The Morris boy was taken away—there was a row."

Franz's buoyant face fell.

"I knew he'd left. I met Lladislau on the veranda."

"What did Lladislau say?"

"Just that young Morris had gone—that you'd tell me about it. What about it?"

"The usual incoherent reasons."

"He was a devil, that boy."

"He was a case for anesthesia," Dick agreed. "Anyhow, the father had beaten Lladislau into a colonial subject by the time I came along. What about Lladislau? Do we keep him? I say no—he's not much of a man, he can't seem to cope with anything." Dick hesitated on the verge of the truth, swung away to give himself space within which to recapitulate. Franz perched on the edge of a desk, still in his linen duster and traveling gloves. Dick said:

"One of the remarks the boy made to his father was that your distinguished collaborator was a drunkard. The man is a fanatic, and the descendant seems to have caught traces of *vin du pays* on me."

Franz sat down, musing on his lower lip. "You can tell me at length," he said finally.

"Why not now?" Dick suggested. "You must know I'm the last man to abuse liquor." His eyes and Franz's glinted on each other, pair on pair. "Lladislau let the man get so worked up that I was on the defensive. It might have happened in front of patients, and you can imagine how hard it could be to defend yourself in a situation like that!"

Franz took off his gloves and coat. He went to the door and told the secretary, "Don't disturb us." Coming back into the room he flung himself at the long table and fooled with his mail, reasoning as little as is characteristic of people in such postures, rather summoning up a suitable mask for what he had to say.

"Dick, I know well that you are a temperate, well-balanced man, even though we do not entirely agree on the subject of alcohol. But a time has come—Dick, I must say frankly that I have been aware several times that you have had a drink when it was not the moment to have one. There is some reason. Why not try another leave of abstinence?"

"Absence," Dick corrected him automatically. "It's no solution for me to go away."

They were both chafed, Franz at having his return marred and blurred.

"Sometimes you don't use your common sense, Dick."

"I never understood what common sense meant applied to complicated problems—unless it means that a general practitioner can perform a better operation than a specialist."

He was seized by an overwhelming disgust for the situation. To explain, to patch—these were not natural functions at their age—better to continue with the cracked echo of an old truth in the ears.

"This is no go," he said suddenly.

"Well, that's occurred to me," Franz admitted. "Your heart isn't in this project any more, Dick."

"I know. I want to leave—we could strike some arrangement about taking Nicole's money out gradually."

"I have thought about that too, Dick—I have seen this coming. I am able to arrange other backing, and it will be possible to take all your money out by the end of the year."

Dick had not intended to come to a decision so quickly, nor was he prepared for Franz's so ready acquiescence in the break, yet he was relieved. Not without desperation he had long felt the ethics of his profession dissolving into a lifeless mass.

IV

THE Divers would return to the Riviera, which was home. The Villa Diana had been rented again for the summer, so they divided the intervening time between German spas and French cathedral towns where they were always happy for a few days. Dick wrote a little with no particular method; it was one of those parts of life that is an awaiting; not upon Nicole's health, which seemed to thrive on travel, nor upon work, but simply an awaiting. The factor that gave purposefulness to the period was the children.

Dick's interest in them increased with their ages, now eleven and nine. He managed to reach them over the heads of employees on the principle that both the forcing of children and the fear of forcing them were inadequate substitutes for the long, careful watchfulness, the checking and balancing and reckoning of accounts, to the end that there should be no slip below a certain level of duty. He came to know them much better than Nicole did, and in expansive moods over the wines of several countries he talked and played with them at length. They had that wistful charm, almost sadness, peculiar to children who have learned early not to cry or laugh with abandon; they were apparently moved to no extremes of emotion, but content with a simple regimentation and the simple pleasures allowed them. They lived on the even tenor found advisable in the experience of old families of the Western world, brought up rather than brought out. Dick thought, for example, that nothing was more conducive to the development of observation than compulsory silence.

Lanier was an unpredictable boy with an inhuman curiosity. "Well, how many Pomeranians would it take to lick a lion, father?" was typical of the questions with which he harassed Dick. Topsy was easier. She was nine and very fair and exquisitely made like Nicole, and in the past Dick had worried about that. Lately she had become as robust as any American child. He was satisfied with them both, but conveyed the fact to them only in a tacit way. They were not let off breaches of good conduct—"Either one learns politeness at home," Dick said, "or the world teaches it to you with a whip and you may get hurt in the process. What do I care whether Topsy 'adores' me or not? I'm not bringing her up to be my wife."

Another element that distinguished this summer and autumn for the Divers was a plenitude of money. Due to the sale of their interest in the clinic, and to developments in America, there was now so much that the mere spending of it, the care of goods, was an absorption in itself. The style in which they traveled seemed fabulous.

Regard them, for example, as the train slows up at Boyen where they are to spend a fortnight visiting. The shifting from the *wagon-lit* has begun at the Italian frontier. The governess's maid and Madame Diver's maid have come up from second class to help with the baggage and the dogs. Mlle. Bellois will superintend the hand-luggage, leaving the Sealyhams to one maid and the pair of Pekinese to the other. It is not necessarily poverty of spirit that makes a woman surround herself with life—it can be a superabundance of interest, and, except during her flashes of illness, Nicole was capable of being curator of it all. For example with the great quantity of heavy baggage—presently from the van would be unloaded four wardrobe trunks, a shoe trunk, three hat trunks, and two hat boxes, a chest of servants' trunks, a portable filing-cabinet, a medicine case, a spirit lamp container, a picnic set, four tennis rackets in presses and cases, a phonograph, a typewriter. Distributed among the spaces reserved for family and entourage were two dozen supplementary grips, satchels and packages, each one numbered, down to the tag on the cane case. Thus all of it could be checked up in two minutes on any station platform, some for storage, some for accompaniment from the "light trip list" or the "heavy trip list," constantly revised, and carried on metal-edged plaques in Nicole's purse. She had devised the system as a child when traveling with her failing mother. It was equivalent to the system of a regimental supply officer who must think of the bellies and equipment of three thousand men.

The Divers flocked from the train into the early gathered twilight of the valley. The village people watched the debarkation with an awe akin to that which followed the Italian pilgrimages of Lord Byron a century before. Their hostess was the Contessa di Minghetti, lately Mary North. The journey that had begun in a room over the shop of a paperhanger in Newark had ended in an extraordinary marriage.

"Conte di Minghetti" was merely a papal title—the wealth of Mary's husband flowed from his being ruler-owner of manganese deposits in southwestern Asia. He was not quite light enough to travel in a Pullman south of Mason-Dixon; he was of the Kyble-Berber-Sabaean-Hindu strain that belts across north Africa and Asia, more sympathetic to the European than the mongrel faces of the ports.

When these princely households, one of the East, one of the West, faced each other on the station platform, the splendor of the Divers seemed pioneer simplicity by comparison. Their hosts were accompanied by an Italian major-domo carrying a staff, by a quartet of turbaned retainers on motorcycles, and by two half-veiled females who stood respectfully a little behind Mary and salaamed at Nicole, making her jump with the gesture.

To Mary as well as to the Divers the greeting was faintly comic; Mary gave an apologetic, belittling giggle; yet her voice, as she introduced her husband by his Asiatic title, flew proud and high.

In their rooms as they dressed for dinner, Dick and Nicole grimaced at each other in an awed way: such rich as want to be thought democratic pretend in private to be swept off their feet by swank.

"Little Mary North knows what she wants," Dick muttered through his shaving cream. "Abe educated her, and now she's married to a Buddha. If Europe ever goes Bolshevik she'll turn up as the bride of Stalin."

Nicole looked around from her dressing-case. "Watch your tongue, Dick, will you?" But she laughed. "They're very swell. The warships all fire at them or salute them or something. Mary rides in the royal bus in London."

"All right," he agreed. As he heard Nicole at the door asking for pins, he called, "I wonder if I could have some whiskey; I feel the mountain air!"

"She'll see to it," presently Nicole called through the bathroom door. "It was one of those women who were at the station. She has her veil off."

"What did Mary tell you about life?" he asked.

"She didn't say so much—she was interested in high life—she asked me a lot of questions about my genealogy and all that sort of thing, as if I knew anything about it. But it seems the bridegroom has two very tan children by another marriage—one of them ill with some Asiatic thing they can't diagnose. I've got to warn the children. Sounds very peculiar to me. Mary will see how we'd feel about it." She stood worrying a minute.

"She'll understand," Dick reassured her. "Probably the child's in bed."

At dinner Dick talked to Hosain, who had been at an English public school. Hosain wanted to know about stocks and about Hollywood and Dick, whipping up his imagination with champagne, told him preposterous tales.

"Billions?" Hosain demanded.

"Trillions," Dick assured him.

"I didn't truly realize——"

"Well, perhaps millions," Dick conceded. "Every hotel guest is assigned a harem—or what amounts to a harem."

"Other than the actors and directors?"

"Every hotel guest—even traveling salesmen. Why, they tried to send me up a dozen candidates, but Nicole wouldn't stand for it."

Nicole reproved him when they were in their room alone. "Why so many highballs? Why did you use your word spic in front of him?"

"Excuse me, I meant smoke. The tongue slipped."

"Dick, this isn't faintly like you."

"Excuse me again. I'm not much like myself any more."

That night Dick opened a bathroom window, giving on a narrow and tubular court of the château, gray as rats but echoing at the moment to plaintive and peculiar music, sad as a flute. Two men were chanting in an Eastern language or dialect full of k's and l's—he leaned out but he could not see them; there was obviously a religious significance in the sounds, and tired and emotionless he let them pray for him too, but what for, save that he should not lose himself in his increasing melancholy, he did not know.

Next day, over a thinly wooded hillside they shot scrawny birds, distant poor relations to the partridge. It was done in a vague imitation of the English manner, with a corps of inexperienced beaters whom Dick managed to miss by firing only directly overhead.

On their return Lanier was waiting in their suite.

"Father, you said tell you immediately if we were near the sick boy."

Nicole whirled about, immediately on guard.

"—so, Mother," Lanier continued, turning to her, "the boy takes a bath every evening and tonight he took his bath just before mine and I had to take mine in his water, and it was dirty."

"What? Now what?"

"I saw them take Tony out of it, and then they called me into it and the water was dirty."

"But—did you take it?"

"Yes, Mother."

"Heavens!" she exclaimed to Dick.

He demanded: "Why didn't Lucienne draw your bath?"

"Lucienne can't. It's a funny heater—it reached out of herself and burned her arm last night and she's afraid of it, so one of those two women——"

"You go in this bathroom and take a bath now."

"Don't say *I* told you," said Lanier from the doorway.

Dick went in and sprinkled the tub with sulphur; closing the door he said to Nicole:

"Either we speak to Mary or we'd better get out."

She agreed and he continued: "People think their children are constitutionally cleaner than other people's, and their diseases are less contagious."

Dick came in and helped himself from the decanter, chewing a biscuit savagely in the rhythm of the pouring water in the bathroom.

"Tell Lucienne that she's got to learn about the heater—" he suggested. At that moment the Asiatic woman came in person to the door.

"*El Contessa*——"

Dick beckoned her inside and closed the door.

"Is the little sick boy better?" he inquired pleasantly.

"Better, yes, but he still has the eruptions frequently."

"That's too bad—I'm very sorry. But you see our children mustn't be bathed in his water. That's out of the question—I'm sure your mistress would be furious if she had known you had done a thing like that."

"I?" She seemed thunderstruck. "Why, I merely saw your maid had difficulty with the heater—I told her about it and started the water."

"But with a sick person you must empty the bath-water entirely out, and clean the tub."

"I?"

Chokingly the woman drew a long breath, uttered a convulsed sob and rushed from the room.

"She mustn't get up on western civilization at our expense," he said grimly.

At dinner that night he decided that it must inevitably be a truncated visit: about his own country Hosain seemed to have observed only that there were many mountains and some goats and herders of goats. He was a reserved young man—to draw him out would have required the sincere effort that Dick now reserved for his family. Soon after dinner Hosain left Mary and the Divers to themselves, but the old unity was split—between them lay the restless social fields that Mary was about to conquer. Dick was relieved when, at nine-thirty, Mary received and read a note and got up.

"You'll have to excuse me. My husband is leaving on a short trip—and I must be with him."

Next morning, hard on the heels of the servant bringing coffee, Mary entered their room. She was dressed and they were not dressed, and she had the air of having been up for some time. Her face was toughened with quiet jerky fury.

"What is this story about Lanier having been bathed in a dirty bath?"

Dick began to protest, but she cut through:

"*What* is this story that you commanded my husband's sister to clean Lanier's tub?"

She remained on her feet staring at them, as they sat

impotent as idols in their beds, weighted by their trays. Together they exclaimed: "His *sister!*"

"That you ordered one of his sisters to clean out a tub!"

"We didn't—" their voices rang together saying the same thing, "—I spoke to the native servant——"

"You spoke to Hosain's sister."

Dick could only say: "I supposed they were two maids."

"You were told they were Himadoun."

"What?" Dick got out of bed and into a robe.

"I explained it to you at the piano night before last. Don't tell me you were too merry to understand."

"Was that what you said? I didn't hear the beginning. I didn't connect the—we didn't make any connection, Mary. Well, all we can do is see her and apologize."

"See her and apologize! I explained to you that when the oldest member of the family—when the oldest one marries, well, the two oldest sisters consecrate themselves to being Himadoun, to being his wife's ladies-in-waiting."

"Was that why Hosain left the house last night?"

Mary hesitated; then nodded.

"He had to—they all left. His honor makes it necessary."

Now both the Divers were up and dressing; Mary went on:

"And what's all that about the bathwater. As if a thing like that could happen in this house! We'll ask Lanier about it."

Dick sat on the bedside indicating in a private gesture to Nicole that she should take over. Meanwhile Mary went to the door and spoke to an attendant in Italian.

"Wait a minute," Nicole said. "I won't have that."

"You accused us," answered Mary, in a tone she had never used to Nicole before. "Now I have a right to see."

"I won't have the child brought in." Nicole threw on her clothes as though they were chain mail.

"That's all right," said Dick. "Bring Lanier in. We'll settle this bathtub matter—fact or myth."

Lanier, half clothed mentally and physically, gazed at the angered faces of the adults.

"Listen, Lanier," Mary demanded, "how did you come to think you were bathed in water that had been used before?"

"Speak up," Dick added.

"It was just dirty, that was all."

"Couldn't you hear the new water running, from your room, next door?"

Lanier admitted the possibility but reiterated his point—the water was dirty. He was a little awed; he tried to see ahead:

"It couldn't have been running, because——"

They pinned him down.

"Why not?"

He stood in his little kimono arousing the sympathy of his parents and further arousing Mary's impatience—then he said:

"The water was dirty, it was full of soap-suds."

"When you're not sure what you're saying—" Mary began, but Nicole interrupted.

"Stop it, Mary. If there were dirty suds in the water it was logical to think it was dirty. His father told him to come——"

"There couldn't have been dirty suds in the water."

Lanier looked reproachfully at his father, who had betrayed him. Nicole turned him about by the shoulders and sent him out of the room; Dick broke the tensity with a laugh.

Then, as if the sound recalled the past, the old friendship, Mary guessed how far away from them she had gone and said in a mollifying tone: "It's always like that with children."

Her uneasiness grew as she remembered the past. "You'd be silly to go—Hosain wanted to make this trip anyhow. After all, you're my guests and you just blundered into the thing." But Dick, made more angry by this obliqueness and the use of the word blunder, turned away and began arranging his effects, saying:

"It's too bad about the young women. I'd like to apologize to the one who came in here."

"If you'd only listened on the piano seat!"

"But you've gotten so damned dull, Mary. I listened as long as I could."

"Be quiet!" Nicole advised him.

"I return his compliment," said Mary bitterly. "Good-by, Nicole." She went out.

After all that there was no question of her coming to see them off; the major-domo arranged the departure. Dick left formal notes for Hosain and the sisters. There was nothing to do except to go, but all of them, especially Lanier, felt bad about it.

"I insist," insisted Lanier on the train, "that it was dirty bathwater."

"That'll do," his father said. "You better forget it—unless you want me to divorce you. Did you know there was a new law in France that you can divorce a child?"

Lanier roared with delight and the Divers were unified again—Dick wondered how many more times it could be done.

V

NICOLE went to the window and bent over the sill to take a look at the rising altercation on the terrace; the April sun shone pink on the saintly face of Augustine, the cook, and blue on the butcher's knife she waved in her drunken hand. She had been with them since their return to Villa Diana in February.

Because of an obstruction of an awning she could see only Dick's head and his hand holding one of his heavy canes with a bronze knob on it. The knife and the cane, menacing each other, were like tripos and short sword in a gladiatorial combat. Dick's words reached her first:

"—care how much kitchen wine you drink but when I find you digging into a bottle of Chablis Moutonne——"

"You talk about drinking!" Augustine cried, flourishing her saber. "You drink—all the time!"

Nicole called over the awning: "What's the matter, Dick?" and he answered in English:

"The old girl has been polishing off the vintage wines. I'm firing her—at least I'm trying to."

"Heavens! Well, don't let her reach you with that knife."

Augustine shook her knife up at Nicole. Her old mouth was made of two small intersecting cherries.

"I would like to say, Madame, if you knew that your husband drinks over at his Bastide comparatively as a day laborer——"

"Shut up and get out!" interrupted Nicole. "We'll get the gendarmes."

"*You'll* get the gendarmes! With my brother in the corps! You—a disgusting American?"

In English Dick called up to Nicole:

"Get the children away from the house till I settle this."

"—disgusting Americans who come here and drink up our finest wines," screamed Augustine with the voice of the commune.

Dick mastered a firmer tone.

"You must leave now! I'll pay you what we owe you."

"Very sure you'll pay me! And let me tell you—" she came close and waved the knife so furiously that Dick raised his stick, whereupon she rushed into the kitchen and returned with the carving knife reinforced by a hatchet.

The situation was not prepossessing—Augustine was a strong woman and could be disarmed only at the risk of serious results to herself—and severe legal complications which were the lot of one who molested a French citizen. Trying a bluff Dick called up to Nicole:

"Phone the *poste de police.*" Then to Augustine, indicating her armament, "This means arrest for you."

"Ha-*ha!*" she laughed demoniacally; nevertheless she came no nearer. Nicole phoned the police but was answered with what was almost an echo of Augustine's laugh. She heard mumbles and passings of the word around—the connection was suddenly broken.

Returning to the window she called down to Dick: "Give her something extra!"

"If I could get to that phone!" As this seemed impracticable, Dick capitulated. For fifty francs, increased to a hundred as he succumbed to the idea of getting her out hastily, Augustine yielded her fortress, covering the retreat with stormy grenades of "*Salud!*" She would leave only when her nephew could come for her baggage. Waiting cautiously in the neighborhood of the kitchen Dick heard a cork pop, but he yielded the point.

There was no further trouble—when the nephew arrived, all apologetic, Augustine bade Dick a cheerful, convivial good-by and called up *"Au revoir, Madame! Bonne chance!"* to Nicole's window.

The Divers went to Nice and dined on a bouillabaisse, which is a stew of rock fish and small lobsters, highly seasoned with saffron, and a bottle of cold Chablis. He expressed pity for Augustine.

"I'm not sorry a bit," said Nicole.

"I'm sorry—and yet I wish I'd shoved her over the cliff."

There was little they dared talk about in these days; seldom did they find the right word when it counted, it arrived always a moment too late when one could not reach the other any more. Tonight Augustine's outburst had shaken them from their separate reveries; with the burn and chill of the spiced broth and the parching wine they talked.

"We can't go on like this," Nicole suggested. "Or can we?—what do you think?" Startled that for the moment Dick did not deny it, she continued, "Some of the time I think it's my fault—I've ruined you."

"So I'm ruined, am I?" he inquired pleasantly.

"I didn't mean that. But you used to want to create things—now you seem to want to smash them up."

She trembled at criticizing him in these broad terms—but his enlarging silence frightened her even more. She guessed that something was developing behind the silence, behind the hard, blue eyes, the almost unnatural interest in the children. Uncharacteristic bursts of temper surprised her—he would suddenly unroll a long scroll of contempt for some person, race, class, way of life, way of thinking. It was as though an incalculable story was telling itself inside him, about which she could only guess at in the moments when it broke through the surface.

"After all, what do you get out of this?" she demanded.

"Knowing you're stronger every day. Knowing that your illness follows the law of diminishing returns."

His voice came to her from far off, as though he were speaking of something remote and academic; her alarm made her exclaim, "Dick!" and she thrust her hand forward to his across the table. A reflex pulled Dick's hand back and he added:

"There's the whole situation to think of, isn't there? There's not just you." He covered her hand with his and said in the old pleasant voice of a conspirator for pleasure, mischief, profit, and delight: "See that boat out there?"

It was the motor yacht of T. F. Golding lying placid among the little swells of the Nicean Bay, constantly bound upon a romantic voyage that was not dependent upon actual motion. "We'll go out there now and ask the people on board what's the matter with them. We'll find out if they're happy."

"We hardly know him," Nicole objected.

"He urged us. Besides, Baby knows him—she practically married him, doesn't she—didn't she?"

When they put out from the port in a hired launch it was already summer dusk and lights were breaking out in spasms along the rigging of the Margin. As they drew up alongside, Nicole's doubts reasserted themselves.

"He's having a party——"

"It's only a radio," he guessed.

They were hailed—a huge white-haired man in a white suit looked down at them, calling:

"Do I recognize the Divers?"

"Boat ahoy, Margin!"

Their boat moved under the companionway; as they mounted Golding doubled his huge frame to give Nicole a hand.

"Just in time for dinner."

A small orchestra was playing astern.

"I'm yours for the asking—
but till then you can't ask me to behave——"

And as Golding's cyclonic arms blew them aft without touching them, Nicole was sorrier they had come, and more impatient at Dick. Having taken up an attitude of aloofness from the gay people here, at the time when Dick's work and her health were incompatible with going about, they had a reputation as refusers. Riviera replacements during the ensuing years interpreted this as a vague unpopularity. Nevertheless, having taken such a stand, Nicole felt it should not be cheaply compromised for a momentary self-indulgence.

As they passed through the principal salon they saw ahead of them figures that seemed to dance in the half light of the circular stern. This was an illusion made by the enchantment of the music, the unfamiliar lighting, and the surrounding presence of water. Actually, save for some busy stewards, the guests loafed on a wide divan that followed the curve of the deck. There were a white, a red, a blurred dress, the laundered chests of several men, of whom one, detaching and identifying himself, brought from Nicole a rare little cry of delight.

"Tommy!"

Brushing aside the Gallicism of his formal dip at her hand, Nicole pressed her face against his. They sat, or rather lay down together on the Antoninian bench.

His handsome face was so dark as to have lost the pleasantness of deep tan, without attaining the blue beauty of Negroes—it was just worn leather. The foreignness of his pigmentation by unknown suns, his nourishment by strange soils, his tongue awkward with the curl of many dialects, his reactions attuned to odd alarms—these things fascinated and rested Nicole—in the moment of meeting she lay on his bosom, spiritually, going out and out. . . . Then self-preservation reasserted itself and retiring to her own world she spoke lightly.

"You look just like all the adventurers in the movies—but why do you have to stay away so long?"

Tommy Barban looked at her, uncomprehending but alert; the pupils of his eyes flashed.

"Five years," she continued, in throaty mimicry of nothing. "*Much* too long. Couldn't you only slaughter a certain number of creatures and then come back, and breathe our air for a while?"

In her cherished presence Tommy Europeanized himself quickly.

"*Mais pour nous héros,*" he said, "*il nous faut du temps, Nicole. Nous ne pouvons pas faire de petits exercises d'héroisme—il faut faire les grandes compositions.*"

"Talk English to me, Tommy."

"*Parlez français avec moi, Nicole.*"

"But the meanings are different—in French you can be heroic and gallant with dignity, and you know it. But in English you can't be heroic and gallant without being a little absurd, and you know that too. That gives me an advantage."

"But after all—" He chuckled suddenly. "Even in English I'm brave, heroic and all that."

She pretended to be groggy with wonderment but he was not abashed.

"I only know what I see in the cinema," he said.

"Is it all like the movies?"

"The movies aren't so bad—now this Ronald Colman —have you seen his pictures about the Corps d'Afrique du Nord? They're not bad at all."

"Very well, whenever I go to the movies I'll know you're going through just that sort of thing at that moment."

As she spoke, Nicole was aware of a small, pale, pretty young woman with lovely metallic hair, almost green in the deck lights, who had been sitting on the other side of Tommy and might have been part either of their conversation or of the one next to them. She had obviously had a monopoly of Tommy, for now she abandoned hope of his attention with what was once called ill grace, and petulantly crossed the crescent of the deck.

"After all, I am a hero," Tommy said calmly, only half joking. "I have ferocious courage, *us*ually, something like a lion, something like a drunken man."

Nicole waited until the echo of his boast had died away in his mind—she knew he had probably never made such a statement before. Then she looked among the strangers, and found as usual, the fierce neurotics, pretending calm, liking the country only in horror of the city, of the sound of their own voices which had set the tone and pitch. . . . She asked:

"Who is the woman in white?"

"The one who was beside me? Lady Caroline Sibly-Biers."—They listened for a moment to her voice across the way:

"The man's a scoundrel, but he's a cat of the stripe. We sat up all night playing two-handed chemin-de-fer, and he owes me a mille Swiss."

Tommy laughed and said: "She is now the wickedest

woman in London—whenever I come back to Europe there is a new crop of the wickedest women from London. She's the very latest—though I believe there is now one other who's considered almost as wicked."

Nicole glanced again at the woman across the deck—she was fragile, tubercular—it was incredible that such narrow shoulders, such puny arms could bear aloft the pennon of decadence, last ensign of the fading empire. Her resemblance was rather to one of John Held's flat-chested flappers than to the hierarchy of tall languid blondes who had posed for painters and novelists since before the war.

Golding approached, fighting down the resonance of his huge bulk, which transmitted his will as through a gargantuan amplifier, and Nicole, still reluctant, yielded to his reiterated points: that the Margin was starting for Cannes immediately after dinner; that they could always pack in some caviare and champagne, even though they had dined; that in any case Dick was now on the phone, telling their chauffeur in Nice to drive their car back to Cannes and leave it in front of the Café des Alliés where the Divers could retrieve it.

They moved into the dining salon and Dick was placed next to Lady Sibly-Biers. Nicole saw that his usually ruddy face was drained of blood; he talked in a dogmatic voice, of which only snatches reached Nicole:

". . . It's all right for you English, you're doing a dance of death. . . . Sepoys in the ruined fort, I mean Sepoys at the gate and gaiety in the fort and all that. The green hat, the crushed hat, no future."

Lady Caroline answered him in short sentences spotted with the terminal "What?" the double-edged "Quite!" the depressing "Cheerio!" that always had a connotation of imminent peril, but Dick appeared oblivious to the warning signals. Suddenly he made a particularly vehement pronouncement, the purport of which eluded Nicole, but she saw the young woman turn dark and sinewy, and heard her answer sharply:

"After all a chep's a chep and a chum's a chum."

Again he had offended some one—couldn't he hold his tongue a little longer? How long? To death then.

At the piano, a fair-haired young Scotsman from the orchestra (entitled by its drum "The Ragtime College Jazzes of Edinboro") had begun singing in a Danny Deever monotone, accompanying himself with low chords on the piano. He pronounced his words with great precision, as though they impressed him almost intolerably.

"There was a young lady from hell,
Who jumped at the sound of a bell,
Because she was bad—bad—bad,
She jumped at the sound of a bell,
From hell (BOOMBOOM)
From hell (TOOTTOOT)
There was a young lady from hell——"

"What is all this?" whispered Tommy to Nicole.

The girl on the other side of him supplied the answer:

"Caroline Sibly-Biers wrote the words. He wrote the music."

"Quelle enfanterie!" Tommy murmured as the next verse began, hinting at the jumpy lady's further predilections. *"On dirait qu'il récite Racine!"*

On the surface at least, Lady Caroline was paying no attention to the performance of her work. Glancing at her again Nicole found herself impressed, neither with the character nor the personality, but with the sheer strength derived from an attitude; Nicole thought that she was formidable, and she was confirmed in this point of view as the party rose from table. Dick remained in his seat wearing an odd expression; then he crashed into words with a harsh ineptness.

"I don't like innuendo in these deafening English whispers."

Already half-way out of the room Lady Caroline turned and walked back to him; she spoke in a low clipped voice purposely audible to the whole company.

"You came to me asking for it—disparaging my countrymen, disparaging my friend, Mary Minghetti. I simply said you were observed associating with a questionable crowd in Lausanne. Is that a deafening whisper? Or does it simply deafen *you?*"

"It's still not loud enough," said Dick, a little too late. "So I am actually a notorious——"

Golding crushed out the phrase with his voice saying: "What! What!" and moved his guests on out, with the threat of his powerful body. Turning the corner of the door Nicole saw that Dick was still sitting at the table. She was furious at the woman for her preposterous statement, equally furious at Dick for having brought them here, for having become fuddled, for having untipped the capped barbs of his irony, for having come off humiliated—she was a little more annoyed because she knew that her taking possession of Tommy Barban on their arrival had first irritated the Englishwoman.

A moment later she saw Dick standing in the gangway, apparently in complete control of himself as he talked with Golding; then for half an hour she did not see him anywhere about the deck and she broke out of an intricate Malay game, played with string and coffee beans, and said to Tommy:

"I've got to find Dick."

Since dinner the yacht had been in motion westward. The fine night streamed away on either side, the Diesel engines pounded softly, there was a spring wind that blew Nicole's hair abruptly when she reached the bow, and she had a sharp lesion of anxiety at seeing Dick standing in the angle by the flagstaff. His voice was serene as he recognized her.

"It's a nice night."

"I was worried."

"Oh, you were worried?"

"Oh, don't talk that way. It would give me so much pleasure to think of a little something I could do for you, Dick."

He turned away from her, toward the veil of starlight over Africa.

"I believe that's true, Nicole. And sometimes I believe that the littler it was, the more pleasure it would give you."

"Don't talk like that—don't say such things."

His face, wan in the light that the white spray caught and tossed back to the brilliant sky had none of the lines of annoyance she had expected. It was even detached; his eyes focused upon her gradually as upon a chessman to be moved; in the same slow manner he caught her wrist and drew her near.

"You ruined me, did you?" he inquired blandly. "Then we're both ruined. So——"

Cold with terror she put her other wrist into his grip. All right, she would go with him—again she felt the beauty of the night vividly in one moment of complete response and abnegation—all right, then——

—But now she was unexpectedly free and Dick turned his back sighing, "Tch! tch!"

Tears streamed down Nicole's face—in a moment she heard some one approaching; it was Tommy.

"You found him! Nicole thought maybe you jumped overboard, Dick," he said, "because that little English *poule* slanged you."

"It'd be a good setting to jump overboard," said Dick mildly.

"Wouldn't it?" agreed Nicole hastily. "Let's borrow life-preservers and jump over. I think we should do something spectacular. I feel that all our lives have been too restrained."

Tommy sniffed from one to the other trying to breathe in the situation with the night. "We'll go ask the Lady Beer-and-Ale what to do—she should know the latest things. And we should memorize her song 'There was a young lady from *l'enfer*.' I shall translate it, and make a fortune from its success at the Casino."

"Are you rich, Tommy?" Dick asked him, as they retraced the length of the boat.

"Not as things go now. I got tired of the brokerage business and went away. But I have good stocks in the hands of friends who are holding it for me. All goes well."

"Dick's getting rich," Nicole said. In reaction her voice had begun to tremble.

On the after deck Golding had fanned three pairs of dancers into action with his colossal paws. Nicole and Tommy joined them and Tommy remarked: "Dick seems to be drinking."

"Only moderately," she said loyally.

"There are those who can drink and those who can't. Obviously Dick can't. You ought to tell him not to."

"I!" she exclaimed in amazement. "*I* tell Dick what he should do or shouldn't do!"

But in a reticent way Dick was still vague and sleepy when they reached the pier at Cannes. Golding buoyed him down into the launch of the Margin whereupon Lady Caroline shifted her place conspicuously. On the dock he bowed good-by with exaggerated formality, and for a moment he seemed about to speed her with a salty epigram, but the bone of Tommy's arm went into the soft part of his and they walked to the attendant car.

"I'll drive you home," Tommy suggested.

"Don't bother—we can get a cab."

"I'd like to, if you can put me up."

On the back seat of the car Dick remained quiescent until the yellow monolith of Golfe Juan was passed, and then the constant carnival at Juan les Pins where the night was musical and strident in many languages. When the car turned up the hill toward Tarmes, he sat up suddenly, prompted by the tilt of the vehicle and delivered a peroration:

"A charming representative of the—" he stumbled momentarily, "—a firm of—bring me Brains addled *à l'Anglaise.*" Then he went into an appeased sleep, belching now and then contentedly into the soft warm darkness.

VI

NEXT morning Dick came early into Nicole's room. "I waited till I heard you up. Needless to say I feel badly about the evening—but how about no post-mortems?"

"I'm agreed," she answered coolly, carrying her face to the mirror.

"Tommy drove us home? Or did I dream it?"

"You know he did."

"Seems probable," he admitted, "since I just heard him coughing. I think I'll call on him."

She was glad when he left her, for almost the first time in her life—his awful faculty of being right seemed to have deserted him at last.

Tommy was stirring in his bed, waking for café au lait.

"Feel all right?" Dick asked.

When Tommy complained of a sore throat he seized at a professional attitude.

"Better have a gargle or something."

"You have one?"

"Oddly enough I haven't—probably Nicole has."

"Don't disturb her."

"She's up."

"How is she?"

Dick turned around slowly. "Did you expect her to be dead because I was tight?" His tone was pleasant. "Nicole is now made of—of Georgia pine, which is the hardest wood known, except lignum vitæ from New Zealand——"

Nicole, going downstairs, heard the end of the conversation. She knew, as she had always known, that Tommy loved her; she knew he had come to dislike Dick, and that Dick had realized it before he did, and would react in some positive way to the man's lonely passion. This thought was succeeded by a moment of sheerly feminine satisfaction. She leaned over her children's breakfast table and told off instructions to the governess, while upstairs two men were concerned about her.

Later in the garden she was happy; she did not want anything to happen, but only for the situation to remain in suspension as the two men tossed her from one mind to another; she had not existed for a long time, even as a ball.

"Nice, Rabbits, isn't it— Or is it? Hey, Rabbit—hey you! Is it nice?—hey? Or does it sound very peculiar to you?"

The rabbit, after an experience of practically nothing else and cabbage leaves, agreed after a few tentative shiftings of the nose.

Nicole went on through her garden routine. She left

the flowers she cut in designated spots to be brought to the house later by the gardener. Reaching the sea wall she fell into a communicative mood and no one to communicate with; so she stopped and deliberated. She was somewhat shocked at the idea of being interested in another man—but other women have lovers—why not me? In the fine spring morning the inhibitions of the male world disappeared and she reasoned as gaily as a flower, while the wind blew her hair until her head moved with it. Other women have had lovers—the same forces that last night had made her yield to Dick up to the point of death, now kept her head nodding to the wind, content and happy with the logic of, Why shouldn't I?

She sat upon the low wall and looked down upon the sea. But from another sea, the wide swell of fantasy, she had fished out something tangible to lay beside the rest of her loot. If she need not, in her spirit, be forever one with Dick as he had appeared last night, she must be something in addition, not just an image on his mind, condemned to endless parades around the circumference of a medal.

Nicole had chosen this part of the wall on which to sit, because the cliff shaded to a slanting meadow with a cultivated vegetable garden. Through a cluster of boughs she saw two men carrying rakes and spades and talking in a counterpoint of Niçoise and Provençal. Attracted by their words and gestures she caught the sense:

"I laid her down here."

"I took her behind the vines there."

"She doesn't care—neither does he. It was that sacred dog. Well, I laid her down here——"

"You got the rake?"

"You got it yourself, you clown."

"Well, I don't care where you laid her down. Until that night I never even felt a woman's breast against my chest since I married—twelve years ago. And now you tell me——"

"But listen about the dog——"

Nicole watched them through the boughs; it seemed all right what they were saying—one thing was good for one person, another for another. Yet it was a man's world she had overheard; going back to the house she became doubtful again.

Dick and Tommy were on the terrace. She walked through them and into the house, brought out a sketch pad and began a head of Tommy.

"Hands never idle—distaff flying," Dick said lightly. How could he talk so trivially with the blood still drained down from his cheeks so that the auburn lather of beard showed red as his eyes? She turned to Tommy saying:

"I can always do something. I used to have a nice active little Polynesian ape and juggle him around for hours till people began to make the most dismal rough jokes——"

She kept her eyes resolutely away from Dick. Presently he excused himself and went inside—she saw him pour himself two glasses of water, and she hardened further.

"Nicole—" Tommy began but interrupted himself to clear the harshness from his throat.

"I'm going to get you some special camphor rub," she suggested. "It's American—Dick believes in it. I'll be just a minute."

"I must go really."

Dick came out and sat down. "Believes in what?"

When she returned with the jar neither of the men had moved, though she gathered they had had some sort of excited conversation about nothing.

The chauffeur was at the door, with a bag containing Tommy's clothes of the night before. The sight of Tommy in clothes borrowed from Dick moved her sadly, falsely, as though Tommy were not able to afford such clothes.

"When you get to the hotel rub this into your throat and chest and then inhale it," she said.

"Say, there," Dick murmured as Tommy went down the steps, "don't give Tommy the whole jar—it has to be ordered from Paris—it's out of stock down here."

Tommy came back within hearing and the three of them stood in the sunshine, Tommy squarely before the car so that it seemed by leaning forward he would tip it upon his back.

Nicole stepped down to the path.

"Now catch it," she advised him. "It's extremely rare."

She heard Dick grow silent at her side; she took a step off from him and waved as the car drove off with Tommy and the special camphor rub. Then she turned to take her own medicine.

"There was no necessity for that gesture," Dick said. "There are four of us here—and for years whenever there's a cough——"

They looked at each other.

"We can always get another jar—" then she lost her nerve and presently followed him upstairs where he lay down on his own bed and said nothing.

"Do you want lunch to be brought up to you?" she asked.

He nodded and continued to lie quiescent, staring at the ceiling. Doubtfully she went to give the order. Upstairs again she looked into his room—the blue eyes, like searchlights, played on a dark sky. She stood a minute in the doorway, aware of the sin she had committed against him, half afraid to come in. . . . She put out her hand as if to rub his head, but he turned away like a suspicious animal. Nicole could stand the situation no longer; in a kitchen-maid's panic she ran downstairs, afraid of what the stricken man above would feed on while she must still continue her dry suckling at his lean chest.

In a week Nicole forgot her flash about Tommy—she had not much memory for people and forgot them easily. But in the first hot blast of June she heard he was in Nice. He wrote a little note to them both—and she opened it under the parasol, together with other mail they had brought from the house. After reading it she tossed it over to Dick, and in exchange he threw a telegram into the lap of her beach pajamas:

"Dears will be at Gausses to-morrow unfortunately without mother am counting on seeing you.

ROSEMARY."

"I'll be glad to see her," said Nicole, grimly.

VII

BUT she went to the beach with Dick next morning with a renewal of her apprehension that Dick was contriving at some desperate solution. Since the evening on Golding's yacht she had sensed what was going on. So delicately balanced was she between an old foothold that had always guaranteed her security, and the imminence of a leap from which she must alight changed in the very chemistry of blood and muscle, that she did not dare bring the matter into the true forefront of consciousness. The figures of Dick and herself, mutating, undefined, appeared as spooks caught up into a fantastic dance. For months every word had seemed to have an overtone of some other meaning, soon to be resolved under circumstances that Dick would determine. Though this state of mind was perhaps more hopeful,—the long years of sheer being had had an enlivening effect on the parts of her nature that early illness had killed, that Dick had not reached—through no fault of his but simply because no one nature can extend entirely inside another—it was still disquieting. The most unhappy aspect of their relations was Dick's growing indifference, at present personified by too much drink; Nicole did not know whether she was to be crushed or spared—Dick's voice, throbbing with insincerity, confused the issue; she couldn't guess how he was going to behave next upon the tortuously slow unrolling of the carpet, nor what would happen at the end, at the moment of the leap.

For what might occur thereafter she had no anxiety—she suspected that that would be the lifting of a burden, an unblinding of eyes. Nicole had been designed for change, for flight, with money as fins and wings. The new state of things would be no more than if a racing chassis, concealed for years under the body of a family limousine, should be stripped to its original self. Nicole could feel the fresh breeze already—the wrench it was she feared, and the dark manner of its coming.

The Divers went out on the beach with her white suit and his white trunks very white against the color of their bodies. Nicole saw Dick peer about for the children among the confused shapes and shadows of many umbrellas, and as his mind temporarily left her, ceasing to grip her, she looked at him with detachment, and decided that he was seeking his children, not protectively but for protection. Probably it was the beach he feared, like a deposed ruler secretly visiting an old court. She had come to hate his world with its delicate jokes and politenesses, forgetting that for many years it was the only world open to her. Let him look at it—his beach, perverted now to the tastes of the tasteless; he could search it for a day and find no stone of the Chinese Wall he had once erected around it, no footprint of an old friend.

For a moment Nicole was sorry it was so; remembering the glass he had raked out of the old trash heap, remembering the sailor trunks and sweaters they had bought in a Nice back street—garments that afterward ran through a vogue in silk among the Paris *couturiers,* remembering the simple little French girls climbing on the breakwaters crying *"Dîtes donc! Dîtes donc!"* like birds, and the ritual of the morning time, the quiet restful extraversion toward sea and sun—many inventions of his, buried deeper than the sand under the span of so few years. . . .

Now the swimming place was a "club," though, like the international society it represented, it would be hard to say who was not admitted.

Nicole hardened again as Dick knelt on the straw mat and looked about for Rosemary. Her eyes followed his, searching among the new paraphernalia, the trapezes over the water, the swinging rings, the portable bathhouses, the floating towers, the searchlights from last night's fêtes, the modernistic buffet, white with a hackneyed motif of endless handlebars.

The water was almost the last place he looked for Rosemary, because few people swam any more in that blue paradise, children and one exhibitionistic valet who punctuated the morning with spectacular dives from a fifty-foot rock—most of Gausse's guests stripped the concealing pajamas from their flabbiness only for a short hangover dip at one o'clock.

"There she is," Nicole remarked.

She watched Dick's eyes following Rosemary's track from raft to raft; but the sigh that rocked out of her bosom was something left over from five years ago.

"Let's swim out and speak to Rosemary," he suggested.

"You go."

"We'll both go." She struggled a moment against his pronouncement, but eventually they swam out together, tracing Rosemary by the school of little fish who followed her, taking their dazzle from her, the shining spoon of a trout hook.

Nicole stayed in the water while Dick hoisted himself up beside Rosemary, and the two sat dripping and talking, exactly as if they had never loved or touched each other. Rosemary was beautiful—her youth was a shock to Nicole, who rejoiced, however, that the young girl was less slender by a hairline than herself. Nicole swam around in little rings, listening to Rosemary who was acting amusement, joy, and expectation—more confident than she had been five years ago.

"I miss Mother so, but she's meeting me in Paris, Monday."

"Five years ago you came here," said Dick. "And what a funny little thing you were, in one of those hotel peignoirs!"

"How you remember things! You always did—and always the nice things."

Nicole saw the old game of flattery beginning again and she dove under water, coming up again to hear:

"I'm going to pretend it's five years ago and I'm a girl of eighteen again. You could always make me feel some you know, kind of, you know, kind of happy way—you and Nicole. I feel as if you're still on the beach there, under one of those umbrellas—the nicest people I'd ever known, maybe ever will."

Swimming away, Nicole saw that the cloud of Dick's heartsickness had lifted a little as he began to play with Rosemary, bringing out his old expertness with people, a tarnished object of art; she guessed that with a drink or so he would have done his stunts on the swinging rings for her, fumbling through stunts he had once done with ease. She noticed that this summer, for the first time, he avoided high diving.

Later, as she dodged her way from raft to raft, Dick overtook her.

"Some of Rosemary's friends have a speed boat, the one out there. Do you want to aquaplane? I think it would be amusing."

Remembering that once he could stand on his hands on a chair at the end of a board, she indulged him as she might have indulged Lanier. Last summer on the Zugersee they had played at that pleasant water game, and Dick had lifted a two-hundred-pound man from the board onto his shoulders and stood up. But women marry all their husbands' talents and naturally, afterward, are not so impressed with them as they may keep up the pretense of being. Nicole had not even pretended to be impressed, though she had said "Yes" to him, and "Yes, I thought so too."

She knew, though, that he was somewhat tired, that it was only the closeness of Rosemary's exciting youth that prompted the impending effort—she had seen him draw the same inspiration from the new bodies of her children and she wondered coldly if he would make a spectacle of himself. The Divers were older than the others in the boat—the young people were polite, deferential, but Nicole felt an undercurrent of "Who are these Numbers anyhow?" and she missed Dick's easy talent of taking control of situations and making them all right—he had concentrated on what he was going to try to do.

The motor throttled down two hundred yards from shore and one of the young men dove flat over the edge. He swam at the aimless twisting board, steadied it, climbed slowly to his knees on it—then got on his feet as the boat accelerated. Leaning back he swung his light vehicle ponderously from side to side in slow, breathless arcs that rode the trailing side-swell at the end of each swing. In the direct wake of the boat he let go his rope, balanced for a moment, then back-flipped into the water, disappearing like a statue of glory, and reappearing as an insignificant head while the boat made the circle back to him.

Nicole refused her turn; then Rosemary rode the board neatly and conservatively, with facetious cheers from her admirers. Three of them scrambled egotistically for the honor of pulling her into the boat, managing, among them, to bruise her knee and hip against the side.

"Now you, Doctor," said the Mexican at the wheel.

Dick and the last young man dove over the side and swam to the board. Dick was going to try his lifting trick and Nicole began to watch with smiling scorn. This physical showing-off for Rosemary irritated her most of all.

When the men had ridden long enough to find their balance, Dick knelt, and putting the back of his neck in the other man's crotch, found the rope through his legs, and slowly began to rise.

The people in the boat, watching closely, saw that he was having difficulties. He was on one knee; the trick was to straighten all the way up in the same motion with which he left his kneeling position. He rested for a moment, then his face contracted as he put his heart into the strain, and lifted.

The board was narrow, the man, though weighing less than a hundred and fifty, was awkward with his weight and grabbed clumsily at Dick's head. When, with a last wrenching effort of his back, Dick stood upright, the board slid sidewise and the pair toppled into the sea.

In the boat Rosemary exclaimed: "Wonderful! They almost had it."

But as they came back to the swimmers Nicole watched for a sight of Dick's face. It was full of annoyance as she expected, because he had done the thing with ease only two years ago.

The second time he was more careful. He rose a little, testing the balance of his burden, settled down again on his knee; then, grunting "Alley oop!" began to rise —but before he could really straighten out, his legs suddenly buckled and he shoved the board away with his feet to avoid being struck as they fell off.

This time when the Baby Gar came back it was apparent to all the passengers that he was angry.

"Do you mind if I try that once more?" he called, treading water. "We almost had it then."

"Sure. Go ahead."

To Nicole he looked white-around-the-gills, and she cautioned him:

"Don't you think that's enough for now?"

He didn't answer. The first partner had had plenty and was hauled over the side, the Mexican driving the motor boat obligingly took his place.

He was heavier than the first man. As the boat gathered motion, Dick rested for a moment, belly-down on the board. Then he got beneath the man and took the rope, and his muscles flexed as he tried to rise.

He could not rise. Nicole saw him shift his position and strain upward again but at the instant when the weight of his partner was full upon his shoulders he became immovable. He tried again—lifting an inch, two inches—Nicole felt the sweat glands of her forehead open as she strained with him—then he was simply holding his ground, then he collapsed back down on his knees with a smack, and they went over, Dick's head barely missing a kick of the board.

"Hurry back!" Nicole called to the driver; even as she spoke she saw him slide under water and she gave a little cry; but he came up again and turned on his back, and "Château" swam near to help. It seemed forever till the boat reached them but when they came alongside at last and Nicole saw Dick floating exhausted and expressionless, alone with the water and the sky, her panic changed suddenly to contempt.

"We'll help you up, Doctor. . . . Get his foot . . . all right . . . now altogether. . . ."

Dick sat panting and looking at nothing.

"I knew you shouldn't have tried it," Nicole could not help saying.

"He'd tired himself the first two times," said the Mexican.

"It was a foolish thing," Nicole insisted. Rosemary tactfully said nothing.

After a minute Dick got his breath, panting, "I couldn't have lifted a paper doll that time."

An explosive little laugh relieved the tension caused by his failure. They were all attentive to Dick as he disembarked at the dock. But Nicole was annoyed—everything he did annoyed her now.

She sat with Rosemary under an umbrella while Dick

went to the buffet for a drink—he returned presently with some sherry for them.

"The first drink I ever had was with you," Rosemary said, and with a spurt of enthusiasm she added, "Oh, I'm so glad to see you and *know* you're all right. I was worried—" Her sentence broke as she changed direction "that maybe you wouldn't be."

"Did you hear I'd gone into a process of deterioration?"

"Oh, no. I simply—just heard you'd changed. And I'm glad to see with my own eyes it isn't true."

"It is true," Dick answered, sitting down with them. "The change came a long way back—but at first it didn't show. The manner remains intact for some time after the morale cracks."

"Do you practise on the Riviera?" Rosemary demanded hastily.

"It'd be a good ground to find likely specimens." He nodded here and there at the people milling about in the golden sand. "Great candidates. Notice our old friend, Mrs. Abrams, playing duchess to Mary North's queen? Don't get jealous about it—think of Mrs. Abram's long climb up the back stairs of the Ritz on her hands and knees and all the carpet dust she had to inhale."

Rosemary interrupted him. "But is that really Mary North?" She was regarding a woman sauntering in their direction followed by a small group who behaved as if they were accustomed to being looked at. When they were ten feet away, Mary's glance flickered fractionally over the Divers, one of those unfortunate glances that indicate to the glanced-upon that they have been observed but are to be overlooked, the sort of glance that neither the Divers nor Rosemary Hoyt had ever permitted themselves to throw at any one in their lives.

Dick was amused when Mary perceived Rosemary, changed her plans and came over. She spoke to Nicole with pleasant heartiness, nodded unsmilingly to Dick as if he were somewhat contagious—whereupon he bowed in ironic respect—as she greeted Rosemary.

"I heard you were here. For how long?"

"Until tomorrow," Rosemary answered.

She, too, saw how Mary had walked through the Divers to talk to her, and a sense of obligation kept her unenthusiastic. No, she could not dine tonight.

Mary turned to Nicole, her manner indicating affection blended with pity.

"How are the children?" she asked.

They came up at the moment, and Nicole gave ear to a request that she overrule the governess on a swimming point.

"No," Dick answered for her. "What Mademoiselle says must go."

Agreeing that one must support delegated authority, Nicole refused their request, whereupon Mary—who in the manner of an Anita Loos' heroine had dealings only with *faits accomplis,* who indeed could not have house-broken a French poodle puppy—regarded Dick as though he were guilty of a most flagrant bullying. Dick, chafed by the tiresome performance, inquired with mock solicitude:

"How are your children—and their aunts?"

Mary did not answer; she left them, first draping a sympathetic hand over Lanier's reluctant head. After she had gone Dick said: "When I think of the time I spent working over her."

"I like her," said Nicole.

Dick's bitterness had surprised Rosemary, who had thought of him as all-forgiving, all-comprehending. Suddenly she recalled what it was she had heard about him. In conversation with some State Department people on the boat,—Europeanized Americans who had reached a position where they could scarcely have been said to belong to any nation at all, at least not to any great power though perhaps to a Balkan-like state composed of similar citizens—the name of the ubiquitously renowned Baby Warren had occurred and it was remarked that Baby's younger sister had thrown herself away on a dissipated doctor. "He's not received anywhere any more," the woman said.

The phrase disturbed Rosemary, though she could not place the Divers as living in any relation to society where such a fact, if fact it was, could have any meaning, yet the hint of a hostile and organized public opinion rang in her ears. "He's not received anywhere any more." She pictured Dick climbing the steps of a mansion, presenting cards and being told by a butler: "We're not receiving you any more"; then proceeding down an avenue only to be told the same thing by the countless other butlers of countless Ambassadors, Ministers, Chargés d'Affaires. . . .

Nicole wondered how she could get away. She guessed that Dick, stung into alertness, would grow charming and would make Rosemary respond to him. Sure enough, in a moment his voice managed to qualify everything unpleasant he had said:

"Mary's all right—she's done very well. But it's hard to go on liking people who don't like you."

Rosemary, falling into line, swayed toward Dick and crooned:

"Oh, you're so nice. I can't imagine anybody not forgiving you anything, no matter what you did to them." Then feeling that her exuberance had transgressed on Nicole's rights, she looked at the sand exactly between them: "I wanted to ask you both what you thought of my latest pictures—if you saw them."

Nicole said nothing, having seen one of them and thought little about it.

"It'll take a few minutes to tell you," Dick said. "Let's suppose that Nicole says to you that Lanier is ill. What do you do in life? What does anyone do? They *act*—face, voice, words—the face shows sorrow, the voice shows shock, the words show sympathy."

"Yes—I understand."

"But, in the theater, No. In the theater all the best comédiennes have built up their reputations by bur*les*quing the correct emotional responses—fear and love and sympathy."

"I see." Yet she did not quite see.

Losing the thread of it, Nicole's impatience increased as Dick continued:

"The danger to an actress is in responding. Again, let's suppose that somebody told you, 'Your lover is dead.' In life you'd probably go to pieces. But on the stage you're trying to entertain—the audience can do the 'responding' for themselves. First the actress has lines to follow, then she has to get the audience's attention back on herself, away from the murdered Chinese or whatever the thing is. So she must do something unexpected. If the audience thinks the character is hard she goes soft on them—if they think she's soft she goes hard. You go all *out* of character—you understand?"

"I don't quite," admitted Rosemary. "How do you mean out of character?"

"You do the unexpected thing until you've manœuvred the audience back from the objective fact to yourself. *Then* you slide into character again."

Nicole could stand no more. She stood up sharply,

making no attempt to conceal her impatience. Rosemary, who had been for a few minutes half-conscious of this, turned in a conciliatory way to Topsy.

"Would you like to be an actress when you grow up? I think you'd make a fine actress."

Nicole stared at her deliberately and in her grandfather's voice said, slow and distinct:

"It's absolutely *out* to put such ideas in the heads of other people's children. Remember, we may have quite different plans for them." She turned sharply to Dick. "I'm going to take the car home. I'll send Michelle for you and the children."

"You haven't driven for months," he protested.

"I haven't forgotten how."

Without a glance at Rosemary whose face was "responding" violently, Nicole left the umbrella.

In the bathhouse, she changed to pajamas, her expression still hard as a plaque. But as she turned into the road of arched pines and the atmosphere changed, —with a squirrel's flight on a branch, a wind nudging at the leaves, a cock splitting distant air, with a creep of sunlight transpiring through the immobility, then the voices of the beach receded—Nicole relaxed and felt new and happy; her thoughts were clear as good bells—she had a sense of being cured and in a new way. Her ego began blooming like a great rich rose as she scrambled back along the labyrinths in which she had wandered for years. She hated the beach, resented the places where she had played planet to Dick's sun.

"Why, I'm almost complete," she thought. "I'm practically standing alone, without him." And like a happy child, wanting the completion as soon as possible, and knowing vaguely that Dick had planned for her to have it, she lay on her bed as soon as she got home and wrote Tommy Barban in Nice a short provocative letter.

But that was for the daytime—toward evening with the inevitable diminution of nervous energy, her spirits flagged, and the arrows flew a little in the twilight. She was afraid of what was in Dick's mind; again she felt that a plan underlay his current actions and she was afraid of his plans—they worked well and they had an all-inclusive logic about them which Nicole was not able to command. She had somehow given over the thinking to him, and in his absences her every action seemed automatically governed by what he would like, so that now she felt inadequate to match her intentions against his. Yet think she must; she knew at last the number on the dreadful door of fantasy, the threshold to the escape that was no escape; she knew that for her the greatest sin now and in the future was to delude herself. It had been a long lesson but she had learned it. Either you think—or else others have to think for you and take power from you, pervert and discipline your natural tastes, civilize and sterilize you.

They had a tranquil supper with Dick drinking much beer and being cheerful with the children in the dusky room. Afterward he played some Schubert songs and some new jazz from America that Nicole hummed in her harsh, sweet contralto over his shoulder.

"Thank y' father-r
Thank y' mother-r
Thanks for meetingup with one another——"

"I don't like that one," Dick said, starting to turn the page.

"Oh, play it!" she exclaimed. "Am I going through the rest of life flinching at the word 'father'?"

"—Thank the horse that pulled the buggy that night!
Thank you both for being justabit tight——"

Later they sat with the children on the Moorish roof and watched the fireworks of two casinos, far apart, far down on the shore. It was lonely and sad to be so empty-hearted toward each other.

Next morning, back from shopping in Cannes, Nicole found a note saying that Dick had taken the small car and gone up into Provence for a few days by himself. Even as she read it the phone rang—it was Tommy Barban from Monte Carlo, saying that he had received her letter and was driving over. She felt her lips' warmth in the receiver as she welcomed his coming.

VIII

SHE bathed and anointed herself and covered her body with a layer of powder, while her toes crunched another pile on a bath towel. She looked microscopically at the lines of her flanks, wondering how soon the fine, slim edifice would begin to sink squat and earthward. In about six years, but now I'll do—in fact I'll do as well as anyone I know.

She was not exaggerating. The only physical disparity between Nicole at present and the Nicole of five years before was simply that she was no longer a young girl. But she was enough ridden by the current youth worship, the moving pictures with their myriad faces of girl-children, blandly represented as carrying on the work and wisdom of the world, to feel a jealousy of youth.

She put on the first ankle-length day dress that she had owned for many years, and crossed herself reverently with Chanel Sixteen. When Tommy drove up at one o'clock she had made her person into the trimmest of gardens.

How good to have things like this, to be worshiped

again, to pretend to have a mystery! She had lost two of the great arrogant years in the life of a pretty girl—now she felt like making up for them; she greeted Tommy as if he were one of many men at her feet, walking ahead of him instead of beside him as they crossed the garden toward the market umbrella. Attractive women of nineteen and of twenty-nine are alike in their breezy confidence; on the contrary, the exigent womb of the twenties does not pull the outside world centripetally around itself. The former are ages of insolence, comparable the one to a young cadet, the other to a fighter strutting after combat.

But whereas a girl of nineteen draws her confidence from a surfeit of attention, a woman of twenty-nine is nourished on subtler stuff. Desirous, she chooses her *apéritifs* wisely, or, content, she enjoys the caviare of potential power. Happily she does not seem, in either case, to anticipate the subsequent years when her insight will often be blurred by panic, by the fear of stopping or the fear of going on. But on the landings of nineteen or twenty-nine she is pretty sure that there are no bears in the hall.

Nicole did not want any vague spiritual romance—she wanted an "affair"; she wanted a change. She realized, thinking with Dick's thoughts, that from a superficial view it was a vulgar business to enter, without emotion, into an indulgence that menaced all of them. On the other hand, she blamed Dick for the immediate situation, and honestly thought that such an experiment might have a therapeutic value. All summer she had been stimulated by watching people do exactly what they were tempted to do and pay no penalty for it—moreover, in spite of her intention of no longer lying to herself, she preferred to consider that she was merely feeling her way and that at any moment she could withdraw. . . .

In the light shade Tommy caught her up in his white-duck arms and pulled her around to him, looking at her eyes.

"Don't move," he said. "I'm going to look at you a great deal from now on."

There was some scent on his hair, a faint aura of soap from his white clothes. Her lips were tight, not smiling and they both simply looked for a moment.

"Do you like what you see?" she murmured.

"Parle français."

"Very well," and she asked again in French. "Do you like what you see?"

He pulled her closer.

"I like whatever I see about you." He hesitated. "I thought I knew your face but it seems there are some things I didn't know about it. When did you begin to have white crook's eyes?"

She broke away, shocked and indignant, and cried in English:

"Is that why you wanted to talk French?" Her voice quieted as the butler came with sherry. "So you could be offensive more accurately?"

She parked her small seat violently on the cloth-of-silver chair cushion.

"I have no mirror here," she said, again in French, but decisively, "but if my eyes have changed it's because I'm well again. And being well perhaps I've gone back to my true self—I suppose my grandfather was a crook and I'm a crook by heritage, so there we are. Does that satisfy your logical mind?"

He scarcely seemed to know what she was talking about.

"Where's Dick—is he lunching with us?"

Seeing that his remark had meant comparatively little to him she suddenly laughed away its effect.

"Dick's on a tour," she said. "Rosemary Hoyt turned up, and either they're together or she upset him so much that he wants to go away and dream about her."

"You know, you're a little complicated after all."

"Oh no," she assured him hastily. "No, I'm not really —I'm just a—I'm just a whole lot of different simple people."

Marius brought out melon and an ice pail, and Nicole, thinking irresistibly about her crook's eyes did not answer; he gave one an entire nut to crack, this man, instead of giving it in fragments to pick at for meat.

"Why didn't they leave you in your natural state?" Tommy demanded presently. "You are the most dramatic person I have known."

She had no answer.

"All this taming of women!" he scoffed.

"In any society there are certain—" She felt Dick's ghost prompting at her elbow but she subsided at Tommy's overtone:

"I've brutalized many men into shape but I wouldn't take a chance on half the number of women. Especially this 'kind' bullying—what good does it do anybody?— you or him or anybody?"

Her heart leaped and then sank faintly with a sense of what she owed Dick.

"I suppose I've got——"

"You've got too much money," he said impatiently. "That's the crux of the matter. Dick can't beat that."

She considered while the melons were removed.

"What do you think I ought to do?"

For the first time in ten years she was under the sway

of a personality other than her husband's. Everything Tommy said to her became part of her forever.

They drank the bottle of wine while a faint wind rocked the pine needles and the sensuous heat of early afternoon made blinding freckles on the checkered luncheon cloth. Tommy came over behind her and laid his arms along hers, clasping her hands. Their cheeks touched and then their lips and she gasped half with passion for him, half with the sudden surprise of its force. . . .

"Can't you send the governess and the children away for the afternoon?"

"They have a piano lesson. Anyhow I don't want to stay here."

"Kiss me again."

A little later, riding toward Nice, she thought: So I have white crook's eyes, have I? Very well then, better a sane crook than a mad puritan.

His assertion seemed to absolve her from all blame or responsibility and she had a thrill of delight in thinking of herself in a new way. New vistas appeared ahead, peopled with the faces of many men, none of whom she need obey or even love. She drew in her breath, hunched her shoulders with a wriggle and turned to Tommy.

"Have we *got* to go all the way to your hotel at Monte Carlo?"

He brought the car to a stop with a squeak of tires.

"No!" he answered. "And, my God, I have never been so happy as I am this minute."

They had passed through Nice following the blue coast and begun to mount to the middling-high Corniche. Now Tommy turned sharply down to the shore, ran out a blunt peninsula, and stopped in the rear of a small shore hotel.

Its tangibility frightened Nicole for a moment. At the desk an American was arguing interminably with the clerk about the rate of exchange. She hovered, outwardly tranquil but inwardly miserable, as Tommy filled out the police blanks—his real, hers false. Their room was a Mediterranean room, almost ascetic, almost clean, darkened to the glare of the sea. Simplest of pleasures—simplest of places. Tommy ordered two cognacs, and when the door closed behind the waiter, he sat in the only chair, dark, scarred and handsome, his eyebrows arched and upcurling, a fighting Puck, an earnest Satan.

Before they had finished the brandy they suddenly moved together and met standing up; then they were sitting on the bed and he kissed her hardy knees. Struggling a little still, like a decapitated animal she forgot about Dick and her new white eyes, forgot Tommy himself and sank deeper and deeper into the minutes and the moment.

. . . When he got up to open a shutter and find out what caused the increasing clamor below their windows, his figure was darker and stronger than Dick's, with high lights along the rope-twists of muscle. Momentarily he had forgotten her too—almost in the second of his flesh breaking from hers she had a foretaste that things were going to be different than she had expected. She felt the nameless fear which precedes all emotions, joyous or sorrowful, inevitably as a hum of thunder precedes a storm.

Tommy peered cautiously from the balcony and reported.

"All I can see is two women on the balcony below this. They're talking about weather and tipping back and forth in American rocking-chairs."

"Making all that noise?"

"The noise is coming from somewhere below them. Listen."

"Oh, way down South in the land of cotton
Hotels bum and business rotten
Look away——"

"It's Americans."

Nicole flung her arms wide on the bed and stared at the ceiling; the powder had dampened on her to make a milky surface. She liked the bareness of the room, the sound of the single fly navigating overhead. Tommy brought the chair over to the bed and swept the clothes off it to sit down; she liked the economy of the weightless dress and *espadrilles* that mingled with his ducks upon the floor.

He inspected the oblong white torso joined abruptly to the brown limbs and head, and said, laughing gravely:

"You are all new like a baby."

"With white eyes."

"I'll take care of that."

"It's very hard taking care of white eyes—especially the ones made in Chicago."

"I know all the old Languedoc peasant remedies."

"Kiss me, on the lips, Tommy."

"That's so American," he said, kissing her nevertheless. "When I was in America last there were girls who would tear you apart with their lips, tear themselves too, until their faces were scarlet with the blood around the lips all brought out in a patch—but nothing further."

Nicole leaned up on one elbow.

"I like this room," she said.

He looked around.

"I find it somewhat meager. Darling, I'm glad you wouldn't wait until we got to Monte Carlo."

"Why only meager? Why, this is a wonderful room, Tommy—like the bare tables in so many Cézannes and Picassos."

"I don't know." He did not try to understand her. "There's that noise again. My God, has there been a murder?"

He went to the window and reported once more:

"It seems to be two American sailors fighting and a lot more cheering them on. They are from your battleship off shore." He wrapped a towel around himself and went farther out on the balcony. "They have *poules* with them. I have heard about this now—the women follow them from place to place wherever the ship goes. But what women! One would think with their pay they could find better women! Why the women who followed Korniloff! Why we never looked at anything less than a ballerina!"

Nicole was glad he had known so many women, so that the word itself meant nothing to him; she would be able to hold him so long as the person in her transcended the universals of her body.

"Hit him where it hurts!"

"Yah-h-h-h!"

"Hey, what I tell you get inside that right!"

"Come on, Dulschmit, you son!"

"Yaa-Yaa!"

"YA-YEH-YAH!"

Tommy turned away.

"This place seems to have outlived its usefulness, you agree?"

She agreed, but they clung together for a moment

before dressing, and then for a while longer it seemed as good enough a place as any. . . .

Dressing at last Tommy exclaimed:

"*My God,* those two women in the rocking-chairs on the balcony below us haven't moved. They're trying to talk this matter out of existence. They're here on an economical holiday, and all the American navy and all the whores in Europe couldn't spoil it."

He came over gently and surrounded her, pulling the shoulder strap of her slip into place with his teeth; then a sound split the air outside: Cr-ACK—BOOM-M-m-*m!* It was the battleship sounding a recall.

Now, down below their window, it was pandemonium indeed—for the boat was moving to shores as yet unannounced. Waiters called accounts and demanded settlements in impassioned voices, there were oaths and denials; the tossing of bills too large and change too small; passouts were assisted to the boats, and the voices of the naval police chopped with quick commands through all voices. There were cries, tears, shrieks, promises as the first launch shoved off and the women crowded forward on the wharf, screaming and waving.

Tommy saw a girl rush out upon the balcony below waving a napkin, and before he could see whether or not the rocking Englishwomen gave in at last and acknowledged her presence, there was a knock at their own door. Outside, excited female voices made them agree to unlock it, disclosing two girls, young, thin and barbaric, unfound rather than lost, in the hall. One of them wept chokingly.

"Kwee wave off your porch?" implored the other in passionate American. "Kwee please? Wave at the boy friends? Kwee, please. The other rooms is all locked."

"With pleasure," Tommy said.

The girls rushed out on the balcony and presently their voices struck a loud treble over the din.

"'By, Charlie! Charlie, look *up!*"

"Send a wire gen'al alivery Nice!"

"Charlie! He don't see me."

One of the girls hoisted her skirt suddenly, pulled and ripped at her pink step-ins and tore them to a sizable flag; then, screaming "Ben! Ben!" she waved it wildly. As Tommy and Nicole left the room it still fluttered against the blue sky. Oh, say can you see the tender color of remembered flesh?—while at the stern of the battleship arose in rivalry the Star-Spangled Banner.

They dined at the new Beach Casino at Monte Carlo . . . much later they swam in Beaulieu in a roofless cavern of white moonlight formed by a circlet of pale boulders about a cup of phosphorescent water, facing Monaco and the blur of Mentone. She liked his bringing her there to the eastward vision and the novel tricks of wind and water; it was all as new as they were to each other. Symbolically she lay across his saddlebow as surely as if he had wolfed her away from Damascus and they had come out upon the Mongolian plain. Moment by moment all that Dick had taught her fell away and she was ever nearer to what she had been in the beginning, prototype of that obscure yielding up of swords that was going on in the world about her. Tangled with love in the moonlight she welcomed the anarchy of her lover.

They awoke together finding the moon gone down and the air cool. She struggled up demanding the time and Tommy called it roughly at three.

"I've got to go home then."

"I thought we'd sleep in Monte Carlo."

"No. There's a governess and the children. I've got to roll in before daylight."

"As you like."

They dipped for a second, and when he saw her shivering he rubbed her briskly with a towel. As they got into the car with their heads still damp, their skins fresh and glowing, they were loath to start back. It was very bright where they were and as Tommy kissed her she felt him losing himself in the whiteness of her cheeks and her white teeth and her cool brow and the hand that touched his face. Still attuned to Dick, she waited for interpretation or qualification; but none was forthcoming. Reassured sleepily and happily that none would be, she sank low in the seat and drowsed until the sound of the motor changed and she felt them climbing toward Villa Diana. At the gate she kissed him an almost automatic good-by. The sound of her feet on the walk was changed, the night noises of the garden were suddenly in the past but she was glad, none the less, to be back. The day had progressed at a staccato rate, and in spite of its satisfactions she was not habituated to such strain.

IX

AT FOUR o'clock next afternoon a station taxi stopped at the gate and Dick got out. Suddenly off balance, Nicole ran from the terrace to meet him, breathless with her effort at self-control.

"Where's the car?" she asked.

"I left it in Arles. I didn't feel like driving any more."

"I thought from your note that you'd be several days."

"I ran into a mistral and some rain."

"Did you have fun?"

"Just as much fun as anybody has running away from

things. I drove Rosemary as far as Avignon and put her on her train there." They walked toward the terrace together, where he deposited his bag. "I didn't tell you in the note because I thought you'd imagine a lot of things."

"That was very considerate of you." Nicole felt surer of herself now.

"I wanted to find out if she had anything to offer—the only way was to see her alone."

"Did she have—anything to offer?"

"Rosemary didn't grow up," he answered. "It's probably better that way. What have you been doing?"

She felt her face quiver like a rabbit's.

"I went dancing last night—with Tommy Barban. We went——"

He winced, interrupting her.

"Don't tell me about it. It doesn't matter what you do, only I don't want to know anything definitely."

"There isn't anything to know."

"All right, all right." Then as if he had been away a week: "How are the children?"

The phone rang in the house.

"If it's for me I'm not home," said Dick turning away quickly. "I've got some things to do over in the workroom."

Nicole waited till he was out of sight behind the well; then she went into the house and took up the phone.

"*Nicole, comment va-tu?*"

"Dick's home."

He groaned.

"Meet me here in Cannes," he suggested. "I've got to talk to you."

"I can't."

"Tell me you love me." Without speaking she nodded at the receiver; he repeated, "Tell me you love me."

"Oh, I do," she assured him. "But there's nothing to be done right now."

"Of course there is," he said impatiently. "Dick sees it's over between you two—it's obvious he has quit. What does he expect you to do?"

"I don't know. I'll have to—" She stopped herself from saying "—to wait until I can ask Dick," and instead finished with: "I'll write and I'll phone you tomorrow."

She wandered about the house rather contentedly, resting on her achievement. She was a mischief, and that was a satisfaction; no longer was she a huntress of corralled game. Yesterday came back to her now in innumerable detail—detail that began to overlay her memory of similar moments when her love for Dick was fresh and intact. She began to slight that love, so that it seemed to have been tinged with sentimental habit from the first. With the opportunistic memory of women she scarcely recalled how she had felt when she and Dick had possessed each other in secret places around the corners of the world, during the month before they were married. Just so had she lied to Tommy last night, swearing to him that never before had she so entirely, so completely, so utterly. . . .

. . . then remorse for this moment of betrayal, which so cavalierly belittled a decade of her life, turned her walk toward Dick's sanctuary.

Approaching noiselessly she saw him behind his cottage, sitting in a steamer chair by the cliff wall, and for a moment she regarded him silently. He was thinking, he was living a world completely his own and in the small motions of his face, the brow raised or lowered, the eyes narrowed or widened, the lips set and reset, the play of his hands, she saw him progress from phase to phase of his own story spinning out inside him, his own, not hers. Once he clenched his fists and leaned forward, once it brought into his face an expression of torment and despair—when this passed its stamp lingered in his eyes. For almost the first time in her life she was sorry for him—it is hard for those who have once been mentally afflicted to be sorry for those who are well, and though Nicole often paid lip service to the fact that he had led her back to the world she had forfeited, she had thought of him really as an inexhaustible energy, incapable of fatigue—she forgot the troubles she caused him at the moment when she forgot the troubles of her own that had prompted her. That he no longer controlled her—did he know that? Had he willed it all?—she felt as sorry for him as she had sometimes felt for Abe North and his ignoble destiny, sorry as for the helplessness of infants and the old.

She went up putting her arm around his shoulder and touching their heads together said:

"Don't be sad."

He looked at her coldly.

"Don't touch me!" he said.

Confused she moved a few feet away.

"Excuse me," he continued abstractedly. "I was just thinking what I thought of you——"

"Why not add the new classification to your book?"

"I have thought of it—'Furthermore and beyond the psychoses and neuroses——' "

"I didn't come over here to be disagreeable."

"Then why *did* you come, Nicole? I can't do anything for you any more. I'm trying to save myself."

"From my contamination?"

"Profession throws me in contact with questionable company sometimes."

She wept with anger at the abuse.

"You're a coward! You've made a failure of your life, and you want to blame it on me."

While he did not answer she began to feel the old hypnotism of his intelligence, sometimes exercised without power but always with substrata of truth under truth which she could not break or even crack. Again she struggled with it, fighting him with her small, fine eyes, with the plush arrogance of a top dog, with her nascent transference to another man, with the accumulated resentment of years; she fought him with her money and her faith that her sister disliked him and was behind her now; with the thought of the new enemies he was making with his bitterness, with her quick guile against his wine-ing and dine-ing slowness, her health and beauty against his physical deterioration, her unscrupulousness against his moralities—for this inner battle she used even her weaknesses—fighting bravely and courageously with the old cans and crockery and bottles, empty receptables of her expiated sins, outrages, mistakes. And suddenly, in the space of two minutes she achieved her victory and justified herself to herself without lie or subterfuge, cut the cord forever. Then she walked, weak in the legs, and sobbing coolly, toward the household that was hers at last.

Dick waited until she was out of sight. Then he leaned his head forward on the parapet. The case was finished. Doctor Diver was at liberty.

X

AT TWO o'clock that night the phone woke Nicole and she heard Dick answer it from what they called the restless bed, in the next room.

"*Oui, oui . . . mais à qui est-ce-que je parle? . . . Oui . . .*" His voice woke up with surprise. "But can I speak to one of the ladies, Sir the Officer? They are both ladies of the very highest prominence, ladies of connections that might cause political complications of the most serious. . . . It is a fact, I swear to you. . . . Very well, you will see."

He got up and, as he absorbed the situation, his self-knowledge assured him that he would undertake to deal with it—the old fatal pleasingness, the old forceful charm, swept back with its cry of "Use me!" He would have to go fix this thing that he didn't care a damn about, because it had early become a habit to be loved, perhaps from the moment when he had realized that he was the last hope of a decaying clan. On an almost parallel occasion, back in Dohmler's clinic on the Zürichsee, realizing this power, he had made his choice, chosen Ophelia, chosen the sweet poison and drunk it. Wanting above all to be brave and kind, he had wanted, even more than that, to be loved. So it had been. So it would ever be, he saw, simultaneously with the slow archaic tinkle from the phone box as he rang off.

There was a long pause. Nicole called, "What is it? Who is it?"

Dick had begun to dress even as he hung up the phone.

"It's the *poste de police* in Antibes—they're holding Mary North and that Sibley-Biers. It's something serious—the agent wouldn't tell me; he kept saying '*pas de mortes—pas d'automobiles*,' but he implied it was just about everything else."

"Why on earth did they call on *you*? It sounds very peculiar to me."

"They've got to get out on bail to save their faces; and only some property owner in the Alpes Maritimes can give bail."

"They had their nerve."

"I don't mind. However I'll pick up Gausse at the hotel——"

Nicole stayed awake after he had departed wondering what offense they could have committed; then she slept. A little after three when Dick came in she sat up stark awake saying, "What?" as if to a character in her dream.

"It was an extraordinary story—" Dick said. He sat on the foot of her bed, telling her how he had roused old Gausse from an Alsatian coma, told him to clean out his cash drawer, and driven with him to the police station.

"I don't like to do something for that *Anglaise,*" Gausse grumbled.

Mary North and Lady Caroline, dressed in the costume of French sailors, lounged on a bench outside the two dingy cells. The latter had the outraged air of a Briton who momentarily expected the Mediterranean fleet to steam up to her assistance. Mary Minghetti was in a condition of panic and collapse—she literally flung herself at Dick's stomach as though that were the point of greatest association, imploring him to do something. Meanwhile the chief of police explained the matter to Gausse who listened to each word with reluctance, divided between being properly appreciative of the officer's narrative gift and showing that, as the perfect servant, the story had no shocking effect on him.

"It was merely a lark," said Lady Caroline with scorn. "We were pretending to be sailors on leave, and we picked up two silly girls. They got the wind up and made a rotten scene in a lodging house."

Dick nodded gravely, looking at the stone floor, like a priest in the confessional—he was torn between a tendency to ironic laughter and another tendency to order fifty stripes of the cat and a fortnight of bread and water. The lack, in Lady Caroline's face, of any sense of evil, except the evil wrought by cowardly Provençal girls and stupid police, confounded him; yet he had long concluded that certain classes of English people lived upon a concentrated essence of the anti-social that, in comparison, reduced the gorgings of New York to something like a child contracting indigestion from ice cream.

"I've got to get out before Hosain hears about this," Mary pleaded. "Dick, you can always arrange things—you always could. Tell 'em we'll go right home, tell 'em we'll pay anything."

"I shall not," said Lady Caroline disdainfully. "Not a shilling. But I shall jolly well find out what the Consulate in Cannes has to say about this."

"No, no!" insisted Mary. "We've got to get out to-night."

"I'll see what I can do," said Dick, and added, "but money will certainly have to change hands." Looking at them as though they were the innocents that he knew they were not, he shook his head: "Of all the crazy stunts!"

Lady Caroline smiled complacently.

"You're an insanity doctor, aren't you? You ought to be able to help us—and Gausse has *got* to!"

At this point Dick went aside with Gausse and talked over the old man's findings. The affair was more serious than had been indicated—one of the girls whom they had picked up was of a respectable family. The family were furious, or pretended to be; a settlement would have to be made with them. The other girl, a girl of the port, could be more easily dealt with. There were French statutes that would make conviction punishable by imprisonment or, at the very least, public expulsion from the country. In addition to the difficulties, there was a growing difference in tolerance between such townspeople as benefited by the foreign colony and the ones who were annoyed by the consequent rise of prices. Gausse, having summarized the situation, turned it over to Dick. Dick called the chief of police into conference.

"Now you know that the French government wants to encourage American touring—so much so that in Paris this summer there's an order that Americans can't be arrested except for the most serious offenses."

"This is serious enough, my God."

"But look now—you have their *cartes d'identité?*"

"They had none. They had nothing—two hundred francs and some rings. Not even shoe-laces that they could have hung themselves with!"

Relieved that there had been no *cartes d'identité* Dick continued.

"The Italian Countess is still an American citizen. She is the grand-daughter—" he told a string of lies slowly and portentously, "of John D. Rockefeller Mellon. You have heard of him?"

"Yes, oh heavens, yes. You mistake me for a nobody?"

"In addition she is the niece of Lord Henry Ford and so connected with the Renault and Citroën companies—" He thought he had better stop here. However the sincerity of his voice had begun to affect the officer, so he continued: "To arrest her is just as if you arrested a great royalty of England. It might mean—War!"

"But how about the Englishwoman?"

"I'm coming to that. She is affianced to the brother of the Prince of Wales—the Duke of Buckingham."

"She will be an exquisite bride for him."

"Now we are prepared to give—" Dick calculated quickly, "one thousand francs to each of the girls—and an additional thousand to the father of the 'serious' one. Also two thousand in addition, for you to distribute as you think best—" he shrugged his shoulders, "—among the men who made the arrest, the lodging-house keeper and so forth. I shall hand you the five thousand and expect you to do the negotiating immediately. Then they can be released on bail on some charge like disturbing the peace, and whatever fine there is will be paid before the magistrate tomorrow—by messenger."

Before the officer spoke Dick saw by his expression that it would be all right. The man said hesitantly, "I have made no entry because they have no *cartes d'identité*. I must see—give me the money."

An hour later Dick and M. Gausse dropped the women by the Majestic Hotel, where Lady Caroline's chauffeur slept in her landaulet.

"Remember," said Dick, "you owe Monsieur Gausse a hundred dollars apiece."

"All right," Mary agreed, "I'll give him a check tomorrow—and something more."

"Not I!" Startled, they all turned to Lady Caroline, who, now entirely recovered, was swollen with righteousness. "The whole thing was an outrage. By no means did I authorize you to give a hundred dollars to those people."

Little Gausse stood beside the car, his eyes blazing suddenly.

"You won't pay me?"

"Of course she will," said Dick.

Suddenly the abuse that Gausse had once endured as a bus boy in London flamed up and he walked through the moonlight up to Lady Caroline.

He whipped a string of condemnatory words about her, and as she turned away with a frozen laugh, he took a step after her and swiftly planted his little foot in the most celebrated of targets. Lady Caroline, taken by surprise, flung up her hands like a person shot as her sailor-clad form sprawled forward on the sidewalk.

Dick's voice cut across her raging: "Mary, you quiet her down! or you'll both be in leg-irons in ten minutes!"

On the way back to the hotel old Gausse said not a word, until they passed the Juan-les-Pins Casino, still sobbing and coughing with jazz; then he sighed forth:

"I have never seen women like this sort of women. I have known many of the great courtesans of the world, and for them I have much respect often, but women like these women I have never seen before."

XI

DICK and Nicole were accustomed to go together to the barber, and have haircuts and shampoos in adjoining rooms. From Dick's side Nicole could hear the snip of shears, the count of change, the *voilàs* and *pardons*. The day after his return they went down to be shorn and washed in the perfumed breeze of the fans.

In front of the Carleton Hotel, its windows as stubbornly blank to the summer as so many cellar doors, a car passed them and Tommy Barban was in it. Nicole's momentary glimpse of his expression, taciturn and thoughtful and, in the second of seeing her, wide-eyed and alert, disturbed her. She wanted to be going where he was going. The hour with the hair-dresser seemed one of the wasteful intervals that composed her life, another little prison. The *coiffeuse* in her white uniform, faintly sweating lip-rouge and cologne reminded her of many nurses.

In the next room Dick dozed under an apron and a lather of soap. The mirror in front of Nicole reflected the passage between the men's side and the women's, and Nicole started up at the sight of Tommy entering and wheeling sharply into the men's shop. She knew with a flush of joy that there was going to be some sort of showdown.

She heard fragments of its beginning.

"Hello, I want to see you."

". . . serious."

". . . serious."

". . . perfectly agreeable."

In a minute Dick came into Nicole's booth, his expression emerging annoyed from behind the towel of his hastily rinsed face.

"Your friend has worked himself up into a state. He wants to see us together, so I agreed to have it over with. Come along!"

"But my hair—it's half-cut."

"Never mind—come along!"

Resentfully she had the staring coiffeuse remove the towels.

Feeling messy and unadorned she followed Dick from the hotel. Outside Tommy bent over her hand.

"We'll go to the Café des Alliés," said Dick.

"Wherever we can be alone," Tommy agreed.

Under the arching trees, central in summer, Dick asked: "Will you take anything, Nicole?"

"A citron pressé."

"For me a demi," said Tommy.

"The Blackenwite with siphon," said Dick.

"Il n'y a plus de Blackenwite. Nous n'avons que le Johnny Walkair."

"Ça va."

"She's—not—wired for sound
but on the quiet
you ought to try it——"

"Your wife does not love you," said Tommy suddenly. "She loves me."

The two men regarded each other with a curious impotence of expression. There can be little communication between men in that position, for their relation is indirect, and consists of how much each of them has possessed or will possess of the woman in question, so that their emotions pass through her divided self as through a bad telephone connection.

"Wait a minute," Dick said. "*Donnez moi du gin et du siphon.*"

"*Bien, Monsieur.*"

"All right, go on, Tommy."

"It's very plain to me that your marriage to Nicole has run its course. She is through. I've waited five years for that to be so."

"What does Nicole say?"

They both looked at her.

"I've gotten very fond of Tommy, Dick."

He nodded.

"You don't care for me any more," she continued. "It's all just habit. Things were never the same after Rosemary."

Unattracted to this angle, Tommy broke in sharply with:

"You don't understand Nicole. You treat her always like a patient because she was once sick."

They were suddenly interrupted by an insistent American, of sinister aspect, vending copies of the *Herald* and of the *Times* fresh from New York.

"Got everything here, Buddies," he announced. "Been here long?"

"*Cessez cela! Allez ouste!*" Tommy cried and then to Dick, "Now no woman would stand such——"

"Buddies," interrupted the American again. "You think I'm wasting my time—but lots of others don't." He brought a gray clipping from his purse—and Dick recognized it as he saw it. It cartooned millions of Americans pouring from liners with bags of gold. "You think I'm not going to get part of that? Well, I am. I'm just over from Nice for the Tour de France."

As Tommy got him off with a fierce *"allez-vous-en,"* Dick identified him as the man who had once hailed him in the Rue des Saints-Anges, five years before.

"When does the Tour de France get here?" he called after him.

"Any minute now, Buddy."

He departed at last with a cheery wave and Tommy returned to Dick.

"Elle doit avoir plus avec moi qu'avec vous."

"Speak English! What do you mean *'doit avoir'*?"

"*'Doit avoir?'* Would have more happiness with me."

"You'd be new to each other. But Nicole and I have had much happiness together, Tommy."

"L'amour de famille," Tommy said, scoffing.

"If you and Nicole married won't that be *'l'amour de famille'*?" The increasing commotion made him break off; presently it came to a serpentine head on the promenade and a group, presently a crowd, of people sprung from hidden siestas, lined the curbstone.

Boys sprinted past on bicycles, automobiles jammed with elaborate betasseled sportsmen slid up the street, high horns tooted to announce the approach of the race, and unsuspected cooks in undershirts appeared at restaurant doors as around a bend a procession came into sight. First was a lone cyclist in a red jersey, toiling intent and confident out of the westering sun, passing to the melody of a high chattering cheer. Then three together in a harlequinade of faded color, legs caked yellow with dust and sweat, faces expressionless, eyes heavy and endlessly tired.

Tommy faced Dick, saying: "I think Nicole wants a divorce—I suppose you'll make no obstacles?"

A troupe of fifty more swarmed after the first bicycle racers, strung out over two hundred yards; a few were smiling and self-conscious, a few obviously exhausted, most of them indifferent and weary. A retinue of small boys passed, a few defiant stragglers, a light truck carried the dupes of accident and defeat. They were back at the table. Nicole wanted Dick to take the initiative, but he seemed content to sit with his face half-shaved matching her hair half-cut.

"Isn't it true you're not happy with me any more?" Nicole continued. "Without me you could get to your work again—you could work better if you didn't worry about me."

Tommy moved impatiently.

"That is so useless. Nicole and I love each other, that's all there is to it."

"Well, then," said the Doctor, "since it's all settled, suppose we go back to the barber shop."

Tommy wanted a row: "There are several points——"

"Nicole and I will talk things over," said Dick equitably. "Don't worry—I agree in principal, and Nicole and I understand each other. There's less chance of unpleasantness if we avoid a three-cornered discussion."

Unwillingly acknowledging Dick's logic, Tommy was moved by an irresistible racial tendency to chisel for an advantage.

"Let it be understood that from this moment," he said, "I stand in the position of Nicole's protector until details can be arranged. And I shall hold you strictly accountable for any abuse of the fact that you continue to inhabit the same house."

"I never did go in for making love to dry loins," said Dick.

He nodded, and walked off toward the hotel with Nicole's whitest eyes following him.

"He was fair enough," Tommy conceded. "Darling, will we be together tonight?"

"I suppose so."

So it had happened—and with a minimum of drama; Nicole felt outguessed, realizing that from the episode of the camphor-rub, Dick had anticipated everything. But also she felt happy and excited, and the odd little wish that she could tell Dick all about it faded quickly. But her eyes followed his figure until it became a dot and mingled with the other dots in the summer crowd.

XII

THE day before Doctor Diver left the Riviera he spent all his time with his children. He was not young any more with a lot of nice thoughts and dreams to have about himself, so he wanted to remember them well. The children had been told that this winter they would be with their aunt in London and that soon they were going to come and see him in America. Fräulein was not to be discharged without his consent.

He was glad he had given so much to the little girl—about the boy he was more uncertain—always he had been uneasy about what he had to give to the ever-climbing, ever-clinging, breast-searching young. But, when he said good-by to them, he wanted to lift their beautiful heads off their necks and hold them close for hours.

He embraced the old gardener who had made the

first garden at Villa Diana six years ago; he kissed the Provençal girl who helped with the children. She had been with them for almost a decade and she fell on her knees and cried until Dick jerked her to her feet and gave her three hundred francs. Nicole was sleeping late, as had been agreed upon—he left a note for her, and one for Baby Warren who was just back from Sardinia and staying at the house. Dick took a big drink from a bottle of brandy three feet high, holding ten quarts, that some one had presented them with.

Then he decided to leave his bags by the station in Cannes and take a last look at Gausse's beach.

The beach was peopled with only an advance guard of children when Nicole and her sister arrived that morning. A white sun, chivied of outline by a white sky, boomed over a windless day. Waiters were putting extra ice into the bar; an American photographer from the AP worked with his equipment in a precarious shade and looked up quickly at every footfall descending the stone steps. At the hotel his prospective subjects slept late in darkened rooms upon their recent opiate of dawn.

When Nicole started out on the beach she saw Dick, not dressed for swimming, sitting on a rock above. She shrank back in the shadow of her dressing-tent. In a minute Baby joined her, saying:

"Dick's still there."

"I saw him."

"I think he might have the delicacy to go."

"This is his place—in a way, he discovered it. Old Gausse always says he owes everything to Dick."

Baby looked calmly at her sister.

"We should have let him confine himself to his bicycle excursions," she remarked. "When people are taken out of their depths they lose their heads, no matter how charming a bluff they put up."

"Dick was a good husband to me for six years," Nicole said. "All that time I never suffered a minute's pain because of him, and he always did his best never to let anything hurt me."

Baby's lower jaw projected slightly as she said:

"That's what he was educated for."

The sisters sat in silence; Nicole wondering in a tired way about things; Baby considering whether or not to marry the latest candidate for her hand and money, an authenticated Hapsburg. She was not quite *think*ing about it. Her affairs had long shared such a sameness, that, as she dried out, they were more important for their conversational value than for themselves. Her emotions had their truest existence in the telling of them.

"Is he gone?" Nicole asked after a while. "I think his train leaves at noon."

Baby looked.

"No. He's moved up higher on the terrace and he's talking to some women. Anyhow there are so many people now that he doesn't *have* to see us."

He had seen them though, as they left their pavilion, and he followed them with his eyes until they disappeared again. He sat with Mary Minghetti, drinking anisette.

"You were like you used to be the night you helped us," she was saying, "except at the end, when you were horrid about Caroline. Why aren't you nice like that always? You can be."

It seemed fantastic to Dick to be in a position where Mary North could tell him about things.

"Your friends still like you, Dick. But you say awful things to people when you've been drinking. I've spent most of my time defending you this summer."

"That remark is one of Doctor Eliot's classics."

"It's true. Nobody cares whether you drink or not—" She hesitated, "even when Abe drank hardest, he never offended people like you do."

"You're all so dull," he said.

"But we're all there is!" cried Mary. "If you don't like nice people, try the ones who aren't nice, and see how you like that! All people want is to have a good time and if you make them unhappy you cut yourself off from nourishment."

"Have I been nourished?" he asked.

Mary was having a good time, though she did not know it, as she had sat down with him only out of fear. Again she refused a drink and said: "Self-indulgence is back of it. Of course, after Abe you can imagine how I feel about it—since I watched the progress of a good man toward alcoholism——"

Down the steps tripped Lady Caroline Sibly-Biers with blithe theatricality.

Dick felt fine—he was already well in advance of the day; arrived at where a man should be at the end of a good dinner, yet he showed only a fine, considered, restrained interest in Mary. His eyes, for the moment clear as a child's, asked her sympathy and stealing over him he felt the old necessity of convincing her that he was the last man in the world and she was the last woman.

. . . Then he would not have to look at those two other figures, a man and a woman, black and white and metallic against the sky. . . .

"You once liked me, didn't you?" he asked.

"*Liked* you—I *loved* you. Everybody loved you. You

could've had anybody you wanted for the asking——"

"There has always been something between you and me."

She bit eagerly. "Has there, Dick?"

"Always—I knew your troubles and how brave you were about them." But the old interior laughter had begun inside him and he knew he couldn't keep it up much longer.

"I always thought you knew a lot," Mary said enthusiastically. "More about me than anyone has ever known. Perhaps that's why I was so afraid of you when we didn't get along so well."

His glance fell soft and kind upon hers, suggesting an emotion underneath; their glances married suddenly, bedded, strained together. Then, as the laughter inside of him became so loud that it seemed as if Mary must hear it, Dick switched off the light and they were back in the Riviera sun.

"I must go," he said. As he stood up he swayed a little; he did not feel well any more—his blood raced slow. He raised his right hand and with a papal cross he blessed the beach from the high terrace. Faces turned upward from several umbrellas.

"I'm going to him." Nicole got to her knees.

"No, you're not," said Tommy, pulling her down firmly. "Let well enough alone."

XIII

NICOLE kept in touch with Dick after her new marriage; there were letters on business matters, and about the children. When she said, as she often did, "I loved Dick and I'll never forget him," Tommy answered, "Of course not—why should you?"

Dick opened an office in Buffalo, but evidently without success. Nicole did not find what the trouble was, but she heard a few months later that he was in a little town named Batavia, New York, practicing general medicine, and later that he was in Lockport, doing the same thing. By accident she heard more about his life there than anywhere: that he bicycled a lot, was much admired by the ladies, and always had a big stack of papers on his desk that were known to be an important treatise on some medical subject, almost in process of completion. He was considered to have fine manners and once made a good speech at a public health meeting on the subject of drugs; but he became entangled with a girl who worked in a grocery store, and he was also involved in a lawsuit about some medical question; so he left Lockport.

After that he didn't ask for the children to be sent to America and didn't answer when Nicole wrote asking him if he needed money. In the last letter she had from him he told her that he was practicing in Geneva, New York, and she got the impression that he had settled down with some one to keep house for him. She looked up Geneva in an atlas and found it was in the heart of the Finger Lakes Section and considered a pleasant place. Perhaps, so she liked to think, his career was biding its time, again like Grant's in Galena; his latest note was post-marked from Hornell, New York, which is some distance from Geneva and a very small town; in any case he is almost certainly in that section of the country, in one town or another.

out success. Nicole didn't know what the trouble was but she heard a few months later that he was in a little town named Batavia, New York, practicing general medicine, and later that he was in Lockport, doing the same thing. By accident she heard more about his life there than anywhere, that he bicycled a lot, was much admired by the ladies, and always had a big stack of papers on his desk that were known to be an important treatise on some medical subject, almost in process of completion. He was considered to have fine manners and once made a good speech at a public health meeting on the subject of drugs; but he became entangled with a girl who worked in a grocery store, and he was also involved in a lawsuit about some medical question; so he left Lockport.

After that he didn't ask for the children to be sent to America and didn't answer when Nicole wrote asking him if he needed money. In the last letter she had from him he told her that he was practicing in Geneva, New York, and she got the impression that he had settled down with some one to keep house for him. She looked up Geneva in an atlas and found it was in the heart of the Finger Lakes Section and considered a pleasant place. Perhaps, so she liked to think, his career was biding its time, again like Grant's in Galena; his latest note was post-marked from Hornell, New York, which is some distance from Geneva and a very small town; in any case he is almost certainly in that section of the country, in one town or another.

STORIES

ABSOLUTION

THERE was once a priest with cold, watery eyes, who, in the still of the night, wept cold tears. He wept because the afternoons were warm and long, and he was unable to attain a complete mystical union with our Lord. Sometimes, near four o'clock, there was a rustle of Swede girls along the path by his window, and in their shrill laughter he found a terrible dissonance that made him pray aloud for the twilight to come. At twilight the laughter and the voices were quieter, but several times he had walked past Romberg's Drug Store when it was dusk and the yellow lights shone inside and the nickel taps of the soda-fountain were gleaming, and he had found the scent of cheap toilet soap desperately sweet upon the air. He passed that way when he returned from hearing confessions on Saturday nights, and he grew careful to walk on the other side of the street so that the smell of the soap would float upward before it reached his nostrils as it drifted, rather like incense, toward the summer moon.

But there was no escape from the hot madness of four o'clock. From his window, as far as he could see, the Dakota wheat thronged the valley of the Red River. The wheat was terrible to look upon and the carpet pattern to which in agony he bent his eyes sent his thought brooding through grotesque labyrinths, open always to the unavoidable sun.

One afternoon when he had reached the point where

the mind runs down like an old clock, his housekeeper brought into his study a beautiful, intense little boy of eleven named Rudolph Miller. The little boy sat down in a patch of sunshine, and the priest, at his walnut desk, pretended to be very busy. This was to conceal his relief that someone had come into his haunted room.

Presently he turned around and found himself staring into two enormous, staccato eyes, lit with gleaming points of cobalt light. For a moment their expression startled him—then he saw that his visitor was in a state of abject fear.

"Your mouth is trembling," said Father Schwartz, in a haggard voice.

The little boy covered his quivering mouth with his hand.

"Are you in trouble?" asked Father Schwartz, sharply. "Take your hand away from your mouth and tell me what's the matter."

The boy—Father Schwartz recognized him now as the son of a parishioner, Mr. Miller, the freight-agent—moved his hand reluctantly off his mouth and became articulate in a despairing whisper.

"Father Schwartz—I've committed a terrible sin."

"A sin against purity?"

"No, Father . . . worse."

Father Schwartz's body jerked sharply.

"Have you killed somebody?"

"No—but I'm afraid—" the voice rose to a shrill whimper.

"Do you want to go to confession?"

The little boy shook his head miserably. Father Schwartz cleared his throat so that he could make his voice soft and say some quiet, kind thing. In this moment he should forget his own agony, and try to act like God. He repeated to himself a devotional phrase, hoping that in return God would help him to act correctly.

"Tell me what you've done," said his new soft voice.

The little boy looked at him through his tears, and was reassured by the impression of moral resiliency which the distraught priest had created. Abandoning as much of himself as he was able to this man, Rudolph Miller began to tell his story.

"On Saturday, three days ago, my father he said I had to go to confession, because I hadn't been for a month, and the family they go every week, and I hadn't been. So I just as leave go, I didn't care. So I put it off till after supper because I was playing with a bunch of kids and father asked me if I went, and I said 'no,' and he took me by the neck and he said 'You go now,' so I said 'All right,' so I went over to church. And he yelled after me: 'Don't come back till you go.' . . ."

II

"On Saturday, Three Days Ago."

THE plush curtain of the confessional rearranged its dismal creases, leaving exposed only the bottom of an old man's old shoe. Behind the curtain an immortal soul was alone with God and the Reverend Adolphus Schwartz, priest of the parish. Sound began, a labored whispering, sibilant and discreet, broken at intervals by the voice of the priest in audible question.

Rudolph Miller knelt in the pew beside the confessional and waited, straining nervously to hear, and yet not to hear what was being said within. The fact that the priest was audible alarmed him. His own turn came next, and the three or four others who waited might listen unscrupulously while he admitted his violations of the Sixth and Ninth Commandments.

Rudolph had never committed adultery, nor even coveted his neighbor's wife—but it was the confession of the associate sins that was particularly hard to contemplate. In comparison he relished the less shameful fallings away—they formed a grayish background which relieved the ebony mark of sexual offenses upon his soul.

He had been covering his ears with his hands, hoping that his refusal to hear would be noticed, and a like courtesy rendered to him in turn, when a sharp movement of the penitent in the confessional made him sink his face precipitately into the crook of his elbow. Fear assumed solid form, and pressed out a lodging between his heart and his lungs. He must try now with all his might to be sorry for his sins—not because he was afraid, but because he had offended God. He must convince God that he was sorry and to do so he must first convince himself. After a tense emotional struggle he achieved a tremulous self-pity, and decided that he was now ready. If, by allowing no other thought to enter his head, he could preserve this state of emotion unimpaired until he went into that large coffin set on end, he would have survived another crisis in his religious life.

For some time, however, a demoniac notion had partially possessed him. He could go home now, before his turn came, and tell his mother that he had arrived too late, and found the priest gone. This, unfortunately, involved the risk of being caught in a lie. As an alternative he could say that he *had* gone to confession, but this meant that he must avoid communion next day, for communion taken upon an uncleansed soul would turn to poison in his mouth, and he would crumple limp and damned from the altar-rail.

Again Father Schwartz's voice became audible.

"And for your——"

The words blurred to a husky mumble, and Rudolph got excitedly to his feet. He felt that it was impossible for him to go to confession this afternoon. He hesitated tensely. Then from the confessional came a tap, a creak, and a sustained rustle. The slide had fallen and the plush curtain trembled. Temptation had come to him too late. . . .

"Bless me, Father, for I have sinned. . . . I confess to Almighty God and to you, Father, that I have sinned. . . . Since my last confession it has been one month and three days. . . . I accuse myself of—taking the Name of the Lord in vain. . . ."

This was an easy sin. His curses had been but bravado—telling of them was little less than a brag.

". . . of being mean to an old lady."

The wan shadow moved a little on the latticed slat.

"How, my child?"

"Old lady Swenson," Rudolph's murmur soared jubilantly. "She got our baseball that we knocked in her window, and she wouldn't give it back, so we yelled 'Twenty-three, Skidoo,' at her all afternoon. Then about five o'clock she had a fit, and they had to have the doctor."

"Go on, my child."

"Of—of not believing I was the son of my parents."

"What?" The interrogation was distinctly startled.

"Of not believing that I was the son of my parents."

"Why not?"

"Oh, just pride," answered the penitent airily.

"You mean you thought you were too good to be the son of your parents?"

"Yes, Father." On a less jubilant note.

"Go on."

"Of being disobedient and calling my mother names. Of slandering people behind my back. Of smoking——"

Rudolph had now exhausted the minor offenses, and was approaching the sins it was agony to tell. He held his fingers against his face like bars as if to press out between them the shame in his heart.

"Of dirty words and immodest thoughts and desires," he whispered very low.

"How often?"

"I don't know."

"Once a week? Twice a week?"

"Twice a week."

"Did you yield to these desires?"

"No, Father."

"Were you alone when you had them?"

"No, Father. I was with two boys and a girl."

"Don't you know, my child, that you should avoid the occasions of sin as well as the sin itself? Evil companionship leads to evil desires and evil desires to evil actions. Where were you when this happened?"

"In a barn in back of——"

"I don't want to hear any names," interrupted the priest sharply.

"Well, it was up in the loft of this barn and this girl and—a fella, they were saying things—saying immodest things, and I stayed."

"You should have gone—you should have told the girl to go."

He should have gone! He could not tell Father Schwartz how his pulse had bumped in his wrist, how a strange, romantic excitement had possessed him when those curious things had been said. Perhaps in the houses of delinquency among the dull and hard-eyed incorrigible girls can be found those for whom has burned the whitest fire.

"Have you anything else to tell me?"

"I don't think so, Father."

Rudolph felt a great relief. Perspiration had broken out under his tight-pressed fingers.

"Have you told any lies?"

The question startled him. Like all those who habitually and instinctively lie, he had an enormous respect and awe for the truth. Something almost exterior to himself dictated a quick, hurt answer.

"Oh, no, Father, I never tell lies."

For a moment, like the commoner in the king's chair, he tasted the pride of the situation. Then as the priest began to murmur conventional admonitions he realized that in heroically denying he had told lies, he had committed a terrible sin—he had told a lie in confession.

In automatic response to Father Schwartz's "Make an act of contrition," he began to repeat aloud meaninglessly:

"Oh, my God, I am heartily sorry for having offended Thee. . . ."

He must fix this now—it was a bad mistake—but as his teeth shut on the last words of his prayer there was a sharp sound, and the slat was closed.

A minute later when he emerged into the twilight the relief in coming from the muggy church into an open world of wheat and sky postponed the full realization of what he had done. Instead of worrying he took a deep breath of the crisp air and began to say over and over to himself the words "Blatchford Sarnemington, Blatchford Sarnemington!"

Blatchford Sarnemington was himself, and these

words were in effect a lyric. When he became Blatchford Sarnemington a suave nobility flowed from him. Blatchford Sarnemington lived in great sweeping triumphs. When Rudolph half closed his eyes it meant that Blatchford had established dominance over him and, as he went by, there were envious mutters in the air: "Blatchford Sarnemington! There goes Blatchford Sarnemington."

He was Blatchford now for a while as he strutted homeward along the staggering road, but when the road braced itself in macadam in order to become the main street of Ludwig, Rudolph's exhilaration faded out and his mind cooled, and he felt the horror of his lie. God, of course, already knew of it—but Rudolph reserved a corner of his mind where he was safe from God, where he prepared the subterfuges with which he often tricked God. Hiding now in this corner he considered how he could best avoid the consequences of his misstatement.

At all costs he must avoid communion next day. The risk of angering God to such an extent was too great. He would have to drink water "by accident" in the morning, and thus, in accordance with a church law, render himself unfit to receive communion that day. In spite of its flimsiness this subterfuge was the most feasible that occurred to him. He accepted its risks and was concentrating on how best to put it into effect, as he turned the corner by Romberg's Drug Store and came in sight of his father's house.

III

RUDOLPH'S father, the local freight-agent, had floated with the second wave of German and Irish stock to the Minnesota-Dakota country. Theoretically, great opportunities lay ahead of a young man of energy in that day and place, but Carl Miller had been incapable of establishing either with his superiors or his subordinates the reputation for approximate immutability which is essential to success in a hierarchic industry. Somewhat gross, he was, nevertheless, insufficiently hard-headed and unable to take fundamental relationships for granted, and this inability made him suspicious, unrestful, and continually dismayed.

His two bonds with the colorful life were his faith in the Roman Catholic Church and his mystical worship of the Empire Builder, James J. Hill. Hill was the apotheosis of that quality in which Miller himself was deficient—the sense of things, the feel of things, the hint of rain in the wind on the cheek. Miller's mind worked late on the old decisions of other men, and he had never in his life felt the balance of any single thing in his hands. His weary, sprightly, undersized body was growing old in Hill's gigantic shadow. For twenty years he had lived alone with Hill's name and God.

On Sunday morning Carl Miller awoke in the dustless quiet of six o'clock. Kneeling by the side of the bed he bent his yellow-gray hair and the full dapple bangs of his mustache into the pillow, and prayed for several minutes. Then he drew off his night-shirt—like the rest of his generation he had never been able to endure pajamas—and clothed his thin, white, hairless body in woolen underwear.

He shaved. Silence in the other bedroom where his wife lay nervously asleep. Silence from the screened-off corner of the hall where his son's cot stood, and his son slept among his Alger books, his collection of cigar-bands, his mothy pennants—"Cornell," "Hamlin," and "Greetings from Pueblo, New Mexico"—and the other possessions of his private life. From outside Miller could hear the shrill birds and the whirring movement of the poultry, and, as an undertone, the low, swelling click-a-tick of the six-fifteen through-train for Montana and the green coast beyond. Then as the cold water dripped from the wash-rag in his hand he raised his head suddenly—he had heard a furtive sound from the kitchen below.

He dried his razor hastily, slipped his dangling suspenders to his shoulder, and listened. Some one was walking in the kitchen, and he knew by the light footfall that it was not his wife. With his mouth faintly ajar he ran quickly down the stairs and opened the kitchen door.

Standing by the sink, with one hand on the still dripping faucet and the other clutching a full glass of water, stood his son. The boy's eyes, still heavy with sleep, met his father's with a frightened, reproachful beauty. He was barefooted, and his pajamas were rolled up at the knees and sleeves.

For a moment they both remained motionless—Carl Miller's brow went down and his son's went up, as though they were striking a balance between the extremes of emotion which filled them. Then the bangs of the parent's mustache descended portentously until they obscured his mouth, and he gave a short glance around to see if anything had been disturbed.

The kitchen was garnished with sunlight which beat on the pans and made the smooth boards of the floor and table yellow and clean as wheat. It was the center of the house where the fire burned and the tins fitted into tins like toys, and the steam whistled all day on a thin pastel note. Nothing was moved, nothing touched —except the faucet where beads of water still formed and dripped with a white flash into the sink below.

"What are you doing?"

"I got awful thirsty, so I thought I'd just come down and get——"

"I thought you were going to communion."

A look of vehement astonishment spread over his son's face.

"I forgot all about it."

"Have you drunk any water?"

"No——"

As the word left his mouth Rudolph knew it was the wrong answer, but the faded indignant eyes facing him had signaled up the truth before the boy's will could act. He realized, too, that he should never have come downstairs; some vague necessity for verisimilitude had made him want to leave a wet glass as evidence by the sink; the honesty of his imagination had betrayed him.

"Pour it out," commanded his father, "that water!"

Rudolph despairingly inverted the tumbler.

"What's the matter with you, anyways?" demanded Miller angrily.

"Nothing."

"Did you go to confession yesterday?"

"Yes."

"Then why were you going to drink water?"

"I don't know—I forgot."

"Maybe you care more about being a little bit thirsty than you do about your religion."

"I forgot." Rudolph could feel the tears straining in his eyes.

"That's no answer."

"Well, I did."

"You better look out!" His father held to a high, persistent, inquisitory note: "If you're so forgetful that you can't remember your religion something better be done about it."

Rudolph filled a sharp pause with:

"I can remember it all right."

"First you begin to neglect your religion," cried his father, fanning his own fierceness, "the next thing you'll begin to lie and steal, and the *next* thing is the *reform* school!"

Not even this familiar threat could deepen the abyss that Rudolph saw before him. He must either tell all now, offering his body for what he knew would be a ferocious beating, or else tempt the thunderbolts by receiving the Body and Blood of Christ with sacrilege upon his soul. And of the two the former seemed more terrible—it was not so much the beating he dreaded as the savage ferocity, outlet of the ineffectual man, which would lie behind it.

"Put down that glass and go upstairs and dress!" his father ordered, "and when we get to church, before you go to communion, you better kneel down and ask God to forgive you for your carelessness."

Some accidental emphasis in the phrasing of this command acted like a catalytic agent on the confusion and terror of Rudolph's mind. A wild, proud anger rose in him, and he dashed the tumbler passionately into the sink.

His father uttered a strained, husky sound, and sprang for him. Rudolph dodged to the side, tipped over a chair, and tried to get beyond the kitchen table. He cried out sharply when a hand grasped his pajama shoulder, then he felt the dull impact of a fist against the side of his head, and glancing blows on the upper part of his body. As he slipped here and there in his father's grasp, dragged or lifted when he clung instinctively to an arm, aware of sharp smarts and strains, he made no sound except that he laughed hysterically several times. Then in less than a minute the blows abruptly ceased. After a lull during which Rudolph was tightly held, and during which they both trembled violently and uttered strange, truncated words, Carl Miller half dragged, half threatened his son upstairs.

"Put on your clothes!"

Rudolph was now both hysterical and cold. His head hurt him, and there was a long, shallow scratch on his neck from his father's finger-nail, and he sobbed and trembled as he dressed. He was aware of his mother standing at the doorway in a wrapper, her wrinkled face compressing and squeezing and opening out into new series of wrinkles which floated and eddied from neck to brow. Despising her nervous ineffectuality and avoiding her rudely when she tried to touch his neck with witch-hazel, he made a hasty, choking toilet. Then he followed his father out of the house and along the road toward the Catholic church.

IV

THEY walked without speaking except when Carl Miller acknowledged automatically the existence of passers-by. Rudolph's uneven breathing alone ruffled the hot Sunday silence.

His father stopped decisively at the door of the church.

"I've decided you'd better go to confession again. Go in and tell Father Schwartz what you did and ask God's pardon."

"You lost your temper, too!" said Rudolph quickly.

Carl Miller took a step toward his son, who moved cautiously backward.

"All right, I'll go."

"Are you going to do what I say?" cried his father in a hoarse whisper.

"All right."

Rudolph walked into the church, and for the second

time in two days entered the confessional and knelt down. The slat went up almost at once.

"I accuse myself of missing my morning prayers."

"Is that all?"

"That's all."

A maudlin exultation filled him. Not easily ever again would he be able to put an abstraction before the necessities of his ease and pride. An invisible line had been crossed, and he had become aware of his isolation—aware that it applied not only to those moments when he was Blatchford Sarnemington but that it applied to all his inner life. Hitherto such phenomena as "crazy" ambitions and petty shames and fears had been but private reservations, unacknowledged before the throne of his official soul. Now he realized unconsciously that his private reservations were himself—and all the rest a garnished front and a conventional flag. The pressure of his environment had driven him into the lonely secret road of adolescence.

He knelt in the pew beside his father. Mass began. Rudolph knelt up—when he was alone he slumped his posterior back against the seat—and tasted the consciousness of a sharp, subtle revenge. Beside him his father prayed that God would forgive Rudolph, and asked also that his own outbreak of temper would be pardoned. He glanced sidewise at this son, and was relieved to see that the strained, wild look had gone from his face and that he had ceased sobbing. The Grace of God, inherent in the Sacrament, would do the rest, and perhaps after Mass everything would be better. He was proud of Rudolph in his heart, and beginning to be truly as well as formally sorry for what he had done.

Usually, the passing of the collection box was a

significant point for Rudolph in the services. If, as was often the case, he had no money to drop in he would be furiously ashamed and bow his head and pretend not to see the box, lest Jeanne Brady in the pew behind should take notice and suspect an acute family poverty. But today he glanced coldly into it as it skimmed under his eyes, noting with casual interest the large number of pennies it contained.

When the bell rang for communion, however, he quivered. There was no reason why God should not stop his heart. During the past twelve hours he had committed a series of mortal sins increasing in gravity, and he was now to crown them all with a blasphemous sacrilege.

"Domini, non sum dignus; ut interes sub tectum meum; sed tantum dic verbo, et sanabitur anima mea. . . ."

There was a rustle in the pews, and the communicants worked their ways into the aisle with downcast eyes and joined hands. Those of larger piety pressed together their finger-tips to form steeples. Among these latter was Carl Miller. Rudolph followed him toward the altar-rail and knelt down, automatically taking up the napkin under his chin. The bell rang sharply, and the priest turned from the altar with the white Host held above the chalice:

"Corpus Domini nostri Jesu Christi custodiat animam meam in vitam æternam."

A cold sweat broke out on Rudolph's forehead as the communion began. Along the line Father Schwartz moved, and with gathering nausea Rudolph felt his heart-valves weakening at the will of God. It seemed to him that the church was darker and that a great quiet had fallen, broken only by the inarticulate mumble which announced the approach of the Creator of Heaven and Earth. He dropped his head down between his shoulders and waited for the blow.

Then he felt a sharp nudge in his side. His father was poking him to sit up, not to slump against the rail; the priest was only two places away.

"Corpus Domini nostri Jesu Christi custodiat animam meam in vitam æternam."

Rudolph opened his mouth. He felt the sticky wax taste of the wafer on his tongue. He remained motionless for what seemed an interminable period of time, his head still raised, the wafer undissolved in his mouth. Then again he started at the pressure of his father's elbow, and saw that the people were falling away from the altar like leaves and turning with blind downcast eyes to their pews, alone with God.

Rudolph was alone with himself, drenched with perspiration and deep in mortal sin. As he walked back to his pew the sharp taps of his cloven hoofs were loud upon the floor, and he knew that it was a dark poison he carried in his heart.

V

"Sagitta Volante in Dei"

THE beautiful little boy with eyes like blue stones, and lashes that sprayed open from them like flower-petals had finished telling his sin to Father Schwartz—and the square of sunshine in which he sat had moved forward half an hour into the room. Rudolph had become less frightened now; once eased of the story a reaction had set in. He knew that as long as he was in the room with this priest God would not stop his heart, so he sighed and sat quietly, waiting for the priest to speak.

Father Schwartz's cold watery eyes were fixed upon the carpet pattern on which the sun had brought out the swastikas and the flat bloomless vines and the pale echoes of flowers. The hall-clock ticked insistently toward sunset, and from the ugly room and from the afternoon outside the window arose a stiff monotony, shattered now and then by the reverberate clapping of a far-away hammer on the dry air. The priest's nerves were strung thin and the beads of his rosary were crawling and squirming like snakes upon the green felt of his table top. He could not remember now what it was he should say.

Of all the things in this lost Swede town he was most aware of this little boy's eyes—the beautiful eyes, with lashes that left them reluctantly and curved back as though to meet them once more.

For a moment longer the silence persisted while Rudolph waited, and the priest struggled to remember something that was slipping farther and farther away from him, and the clock ticked in the broken house. Then Father Schwartz stared hard at the little boy and remarked in a peculiar voice:

"When a lot of people get together in the best places things go glimmering."

Rudolph started and looked quickly at Father Schwartz's face.

"I said—" began the priest, and paused, listening. "Do you hear the hammer and the clock ticking and the bees? Well, that's no good. The thing is to have a lot of people in the center of the world, wherever that happens to be. Then"—his watery eyes widened knowingly—"things go glimmering."

"Yes, Father," agreed Rudolph, feeling a little frightened.

"What are you going to be when you grow up?"

"Well, I was going to be a baseball-player for a while," answered Rudolph nervously, "but I don't think that's a very good ambition, so I think I'll be an actor or a Navy officer."

Again the priest stared at him.

"I see *exactly* what you mean," he said, with a fierce air.

Rudolph had not meant anything in particular, and at the implication that he had, he became more uneasy.

"This man is crazy," he thought, "and I'm scared of him. He wants me to help him out some way, and I don't want to."

"You look as if things went glimmering," cried Father Schwartz wildly. "Did you ever go to a party?"

"Yes, Father."

"And did you notice that everybody was properly dressed? That's what I mean. Just as you went into the party there was a moment when everybody was properly dressed. Maybe two little girls were standing by the door and some boys were leaning over the banisters, and there were bowls around full of flowers."

"I've been to a lot of parties," said Rudolph, rather relieved that the conversation had taken this turn.

"Of course," continued Father Schwartz triumphantly, "I knew you'd agree with me. But my theory is that when a whole lot of people get together in the best places things go glimmering all the time."

Rudolph found himself thinking of Blatchford Sarnemington.

"Please listen to me!" commanded the priest impatiently. "Stop worrying about last Saturday. Apostasy implies an absolute damnation only on the supposition of a previous perfect faith. Does that fix it?"

Rudolph had not the faintest idea what Father Schwartz was talking about, but he nodded and the priest nodded back at him and returned to his mysterious preoccupation.

"Why," he cried, "they have lights now as big as stars—do you realize that? I heard of one light they had in Paris or somewhere that was as big as a star. A lot of people had it—a lot of gay people. They have all sorts of things now that you never dreamed of."

"Look here—" He came nearer to Rudolph, but the boy drew away, so Father Schwartz went back and sat down in his chair, his eyes dried out and hot. "Did you ever see an amusement park?"

"No, Father."

"Well, go and see an amusement park." The priest waved his hand vaguely. "It's a thing like a fair, only much more glittering. Go to one at night and stand a little way off from it in a dark place—under dark trees. You'll see a big wheel made of lights turning in the air, and a long slide shooting boats down into the water. A band playing somewhere, and a smell of peanuts—and everything will twinkle. But it won't remind you of anything, you see. It will all just hang out there in the night like a colored balloon—like a big yellow lantern on a pole."

Father Schwartz frowned as he suddenly thought of something.

"But don't get up close," he warned Rudolph, "because if you do you'll only feel the heat and the sweat and the life."

All this talking seemed particularly strange and awful to Rudolph, because this man was a priest. He sat there, half terrified, his beautiful eyes open wide and staring at Father Schwartz. But underneath his terror he felt that his own inner convictions were confirmed. There was something ineffably gorgeous somewhere that had nothing to do with God. He no longer thought that God was angry at him about the original lie, because He must have understood that Rudolph had done it to make things finer in the confessional, brightening up the dinginess of his admissions by saying a thing radiant and proud. At the moment when he had affirmed immaculate honor a silver pennon had flapped out into the breeze somewhere and there had been the crunch of leather and the shine of silver spurs and a troop of horsemen waiting for dawn on a low green hill. The sun had made stars of light on their breastplates like the picture at home of the German cuirassiers at Sedan.

But now the priest was muttering inarticulate and heart-broken words, and the boy became wildly afraid. Horror entered suddenly in at the open window, and the atmosphere of the room changed. Father Schwartz collapsed precipitously down on his knees, and let his body settle back against a chair.

"Oh, my God!" he cried out, in a strange voice, and wilted to the floor.

Then a human oppression rose from the priest's worn clothes, and mingled with the faint smell of old food in the corners. Rudolph gave a sharp cry and ran in a panic from the house—while the collapsed man lay there quite still, filling his room, filling it with voices and faces until it was crowded with echolalia, and rang loud with a steady, shrill note of laughter.

Outside the window the blue sirocco trembled over the wheat, and girls with yellow hair walked sensuously along roads that bounded the fields, calling innocent, exciting things to the young men who were working in the lines between the grain. Legs were shaped under starchless gingham, and rims of the necks of dresses were warm and damp. For five hours now hot fertile life had burned in the afternoon. It would be night in three hours, and all along the land there would be these blonde Northern girls and the tall young men from the farms lying out beside the wheat, under the moon.

THE BABY PARTY

WHEN John Andros felt old he found solace in the thought of life continuing through his child. The dark trumpets of oblivion were less loud at the patter of his child's feet or at the sound of his child's voice babbling mad non sequiturs to him over the telephone. The latter incident occurred every afternoon at three when his wife called the office from the country, and he came to look forward to it as one of the vivid minutes of his day.

He was not physically old, but his life had been a series of struggles up a series of rugged hills, and here at thirty-eight having won his battles against ill-health and poverty he cherished less than the usual number of illusions. Even his feeling about his little girl was qualified. She had interrupted his rather intense love-affair with his wife, and she was the reason for their living in a suburban town, where they paid for country air with endless servant troubles and the weary merry-go-round of the commuting train.

It was little Ede as a definite piece of youth that chiefly interested him. He liked to take her on his lap and examine minutely her fragrant, downy scalp and her eyes with their irises of morning blue. Having paid this homage John was content that the nurse should take her away. After ten minutes the very vitality of the child irritated him; he was inclined to lose his temper when things were broken, and one Sunday afternoon when she had disrupted a bridge game by permanently hiding up the ace of spades, he had made a scene that had reduced his wife to tears.

This was absurd and John was ashamed of himself. It was inevitable that such things would happen, and it was impossible that little Ede should spend all her indoor hours in the nursery upstairs when she was becoming, as her mother said, more nearly a "real person" every day.

She was two and a half, and this afternoon, for instance, she was going to a baby party. Grown-up Edith, her mother, had telephoned the information to the office, and little Ede had confirmed the business by shouting "I yam going to a *pantry!*" into John's unsuspecting left ear.

"Drop in at the Markeys' when you get home, won't you, dear?" resumed her mother. "It'll be funny. Ede's going to be all dressed up in her new pink dress——"

The conversation terminated abruptly with a squawk which indicated that the telephone had been pulled violently to the floor. John laughed and decided to get an early train out; the prospect of a baby party in some one else's house amused him.

"What a peach of a mess!" he thought humorously. "A dozen mothers, and each one looking at nothing but her own child. All the babies breaking things and grabbing at the cake, and each mamma going home thinking about the subtle superiority of her own child to every other child there."

He was in a good humor today—all the things in his life were going better than they had ever gone before. When he got off the train at his station he shook his head at an importunate taxi man, and began to walk up the long hill toward his house through the crisp December twilight. It was only six o'clock but the moon was out, shining with proud brilliance on the thin sugary snow that lay over the lawns.

As he walked along drawing his lungs full of cold air his happiness increased, and the idea of a baby party appealed to him more and more. He began to wonder how Ede compared to other children of her own age, and if the pink dress she was to wear was something radical and mature. Increasing his gait he came in sight of his own house, where the lights of a defunct Christmas tree still blossomed in the window, but he continued on past the walk. The party was at the Markeys' next door.

As he mounted the brick step and rang the bell he became aware of voices inside, and he was glad he was not too late. Then he raised his head and listened—the voices were not children's voices, but they were loud and pitched high with anger; there were at least three of them and one, which rose as he listened to a hysterical sob, he recognized immediately as his wife's.

"There's been some trouble," he thought quickly.

Trying the door, he found it unlocked and pushed it open.

The baby party began at half past four, but Edith Andros, calculating shrewdly that the new dress would stand out more sensationally against vestments already rumpled, planned the arrival of herself and little Ede for five. When they appeared it was already a flourishing affair. Four baby girls and nine baby boys, each one curled and washed and dressed with all the care of a proud and jealous heart, were dancing to the music of a phonograph. Never more than two or three were dancing at once, but as all were continually in motion running to and from their mothers for encouragement, the general effect was the same.

As Edith and her daughter entered, the music was temporarily drowned out by a sustained chorus, consisting largely of the word *cute* and directed toward little Ede, who stood looking timidly about and fingering the edges of her pink dress. She was not kissed—this is the sanitary age—but she was passed along a row of mammas each one of whom said "cu-u-ute" to her and held her pink little hand before passing her on to the next. After some encouragement and a few mild pushes she was absorbed into the dance, and became an active member of the party.

Edith stood near the door talking to Mrs. Markey, and keeping one eye on the tiny figure in the pink dress. She did not care for Mrs. Markey; she considered her both snippy and common, but John and Joe Markey were congenial and went in together on the commuting train every morning, so the two women kept up an elaborate pretense of warm amity. They were always reproaching each other for "not coming to see me," and they were always planning the kind of parties that began with "You'll have to come to dinner with us soon, and we'll go in to the theatre," but never matured further.

"Little Ede looks perfectly darling," said Mrs. Markey, smiling and moistening her lips in a way that Edith found particularly repulsive. "So *grown-up*—I can't *believe* it!"

Edith wondered if "little Ede" referred to the fact that Billy Markey, though several months younger, weighed almost five pounds more. Accepting a cup of tea she took a seat with two other ladies on a divan and launched into the real business of the afternoon, which of course lay in relating the recent accomplishments and insouciances of her child.

An hour passed. Dancing palled and the babies took to sterner sport. They ran into the dining-room, rounded the big table, and essayed the kitchen door, from which they were rescued by an expeditionary force of mothers. Having been rounded up they immediately broke loose, and rushing back to the dining-room tried the familiar swinging door again. The word "overheated" began to be used, and small white brows were dried with small white handkerchiefs. A general attempt to make the babies sit down began, but the babies squirmed off laps with peremptory cries of "Down! Down!" and the rush into the fascinating dining-room began anew.

This phase of the party came to an end with the arrival of refreshments, a large cake with two candles, and saucers of vanilla ice cream. Billy Markey, a stout laughing baby with red hair and legs somewhat bowed, blew out the candles, and placed an experimental thumb on the white frosting. The refreshments were distributed, and the children ate, greedily but without confusion—they had behaved remarkably well all afternoon. They were modern babies who ate and slept at regular hours, so their dispositions were good, and their faces healthy and pink—such a peaceful party would not have been possible thirty years ago.

After the refreshments a gradual exodus began. Edith glanced anxiously at her watch—it was almost six, and John had not arrived. She wanted him to see Ede with the other children—to see how dignified and polite and intelligent she was, and how the only ice-cream spot on her dress was some that had dropped from her chin when she was joggled from behind.

"You're a darling," she whispered to her child, drawing her suddenly against her knee. "Do you know you're a darling? Do you *know* you're a darling?"

Ede laughed. "Bow-wow," she said suddenly.

"Bow-wow?" Edith looked around. "There isn't any bow-wow."

"Bow-wow," repeated Ede. "I want a bow-wow."

Edith followed the small pointing finger.

"That isn't a bow-wow, dearest, that's a teddy-bear."

"Bear?"

"Yes, that's a teddy-bear, and it belongs to Billy Markey. You don't want Billy Markey's teddy-bear, do you?"

Ede did want it.

She broke away from her mother and approached Billy Markey, who held the toy closely in his arms. Ede stood regarding him with inscrutable eyes, and Billy laughed.

Grown-up Edith looked at her watch again, this time impatiently.

The party had dwindled until, besides Ede and Billy, there were only two babies remaining—and one of the two remained only by virtue of having hidden himself under the dining-room table. It was selfish of John not to come. It showed so little pride in the child. Other fathers had come, half a dozen of them, to call for their wives, and they had stayed for a while and looked on.

There was a sudden wail. Ede had obtained Billy's teddy-bear by pulling it forcibly from his arms, and on Billy's attempt to recover it, she had pushed him casually to the floor.

"Why, Ede!" cried her mother, repressing an inclination to laugh.

Joe Markey, a handsome, broad-shouldered man of

thirty-five, picked up his son and set him on his feet. "You're a fine fellow," he said jovially. "Let a girl knock you over! You're a fine fellow."

"Did he bump his head?" Mrs. Markey returned anxiously from bowing the next to last remaining mother out the door.

"No-o-o-o," exclaimed Markey. "He bumped something else, didn't you, Billy? He bumped something else."

Billy had so far forgotten the bump that he was already making an attempt to recover his property. He seized a leg of the bear which projected from Ede's enveloping arms and tugged at it but without success.

"No," said Ede emphatically.

Suddenly, encouraged by the success of her former half-accidental manœuvre, Ede dropped the teddy-bear, placed her hands on Billy's shoulders and pushed him backward off his feet.

This time he landed less harmlessly; his head hit the bare floor just off the rug with a dull hollow sound, whereupon he drew in his breath and delivered an agonized yell.

Immediately the room was in confusion. With an exclamation Markey hurried to his son, but his wife was first to reach the injured baby and catch him up into her arms.

"Oh, *Billy,*" she cried, "what a terrible bump! She ought to be spanked."

Edith, who had rushed immediately to her daughter, heard this remark, and her lips came sharply together.

"Why, Ede," she whispered perfunctorily, "you bad girl!"

Ede put back her little head suddenly and laughed. It was a loud laugh, a triumphant laugh with victory in it and challenge and contempt. Unfortunately it was also an infectious laugh. Before her mother realized the delicacy of the situation, she too had laughed, an audible, distinct laugh not unlike the baby's, and partaking of the same overtones.

Then, as suddenly, she stopped.

Mrs. Markey's face had grown red with anger, and Markey, who had been feeling the back of the baby's head with one finger, looked at her, frowning.

"It's swollen already," he said with a note of reproof in his voice. "I'll get some witch-hazel."

But Mrs. Markey had lost her temper. "I don't see anything funny about a child being hurt!" she said in a trembling voice.

Little Ede meanwhile had been looking at her mother curiously. She noted that her own laugh had produced her mother's, and she wondered if the same cause would always produce the same effect. So she chose this moment to throw back her head and laugh again.

To her mother the additional mirth added the final touch of hysteria to the situation. Pressing her handkerchief to her mouth she giggled irrepressibly. It was more than nervousness—she felt that in a peculiar way she was laughing with her child—they were laughing together.

It was in a way a defiance—those two against the world.

While Markey rushed upstairs to the bathroom for ointment, his wife was walking up and down rocking the yelling boy in her arms.

"Please go home!" she broke out suddenly. "The child's badly hurt, and if you haven't the decency to be quiet, you'd better go home."

"Very well," said Edith, her own temper rising. "I've never seen any one make such a mountain out of——"

"Get out!" cried Mrs. Markey frantically. "There's the door, get out—I never want to see you in our house again. You or your brat either!"

Edith had taken her daughter's hand and was moving quickly toward the door, but at this remark she stopped and turned around, her face contracting with indignation.

"Don't you dare call her that!"

Mrs. Markey did not answer but continued walking up and down, muttering to herself and to Billy in an inaudible voice.

Edith began to cry.

"I will get out!" she sobbed, "I've never heard anybody so rude and c-common in my life. I'm glad your baby did get pushed down—he's nothing but a f-fat little fool anyhow."

Joe Markey reached the foot of the stairs just in time to hear this remark.

"Why, Mrs. Andros," he said sharply, "can't you see the child's hurt? You really ought to control yourself."

"Control m-myself!" exclaimed Edith brokenly. "You better ask her to c-control herself. I've never heard anybody so c-common in my life."

"She's insulting me!" Mrs. Markey was now livid with rage. "Did you hear what she said, Joe? I wish you'd put her out. If she won't go, just take her by the shoulders and put her out!"

"Don't you dare touch me!" cried Edith. "I'm going just as quick as I can find my c-coat!"

Blind with tears she took a step toward the hall. It was just at this moment that the door opened and John Andros walked anxiously in.

"John!" cried Edith, and fled to him wildly.

"What's the matter? Why, what's the matter?"

"They're—they're putting me out!" she wailed, collapsing against him. "He'd just started to take me by the shoulders and put me out. I want my coat!"

"That's not true," objected Markey hurriedly. "Nobody's going to put you out." He turned to John. "Nobody's going to put her out," he repeated. "She's——"

"What do you mean 'put her out'?" demanded John abruptly. "What's all this talk, anyhow?"

"Oh, let's go!" cried Edith. "I want to go. They're so *common*, John!"

"Look here!" Markey's face darkened. "You've said that about enough. You're acting sort of crazy."

"They called Ede a brat!"

For the second time that afternoon little Ede expressed emotion at an inopportune moment. Confused and frightened at the shouting voices, she began to cry, and her tears had the effect of conveying that she felt the insult in her heart.

"What's the idea of this?" broke out John. "Do you insult your guests in your own house?"

"It seems to me it's your wife that's done the insulting!" answered Markey crisply. "In fact, your baby there started all the trouble."

John gave a contemptuous snort. "Are you calling names at a little baby?" he inquired. "That's a fine manly business!"

"Don't talk to him, John," insisted Edith. "Find my coat!"

"You must be in a bad way," went on John angrily "if you have to take out your temper on a helpless little baby."

"I never heard anything so damn twisted in my life," shouted Markey. "If that wife of yours would shut her mouth for a minute——"

"Wait a minute! You're not talking to a woman and child now——"

There was an incidental interruption. Edith had been fumbling on a chair for her coat, and Mrs. Markey had been watching her with hot, angry eyes. Suddenly she laid Billy down on the sofa, where he immediately stopped crying and pulled himself upright, and coming into the hall she quickly found Edith's coat and handed it to her without a word. Then she went back to the sofa, picked up Billy, and rocking him in her arms looked again at Edith with hot, angry eyes. The interruption had taken less than half a minute.

"Your wife comes in here and begins shouting around about how common we are!" burst out Markey violently. "Well, if we're so damn common, you'd better stay away! And, what's more, you'd better get out now!"

Again John gave a short, contemptuous laugh.

"You're not only common," he returned, "you're evidently an awful bully—when there's any helpless women and children around." He felt for the knob and swung the door open. "Come on, Edith."

Taking up her daughter in her arms, his wife stepped outside and John, still looking contemptuously at Markey, started to follow.

"Wait a minute!" Markey took a step forward; he was trembling slightly, and two large veins on his temple were suddenly full of blood. "You don't think you can get away with that, do you? With me?"

Without a word John walked out the door, leaving it open.

Edith, still weeping, had started for home. After following her with his eyes until she reached her own walk, John turned back toward the lighted doorway where Markey was slowly coming down the slippery steps. He took off his overcoat and hat, tossed them off the path onto the snow. Then, sliding a little on the iced walk, he took a step forward.

At the first blow, they both slipped and fell heavily to the sidewalk, half rising then, and again pulling each other to the ground. They found a better foothold in the thin snow to the side of the walk and rushed at each other, both swinging wildly and pressing out the snow into a pasty mud underfoot.

The street was deserted, and except for their short tired gasps and the padded sound as one or the other slipped down into the slushy mud, they fought in silence, clearly defined to each other by the full moonlight as well as by the amber glow that shone out of the open door. Several times they both slipped down together, and then for a while the conflict threshed about wildly on the lawn.

For ten, fifteen, twenty minutes they fought there senselessly in the moonlight. They had both taken off coats and vests at some silently agreed upon interval and now their shirts dripped from their backs in wet pulpy shreds. Both were torn and bleeding and so exhausted that they could stand only when by their position they mutually supported each other—the impact, the mere effort of a blow, would send them both to their hands and knees.

But it was not weariness that ended the business, and the very meaninglessness of the fight was a reason for not stopping. They stopped because once when they were straining at each other on the ground, they heard a man's footsteps coming along the sidewalk. They had rolled somehow into the shadow, and when they heard these footsteps they stopped fighting, stopped moving, stopped breathing, lay huddled together like two boys playing Indian until the footsteps had passed. Then, staggering to their feet, they looked at each other like two drunken men.

"I'll be damned if I'm going on with this thing any more," cried Markey thickly.

"I'm not going on any more either," said John Andros. "I've had enough of this thing."

Again they looked at each other, sulkily this time, as if each suspected the other of urging him to a renewal of the fight. Markey spat out a mouthful of blood from a cut lip; then he cursed softly, and picking up his coat and vest, shook off the snow from them in a surprised way, as if their comparative dampness was his only worry in the world.

"Want to come in and wash up?" he asked suddenly.

"No, thanks," said John. "I ought to be going home—my wife'll be worried."

He too picked up his coat and vest and then his overcoat and hat. Soaking wet and dripping with perspiration, it seemed absurd that less than half an hour ago he had been wearing all these clothes.

"Well—good night," he said hesitantly.

Suddenly they both walked toward each other and shook hands. It was no perfunctory hand-shake: John Andros's arm went around Markey's shoulder, and he patted him softly on the back for a little while.

"No harm done," he said brokenly.

"No—you?"

"No, no harm done."

"Well," said John Andros after a minute, "I guess I'll say good night."

"Good night."

Limping slightly and with his clothes over his arm, John Andros turned away. The moonlight was still bright as he left the dark patch of trampled ground and walked over the intervening lawn. Down at the station, half a mile away, he could hear the rumble of the seven o'clock train.

"But you must have been crazy," cried Edith brokenly. "I thought you were going to fix it all up there and shake hands. That's why I went away."

"Did you want us to fix it up?"

"Of course not, I never want to see them again. But I thought of course that was what you were going to do." She was touching the bruises on his neck and back with iodine as he sat placidly in a hot bath. "I'm going to get the doctor," she said insistently. "You may be hurt internally."

He shook his head. "Not a chance," he answered. "I don't want this to get all over town."

"I don't understand yet how it all happened."

"Neither do I." He smiled grimly. "I guess these baby parties are pretty rough affairs."

"Well, one thing—" suggested Edith hopefully, "I'm certainly glad we have beefsteak in the house for to-morrow's dinner."

"Why?"

"For your eye, of course. Do you know I came within an ace of ordering veal? Wasn't that the luckiest thing?"

Half an hour later, dressed except that his neck would accommodate no collar, John moved his limbs experimentally before the glass. "I believe I'll get my-self in better shape," he said thoughtfully. "I must be getting old."

"You mean so that next time you can beat him?"

"I did beat him," he announced. "At least, I beat him as much as he beat me. And there isn't going to be any next time. Don't you go calling people common any more. If you get in any trouble, you just take your coat and go home. Understand?"

"Yes, dear," she said meekly. "I was very foolish and now I understand."

Out in the hall, he paused abruptly by the baby's door.

"Is she asleep?"

"Sound asleep. But you can go in and peek at her —just to say good night."

They tiptoed in and bent together over the bed. Little Ede, her cheeks flushed with health, her pink hands clasped tight together, was sleeping soundly in the cool, dark room. John reached over the railing of the bed and passed his hand lightly over the silken hair.

"She's asleep," he murmured in a puzzled way.

"Naturally, after such an afternoon."

"Miz Andros," the colored maid's stage whisper floated in from the hall, "Mr. and Miz Markey downstairs an' want to see you. Mr. Markey he's all cut up in pieces, ma'am. His face look like a roast beef. An' Miz Markey she 'pear mighty mad."

"Why, what incomparable nerve!" exclaimed Edith. "Just tell them we're not home. I wouldn't go down for anything in the world."

"You most certainly will." John's voice was hard and set.

"What?"

"You'll go down right now, and, what's more, whatever that other woman does, you'll apologize for what you said this afternoon. After that you don't ever have to see her again."

"Why—John, I can't."

"You've got to. And just remember that she probably hated to come over here just twice as much as you hate to go downstairs."

"Aren't you coming? Do I have to go alone?"

"I'll be down—in just a minute."

John Andros waited until she had closed the door behind her; then he reached over into the bed, and picking up his daughter, blankets and all, sat down in the rocking-chair holding her tightly in his arms. She moved a little, and he held his breath, but she was sleeping soundly, and in a moment she was resting quietly in the hollow of his elbow. Slowly he bent his head until his cheek was against her bright hair. "Dear little girl," he whispered. "Dear little girl, dear little girl."

John Andros knew at length what it was he had fought for so savagely that evening. He had it now, he possessed it forever, and for some time he sat there rocking very slowly to and fro in the darkness.

THE RICH BOY

BEGIN with an individual, and before you know it you find that you have created a type; begin with a type, and you find that you have created—nothing. That is because we are all queer fish, queerer behind our faces and voices than we want any one to know or than we know ourselves. When I hear a man proclaiming himself an "average, honest, open fellow," I feel pretty sure that he has some definite and perhaps terrible abnormality which he has agreed to conceal—and his protestation of being average and honest and open is his way of reminding himself of his misprision.

There are no types, no plurals. There is a rich boy,

and this is his and not his brothers' story. All my life I have lived among his brothers but this one has been my friend. Besides, if I wrote about his brothers I should have to begin by attacking all the lies that the poor have told about the rich and the rich have told about themselves—such a wild structure they have erected that when we pick up a book about the rich, some instinct prepares us for unreality. Even the intelligent and impassioned reporters of life have made the country of the rich as unreal as fairy-land.

Let me tell you about the very rich. They are different from you and me. They possess and enjoy early, and it does something to them, makes them soft where we are hard, and cynical where we are trustful, in a way that, unless you were born rich, it is very difficult to understand. They think, deep in their hearts, that they are better than we are because we had to discover the compensations and refuges of life for ourselves. Even when they enter deep into our world or sink below us, they still think that they are better than we are. They are different. The only way I can describe young Anson Hunter is to approach him as if he were a foreigner and cling stubbornly to my point of view. If I accept his for a moment I am lost—I have nothing to show but a preposterous movie.

II

ANSON was the eldest of six children who would some day divide a fortune of fifteen million dollars, and he reached the age of reason—is it seven?—at the beginning of the century when daring young women were already gliding along Fifth Avenue in electric "mobiles." In those days he and his brother had an English governess who spoke the language very clearly and crisply and well, so that the two boys grew to speak as she did—their words and sentences were all crisp and clear and not run together as ours are. They didn't talk exactly like English children but acquired an accent that is peculiar to fashionable people in the city of New York.

In the summer the six children were moved from the house on Seventy-first Street to a big estate in northern Connecticut. It was not a fashionable locality—Anson's father wanted to delay as long as possible his children's knowledge of that side of life. He was a man somewhat superior to his class, which composed New York society, and to his period, which was the snobbish and formalized vulgarity of the Gilded Age, and he wanted his sons to learn habits of concentration and have sound constitutions and grow up into right-living and successful men. He and his wife kept an eye on them as well as they were able until the two older boys went away to school, but in huge establishments this is difficult—it was much simpler in the series of small and medium-sized houses in which my own youth was spent—I was never far out of the reach of my mother's voice, of the sense of her presence, her approval or disapproval.

Anson's first sense of his superiority came to him when he realized the half-grudging American deference that was paid to him in the Connecticut village. The parents of the boys he played with always inquired after his father and mother, and were vaguely excited when their own children were asked to the Hunters' house. He accepted this as the natural state of things, and a sort of impatience with all groups of which he was not the center—in money, in position, in authority—remained with him for the rest of his life. He disdained to struggle with other boys for precedence—he expected it to be given him freely, and when it wasn't he withdrew into his family. His family was sufficient, for in the East money is still a somewhat feudal thing, a clan-forming thing. In the snobbish West, money separates families to form "sets."

At eighteen, when he went to New Haven, Anson was tall and thick-set, with a clear complexion and a healthy color from the ordered life he had led in school. His hair was yellow and grew in a funny way on his head, his nose was beaked—these two things kept him from being handsome—but he had a confident charm and a certain brusque style, and the upper-class men who passed him on the street knew without being told that he was a rich boy and had gone to one of the best schools. Nevertheless, his very superiority kept him from being a success in college—the independence was mistaken for egotism, and the refusal to accept Yale standards with the proper awe seemed to belittle all those who had. So, long before he graduated, he began to shift the center of his life to New York.

He was at home in New York—there was his own house with "the kind of servants you can't get any more"—and his own family, of which, because of his good humor and a certain ability to make things go, he was rapidly becoming the centre, and the débutante parties, and the correct manly world of the men's clubs, and the occasional wild spree with the gallant girls whom New Haven only knew from the fifth row. His aspirations were conventional enough—they included even the irreproachable shadow he would some day marry, but they differed from the aspirations of the majority of young men in that there was no mist over them, none of that quality which is variously known as "idealism" or "illusion." Anson accepted without reservation the world of high finance and high extravagance, of divorce and dissipation, of snobbery and of privilege.

Most of our lives end as a compromise—it was as a compromise that his life began.

He and I first met in the late summer of 1917 when he was just out of Yale, and, like the rest of us, was swept up into the systematized hysteria of the war. In the blue-green uniform of the naval aviation he came down to Pensacola, where the hotel orchestras played "I'm sorry, dear," and we young officers danced with the girls. Every one liked him, and though he ran with the drinkers and wasn't an especially good pilot, even the instructors treated him with a certain respect. He was always having long talks with them in his confident, logical voice—talks which ended by his getting himself, or, more frequently, another officer, out of some impending trouble. He was convivial, bawdy, robustly avid for pleasure, and we were all surprised when he fell in love with a conservative and rather proper girl.

Her name was Paula Legendre, a dark, serious beauty from somewhere in California. Her family kept a winter residence just outside of town, and in spite of her primness she was enormously popular; there is a large class of men whose egotism can't endure humor in a woman. But Anson wasn't that sort, and I couldn't understand the attraction of her "sincerity"—that was the thing to say about her—for his keen and somewhat sardonic mind.

Nevertheless, they fell in love—and on her terms. He no longer joined the twilight gathering at the De Sota bar, and whenever they were seen together they were engaged in a long, serious dialogue, which must have gone on several weeks. Long afterward he told me that it was not about anything in particular but was composed on both sides of immature and even meaningless statements—the emotional content that gradually came to fill it grew up not out of the words but out of its enormous seriousness. It was a sort of hypnosis. Often it was interrupted, giving way to that emasculated humor we call fun; when they were alone it was resumed again, solemn, low-keyed, and pitched so as to give each other a sense of unity in feeling and thought. They came to resent any interruptions of it, to be unresponsive to facetiousness about life, even to the mild cynicism of their contemporaries. They were only happy when the dialogue was going on, and its seriousness bathed them like the amber glow of an open fire. Toward the end there came an interruption they did not resent—it began to be interrupted by passion.

Oddly enough, Anson was as engrossed in the dialogue as she was and as profoundly affected by it, yet at the same time aware that on his side much was insincere, and on hers much was merely simple. At first, too, he despised her emotional simplicity as well, but with his love her nature deepened and blossomed, and he could despise it no longer. He felt that if he could enter into Paula's warm safe life he would be happy. The long preparation of the dialogue removed any constraint—he taught her some of what he had learned from more adventurous women, and she responded with a rapt holy intensity. One evening after a dance they agreed to marry, and he wrote a long letter about her to his mother. The next day Paula told him that she was rich, that she had a personal fortune of nearly a million dollars.

III

IT WAS exactly as if they could say "Neither of us has anything: we shall be poor together"—just as delightful that they should be rich instead. It gave them the same communion of adventure. Yet when Anson got leave in April, and Paula and her mother accompanied him North, she was impressed with the standing of his family in New York and with the scale on which they lived. Alone with Anson for the first time in the rooms where he had played as a boy, she was filled with a comfortable emotion, as though she were preeminently safe and taken care of. The pictures of Anson in a skull cap at his first school, of Anson on horseback with the sweetheart of a mysterious forgotten summer, of Anson in a gay group of ushers and bridesmaids at a wedding, made her jealous of his life apart from her in the past, and so completely did his authoritative person seem to sum up and typify these possessions of his that she was inspired with the idea of being married immediately and returning to Pensacola as his wife.

But an immediate marriage wasn't discussed—even the engagement was to be secret until after the war. When she realized that only two days of his leave remained, her dissatisfaction crystallized in the intention of making him as unwilling to wait as she was. They were driving to the country for dinner, and she determined to force the issue that night.

Now a cousin of Paula's was staying with them at the Ritz, a severe, bitter girl who loved Paula but was somewhat jealous of her impressive engagement, and as Paula was late in dressing, the cousin, who wasn't going to the party, received Anson in the parlor of the suite.

Anson had met friends at five o'clock and drunk freely and indiscreetly with them for an hour. He left the Yale Club at a proper time, and his mother's chauffeur drove him to the Ritz, but his usual capacity was not in evidence, and the impact of the steam-heated sitting-room made him suddenly dizzy. He knew it, and he was both amused and sorry.

Paula's cousin was twenty-five, but she was exceptionally naïve, and at first failed to realize what was up. She had never met Anson before, and she was surprised when he mumbled strange information and nearly fell off his chair, but until Paula appeared it didn't occur to her that what she had taken for the odor of a dry-cleaned uniform was really whisky. But Paula understood as soon as she appeared; her only thought was to get Anson away before her mother saw him, and at the look in her eyes the cousin understood too.

When Paula and Anson descended to the limousine they found two men inside, both asleep; they were the men with whom he had been drinking at the Yale Club, and they were also going to the party. He had entirely forgotten their presence in the car. On the way to Hempstead they awoke and sang. Some of the songs were rough, and though Paula tried to reconcile herself to the fact that Anson had few verbal inhibitions, her lips tightened with shame and distaste.

Back at the hotel the cousin, confused and agitated, considered the incident, and then walked into Mrs. Legendre's bedroom, saying: "Isn't he funny?"

"Who is funny?"

"Why—Mr. Hunter. He seemed so funny."

Mrs. Legendre looked at her sharply.

"How is he funny?"

"Why, he said he was French. I didn't know he was French."

"That's absurd. You must have misunderstood." She smiled: "It was a joke."

The cousin shook her head stubbornly.

"No. He said he was brought up in France. He said he couldn't speak any English, and that's why he couldn't talk to me. And he couldn't!"

Mrs. Legendre looked away with impatience just as

the cousin added thoughtfully, "Perhaps it was because he was so drunk," and walked out of the room.

This curious report was true. Anson, finding his voice thick and uncontrollable, had taken the unusual refuge of announcing that he spoke no English. Years afterward he used to tell that part of the story, and he invariably communicated the uproarious laughter which the memory aroused in him.

Five times in the next hour Mrs. Legendre tried to get Hempstead on the phone. When she succeeded, there was a ten-minute delay before she heard Paula's voice on the wire.

"Cousin Jo told me Anson was intoxicated."

"Oh, no. . . ."

"Oh, yes. Cousin Jo says he was intoxicated. He told her he was French, and fell off his chair and behaved as if he was very intoxicated. I don't want you to come home with him."

"Mother, he's all right! Please don't worry about——"

"But I do worry. I think it's dreadful. I want you to promise me not to come home with him."

"I'll take care of it, mother. . . ."

"I don't want you to come home with him."

"All right, mother. Good-by."

"Be sure now, Paula. Ask some one to bring you."

Deliberately Paula took the receiver from her ear and hung it up. Her face was flushed with helpless annoyance. Anson was stretched asleep out in a bedroom upstairs, while the dinner-party below was proceeding lamely toward conclusion.

The hour's drive had sobered him somewhat—his arrival was merely hilarious—and Paula hoped that the evening was not spoiled, after all, but two imprudent cocktails before dinner completed the disaster. He talked boisterously and somewhat offensively to the party at large for fifteen minutes, and then slid silently under the table; like a man in an old print—but, unlike an old print, it was rather horrible without being at all quaint. None of the young girls present remarked upon the incident—it seemed to merit only silence. His uncle and two other men carried him upstairs, and it was just after this that Paula was called to the phone.

An hour later Anson awoke in a fog of nervous agony, through which he perceived after a moment the figure of his uncle Robert standing by the door.

". . . I said are you better?"

"What?"

"Do you feel better, old man?"

"Terrible," said Anson.

"I'm going to try you on another Bromo-seltzer. If you can hold it down, it'll do you good to sleep."

With an effort Anson slid his legs from the bed and stood up.

"I'm all right," he said dully.

"Take it easy."

"I thin' if you gave me a glassbrandy I could go downstairs."

"Oh, no——"

"Yes, that's the only thin'. I'm all right now. . . . I suppose I'm in dutch dow' there."

"They know you're a little under the weather," said his uncle deprecatingly. "But don't worry about it. Schuyler didn't even get here. He passed away in the locker-room over at the Links."

Indifferent to any opinion, except Paula's, Anson was nevertheless determined to save the débris of the evening, but when after a cold bath he made his appearance most of the party had already left. Paula got up immediately to go home.

In the limousine the old serious dialogue began. She

had known that he drank, she admitted, but she had never expected anything like this—it seemed to her that perhaps they were not suited to each other, after all. Their ideas about life were too different, and so forth. When she finished speaking, Anson spoke in turn, very soberly. Then Paula said she'd have to think it over; she wouldn't decide tonight; she was not angry but she was terribly sorry. Nor would she let him come into the hotel with her, but just before she got out of the car she leaned and kissed him unhappily on the cheek.

The next afternoon Anson had a long talk with Mrs. Legendre while Paula sat listening in silence. It was agreed that Paula was to brood over the incident for a proper period and then, if mother and daughter thought it best, they would follow Anson to Pensacola. On his part he apologized with sincerity and dignity—that was all; with every card in her hand Mrs. Legendre was unable to establish any advantage over him. He made no promises, showed no humility, only delivered a few serious comments on life which brought him off with rather a moral superiority at the end. When they came South three weeks later, neither Anson in his satisfaction nor Paula in her relief at the reunion realized that the psychological moment had passed forever.

IV

HE DOMINATED and attracted her, and at the same time filled her with anxiety. Confused by his mixture of solidity and self-indulgence, of sentiment and cynicism—incongruities which her gentle mind was unable to resolve—Paula grew to think of him as two alternating personalities. When she saw him alone, or at a formal party, or with his casual inferiors, she felt a tremendous pride in his strong, attractive presence, the paternal, understanding stature of his mind. In other company she became uneasy when what had been a fine imperviousness to mere gentility showed its other face. The other face was gross, humorous, reckless of everything but pleasure. It startled her mind temporarily away from him, even led her into a short covert experiment with an old beau, but it was no use—after four months of Anson's enveloping vitality there was an anæmic pallor in all other men.

In July he was ordered abroad, and their tenderness and desire reached a crescendo. Paula considered a last-minute marriage—decided against it only because there were always cocktails on his breath now, but the parting itself made her physically ill with grief. After his departure she wrote him long letters of regret for the days of love they had missed by waiting. In August Anson's plane slipped down into the North Sea. He was pulled onto a destroyer after a night in the water and sent to hospital with pneumonia; the armistice was signed before he was finally sent home.

Then, with every opportunity given back to them, with no material obstacle to overcome, the secret weavings of their temperaments came between them, drying up their kisses and their tears, making their voices less loud to one another, muffling the intimate chatter of their hearts until the old communication was only possible by letters, from far away. One afternoon a society reporter waited for two hours in the Hunters' house for a confirmation of their engagement. Anson denied it; nevertheless an early issue carried the report as a leading paragraph—they were "constantly seen together at Southampton, Hot Springs, and Tuxedo Park." But the serious dialogue had turned a corner into a long-sustained quarrel, and the affair was almost played out. Anson got drunk flagrantly and missed an engagement with her, whereupon Paula made certain behavioristic demands. His despair was helpless before his pride and his knowledge of himself: the engagement was definitely broken.

"Dearest," said their letters now, "Dearest, Dearest, when I wake up in the middle of the night and realize that after all it was not to be, I feel that I want to die. I can't go on living any more. Perhaps when we meet this summer we may talk things over and decide differently—we were so excited and sad that day, and I don't feel that I can live all my life without you. You speak of other people. Don't you know there are no other people for me, but only you. . . ."

But as Paula drifted here and there around the East she would sometimes mention her gaieties to make him wonder. Anson was too acute to wonder. When he saw a man's name in her letters he felt more sure of her and a little disdainful—he was always superior to such things. But he still hoped that they would some day marry.

Meanwhile he plunged vigorously into all the movement and glitter of post-bellum New York, entering a brokerage house, joining half a dozen clubs, dancing late, and moving in three worlds—his own world, the world of young Yale graduates, and that section of the half-world which rests one end on Broadway. But there was always a thorough and infractible eight hours devoted to his work in Wall Street, where the combination of his influential family connection, his sharp intelligence, and his abundance of sheer physical energy brought him almost immediately forward. He had one of those invaluable minds with partitions in it; sometimes he appeared at his office refreshed by less than an hour's sleep, but such occurrences were rare. So early as 1920 his income in salary and commissions exceeded twelve thousand dollars.

As the Yale tradition slipped into the past he became more and more of a popular figure among his classmates in New York, more popular than he had ever been in college. He lived in a great house, and had the means of introducing young men into other great houses. Moreover, his life already seemed secure, while theirs, for the most part, had arrived again at precarious beginnings. They commenced to turn to him for amusement and escape, and Anson responded readily, taking pleasure in helping people and arranging their affairs.

There were no men in Paula's letters now, but a note of tenderness ran through them that had not been there before. From several sources he heard that she had "a heavy beau," Lowell Thayer, a Bostonian of wealth and position, and though he was sure she still loved him, it made him uneasy to think that he might lose her, after all. Save for one unsatisfactory day she had not been in New York for almost five months, and as the rumors multiplied he became increasingly anxious to see her. In February he took his vacation and went down to Florida.

Palm Beach sprawled plump and opulent between the sparkling sapphire of Lake Worth, flawed here and there by houseboats at anchor, and the great turquoise bar of the Atlantic Ocean. The huge bulks of the Breakers and the Royal Poinciana rose as twin paunches from the bright level of the sand, and around them clustered the Dancing Glade, Bradley's House of Chance, and a dozen modistes and milliners with goods at triple prices from New York. Upon the trellissed veranda of the Breakers two hundred women stepped right, stepped left, wheeled, and slid in that then celebrated calisthenic known as the double-shuffle, while in half-time to the music two thousand bracelets clicked up and down on two hundred arms.

At the Everglades Club after dark Paula and Lowell Thayer and Anson and a casual fourth played bridge with hot cards. It seemed to Anson that her kind, serious face was wan and tired—she had been around now for four, five, years. He had known her for three.

"Two spades."

"Cigarette? . . . Oh, I beg your pardon. By me."

"By."

"I'll double three spades."

There were a dozen tables of bridge in the room, which was filling up with smoke. Anson's eyes met Paula's, held them persistently even when Thayer's glance fell between them. . . .

"What was bid?" he asked abstractedly.

"Rose of Washington Square"

sang the young people in the corners:

"I'm withering there
In basement air——"

The smoke banked like fog, and the opening of a door filled the room with blown swirls of ectoplasm. Little Bright Eyes streaked past the tables seeking Mr. Conan Doyle among the Englishmen who were posing as Englishmen about the lobby.

"You could cut it with a knife."

". . . cut it with a knife."

". . . a knife."

At the end of the rubber Paula suddenly got up and spoke to Anson in a tense, low voice. With scarcely a glance at Lowell Thayer, they walked out the door and descended a long flight of stone steps—in a moment they were walking hand in hand along the moonlit beach.

"Darling, darling. . . ." They embraced recklessly, passionately, in a shadow. . . . Then Paula drew back her face to let his lips say what she wanted to hear—she could feel the words forming as they kissed again. . . . Again she broke away, listening, but as he pulled her close once more she realized that he had said nothing—only *"Darling! Darling!"* in that deep, sad whisper that always made her cry. Humbly, obediently, her emotions yielded to him and the tears streamed down her face, but her heart kept on crying: "Ask me—oh, Anson, dearest, ask me!"

"Paula. . . . *Paula!*"

The words wrung her heart like hands, and Anson, feeling her tremble, knew that emotion was enough. He need say no more, commit their destinies to no practical enigma. Why should he, when he might hold her so, biding his own time, for another year—forever? He was considering them both, her more than himself. For a moment, when she said suddenly that she must go back to her hotel, he hesitated, thinking, first, "This is the moment, after all," and then: "No, let it wait—she is mine. . . ."

He had forgotten that Paula too was worn away inside with the strain of three years. Her mood passed forever in the night.

He went back to New York next morning filled with a certain restless dissatisfaction. Late in April, without warning, he received a telegram from Bar Harbor in which Paula told him that she was engaged to Lowell Thayer, and that they would be married immediately in Boston. What he never really believed could happen had happened at last.

Anson filled himself with whisky that morning, and going to the office, carried on his work without a break—rather with a fear of what would happen if he stopped. In the evening he went out as usual, saying nothing of what had occurred; he was cordial, humorous, unabstracted. But one thing he could not help—for three days, in any place, in any company, he would suddenly bend his head into his hands and cry like a child.

V

IN 1922 when Anson went abroad with the junior partner to investigate some London loans, the journey intimated that he was to be taken into the firm. He was twenty-seven now, a little heavy without being definitely stout, and with a manner older than his years. Old people and young people liked him and trusted him, and mothers felt safe when their daughters were in his charge, for he had a way, when he came into a room, of putting himself on a footing with the oldest and most conservative people there. "You and I," he seemed to say, "we're solid. We understand."

He had an instinctive and rather charitable knowledge of the weaknesses of men and women, and, like a priest, it made him the more concerned for the maintenance of outward forms. It was typical of him that every Sunday morning he taught in a fashionable Episcopal Sunday school—even though a cold shower and a quick change into a cutaway coat were all that separated him from the wild night before.

After his father's death he was the practical head of his family, and, in effect, guided the destinies of the younger children. Through a complication his authority did not extend to his father's estate, which was administrated by his Uncle Robert, who was the horsy member of the family, a good-natured, hard-drinking member of that set which centers about Wheatley Hills.

Uncle Robert and his wife, Edna, had been great friends of Anson's youth, and the former was disappointed when his nephew's superiority failed to take a horsey form. He backed him for a city club which was the most difficult in America to enter—one could only join if one's family had "helped to build up New York (or, in other words, were rich before 1880)—and when Anson, after his election, neglected it for the Yale Club, Uncle Robert gave him a little talk on the subject. But when on top of that Anson declined to enter Robert Hunter's own conservative and somewhat neglected brokerage house, his manner grew cooler. Like a primary teacher who has taught all he knew, he slipped out of Anson's life.

There were so many friends in Anson's life—scarcely one for whom he had not done some unusual kindness and scarcely one whom he did not occasionally embarrass by his bursts of rough conversation or his habit of getting drunk whenever and however he liked. It annoyed him when any one else blundered in that regard—about his own lapses he was always humorous. Odd things happened to him and he told them with infectious laughter.

I was working in New York that spring, and I used to lunch with him at the Yale Club, which my university was sharing until the completion of our own. I had read of Paula's marriage, and one afternoon, when I asked him about her, something moved him to tell me the story. After that he frequently invited me to family dinners at his house and behaved as though there was a special relation between us, as though with his confidence a little of that consuming memory had passed into me.

I found that despite the trusting mothers, his attitude toward girls was not indiscriminately protective. It was up to the girl—if she showed an inclination toward looseness, she must take care of herself, even with him.

"Life," he would explain sometimes, "has made a cynic of me."

By life he meant Paula. Sometimes, especially when he was drinking, it became a little twisted in his mind, and he thought that she had callously thrown him over.

This "cynicism," or rather his realization that naturally fast girls were not worth sparing, led to his affair with Dolly Karger. It wasn't his only affair in those years, but it came nearest to touching him deeply, and it had a profound effect upon his attitude toward life.

Dolly was the daughter of a notorious "publicist" who had married into society. She herself grew up into the Junior League, came out at the Plaza, and went to the Assembly; and only a few old families like the Hunters could question whether or not she "belonged," for her picture was often in the papers, and she had more enviable attention than many girls who undoubtedly did. She was dark-haired, with carmine lips and a high, lovely color, which she concealed under pinkish-gray powder all through the first year out, because high color was unfashionable—Victorian-pale was the thing to be. She wore black, severe suits and stood with her hands in her pockets leaning a little forward, with a humorous restraint on her face. She danced exquisitely—better than anything she liked to dance—better than anything except making love. Since she was ten she had always been in love, and, usually, with some boy who didn't respond to her. Those who did—and there were many—bored her after a brief encounter, but for her failures she reserved the warmest spot in her heart. When she met them she would always try once more—sometimes she succeeded, more often she failed.

It never occurred to this gypsy of the unattainable that there was a certain resemblance in those who refused to love her—they shared a hard intuition that saw through to her weakness, not a weakness of emotion but a weakness of rudder. Anson perceived this when he first met her, less than a month after Paula's marriage. He was drinking rather heavily, and he pretended for a week that he was falling in love with her. Then he dropped her abruptly and forgot—immediately he took up the commanding position in her heart.

Like so many girls of that day Dolly was slackly and indiscreetly wild. The unconventionality of a slightly older generation had been simply one facet of a post-war movement to discredit obsolete manners—Dolly's was both older and shabbier, and she saw in Anson the two extremes which the emotionally shiftless woman seeks, an abandon to indulgence alternating with a protective strength. In his character she felt both the sybarite and the solid rock, and these two satisfied every need of her nature.

She felt that it was going to be difficult, but she mistook the reason—she thought that Anson and his family expected a more spectacular marriage, but she guessed immediately that her advantage lay in his tendency to drink.

They met at the large débutante dances, but as her infatuation increased they managed to be more and more together. Like most mothers, Mrs. Karger believed that Anson was exceptionally reliable, so she allowed Dolly to go with him to distant country clubs and suburban houses without inquiring closely into their activities or questioning her explanations when they came in late. At first these explanations might have been accurate, but Dolly's worldly ideas of capturing Anson were soon engulfed in the rising sweep of her emotion. Kisses in the back of taxis and motor-cars were no longer enough; they did a curious thing:

They dropped out of their world for a while and made another world just beneath it where Anson's tippling and Dolly's irregular hours would be less noticed and commented on. It was composed, this world, of varying elements—several of Anson's Yale friends and their wives, two or three young brokers and bond salesmen and a handful of unattached men, fresh from college, with money and a propensity to dissipation. What this world lacked in spaciousness and scale it made up for by allowing them a liberty that it scarcely permitted itself. Moreover, it centered around them and permitted Dolly the pleasure of a faint condescension—a pleasure which Anson, whose whole life was a condescension from the certitudes of his childhood, was unable to share.

He was not in love with her, and in the long feverish winter of their affair he frequently told her so. In the spring he was weary—he wanted to renew his life at some other source—moreover, he saw that either he must break with her now or accept the responsibility of a definite seduction. Her family's encouraging attitude precipitated his decision—one evening when Mr. Karger knocked discreetly at the library door to announce that he had left a bottle of old brandy in the dining-room, Anson felt that life was hemming him in. That night he wrote her a short letter in which he told her that he was going on his vacation, and that in view of all the circumstances they had better meet no more.

It was June. His family had closed up the house and gone to the country, so he was living temporarily at the Yale Club. I had heard about his affair with Dolly as it developed—accounts salted with humor, for he despised unstable women, and granted them no place in the social edifice in which he believed—and when he told me that night that he was definitely breaking with her I was glad. I had seen Dolly here and there, and each time with a feeling of pity at the hopelessness of her struggle, and of shame at knowing so much about her that I had no right to know. She was what is known as "a pretty little thing," but there was a certain recklessness which rather fascinated me. Her dedication to the goddess of waste would have been less obvious had she been less spirited—she would most certainly throw herself away, but I was glad when I heard that the sacrifice would not be consummated in my sight.

Anson was going to leave the letter of farewell at her house next morning. It was one of the few houses left open in the Fifth Avenue district, and he knew that the Kargers, acting upon erroneous information from Dolly, had foregone a trip abroad to give their daughter her chance. As he stepped out the door of the Yale Club into Madison Avenue the postman passed him, and he followed back inside. The first letter that caught his eye was in Dolly's hand.

He knew what it would be—a lonely and tragic monologue, full of the reproaches he knew, the invoked memories, the "I wonder if's"—all the immemorial intimacies that he had communicated to Paula Legendre in what seemed another age. Thumbing over some bills, he brought it on top again and opened it. To his surprise it was a short, somewhat formal note, which said that Dolly would be unable to go to the country with him for the week-end, because Perry Hull from Chicago had unexpectedly come to town. It added that Anson had brought this on himself: "—if I felt that you loved me as I love you I would go with you at any time, any place, but Perry is *so* nice, and he so much wants me to marry him——"

Anson smiled contemptuously—he had had experience with such decoy epistles. Moreover, he knew how

Dolly had labored over this plan, probably sent for the faithful Perry and calculated the time of his arrival—even labored over the note so that it would make him jealous without driving him away. Like most compromises, it had neither force nor vitality but only a timorous despair.

Suddenly he was angry. He sat down in the lobby and read it again. Then he went to the phone, called Dolly and told her in his clear, compelling voice that he had received her note and would call for her at five o'clock as they had previously planned. Scarcely waiting for the pretended uncertainty of her "Perhaps I can see you for an hour," he hung up the receiver and went down to his office. On the way he tore his own letter into bits and dropped it in the street.

He was not jealous—she meant nothing to him—but at her pathetic ruse everything stubborn and self-indulgent in him came to the surface. It was a presumption from a mental inferior and it could not be overlooked. If she wanted to know to whom she belonged she would see.

He was on the door-step at quarter past five. Dolly was dressed for the street, and he listened in silence to the paragraph of "I can only see you for an hour," which she had begun on the phone.

"Put on your hat, Dolly," he said, "we'll take a walk."

They strolled up Madison Avenue and over to Fifth while Anson's shirt dampened upon his portly body in the deep heat. He talked little, scolding her, making no love to her, but before they had walked six blocks she was his again, apologizing for the note, offering not to see Perry at all as an atonement, offering anything. She thought that he had come because he was beginning to love her.

"I'm hot," he said when they reached 71st Street.

"This is a winter suit. If I stop by the house and change, would you mind waiting for me downstairs? I'll only be a minute."

She was happy; the intimacy of his being hot, of any physical fact about him, thrilled her. When they came to the iron-grated door and Anson took out his key she experienced a sort of delight.

Downstairs it was dark, and after he ascended in the lift Dolly raised a curtain and looked out through opaque lace at the houses over the way. She heard the lift machinery stop, and with the notion of teasing him pressed the button that brought it down. Then on what was more than an impulse she got into it and sent it up to what she guessed was his floor.

"Anson," she called, laughing a little.

"Just a minute," he answered from his bedroom . . . then after a brief delay: "Now you can come in."

He had changed and was buttoning his vest. "This is my room," he said lightly. "How do you like it?"

She caught sight of Paula's picture on the wall and stared at it in fascination, just as Paula had stared at the pictures of Anson's childish sweethearts five years before. She knew something about Paula—sometimes she tortured herself with fragments of the story.

Suddenly she came close to Anson, raising her arms. They embraced. Outside the area window a soft artificial twilight already hovered, though the sun was still bright on a back roof across the way. In half an hour the room would be quite dark. The uncalculated opportunity overwhelmed them, made them both breathless, and they clung more closely. It was eminent, inevitable. Still holding one another, they raised their heads—their eyes fell together upon Paula's picture, staring down at them from the wall.

Suddenly Anson dropped his arms, and sitting down at his desk tried the drawer with a bunch of keys.

"Like a drink?" he asked in a gruff voice.

"No, Anson."

He poured himself half a tumbler of whisky, swallowed it, and then opened the door into the hall.

"Come on," he said.

Dolly hesitated.

"Anson—I'm going to the country with you tonight, after all. You understand that, don't you?"

"Of course," he answered brusquely.

In Dolly's car they rode on to Long Island, closer in their emotions than they had ever been before. They knew what would happen—not with Paula's face to remind them that something was lacking, but when they were alone in the still, hot Long Island night they did not care.

The estate in Port Washington where they were to spend the week-end belonged to a cousin of Anson's who had married a Montana copper operator. An interminable drive began at the lodge and twisted under imported poplar saplings toward a huge, pink, Spanish house. Anson had often visited there before.

After dinner they danced at the Linx Club. About midnight Anson assured himself that his cousins would not leave before two—then he explained that Dolly was tired; he would take her home and return to the dance later. Trembling a little with excitement, they got into a borrowed car together and drove to Port Washington. As they reached the lodge he stopped and spoke to the night-watchman.

"When are you making a round, Carl?"

"Right away."

"Then you'll be here till everybody's in?"

"Yes, sir."

"All right. Listen: if any automobile, no matter whose it is, turns in at this gate, I want you to phone the house immediately." He put a five-dollar bill into Carl's hand. "Is that clear?"

"Yes, Mr. Anson." Being of the Old World, he neither winked nor smiled. Yet Dolly sat with her face turned slightly away.

Anson had a key. Once inside he poured a drink for both of them—Dolly left hers untouched—then he ascertained definitely the location of the phone, and found that it was within easy hearing distance of their rooms, both of which were on the first floor.

Five minutes later he knocked at the door of Dolly's room.

"Anson?" He went in, closing the door behind him. She was in bed, leaning up anxiously with elbows on the pillow; sitting beside her he took her in his arms.

"Anson, darling."

He didn't answer.

"Anson. . . . Anson! I love you. . . . Say you love me. Say it now—can't you say it now? Even if you don't mean it?"

He did not listen. Over her head he perceived that the picture of Paula was hanging here upon this wall.

He got up and went close to it. The frame gleamed faintly with thrice-reflected moonlight—within was a blurred shadow of a face that he saw he did not know. Almost sobbing, he turned around and stared with abomination at the little figure on the bed.

"This is all foolishness," he said thickly. "I don't know what I was thinking about. I don't love you and you'd better wait for somebody that loves you. I don't love you a bit, can't you understand?"

His voice broke, and he went hurriedly out. Back in the salon he was pouring himself a drink with uneasy fingers, when the front door opened suddenly, and his cousin came in.

"Why, Anson, I hear Dolly's sick," she began solicitously. "I hear she's sick. . . ."

"It was nothing," he interrupted, raising his voice so that it would carry into Dolly's room. "She was a little tired. She went to bed."

For a long time afterward Anson believed that a protective God sometimes interfered in human affairs. But Dolly Karger, lying awake and staring at the ceiling, never again believed in anything at all.

VI

WHEN Dolly married during the following autumn, Anson was in London on business. Like Paula's marriage, it was sudden, but it affected him in a different way. At first he felt that it was funny, and had an inclination to laugh when he thought of it. Later it depressed him—it made him feel old.

There was something repetitive about it—why, Paula and Dolly had belonged to different generations. He had a foretaste of the sensation of a man of forty who hears that the daughter of an old flame has married. He wired congratulations and, as was not the case with Paula, they were sincere—he had never really hoped that Paula would be happy.

When he returned to New York, he was made a partner in the firm, and, as his responsibilities increased, he had less time on his hands. The refusal of a life-insurance company to issue him a policy made such an impression on him that he stopped drinking for a year, and claimed that he felt better physically, though I think he missed the convivial recounting of those Celliniesque adventures which, in his early twenties, had played such a part of his life. But he never abandoned the Yale Club. He was a figure there, a personality, and the tendency of his class, who were now seven years out of college, to drift away to more sober haunts was checked by his presence.

His day was never too full nor his mind too weary to give any sort of aid to any one who asked it. What had been done at first through pride and superiority had become a habit and a passion. And there was always something—a younger brother in trouble at New Haven, a quarrel to be patched up between a friend and his wife, a position to be found for this man, an investment for that. But his specialty was the solving of problems for young married people. Young married people fascinated him and their apartments were almost sacred to him—he knew the story of their love-affair, advised them where to live and how, and remembered their babies' names. Toward young wives his attitude was circumspect: he never abused the trust which their husbands—strangely enough in view of his unconcealed irregularities—invariably reposed in him.

He came to take a vicarious pleasure in happy marriages, and to be inspired to an almost equally pleasant melancholy by those that went astray. Not a season passed that he did not witness the collapse of an affair that perhaps he himself had fathered. When Paula was divorced and almost immediately remarried to another Bostonian, he talked about her to me all one afternoon. He would never love any one as he had loved Paula, but he insisted that he no longer cared.

"I'll never marry," he came to say; "I've seen too much of it, and I know a happy marriage is a very rare thing. Besides, I'm too old."

But he did believe in marriage. Like all men who spring from a happy and successful marriage, he believed in it passionately—nothing he had seen would change his belief, his cynicism dissolved upon it like air. But he did really believe he was too old. At twenty-eight he began to accept with equanimity the prospect of marrying without romantic love; he resolutely chose a New York girl of his own class, pretty, intelligent, congenial, above reproach—and set about falling in love with her. The things he had said to Paula with sincerity, to other girls with grace, he could no longer say at all without smiling, or with the force necessary to convince.

"When I'm forty," he told his friends, "I'll be ripe. I'll fall for some chorus girl like the rest."

Nevertheless, he persisted in his attempt. His mother wanted to see him married, and he could now well afford it—he had a seat on the Stock Exchange, and his earned income came to twenty-five thousand a year. The idea was agreeable: when his friends—he spent most of his time with the set he and Dolly had evolved—closed themselves in behind domestic doors at night, he no longer rejoiced in his freedom. He even wondered if he should have married Dolly. Not even Paula had loved him more, and he was learning the rarity, in a single life, of encountering true emotion.

Just as this mood began to creep over him a disquieting story reached his ear. His aunt Edna, a woman just this side of forty, was carrying on an open intrigue with a dissolute, hard-drinking young man named Cary Sloane. Every one knew of it except Anson's Uncle Robert, who for fifteen years had talked long in clubs and taken his wife for granted.

Anson heard the story again and again with increasing annoyance. Something of his old feeling for his uncle came back to him, a feeling that was more than personal, a reversion toward that family solidarity on which he had based his pride. His intuition singled out the essential point of the affair, which was that his uncle shouldn't be hurt. It was his first experiment in unsolicited meddling, but with his knowledge of Edna's character he felt that he could handle the matter better than a district judge or his uncle.

His uncle was in Hot Springs. Anson traced down the sources of the scandal so that there should be no possibility of mistake and then he called Edna and asked her to lunch with him at the Plaza next day. Something in his tone must have frightened her, for she was reluctant, but he insisted, putting off the date until she had no excuse for refusing.

She met him at the appointed time in the Plaza lobby, a lovely, faded, gray-eyed blonde in a coat of Russian sable. Five great rings, cold with diamonds and emeralds, sparkled on her slender hands. It occurred to Anson that it was his father's intelligence and not his uncle's that had earned the fur and the stones, the rich brilliance that buoyed up her passing beauty.

Though Edna scented his hostility, she was unprepared for the directness of his approach.

"Edna, I'm astonished at the way you've been acting," he said in a strong, frank voice. "At first I couldn't believe it."

"Believe what?" she demanded sharply.

"You needn't pretend with me, Edna. I'm talking about Cary Sloane. Aside from any other consideration, I didn't think you could treat Uncle Robert——"

"Now look here, Anson—" she began angrily, but his peremptory voice broke through hers:

"—and your children in such a way. You've been married eighteen years, and you're old enough to know better."

"You can't talk to me like that! You——"

"Yes, I can. Uncle Robert has always been my best

friend." He was tremendously moved. He felt a real distress about his uncle, about his three young cousins.

Edna stood up, leaving her crab-flake cocktail untasted.

"This is the silliest thing——"

"Very well, if you won't listen to me I'll go to Uncle Robert and tell him the whole story—he's bound to hear it sooner or later. And afterward I'll go to old Moses Sloane."

Edna faltered back into her chair.

"Don't talk so loud," she begged him. Her eyes blurred with tears. "You have no idea how your voice carries. You might have chosen a less public place to make all these crazy accusations."

He didn't answer.

"Oh, you never liked me, I know," she went on. "You're just taking advantage of some silly gossip to try and break up the only interesting friendship I've ever had. What did I ever do to make you hate me so?"

Still Anson waited. There would be the appeal to his chivalry, then to his pity, finally to his superior sophistication—when he had shouldered his way through all these there would be admissions, and he could come to grips with her. By being silent, by being impervious, by returning constantly to his main weapon, which was his own true emotion, he bullied her into frantic despair as the luncheon hour slipped away. At two o'clock she took out a mirror and a handkerchief, shined away the marks of her tears and powdered the slight hollows where they had lain. She had agreed to meet him at her own house at five.

When he arrived she was stretched on a chaise longue which was covered with cretonne for the summer, and the tears he had called up at luncheon seemed still to be standing in her eyes. Then he was aware of Cary Sloane's dark anxious presence upon the cold hearth.

"What's this idea of yours?" broke out Sloane immediately. "I understand you invited Edna to lunch and then threatened her on the basis of some cheap scandal."

Anson sat down.

"I have no reason to think it's only scandal."

"I hear you're going to take it to Robert Hunter, and to my father."

Anson nodded.

"Either you break it off—or I will," he said.

"What God damned business is it of yours, Hunter?"

"Don't lose your temper, Cary," said Edna nervously. "It's only a question of showing him how absurd——"

"For one thing, it's my name that's being handed around," interrupted Anson. "That's all that concerns you, Cary."

"Edna isn't a member of your family."

"She most certainly is!" His anger mounted. "Why—she owes this house and the rings on her fingers to my father's brains. When Uncle Robert married her she didn't have a penny."

They all looked at the rings as if they had a significant bearing on the situation. Edna made a gesture to take them from her hand.

"I guess they're not the only rings in the world," said Sloane.

"Oh, this is absurd," cried Edna. "Anson, will you listen to me? I've found out how the silly story started. It was a maid I discharged who went right to the Chilicheffs—all these Russians pump things out of their servants and then put a false meaning on them." She brought down her fist angrily on the table: "And after Tom lent them the limousine for a whole month when we were South last winter——"

"Do you see?" demanded Sloane eagerly. "This maid got hold of the wrong end of the thing. She knew that Edna and I were friends, and she carried it to the Chilicheffs. In Russia they assume that if a man and a woman——"

He enlarged the theme to a disquisition upon social relations in the Caucasus.

"If that's the case it better be explained to Uncle Robert," said Anson dryly, "so that when the rumors do reach him he'll know they're not true."

Adopting the method he had followed with Edna at luncheon he let them explain it all away. He knew that they were guilty and that presently they would cross the line from explanation into justification and convict themselves more definitely than he could ever do. By seven they had taken the desperate step of telling him the truth—Robert Hunter's neglect, Edna's empty life, the casual dalliance that had flamed up into passion—but like so many true stories it had the misfortune of being old, and its enfeebled body beat helplessly against the armor of Anson's will. The threat to go to Sloane's father sealed their helplessness, for the latter, a retired cotton broker out of Alabama, was a notorious fundamentalist who controlled his son by a rigid allowance and the promise that at his next vagary the allowance would stop forever.

They dined at a small French restaurant, and the discussion continued—at one time Sloane resorted to physical threats, a little later they were both imploring him to give them time. But Anson was obdurate. He saw that Edna was breaking up, and that her spirit must not be refreshed by any renewal of their passion.

At two o'clock in a small night-club on 53d Street, Edna's nerves suddenly collapsed, and she cried to go home. Sloane had been drinking heavily all evening, and he was faintly maudlin, leaning on the table and weeping a little with his face in his hands. Quickly Anson gave them his terms. Sloane was to leave town for six months, and he must be gone within forty-eight hours. When he returned there was to be no resumption of the affair, but at the end of a year Edna might, if she wished, tell Robert Hunter that she wanted a divorce and go about it in the usual way.

He paused, gaining confidence from their faces for his final word.

"Or there's another thing you can do," he said slowly, "if Edna wants to leave her children, there's nothing I can do to prevent your running off together."

"I want to go home!" cried Edna again. "Oh, haven't you done enough to us for one day?"

Outside it was dark, save for a blurred glow from Sixth Avenue down the street. In that light those two who had been lovers looked for the last time into each other's tragic faces, realizing that between them there was not enough youth and strength to avert their eternal parting. Sloane walked suddenly off down the street and Anson tapped a dozing taxi-driver on the arm.

It was almost four; there was a patient flow of cleaning water along the ghostly pavement of Fifth Avenue, and the shadows of two night women flitted over the dark façade of St. Thomas's church. Then the desolate shrubbery of Central Park where Anson had often played as a child, and the mounting numbers, significant as names, of the marching streets. This was his city, he thought, where his name had flourished through five generations. No change could alter the permanence of its place here, for change itself was the essential substratum by which he and those of his name identified themselves with the spirit of New York. Resourcefulness and a powerful will—for his threats in weaker hands would have been less than nothing—had beaten the gathering dust from his uncle's name, from the name of his family, from even this shivering figure that sat beside him in the car.

Cary Sloane's body was found next morning on the lower shelf of a pillar of Queensboro Bridge. In the darkness and in his excitement he had thought that it was the water flowing black beneath him, but in less than a second it made no possible difference—unless he had planned to think one last thought of Edna, and call out her name as he struggled feebly in the water.

VII

ANSON never blamed himself for his part in this affair—the situation which brought it about had not been of his making. But the just suffer with the unjust, and he found that his oldest and somehow his most precious friendship was over. He never knew what distorted story Edna told, but he was welcome in his uncle's house no longer.

Just before Christmas Mrs. Hunter retired to a select Episcopal heaven, and Anson became the responsible head of his family. An unmarried aunt who had lived with them for years ran the house, and attempted with helpless inefficiency to chaperone the younger girls. All the children were less self-reliant than Anson, more conventional both in their virtues and in their shortcomings. Mrs. Hunter's death had postponed the début of one daughter and the wedding of another. Also it had taken something deeply material from all of them, for with her passing the quiet, expensive superiority of the Hunters came to an end.

For one thing, the estate, considerably diminished by two inheritance taxes and soon to be divided among six children, was not a notable fortune any more. Anson saw a tendency in his youngest sisters to speak rather respectfully of families that hadn't "existed" twenty years ago. His own feeling of precedence was not echoed in them—sometimes they were conventionally snobbish, that was all. For another thing, this was the last summer they would spend on the Connecticut estate; the clamor against it was too loud: "Who wants to waste the best months of the year shut up in that dead old town?" Reluctantly he yielded—the house would go into the market in the fall, and next summer they would rent a smaller place in Westchester County. It was a step down from the expensive simplicity of his father's idea, and, while he sympathized with the revolt, it also annoyed him; during his mother's lifetime he had gone up there at least every other week-end—even in the gayest summers.

Yet he himself was part of this change, and his strong instinct for life had turned him in his twenties from the hollow obsequies of that abortive leisure class. He did not see this clearly—he still felt that there was a norm, a standard of society. But there was no norm, it was doubtful if there had ever been a true norm in New York. The few who still paid and fought to enter a particular set succeeded only to find that as a society it scarcely functioned—or, what was more alarming, that the Bohemia from which they fled sat above them at table.

At twenty-nine Anson's chief concern was his own growing loneliness. He was sure now that he would never marry. The number of weddings at which he had officiated as best man or usher was past all counting—there was a drawer at home that bulged with the official neckties of this or that wedding-party, neckties standing for romances that had not endured a year, for couples who had passed completely from his life. Scarf-pins, gold pencils, cuff-buttons, presents from a generation of grooms had passed through his jewel-box and been lost—and with every ceremony he was less and less able to imagine himself in the groom's place. Under his hearty good-will toward all those marriages there was despair about his own.

And as he neared thirty he became not a little depressed at the inroads that marriage, especially lately, had made upon his friendships. Groups of people had a disconcerting tendency to dissolve and disappear. The men from his own college—and it was upon them he had expended the most time and affection—were the most elusive of all. Most of them were drawn deep into domesticity, two were dead, one lived abroad, one was in Hollywood writing continuities for pictures that Anson went faithfully to see.

Most of them, however, were permanent commuters with an intricate family life centering around some suburban country club, and it was from these that he felt his estrangement most keenly.

In the early days of their married life they had all needed him; he gave them advice about their slim finances, he exorcised their doubts about the advisability of bringing a baby into two rooms and a bath, especially he stood for the great world outside. But now their financial troubles were in the past and the fearfully expected child had evolved into an absorbing family. They were always glad to see old Anson, but they dressed up for him and tried to impress him with their present importance, and kept their troubles to themselves. They needed him no longer.

A few weeks before his thirtieth birthday the last of his early and intimate friends was married. Anson acted in his usual rôle of best man, gave his usual silver tea-service, and went down to the usual *Homeric* to say good-by. It was a hot Friday afternoon in May, and as he walked from the pier he realized that Saturday closing had begun and he was free until Monday morning.

"Go where?" he asked himself.

The Yale Club, of course; bridge until dinner, then four or five raw cocktails in somebody's room and a pleasant confused evening. He regretted that this afternoon's groom wouldn't be along—they had always been able to cram so much into such nights: they knew how to attach women and how to get rid of them, how much consideration any girl deserved from their intelligent hedonism. A party was an adjusted thing—you took certain girls to certain places and spent just so much on their amusement; you drank a little, not much, more than you ought to drink, and at a certain time in the morning you stood up and said you were going home. You avoided college boys, sponges, future engagements, fights, sentiment, and indiscretions. That was the way it was done. All the rest was dissipation.

In the morning you were never violently sorry—you made no resolutions, but if you had overdone it and your heart was slightly out of order, you went on the wagon for a few days without saying anything about it, and waited until an accumulation of nervous boredom projected you into another party.

The lobby of the Yale Club was unpopulated. In the bar three very young alumni looked up at him, momentarily and without curiosity.

"Hello there, Oscar," he said to the bartender. "Mr. Cahill been around this afternoon?"

"Mr. Cahill's gone to New Haven."

"Oh . . . that so?"

"Gone to the ball game. Lot of men gone up."

Anson looked once again into the lobby, considered for a moment, and then walked out and over to Fifth Avenue. From the broad window of one of his clubs—one that he had scarcely visited in five years—a gray man with watery eyes stared down at him. Anson looked quickly away—that figure sitting in vacant resignation, in supercilious solitude, depressed him. He stopped and, retracing his steps, started over 47th Street toward Teak Warden's apartment. Teak and his wife had once been his most familiar friends—it was a household where he and Dolly Karger had been used to go in the days of their affair. But Teak had taken to drink, and his wife had remarked publicly that Anson was a bad influence on him. The remark reached Anson in an exaggerated form—when it was finally cleared up, the delicate spell of intimacy was broken, never to be renewed.

"Is Mr. Warden at home?" he inquired.

"They've gone to the country."

The fact unexpectedly cut at him. They were gone to the country and he hadn't known. Two years before he would have known the date, the hour, come up at the last moment for a final drink, and planned his first visit to them. Now they had gone without a word.

Anson looked at his watch and considered a week-end with his family, but the only train was a local that would jolt through the aggressive heat for three hours. And tomorrow in the country, and Sunday—he was in no mood for porch-bridge with polite undergraduates, and dancing after dinner at a rural road-house, a diminutive of gaiety which his father had estimated too well.

"Oh, no," he said to himself. . . . "No."

He was a dignified, impressive young man, rather stout now, but otherwise unmarked by dissipation. He could have been cast for a pillar of something—at times you were sure it was not society, at others nothing else—for the law, for the church. He stood for a few minutes motionless on the sidewalk in front of a 47th Street apartment-house; for almost the first time in his life he had nothing whatever to do.

Then he began to walk briskly up Fifth Avenue, as if he had just been reminded of an important engagement there. The necessity of dissimulation is one of the few characteristics that we share with dogs, and I think of Anson on that day as some well-bred specimen who had been disappointed at a familiar back door. He was going to see Nick, once a fashionable bartender in demand at all private dances, and now employed in cooling non-alcoholic champagne among the labyrinthine cellars of the Plaza Hotel.

"Nick," he said, "what's happened to everything?"

"Dead," Nick said.

"Make me a whisky sour." Anson handed a pint bottle over the counter. "Nick, the girls are different; I had a little girl in Brooklyn and she got married last week without letting me know."

"That a fact? Ha-ha-ha," responded Nick diplomatically. "Slipped it over on you."

"Absolutely," said Anson. "And I was out with her the night before."

"Ha-ha-ha," said Nick, "ha-ha-ha!"

"Do you remember the wedding, Nick, in Hot Springs where I had the waiters and the musicians singing 'God save the King'?"

"Now where was that, Mr. Hunter?" Nick concentrated doubtfully. "Seems to me that was——"

"Next time they were back for more, and I began to wonder how much I'd paid them," continued Anson.

"—seems to me that was at Mr. Trenholm's wedding."

"Don't know him," said Anson decisively. He was offended that a strange name should intrude upon his reminiscences; Nick perceived this.

"Naw—aw—" he admitted, "I ought to know that. It was one of *your* crowd—Brakins. . . . Baker——"

"Bicker Baker," said Anson responsively. "They put me in a hearse after it was over and covered me up with flowers and drove me away."

"Ha-ha-ha," said Nick. "Ha-ha-ha."

Nick's simulation of the old family servant paled presently and Anson went upstairs to the lobby. He looked around—his eyes met the glance of an unfamiliar clerk at the desk, then fell upon a flower from the morning's marriage hesitating in the mouth of a brass cuspidor. He went out and walked slowly toward the blood-red sun over Columbus Circle. Suddenly he turned around and, retracing his steps to the Plaza, immured himself in a telephone-booth.

Later he said that he tried to get me three times that afternoon, that he tried every one who might be in New York—men and girls he had not seen for years, an artist's model of his college days whose faded number was still in his address book—Central told him that even the exchange existed no longer. At length his quest roved into the country, and he held brief disappointing conversations with emphatic butlers and maids. So-and-so was out, riding, swimming, playing golf, sailed to Europe last week. Who shall I say phoned?

It was intolerable that he should pass the evening alone—the private reckonings which one plans for a moment of leisure lose every charm when the solitude is enforced. There were always women of a sort, but the ones he knew had temporarily vanished, and to pass a New York evening in the hired company of a stranger never occurred to him—he would have considered that that was something shameful and secret, the diversion of a traveling salesman in a strange town.

Anson paid the telephone bill—the girl tried unsuccessfully to joke with him about its size—and for the second time that afternoon started to leave the Plaza and go he knew not where. Near the revolving door the figure of a woman, obviously with child, stood sideways to the light—a sheer beige cape fluttered at her shoulders when the door turned and, each time, she looked impatiently toward it as if she were weary of waiting. At the first sight of her a strong nervous thrill of familiarity went over him, but not until he was within five feet of her did he realize that it was Paula.

"Why, Anson Hunter!"

His heart turned over.

"Why, Paula——"

"Why, this is wonderful. I can't believe it, *Anson!*"

She took both his hands, and he saw in the freedom of the gesture that the memory of him had lost poignancy to her. But not to him—he felt that old mood that she evoked in him stealing over his brain, that gentleness with which he had always met her optimism as if afraid to mar its surface.

"We're at Rye for the summer. Pete had to come East on business—you know of course I'm Mrs. Peter Hagerty now—so we brought the children and took a house. You've got to come out and see us."

"Can I?" he asked directly. "When?"

"When you like. Here's Pete." The revolving door functioned, giving up a fine tall man of thirty with a tanned face and a trim mustache. His immaculate fitness made a sharp contrast with Anson's increasing bulk, which was obvious under the faintly tight cutaway coat.

"You oughtn't to be standing," said Hagerty to his wife. "Let's sit down here." He indicated lobby chairs, but Paula hesitated.

"I've got to go right home," she said. "Anson, why don't you—why don't you come out and have dinner with us tonight? We're just getting settled, but if you can stand that——"

Hagerty confirmed the invitation cordially.

"Come out for the night."

Their car waited in front of the hotel, and Paula with a tired gesture sank back against silk cushions in the corner.

"There's so much I want to talk to you about," she said, "it seems hopeless."

"I want to hear about you."

"Well"—she smiled at Hagerty—"that would take a long time too. I have three children—by my first marriage. The oldest is five, then four, then three." She smiled again. "I didn't waste much time having them, did I?"

"Boys?"

"A boy and two girls. Then—oh, a lot of things happened, and I got a divorce in Paris a year ago and married Pete. That's all—except that I'm awfully happy."

In Rye they drove up to a large house near the Beach Club, from which there issued presently three dark, slim children who broke from an English governess and approached them with an esoteric cry. Abstractedly and with difficulty Paula took each one into her arms, a caress which they accepted stiffly, as they had evidently been told not to bump into Mummy. Even against their fresh faces Paula's skin showed scarcely any weariness—for all her physical languor she seemed younger than when he had last seen her at Palm Beach seven years ago.

At dinner she was preoccupied, and afterward, during the homage to the radio, she lay with closed eyes on the sofa, until Anson wondered if his presence at this time were not an intrusion. But at nine o'clock, when Hagerty rose and said pleasantly that he was going to leave them by themselves for a while, she began to talk slowly about herself and the past.

"My first baby," she said—"the one we call Darling, the biggest little girl—I wanted to die when I knew I was going to have her, because Lowell was like a stranger to me. It didn't seem as though she could be my own. I wrote you a letter and tore it up. Oh, you were *so* bad to me, Anson."

It was the dialogue again, rising and falling. Anson felt a sudden quickening of memory.

"Weren't you engaged once?" she asked—"a girl named Dolly something?"

"I wasn't ever engaged. I tried to be engaged, but I never loved anybody but you, Paula."

"Oh," she said. Then after a moment: "This baby is the first one I ever really wanted. You see, I'm in love now—at last."

He didn't answer, shocked at the treachery of her remembrance. She must have seen that the "at last" bruised him, for she continued:

"I was infatuated with you, Anson—you could make me do anything you liked. But we wouldn't have been happy. I'm not smart enough for you. I don't like things to be complicated like you do." She paused. "You'll never settle down," she said.

The phrase struck at him from behind—it was an accusation that of all accusations he had never merited.

"I could settle down if women were different," he said. "If I didn't understand so much about them, if women didn't spoil you for other women, if they had only a little pride. If I could go to sleep for a while and wake up into a home that was really mine—why, that's what I'm made for, Paula, that's what women have seen in me and liked in me. It's only that I can't get through the preliminaries any more."

Hagerty came in a little before eleven; after a whisky Paula stood up and announced that she was going to bed. She went over and stood by her husband.

"Where did you go, dearest?" she demanded.

"I had a drink with Ed Saunders."

"I was worried. I thought maybe you'd run away."

She rested her head against his coat.

"He's sweet, isn't he, Anson?" she demanded.

"Absolutely," said Anson, laughing.

She raised her face to her husband.

"Well, I'm ready," she said. She turned to Anson: "Do you want to see our family gymnastic stunt?"

"Yes," he said in an interested voice.

"All right. Here we go!"

Hagerty picked her up easily in his arms.

"This is called the family acrobatic stunt," said Paula. "He carries me upstairs. Isn't it sweet of him?"

"Yes," said Anson.

Hagerty bent his head slightly until his face touched Paula's.

"And I love him," she said. "I've just been telling you, haven't I, Anson?"

"Yes," he said.

"He's the dearest thing that ever lived in this world; aren't you, darling? . . . Well, good night. Here we go. Isn't he strong?"

"Yes," Anson said.

"You'll find a pair of Pete's pajamas laid out for you. Sweet dreams—see you at breakfast."

"Yes," Anson said.

VIII

THE older members of the firm insisted that Anson should go abroad for the summer. He had scarcely had a vacation in seven years, they said. He was stale and needed a change. Anson resisted.

"If I go," he declared, "I won't come back any more."

"That's absurd, old man. You'll be back in three months with all this depression gone. Fit as ever."

"No." He shook his head stubbornly. "If I stop, I won't go back to work. If I stop, that means I've given up—I'm through."

"We'll take a chance on that. Stay six months if you like—we're not afraid you'll leave us. Why, you'd be miserable if you didn't work."

They arranged his passage for him. They liked Anson—every one liked Anson—and the change that had been coming over him cast a sort of pall over the office. The enthusiasm that had invariably signaled up business, the consideration toward his equals and his inferiors, the lift of his vital presence—within the past four months his intense nervousness had melted down these qualities into the fussy pessimism of a man of forty. On every transaction in which he was involved he acted as a drag and a strain.

"If I go I'll never come back," he said.

Three days before he sailed Paula Legendre Hagerty died in childbirth. I was with him a great deal then, for we were crossing together, but for the first time in our friendship he told me not a word of how he felt, nor did I see the slightest sign of emotion. His chief preoccupation was with the fact that he was thirty years old—he would turn the conversation to the point where he could remind you of it and then fall silent, as if he assumed that the statement would start a chain of thought sufficient to itself. Like his partners, I was amazed at the change in him, and I was glad when the *Paris* moved off into the wet space between the worlds, leaving his principality behind.

"How about a drink?" he suggested.

We walked into the bar with that defiant feeling that characterizes the day of departure and ordered four Martinis. After one cocktail a change came over him—he suddenly reached across and slapped my knee with the first joviality I had seen him exhibit for months.

"Did you see that girl in the red tam?" he demanded, "the one with the high color who had the two police dogs down to bid her good-by."

"She's pretty," I agreed.

"I looked her up in the purser's office and found out that she's alone. I'm going down to see the steward in a few minutes. We'll have dinner with her tonight."

After a while he left me, and within an hour he was walking up and down the deck with her, talking to her in his strong, clear voice. Her red tam was a bright spot of color against the steel-green sea, and from time to time she looked up with a flashing bob of her head, and smiled with amusement and interest, and anticipation. At dinner we had champagne, and were very joyous—afterward Anson ran the pool with infectious gusto, and several people who had seen me with him asked me his name. He and the girl were talking and laughing together on a lounge in the bar when I went to bed.

I saw less of him on the trip than I had hoped. He wanted to arrange a foursome, but there was no one available, so I saw him only at meals. Sometimes, though, he would have a cocktail in the bar, and he told me about the girl in the red tam, and his adventures with her, making them all bizarre and amusing, as he had a way of doing, and I was glad that he was himself again, or at least the self that I knew, and with which I felt at home. I don't think he was ever happy unless some one was in love with him, responding to him like filings to a magnet, helping him to explain himself, promising him something. What it was I do not know. Perhaps they promised that there would always be women in the world who would spend their brightest, freshest, rarest hours to nurse and protect that superiority he cherished in his heart.

MAY DAY

THERE had been a war fought and won and the great city of the conquering people was crossed with triumphal arches and vivid with thrown flowers of white, red, and rose. All through the long spring days the returning soldiers marched up the chief highway behind the strump of drums and the joyous, resonant wind of the brasses, while merchants and clerks left their bickerings and figurings and, crowding to the windows, turned their white-bunched faces gravely upon the passing battalions.

Never had there been such splendor in the great city, for the victorious war had brought plenty in its train, and the merchants had flocked thither from the South and West with their households to taste of all the luscious feasts and witness the lavish entertainments prepared—and to buy for their women furs against the next winter and bags of golden mesh and varicolored slippers of silk and silver and rose satin and cloth of gold.

So gaily and noisily were the peace and prosperity impending hymned by the scribes and poets of the conquering people that more and more spenders had gathered from the provinces to drink the wine of excitement, and faster and faster did the merchants dispose of their trinkets and slippers until they sent up a mighty cry for more trinkets and more slippers in order that they might give in barter what was demanded of them. Some even of them flung up their hands helplessly, shouting:

"Alas! I have no more slippers! and alas! I have no more trinkets! May Heaven help me, for I know not what I shall do!"

But no one listened to their great outcry, for the throngs were far too busy—day by day, the foot-soldiers trod jauntily the highway and all exulted because the young men returning were pure and brave, sound of tooth and pink of cheek, and the young women of the land were virgins and comely both of face and of figure.

So during all this time there were many adventures that happened in the great city, and, of these, several—or perhaps one—are here set down.

I

AT NINE O'CLOCK on the morning of the first of May, 1919, a young man spoke to the room clerk at the Biltmore Hotel, asking if Mr. Philip Dean were registered there, and if so, could he be connected with Mr. Dean's rooms. The inquirer was dressed in a well-cut, shabby suit. He was small, slender, and darkly handsome; his eyes were framed above with unusually long eyelashes and below with the blue semicircle of ill health, this latter effect heightened by an unnatural glow which colored his face like a low, incessant fever.

Mr. Dean was staying there. The young man was directed to a telephone at the side.

After a second his connection was made; a sleepy voice hello'd from somewhere above.

"Mr. Dean?"—this very eagerly—"it's Gordon, Phil. It's Gordon Sterrett. I'm downstairs. I heard you were in New York and I had a hunch you'd be here."

The sleepy voice became gradually enthusiastic. Well, how was Gordy, old boy! Well, he certainly was surprised and tickled! Would Gordy come right up, for Pete's sake!

A few minutes later Philip Dean, dressed in blue silk pajamas, opened his door and the two young men greeted each other with a half-embarrassed exuberance. They were both about twenty-four, Yale graduates of the year before the war; but there the resemblance stopped abruptly. Dean was blond, ruddy, and rugged under his thin pajamas. Everything about him radiated fitness and bodily comfort. He smiled frequently, showing large and prominent teeth.

"I was going to look you up," he cried enthusiastically. "I'm taking a couple of weeks off. If you'll sit down a sec I'll be right with you. Going to take a shower."

As he vanished into the bathroom his visitor's dark eyes roved nervously around the room, resting for a moment on a great English traveling bag in the corner and on a family of thick silk shirts littered on the chairs amid impressive neckties and soft woollen socks.

Gordon rose and, picking up one of the shirts, gave it a minute examination. It was of very heavy silk, yellow, with a pale blue stripe—and there were nearly a dozen of them. He stared involuntarily at his own shirt-cuffs—they were ragged and linty at the edges and soiled to a faint gray. Dropping the silk shirt, he held his coat-sleeves down and worked the frayed shirt-cuffs up till they were out of sight. Then he went to the mirror and looked at himself with listless, unhappy interest. His tie, of former glory, was faded and thumb-creased—it served no longer to hide the jagged button-holes of his collar. He thought, quite without amusement, that only three years before he had received a scattering vote in the senior elections at college for being the best-dressed man in his class.

Dean emerged from the bathroom polishing his body.

"Saw an old friend of yours last night," he remarked. "Passed her in the lobby and couldn't think of her name to save my neck. That girl you brought up to New Haven senior year."

Gordon started.

"Edith Bradin? That whom you mean?"

"'At's the one. Damn good looking. She's still sort of a pretty doll—you know what I mean: as if you touched her she'd smear."

He surveyed his shining self complacently in the mirror, smiled faintly, exposing a section of teeth.

"She must be twenty-three anyway," he continued.

"Twenty-two last month," said Gordon absently.

"What? Oh, last month. Well, I imagine she's down for the Gamma Psi dance. Did you know we're having a Yale Gamma Psi dance tonight at Delmonico's? You better come up, Gordy. Half of New Haven'll probably be there. I can get you an invitation."

Draping himself reluctantly in fresh underwear, Dean lit a cigarette and sat down by the open window, inspecting his calves and knees under the morning sunshine which poured into the room.

"Sit down, Gordy," he suggested, "and tell me all about what you've been doing and what you're doing now and everything."

Gordon collapsed unexpectedly upon the bed; lay there inert and spiritless. His mouth, which habitually dropped a little open when his face was in repose, became suddenly helpless and pathetic.

"What's the matter?" asked Dean quickly.

"Oh, God!"

"What's the matter?"

"Every God damn thing in the world," he said miserably. "I've absolutely gone to pieces, Phil. I'm all in."

"Huh?"

"I'm all in." His voice was shaking.

Dean scrutinized him more closely with appraising blue eyes.

"You certainly look all shot."

"I am. I've made a hell of a mess of everything." He paused. "I'd better start at the beginning—or will it bore you?"

"Not at all; go on." There was, however, a hesitant note in Dean's voice. This trip East had been planned for a holiday—to find Gordon Sterrett in trouble exasperated him a little.

"Go on," he repeated, and then added half under his breath, "Get it over with."

"Well," began Gordon unsteadily, "I got back from France in February, went home to Harrisburg for a month, and then came down to New York to get a job. I got one—with an export company. They fired me yesterday."

"Fired you?"

"I'm coming to that, Phil. I want to tell you frankly. You're about the only man I can turn to in a matter like this. You won't mind if I just tell you frankly, will you, Phil?"

Dean stiffened a bit more. The pats he was bestowing on his knees grew perfunctory. He felt vaguely that he was being unfairly saddled with responsibility; he was not even sure he wanted to be told. Though never surprised at finding Gordon Sterrett in mild difficulty, there was something in this present misery that repelled him and hardened him, even though it excited his curiosity.

"Go on."

"It's a girl."

"Hm." Dean resolved that nothing was going to spoil his trip. If Gordon was going to be depressing, then he'd have to see less of Gordon.

"Her name is Jewel Hudson," went on the distressed voice from the bed. "She used to be 'pure,' I guess, up to about a year ago. Lived here in New York—poor family. Her people are dead now and she lives with an old aunt. You see it was just about the time I met her that everybody began to come back from France in droves—and all I did was to welcome the newly arrived and go on parties with 'em. That's the way it started, Phil, just from being glad to see everybody and having them glad to see me."

"You ought to've had more sense."

"I know," Gordon paused, and then continued listlessly. "I'm on my own now, you know, and Phil, I can't stand being poor. Then came this darn girl. She sort of fell in love with me for a while and, though I never intended to get so involved, I'd always seem to run into her somewhere. You can imagine the sort of work I was doing for those exporting people—of course, I always intended to draw; do illustrating for magazines; there's a pile of money in it."

"Why didn't you? You've got to buckle down if you want to make good," suggested Dean with cold formalism.

"I tried, a little, but my stuff's crude. I've got talent, Phil; I can draw—but I just don't know how. I ought to go to art school and I can't afford it. Well, things came to a crisis about a week ago. Just as I was down to about my last dollar this girl began bothering me. She wants some money; claims she can make trouble for me if she doesn't get it."

"Can she?"

"I'm afraid she can. That's one reason I lost my job—she kept calling up the office all the time, and that was sort of the last straw down there. She's got a letter all written to send to my family. Oh, she's got me, all right. I've got to have some money for her."

There was an awkward pause. Gordon lay very still, his hands clenched by his side.

"I'm all in," he continued, his voice trembling. "I'm half crazy, Phil. If I hadn't known you were coming East, I think I'd have killed myself. I want you to lend me three hundred dollars."

Dean's hands, which had been patting his bare ankles, were suddenly quiet—and the curious uncertainty playing between the two became taut and strained.

After a second Gordon continued:

"I've bled the family until I'm ashamed to ask for another nickel."

Still Dean made no answer.

"Jewel says she's got to have two hundred dollars."

"Tell her where she can go."

"Yes, that sounds easy, but she's got a couple of drunken letters I wrote her. Unfortunately she's not at all the flabby sort of person you'd expect."

Dean made an expression of distaste.

"I can't stand that sort of woman. You ought to have kept away."

"I know," admitted Gordon wearily.

"You've got to look at things as they are. If you haven't got money you've got to work and stay away from women."

"That's easy for you to say," began Gordon, his eyes narrowing. "You've got all the money in the world."

"I most certainly have not. My family keep darn close tab on what I spend. Just because I have a little leeway I have to be extra careful not to abuse it."

He raised the blind and let in a further flood of sunshine.

"I'm no prig, Lord knows," he went on deliberately. "I like pleasure—and I like a lot of it on a vacation like this, but you're—you're in awful shape. I never heard you talk just this way before. You seem to be sort of bankrupt—morally as well as financially."

"Don't they usually go together?"

Dean shook his head impatiently.

"There's a regular aura about you that I don't understand. It's a sort of evil."

"It's an air of worry and poverty and sleepless nights," said Gordon, rather defiantly.

"I don't know."

"Oh, I admit I'm depressing. I depress myself. But, my God, Phil, a week's rest and a new suit and some ready money and I'd be like—like I was. Phil, I can draw like a streak, and you know it. But half the time I haven't had the money to buy decent drawing materials—and I can't draw when I'm tired and discouraged and all in. With a little ready money I can take a few weeks off and get started."

"How do I know you wouldn't use it on some other woman?"

"Why rub it in?" said Gordon quietly.

"I'm not rubbing it in. I hate to see you this way."

"Will you lend me the money, Phil?"

"I can't decide right off. That's a lot of money and it'll be darn inconvenient for me."

"It'll be hell for me if you can't—I know I'm whining, and it's all my own fault but—that doesn't change it."

"When could you pay it back?"

This was encouraging. Gordon considered. It was probably wisest to be frank.

"Of course, I could promise to send it back next month, but—I'd better say three months. Just as soon as I start to sell drawings."

"How do I know you'll sell any drawings?"

A new hardness in Dean's voice sent a faint chill of doubt over Gordon. Was it possible that he wouldn't get the money?

"I supposed you had a little confidence in me."

"I did have—but when I see you like this I begin to wonder."

"Do you suppose if I wasn't at the end of my rope I'd come to you like this? Do you think I'm enjoying it?" He broke off and bit his lip, feeling that he had better subdue the rising anger in his voice. After all, he was the suppliant.

"You seem to manage it pretty easily," said Dean angrily. "You put me in the position where, if I don't lend it to you, I'm a sucker—oh, yes, you do. And let me tell you it's no easy thing for me to get hold of three hundred dollars. My income isn't so big but that a slice like that won't play the deuce with it."

He left his chair and began to dress, choosing his clothes carefully. Gordon stretched out his arms and clenched the edges of the bed, fighting back a desire to cry out. His head was splitting and whirring, his mouth was dry and bitter and he could feel the fever in his blood resolving itself into innumerable regular counts like a slow dripping from a roof.

Dean tied his tie precisely, brushed his eyebrows, and removed a piece of tobacco from his teeth with solemnity. Next he filled his cigarette case, tossed the empty box thoughtfully into the waste basket, and settled the case in his vest pocket.

"Had breakfast?" he demanded.

"No; I don't eat it any more."

"Well, we'll go out and have some. We'll decide about that money later. I'm sick of the subject. I came East to have a good time."

"Let's go over to the Yale Club," he continued moodily, and then added with an implied reproof: "You've given up your job. You've got nothing else to do."

"I'd have a lot to do if I had a little money," said Gordon pointedly.

"Oh, for Heaven's sake drop the subject for a while! No point in glooming on my whole trip. Here, here's some money."

He took a five-dollar bill from his wallet and tossed it over to Gordon, who folded it carefully and put it in his pocket. There was an added spot of color in his cheeks, an added glow that was not fever. For an instant before they turned to go out their eyes met, and in that instant each found something that made him lower his own glance quickly. For in that instant they quite suddenly and definitely hated each other.

II

FIFTH AVENUE and Forty-fourth Street swarmed with the noon crowd. The wealthy, happy sun glittered in transient gold through the thick windows of the smart shops, lighting upon mesh bags and purses and strings of pearls in gray velvet cases; upon gaudy feather fans of many colors; upon the laces and silks of expensive dresses; upon the bad paintings and the fine period furniture in the elaborate show rooms of interior decorators.

Working-girls, in pairs and groups and swarms, loitered by these windows, choosing their future boudoirs from some resplendent display which included even a man's silk pajamas laid domestically across the bed. They stood in front of the jewelry stores and picked out their engagement rings, and their wedding rings and their platinum wrist watches, and then drifted on to inspect the feather fans and opera cloaks; meanwhile digesting the sandwiches and sundaes they had eaten for lunch.

All through the crowd were men in uniform, sailors from the great fleet anchored in the Hudson, soldiers with divisional insignia from Massachusetts to California, wanting fearfully to be noticed, and finding the great city thoroughly fed up with soldiers unless they were nicely massed into pretty formations and uncomfortable under the weight of a pack and rifle.

Through this medley Dean and Gordon wandered; the former interested, made alert by the display of humanity at its frothiest and gaudiest; the latter reminded of how often he had been one of the crowd, tired, casually fed, overworked, and dissipated. To Dean the struggle was significant, young, cheerful; to Gordon it was dismal, meaningless, endless.

In the Yale Club they met a group of their former classmates who greeted the visiting Dean vociferously. Sitting in a semicircle of lounges and great chairs, they had a highball all around.

Gordon found the conversation tiresome and interminable. They lunched together en masse, warmed with liquor as the afternoon began. They were all going to the Gamma Psi dance that night—it promised to be the best party since the war.

"Edith Bradin's coming," said some one to Gordon. "Didn't she used to be an old flame of yours? Aren't you both from Harrisburg?"

"Yes." He tried to change the subject. "I see her brother occasionally. He's sort of a socialistic nut. Runs a paper or something here in New York."

"Not like his gay sister, eh?" continued his eager informant. "Well, she's coming tonight with a junior named Peter Himmel."

Gordon was to meet Jewel Hudson at eight o'clock—he had promised to have some money for her. Several times he glanced nervously at his wrist watch. At four, to his relief, Dean rose and announced that he was going over to Rivers Brothers to buy some collars and ties. But as they left the Club another of the party joined them, to Gordon's great dismay. Dean was in a jovial mood now, happy, expectant of the evening's party, faintly hilarious. Over in Rivers' he chose a dozen neckties, selecting each one after long consultations with the other man. Did he think narrow ties were coming back? And wasn't it a shame that Rivers couldn't get any more Welsh Margotson collars? There never was a collar like the "Covington."

Gordon was in something of a panic. He wanted the money immediately. And he was now inspired also with a vague idea of attending the Gamma Psi dance. He wanted to see Edith—Edith whom he hadn't met since one romantic night at the Harrisburg Country Club just before he went to France. The affair had died, drowned in the turmoil of the war and quite forgotten in the arabesque of these three months, but a picture of her, poignant, debonaire, immersed in her own inconsequential chatter, recurred to him unexpectedly and brought a hundred memories with it. It was Edith's face that he had cherished through college with a sort of detached yet affectionate admiration. He had loved to draw her—around his room had been a dozen sketches of her—playing golf, swimming—he could draw her pert, arresting profile with his eyes shut.

They left Rivers' at five-thirty and paused for a moment on the sidewalk.

"Well," said Dean genially, "I'm all set now. Think I'll go back to the hotel and get a shave, haircut, and massage."

"Good enough," said the other man, "I think I'll join you."

Gordon wondered if he was to be beaten after all. With difficulty he restrained himself from turning to the man and snarling out, "Go on away, damn you!" In despair he suspected that perhaps Dean had spoken to him, was keeping him along in order to avoid a dispute about the money.

They went into the Biltmore—a Biltmore alive with girls—mostly from the West and South, the stellar débutantes of many cities gathered for the dance of a famous fraternity of a famous university. But to Gordon they were faces in a dream. He gathered together his forces for a last appeal, was about to come out with he knew not what, when Dean suddenly excused himself to the other man and taking Gordon's arm led him aside.

"Gordy," he said quickly, "I've thought the whole thing over carefully and I've decided that I can't lend you that money. I'd like to oblige you, but I don't feel I ought to—it'd put a crimp in me for a month."

Gordon, watching him dully, wondered why he had never before noticed how much those upper teeth projected.

"—I'm mighty sorry, Gordon," continued Dean, "but that's the way it is."

He took out his wallet and deliberately counted out seventy-five dollars in bills.

"Here," he said, holding them out, "here's seventy-five; that makes eighty all together. That's all the actual cash I have with me, besides what I'll actually spend on the trip."

Gordon raised his clenched hand automatically, opened it as though it were a tongs he was holding, and clenched it again on the money.

"I'll see you at the dance," continued Dean. "I've got to get along to the barber shop."

"So-long," said Gordon in a strained and husky voice. "So-long."

Dean began to smile, but seemed to change his mind. He nodded briskly and disappeared.

But Gordon stood there, his handsome face awry with distress, the roll of bills clenched tightly in his hand. Then, blinded by sudden tears, he stumbled clumsily down the Biltmore steps.

III

ABOUT nine o'clock of the same night two human beings came out of a cheap restaurant in Sixth Avenue. They were ugly, ill-nourished, devoid of all except the very lowest form of intelligence, and without even that animal exuberance that in itself brings color into life; they were lately vermin-ridden, cold, and hungry in a dirty town of a strange land; they were poor, friendless; tossed as driftwood from their births, they would be tossed as driftwood to their deaths. They were dressed in the uniform of the United States Army, and on the shoulder of each was the insignia of a drafted division from New Jersey, landed three days before.

The taller of the two was named Carrol Key, a name hinting that in his veins, however thinly diluted by generations of degeneration, ran blood of some potentiality. But one could stare endlessly at the long, chinless face, the dull, watery eyes, and high cheek-bones, without finding a suggestion of either ancestral worth or native resourcefulness.

His companion was swart and bandy-legged, with rat-eyes and a much-broken hooked nose. His defiant air was obviously a pretense, a weapon of protection borrowed from that world of snarl and snap, of physical bluff and physical menace, in which he had always lived. His name was Gus Rose.

Leaving the café they sauntered down Sixth Avenue, wielding toothpicks with great gusto and complete detachment.

"Where to?" asked Rose, in a tone which implied that he would not be surprised if Key suggested the South Sea Islands.

"What you say we see if we can getta holda some

liquor?" Prohibition was not yet. The ginger in the suggestion was caused by the law forbidding the selling of liquor to soldiers.

Rose agreed enthusiastically.

"I got an idea," continued Key, after a moment's thought, "I got a brother somewhere."

"In New York?"

"Yeah. He's an old fella." He meant that he was an elder brother. "He's a waiter in a hash joint."

"Maybe he can get us some."

"I'll say he can!"

"B'lieve me, I'm goin' to get this darn uniform off me tomorra. Never get me in it again, neither. I'm goin' to get me some regular clothes."

"Say, maybe I'm not."

As their combined finances were something less than five dollars, this intention can be taken largely as a pleasant game of words, harmless and consoling. It seemed to please both of them, however, for they reinforced it with chuckling and mention of personages high in Biblical circles, adding such further emphasis as "Oh, boy!" "You know!" and "I'll say so!" repeated many times over.

The entire mental pabulum of these two men consisted of an offended nasal comment extended through the years upon the institution—army, business, or poorhouse—which kept them alive, and toward their immediate superior in that institution. Until that very morning the institution had been the "government" and the immediate superior had been the "Cap'n"—from these two they had glided out and were now in the vaguely uncomfortable state before they should adopt their next bondage. They were uncertain, resentful, and somewhat ill at ease. This they hid by pretending an elaborate relief at being out of the army, and by assuring each other that military discipline should never again rule their stubborn, liberty-loving wills. Yet, as a matter of fact, they would have felt more at home in a prison than in this new-found and unquestionable freedom.

Suddenly Key increased his gait. Rose, looking up and following his glance, discovered a crowd that was collecting fifty yards down the street. Key chuckled and began to run in the direction of the crowd; Rose thereupon also chuckled and his short bandy legs twinkled beside the long, awkward strides of his companion.

Reaching the outskirts of the crowd they immediately became an indistinguishable part of it. It was composed of ragged civilians somewhat the worse for liquor, and of soldiers representing many divisions and many stages of sobriety, all clustered around a gesticulating little Jew with long black whiskers, who was waving his arms and delivering an excited but succinct harangue. Key and Rose, having wedged themselves into the approximate parquet, scrutinized him with acute suspicion, as his words penetrated their common consciousness.

"—What have you got outa the war?" he was crying fiercely. "Look arounja, look arounja! Are you rich? Have you got a lot of money offered you?—no; you're lucky if you're alive and got both your legs; you're lucky if you came back an' find your wife ain't gone off with some other fella that had the money to buy himself out of the war! That's when you're lucky! Who got anything out of it except J. P. Morgan an' John D. Rockefeller?"

At this point the little Jew's oration was interrupted by the hostile impact of a fist upon the point of his bearded chin and he toppled backward to a sprawl on the pavement.

"God damn Bolsheviki!" cried the big soldier-blacksmith who had delivered the blow. There was a rumble of approval, the crowd closed in nearer.

The Jew staggered to his feet, and immediately went down again before a half-dozen reaching-in fists. This time he stayed down, breathing heavily, blood oozing from his lip where it was cut within and without.

There was a riot of voices, and in a minute Rose and Key found themselves flowing with the jumbled crowd down Sixth Avenue under the leadership of a thin civilian in a slouch hat and the brawny soldier who had summarily ended the oration. The crowd had marvelously swollen to formidable proportions and a stream of more noncommittal citizens followed it along the sidewalks lending their moral support by intermittent huzzas.

"Where we goin'?" yelled Key to the man nearest him.

His neighbor pointed up to the leader in the slouch hat.

"That guy knows where there's a lot of 'em. We're goin' to show 'em!"

"We're goin' to show 'em!" whispered Key delightedly to Rose, who repeated the phrase rapturously to a man on the other side.

Down Sixth Avenue swept the procession, joined here and there by soldiers and marines, and now and then by civilians, who came up with the inevitable cry that they were just out of the army themselves, as if presenting it as a card of admission to a newly formed Sporting and Amusement Club.

Then the procession swerved down a cross street and headed for Fifth Avenue and the word filtered here and there that they were bound for a Red meeting at Tolliver Hall.

"Where is it?"

The question went up the line and a moment later the answer floated back. Tolliver Hall was down on Tenth Street. There was a bunch of other sojers who was goin' to break it up and was down there now!

But Tenth Street had a faraway sound and at the word a general groan went up and a score of the procession dropped out. Among these were Rose and Key, who slowed down to a saunter and let the more enthusiastic sweep on by.

"I'd rather get some liquor," said Key as they halted and made their way to the sidewalk amid cries of "Shell hole!" and "Quitters!"

"Does your brother work around here?" asked Rose, assuming the air of one passing from the superficial to the eternal.

"He oughta," replied Key. "I ain't seen him for a coupla years. I been out to Pennsylvania since. Maybe he don't work at night anyhow. It's right along here. He can get us some o'right if he ain't gone."

They found the place after a few minutes' patrol of the street—a shoddy tablecloth restaurant between Fifth Avenue and Broadway. Here Key went inside to inquire for his brother George, while Rose waited on the sidewalk.

"He ain't here no more," said Key emerging. "He's a waiter up to Delmonico's."

Rose nodded wisely, as if he'd expected as much. One should not be surprised at a capable man changing jobs occasionally. He knew a waiter once—there ensued a long conversation as they walked as to whether waiters made more in actual wages than in tips—it was decided that it depended on the social tone of the joint wherein the waiter labored. After having given each other vivid pictures of millionaires dining at Delmonico's and throwing away fifty-dollar bills after their first quart of champagne, both men thought privately of becoming waiters. In fact, Key's narrow brow was secreting a resolution to ask his brother to get him a job.

"A waiter can drink up all the champagne those fellas leave in bottles," suggested Rose with some relish, and then added as an afterthought, "Oh, boy!"

By the time they reached Delmonico's it was half past ten, and they were surprised to see a stream of taxis driving up to the door one after the other and emitting marvelous, hatless young ladies, each one attended by a stiff young gentleman in evening clothes.

"It's a party," said Rose with some awe. "Maybe we better not go in. He'll be busy."

"No, he won't. He'll be o'right."

After some hesitation they entered what appeared to them to be the least elaborate door and, indecision falling upon them immediately, stationed themselves nervously in an inconspicuous corner of the small dining-room in which they found themselves. They took off their caps and held them in their hands. A cloud of gloom fell upon them and both started when a door at one end of the room crashed open, emitting a comet-like waiter who streaked across the floor and vanished through another door on the other side.

There had been three of these lightning passages before the seekers mustered the acumen to hail a waiter. He turned, looked at them suspiciously, and then approached with soft, catlike steps, as if prepared at any moment to turn and flee.

"Say," began Key, "say, do you know my brother? He's a waiter here."

"His name is Key," annotated Rose.

Yes, the waiter knew Key. He was upstairs, he

thought. There was a big dance going on in the main ballroom. He'd tell him.

Ten minutes later George Key appeared and greeted his brother with the utmost suspicion; his first and most natural thought being that he was going to be asked for money.

George was tall and weak chinned, but there his resemblance to his brother ceased. The waiter's eyes were not dull, they were alert and twinkling, and his manner was suave, indoor, and faintly superior. They exchanged formalities. George was married and had three children. He seemed fairly interested, but not impressed by the news that Carrol had been abroad in the army. This disappointed Carrol.

"George," said the younger brother, these amenities having been disposed of, "we want to get some booze, and they won't sell us none. Can you get us some?"

George considered.

"Sure. Maybe I can. It may be half an hour, though."

"All right," agreed Carrol, "we'll wait."

At this Rose started to sit down in a convenient chair, but was haled to his feet by the indignant George.

"Hey! Watch out, you! Can't sit down here! This room's all set for a twelve o'clock banquet."

"I ain't goin' to hurt it," said Rose resentfully. "I been through the delouser."

"Never mind," said George sternly, "if the head waiter seen me here talkin' he'd romp all over me."

"Oh."

The mention of the head waiter was full explanation to the other two; they fingered their overseas caps nervously and waited for a suggestion.

"I tell you," said George, after a pause, "I got a place you can wait; you just come here with me."

They followed him out the far door, through a deserted pantry and up a pair of dark winding stairs, emerging finally into a small room chiefly furnished by piles of pails and stacks of scrubbing brushes, and illuminated by a single dim electric light. There he left them, after soliciting two dollars and agreeing to return in half an hour with a quart of whisky.

"George is makin' money, I bet," said Key gloomily as he seated himself on an inverted pail. "I bet he's making fifty dollars a week."

Rose nodded his head and spat.

"I bet he is, too."

"What'd he say the dance was of?"

"A lot of college fellas. Yale College."

They both nodded solemnly at each other.

"Wonder where that crowda sojers is now?"

"I don't know. I know that's too damn long to walk for me."

"Me too. You don't catch me walkin' that far."

Ten minutes later restlessness seized them.

"I'm goin' to see what's out here," said Rose, stepping cautiously toward the other door.

It was a swinging door of green baize and he pushed it open a cautious inch.

"See anything?"

For answer Rose drew in his breath sharply.

"Doggone! Here's some liquor I'll say!"

"Liquor?"

Key joined Rose at the door, and looked eagerly.

"I'll tell the world that's liquor," he said, after a moment of concentrated gazing.

It was a room about twice as large as the one they were in—and in it was prepared a radiant feast of spirits. There were long walls of alternating bottles set along two white-covered tables; whisky, gin, brandy, French and Italian vermouths, and orange juice, not to mention an array of siphons and two great empty punch bowls. The room was as yet uninhabited.

"It's for this dance they're just starting," whispered Key; "hear the violins playin'? Say, boy, I wouldn't mind havin' a dance."

They closed the door softly and exchanged a glance of mutual comprehension. There was no need of feeling each other out.

"I'd like to get my hands on a coupla those bottles," said Rose emphatically.

"Me too."

"Do you suppose we'd get seen?"

Key considered.

"Maybe we better wait till they start drinkin' 'em. They got 'em all laid out now, and they know how many of them there are."

They debated this point for several minutes. Rose was all for getting his hands on a bottle now and tucking it under his coat before any one came into the room. Key, however, advocated caution. He was afraid he might get his brother in trouble. If they waited till some of the bottles were opened it'd be all right to take one, and everybody'd think it was one of the college fellas.

While they were still engaged in argument George Key hurried through the room and, barely grunting at them, disappeared by way of the green baize door. A minute later they heard several corks pop, and then the sound of cracking ice and splashing liquid. George was mixing the punch.

The soldiers exchanged delighted grins.

"Oh, boy!" whispered Rose.

George reappeared.

"Just keep low, boys," he said quickly. "I'll have your stuff for you in five minutes."

He disappeared through the door by which he had come.

As soon as his footsteps receded down the stairs, Rose, after a cautious look, darted into the room of delights and reappeared with a bottle in his hand.

"Here's what I say," he said, as they sat radiantly digesting their first drink. "We'll wait till he comes up, and we'll ask him if we can't just stay here and drink what he brings us—see. We'll tell him we haven't got any place to drink it—see. Then we can sneak in there whenever there ain't nobody in that there room and tuck a bottle under our coats. We'll have enough to last us a couple days—see?"

"Sure," agreed Rose enthusiastically. "Oh, boy! And if we want to we can sell it to sojers any time we want to."

They were silent for a moment thinking rosily of this idea. Then Key reached up and unhooked the collar of his O. D. coat.

"It's hot in here, ain't it?"

Rose agreed earnestly.

"Hot as hell."

IV

SHE was still quite angry when she came out of the dressing-room and crossed the intervening parlor of politeness that opened onto the hall—angry not so much at the actual happening which was, after all, the merest commonplace of her social existence, but because it had occurred on this particular night. She had no quarrel with herself. She had acted with that correct mixture of dignity and reticent pity which she always employed. She had succinctly and deftly snubbed him.

It had happened when their taxi was leaving the

Biltmore—hadn't gone half a block. He had lifted his right arm awkwardly—she was on his right side—and attempted to settle it snugly around the crimson fur-trimmed opera cloak she wore. This in itself had been a mistake. It was inevitably more graceful for a young man attempting to embrace a young lady of whose acquiescence he was not certain, to first put his far arm around her. It avoided that awkward movement of raising the near arm.

His second *faux pas* was unconscious. She had spent the afternoon at the hairdresser's; the idea of any calamity overtaking her hair was extremely repugnant—yet as Peter made his unfortunate attempt the point of his elbow had just faintly brushed it. That was his second *faux pas*. Two were quite enough.

He had begun to murmur. At the first murmur she had decided that he was nothing but a college boy—Edith was twenty-two, and anyhow, this dance, first of its kind since the war, was reminding her, with the accelerating rhythm of its associations, of something else—of another dance and another man, a man for whom her feelings had been little more than a sad-eyed, adolescent mooniness. Edith Bradin was falling in love with her recollection of Gordon Sterrett.

So she came out of the dressing-room at Delmonico's and stood for a second in the doorway looking over the shoulders of a black dress in front of her at the groups of Yale men who flitted like dignified black moths around the head of the stairs. From the room she had left drifted out the heavy fragrance left by the passage to and fro of many scented young beauties—rich perfumes and the fragile memory-laden dust of fragrant powders. This odor drifting out acquired the tang of cigarette smoke in the hall, and then settled sensuously down the stairs and permeated the ballroom where the Gamma

Psi dance was to be held. It was an odor she knew well, exciting, stimulating, restlessly sweet—the odor of a fashionable dance.

She thought of her own appearance. Her bare arms and shoulders were powdered to a creamy white. She knew they looked very soft and would gleam like milk against the black backs that were to silhouette them tonight. The hairdressing had been a success; her reddish mass of hair was piled and crushed and creased to an arrogant marvel of mobile curves. Her lips were finely made of deep carmine; the irises of her eyes were delicate, breakable blue, like china eyes. She was a complete, infinitely delicate, quite perfect thing of beauty, flowing in an even line from a complex coiffure to two small slim feet.

She thought of what she would say tonight at this revel, faintly presaged already by the sounds of high and low laughter and slippered footsteps, and movements of couples up and down the stairs. She would talk the language she had talked for many years—her line—made up of the current expressions, bits of journalese and college slang strung together into an intrinsic whole, careless, faintly provocative, delicately sentimental. She smiled faintly as she heard a girl sitting on the stairs near her say: "You don't know the half of it, dearie!"

And as she smiled her anger melted for a moment, and closing her eyes she drew in a deep breath of pleasure. She dropped her arms to her side until they were faintly touching the sleek sheath that covered and suggested her figure. She had never felt her own softness so much nor so enjoyed the whiteness of her own arms.

"I smell sweet," she said to herself simply, and then came another thought—"I'm made for love."

She liked the sound of this and thought it again; then in inevitable succession came her new-born riot of dreams about Gordon. The twist of her imagination which, two months before, had disclosed to her her unguessed desire to see him again, seemed now to have been leading up to this dance, this hour.

For all her sleek beauty, Edith was a grave, slow-thinking girl. There was a streak in her of that same desire to ponder, of that adolescent idealism that had turned her brother socialist and pacifist. Henry Bradin had left Cornell, where he had been an instructor in economics, and had come to New York to pour the latest cures for incurable evils into the columns of a radical weekly newspaper.

Edith, less fatuously, would have been content to cure Gordon Sterrett. There was a quality of weakness in Gordon that she wanted to take care of; there was a helplessness in him that she wanted to protect. And she wanted someone she had known a long while, someone who had loved her a long while. She was a little tired; she wanted to get married. Out of a pile of letters, half a dozen pictures and as many memories, and this weariness, she had decided that next time she saw Gordon their relations were going to be changed. She would say something that would change them. There was this evening. This was her evening. All evenings were her evenings.

Then her thoughts were interrupted by a solemn undergraduate with a hurt look and an air of strained formality who presented himself before her and bowed unusually low. It was the man she had come with, Peter Himmel. He was tall and humorous, with horn-rimmed glasses and an air of attractive whimsicality. She suddenly rather disliked him—probably because he had not succeeded in kissing her.

"Well," she began, "are you still furious at me?"

"Not at all."

She stepped forward and took his arm.

"I'm sorry," she said softly. "I don't know why I snapped out that way. I'm in a bum humor tonight for some strange reason. I'm sorry."

"S'all right," he mumbled, "don't mention it."

He felt disagreeably embarrassed. Was she rubbing in the fact of his late failure?

"It was a mistake," she continued, on the same consciously gentle key. "We'll both forget it." For this he hated her.

A few minutes later they drifted out on the floor while the dozen swaying, sighing members of the specially hired jazz orchestra informed the crowded ballroom that "if a saxophone and me are left alone, why then two is com-pan-ee!"

A man with a mustache cut in.

"Hello," he began reprovingly. "You don't remember me."

"I can't just think of your name," she said lightly—"and I know you so well."

"I met you up at—" His voice trailed disconsolately off as a man with very fair hair cut in. Edith murmured a conventional "Thanks, loads—cut in later," to the *inconnu.*

The very fair man insisted on shaking hands enthusiastically. She placed him as one of the numerous Jims of her acquaintance—last name a mystery. She remembered even that he had a peculiar rhythm in dancing and found as they started that she was right.

"Going to be here long?" he breathed confidentially.

She leaned back and looked up at him.

"Couple of weeks."

"Where are you?"

"Biltmore. Call me up some day."

"I mean it," he assured her. "I will. We'll go to tea."

"So do I—Do."

A dark man cut in with intense formality.

"You don't remember me, do you?" he said gravely.

"I should say I do. Your name's Harlan."

"No-ope. Barlow."

"Well, I knew there were two syllables anyway. You're the boy that played the ukulele so well up at Howard Marshall's house party."

"I played—but not——"

A man with prominent teeth cut in. Edith inhaled a slight cloud of whisky. She liked men to have had something to drink; they were so much more cheerful, and appreciative and complimentary—much easier to talk to.

"My name's Dean, Philip Dean," he said cheerfully. "You don't remember me, I know, but you used to come up to New Haven with a fellow I roomed with senior year, Gordon Sterrett."

Edith looked up quickly.

"Yes, I went up with him twice—to the Pump and Slipper and the Junior prom."

"You've seen him, of course," said Dean carelessly. "He's here tonight. I saw him just a minute ago."

Edith started. Yet she had felt quite sure he would be here.

"Why, no, I haven't——"

A fat man with red hair cut in.

"Hello, Edith," he began.

"Why—hello there——"

She slipped, stumbled lightly.

"I'm sorry, dear," she murmured mechanically.

She had seen Gordon—Gordon very white and listless, leaning against the side of a doorway, smoking and looking into the ballroom. Edith could see that his face was thin and wan—that the hand he raised to his lips with a cigarette was trembling. They were dancing quite close to him now.

"—They invite so darn many extra fellas that you—" the short man was saying.

"Hello, Gordon," called Edith over her partner's shoulder. Her heart was pounding wildly.

His large dark eyes were fixed on her. He took a step in her direction. Her partner turned her away—she heard his voice bleating——

"—but half the stags get lit and leave before long, so——"

Then a low tone at her side.

"May I, please?"

She was dancing suddenly with Gordon; one of his arms was around her; she felt it tighten spasmodically; felt his hand on her back with the fingers spread. Her hand holding the little lace handkerchief was crushed in his.

"Why Gordon," she began breathlessly.

"Hello, Edith."

She slipped again—was tossed forward by his recovery until her face touched the black cloth of his dinner coat. She loved him—she knew she loved him—then for a minute there was silence while a strange feeling of uneasiness crept over her. Something was wrong.

Of a sudden her heart wrenched, and turned over as she realized what it was. He was pitiful and wretched, a little drunk, and miserably tired.

"Oh—" she cried involuntarily.

His eyes looked down at her. She saw suddenly that they were blood-streaked and rolling uncontrollably.

"Gordon," she murmured, "we'll sit down; I want to sit down."

They were nearly in mid-floor, but she had seen two men start toward her from opposite sides of the room, so she halted, seized Gordon's limp hand and led him bumping through the crowd, her mouth tight shut, her face a little pale under her rouge, her eyes trembling with tears.

She found a place high up on the soft-carpeted stairs, and he sat down heavily beside her.

"Well," he began, staring at her unsteadily, "I certainly am glad to see you, Edith."

She looked at him without answering. The effect of this on her was immeasurable. For years she had seen men in various stages of intoxication, from uncles all the way down to chauffeurs, and her feelings had varied from amusement to disgust, but here for the first time she was seized with a new feeling—an unutterable horror.

"Gordon," she said accusingly and almost crying, "you look like the devil."

He nodded. "I've had trouble, Edith."

"Trouble?"

"All sorts of trouble. Don't you say anything to the family, but I'm all gone to pieces. I'm a mess, Edith."

His lower lip was sagging. He seemed scarcely to see her.

"Can't you—can't you," she hesitated, "can't you tell me about it, Gordon? You know I'm always interested in you."

She bit her lip—she had intended to say something stronger, but found at the end that she couldn't bring it out.

Gordon shook his head dully. "I can't tell you. You're

a good woman. I can't tell a good woman the story."

"Rot," she said defiantly. "I think it's a perfect insult to call any one a good woman in that way. It's a slam. You've been drinking, Gordon."

"Thanks." He inclined his head gravely. "Thanks for the information."

"Why do you drink?"

"Because I'm so damn miserable."

"Do you think drinking's going to make it any better?"

"What you doing—trying to reform me?"

"No; I'm trying to help you, Gordon. Can't you tell me about it?"

"I'm in an awful mess. Best thing you can do is to pretend not to know me."

"Why, Gordon?"

"I'm sorry I cut in on you—it's unfair to you. You're pure woman—and all that sort of thing. Here, I'll get someone else to dance with you."

He rose clumsily to his feet, but she reached up and pulled him down beside her on the stairs.

"Here, Gordon. You're ridiculous. You're hurting me. You're acting like a—like a crazy man——"

"I admit it. I'm a little crazy. Something's wrong with me, Edith. There's something left me. It doesn't matter."

"It does, tell me."

"Just that. I was always queer—little bit different from other boys. All right in college, but now it's all wrong. Things have been snapping inside me for four months like little hooks on a dress, and it's about to come off when a few more hooks go. I'm very gradually going loony."

He turned his eyes full on her and began to laugh, and she shrank away from him.

"What *is* the matter?"

"Just me," he repeated. "I'm going loony. This whole place is like a dream to me—this Delmonico's——"

As he talked she saw he had changed utterly. He wasn't at all light and gay and careless—a great lethargy and discouragement had come over him. Revulsion seized her, followed by a faint, surprising boredom. His voice seemed to come out of a great void.

"Edith," he said, "I used to think I was clever, talented, an artist. Now I know I'm nothing. Can't draw, Edith. Don't know why I'm telling you this."

She nodded absently.

"I can't draw, I can't do anything. I'm poor as a church mouse." He laughed bitterly and rather too loud. "I've become a damn beggar, a leech on my friends. I'm a failure. I'm poor as hell."

Her distaste was growing. She barely nodded this time, waiting for her first possible cue to rise.

Suddenly Gordon's eyes filled with tears.

"Edith," he said, turning to her with what was evidently a strong effort at self-control, "I can't tell you what it means to me to know there's one person left who's interested in me."

He reached out and patted her hand, and involuntarily she drew it away.

"It's mighty fine of you," he repeated.

"Well," she said slowly, looking him in the eye, "any one's always glad to see an old friend—but I'm sorry to see you like this, Gordon."

There was a pause while they looked at each other, and the momentary eagerness in his eyes wavered. She rose and stood looking at him, her face quite expressionless.

"Shall we dance?" she suggested coolly.

—Love is fragile—she was thinking—but perhaps

the pieces are saved, the things that hovered on lips, that might have been said. The new love words, the tendernesses learned, are treasured up for the next lover.

V

PETER HIMMEL, escort to the lovely Edith, was unaccustomed to being snubbed; having been snubbed, he was hurt and embarrassed, and ashamed of himself. For a matter of two months he had been on special delivery terms with Edith Bradin, and knowing that the one excuse and explanation of the special delivery letter is its value in sentimental correspondence, he had believed himself quite sure of his ground. He searched in vain for any reason why she should have taken this attitude in the matter of a simple kiss.

Therefore when he was cut in on by the man with the mustache he went out into the hall and, making up a sentence, said it over to himself several times. Considerably deleted, this was it:

"Well, if any girl ever led a man on and then jolted him, she did—and she has no kick coming if I go out and get beautifully boiled."

So he walked through the supper room into a small room adjoining it, which he had located earlier in the evening. It was a room in which there were several large bowls of punch flanked by many bottles. He took a seat beside the table which held the bottles.

At the second highball, boredom, disgust, the monotony of time, the turbidity of events, sank into a vague background before which glittering cobwebs formed. Things became reconciled to themselves, things lay quietly on their shelves; the troubles of the day arranged themselves in trim formation and at his curt wish of dismissal, marched off and disappeared. And with the departure of worry came brilliant, permeating symbolism. Edith became a flighty, negligible girl, not to be worried over; rather to be laughed at. She fitted like a figure of his own dream into the surface world forming about him. He himself became in a measure symbolic, a type of the continent bacchanal, the brilliant dreamer at play.

Then the symbolic mood faded and as he sipped his third highball his imagination yielded to the warm glow and he lapsed into a state similar to floating on his back in pleasant water. It was at this point that he noticed that a green baize door near him was open about two inches, and that through the aperture a pair of eyes were watching him intently.

"Hm," murmured Peter calmly.

The green door closed—and then opened again—a bare half inch this time.

"Peek-a-boo," murmured Peter.

The door remained stationary and then he became aware of a series of tense intermittent whispers.

"One guy."

"What's he doin'?"

"He's sittin' lookin'."

"He better beat it off. We gotta get another li'l' bottle."

Peter listened while the words filtered into his consciousness.

"Now this," he thought, "is most remarkable."

He was excited. He was jubilant. He felt that he had stumbled upon a mystery. Affecting an elaborate carelessness he arose and walked around the table—then, turning quickly, pulled open the green door, precipitating Private Rose into the room.

"How do you do?" he said.

Private Rose set one foot slightly in front of the other, poised for fight, flight, or compromise.

"How do you do?" repeated Peter politely.

"I'm o'right."

"Can I offer you a drink?"

Private Rose looked at him searchingly, suspecting possible sarcasm.

"O'right," he said finally.

Peter indicated a chair.

"Sit down."

"I got a friend," said Rose, "I got a friend in there." He pointed to the green door.

"By all means let's have him in."

Peter crossed over, opened the door and welcomed in Private Key, very suspicious and uncertain and guilty. Chairs were found and the three took their seats around the punch bowl. Peter gave them each a highball and offered them a cigarette from his case. They accepted both with some diffidence.

"Now," continued Peter easily, "may I ask why you gentlemen prefer to lounge away your leisure hours in a room which is chiefly furnished, as far as I can see, with scrubbing brushes. And when the human race has progressed to the stage where seventeen thousand chairs are manufactured on every day except Sunday—" he paused. Rose and Key regarded him vacantly. "Will you tell me," went on Peter, "why you choose to rest yourselves on articles intended for the transportation of water from one place to another?"

At this point Rose contributed a grunt to the conversation.

"And lastly," finished Peter, "will you tell me why, when you are in a building beautifully hung with enormous candelabra, you prefer to spend these evening hours under one anemic electric light?"

Rose looked at Key; Key looked at Rose. They laughed; they laughed uproariously; they found it was impossible to look at each other without laughing. But they were not laughing with this man—they were laughing at him. To them a man who talked after this fashion was either raving drunk or raving crazy.

"You are Yale men, I presume," said Peter, finishing his highball and preparing another.

They laughed again.

"Na-ah."

"So? I thought perhaps you might be members of that lowly section of the university known as the Sheffield Scientific School."

"Na-ah."

"Hm. Well, that's too bad. No doubt you are Harvard men, anxious to preserve your incognito in this—this paradise of violet blue, as the newspapers say."

"Na-ah," said Key scornfully, "we was just waitin' for somebody."

"Ah," exclaimed Peter, rising and filling their glasses, "very interestin'. Had a date with a scrublady, eh?"

They both denied this indignantly.

"It's all right," Peter reassured them, "don't apologize. A scrublady's as good as any lady in the world. Kipling says 'Any lady and Judy O'Grady under the skin.' "

"Sure," said Key, winking broadly at Rose.

"My case, for instance," continued Peter, finishing his glass. "I got a girl up here that's spoiled. Spoiledest darn girl I ever saw. Refused to kiss me; no reason whatsoever. Led me on deliberately to think sure I want to kiss you and then plunk! Threw me over! What's the younger generation comin' to?"

"Say tha's hard luck," said Key—"that's awful hard luck."

"Oh, boy!" said Rose.

"Have another?" said Peter.

"We got in a sort of fight for a while," said Key after a pause, "but it was too far away."

"A fight?—tha's stuff!" said Peter, seating himself unsteadily. "Fight 'em all! I was in the army."

"This was with a Bolshevik fella."

"Tha's stuff!" exclaimed Peter, enthusiastic. "That's what I say! Kill the Bolshevik! Exterminate 'em!"

"We're Americuns," said Rose, implying a sturdy, defiant patriotism.

"Sure," said Peter. "Greatest race in the world! We're all Americuns! Have another."

They had another.

VI

AT ONE O'CLOCK a special orchestra, special even in a day of special orchestras, arrived at Delmonico's, and its members, seating themselves arrogantly around the piano, took up the burden of providing music for the Gamma Psi Fraternity. They were headed by a famous flute-player, distinguished throughout New York for his feat of standing on his head and shimmying with his shoulders while he played the latest jazz on his flute. During his performance the lights were extinguished except for the spotlight on the flute-player and another roving beam that threw flickering shadows and changing kaleidoscopic colors over the massed dancers.

Edith had danced herself into that tired, dreamy state habitual only with débutantes, a state equivalent to the glow of a noble soul after several long highballs. Her mind floated vaguely on the bosom of her music; her partners changed with the unreality of phantoms under the colorful shifting dusk, and to her present coma it seemed as if days had passed since the dance began. She had talked on many fragmentary subjects with many men. She had been kissed once and made love to six times. Earlier in the evening different undergraduates had danced with her, but now, like all the more popular girls there, she had her own entourage—that is, half a dozen gallants had singled her out or were alternating her charms with those of some other chosen beauty; they cut in on her in regular, inevitable succession.

Several times she had seen Gordon—he had been sitting a long time on the stairway with his palm to his head, his dull eyes fixed at an infinite speck on the floor before him, very depressed, he looked, and quite drunk—but Edith each time had averted her glance hurriedly. All that seemed long ago; her mind was passive now, her senses were lulled to trance-like sleep; only her feet danced and her voice talked on in hazy sentimental banter.

But Edith was not nearly so tired as to be incapable of moral indignation when Peter Himmel cut in on her, sublimely and happily drunk. She gasped and looked up at him.

"Why, *Peter!*"

"I'm a li'l' stewed, Edith."

"Why, Peter, you're a *peach*, you are! Don't you think it's a bum way of doing—when you're with me?"

Then she smiled unwillingly, for he was looking at her with owlish sentimentality varied with a silly spasmodic smile.

"Darlin' Edith," he began earnestly, "you know I love you, don't you?"

"You tell it well."

"I love you—and I merely wanted you to kiss me," he added sadly.

His embarrassment, his shame, were both gone. She was a mos' beautiful girl in whole worl'. Mos' beautiful eyes, like stars above. He wanted to 'pologize—firs', for presuming try to kiss her; second, for drinking—but he'd been so discouraged 'cause he had thought she was mad at him——

The red-fat man cut in, and looking up at Edith smiled radiantly.

"Did you bring any one?" she asked.

No. The red-fat man was a stag.

"Well, would you mind—would it be an awful bother for you to—to take me home tonight?" (this extreme diffidence was a charming affectation on Edith's part—she knew that the red-fat man would immediately dissolve into a paroxysm of delight).

"Bother? Why, good Lord, I'd be darn glad to! You know I'd be darn glad to."

"Thanks *loads!* You're awfully sweet."

She glanced at her wrist-watch. It was half past one. And, as she said "half past one" to herself, it floated vaguely into her mind that her brother had told her at luncheon that he worked in the office of his newspaper until after one-thirty every evening.

Edith turned suddenly to her current partner.

"What street is Delmonico's on, anyway?"

"Street? Oh, why Fifth Avenue, of course."

"I mean, what cross street?"

"Why—let's see—it's on Forty-fourth Street."

This verified what she had thought. Henry's office must be across the street and just around the corner, and it occurred to her immediately that she might slip over for a moment and surprise him, float in on him, a shimmering marvel in her new crimson opera cloak and "cheer him up." It was exactly the sort of thing Edith reveled in doing—an unconventional, jaunty thing. The idea reached out and gripped at her imagination—after an instant's hesitation she had decided.

"My hair is just about to tumble entirely down," she said pleasantly to her partner; "would you mind if I go and fix it?"

"Not at all."

"You're a peach."

A few minutes later, wrapped in her crimson opera cloak, she flitted down a side-stairs, her cheeks glowing with excitement at her little adventure. She ran by a couple who stood at the door—a weak-chinned waiter and an over-rouged young lady, in hot dispute—and opening the outer door stepped into the warm May night.

VII

THE over-rouged young lady followed her with a brief, bitter glance—then turned again to the weak-chinned waiter and took up her argument.

"You better go up and tell him I'm here," she said defiantly, "or I'll go up myself."

"No, you don't!" said George sternly.

The girl smiled sardonically.

"Oh, I don't, don't I? Well, let me tell you I know more college fellas and more of 'em know me, and are glad to take me out on a party, than you ever saw in your whole life."

"Maybe so——"

"Maybe so," she interrupted. "Oh, it's all right for any of 'em like that one that just ran out—God knows where *she* went—it's all right for them that are asked here to come or go as they like—but when I want to see a friend they have some cheap, ham-slinging, bring-me-a-doughnut waiter to stand here and keep me out."

"See here," said the elder Key indignantly, "I can't lose my job. Maybe this fella you're talkin' about doesn't want to see you."

"Oh, he wants to see me all right."

"Anyways, how could I find him in all that crowd?"

"Oh, he'll be there," she asserted confidently. "You just ask anybody for Gordon Sterrett and they'll point him out to you. They all know each other, those fellas."

She produced a mesh bag, and taking out a dollar bill handed it to George.

"Here," she said, "here's a bribe. You find him and give him my message. You tell him if he isn't here in five minutes I'm coming up."

George shook his head pessimistically, considered the question for a moment, wavered violently, and then withdrew.

In less than the allotted time Gordon came downstairs. He was drunker than he had been earlier in the evening and in a different way. The liquor seemed to have hardened on him like a crust. He was heavy and lurching—almost incoherent when he talked.

"'Lo, Jewel," he said thickly. "Came right away. Jewel, I couldn't get that money. Tried my best."

"Money nothing!" she snapped. "You haven't been near me for ten days. What's the matter?"

He shook his head slowly.

"Been very low, Jewel. Been sick."

"Why didn't you tell me if you were sick. I don't care about the money that bad. I didn't start bothering you about it at all until you began neglecting me."

Again he shook his head.

"Haven't been neglecting you. Not at all."

"Haven't! You haven't been near me for three weeks,

unless you been so drunk you didn't know what you were doing."

"Been sick, Jewel," he repeated, turning his eyes upon her wearily.

"You're well enough to come and play with your society friends here all right. You told me you'd meet me for dinner, and you said you'd have some money for me. You didn't even bother to ring me up."

"I couldn't get any money."

"Haven't I just been saying that doesn't matter? I wanted to see *you*, Gordon, but you seem to prefer your somebody else."

He denied this bitterly.

"Then get your hat and come along," she suggested.

Gordon hesitated—and she came suddenly close to him and slipped her arms around his neck.

"Come on with me, Gordon," she said in a half whisper. "We'll go over to Devineries' and have a drink, and then we can go up to my apartment."

"I can't, Jewel——"

"You can," she said intensely.

"I'm sick as a dog!"

"Well, then, you oughtn't to stay here and dance."

With a glance around him in which relief and despair were mingled, Gordon hesitated; then she suddenly pulled him to her and kissed him with soft, pulpy lips.

"All right," he said heavily. "I'll get my hat."

VIII

WHEN Edith came out into the clear blue of the May night she found the Avenue deserted. The windows of the big shops were dark; over their doors were drawn great iron masks until they were only shadowy tombs of the late day's splendor. Glancing down toward Forty-second Street she saw a commingled blur of lights from the all-night restaurants. Over on Sixth Avenue the elevated, a flare of fire, roared across the street between the glimmering parallels of light at the station and streaked along into the crisp dark. But at Forty-fourth Street it was very quiet.

Pulling her cloak close about her Edith darted across the Avenue. She started nervously as a solitary man passed her and said in a hoarse whisper—"Where bound, kiddo?" She was reminded of a night in her childhood when she had walked around the block in her pajamas and a dog had howled at her from a mystery-big back yard.

In a minute she had reached her destination, a two-story, comparatively old building on Forty-fourth, in the upper window of which she thankfully detected a wisp of light. It was bright enough outside for her to make out the sign beside the window—the *New York Trumpet*. She stepped inside a dark hall and after a second saw the stairs in the corner.

Then she was in a long, low room furnished with many desks and hung on all sides with file copies of newspapers. There were only two occupants. They were sitting at different ends of the room, each wearing a green eye-shade and writing by a solitary desk light.

For a moment she stood uncertainly in the doorway, and then both men turned around simultaneously and she recognized her brother.

"Why, Edith!" He rose quickly and approached her in surprise, removing his eye-shade. He was tall, lean, and dark, with black, piercing eyes under very thick glasses. They were far-away eyes that seemed always fixed just over the head of the person to whom he was talking.

He put his hands on her arms and kissed her cheek.

"What is it?" he repeated in some alarm.

"I was at a dance across at Delmonico's, Henry," she said excitedly, "and I couldn't resist tearing over to see you."

"I'm glad you did." His alertness gave way quickly to a habitual vagueness. "You oughtn't to be out alone at night though, ought you?"

The man at the other end of the room had been looking at them curiously, but at Henry's beckoning gesture he approached. He was loosely fat with little twinkling eyes, and, having removed his collar and tie, he gave the impression of a Middle-Western farmer on a Sunday afternoon.

"This is my sister," said Henry. "She dropped in to see me."

"How do you do?" said the fat man, smiling. "My name's Bartholomew, Miss Bradin. I know your brother has forgotten it long ago."

Edith laughed politely.

"Well," he continued, "not exactly gorgeous quarters we have here, are they?"

Edith looked around the room.

"They seem very nice," she replied. "Where do you keep the bombs?"

"The bombs?" repeated Bartholomew, laughing. "That's pretty good—the bombs. Did you hear her, Henry? She wants to know where we keep the bombs. Say, that's pretty good."

Edith swung herself onto a vacant desk and sat dangling her feet over the edge. Her brother took a seat beside her.

"Well," he asked, absent-mindedly, "how do you like New York this trip?"

"Not bad. I'll be over at the Biltmore with the Hoyts until Sunday. Can't you come to luncheon tomorrow?"

He thought a moment.

"I'm especially busy," he objected, "and I hate women in groups."

"All right," she agreed, unruffled. "Let's you and me have luncheon together."

"Very well."

"I'll call for you at twelve."

Bartholomew was obviously anxious to return to his desk, but apparently considered that it would be rude to leave without some parting pleasantry.

"Well"—he began awkwardly.

They both turned to him.

"Well, we—we had an exciting time earlier in the evening."

The two men exchanged glances.

"You should have come earlier," continued Bartholomew, somewhat encouraged. "We had a regular vaudeville."

"Did you really?"

"A serenade," said Henry. "A lot of soldiers gathered down there in the street and began to yell at the sign."

"Why?" she demanded.

"Just a crowd," said Henry, abstractedly. "All crowds have to howl. They didn't have anybody with much initiative in the lead, or they'd probably have forced their way in here and smashed things up."

"Yes," said Bartholomew, turning again to Edith, "you should have been here."

He seemed to consider this a sufficient cue for withdrawal, for he turned abruptly and went back to his desk.

"Are the soldiers all set against the Socialists?" demanded Edith of her brother. "I mean do they attack you violently and all that?"

Henry replaced his eye-shade and yawned.

"The human race has come a long way," he said casually, "but most of us are throw-backs; the soldiers don't know what they want, or what they hate, or what they like. They're used to acting in large bodies, and they seem to have to make demonstrations. So it happens to be against us. There've been riots all over the city tonight. It's May Day, you see."

"Was the disturbance here pretty serious?"

"Not a bit," he said scornfully. "About twenty-five of them stopped in the street about nine o'clock, and began to bellow at the moon."

"Oh"—She changed the subject. "You're glad to see me, Henry?"

"Why, sure."

"You don't seem to be."

"I am."

"I suppose you think I'm a—a waster. Sort of the World's Worst Butterfly."

Henry laughed.

"Not at all. Have a good time while you're young. Why? Do I seem like the priggish and earnest youth?"

"No—" She paused, "—but somehow I began thinking how absolutely different the party I'm on is from—from all your purposes. It seems sort of—of incongruous, doesn't it?—me being at a party like that, and you over here working for a thing that'll make that sort of party impossible ever any more, if your ideas work."

"I don't think of it that way. You're young, and you're acting just as you were brought up to act. Go ahead—have a good time?"

Her feet, which had been idly swinging, stopped and her voice dropped a note.

"I wish you'd—you'd come back to Harrisburg and have a good time. Do you feel sure that you're on the right track——"

"You're wearing beautiful stockings," he interrupted. "What on earth are they?"

"They're embroidered," she replied, glancing down. "Aren't they cunning?" She raised her skirts and uncovered slim, silk-sheathed calves. "Or do you disapprove of silk stockings?"

He seemed slightly exasperated, bent his dark eyes on her piercingly.

"Are you trying to make me out as criticizing you in any way, Edith?"

"Not at all——"

She paused. Bartholomew had uttered a grunt. She turned and saw that he had left his desk and was standing at the window.

"What is it?" demanded Henry.

"People," said Bartholomew, and then after an instant: "Whole jam of them. They're coming from Sixth Avenue."

"People?"

The fat man pressed his nose to the pane.

"Soldiers, by God!" he said emphatically. "I had an idea they'd come back."

Edith jumped to her feet, and running over joined Bartholomew at the window.

"There's a lot of them!" she cried excitedly. "Come here, Henry!"

Henry readjusted his shade, but kept his seat.

"Hadn't we better turn out the lights?" suggested Bartholomew.

"No. They'll go away in a minute."

"They're not," said Edith, peering from the window. "They're not even thinking of going away. There's more of them coming. Look—there's a whole crowd turning the corner of Sixth Avenue."

By the yellow glow and blue shadows of the street lamp she could see that the sidewalk was crowded with men. They were mostly in uniform, some sober, some enthusiastically drunk, and over the whole swept an incoherent clamor and shouting.

Henry rose, and going to the window exposed himself as a long silhouette against the office lights. Immediately the shouting became a steady yell, and a rattling fusillade of small missiles, corners of tobacco plugs, cigarette-boxes, and even pennies beat against the window. The sounds of the racket now began floating up the stairs as the folding doors revolved.

"They're coming up!" cried Bartholomew.

Edith turned anxiously to Henry.

"They're coming up, Henry."

From downstairs in the lower hall their cries were now quite audible.

"—God damn Socialists!"

"Pro-Germans, Boche-lovers!"

"Second floor, front! Come on!"

"We'll get the sons——"

The next five minutes passed in a dream. Edith was conscious that the clamor burst suddenly upon the three of them like a cloud of rain, that there was a thunder of many feet on the stairs, that Henry had seized her arm and drawn her back toward the rear of the office. Then the door opened and an overflow of men were forced into the room—not the leaders, but simply those who happened to be in front.

"Hello, Bo!"

"Up late, ain't you?"

"You an' your girl. Damn *you!*"

She noticed that two very drunken soldiers had been

forced to the front, where they wobbled fatuously—one of them was short and dark, the other was tall and weak of chin.

Henry stepped forward and raised his hand.

"Friends!" he said.

The clamor faded into a momentary stillness, punctuated with mutterings.

"Friends!" he repeated, his faraway eyes fixed over the heads of the crowd, "you're injuring no one but yourselves by breaking in here tonight. Do we look like rich men? Do we look like Germans? I ask you in all fairness——"

"Pipe down!"

"I'll say you do!"

"Say, who's your lady friend, buddy?"

A man in civilian clothes, who had been pawing over a table, suddenly held up a newspaper.

"Here it is!" he shouted. "They wanted the Germans to win the war!"

A new overflow from the stairs was shouldered in and of a sudden the room was full of men all closing around the pale little group at the back. Edith saw that the tall soldier with the weak chin was still in front. The short dark one had disappeared.

She edged slightly backward, stood close to the open window, through which came a clear breath of cool night air.

Then the room was a riot. She realized that the soldiers were surging forward, glimpsed the fat man swinging a chair over his head—instantly the lights went out, and she felt the push of warm bodies under rough cloth, and her ears were full of shouting and trampling and hard breathing.

A figure flashed by her out of nowhere, tottered, was edged sideways, and of a sudden disappeared helplessly out through the open window with a frightened, fragmentary cry that died staccato on the bosom of the clamor. By the faint light streaming from the building backing on the area Edith had a quick impression that it had been the tall soldier with the weak chin.

Anger rose astonishingly in her. She swung her arms wildly, edged blindly toward the thickest of the scuffling. She heard grunts, curses, the muffled impact of fists.

"Henry!" she called frantically, "Henry!"

Then, it was minutes later, she felt suddenly that there were other figures in the room. She heard a voice, deep, bullying, authoritative; she saw yellow rays of light sweeping here and there in the fracas. The cries became more scattered. The scuffling increased and then stopped.

Suddenly the lights were on and the room was full of policemen, clubbing left and right. The deep voice boomed out:

"Here now! Here now! Here now!"

And then:

"Quiet down and get out! Here now!"

The room seemed to empty like a wash-bowl. A policeman fast-grappled in the corner released his hold on his soldier antagonist and started him with a shove toward the door. The deep voice continued. Edith perceived now that it came from a bull-necked police captain standing near the door.

"Here now! This is no way! One of your own sojers got shoved out of the back window an' killed hisself!"

"Henry!" called Edith, "Henry!"

She beat wildly with her fists on the back of the man in front of her; she brushed between two others; fought, shrieked, and beat her way to a very pale figure sitting on the floor close to a desk.

"Henry," she cried passionately, "what's the matter? What's the matter? Did they hurt you?"

His eyes were shut. He groaned and then looking up said disgustedly——

"They broke my leg. My God, the fools!"

"Here now!" called the police captain. "Here now! Here now!"

IX

"CHILDS', Fifty-ninth Street," at eight o'clock of any morning differs from its sisters by less than the width of their marble tables or the degree of polish on the frying-pans. You will see there a crowd of poor people with sleep in the corners of their eyes, trying to look straight before them at their food so as not to see the other poor people. But Childs', Fifty-ninth, four hours earlier is quite unlike any Childs' restaurant from Portland, Oregon, to Portland, Maine. Within its pale but sanitary walls one finds a noisy medley of chorus girls, college boys, débutantes, rakes, *filles de joie*—a not unrepresentative mixture of the gayest of Broadway, and even of Fifth Avenue.

In the early morning of May the second it was unusually full. Over the marble-topped tables were bent the excited faces of flappers whose fathers owned individual villages. They were eating buckwheat cakes and scrambled eggs with relish and gusto, an accomplishment that it would have been utterly impossible for them to repeat in the same place four hours later.

Almost the entire crowd were from the Gamma Psi dance at Delmonico's, except for several chorus girls from a midnight revue who sat at a side table and wished they'd taken off a little more make-up after the show. Here and there a drab, mouse-like figure, desperately out of place, watched the butterflies with a weary, puzzled curiosity. But the drab figure was the exception. This was the morning after May Day, and celebration was still in the air.

Gus Rose, sober but a little dazed, must be classed as one of the drab figures. How he had got himself from Forty-fourth Street to Fifty-ninth Street after the riot was only a hazy half-memory. He had seen the body of Carrol Key put in an ambulance and driven off, and then he had started uptown with two or three soldiers. Somewhere between Forty-fourth Street and Fifty-ninth Street the other soldiers had met some women and disappeared. Rose had wandered to Columbus Circle and chosen the gleaming lights of Childs' to minister to his craving for coffee and doughnuts. He walked in and sat down.

All around him floated airy, inconsequential chatter and high-pitched laughter. At first he failed to understand, but after a puzzled five minutes he realized that this was the aftermath of some gay party. Here and there a restless, hilarious young man wandered fraternally and familiarly between the tables, shaking hands indiscriminately and pausing occasionally for a facetious chat, while excited waiters, bearing cakes and eggs aloft, swore at him silently, and bumped him out of the way. To Rose, seated at the most inconspicuous and least crowded table, the whole scene was a colorful circus of beauty and riotous pleasure.

He became gradually aware, after a few moments, that the couple seated diagonally across from him, with their backs to the crowd, were not the least interesting pair in the room. The man was drunk. He wore a dinner coat with a dishevelled tie and shirt swollen by spillings of water and wine. His eyes, dim and blood-shot, moved unnaturally from side to side. His breath came short between his lips.

"He's been on a spree!" thought Rose.

The woman was almost if not quite sober. She was pretty, with dark eyes and feverish high color, and she kept her active eyes fixed on her companion with the alertness of a hawk. From time to time she would lean and whisper intently to him, and he would answer by inclining his head heavily or by a particularly ghoulish and repellent wink.

Rose scrutinized them dumbly for some minutes, until the woman gave him a quick, resentful look; then he shifted his gaze to two of the most conspicuously hilarious of the promenaders who were on a protracted circuit of the tables. To his surprise he recognized in one of them the young man by whom he had been so ludicrously entertained at Delmonico's. This started him thinking of Key with a vague sentimentality, not unmixed with awe. Key was dead. He had fallen thirty-five feet and split his skull like a cracked coconut.

"He was a darn good guy," thought Rose mournfully. "He was a darn good guy, o'right. That was awful hard luck about him."

The two promenaders approached and started down between Rose's table and the next, addressing friends and strangers alike with jovial familiarity. Suddenly Rose saw the fair-haired one with the prominent teeth stop, look unsteadily at the man and girl opposite, and then begin to move his head disapprovingly from side to side.

The man with the bloodshot eyes looked up.

"Gordy," said the promenader with the prominent teeth, "Gordy."

"Hello," said the man with the stained shirt thickly.

Prominent Teeth shook his finger pessimistically at the pair, giving the woman a glance of aloof condemnation.

"What'd I tell you, Gordy?"

Gordon stirred in his seat.

"Go to hell!" he said.

Dean continued to stand there shaking his finger. The woman began to get angry.

"You go way!" she cried fiercely. "You're drunk, that's what you are!"

"So's he," suggested Dean, staying the motion of his finger and pointing it at Gordon.

Peter Himmel ambled up, owlish now and oratorically inclined.

"Here now," he began as if called upon to deal with some petty dispute between children. "Wha's all trouble?"

"You take your friend away," said Jewel tartly. "He's bothering us."

"What's at?"

"You heard me!" she said shrilly. "I said to take your drunken friend away."

Her rising voice rang out above the clatter of the restaurant and a waiter came hurrying up.

"You gotta be more quiet!"

"That fella's drunk," she cried. "He's insulting us."

"Ah-ha, Gordy," persisted the accused. "What'd I tell you." He turned to the waiter. "Gordy an I friends. Been tryin' help him, haven't I, Gordy?"

Gordy looked up.

"Help me? Hell, no!"

Jewel rose suddenly, and seizing Gordon's arm assisted him to his feet.

"Come on, Gordy!" she said, leaning toward him and speaking in a half whisper. "Let's us get out of here. This fella's got a mean drunk on."

Gordon allowed himself to be urged to his feet and started toward the door. Jewel turned for a second and addressed the provoker of their flight.

"I know all about *you!*" she said fiercely. "Nice friend, you are, I'll say. He told me about you."

Then she seized Gordon's arm, and together they made their way through the curious crowd, paid their check and went out.

"You'll have to sit down," said the waiter to Peter after they had gone.

"What's 'at? Sit down?"

"Yes—or get out."

Peter turned to Dean.

"Come on," he suggested. "Let's beat up this waiter."

"All right."

They advanced toward him, their faces grown stern. The waiter retreated.

Peter suddenly reached over to a plate on the table beside him and picking up a handful of hash tossed it into the air. It descended as a languid parabola in snowflake effect on the heads of those near by.

"Hey! Ease up!"

"Put him out!"

"Sit down, Peter!"

"Cut out that stuff!"

Peter laughed and bowed.

"Thank you for your kind applause, ladies and gents. If someone will lend me some more hash and a tall hat we will go on with the act."

The bouncer bustled up.

"You've gotta get out!" he said to Peter.

"Hell, no!"

"He's my friend!" put in Dean indignantly.

A crowd of waiters were gathering. "Put him out!"

"Better go, Peter."

There was a short struggle and the two were edged and pushed toward the door.

"I got a hat and a coat here!" cried Peter.

"Well, go get 'em and be spry about it!"

The bouncer released his hold on Peter, who, adopting a ludicrous air of extreme cunning, rushed immediately around to the other table, where he burst into derisive laughter and thumbed his nose at the exasperated waiters.

"Think I just better wait a l'il' longer," he announced.

The chase began. Four waiters were sent around one way and four another. Dean caught hold of two of them by the coat, and another struggle took place before the pursuit of Peter could be resumed; he was finally pinioned after overturning a sugar-bowl and several cups of coffee. A fresh argument ensued at the cashier's desk, where Peter attempted to buy another dish of hash to take with him and throw at policemen.

But the commotion upon his exit proper was dwarfed by another phenomenon which drew admiring glances and a prolonged involuntary "Oh-h-h!" from every person in the restaurant.

The great plate-glass front had turned to a deep creamy blue, the color of a Maxfield Parrish moonlight —a blue that seemed to press close upon the pane as if to crowd its way into the restaurant. Dawn had come up in Columbus Circle, magical, breathless dawn, silhouetting the great statue of the immortal Christopher, and mingling in a curious and uncanny manner with the fading yellow electric light inside.

X

MR. IN and Mr. Out are not listed by the census-taker. You will search for them in vain through the social register or the births, marriages, and deaths, or the grocer's credit list. Oblivion has swallowed them and the testimony that they ever existed at all is vague and shadowy, and inadmissible in a court of law. Yet I have it upon the best authority that for a brief space Mr. In and Mr. Out lived, breathed, answered to their names and radiated vivid personalities of their own.

During the brief span of their lives they walked in their native garments down the great highway of a great nation; were laughed at, sworn at, chased, and fled from. Then they passed and were heard of no more.

They were already taking form dimly, when a taxicab with the top open breezed down Broadway in the faintest glimmer of May dawn. In this car sat the souls of Mr. In and Mr. Out discussing with amazement the blue light that had so precipitately colored the sky behind the statue of Christopher Columbus, discussing with bewilderment the old, gray lake. They were agreed on all things, from the absurdity of the bouncer in Childs' to the absurdity of the business of life. They were dizzy with the extreme maudlin happiness that the morning had awakened in their glowing souls. Indeed, so fresh and vigorous was their pleasure in living that they felt it should be expressed by loud cries.

"Ye-ow-ow!" hooted Peter, making a megaphone with his hands—and Dean joined in with a call that, though equally significant and symbolic, derived its resonance from its very inarticulateness.

"Yo-ho! Yea! Yoho! Yo-buba!"

Fifty-third Street was a bus with a dark, bobbed-hair beauty atop; Fifty-second was a street cleaner who dodged, escaped, and sent up a yell of, "Look where you're aimin'!" in a pained and grieved voice. At Fiftieth Street a group of men on a very white sidewalk in front of a very white building turned to stare after them, and shouted:

"Some party, boys!"

At Forty-ninth Street Peter turned to Dean. "Beautiful morning," he said gravely, squinting up his owlish eyes.

"Probably is."

"Go get some breakfast, hey?"

Dean agreed—with additions.

"Breakfast and liquor."

"Breakfast and liquor," repeated Peter, and they looked at each other, nodding. "That's logical."

Then they both burst into loud laughter.

"Breakfast and liquor! Oh, gosh!"

"No such thing," announced Peter.

"Don't serve it? Ne'mind. We force 'em serve it. Bring pressure bear."

"Bring logic bear."

The taxi cut suddenly off Broadway, sailed along a cross street, and stopped in front of a heavy tomb-like building in Fifth Avenue.

"What's idea?"

The taxi-driver informed them that this was Delmonico's.

This was somewhat puzzling. They were forced to devote several minutes to intense concentration, for if such an order had been given there must have been a reason for it.

"Somep'm 'bouta coat," suggested the taxi-man.

That was it. Peter's overcoat and hat. He had left them at Delmonico's. Having decided this, they disembarked from the taxi and strolled toward the entrance arm in arm.

"Hey!" said the taxi-driver.

"Huh?"

"You better pay me."

They shook their heads in shocked negation.

"Later, not now—we give orders, you wait."

The taxi-driver objected; he wanted his money now.

With the scornful condescension of men exercising tremendous self-control they paid him.

Inside Peter groped in vain through a dim, deserted check-room in search of his coat and derby.

"Gone, I guess. Somebody stole it."

"Some Sheff student."

"All probability."

"Never mind," said Dean, nobly. "I'll leave mine here too—then we'll both be dressed the same."

He removed his overcoat and hat and was hanging them up when his roving glance was caught and held magnetically by two large squares of cardboard tacked to the two coat-room doors. The one on the left-hand door bore the word "In" in big black letters, and the one on the right-hand door flaunted the equally emphatic word "Out."

"Look!" he exclaimed happily——

Peter's eyes followed his pointing finger.

"What?"

"Look at the signs. Let's take 'em."

"Good idea."

"Probably pair very rare an' valuable signs. Probably come in handy."

Peter removed the left-hand sign from the door and endeavored to conceal it about his person. The sign being of considerable proportions, this was a matter of some difficulty. An idea flung itself at him, and with an air of dignified mystery he turned his back. After an instant he wheeled dramatically around, and stretching out his arms displayed himself to the admiring Dean. He had inserted the sign in his vest, completely covering his shirt front. In effect, the word "In" had been painted upon his shirt in large black letters.

"Yoho!" cheered Dean. "Mister In."

He inserted his own sign in like manner.

"Mister Out!" he announced triumphantly. "Mr. In meet Mr. Out."

They advanced and shook hands. Again laughter overcame them and they rocked in a shaken spasm of mirth.

"Yoho!"

"We probably get a flock of breakfast."

"We'll go—go to the Commodore."

Arm in arm they sallied out the door, and turning east in Forty-fourth Street set out for the Commodore.

As they came out a short dark soldier, very pale and tired, who had been wandering listlessly along the sidewalk, turned to look at them.

He started over as though to address them, but as they immediately bent on him glances of withering unrecognition, he waited until they had started unsteadily down the street, and then followed at about forty paces, chuckling to himself and saying "Oh, boy!" over and over under his breath, in delighted, anticipatory tones.

Mr. In and Mr. Out were meanwhile exchanging pleasantries concerning their future plans.

"We want liquor; we want breakfast. Neither without the other. One and indivisible."

"We want both 'em!"

"Both 'em!"

It was quite light now, and passers-by began to bend curious eyes on the pair. Obviously they were engaged in a discussion, which afforded each of them intense amusement, for occasionally a fit of laughter would seize upon them so violently that, still with their arms interlocked, they would bend nearly double.

Reaching the Commodore, they exchanged a few spicy epigrams with the sleepy-eyed doorman, navigated the revolving door with some difficulty, and then made their way through a thinly populated but startled lobby to the dining-room, where a puzzled waiter showed them an obscure table in a corner. They studied the bill of fare helplessly, telling over the items to each other in puzzled mumbles.

"Don't see any liquor here," said Peter reproachfully.

The waiter became audible but unintelligible.

"Repeat," continued Peter, with patient tolerance, "that there seems to be unexplained and quite distasteful lack of liquor upon bill of fare."

"Here!" said Dean confidently, "let me handle him." He turned to the waiter—"Bring us—bring us—" he scanned the bill of fare anxiously. "Bring us a quart of champagne and a—a—probably ham sandwich."

The waiter looked doubtful.

"Bring it!" roared Mr. In and Mr. Out in chorus.

The waiter coughed and disappeared. There was a short wait during which they were subjected without their knowledge to a careful scrutiny by the headwaiter. Then the champagne arrived, and at the sight of it Mr. In and Mr. Out became jubilant.

"Imagine their objecting to us having champagne for breakfast—jus' imagine."

They both concentrated upon the vision of such an awesome possibility, but the feat was too much for them. It was impossible for their joint imaginations to conjure up a world where anyone might object to anyone else having champagne for breakfast. The waiter drew the cork with an enormous *pop*—and their glasses immediately foamed with pale yellow froth.

"Here's health, Mr. In."

"Here's same to you, Mr. Out."

The waiter withdrew; the minutes passed; the champagne became low in the bottle.

"It's—it's mortifying," said Dean suddenly.

"What's mortifying?"

"The idea their objecting us having champagne breakfast."

"Mortifying?" Peter considered. "Yes, tha's word—mortifying."

Again they collapsed into laughter, howled, swayed, rocked back and forth in their chairs, repeating the word "mortifying" over and over to each other—each repetition seeming to make it only more brilliantly absurd.

After a few more gorgeous minutes they decided on another quart. Their anxious waiter consulted his immediate superior, and this discreet person gave explicit instructions that no more champagne should be served. Their check was brought.

Five minutes later, arm in arm, they left the Commodore and made their way through a curious, staring crowd along Forty-second Street, and up Vanderbilt Avenue to the Biltmore. There, with sudden cunning, they rose to the occasion and traversed the lobby, walking fast and standing unnaturally erect.

Once in the dining-room they repeated their performance. They were torn between intermittent convulsive laughter and sudden spasmodic discussions of politics, college, and the sunny state of their dispositions. Their watches told them that it was now nine o'clock, and a dim idea was born in them that they were on a memorable party, something that they would remember always. They lingered over the second bottle. Either of them had only to mention the word "mortifying" to send them both into riotous gasps. The dining-room was whirring and shifting now; a curious lightness permeated and rarefied the heavy air.

They paid their check and walked out into the lobby.

It was at this moment that the exterior doors revolved for the thousandth time that morning, and admitted into the lobby a very pale young beauty with dark circles under her eyes, attired in a much-rumpled evening dress. She was accompanied by a plain stout man, obviously not an appropriate escort.

At the top of the stairs this couple encountered Mr. In and Mr. Out.

"Edith," began Mr. In, stepping toward her hilariously, and making a sweeping bow, "darling, good morning."

The stout man glanced questioningly at Edith, as if merely asking her permission to throw this man summarily out of the way.

"Scuse familiarity," added Peter, as an afterthought. "Edith, good-morning."

He seized Dean's elbow and impelled him into the foreground.

"Meet Mr. In, Edith, my bes' frien'. Inseparable. Mr. In and Mr. Out."

Mr. Out advanced and bowed; in fact, he advanced so far and bowed so low that he tipped slightly forward and only kept his balance by placing a hand lightly on Edith's shoulder.

"I'm Mr. Out, Edith," he mumbled pleasantly, "S'misterin Misterout."

"'Smisterinanout," said Peter proudly.

But Edith stared straight by them, her eyes fixed on some infinite speck in the gallery above her. She nodded slightly to the stout man, who advanced bull-like and with a sturdy brisk gesture pushed Mr. In and Mr. Out to either side. Through this alley he and Edith walked.

But ten paces farther on Edith stopped again—stopped and pointed to a short, dark soldier who was eying the crowd in general, and the tableau of Mr. In and Mr. Out in particular, with a sort of puzzled, spellbound awe.

"There," cried Edith. "See there!"

Her voice rose, became somewhat shrill. Her pointing finger shook slightly.

"There's the soldier who broke my brother's leg."

There were a dozen exclamations; a man in a cutaway coat left his place near the desk and advanced alertly; the stout person made a sort of lightning-like spring toward the short, dark soldier, and then the lobby closed around the little group and blotted them from the sight of Mr. In and Mr. Out.

But to Mr. In and Mr. Out this event was merely a particolored iridescent segment of a whirring, spinning world.

They heard loud voices; they saw the stout man spring; the picture suddenly blurred.

Then they were in an elevator bound skyward.

"What floor, please?" said the elevator man.

"Any floor," said Mr. In.

"Top floor," said Mr. Out.

"This is the top floor," said the elevator man.

"Have another floor put on," said Mr. Out.

"Higher," said Mr. In.

"Heaven," said Mr. Out.

XI

IN A BEDROOM of a small hotel just off Sixth Avenue Gordon Sterrett awoke with a pain in the back of his head and a sick throbbing in all his veins. He looked at the dusky gray shadows in the corners of the room and at a raw place on a large leather chair in the corner where it had long been in use. He saw clothes, disheveled, rumpled clothes on the floor and he smelt stale cigarette smoke and stale liquor. The windows were tight shut. Outside the bright sunlight had thrown a dust-filled beam across the sill—a beam broken by the head of the wide wooden bed in which he had slept. He lay very quiet—comatose, drugged, his eyes wide, his mind clicking wildly like an unoiled machine.

It must have been thirty seconds after he perceived the sunbeam with the dust on it and the rip on the large leather chair that he had the sense of life close beside him, and it was another thirty seconds after that before he realized that he was irrevocably married to Jewel Hudson.

He went out half an hour later and bought a revolver at a sporting goods store. Then he took a taxi to the room where he had been living on East Twenty-seventh Street, and, leaning across the table that held his drawing materials, fired a cartridge into his head just behind the temple.

THE CUT-GLASS BOWL

THERE was a rough stone age and a smooth stone age and a bronze age, and many years afterward a cut-glass age. In the cut-glass age, when young ladies had persuaded young men with long, curly mustaches to marry them, they sat down several months afterward and wrote thank-you notes for all sorts of cut-glass presents—punch-bowls, finger-bowls, dinner-glasses, wine-glasses, ice-cream dishes, bonbon dishes, decanters, and vases—for, though cut glass was nothing new in the nineties, it was then especially busy reflecting the dazzling light of fashion from the Back Bay to the fastnesses of the Middle West.

After the wedding the punch-bowls were arranged on the sideboard with the big bowl in the center; the glasses were set up in the china-closet; the candlesticks were put at both ends of things—and then the struggle for existence began. The bonbon dish lost its little handle and became a pin-tray upstairs; a promenading cat knocked the little bowl off the sideboard, and the hired girl chipped the middle-sized one with the sugar-dish; then the wine-glasses succumbed to leg fractures, and even the dinner-glasses disappeared one by one like the ten little niggers, the last one ending up, scarred and maimed, as a tooth-brush holder among other shabby genteels on the bathroom shelf. But by the time all this had happened the cut-glass age was over, anyway.

It was well past its first glory on the day the curious Mrs. Roger Fairboalt came to see the beautiful Mrs. Harold Piper.

"My *dear,*" said the curious Mrs. Roger Fairboalt, "I *love* your house. I think it's *quite* artistic."

"I'm *so* glad," said the beautiful Mrs. Harold Piper, lights appearing in her young, dark eyes; "and you *must* come often. I'm almost *always* alone in the afternoon."

Mrs. Fairboalt would have liked to remark that she didn't believe this at all and couldn't see how she'd be expected to—it was all over town that Mr. Freddy Gedney had been dropping in on Mrs. Piper five afternoons a week for the past six months. Mrs. Fairboalt was at that ripe age where she distrusted all beautiful women——

"I love the dining-room *most,*" she said, "all that *marvelous* china, and that *huge* cut-glass bowl."

Mrs. Piper laughed, so prettily that Mrs. Fairboalt's lingering reservations about the Freddy Gedney story quite vanished.

"Oh, that big bowl!" Mrs. Piper's mouth forming the words was a vivid rose petal. "There's a story about that bowl——"

"Oh——"

"You remember young Carleton Canby? Well, he was very attentive at one time, and the night I told him I was going to marry Harold, seven years ago, in ninety-two, he drew himself way up and said: 'Evylyn, I'm going to give a present that's as hard as you are and as beautiful and as empty and as easy to see through.' He frightened me a little—his eyes were so black. I thought he was going to deed me a haunted house or something that would explode when you opened it. That bowl came, and of course it's beautiful. Its diameter or circumference or something is two and a half feet—or perhaps it's three and a half. Anyway, the sideboard is really too small for it; it sticks way out."

"My *dear*, wasn't that *odd!* And he left town about then, didn't he?" Mrs. Fairboalt was scribbling italicized notes on her memory—"hard, beautiful, empty, and easy to see through."

"Yes, he went West—or South—or somewhere," answered Mrs. Piper, radiating that divine vagueness that helps to lift beauty out of time.

Mrs. Fairboalt drew on her gloves, approving the effect of largeness given by the open sweep from the spacious music-room through the library, disclosing a part of the dining-room beyond. It was really the nicest smaller house in town, and Mrs. Piper had talked of moving to a larger one on Devereaux Avenue. Harold Piper must be *coining* money.

As she turned into the sidewalk under the gathering autumn dusk she assumed that disapproving, faintly unpleasant expression that almost all successful women of forty wear on the street.

If *I* were Harold Piper, she thought, I'd spend a *little* less time on business and a *little* more time at home. Some *friend* should speak to him.

But if Mrs. Fairboalt had considered it a successful afternoon she would have named it a triumph had she waited two minutes longer. For while she was still a black receding figure a hundred yards down the street, a very good-looking distraught young man turned up the walk to the Piper house. Mrs. Piper answered the door-bell herself, and with a rather dismayed expression led him quickly into the library.

"I had to see you," he began wildly; "your note played the devil with me. Did Harold frighten you into this?"

She shook her head.

"I'm through, Fred," she said slowly, and her lips had never looked to him so much like tearings from a rose. "He came home last night sick with it. Jessie Piper's sense of duty was too much for her, so she went down to his office and told him. He was hurt and—oh, I can't help seeing it his way, Fred. He says we've been club gossip all summer and he didn't know it, and now he understands snatches of conversation he's caught and veiled hints people have dropped about me. He's mighty angry, Fred, and he loves me and I love him—rather."

Gedney nodded slowly and half closed his eyes.

"Yes," he said, "yes, my trouble's like yours. I can see other people's points of view too plainly." His gray eyes met her dark ones frankly. "The blessed thing's over. My God, Evylyn, I've been sitting down at the office all day looking at the outside of your letter, and looking at it and looking at it——"

"You've got to go, Fred," she said steadily, and the slight emphasis of hurry in her voice was a new thrust for him. "I gave him my word of honor I wouldn't see you. I know just how far I can go with Harold, and being here with you this evening is one of the things I can't do."

They were still standing, and as she spoke she made a little movement toward the door. Gedney looked at her miserably, trying, here at the end, to treasure up a last picture of her—and then suddenly both of them were stiffened into marble at the sound of steps on the walk outside. Instantly her arm reached out grasping the lapel of his coat—half urged, half swung him through the big door into the dark dining-room.

"I'll make him go upstairs," she whispered close to his ear; "don't move till you hear him on the stairs. Then go out the front way."

Then he was alone listening as she greeted her husband in the hall.

Harold Piper was thirty-six, nine years older than his wife. He was handsome—with marginal notes: these being eyes that were too close together, and a certain woodenness when his face was in repose. His attitude toward this Gedney matter was typical of all his attitudes. He had told Evylyn that he considered the subject closed and would never reproach her nor allude to it in any form; and he told himself that this was rather a big way of looking at it—that she was not a little impressed. Yet, like all men who are preoccupied with their own broadness, he was exceptionally narrow.

He greeted Evylyn with emphasized cordiality this evening.

"You'll have to hurry and dress, Harold," she said eagerly; "we're going to the Bronsons'."

He nodded.

"It doesn't take me long to dress, dear," and, his

words trailing off, he walked on into the library. Evylyn's heart clattered loudly.

"Harold—" she began, with a little catch in her voice, and followed him in. He was lighting a cigarette. "You'll have to hurry, Harold," she finished, standing in the doorway.

"Why?" he asked, a trifle impatiently; "you're not dressed yourself yet, Evie."

He stretched out in a Morris chair and unfolded a newspaper. With a sinking sensation Evylyn saw that this meant at least ten minutes—and Gedney was standing breathless in the next room. Supposing Harold decided that before he went upstairs he wanted a drink from the decanter on the sideboard. Then it occurred to her to forestall this contingency by bringing him the decanter and a glass. She dreaded calling his attention to the dining-room in any way, but she couldn't risk the other chance.

But at the same moment Harold rose and, throwing his paper down, came toward her.

"Evie, dear," he said, bending and putting his arms about her, "I hope you're not thinking about last night—" She moved close to him, trembling. "I know," he continued, "it was just an imprudent friendship on your part. We all make mistakes."

Evylyn hardly heard him. She was wondering if by sheer clinging to him she could draw him out and up the stairs. She thought of playing sick, asking to be carried up—unfortunately, she knew he would lay her on the couch and bring her whisky.

Suddenly her nervous tension moved up a last impossible notch. She had heard a very faint but quite unmistakable creak from the floor of the dining-room. Fred was trying to get out the back way.

Then her heart took a flying leap as a hollow ringing note like a gong echoed and re-echoed through the house. Gedney's arm had struck the big cut-glass bowl.

"What's that!" cried Harold. "Who's there?"

She clung to him but he broke away, and the room seemed to crash about her ears. She heard the pantry-door swing open, a scuffle, the rattle of a tin pan, and in wild despair she rushed into the kitchen and pulled up the gas. Her husband's arm slowly unwound from Gedney's neck, and he stood there very still, first in amazement, then with pain dawning in his face.

"My golly!" he said in bewilderment, and then repeated: "My *golly!*"

He turned as if to jump again at Gedney, stopped, his muscles visibly relaxed, and he gave a bitter little laugh.

"You people—you people—" Evylyn's arms were around him and her eyes were pleading with him frantically, but he pushed her away and sank dazed into a kitchen chair, his face like porcelain. "You've been doing things to me, Evylyn. Why, you little devil! You little *devil!*"

She had never felt so sorry for him; she had never loved him so much.

"It wasn't her fault," said Gedney rather humbly. "I just came." But Piper shook his head, and his expression when he stared up was as if some physical accident had jarred his mind into a temporary inability to function. His eyes, grown suddenly pitiful, struck a deep, unsounded chord in Evylyn—and simultaneously a furious anger surged in her. She felt her eyelids burning; she stamped her foot violently; her hands scurried nervously over the table as if searching for a weapon, and then she flung herself wildly at Gedney.

"Get out!" she screamed, dark eyes blazing, little

fists beating helplessly on his outstretched arm. "You did this! Get out of here—get out—get *out! Get out!*"

II

CONCERNING Mrs. Harold Piper at thirty-five, opinion was divided—women said she was still handsome; men said she was pretty no longer. And this was probably because the qualities in her beauty that women had feared and men had followed had vanished. Her eyes were still as large and as dark and as sad, but the mystery had departed; their sadness was no longer eternal, only human, and she had developed a habit, when she was startled or annoyed, of twitching her brows together and blinking several times. Her mouth also had lost: the red had receded and the faint down-turning of its corners when she smiled, that had added to the sadness of the eyes and been vaguely mocking and beautiful, was quite gone. When she smiled now the corners of her lips turned up. Back in the days when she reveled in her own beauty Evylyn had enjoyed that smile of hers—she had accentuated it. When she stopped accentuating it, it faded out and the last of her mystery with it.

Evylyn had ceased accentuating her smile within a month after the Freddy Gedney affair. Externally things had gone on very much as they had before. But in those few minutes during which she had discovered how much she loved her husband Evylyn had realized how indelibly she had hurt him. For a month she struggled against aching silences, wild reproaches and accusations—she pled with him, made quiet, pitiful little love to him, and he laughed at her bitterly—and then she, too, slipped gradually into silence and a shadowy, unpenetrable barrier dropped between them. The surge of love that had risen in her she lavished on

Donald, her little boy, realizing him almost wonderingly as a part of her life.

The next year a piling up of mutual interests and responsibilities and some stray flicker from the past brought husband and wife together again—but after a rather pathetic flood of passion Evylyn realized that her great opportunity was gone. There simply wasn't anything left. She might have been youth and love for both—but that time of silence had slowly dried up the springs of affection and her own desire to drink again of them was dead.

She began for the first time to seek women friends, to prefer books she had read before, to sew a little where she could watch her two children to whom she was devoted. She worried about little things—if she saw crumbs on the dinner-table her mind drifted off the conversation: she was receding gradually into middle age.

Her thirty-fifth birthday had been an exceptionally busy one, for they were entertaining on short notice that night, and as she stood in her bedroom window in the late afternoon she discovered that she was quite tired. Ten years before she would have lain down and slept, but now she had a feeling that things needed watching: maids were cleaning downstairs, bric-à-brac was all over the floor, and there were sure to be grocerymen that had to be talked to imperatively—and then there was a letter to write Donald, who was fourteen and in his first year away at school.

She had nearly decided to lie down, nevertheless, when she heard a sudden familiar signal from little Julie downstairs. She compressed her lips, her brows twitched together, and she blinked.

"Julie!" she called.

"Ah-h-h-ow!" prolonged Julie plaintively. Then the

voice of Hilda, the second maid, floated up the stairs.

"She cut herself a little, Mis' Piper."

Evylyn flew to her sewing-basket, rummaged until she found a torn handkerchief, and hurried downstairs. In a moment Julie was crying in her arms as she searched for the cut, faint, disparaging evidences of which appeared on Julie's dress!

"My *thu*-umb!" explained Julie. "Oh-h-h-h, t'urts."

"It was the bowl here, the he one," said Hilda apologetically. "It was waitin' on the floor while I polished the sideboard, and Julie come along an' went to foolin' with it. She yust scratch herself."

Evylyn frowned heavily at Hilda, and twisting Julie decisively in her lap, began tearing strips off the handkerchief.

"Now—let's see it, dear."

Julie held it up and Evylyn pounced.

"There!"

Julie surveyed her swathed thumb doubtfully. She crooked it; it waggled. A pleased, interested look appeared in her tear-stained face. She sniffled and waggled it again.

"You *precious!*" cried Evylyn and kissed her, but before she left the room she leveled another frown at Hilda. Careless! Servants all that way nowadays. If she could get a good Irishwoman—but you couldn't any more—and these Swedes——

At five o'clock Harold arrived and, coming up to her room, threatened in a suspiciously jovial tone to kiss her thirty-five times for her birthday. Evylyn resisted.

"You've been drinking," she said shortly, and then added qualitatively, "a little. You know I loathe the smell of it."

"Evie," he said, after a pause, seating himself in a chair by the window, "I can tell you something now. I guess you've known things haven't been going quite right down-town."

She was standing at the window combing her hair, but at these words she turned and looked at him.

"How do you mean? You've always said there was room for more than one wholesale hardware house in town." Her voice expressed some alarm.

"There *was*," said Harold significantly, "but this Clarence Ahearn is a smart man."

"I was surprised when you said he was coming to dinner."

"Evie," he went on, with another slap at his knee, "after January first 'The Clarence Ahearn Company' becomes 'The Ahearn, Piper Company'—and 'Piper Brothers' as a company ceases to exist."

Evylyn was startled. The sound of his name in second place was somehow hostile to her; still he appeared jubilant.

"I don't understand, Harold."

"Well, Evie, Ahearn has been fooling around with Marx. If those two had combined we'd have been the little fellow, struggling along, picking up smaller orders, hanging back on risks. It's a question of capital, Evie, and 'Ahearn and Marx' would have had the business just like 'Ahearn and Piper' is going to now." He paused and coughed and a little cloud of whisky floated up to her nostrils. "Tell you the truth, Evie, I've suspected that Ahearn's wife had something to do with it. Ambitious little lady, I'm told. Guess she knew the Marxes couldn't help her much here."

"Is she—common?" asked Evie.

"Never met her, I'm sure—but I don't doubt it. Clarence Ahearn's name's been up at the Country Club five months—no action taken." He waved his hand disparagingly. "Ahearn and I had lunch together today and just about clinched it, so I thought it'd be nice to have him and his wife up tonight—just have nine, mostly family. After all, it's a big thing for me, and of course we'll have to see something of them, Evie."

"Yes," said Evie thoughtfully, "I suppose we will."

Evylyn was not disturbed over the social end of it—but the idea of "Piper Brothers" becoming "The Ahearn, Piper Company" startled her. It seemed like going down in the world.

Half an hour later, as she began to dress for dinner, she heard his voice from downstairs.

"Oh, Evie, come down!"

She went out into the hall and called over the banister:

"What is it?"

"I want you to help me make some of that punch before dinner."

Hurriedly rehooking her dress, she descended the stairs and found him grouping the essentials on the dining-room table. She went to the sideboard and, lifting one of the bowls, carried it over.

"Oh, no," he protested, "let's use the big one. There'll be Ahearn and his wife and you and I and Milton, that's five, and Tom and Jessie, that's seven, and your sister and Joe Ambler, that's nine. You don't know how quick that stuff goes when *you* make it."

"We'll use this bowl," she insisted. "It'll hold plenty. You know how Tom is."

Tom Lowrie, husband to Jessie, Harold's first cousin, was rather inclined to finish anything in a liquid way that he began.

Harold shook his head.

"Don't be foolish. That one holds only about three quarts and there's nine of us, and the servants'll want some—and it isn't strong punch. It's so much more cheerful to have a lot, Evie; we don't have to drink all of it."

"I say the small one."

Again he shook his head obstinately.

"No; be reasonable."

"I *am* reasonable," she said shortly. "I don't want any drunken men in the house."

"Who said you did?"

"Then use the small bowl."

"Now, Evie——"

He grasped the smaller bowl to lift it back. Instantly her hands were on it, holding it down. There was a momentary struggle, and then, with a little exasperated grunt, he raised his side, slipped it from her fingers, and carried it to the sideboard.

She looked at him and tried to make her expression contemptuous, but he only laughed. Acknowledging her defeat but disclaiming all future interest in the punch, she left the room.

III

AT SEVEN-THIRTY, her cheeks glowing and her high-piled hair gleaming with a suspicion of brilliantine, Evylyn descended the stairs. Mrs. Ahearn, a little woman concealing a slight nervousness under red hair and an extreme Empire gown, greeted her volubly. Evylyn disliked her on the spot, but the husband she rather approved of. He had keen blue eyes and a natural gift of pleasing people that might have made him, socially, had he not so obviously committed the blunder of marrying too early in his career.

"I'm glad to know Piper's wife," he said simply. "It looks as though your husband and I are going to see a lot of each other in the future."

She bowed, smiled graciously, and turned to greet

the others: Milton Piper, Harold's quiet, unassertive younger brother; the two Lowries, Jessie and Tom; Irene, her own unmarried sister; and finally Joe Ambler, a confirmed bachelor and Irene's perennial beau.

Harold led the way into dinner.

"We're having a punch evening," he announced jovially—Evylyn saw that he had already sampled his concoction—"so there won't be any cocktails except the punch. It's m' wife's greatest achievement, Mrs. Ahearn; she'll give you the recipe if you want it; but owing to a slight"—he caught his wife's eye and paused—"to a slight indisposition, I'm responsible for this batch. Here's how!"

All through dinner there was punch, and Evylyn, noticing that Ahearn and Milton Piper and all the women were shaking their heads negatively at the maid, knew she had been right about the bowl; it was still half full. She resolved to caution Harold directly afterward, but when the women left the table Mrs. Ahearn cornered her, and she found herself talking cities and dressmakers with a polite show of interest.

"We've moved around a lot," chattered Mrs. Ahearn, her red head nodding violently. "Oh, yes, we've never stayed so long in a town before—but I do hope we're here for good. I like it here; don't you?"

"Well, you see, I've always lived here, so, naturally——"

"Oh, that's true," said Mrs. Ahearn and laughed. "Clarence always used to tell me he had to have a wife he could come home to and say: 'Well, we're going to Chicago tomorrow to live, so pack up.' I got so I never expected to live *any*where." She laughed her little laugh again; Evylyn suspected that it was her society laugh.

"Your husband is a very able man, I imagine."

"Oh, yes," Mrs. Ahearn assured her eagerly. "He's brainy, Clarence is. Ideas and enthusiasm, you know. Finds out what he wants and then goes and gets it."

Evylyn nodded. She was wondering if the men were still drinking punch back in the dining-room. Mrs. Ahearn's history kept unfolding jerkily, but Evylyn had ceased to listen. The first odor of massed cigars began to drift in. It wasn't really a large house, she reflected; on an evening like this the library sometimes grew blue with smoke, and next day one had to leave the windows open for hours to air the heavy staleness out of the curtains. Perhaps this partnership might . . . she began to speculate on a new house. . . .

Mrs. Ahearn's voice drifted in on her:

"I really would like the recipe if you have it written down somewhere——"

Then there was a sound of chairs in the dining-room and the men strolled in. Evylyn saw at once that her worst fears were realized. Harold's face was flushed and his words ran together at the ends of sentences, while Tom Lowrie lurched when he walked and narrowly missed Irene's lap when he tried to sink onto the couch beside her. He sat there blinking dazedly at the company. Evylyn found herself blinking back at him, but she saw no humor in it. Joe Ambler was smiling contentedly and purring on his cigar. Only Ahearn and Milton Piper seemed unaffected.

"It's a pretty fine town, Ahearn," said Ambler, "you'll find that."

"I've found it so," said Ahearn pleasantly.

"You find it more, Ahearn," said Harold, nodding emphatically, "'f I've an'thin' do 'th it."

He soared into a eulogy of the city, and Evylyn wondered uncomfortably if it bored every one as it bored her. Apparently not. They were all listening attentively. Evylyn broke in at the first gap.

"Where've you been living, Mr. Ahearn?" she asked interestedly. Then she remembered that Mrs. Ahearn had told her, but it didn't matter. Harold mustn't talk so much. He was such an *ass* when he'd been drinking. But he plopped directly back in.

"Tell you, Ahearn. Firs' you wanna get a house up here on the hill. Get Stearne house or Ridgeway house. Wanna have it so people say: 'There's Ahearn house.' Solid, you know, tha's effec' it gives."

Evylyn flushed. This didn't sound right at all. Still Ahearn didn't seem to notice anything amiss, only nodded gravely.

"Have you been looking—" But her words trailed off unheard as Harold's voice boomed on.

"Get house—tha's start. Then you get know people. Snobbish town first toward outsider, but not long—not after know you. People like you"—he indicated Ahearn and his wife with a sweeping gesture—"all right. Cordial as an'thin' once get by first barrer-bar-barrer—" He swallowed, and then said "barrier," repeated it masterfully.

Evylyn looked appealingly at her brother-in-law, but before he could intercede a thick mumble had come crowding out of Tom Lowrie, hindered by the dead cigar which he gripped firmly with his teeth.

"Huma uma ho huma ahdy um——"

"What?" demanded Harold earnestly.

Resignedly and with difficulty Tom removed the cigar—that is, he removed part of it, and then blew the remainder with a *whut* sound across the room, where it landed liquidly and limply in Mrs. Ahearn's lap.

"Beg pardon," he mumbled, and rose with the vague intention of going after it. Milton's hand on his coat collapsed him in time, and Mrs. Ahearn not ungracefully flounced the tobacco from her skirt to the floor, never once looking at it.

"I was sayin'," continued Tom thickly, "'fore 'at happened"—he waved his hand apologetically toward Mrs. Ahearn—"I was sayin' I heard all truth that Country Club matter."

Milton leaned and whispered something to him.

"Lemme 'lone," he said petulantly; "know what I'm doin'. 'At's what they came for."

Evylyn sat there in a panic, trying to make her mouth form words. She saw her sister's sardonic expression and Mrs. Ahearn's face turning a vivid red. Ahearn was looking down at his watch-chain, fingering it.

"I heard who's been keepin' y' out, an' he's not a bit better'n you. I can fix whole damn thing up. Would've before, but I didn't know you. Harol' tol' me you felt bad about the thing——"

Milton Piper rose suddenly and awkwardly to his feet. In a second every one was standing tensely and Milton was saying something very hurriedly about having to go early, and the Ahearns were listening with eager intentness. Then Mrs. Ahearn swallowed and turned with a forced smile toward Jessie. Evylyn saw Tom lurch forward and put his hand on Ahearn's shoulder—and suddenly she was listening to a new, anxious voice at her elbow, and, turning, found Hilda, the second maid.

"Please, Mis' Piper, I tank Yulie got her hand poisoned. It's all swole up and her cheeks is hot and she's moanin' an' groanin'——"

"Julie is?" Evylyn asked sharply. The party suddenly

receded. She turned quickly, sought with her eyes for Mrs. Ahearn, slipped toward her.

"If you'll excuse me, Mrs.—" She had momentarily forgotten the name, but she went right on: "My little girl's been taken sick. I'll be down when I can." She turned and ran quickly up the stairs, retaining a confused picture of rays of cigar smoke and a loud discussion in the center of the room that seemed to be developing into an argument.

Switching on the light in the nursery, she found Julie tossing feverishly and giving out odd little cries. She put her hand against the cheeks. They were burning. With an exclamation she followed the arm down under the cover until she found the hand. Hilda was right. The whole thumb was swollen to the wrist and in the center was a little inflamed sore. Blood-poisoning! her mind cried in terror. The bandage had come off the cut and she'd gotten something in it. She'd cut it at three o'clock —it was now nearly eleven. Eight hours. Blood-poisoning couldn't possibly develop so soon. She rushed to the 'phone.

Doctor Martin across the street was out. Doctor Foulke, their family physician, didn't answer. She racked her brains and in desperation called her throat specialist, and bit her lip furiously while he looked up the numbers of two physicians. During that interminable moment she thought she heard loud voices downstairs—but she seemed to be in another world now. After fifteen minutes she located a physician who sounded angry and sulky at being called out of bed. She ran back to the nursery and, looking at the hand, found it was somewhat more swollen.

"Oh, God!" she cried, and kneeling beside the bed began smoothing back Julie's hair over and over. With a vague idea of getting some hot water, she rose and started toward the door, but the lace of her dress caught in the bed-rail and she fell forward on her hands and knees. She struggled up and jerked frantically at the lace. The bed moved and Julie groaned. Then more quietly but with suddenly fumbling fingers she found the pleat in front, tore the whole pannier completely off, and rushed from the room.

Out in the hall she heard a single loud, insistent voice, but as she reached the head of the stairs it ceased and an outer door banged.

The music-room came into view. Only Harold and Milton were there, the former leaning against a chair, his face very pale, his collar open, and his mouth moving loosely.

"What's the matter?"

Milton looked at her anxiously.

"There was a little trouble——"

Then Harold saw her and, straightening up with an effort, began to speak.

"'Sult m'own cousin m'own house. God damn common *nouveau* rish. 'Sult m'own cousin——"

"Tom had trouble with Ahearn and Harold interfered," said Milton.

"My Lord, Milton," cried Evylyn, "couldn't you have done something?"

"I tried; I——"

"Julie's sick," she interrupted; "she's poisoned herself. Get him to bed if you can."

Harold looked up.

"Julie sick?"

Paying no attention, Evylyn brushed by through the dining-room, catching sight, with a burst of horror, of the big punch-bowl still on the table, the liquid from melted ice in its bottom. She heard steps on the front stairs—it was Milton helping Harold up—and then a mumble: "Why, Julie's a'righ'."

"Don't let him go into the nursery!" she shouted.

The hours blurred into a nightmare. The doctor arrived just before midnight and within a half-hour had lanced the wound. He left at two after giving her the addresses of two nurses to call up and promising to return at half past six. It was blood-poisoning.

At four, leaving Hilda by the bedside, she went to her room, and slipping with a shudder out of her evening dress, kicked it into a corner. She put on a house dress and returned to the nursery while Hilda went to make coffee.

Not until noon could she bring herself to look into Harold's room, but when she did it was to find him awake and staring very miserably at the ceiling. He turned blood-shot hollow eyes upon her. For a minute she hated him, couldn't speak. A husky voice came from the bed.

"What time is it?"

"Noon."

"I made a damn fool——"

"It doesn't matter," she said sharply. "Julie's got blood-poisoning. They may"—she choked over the words—"they think she'll have to lose her hand."

"What?"

"She cut herself on that—that bowl."

"Last night?"

"Oh, what does it matter?" she cried; "she's got blood-poisoning. Can't you hear?"

He looked at her bewildered—sat half-way up in bed.

"I'll get dressed," he said.

Her anger subsided and a great wave of weariness

and pity for him rolled over her. After all, it was his trouble, too.

"Yes," she answered listlessly, "I suppose you'd better."

IV

IF EVYLYN'S beauty had hesitated in her early thirties it came to an abrupt decision just afterward and completely left her. A tentative outlay of wrinkles on her face suddenly deepened and flesh collected rapidly on her legs and hips and arms. Her mannerism of drawing her brows together had become an expression—it was habitual when she was reading or speaking and even while she slept. She was forty-six.

As in most families whose fortunes have gone down rather than up, she and Harold had drifted into a colorless antagonism. In repose they looked at each other with the toleration they might have felt for broken old chairs; Evylyn worried a little when he was sick and did her best to be cheerful under the wearying depression of living with a disappointed man.

Family bridge was over for the evening and she sighed with relief. She had made more mistakes than usual this evening and she didn't care. Irene shouldn't have made that remark about the infantry being particularly dangerous. There had been no letter for three weeks now, and, while this was nothing out of the ordinary, it never failed to make her nervous; naturally she hadn't known how many clubs were out.

Harold had gone upstairs, so she stepped out on the porch for a breath of fresh air. There was a bright glamour of moonlight diffusing on the sidewalks and lawns, and with a little half yawn, half laugh, she remembered one long moonlight affair of her youth. It was astonishing to think that life had once been the sum of her current love-affairs. It was now the sum of her current problems.

There was the problem of Julie—Julie was thirteen, and lately she was growing more and more sensitive about her deformity and preferred to stay always in her room reading. A few years before she had been frightened at the idea of going to school, and Evylyn could not bring herself to send her, so she grew up in her mother's shadow, a pitiful little figure with the artificial hand that she made no attempt to use but kept forlornly in her pocket. Lately she had been taking lessons in using it because Evylyn had feared she would cease to lift the arm altogether, but after the lessons, unless she made a move with it in listless obedience to her mother, the little hand would creep back to the pocket of her dress. For a while her dresses were made without pockets, but Julie had moped around the house so miserably at a loss all one month that Evylyn weakened and never tried the experiment again.

The problem of Donald had been different from the start. She had attempted vainly to keep him near her as she had tried to teach Julie to lean less on her—lately the problem of Donald had been snatched out of her hands; his division had been abroad for three months.

She yawned again—life was a thing for youth. What a happy youth she must have had! She remembered her pony, Bijou, and the trip to Europe with her mother when she was eighteen——

"Very, very complicated," she said aloud and severely to the moon, and, stepping inside, was about to close the door when she heard a noise in the library and started.

It was Martha, the middle-aged servant: they kept only one now.

"Why, Martha!" she said in surprise.

Martha turned quickly.

"Oh, I thought you was upstairs. I was jist——"

"Is anything the matter?"

Martha hesitated.

"No; I—" She stood there fidgeting. "It was a letter, Mrs. Piper, that I put somewhere."

"A letter? Your own letter?" asked Evylyn, switching on the light.

"No, it was to you. 'Twas this afternoon, Mrs. Piper, in the last mail. The postman give it to me and then the back door-bell rang. I had it in my hand, so I must have stuck it somewhere. I thought I'd just slip in now and find it."

"What sort of a letter? From Mr. Donald?"

"No, it was an advertisement, maybe, or a business letter. It was a long, narrow one, I remember."

They began a search through the music-room, looking on trays and mantelpieces, and then through the library, feeling on the tops of rows of books. Martha paused in despair.

"I can't think where. I went straight to the kitchen. The dining-room, maybe." She started hopefully for the dining-room, but turned suddenly at the sound of a gasp behind her. Evylyn had sat down heavily in a Morris chair, her brows drawn very close together, eyes blinking furiously.

"Are you sick?"

For a minute there was no answer. Evylyn sat there very still and Martha could see the very quick rise and fall of her bosom.

"Are you sick?" she repeated.

"No," said Evylyn slowly, "but I know where the letter is. Go 'way, Martha. I know."

Wonderingly, Martha withdrew, and still Evylyn sat there, only the muscles around her eyes moving—contracting and relaxing and contracting again. She knew now where the letter was—she knew as well as if she had put it there herself. And she felt instinctively and unquestionably what the letter was. It was long and narrow like an advertisement, but up in the corner in large letters it said "War Department" and, in smaller letters below, "Official Business." She knew it lay there in the big bowl with her name in ink on the outside and her soul's death within.

Rising uncertainly, she walked toward the dining-room, feeling her way along the bookcases and through the doorway. After a moment she found the light and switched it on.

There was the bowl, reflecting the electric light in crimson squares edged with black and yellow squares edged with blue, ponderous and glittering, grotesquely and triumphantly ominous. She took a step forward and paused again; another step and she would see over the top and into the inside—another step and she would see an edge of white—another step—her hands fell on the rough, cold surface——

In a moment she was tearing it open, fumbling with an obstinate fold, holding it before her while the type-written page glared out and struck at her. Then it fluttered like a bird to the floor. The house that had seemed whirring, buzzing a moment since, was suddenly very quiet; a breath of air crept in through the open front door carrying the noise of a passing motor; she heard faint sounds from upstairs and then a grinding racket in the pipe behind the bookcases—her husband turning off a water-tap——

And in that instant it was as if this were not, after all, Donald's hour except in so far as he was a marker in the insidious contest that had gone on in sudden surges and long, listless interludes between Evylyn and this cold, malignant thing of beauty, a gift of enmity from a man whose face she had long since forgotten. With its massive, brooding passivity it lay there in the center of her house as it had lain for years, throwing out the ice-like beams of a thousand eyes, perverse glitterings merging each into each, never aging, never changing.

Evylyn sat down on the edge of the table and stared at it fascinated. It seemed to be smiling now, a very cruel smile, as if to say:

"You see, this time I didn't have to hurt you directly. I didn't bother. You know it was I who took your son away. You know how cold I am and how hard and how beautiful, because once you were just as cold and hard and beautiful."

The bowl seemed suddenly to turn itself over and then to distend and swell until it became a great canopy that glittered and trembled over the room, over the house, and, as the walls melted slowly into mist, Evylyn saw that it was still moving out, out and far away from her, shutting off far horizons and suns and moons and stars except as inky blots seen faintly through it. And under it walked all the people, and the light that came through to them was refracted and twisted until shadow seemed light and light seemed shadow—until the whole panoply of the world became changed and distorted under the twinkling heaven of the bowl.

Then there came a faraway, booming voice like a low, clear bell. It came from the center of the bowl and down the great sides to the ground and then bounced toward her eagerly.

"You see, I am fate," it shouted, "and stronger than your puny plans; and I am how-things-turn-out and I am different from your little dreams, and I am the flight of time and the end of beauty and unfulfilled desire; all the accidents and imperceptions and the little minutes that shape the crucial hours are mine. I am the exception that proves no rules, the limits of your control, the condiment in the dish of life."

The booming sound stopped; the echoes rolled away over the wide land to the edge of the bowl that bounded the world and up the great sides and back to the center where they hummed for a moment and died. Then the great walls began slowly to bear down upon her, growing smaller and smaller, coming closer and closer as if to crush her; and as she clinched her hands and waited for the swift bruise of the cold glass, the bowl gave a sudden wrench and turned over—and lay there on the side-board, shining and inscrutable, reflecting in a hundred prisms, myriad, many-colored glints and gleams and crossings and interlacings of light.

The cold wind blew in again through the front door, and with a desperate, frantic energy Evylyn stretched both her arms around the bowl. She must be quick—she must be strong. She tightened her arms until they ached, tautened the thin strips of muscle under her soft flesh, and with a mighty effort raised it and held it. She felt the wind blow cold on her back where her dress had come apart from the strain of her effort, and as she felt it she turned toward it and staggered under the great weight out through the library and on toward the front door. She must be quick—she must be strong. The blood in her arms throbbed dully and her knees kept giving way under her, but the feel of the cool glass was good.

Out the front door she tottered and over to the stone steps, and there, summoning every fiber of her soul and body for a last effort, swung herself half around—for a second, as she tried to loose her hold, her numb fingers clung to the rough surface, and in that second she slipped and, losing balance, toppled forward with a despairing cry, her arms still around the bowl . . . down. . . .

Over the way lights went on; far down the block the crash was heard, and pedestrians rushed up wonderingly; upstairs a tired man awoke from the edge of sleep and a little girl whimpered in a haunted doze. And all over the moonlit sidewalk around the still, black form, hundreds of prisms and cubes and splinters of glass reflected the light in little gleams of blue, and black edged with yellow, and yellow, and crimson edged with black.

THE OFFSHORE PIRATE

THIS unlikely story begins on a sea that was a blue dream, as colorful as blue-silk stockings, and beneath a sky as blue as the irises of children's eyes. From the western half of the sky the sun was shying little golden disks at the sea—if you gazed intently enough you could see them skip from wave tip to wave tip until they joined a broad collar of golden coin that was collecting half a mile out and would eventually be a dazzling sunset. About half-way between the Florida shore and the golden collar a white steam-yacht, very young and graceful, was riding at anchor and under a blue-and-white awning aft a yellow-haired girl reclined in a wicker settee reading *The Revolt of the Angels,* by Anatole France.

She was about nineteen, slender and supple, with a

spoiled alluring mouth and quick gray eyes full of a radiant curiosity. Her feet, stockingless, and adorned rather than clad in blue-satin slippers which swung nonchalantly from her toes, were perched on the arm of a settee adjoining the one she occupied. And as she read she intermittently regaled herself by a faint application to her tongue of a half-lemon that she held in her hand. The other half, sucked dry, lay on the deck at her feet and rocked very gently to and fro at the almost imperceptible motion of the tide.

The second half-lemon was well-nigh pulpless and the golden collar had grown astonishing in width, when suddenly the drowsy silence which enveloped the yacht was broken by the sound of heavy footsteps, and an elderly man topped with orderly gray hair and clad in a white-flannel suit appeared at the head of the companionway. There he paused for a moment until his eyes became accustomed to the sun, and then seeing the girl under the awning he uttered a long even grunt of disapproval.

If he had intended thereby to obtain a rise of any sort he was doomed to disappointment. The girl calmly turned over two pages, turned back one, raised the lemon mechanically to tasting distance, and then very faintly but quite unmistakably yawned.

"Ardita!" said the gray-haired man sternly.

Ardita uttered a small sound indicating nothing.

"Ardita!" he repeated. "Ardita!"

Ardita raised the lemon languidly, allowing three words to slip out before it reached her tongue.

"Oh, shut up."

"Ardita!"

"What?"

"Will you listen to me—or will I have to get a servant to hold you while I talk to you?"

The lemon descended slowly and scornfully.

"Put it in writing."

"Will you have the decency to close that abominable book and discard that damn lemon for two minutes?"

"Oh, can't you lemme alone for a second?"

"Ardita, I have just received a telephone message from the shore——"

"Telephone?" She showed for the first time a faint interest.

"Yes, it was——"

"Do you mean to say," she interrupted wonderingly, "'at they let you run a wire out here?"

"Yes, and just now——"

"Won't other boats bump into it?"

"No. It's run along the bottom. Five min——"

"Well, I'll be darned! Gosh! Science is golden or something—isn't it?"

"Will you let me say what I started to?"

"Shoot!"

"Well, it seems—well, I am up here—" He paused and swallowed several times distractedly. "Oh, yes. Young woman, Colonel Moreland has called up again to ask me to be sure to bring you in to dinner. His son Toby has come all the way from New York to meet you and he's invited several other young people. For the last time, will you——"

"No," said Ardita shortly, "I won't. I came along on this darn cruise with the one idea of going to Palm Beach, and you knew it, and I absolutely refuse to meet any darn old colonel or any darn young Toby or any darn old young people or to set foot in any other darn old town in this crazy state. So you either take me to Palm Beach or else shut up and go away."

"Very well. This is the last straw. In your infatuation for this man—a man who is notorious for his excesses, a man your father would not have allowed to so much as mention your name—you have reflected the demimonde rather than the circles in which you have presumably grown up. From now on——"

"I know," interrupted Ardita ironically, "from now on you go your way and I go mine. I've heard that story before. You know I'd like nothing better."

"From now on," he announced grandiloquently, "you are no niece of mine. I——"

"O-o-o-oh!" The cry was wrung from Ardita with the agony of a lost soul. "Will you stop boring me! Will you go 'way! Will you jump overboard and drown! Do you want me to throw this book at you!"

"If you dare do any——"

Smack! *The Revolt of the Angels* sailed through the air, missed its target by the length of a short nose, and bumped cheerfully down the companionway.

The gray-haired man made an instinctive step backward and then two cautious steps forward. Ardita jumped to her five feet four and stared at him defiantly, her gray eyes blazing.

"Keep off!"

"How dare you!" he cried.

"Because I darn please!"

"You've grown unbearable! Your disposition——"

"You've made me that way! No child ever has a bad disposition unless it's her family's fault! Whatever I am, you did it."

Muttering something under his breath her uncle turned and, walking forward, called in a loud voice for the launch. Then he returned to the awning, where Ardita had again seated herself and resumed her attention to the lemon.

"I am going ashore," he said slowly. "I will be out again at nine o'clock tonight. When I return we will start back to New York, where I shall turn you over to your aunt for the rest of your natural, or rather unnatural, life."

He paused and looked at her, and then all at once something in the utter childishness of her beauty seemed to puncture his anger like an inflated tire, and render him helpless, uncertain, utterly fatuous.

"Ardita," he said not unkindly, "I'm no fool. I've been round. I know men. And, child, confirmed libertines don't reform until they're tired—and then they're not themselves—they're husks of themselves." He looked at her as if expecting agreement, but receiving no sight or sound of it he continued. "Perhaps the man loves you—that's possible. He's loved many women and he'll love many more. Less than a month ago, one month, Ardita, he was involved in a notorious affair with that red-haired woman, Mimi Merril; promised to give her the diamond bracelet that the Czar of Russia gave his mother. You know—you read the papers."

"Thrilling scandals by an anxious uncle," yawned Ardita. "Have it filmed. Wicked clubman making eyes at virtuous flapper. Virtuous flapper conclusively vamped by his lurid past. Plans to meet him at Palm Beach. Foiled by anxious uncle."

"Will you tell me why the devil you want to marry him?"

"I'm sure I couldn't say," said Ardita shortly. "Maybe because he's the only man I know, good or bad, who has an imagination and the courage of his convictions. Maybe it's to get away from the young fools that spend their vacuous hours pursuing me around the country. But as for the famous Russian bracelet, you can set your mind at rest on that score. He's going to give it to me at Palm Beach—if you'll show a little intelligence."

"How about the—red-haired woman?"

"He hasn't seen her for six months," she said angrily. "Don't you suppose I have enough pride to see to that? Don't you know by this time that I can do any darn thing with any darn man I want to?"

She put her chin in the air like the statue of France Aroused, and then spoiled the pose somewhat by raising the lemon for action.

"Is it the Russian bracelet that fascinates you?"

"No, I'm merely trying to give you the sort of argument that would appeal to your intelligence. And I wish you'd go 'way," she said, her temper rising again. "You know I never change my mind. You've been boring me for three days until I'm about to go crazy. I won't go ashore! Won't! Do you hear? Won't!"

"Very well," he said, "and you won't go to Palm Beach either. Of all the selfish, spoiled, uncontrolled, disagreeable, impossible girls I have——"

Splush! The half-lemon caught him in the neck. Simultaneously came a hail from over the side.

"The launch is ready, Mr. Farnam."

Too full of words and rage to speak, Mr. Farnam cast one utterly condemning glance at his niece and, turning, ran swiftly down the ladder.

II

FIVE o'clock rolled down from the sun and plumped soundlessly into the sea. The golden collar widened into a glittering island; and a faint breeze that had been playing with the edges of the awning and swaying one of the dangling blue slippers became suddenly freighted with song. It was a chorus of men in close harmony and in perfect rhythm to an accompanying sound of oars cleaving the blue waters. Ardita lifted her head and listened.

"Carrots and peas,
Beans on their knees,
Pigs in the seas,
Lucky fellows!
Blow us a breeze,
Blow us a breeze,
Blow us a breeze,
With your bellows."

Ardita's brow wrinkled in astonishment. Sitting very still she listened eagerly as the chorus took up a second verse.

"Onions and beans,
Marshalls and Deans,
Goldbergs and Greens
And Costellos.
Blow us a breeze,
Blow us a breeze,
Blow us a breeze,
With your bellows."

With an exclamation she tossed her book to the deck, where it sprawled at a straddle, and hurried to the rail. Fifty feet away a large rowboat was approaching containing seven men, six of them rowing and one standing up in the stern keeping time to their song with an orchestra leader's baton.

"Oysters and rocks,
Sawdust and socks,
Who could make clocks
Out of cellos?—"

The leader's eyes suddenly rested on Ardita, who was leaning over the rail spellbound with curiosity. He made a quick movement with his baton and the singing instantly ceased. She saw that he was the only white man in the boat—the six rowers were Negroes.

"*Narcissus* ahoy!" he called politely.

"What's the idea of all the discord?" demanded

Ardita cheerfully. "Is this the varsity crew from the county nut farm?"

By this time the boat was scraping the side of the yacht and a great hulking Negro in the bow turned round and grasped the ladder. Thereupon the leader left his position in the stern and before Ardita had realized his intention he ran up the ladder and stood breathless before her on the deck.

"The women and children will be spared!" he said briskly. "All crying babies will be immediately drowned and all males put in double irons!"

Digging her hands excitedly down into the pockets of her dress Ardita stared at him, speechless with astonishment.

He was a young man with a scornful mouth and the bright blue eyes of a healthy baby set in a dark sensitive face. His hair was pitch black, damp and curly—the hair of a Grecian statue gone brunette. He was trimly built, trimly dressed, and graceful as an agile quarter-back.

"Well, I'll be a son of a gun!" she said dazedly.

They eyed each other coolly.

"Do you surrender the ship?"

"Is this an outburst of wit?" demanded Ardita. "Are you an idiot—or just being initiated to some fraternity?"

"I asked you if you surrendered the ship."

"I thought the country was dry," said Ardita disdainfully. "Have you been drinking finger-nail enamel? You better get off this yacht!"

"What?" The young man's voice expressed incredulity.

"Get off the yacht! You heard me!"

He looked at her for a moment as if considering what she had said.

"No," said his scornful mouth slowly; "no, I won't get off the yacht. You can get off if you wish."

Going to the rail he gave a curt command and immediately the crew of the rowboat scrambled up the ladder and ranged themselves in line before him, a coal-black and burly darky at one end and a miniature mulatto of four feet nine at the other. They seemed to be uniformly dressed in some sort of blue costume ornamented with dust, mud, and tatters; over the shoulder of each was slung a small, heavy-looking white sack, and under their arms they carried large black cases apparently containing musical instruments.

" 'Ten-*shun!*" commanded the young man, snapping his own heels together crisply. "Right *driss!* Front! Step out here, Babe!"

The smallest Negro took a quick step forward and saluted.

"Yas-suh!"

"Take command, go down below, catch the crew and tie 'em up—all except the engineer. Bring him up to me. Oh, and pile those bags by the rail there."

"Yas-suh!"

Babe saluted again and wheeling about motioned for the five others to gather about him. Then after a short whispered consultation they all filed noiselessly down the companionway.

"Now," said the young man cheerfully to Ardita, who had witnessed this last scene in withering silence, "if you will swear on your honor as a flapper—which probably isn't worth much—that you'll keep that spoiled little mouth of yours tight shut for forty-eight hours, you can row yourself ashore in our rowboat."

"Otherwise what?"

"Otherwise you're going to sea in a ship."

With a little sigh as for a crisis well passed, the

young man sank into the settee Ardita had lately vacated and stretched his arms lazily. The corners of his mouth relaxed appreciatively as he looked round at the rich striped awning, the polished brass, and the luxurious fittings of the deck. His eye fell on the book, and then on the exhausted lemon.

"Hm," he said, "Stonewall Jackson claimed that lemon-juice cleared his head. Your head feel pretty clear?"

Ardita disdained to answer.

"Because inside of five minutes you'll have to make a clear decision whether it's go or stay."

He picked up the book and opened it curiously.

"*The Revolt of the Angels.* Sounds pretty good. French, eh?" He stared at her with new interest. "You French?"

"No."

"What's your name?"

"Farnam."

"Farnam what?"

"Ardita Farnam."

"Well, Ardita, no use standing up there and chewing out the insides of your mouth. You ought to break those nervous habits while you're young. Come over here and sit down."

Ardita took a carved jade case from her pocket, extracted a cigarette and lit it with a conscious coolness, though she knew her hand was trembling a little; then she crossed over with her supple, swinging walk, and sitting down in the other settee blew a mouthful of smoke at the awning.

"You can't get me off this yacht," she said steadily; "and you haven't got very much sense if you think you'll get far with it. My uncle'll have wirelesses zigzagging all over this ocean by half past six."

"Hm."

She looked quickly at his face, caught anxiety stamped there plainly in the faintest depression of the mouth's corners.

"It's all the same to me," she said, shrugging her shoulders. " 'Tisn't my yacht. I don't mind going for a coupla hours' cruise. I'll even lend you that book so you'll have something to read on the revenue boat that takes you up to Sing Sing."

He laughed scornfully.

"If that's advice you needn't bother. This is part of a plan arranged before I ever knew this yacht existed. If it hadn't been this one it'd have been the next one we passed anchored along the coast."

"Who are you?" demanded Ardita suddenly. "And what are you?"

"You've decided not to go ashore?"

"I never even faintly considered it."

"We're generally known," he said, "all seven of us, as Curtis Carlyle and his Six Black Buddies, late of the Winter Garden and the Midnight Frolic."

"You're singers?"

"We were until today. At present, due to those white bags you see there, we're fugitives from justice, and if the reward offered for our capture hasn't by this time reached twenty thousand dollars I miss my guess."

"What's in the bags?" asked Ardita curiously.

"Well," he said, "for the present we'll call it—mud—Florida mud."

III

WITHIN ten minutes after Curtis Carlyle's interview with a very frightened engineer the yacht *Narcissus* was under way, steaming south through a balmy tropical twilight. The little mulatto,

Babe, who seemed to have Carlyle's implicit confidence, took full command of the situation. Mr. Farnam's valet and the chef, the only members of the crew on board except the engineer, having shown fight, were now reconsidering, strapped securely to their bunks below. Trombone Mose, the biggest Negro, was set busy with a can of paint obliterating the name Narcissus from the bow, and substituting the name Hula Hula, and the others congregated aft and became intently involved in a game of craps.

Having given orders for a meal to be prepared and served on deck at seven-thirty, Carlyle rejoined Ardita, and, sinking back into his settee, half closed his eyes and fell into a state of profound abstraction.

Ardita scrutinized him carefully—and classed him immediately as a romantic figure. He gave the effect of towering self-confidence erected on a slight foundation —just under the surface of each of his decisions she discerned a hesitancy that was in decided contrast to the arrogant curl of his lips.

"He's not like me," she thought. "There's a difference somewhere."

Being a supreme egotist Ardita frequently thought about herself; never having had her egotism disputed she did it entirely naturally and with no detraction from her unquestioned charm. Though she was nineteen she gave the effect of a high-spirited precocious child, and in the present glow of her youth and beauty all the men and women she had known were but driftwood on the ripples of her temperament. She had met other egotists—in fact she found that selfish people bored her rather less than unselfish people—but as yet there had not been one she had not eventually defeated and brought to her feet.

But though she recognized an egotist in the settee

next to her, she felt none of that usual shutting of doors in her mind which meant clearing ship for action; on the contrary her instinct told her that this man was somehow completely pregnable and quite defenseless. When Ardita defied convention—and of late it had been her chief amusement—it was from an intense desire to be herself, and she felt that this man, on the contrary, was preoccupied with his own defiance.

She was much more interested in him than she was in her own situation, which affected her as the prospect of a matinée might affect a ten-year-old child. She had implicit confidence in her ability to take care of herself under any and all circumstances.

The night deepened. A pale new moon smiled misty-eyed upon the sea, and as the shore faded dimly out and dark clouds were blown like leaves along the far horizon a great haze of moonshine suddenly bathed the yacht and spread an avenue of glittering mail in her swift path. From time to time there was the bright flare of a match as one of them lighted a cigarette, but except for the low undertone of the throbbing engines and the even wash of the waves about the stern the yacht was quiet as a dream boat star-bound through the heavens. Round them flowed the smell of the night sea, bringing with it an infinite languor.

Carlyle broke the silence at last.

"Lucky girl," he sighed, "I've always wanted to be rich—and buy all this beauty."

Ardita yawned.

"I'd rather be you," she said frankly.

"You would—for about a day. But you do seem to possess a lot of nerve for a flapper."

"I wish you wouldn't call me that."

"Beg your pardon."

"As to nerve," she continued slowly, "it's my one redeeming feature. I'm not afraid of anything in heaven or earth."

"Hm, I am."

"To be afraid," said Ardita, "a person has either to be very great and strong—or else a coward. I'm neither." She paused for a moment, and eagerness crept into her tone. "But I want to talk about you. What on earth have you done—and how did you do it?"

"Why?" he demanded cynically. "Going to write a movie about me?"

"Go on," she urged. "Lie to me by the moonlight. Do a fabulous story."

A Negro appeared, switched on a string of small lights under the awning, and began setting the wicker table for supper. And while they ate cold sliced chicken, salad, artichokes, and strawberry jam from the plentiful larder below, Carlyle began to talk, hesitatingly at first, but eagerly as he saw she was interested. Ardita scarcely touched her food as she watched his dark young face—handsome, ironic, faintly ineffectual.

He began life as a poor kid in a Tennessee town, he said, so poor that his people were the only white family in their street. He never remembered any white children—but there were inevitably a dozen pickaninnies streaming in his trail, passionate admirers whom he kept in tow by the vividness of his imagination and the amount of trouble he was always getting them in and out of. And it seemed that this association diverted a rather unusual musical gift into a strange channel.

There had been a colored woman named Belle Pope Calhoun who played the piano at parties given for white children—nice white children that would have passed Curtis Carlyle with a sniff. But the ragged little "poh white" used to sit beside her piano by the hour and try to get in an alto with one of those kazoos that boys hum through. Before he was thirteen he was picking up a living teasing ragtime out of a battered violin in little cafés round Nashville. Eight years later the ragtime craze hit the country, and he took six darkies on the Orpheum circuit. Five of them were boys he had grown up with; the other was the little mulatto, Babe Divine, who was a wharf nigger round New York, and long before that a plantation hand in Bermuda, until he stuck an eight-inch stiletto in his master's back. Almost before Carlyle realized his good fortune he was on Broadway, with offers of engagements on all sides, and more money than he had ever dreamed of.

It was about then that a change began in his whole attitude, a rather curious, embittering change. It was when he realized that he was spending the golden years of his life gibbering round a stage with a lot of black men. His act was good of its kind—three trombones, three saxophones, and Carlyle's flute—and it was his own peculiar sense of rhythm that made all the difference; but he began to grow strangely sensitive about it, began to hate the thought of appearing, dreaded it from day to day.

They were making money—each contract he signed called for more—but when he went to managers and told them that he wanted to separate from his sextet and go on as a regular pianist, they laughed at him and told him he was crazy—it would be an artistic suicide. He used to laugh afterward at the phrase "artistic suicide." They all used it.

Half a dozen times they played at private dances at three thousand dollars a night, and it seemed as if these crystallized all his distaste for his mode of livelihood. They took place in clubs and houses that he couldn't have gone into in the daytime. After all, he was merely playing the rôle of the eternal monkey, a sort of sublimated chorus man. He was sick of the very smell of the theater, of powder and rouge and the chatter of the greenroom, and the patronizing approval of the boxes. He couldn't put his heart into it any more. The idea of a slow approach to the luxury of leisure drove him wild. He was, of course, progressing toward it, but, like a child, eating his ice-cream so slowly that he couldn't taste it at all.

He wanted to have a lot of money and time, and opportunity to read and play, and the sort of men and women round him that he could never have—the kind who, if they thought of him at all, would have considered him rather contemptible; in short he wanted all those things which he was beginning to lump under the general head of aristocracy, an aristocracy which it seemed almost any money could buy except money made as he was making it. He was twenty-five then, without family or education or any promise that he would succeed in a business career. He began speculating wildly, and within three weeks he had lost every cent he had saved.

Then the war came. He went to Plattsburg, and even there his profession followed him. A brigadier-general called him up to headquarters and told him he could serve the country better as a band leader—so he spent the war entertaining celebrities behind the line with a headquarters band. It was not so bad—except that when the infantry came limping back from the trenches he wanted to be one of them. The sweat and mud they wore seemed only one of those ineffable symbols of aristocracy that were forever eluding him.

"It was the private dances that did it. After I came

back from the war the old routine started. We had an offer from a syndicate of Florida hotels. It was only a question of time then."

He broke off and Ardita looked at him expectantly, but he shook his head.

"No," he said, "I'm not going to tell you about it. I'm enjoying it too much, and I'm afraid I'd lose a little of that enjoyment if I shared it with any one else. I want to hang on to those few breathless, heroic moments when I stood out before them all and let them know I was more than a damn bobbing, squawking clown."

From up forward came suddenly the low sound of singing. The Negroes had gathered together on the deck and their voices rose together in a haunting melody that soared in poignant harmonics toward the moon. And Ardita listened in enchantment.

"Oh down—
Oh down,
Mammy wanna take me downa milky way,
Oh down—
Oh down,
Pappy say tomorra-a-a-ah!
But mammy say today,
Yes—mammy say today!"

Carlyle sighed and was silent for a moment, looking up at the gathered host of stars blinking like arc lights in the warm sky. The Negroes' song had died away to a plaintive humming and it seemed as if minute by minute the brightness and the great silence were increasing until he could almost hear the midnight toilet of the mermaids as they combed their silver dripping curls under the moon and gossiped to each other of the fine wrecks they lived in on the green opalescent avenues below.

"You see," said Carlyle softly, "this is the beauty I

want. Beauty has got to be astonishing, astounding—it's got to burst in on you like a dream, like the exquisite eyes of a girl."

He turned to her, but she was silent.

"You see, don't you, Anita—I mean, Ardita?"

Again she made no answer. She had been sound asleep for some time.

IV

IN THE dense sun-flooded noon of next day a spot in the sea before them resolved casually into a green-and-gray islet, apparently composed of a great granite cliff at its northern end which slanted south through a mile of vivid coppice and grass to a sandy beach melting lazily into the surf. When Ardita, reading in her favorite seat, came to the last page of *The Revolt of the Angels,* and slamming the book shut looked up and saw it, she gave a little cry of delight, and called to Carlyle, who was standing moodily by the rail.

"Is this it? Is this where you're going?"

Carlyle shrugged his shoulders carelessly.

"You've got me." He raised his voice and called up to the acting skipper: "Oh, Babe, is this your island?"

The mulatto's miniature head appeared from round the corner of the deck-house.

"Yas-suh! This yeah's it."

Carlyle joined Ardita.

"Looks sort of sporting, doesn't it?"

"Yes," she agreed; "but it doesn't look big enough to be much of a hiding-place."

"You still putting your faith in those wirelesses your uncle was going to have zigzagging round?"

"No," said Ardita frankly. "I'm all for you. I'd really like to see you make a get-away."

He laughed.

"You're our Lady Luck. Guess we'll have to keep you with us as a mascot—for the present, anyway."

"You couldn't very well ask me to swim back," she said coolly. "If you do I'm going to start writing dime novels founded on that interminable history of your life you gave me last night."

He flushed and stiffened slightly.

"I'm very sorry I bored you."

"Oh, you didn't—until just at the end with some story about how furious you were because you couldn't dance with the ladies you played music for."

He rose angrily.

"You have got a darn mean little tongue."

"Excuse me," she said, melting into laughter, "but I'm not used to having men regale me with the story of their life ambitions—especially if they've lived such deathly platonic lives."

"Why? What do men usually regale you with?"

"Oh, they talk about me," she yawned. "They tell me I'm the spirit of youth and beauty."

"What do you tell them?"

"Oh, I agree quietly."

"Does every man you meet tell you he loves you?"

Ardita nodded.

"Why shouldn't he? All life is just a progression toward, and then a recession from, one phrase—'I love you.' "

Carlyle laughed and sat down.

"That's very true. That's—that's not bad. Did you make that up?"

"Yes—or rather I found it out. It doesn't mean anything especially. It's just clever."

"It's the sort of remark," he said gravely, "that's typical of your class."

"Oh," she interrupted impatiently, "don't start that

lecture on aristocracy again! I distrust people who can be intense at this hour in the morning. It's a mild form of insanity—a sort of breakfast-food jag. Morning's the time to sleep, swim, and be careless."

Ten minutes later they had swung round in a wide circle as if to approach the island from the north.

"There's a trick somewhere," commented Ardita thoughtfully. "He can't mean just to anchor up against this cliff."

They were heading straight in now toward the solid rock, which must have been well over a hundred feet tall, and not until they were within fifty yards of it did Ardita see their objective. Then she clapped her hands in delight. There was a break in the cliff entirely hidden by a curious overlapping of rock, and through this break the yacht entered and very slowly traversed a narrow channel of crystal-clear water between high gray walls. Then they were riding at anchor in a miniature world of green and gold, a gilded bay smooth as glass and set round with tiny palms, the whole resembling the mirror lakes and twig trees that children set up in sand piles.

"Not so darned bad!" cried Carlyle excitedly. "I guess that little coon knows his way round this corner of the Atlantic."

His exuberance was contagious, and Ardita became quite jubilant.

"It's an absolutely sure-fire hiding-place!"

"Lordy, yes! It's the sort of island you read about."

The rowboat was lowered into the golden lake and they pulled ashore.

"Come on," said Carlyle as they landed in the slushy sand, "we'll go exploring."

The fringe of palms was in turn ringed in by a round mile of flat, sandy country. They followed it south and brushing through a farther rim of tropical vegetation came out on a pearl-gray virgin beach where Ardita kicked off her brown golf shoes—she seemed to have permanently abandoned stockings—and went wading. Then they sauntered back to the yacht, where the indefatigable Babe had luncheon ready for them. He had posted a lookout on the high cliff to the north to watch the sea on both sides, though he doubted if the entrance to the cliff was generally known—he had never even seen a map on which the island was marked.

"What's its name," asked Ardita—"the island, I mean?"

"No name 'tall," chuckled Babe. "Reckin she jus' island, 'at's all."

In the late afternoon they sat with their backs against great boulders on the highest part of the cliff and Carlyle sketched for her his vague plans. He was sure they were hot after him by this time. The total proceeds of the coup he had pulled off, and concerning which he still refused to enlighten her, he estimated as just under a million dollars. He counted on lying up here several weeks and then setting off southward, keeping well outside the usual channels of travel, rounding the Horn and heading for Callao, in Peru. The details of coaling and provisioning he was leaving entirely to Babe, who, it seemed, had sailed these seas in every capacity from cabin-boy aboard a coffee trader to virtual first mate on a Brazilian pirate craft, whose skipper had long since been hung.

"If he'd been white he'd have been king of South America long ago," said Carlyle emphatically. "When it comes to intelligence he makes Booker T. Washington look like a moron. He's got the guile of every race and nationality whose blood is in his veins, and that's half a dozen or I'm a liar. He worships me because I'm the only man in the world who can play better rag-time than he can. We used to sit together on the wharfs down on the New York water-front, he with a bassoon and me with an oboe, and we'd blend minor keys in African harmonics a thousand years old until the rats would crawl up the posts and sit round groaning and squeaking like dogs will in front of a phonograph."

Ardita roared.

"How you can tell 'em!"

Carlyle grinned.

"I swear that's the gos——"

"What you going to do when you get to Callao?" she interrupted.

"Take ship for India. I want to be a rajah. I mean it. My idea is to go up into Afghanistan somewhere, buy up a palace and a reputation, and then after about five years appear in England with a foreign accent and a mysterious past. But India first. Do you know, they say that all the gold in the world drifts very gradually back to India. Something fascinating about that to me. And I want leisure to read—an immense amount."

"How about after that?"

"Then," he answered defiantly, "comes aristocracy. Laugh if you want to—but at least you'll have to admit that I know what I want—which I imagine is more than you do."

"On the contrary," contradicted Ardita, reaching in her pocket for her cigarette case, "when I met you I was in the midst of a great uproar of all my friends and relatives because I did know what I wanted."

"What was it?"

"A man."

He started.

"You mean you were engaged?"

"After a fashion. If you hadn't come aboard I had

every intention of slipping ashore yesterday evening—how long ago it seems—and meeting him in Palm Beach. He's waiting there for me with a bracelet that once belonged to Catharine of Russia. Now don't mutter anything about aristocracy," she put in quickly. "I liked him simply because he had had an imagination and the utter courage of his convictions."

"But your family disapproved, eh?"

"What there is of it—only a silly uncle and a sillier aunt. It seems he got into some scandal with a red-haired woman named Mimi something—it was frightfully exaggerated, he said, and men don't lie to me—and anyway I didn't care what he'd done; it was the future that counted. And I'd see to that. When a man's in love with me he doesn't care for other amusements. I told him to drop her like a hot cake, and he did."

"I feel rather jealous," said Carlyle, frowning—and then he laughed. "I guess I'll just keep you along with us until we get to Callao. Then I'll lend you enough money to get back to the States. By that time you'll have had a chance to think that gentleman over a little more."

"Don't talk to me like that!" fired up Ardita. "I won't tolerate the parental attitude from anybody! Do you understand me?"

He chuckled and then stopped, rather abashed, as her cold anger seemed to fold him about and chill him.

"I'm sorry," he offered uncertainly.

"Oh, don't apologize! I can't stand men who say 'I'm sorry' in that manly, reserved tone. Just shut up!"

A pause ensued, a pause which Carlyle found rather awkward, but which Ardita seemed not to notice at all as she sat contentedly enjoying her cigarette and gazing out at the shining sea. After a minute she crawled out on the rock and lay with her face over the edge looking down. Carlyle, watching her, reflected how it seemed impossible for her to assume an ungraceful attitude.

"Oh, look!" she cried. "There's a lot of sort of ledges down there. Wide ones of all different heights."

He joined her and together they gazed down the dizzy height.

"We'll go swimming tonight!" she said excitedly. "By moonlight."

"Wouldn't you rather go in at the beach on the other end?"

"Not a chance. I like to dive. You can use my uncle's bathing-suit, only it'll fit you like a gunny sack, because he's a very flabby man. I've got a one-piece affair that's shocked the natives all along the Atlantic coast from Biddeford Pool to St. Augustine."

"I suppose you're a shark."

"Yes, I'm pretty good. And I look cute too. A sculptor up at Rye last summer told me my calves were worth five hundred dollars."

There didn't seem to be any answer to this, so Carlyle was silent, permitting himself only a discreet interior smile.

V

WHEN the night crept down in shadowy blue and silver they threaded the shimmering channel in the rowboat and, tying it to a jutting rock, began climbing the cliff together. The first shelf was ten feet up, wide, and furnishing a natural diving platform. There they sat down in the bright moonlight and watched the faint incessant surge of the waters, almost stilled now as the tide set seaward.

"Are you happy?" he asked suddenly.

She nodded.

"Always happy near the sea. You know," she went on,

"I've been thinking all day that you and I are somewhat alike. We're both rebels—only for different reasons. Two years ago, when I was just eighteen, and you were——"

"Twenty-five."

"—well, we were both conventional successes. I was an utterly devastating débutante and you were a prosperous musician just commissioned in the army——"

"Gentleman by act of Congress," he put in ironically.

"Well, at any rate, we both fitted. If our corners were not rubbed off they were at least pulled in. But deep in us both was something that made us require more for happiness. I didn't know what I wanted. I went from man to man, restless, impatient, month by month getting less acquiescent and more dissatisfied. I used to sit sometimes chewing at the insides of my mouth and thinking I was going cray—I had a frightful sense of transiency. I wanted things now—now—now! Here I was—beautiful—I am, aren't I?"

"Yes," agreed Carlyle tentatively.

Ardita rose suddenly.

"Wait a second. I want to try this delightful-looking sea."

She walked to the end of the ledge and shot out over the sea, doubling up in mid-air and then straightening out and entering the water straight as a blade in a perfect jack-knife dive.

In a minute her voice floated up to him.

"You see, I used to read all day and most of the night. I began to resent society——"

"Come on up here," he interrupted. "What on earth are you doing?"

"Just floating round on my back. I'll be up in a minute. Let me tell you. The only thing I enjoyed was shocking people; wearing something quite impossible and quite charming to a fancy-dress party, going round with the fastest men in New York, and getting into some of the most hellish scrapes imaginable."

The sounds of splashing mingled with her words, and then he heard her hurried breathing as she began climbing up the side to the ledge.

"Go on in!" she called.

Obediently he rose and dived. When he emerged, dripping, and made the climb he found that she was no longer on the ledge, but after a frightened second he heard her light laughter from another shelf ten feet up. There he joined her and they both sat quietly for a moment, their arms clasped round their knees, panting a little from the climb.

"The family were wild," she said suddenly. "They tried to marry me off. And then when I'd begun to feel that after all life was scarcely worth living I found something"—her eyes went skyward exultantly—"I found something!"

Carlyle waited and her words came with a rush.

"Courage—just that; courage as a rule of life, and something to cling to always. I began to build up this enormous faith in myself. I began to see that in all my idols in the past some manifestation of courage had unconsciously been the thing that attracted me. I began separating courage from the other things of life. All sorts of courage—the beaten, bloody prize-fighter coming up for more—I used to make men take me to prize-fights; the *déclassée* woman sailing through a nest of cats and looking at them as if they were mud under her feet; the liking what you like always; the utter disregard for other people's opinions—just to live as I liked always and to die in my own way— Did you bring up the cigarettes?"

He handed one over and held a match for her silently.

"Still," Ardita continued, "the men kept gathering—old men and young men, my mental and physical inferiors, most of them, but all intensely desiring to have me—to own this rather magnificent proud tradition I'd built up round me. Do you see?"

"Sort of. You never were beaten and you never apologized."

"Never!"

She sprang to the edge, poised for a moment like a crucified figure against the sky; then describing a dark parabola plunked without a slash between two silver ripples twenty feet below.

Her voice floated up to him again.

"And courage to me meant ploughing through that dull gray mist that comes down on life—not only overriding people and circumstances but overriding the bleakness of living. A sort of insistence on the value of life and the worth of transient things."

She was climbing up now, and at her last words her head, with the damp yellow hair slicked symmetrically back, appeared on his level.

"All very well," objected Carlyle. "You can call it courage, but your courage is really built, after all, on a pride of birth. You were bred to that defiant attitude. On my gray days even courage is one of the things that's gray and lifeless."

She was sitting near the edge, hugging her knees and dazing abstractedly at the white moon; he was farther back, crammed like a grotesque god into a niche in the rock.

"I don't want to sound like Pollyanna," she began, "but you haven't grasped me yet. My courage is faith—faith in the eternal resilience of me—that joy'll come back, and hope and spontaneity. And I feel that till it does I've got to keep my lips shut and my chin high, and my eyes wide—not necessarily any silly smiling. Oh, I've been through hell without a whine quite often —and the female hell is deadlier than the male."

"But supposing," suggested Carlyle, "that before joy and hope and all that came back the curtain was drawn on you for good?"

Ardita rose, and going to the wall climbed with some difficulty to the next ledge, another ten or fifteen feet above.

"Why," she called back, "then I'd have won!"

He edged out till he could see her.

"Better not dive from there! You'll break your back," he said quickly.

She laughed. "Not I!"

Slowly she spread her arms and stood there swan-like, radiating a pride in her young perfection that lit a warm glow in Carlyle's heart.

"We're going through the black air with our arms wide," she called, "and our feet straight out behind like a dolphin's tail, and we're going to think we'll never hit the silver down there till suddenly it'll be all warm round us and full of little kissing, caressing waves."

Then she was in the air, and Carlyle involuntarily held his breath. He had not realized that the dive was nearly forty feet. It seemed an eternity before he heard the swift compact sound as she reached the sea.

And it was with his glad sigh of relief when her light watery laughter curled up the side of the cliff and into his anxious ears that he knew he loved her.

VI

TIME, having no axe to grind, showered down upon them three days of afternoons. When the sun cleared the port-hole of Ardita's cabin an hour after dawn she rose cheerily, donned her bathing-suit, and went up on deck. The Negroes would leave their work when they saw her, and crowd, chuckling and chattering, to the rail as she floated, an agile minnow, on and under the surface of the clear water. Again in the cool of the afternoon she would swim—and loll and smoke with Carlyle upon the cliff; or else they would lie on their sides in the sands of the southern beach, talking little, but watching the day fade colorfully and tragically into the infinite languor of a tropical evening.

And with the long, sunny hours Ardita's idea of the episode as incidental, madcap, a sprig of romance in a desert of reality, gradually left her. She dreaded the time when he would strike off southward; she dreaded all the eventualities that presented themselves to her; thoughts were suddenly troublesome and decisions odious. Had prayers found place in the pagan rituals of her soul she would have asked of life only to be unmolested for a while, lazily acquiescent to the ready, naïf flow of Carlyle's ideas, his vivid boyish imagination, and the vein of monomania that seemed to run crosswise through his temperament and colored his every action.

But this is not a story of two on an island, nor concerned primarily with love bred of isolation. It is merely the presentation of two personalities, and its idyllic setting among the palms of the Gulf Stream is quite incidental. Most of us are content to exist and breed and fight for the right to do both, and the dominant idea, the foredoomed attempt to control one's destiny, is reserved for the fortunate or unfortunate few. To me the interesting thing about Ardita is the courage that will tarnish with her beauty and youth.

"Take me with you," she said late one night as they sat lazily in the grass under the shadowy spreading palms. The Negroes had brought ashore their musical instruments, and the sound of weird ragtime was drifting softly over on the warm breath of the night. "I'd love to reappear in ten years as a fabulously wealthy high-caste Indian lady," she continued.

Carlyle looked at her quickly.

"You can, you know."

She laughed.

"Is it a proposal of marriage? Extra! Ardita Farnam becomes pirate's bride. Society girl kidnaped by ragtime bank robber."

"It wasn't a bank."

"What was it? Why won't you tell me?"

"I don't want to break down your illusions."

"My dear man, I have no illusions about you."

"I mean your illusions about yourself."

She looked up in surprise.

"About myself! What on earth have I got to do with whatever stray felonies you've committed?"

"That remains to be seen."

She reached over and patted his hand.

"Dear Mr. Curtis Carlyle," she said softly, "are you in love with me?"

"As if it mattered."

"But it does—because I think I'm in love with you."

He looked at her ironically.

"Thus swelling your January total to half a dozen," he suggested. "Suppose I call your bluff and ask you to come to India with me?"

"Shall I?"

He shrugged his shoulders.

"We can get married in Callao."

"What sort of life can you offer me? I don't mean that unkindly, but seriously; what would become of me if the people who want that twenty-thousand-dollar reward ever catch up with you?"

"I thought you weren't afraid."

"I never am—but I won't throw my life away just to show one man I'm not."

"I wish you'd been poor. Just a little poor girl dreaming over a fence in a warm cow country."

"Wouldn't it have been nice?"

"I'd have enjoyed astonishing you—watching your eyes open on things. If you only wanted things! Don't you see?"

"I know—like girls who stare into the windows of jewelry-stores."

"Yes—and want the big oblong watch that's platinum and has diamonds all round the edge. Only you'd decide it was too expensive and choose one of white gold for a hundred dollars. Then I'd say: 'Expensive? I should say not!' And we'd go into the store and pretty soon the platinum one would be gleaming on your wrist."

"That sounds so nice and vulgar—and fun, doesn't it?" murmured Ardita.

"Doesn't it? Can't you see us traveling round and spending money right and left, and being worshiped by bell-boys and waiters? Oh, blessed are the simple rich, for they inherit the earth!"

"I honestly wish we were that way."

"I love you, Ardita," he said gently.

Her face lost its childish look for a moment and became oddly grave.

"I love to be with you," she said, "more than with any man I've ever met. And I like your looks and your dark old hair, and the way you go over the side of the rail when we come ashore. In fact, Curtis Carlyle, I like all the things you do when you're perfectly natural. I think you've got nerve, and you know how I feel about that. Sometimes when you're around I've been tempted to kiss you suddenly and tell you that you were just an idealistic boy with a lot of caste nonsense in his head. Perhaps if I were just a little bit older and a little more bored I'd go with you. As it is, I think I'll go back and marry—that other man."

Over across the silver lake the figures of the Negroes writhed and squirmed in the moonlight, like acrobats who, having been too long inactive, must go through their tricks from sheer surplus energy. In single file they marched, weaving in concentric circles, now with their heads thrown back, now bent over their instruments like piping fauns. And from trombone and saxophone ceaselessly whined a blended melody, sometimes riotous and jubilant, sometimes haunting and plaintive as a death-dance from the Congo's heart.

"Let's dance!" cried Ardita. "I can't sit still with that perfect jazz going on."

Taking her hand he led her out into a broad stretch of hard sandy soil that the moon flooded with great splendor. They floated out like drifting moths under the rich hazy light, and as the fantastic symphony wept and exulted and wavered and despaired Ardita's last sense of reality dropped away, and she abandoned her imagination to the dreamy summer scents of tropical flowers and the infinite starry spaces overhead, feeling that if she opened her eyes it would be to find herself dancing with a ghost in a land created by her own fancy.

"This is what I should call an exclusive private dance," he whispered.

"I feel quite mad—but delightfully mad!"

"We're enchanted. The shades of unnumbered generations of cannibals are watching us from high up on the side of the cliff there."

"And I'll bet the cannibal women are saying that we dance too close, and that it was immodest of me to come without my nose-ring."

They both laughed softly—and then their laughter died as over across the lake they heard the trombones stop in the middle of a bar, and the saxophones give a startled moan and fade out.

"What's the matter?" called Carlyle.

After a moment's silence they made out the dark figure of a man rounding the silver lake at a run. As he came closer they saw it was Babe in a state of unusual excitement. He drew up before them and gasped out his news in a breath.

"Ship stan'in' off sho' 'bout half a mile, suh. Mose, he uz on watch, he say look's if she's done ancho'd."

"A ship—what kind of a ship?" demanded Carlyle anxiously.

Dismay was in his voice, and Ardita's heart gave a sudden wrench as she saw his whole face suddenly droop.

"He say he don't know, suh."

"Are they landing a boat?"

"No, suh."

"We'll go up," said Carlyle.

They ascended the hill in silence, Ardita's hand still resting in Carlyle's as it had when they finished dancing. She felt it clinch nervously from time to time as though he were unaware of the contact, but though he hurt her she made no attempt to remove it. It seemed an hour's climb before they reached the top and crept cautiously across the silhouetted plateau to the edge of the cliff. After one short look Carlyle involuntarily gave a little cry. It was a revenue boat with six-inch guns mounted fore and aft.

"They know!" he said with a short intake of breath. "They know! They picked up the trail somewhere."

"Are you sure they know about the channel? They may be only standing by to take a look at the island in the morning. From where they are they couldn't see the opening in the cliff."

"They could with field-glasses," he said hopelessly. He looked at his wrist-watch. "It's nearly two now. They won't do anything until dawn, that's certain. Of course there's always the faint possibility that they're waiting for some other ship to join; or for a coaler."

"I suppose we may as well stay right here."

The hours passed and they lay there side by side, very silently, their chins in their hands like dreaming children. In back of them squatted the Negroes, patient, resigned, acquiescent, announcing now and then with sonorous snores that not even the presence of danger could subdue their unconquerable African craving for sleep.

Just before five o'clock Babe approached Carlyle. There were half a dozen rifles aboard the *Narcissus* he said. Had it been decided to offer no resistance? A pretty good fight might be made, he thought, if they worked out some plan.

Carlyle laughed and shook his head.

"That isn't a Spic army out there, Babe. That's a revenue boat. It'd be like a bow and arrow trying to fight a machine-gun. If you want to bury those bags somewhere and take a chance on recovering them later, go on and do it. But it won't work—they'd dig this island over from one end to the other. It's a lost battle all round, Babe."

Babe inclined his head silently and turned away, and Carlyle's voice was husky as he turned to Ardita.

"There's the best friend I ever had. He'd die for me, and be proud to, if I'd let him."

"You've given up?"

"I've no choice. Of course there's always one way out—the sure way—but that can wait. I wouldn't miss my trial for anything—it'll be an interesting experiment in notoriety. 'Miss Farnam testifies that the pirate's attitude to her was at all times that of a gentleman.' "

"Don't!" she said. "I'm awfully sorry."

When the color faded from the sky and lusterless blue changed to leaden gray a commotion was visible on the ship's deck, and they made out a group of officers clad in white duck, gathered near the rail. They had field-glasses in their hands and were attentively examining the islet.

"It's all up," said Carlyle grimly.

"Damn!" whispered Ardita. She felt tears gathering in her eyes.

"We'll go back to the yacht," he said. "I prefer that to being hunted out up here like a 'possum."

Leaving the plateau they descended the hill, and reaching the lake were rowed out to the yacht by the silent Negroes. Then, pale and weary, they sank into the settees and waited.

Half an hour later in the dim gray light the nose of the revenue boat appeared in the channel and stopped, evidently fearing that the bay might be too shallow. From the peaceful look of the yacht, the man and the girl in the settees, and the Negroes lounging curiously against the rail, they evidently judged that there would be no resistance, for two boats were lowered casually over the side, one containing an officer and six bluejackets, and the other, four rowers and in the stern two gray-haired men in yachting flannels. Ardita and Carlyle stood up, and half unconsciously started toward each other. Then he paused and putting his hand suddenly into his pocket he pulled out a round, glittering object and held it out to her.

"What is it?" she asked wonderingly.

"I'm not positive, but I think from the Russian inscription inside that it's your promised bracelet."

"Where—where on earth——"

"It came out of one of those bags. You see, Curtis Carlyle and his Six Black Buddies, in the middle of their performance in the tea-room of the hotel at Palm Beach, suddenly changed their instruments for automatics and held up the crowd. I took this bracelet from a pretty, overrouged woman with red hair."

Ardita frowned and then smiled.

"So that's what you did! You *have* got nerve!"

He bowed.

"A well-known bourgeois quality," he said.

And then dawn slanted dynamically across the deck and flung the shadows reeling into gray corners. The dew rose and turned to golden mist, thin as a dream, enveloping them until they seemed gossamer relics of the late night, infinitely transient and already fading. For a moment sea and sky were breathless, and dawn held a pink hand over the young mouth of life—then from out in the lake came the complaint of a rowboat and the swish of oars.

Suddenly against the golden furnace low in the east their two graceful figures melted into one, and he was kissing her spoiled young mouth.

"It's a sort of glory," he murmured after a second.

She smiled up at him.

"Happy, are you?"

Her sigh was a benediction—an ecstatic surety that she was youth and beauty now as much as she would ever know. For another instant life was radiant and time a phantom and their strength eternal—then there was a bumping, scraping sound as the rowboat scraped alongside.

Up the ladder scrambled the two gray-haired men, the officer and two of the sailors with their hands on their revolvers. Mr. Farnam folded his arms and stood looking at his niece.

"So," he said, nodding his head slowly.

With a sigh her arms unwound from Carlyle's neck, and her eyes, transfigured and far away, fell upon the boarding party. Her uncle saw her upper lip slowly swell into that arrogant pout he knew so well.

"So," he repeated savagely. "So this is your idea of—of romance. A runaway affair, with a high-seas pirate."

Ardita glanced at him carelessly.

"What an old fool you are!" she said quietly.

"Is that the best you can say for yourself?"

"No," she said as if considering. "No, there's something else. There's that well-known phrase with which I have ended most of our conversations for the past few years—'Shut up!' "

And with that she turned, included the two old men, the officer, and the two sailors in a curt glance of contempt, and walked proudly down the companionway.

But had she waited an instant longer she would have heard a sound from her uncle quite unfamiliar in most of their interviews. He gave vent to a whole-hearted amused chuckle, in which the second old man joined.

The latter turned briskly to Carlyle, who had been regarding this scene with an air of cryptic amusement.

"Well, Toby," he said genially, "you incurable, hare-brained, romantic chaser of rainbows, did you find that she was the person you wanted?"

Carlyle smiled confidently.

"Why—naturally," he said. "I've been perfectly sure ever since I first heard tell of her wild career. That's why I had Babe send up the rocket last night."

"I'm glad you did," said Colonel Moreland gravely. "We've been keeping pretty close to you in case you should have trouble with those six strange niggers. And we hoped we'd find you two in some such compromising position," he sighed. "Well, set a crank to catch a crank!"

"Your father and I sat up all night hoping for the best—or perhaps it's the worst. Lord knows you're welcome to her, my boy. She's run me crazy. Did you give her the Russian bracelet my detective got from that Mimi woman?"

Carlyle nodded.

"Sh!" he said. "She's coming on deck."

Ardita appeared at the head of the companionway and gave a quick involuntary glance at Carlyle's wrists. A puzzled look passed across her face. Back aft the Negroes had begun to sing, and the cool lake, fresh with dawn, echoed serenely to their low voices.

"Ardita," said Carlyle unsteadily.

She swayed a step toward him.

"Ardita," he repeated breathlessly, "I've got to tell you the—the truth. It was all a plant, Ardita. My name isn't Carlyle. It's Moreland, Toby Moreland. The story was invented, Ardita, invented out of thin Florida air."

She stared at him, bewildered amazement, disbelief, and anger flowing in quick waves across her face. The three men held their breaths. Moreland, Senior, took a step toward her; Mr. Farnam's mouth dropped a little open as he waited, panic-stricken, for the expected crash.

But it did not come. Ardita's face became suddenly

radiant, and with a little laugh she went swiftly to young Moreland and looked up at him without a trace of wrath in her gray eyes.

"Will you swear," she said quietly, "that it was entirely a product of your own brain?"

"I swear," said young Moreland eagerly.

She drew his head down and kissed him gently.

"What an imagination!" she said softly and almost enviously. "I want you to lie to me just as sweetly as you know how for the rest of my life."

The Negroes' voices floated drowsily back, mingled in an air that she had heard them sing before.

> "Time is a thief;
> Gladness and grief
> Cling to the leaf
> As it yellows——"

"What was in the bags?" she asked softly.

"Florida mud," he answered. "That was one of the two true things I told you."

"Perhaps I can guess the other one," she said; and reaching up on her tiptoes she kissed him softly in the illustration.

THE FRESHEST BOY

I

IT WAS a hidden Broadway restaurant in the dead of the night, and a brilliant and mysterious group of society people, diplomats and members of the underworld were there. A few minutes ago the sparkling wine had been flowing and a girl had been dancing gaily upon a table, but now the whole crowd were hushed and breathless. All eyes were fixed upon the masked but well-groomed man in the dress suit and opera hat who stood nonchalantly in the door.

"Don't move, please," he said, in a well-bred, cultivated voice that had, nevertheless, a ring of steel in it. "This thing in my hand might—go off."

His glance roved from table to table—fell upon the malignant man higher up with his pale saturnine face, upon Heatherly, the suave secret agent from a foreign power, then rested a little longer, a little more softly perhaps, upon the table where the girl with dark hair and dark tragic eyes sat alone.

"Now that my purpose is accomplished, it might interest you to know who I am." There was a gleam of expectation in every eye. The breast of the dark-eyed girl heaved faintly and a tiny burst of subtle French perfume rose into the air. "I am none other than that elusive gentleman, Basil Lee, better known as the Shadow."

Taking off his well-fitting opera hat, he bowed ironically from the waist. Then, like a flash, he turned and was gone into the night.

"You get up to New York only once a month," Lewis Crum was saying, "and then you have to take a master along."

Slowly, Basil Lee's glazed eyes returned from the barns and billboards of the Indiana countryside to the interior of the Broadway Limited. The hypnosis of the swift telegraph poles faded and Lewis Crum's stolid face took shape against the white slip-cover of the opposite bench.

"I'd just duck the master when I got to New York," said Basil.

"Yes, you would!"

"I bet I would."

"You try it and you'll see."

"What do you mean saying I'll see, all the time, Lewis? What'll I see?"

His very bright dark-blue eyes were at this moment fixed upon his companion with boredom and impatience. The two had nothing in common except their age, which was fifteen, and the lifelong friendship of their fathers—which is less than nothing. Also they were bound from the same Middle-Western city for Basil's first and Lewis' second year at the same Eastern school.

But, contrary to all the best traditions, Lewis the veteran was miserable and Basil the neophyte was happy. Lewis hated school. He had grown entirely dependent on the stimulus of a hearty vital mother, and as he felt her slipping farther and farther away from him, he plunged deeper into misery and homesickness. Basil, on the other hand, had lived with such intensity on so many stories of boarding-school life that, far from being homesick, he had a glad feeling of recognition and familiarity. Indeed, it was with some sense of doing the appropriate thing, having the traditional rough-house, that he had thrown Lewis' comb off the train at Milwaukee last night for no reason at all.

To Lewis, Basil's ignorant enthusiasm was distasteful—his instinctive attempt to dampen it had contributed to the mutual irritation.

"I'll tell you what you'll see," he said ominously. "They'll catch you smoking and put you on bounds."

"No, they won't, because I won't be smoking. I'll be in training for football."

"Football! Yeah! Football!"

"Honestly, Lewis, you don't like anything, do you?"

"I don't like football. I don't like to go out and get a crack in the eye." Lewis spoke aggressively, for his mother had canonized all his timidities as common sense. Basil's answer, made with what he considered kindly intent, was the sort of remark that creates life-long enmities.

"You'd probably be a lot more popular in school if you played football," he suggested patronizingly.

Lewis did not consider himself unpopular. He did not think of it in that way at all. He was astounded.

"You wait!" he cried furiously. "They'll take all that freshness out of you."

"Clam yourself," said Basil, coolly plucking at the creases of his first long trousers. "Just clam yourself."

"I guess everybody knows you were the freshest boy at the Country Day!"

"Clam yourself," repeated Basil, but with less assurance. "Kindly clam yourself."

"I guess I know what they had in the school paper about you——"

Basil's own coolness was no longer perceptible.

"If you don't clam yourself," he said darkly, "I'm going to throw your brushes off the train too."

The enormity of this threat was effective. Lewis sank back in his seat, snorting and muttering, but undoubtedly calmer. His reference had been to one of the most shameful passages in his companion's life. In a periodical issued by the boys of Basil's late school there had appeared, under the heading Personals:

> "If someone will please poison young Basil, or find some other means to stop his mouth, the school at large and myself will be much obliged."

The two boys sat there fuming wordlessly at each other. Then, resolutely, Basil tried to re-inter this unfortunate souvenir of the past. All that was behind him now. Perhaps he had been a little fresh, but he was making a new start. After a moment, the memory passed and with it the train and Lewis' dismal presence—the breath of the East came sweeping over him again with a vast nostalgia. A voice called him out of the fabled world; a man stood beside him with a hand on his sweater-clad shoulder.

"Lee!"

"Yes, sir."

"It all depends on you now. Understand?"

"Yes, sir."

"All right," the coach said, "go in and win."

Basil tore the sweater from his stripling form and dashed out on the field. There were two minutes to play and the score was 3 to 0 for the enemy, but at the sight of young Lee, kept out of the game all year by a malicious plan of Dan Haskins, the school bully, and Weasel Weems, his toady, a thrill of hope went over the St. Regis stand.

"33-12 16-22!" barked Midget Brown, the diminutive little quarterback.

It was his signal——

"Oh, gosh!" Basil spoke aloud, forgetting the late unpleasantness. "I wish we'd get there before tomorrow."

II

St. Regis School, Eastchester,
November 18, 19——

"Dear Mother: There is not much to say today, but I thought I would write you about my allowance. All the boys have a bigger allowance than me, because there are a lot of little things I have to get, such as shoe laces etc. School is still very nice and am having a fine time, but football is over and there is not much to do. I am going to New York this week to see a show. I do not know yet what it will be, but probably the Quacker Girl or little boy Blue as they are both very good. Dr. Bacon is very nice and there is a good phycission in the village. No more now as I have to study Algebra.

"Your Affectionate Son,
"BASIL D. LEE."

As he put the letter in its envelope, a wizened little boy came into the deserted study hall where he sat and stood staring at him.

"Hello," said Basil, frowning.

"I been looking for you," said the little boy, slowly and judicially. "I looked all over—up in your room and out in the gym, and they said you probably might of sneaked off in here."

"What do you want?" Basil demanded.

"Hold your horses, Bossy."

Basil jumped to his feet. The little boy retreated a step.

"Go on, hit me!" he chirped nervously. "Go on, hit me, cause I'm just half your size—Bossy."

Basil winced. "You call me that again and I'll spank you."

"No, you won't spank me. Brick Wales said if you ever touched any of us——"

"But I never did touch any of you."

"Didn't you chase a lot of us one day and didn't Brick Wales——"

"Oh, what do you want?" Basil cried in desperation.

"Doctor Bacon wants you. They sent me after you and somebody said maybe you sneaked in here."

Basil dropped his letter in his pocket and walked out—the little boy and his invective following him through the door. He traversed a long corridor, muggy with that odor best described as the smell of stale caramels that is so peculiar to boys' schools, ascended a stairs and knocked at an unexceptional but formidable door.

Doctor Bacon was at his desk. He was a handsome,

redheaded Episcopal clergyman of fifty whose original real interest in boys was now tempered by the flustered cynicism which is the fate of all headmasters and settles on them like green mould. There were certain preliminaries before Basil was asked to sit down—gold-rimmed glasses had to be hoisted up from nowhere by a black cord and fixed on Basil to be sure that he was not an impostor; great masses of paper on the desk had to be shuffled through, not in search of anything but as a man nervously shuffles a pack of cards.

"I had a letter from your mother this morning—ah—Basil." The use of his first name had come to startle Basil. No one else in school had yet called him anything but Bossy or Lee. "She feels that your marks have been poor. I believe you have been sent here at a certain amount of—ah—sacrifice and she expects——"

Basil's spirit writhed with shame, not at his poor marks but that his financial inadequacy should be so bluntly stated. He knew that he was one of the poorest boys in a rich boys' school.

Perhaps some dormant sensibility in Doctor Bacon became aware of his discomfort; he shuffled through the papers once more and began on a new note.

"However, that was not what I sent for you about this afternoon. You applied last week for permission to go to New York on Saturday, to a matinée. Mr. Davis tells me that for almost the first time since school opened you will be off bounds tomorrow."

"Yes, sir."

"That is not a good record. However, I would allow you to go to New York if it could be arranged. Unfortunately, no masters are available this Saturday."

Basil's mouth dropped ajar. "Why, I—why, Doctor Bacon, I know two parties that are going. Couldn't I go with one of them?"

Doctor Bacon ran through all his papers very quickly. "Unfortunately, one is composed of slightly older boys and the other group made arrangements some weeks ago."

"How about the party that's going to the *Quaker Girl* with Mr. Dunn?"

"It's that party I speak of. They feel that their arrangements are complete and they have purchased seats together."

Suddenly Basil understood. At the look in his eye Doctor Bacon went on hurriedly:

"There's perhaps one thing I can do. Of course there must be several boys in the party so that the expenses of the master can be divided up among all. If you can find two other boys who would like to make up a party, and let me have their names by five o'clock, I'll send Mr. Rooney with you."

"Thank you," Basil said.

Doctor Bacon hesitated. Beneath the cynical incrustations of many years an instinct stirred to look into the unusual case of this boy and find out what made him the most detested boy in school. Among boys and masters there seemed to exist an extraordinary hostility toward him, and though Doctor Bacon had dealt with many sorts of schoolboy crimes, he had neither by himself nor with the aid of trusted sixth-formers been able to lay his hands on its underlying cause. It was probably no single thing, but a combination of things; it was most probably one of those intangible questions of personality. Yet he remembered that when he first saw Basil he had considered him unusually prepossessing.

He sighed. Sometimes these things worked themselves out. He wasn't one to rush in clumsily. "Let us have a better report to send home next month, Basil."

"Yes, sir."

Basil ran quickly downstairs to the recreation room. It was Wednesday and most of the boys had already gone into the village of Eastchester, whither Basil, who was still on bounds, was forbidden to follow. When he looked at those still scattered about the pool tables and piano, he saw that it was going to be difficult to get anyone to go with him at all. For Basil was quite conscious that he was the most unpopular boy at school.

It had begun almost immediately. One day, less than a fortnight after he came, a crowd of the smaller boys, perhaps urged on to it, gathered suddenly around him and began calling him Bossy. Within the next week he had two fights, and both times the crowd was vehemently and eloquently with the other boy. Soon after, when he was merely shoving indiscriminatively, like every one else, to get into the dining room, Carver, the captain of the football team, turned about and, seizing him by the back of the neck, held him and dressed him down savagely. He joined a group innocently at the piano and was told, "Go on away. We don't want you around."

After a month he began to realize the full extent of his unpopularity. It shocked him. One day after a particularly bitter humiliation he went up to his room and cried. He tried to keep out of the way for a while, but it didn't help. He was accused of sneaking off here and there, as if bent on a series of nefarious errands. Puzzled and wretched, he looked at his face in the glass, trying to discover there the secret of their dislike—in the expression of his eyes, his smile.

He saw now that in certain ways he had erred at the outset—he had boasted, he had been considered yellow at football, he had pointed out people's mistakes to them, he had shown off his rather extraordinary fund of general information in class. But he had tried to do better and couldn't understand his failure to atone. It must be too late. He was queered forever.

He had, indeed, become the scapegoat, the immediate villain, the sponge which absorbed all malice and irritability abroad—just as the most frightened person in a party seems to absorb all the others' fear, seems to be afraid for them all. His situation was not helped by the fact, obvious to all, that the supreme self-confidence with which he had come to St. Regis in September was thoroughly broken. Boys taunted him with impunity who would not have dared raise their voices to him several months before.

This trip to New York had come to mean everything to him—surcease from the misery of his daily life as well as a glimpse into the long-awaited heaven of romance. Its postponement for week after week due to his sins—he was constantly caught reading after lights, for example, driven by his wretchedness into such vicarious escapes from reality—had deepened his longing until it was a burning hunger. It was unbearable that he should not go, and he told over the short list of those whom he might get to accompany him. The possibilities were Fat Gaspar, Treadway, and Bugs Brown. A quick journey to their rooms showed that they had all availed themselves of the Wednesday permission to go into Eastchester for the afternoon.

Basil did not hesitate. He had until five o'clock and his only chance was to go after them. It was not the first time he had broken bounds, though the last attempt had ended in disaster and an extension of his confinement. In his room, he put on a heavy sweater—an overcoat was a betrayal of intent—replaced his jacket over it and hid a cap in his back pocket. Then he went downstairs and with an elaborately careless whistle struck out across the lawn for the gymnasium. Once there, he stood for a while as if looking in the windows, first the one close to the walk, then one near the corner of the building. From here he moved quickly, but not too quickly, into a grove of lilacs. Then he dashed around the corner, down a long stretch of lawn that was blind from all windows and, parting the strands of a wire fence, crawled through and stood upon the grounds of a neighboring estate. For the moment he was free. He put on his cap against the chilly November wind, and set out along the half-mile road to town.

Eastchester was a suburban farming community, with a small shoe factory. The institutions which pandered to the factory workers were the ones patronized by the boys—a movie house, a quick-lunch wagon on wheels known as the Dog and the Bostonian Candy Kitchen. Basil tried the Dog first and happened immediately upon a prospect.

This was Bugs Brown, a hysterical boy, subject to fits and strenuously avoided. Years later he became a brilliant lawyer, but at that time he was considered by the boys of St. Regis to be a typical lunatic because of his peculiar series of sounds with which he assuaged his nervousness all day long.

He consorted with boys younger than himself, who were without the prejudices of their elders, and was in the company of several when Basil came in.

"Who-ee!" he cried. "Ee-ee-ee!" He put his hand over his mouth and bounced it quickly, making a wah-wah-wah sound. "It's Bossy Lee! It's Bossy Lee! It's Boss-Boss-Boss-Boss-Bossy Lee!"

"Wait a minute, Bugs," said Basil anxiously, half afraid that Bugs would go finally crazy before he could persuade him to come to town. "Say, Bugs, listen. Don't, Bugs—wait a minute. Can you come up to New York Saturday afternoon?"

"Whe-ee-ee!" cried Bugs to Basil's distress. "Whee-ee-ee!"

"Honestly, Bugs, tell me, can you? We could go up together if you could go."

"I've got to see a doctor," said Bugs, suddenly calm. "He wants to see how crazy I am."

"Can't you have him see about it some other day?" said Basil without humor.

"Whee-ee-ee!" cried Bugs.

"All right then," said Basil hastily. "Have you seen Fat Gaspar in town?"

Bugs was lost in shrill noise, but someone had seen Fat; Basil was directed to the Bostonian Candy Kitchen.

This was a gaudy paradise of cheap sugar. Its odor, heavy and sickly and calculated to bring out a sticky sweat upon an adult's palms, hung suffocatingly over the whole vicinity and met one like a strong moral dissuasion at the door. Inside, beneath a pattern of flies, material as black point lace, a line of boys sat eating heavy dinners of banana splits, maple nut, and chocolate marshmallow nut sundaes. Basil found Fat Gaspar at a table on the side.

Fat Gaspar was at once Basil's most unlikely and most ambitious quest. He was considered a nice fellow—in fact he was so pleasant that he had been courteous to Basil and had spoken to him politely all fall. Basil realized that he was like that to everyone, yet it was just possible that Fat liked him, as people used to in the past, and he was driven desperately to take a chance. But it was undoubtedly a presumption, and as he approached the table and saw the stiffened faces which the other two boys turned toward him, Basil's hope diminished.

"Say, Fat——" he said, and hesitated. Then he burst forth suddenly. "I'm on bounds, but I ran off because I had to see you. Doctor Bacon told me I could go to New York Saturday if I could get two other boys to go. I asked Bugs Brown and he couldn't go, and I thought I'd ask you."

He broke off, furiously embarrassed, and waited. Suddenly the two boys with Fat burst into a shout of laughter.

"Bugs wasn't crazy enough!"

Fat Gaspar hesitated. He couldn't go to New York Saturday and ordinarily he would have refused without offending. He had nothing against Basil; nor, indeed, against anybody; but boys have only a certain resistance to public opinion and he was influenced by the contemptuous laughter of the others.

"I don't want to go," he said indifferently. "Why do you want to ask *me*?"

Then, half in shame, he gave a deprecatory little laugh and bent over his ice cream.

"I just thought I'd ask you," said Basil.

Turning quickly away, he went to the counter and in a hollow and unfamiliar voice ordered a strawberry sundae. He ate it mechanically, hearing occasional whispers and snickers from the table behind. Still in a daze, he started to walk out without paying his check but the clerk called him back and he was conscious of more derisive laughter.

For a moment he hesitated whether to go back to the table and hit one of those boys in the face, but he saw nothing to be gained. They would say the truth—that he had done it because he couldn't get anybody to go to New York. Clenching his fists with impotent rage he walked from the store.

He came immediately upon his third prospect, Treadway. Treadway had entered St. Regis late in the year and had been put in to room with Basil the week before. The fact that Treadway hadn't witnessed his humiliations of the autumn encouraged Basil to behave naturally toward him, and their relations had been, if not intimate, at least tranquil.

"Hey, Treadway," he cried, still excited from the affair in the Bostonian, "can you come up to New York to a show Saturday afternoon?"

He stopped, realizing that Treadway was in the company of Brick Wales, a boy he had had a fight with and one of his bitterest enemies. Looking from one to the other, Basil saw a look of impatience in Treadway's face and a faraway expression in Brick Wales', and he realized what must have been happening. Treadway, making his way into the life of the school, had just been enlightened as to the status of his roommate. Like Fat Gaspar, rather than acknowledge himself eligible to such an intimate request, he preferred to cut their friendly relations short.

"Not on your life," he said briefly. "So long." The two walked past him into the candy kitchen.

Had these slights, so much the bitterer for their lack of passion, been visited upon Basil in September, they would have been unbearable. But since then he had developed a shell of hardness which, while it did not add to his attractiveness, spared him certain delicacies of torture. In misery enough, and despair and self-pity, he went the other way along the street for a little distance until he could control the violent contortions of his face. Then, taking a roundabout route, he started back to school.

He reached the adjoining estate, intending to go back the way he had come. Half-way through a hedge, he heard footsteps approaching along the sidewalk and stood motionless, fearing the proximity of masters. Their voices grew nearer and louder; before he knew it he was listening with horrified fascination:

"—so, after he tried Bugs Brown, the poor nut asked Fat Gaspar to go with him and Fat said, 'What do you ask me for?' It serves him right if he couldn't get anybody at all."

It was the dismal but triumphant voice of Lewis Crum.

III

UP IN his room, Basil found a package lying on his bed. He knew its contents and for a long time he had been eagerly expecting it, but such was his depression that he opened it listlessly. It was a series of eight color reproductions of Harrison Fisher girls "on glossy paper, without printing or advertising matter and suitable for framing."

The pictures were named Dora, Marguerite, Babette, Lucille, Gretchen, Rose, Katherine and Mina. Two of them—Marguerite and Rose—Basil looked at, slowly tore up and dropped in the wastebasket, as one who disposes of the inferior pups from a litter. The other six he pinned at intervals around the room. Then he lay down on his bed and regarded them.

Dora, Lucille and Katherine were blonde; Gretchen was medium; Babette and Mina were dark. After a few minutes, he found that he was looking oftenest at Dora and Babette and, to a lesser extent, at Gretchen, though the latter's Dutch cap seemed unromantic and precluded the element of mystery. Babette, a dark little violet-eyed beauty in a tight-fitting hat, attracted him most; his eyes came to rest on her at last.

"Babette," he whispered to himself—"beautiful Babette."

The sound of the word, so melancholy and suggestive, like "Velia" or "I'm going to Maxime's" on the phonograph, softened him and, turning over on his face, he sobbed into the pillow. He took hold of the bed rails over his head and, sobbing and straining, began to talk to himself brokenly—how he hated them and whom he hated—he listed a dozen—and what he would do to them when he was great and powerful. In previous moments like these he had always rewarded Fat Gaspar for his kindness, but now he was like the rest. Basil set upon him, pummeling him unmercifully, or laughed sneeringly when he passed him blind and begging on the street.

He controlled himself as he heard Treadway come in, but did not move or speak. He listened as the other moved about the room, and after a while became conscious that there was an unusual opening of closets and bureau drawers. Basil turned over, his arm concealing his tear-stained face. Treadway had an armful of shirts in his hand.

"What are you doing?" Basil demanded.

His roommate looked at him stonily. "I'm moving in with Wales," he said.

"Oh!"

Treadway went on with his packing. He carried out a suitcase full, then another, took down some pennants and dragged his trunk into the hall. Basil watched him bundle his toilet things into a towel and take one last survey about the room's new barrenness to see if there was anything forgotten.

"Good-by," he said to Basil, without a ripple of expression on his face.

"Good-by."

Treadway went out. Basil turned over once more and choked into the pillow.

"Oh, poor Babette!" he cried huskily. "Poor little Babette! Poor little Babette!"

Babette, svelte and piquant, looked down at him coquettishly from the wall.

IV

DOCTOR BACON, sensing Basil's predicament and perhaps the extremity of his misery, arranged it that he should go into New York, after all. He went in the company of Mr. Rooney, the football coach and history teacher. At twenty Mr. Rooney had hesitated for some time between joining the police force and having his way paid through a small New England college; in fact he was a hard specimen and Doctor Bacon was planning to get rid of him at Christmas. Mr. Rooney's contempt for Basil was founded on the latter's ambiguous and unreliable conduct on the football field during the past season—he had consented to take him to New York for reasons of his own.

Basil sat meekly beside him on the train, glancing past Mr. Rooney's bulky body at the Sound and the fallow fields of Westchester County. Mr. Rooney finished his newspaper, folded it up and sank into a moody silence. He had eaten a large breakfast and the exigencies of time had not allowed him to work it off with exercise. He remembered that Basil was a fresh boy, and it was time he did something fresh and could be called to account. This reproachless silence annoyed him.

"Lee," he said suddenly, with a thinly assumed air of friendly interest, "why don't you get wise to yourself?"

"What, sir?" Basil was startled from his excited trance of this morning.

"I said why don't you get wise to yourself?" said Mr.

Rooney in a somewhat violent tone. "Do you want to be the butt of the school all your time here?"

"No, I don't," Basil was chilled. Couldn't all this be left behind for just one day?

"You oughtn't to get so fresh all the time. A couple of times in history class I could just about have broken your neck." Basil could think of no appropriate answer. "Then out playing football," continued Mr. Rooney "—you didn't have any nerve. You could play better than a lot of 'em when you wanted, like that day against the Pomfret seconds, but you lost your nerve."

"I shouldn't have tried for the second team," said Basil. "I was too light. I should have stayed on the third."

"You were yellow, that was all the trouble. You ought to get wise to yourself. In class, you're always thinking of something else. If you don't study, you'll never get to college."

"I'm the youngest boy in the fifth form," Basil said rashly.

"You think you're pretty bright, don't you?" He eyed Basil ferociously. Then something seemed to occur to him that changed his attitude and they rode for a while in silence. When the train began to run through the thickly clustered communities near New York, he spoke again in a milder voice and with an air of having considered the matter for a long time:

"Lee, I'm going to trust you."

"Yes, sir."

"You go and get some lunch and then go on to your show. I've got some business of my own I got to attend to, and when I've finished I'll try to get to the show. If I can't, I'll anyhow meet you outside."

Basil's heart leaped up. "Yes, sir."

"I don't want you to open your mouth about this at school—I mean, about me doing some business of my own."

"No, sir."

"We'll see if you can keep your mouth shut for once," he said, making it fun. Then he added, on a note of moral sternness, "And no drinks, you understand that?"

"Oh, no, sir!" The idea shocked Basil. He had never tasted a drink, nor even contemplated the possibility, save the intangible and nonalcoholic champagne of his café dreams.

On the advice of Mr. Rooney he went for luncheon to the Manhattan Hotel, near the station, where he ordered a club sandwich, French fried potatoes and a chocolate parfait. Out of the corner of his eye he watched the nonchalant, debonair, blasé New Yorkers at neighboring tables, investing them with a romance by which these possible fellow citizens of his from the Middle West lost nothing. School had fallen from him like a burden; it was no more than an unheeded clamor, faint and far away. He even delayed opening the letter from the morning's mail which he found in his pocket, because it was addressed to him at school.

He wanted another chocolate parfait, but being reluctant to bother the busy waiter any more, he opened the letter and spread it before him instead. It was from his mother:

"DEAR BASIL: This is written in great haste, as I didn't want to frighten you by telegraphing. Grandfather is going abroad to take the waters and he wants you and me to come too. The idea is that you'll go to school at Grenoble or Montreux for the rest of the year and learn the languages and we'll be close by. That is, if you want to. I know how you like St. Regis and playing football and baseball, and of course there would be none of that; but on the other hand, it would be a nice change, even if it postponed your entering Yale by an extra year. So, as usual, I want you to do just as you like. We will be leaving home almost as soon as you get this and will come to the Waldorf in New York, where you can come in and see us for a few days, even if you decide to stay. Think it over, dear.

"With love to my dearest boy,

"MOTHER."

Basil got up from his chair with a dim idea of walking over to the Waldorf and having himself locked up safely until his mother came. Then, impelled to some gesture, he raised his voice and in one of his first basso notes called boomingly and without reticence for the waiter. No more St. Regis! No more St. Regis! He was almost strangling with happiness.

"Oh, gosh!" he cried to himself. "Oh, golly! Oh, gosh! Oh, gosh!" No more Doctor Bacon and Mr. Rooney and Brick Wales and Fat Gaspar. No more Bugs Brown and on bounds and being called Bossy. He need no longer hate them, for they were impotent shadows in the stationary world that he was sliding away from, sliding past, waving his hand. "Good-by!" He pitied them. "Good-by!"

It required the din of Forty-second Street to sober his maudlin joy. With his hand on his purse to guard against the omnipresent pickpocket, he moved cautiously toward Broadway. What a day! He would tell Mr. Rooney—Why, he needn't ever go back! Or perhaps it would be better to go back and let them know what he was going to do, while they went on and on in the dismal, dreary round of school.

He found the theater and entered the lobby with its powdery feminine atmosphere of a matinée. As he took out his ticket, his gaze was caught and held by a sculptured profile a few feet away. It was that of a well-built blond young man of about twenty with a strong chin and direct gray eyes. Basil's brain spun wildly for a moment and then came to rest upon a name—more than a name—upon a legend, a sign in the sky. What a day! He had never seen the young man before, but from a thousand pictures he knew beyond the possibility of a doubt that it was Ted Fay, the Yale football captain, who had almost single-handed beaten Harvard and Princeton last fall. Basil felt a sort of exquisite pain. The profile turned away; the crowd revolved; the hero disappeared. But Basil would know all through the next hours that Ted Fay was here too.

In the rustling, whispering, sweet-smelling darkness of the theater he read the program. It was the show of all shows that he wanted to see, and until the curtain actually rose the program itself had a curious sacredness—a prototype of the thing itself. But when the curtain rose it became waste paper to be dropped carelessly to the floor.

ACT I. *The Village Green of a Small Town near New York.*

It was too bright and binding to comprehend all at once, and it went so fast that from the very first Basil felt he had missed things; he would make his mother take him again when she came—next week—tomorrow.

An hour passed. It was very sad at this point—a sort of gay sadness, but sad. The girl—the man. What kept them apart even now? Oh, those tragic errors and misconceptions. So sad. Couldn't they look into each other's eyes and *see*?

In a blaze of light and sound, of resolution, anticipation and imminent trouble, the act was over.

He went out. He looked for Ted Fay and thought he saw him leaning rather moodily on the plush wall at the rear of the theater, but he could not be sure. He bought cigarettes and lit one, but fancying at the first puff that he heard a blare of music he rushed back inside.

Act II. *The Foyer of the Hotel Astor.*

Yes, she was, indeed, like that song—a Beautiful Rose of the Night. The waltz buoyed her up, brought her with it to a point of aching beauty and then let her slide back to life across its last bars as a leaf slants to earth across the air. The high life of New York! Who could blame her if she was carried away by the glitter of it all, vanishing into the bright morning of the amber window borders, or into distant and entrancing music as the door opened and closed that led to the ballroom? The toast of the shining town.

Half an hour passed. Her true love brought her roses like herself and she threw them scornfully at his feet. She laughed and turned to the other, and danced—danced madly, wildly. Wait! That delicate treble among the thin horns, the low curving note from the great strings. There it was again, poignant and aching, sweeping like a great gust of emotion across the stage, catching her again like a leaf helpless in the wind:

"Rose—Rose—Rose of the night,
When the spring moon is bright you'll be fair——"

A few minutes later, feeling oddly shaken and exalted, Basil drifted outside with the crowd. The first thing upon which his eyes fell was the almost forgotten and now curiously metamorphosed specter of Mr. Rooney.

Mr. Rooney had, in fact, gone a little to pieces. He was, to begin with, wearing a different and much smaller hat than when he left Basil at noon. Secondly, his face had lost its somewhat gross aspect and turned a pure and even delicate white, and he was wearing his necktie and even portions of his shirt on the outside of his unaccountably wringing-wet overcoat. How, in the short space of four hours, Mr. Rooney had got himself in such shape is explicable only by the pressure of confinement in a boys' school upon a fiery outdoor spirit. Mr. Rooney was born to toil under the clear light of heaven and, perhaps half consciously, he was headed toward his inevitable destiny.

"Lee," he said dimly, "you ought get wise to y'self. I'm going to put you wise y'self."

To avoid the ominous possibility of being put wise to himself in the lobby, Basil uneasily changed the subject.

"Aren't you coming to the show?" he asked, flattering Mr. Rooney by implying that he was in any condition to come to the show. "It's a wonderful show."

Mr. Rooney took off his hat, displaying wringing-wet matted hair. A picture of reality momentarily struggled for development in the back of his brain.

"We got to get back to school," he said in a somber and unconvinced voice.

"But there's another act," protested Basil in horror. "I've got to stay for the last act."

Swaying, Mr. Rooney looked at Basil, dimly realizing that he had put himself in the hollow of this boy's hand.

"All righ'," he admitted. "I'm going to get somethin' to eat. I'll wait for you next door."

He turned abruptly, reeled a dozen steps and curved dizzily into a bar adjoining the theater. Considerably shaken, Basil went back inside.

ACT III. *The Roof Garden of Mr. Van Astor's House. Night.*

Half an hour passed. Everything was going to be all right, after all. The comedian was at his best now, with the glad appropriateness of laughter after tears, and there was a promise of felicity in the bright tropical sky. One lovely plaintive duet, and then abruptly the long moment of incomparable beauty was over.

Basil went into the lobby and stood in thought while the crowd passed out. His mother's letter and the show had cleared his mind of bitterness and vindictiveness—he was his old self and he wanted to do the right thing. He wondered if it was the right thing to get Mr. Rooney back to school. He walked toward the saloon, slowed up as he came to it and, gingerly opening the swinging door, took a quick peer inside. He saw only that Mr. Rooney was not one of those drinking at the bar. He walked down the street a little way, came back and tried again. It was as if he thought the doors were teeth to bite him, for he had the old-fashioned Middle-Western boy's horror of the saloon. The third time he was successful. Mr. Rooney was sound asleep at a table in the back of the room.

Outside again Basil walked up and down, considering. He would give Mr. Rooney half an hour. If, at the end of that time, he had not come out, he would go back to school. After all, Mr. Rooney had laid for him ever since football season—Basil was simply washing his hands of the whole affair, as in a day or so he would wash his hands of school.

He had made several turns up and down, when, glancing up an alley that ran beside the theater his eye was caught by the sign, Stage Entrance. He could watch the actors come forth.

He waited. Women streamed by him, but those were the days before Glorification and he took these drab people for wardrobe women or something. Then suddenly a girl came out and with her a man, and Basil turned and ran a few steps up the street as if afraid they would recognize him—and ran back, breathing as if with a heart attack—for the girl, a radiant little beauty of nineteen, was Her and the young man by her side was Ted Fay.

Arm in arm, they walked past him, and irresistibly Basil followed. As they walked, she leaned toward Ted Fay in a way that gave them a fascinating air of intimacy. They crossed Broadway and turned into the Knickerbocker Hotel, and twenty feet behind them Basil followed, in time to see them go into a long room set for afternoon tea. They sat at a table for two, spoke vaguely to a waiter, and then, alone at last, bent eagerly toward each other. Basil saw that Ted Fay was holding her gloved hand.

The tea room was separated only by a hedge of potted firs from the main corridor. Basil went along this to a lounge which was almost up against their table and sat down.

Her voice was low and faltering, less certain than it had been in the play, and very sad: "Of course I do, Ted." For a long time, as their conversation continued, she repeated "Of course I do" or "But I do, Ted." Ted Fay's remarks were too low for Basil to hear.

"—— says next month, and he won't be put off any more. . . . I do in a way, Ted. It's hard to explain, but he's done everything for mother and me. . . . There's no use kidding myself. It was a fool-proof part and any girl he gave it to was made right then and there. . . . He's been awfully thoughtful. He's done everything for me."

Basil's ears were sharpened by the intensity of his emotion; now he could hear Ted Fay's voice too:

"And you say you love me."

"But don't you see I promised to marry him more than a year ago."

"Tell him the truth—that you love me. Ask him to let you off."

"This isn't musical comedy, Ted."

"That was a mean one," he said bitterly.

"I'm sorry, dear, Ted darling, but you're driving me crazy going on this way. You're making it so hard for me."

"I'm going to leave New Haven, anyhow."

"No, you're not. You're going to stay and play baseball this spring. Why, you're an ideal to all those boys! Why, if you——"

He laughed shortly. "You're a fine one to talk about ideals."

"Why not? I'm living up to my responsibility to Beltzman; you've got to make up your mind just like I have—that we can't have each other."

"Jerry! Think what you're doing! All my life, whenever I hear that waltz——"

Basil got to his feet and hurried down the corridor, through the lobby and out of the hotel. He was in a state of wild emotional confusion. He did not understand all he had heard, but from his clandestine glimpse into the privacy of these two, with all the world that his short experience could conceive of at their feet, he had gathered that life for everybody was a struggle, sometimes magnificent from a distance, but always difficult and surprisingly simple and a little sad.

They would go on. Ted Fay would go back to Yale, put her picture in his bureau drawer and knock out home runs with the bases full this spring—at 8:30 the curtain would go up and She would miss something warm and young out of her life, something she had had this afternoon.

It was dark outside and Broadway was a blazing forest fire as Basil walked slowly along toward the point of brightest light. He looked up at the great intersecting planes of radiance with a vague sense of approval and possession. He would see it a lot now, lay his restless heart upon this greater restlessness of a nation—he would come whenever he could get off from school.

But that was all changed—he was going to Europe. Suddenly Basil realized that he wasn't going to Europe. He could not forego the molding of his own destiny just to alleviate a few months of pain. The conquest of the successive worlds of school, college and New York —why, that was his true dream that he had carried from boyhood into adolescence, and because of the jeers of a few boys he had been about to abandon it and run ignominiously up a back alley! He shivered violently, like a dog coming out of the water, and simultaneously he was reminded of Mr. Rooney.

A few minutes later he walked into the bar, past the quizzical eyes of the bartender and up to the table where Mr. Rooney still sat asleep. Basil shook him gently, then firmly. Mr. Rooney stirred and perceived Basil.

"G'wise to yourself," he muttered drowsily. "G'wise to yourself an' let me alone."

"I am wise to myself," said Basil. "Honest, I am wise to myself, Mr. Rooney. You got to come with me into the washroom and get cleaned up, and then you can sleep on the train again, Mr. Rooney. Come on, Mr. Rooney, please——"

V

IT WAS a long hard time. Basil got on bounds again in December and wasn't free again until March. An indulgent mother had given him no habits of work and this was almost beyond the power of anything but life itself to remedy, but he made numberless new starts and failed and tried again.

He made friends with a new boy named Maplewood after Christmas, but they had a silly quarrel; and through the winter term, when a boys' school is shut in with itself and only partly assuaged from its natural savagery by indoor sports, Basil was snubbed and slighted a good deal for his real and imaginary sins, and he was much alone. But on the other hand, there was Ted Fay, and Rose of the Night on the phonograph—"All my life whenever I hear that waltz"—and the remembered lights of New York, and the thought of what he was going to do in football next autumn and the glamorous mirage of Yale and the hope of spring in the air.

Fat Gasper and a few others were nice to him now. Once when he and Fat walked home together by accident from downtown they had a long talk about actresses—a talk that Basil was wise enough not to presume upon afterward. The smaller boys suddenly decided that they approved of him, and a master who had hitherto disliked him put his hand on his shoulder walking to a class one day. They would all forget eventually—maybe during the summer. There would be new fresh boys in September; he would have a clean start next year.

One afternoon in February, playing basketball, a great thing happened. He and Brick Wales were at forward on the second team and in the fury of the scrimmage the gymnasium echoed with sharp slapping contacts and shrill cries.

"Here yar!"

"Bill! Bill!"

Basil had dribbled the ball down the court and Brick Wales, free, was crying for it.

"Here yar! Lee! Hey! Lee-y!"

Lee-y!

Basil flushed and made a poor pass. He had been called by a nickname. It was a poor makeshift, but it was something more than the stark bareness of his surname or a term of derision. Brick Wales went on playing, unconscious that he had done anything in particular or that he had contributed to the events by which another boy was saved from the army of the bitter, the selfish, the neurasthenic and the unhappy. It isn't given to us to know those rare moments when people are wide open and the lightest touch can wither or heal. A moment too late and we can never reach them any more in this world. They will not be cured by our most efficacious drugs or slain with our sharpest swords.

Lee-y! It could scarcely be pronounced. But Basil took it to bed with him that night, and thinking of it, holding it to him happily to the last, fell easily to sleep.

CRAZY SUNDAY

I

IT WAS Sunday—not a day, but rather a gap between two other days. Behind, for all of them, lay sets and sequences, the long waits under the crane that swung the microphone, the hundred miles a day by automobiles to and fro across a county, the struggles of rival ingenuities in the conference rooms, the ceaseless compromise, the clash and strain of many personalities fighting for their lives. And now Sunday, with individual life starting up again, with a glow kindling in eyes that had been glazed with monotony the afternoon before. Slowly as the hours waned they came awake like "Puppenfeen" in a toy shop: an intense colloquy in a corner, lovers disappearing to neck in a hall. And the feeling of "Hurry, it's not too late, but for God's sake hurry before the blessed forty hours of leisure are over."

Joel Coles was writing continuity. He was twenty-eight and not yet broken by Hollywood. He had had what were considered nice assignments since his arrival six months before and he submitted his scenes and sequences with enthusiasm. He referred to himself modestly as a hack but really did not think of it that way. His mother had been a successful actress; Joel had spent his childhood between London and New York trying to separate the real from the unreal, or at least to keep one guess ahead. He was a handsome man with the pleasant cow-brown eyes that in 1913 had gazed out at Broadway audiences from his mother's face.

When the invitation came it made him sure that he was getting somewhere. Ordinarily he did not go out on Sundays but stayed sober and took work home with him. Recently they had given him a Eugene O'Neill play destined for a very important lady indeed. Everything he had done so far had pleased Miles Calman, and Miles Calman was the only director on the lot who did not work under a supervisor and was responsible to the money men alone. Everything was clicking into place in Joel's career. ("This is Mr. Calman's secretary. Will you come to tea from four to six Sunday—he lives in Beverly Hills, number——.")

Joel was flattered. It would be a party out of the top-drawer. It was a tribute to himself as a young man of promise. The Marion Davies' crowd, the high-hats, the big currency numbers, perhaps even Dietrich and Garbo and the Marquise, people who were not seen everywhere, would probably be at Calman's.

"I won't take anything to drink," he assured himself. Calman was audibly tired of rummies, and thought it was a pity the industry could not get along without them.

Joel agreed that writers drank too much—he did himself, but he wouldn't this afternoon. He wished Miles would be within hearing when the cocktails were passed to hear his succinct, unobtrusive, "No, thank you."

Miles Calman's house was built for great emotional moments—there was an air of listening, as if the far silences of its vistas hid an audience, but this afternoon it was thronged, as though people had been bidden rather than asked. Joel noted with pride that only two other writers from the studio were in the crowd, an ennobled limey and, somewhat to his surprise, Nat Keogh, who had evoked Calman's impatient comment on drunks.

Stella Calman (Stella Walker, of course) did not move on to her other guests after she spoke to Joel. She lingered—she looked at him with the sort of beautiful look that demands some sort of acknowledgment and Joel drew quickly on the dramatic adequacy inherited from his mother:

"Well, you look about sixteen! Where's your kiddy car?"

She was visibly pleased; she lingered. He felt that he should say something more, something confident and easy—he had first met her when she was struggling for bits in New York. At the moment a tray slid up and Stella put a cocktail glass into his hand.

"Everybody's afraid, aren't they?" he said, looking at it absently. "Everybody watches for everybody else's blunders, or tries to make sure they're with people that'll do them credit. Of course that's not true in your house," he covered himself hastily. "I just meant generally in Hollywood."

Stella agreed. She presented several people to Joel as if he were very important. Reassuring himself that Miles was at the other side of the room, Joel drank the cocktail.

"So you have a baby?" he said. "That's the time to look out. After a pretty woman has had her first child, she's very vulnerable, because she wants to be reassured about her own charm. She's got to have some new man's unqualified devotion to prove to herself she hasn't lost anything."

"I never get anybody's unqualified devotion," Stella said rather resentfully.

"They're afraid of your husband."

"You think that's it?" She wrinkled her brow over the idea; then the conversation was interrupted at the exact moment Joel would have chosen.

Her attentions had given him confidence. Not for him to join safe groups, to slink to refuge under the wings of such acquaintances as he saw about the room. He walked to the window and looked out toward the Pacific, colorless under its sluggish sunset. It was good here—the American Riviera and all that, if there were ever time to enjoy it. The handsome, well-dressed people in the room, the lovely girls, and the—well, the lovely girls. You couldn't have everything.

He saw Stella's fresh boyish face, with the tired eyelid that always drooped a little over one eye, moving about among her guests and he wanted to sit with her and talk a long time as if she were a girl instead of a name; he followed her to see if she paid anyone as much attention as she had paid him. He took another cocktail—not because he needed confidence but because she had given him so much of it. Then he sat down beside the director's mother.

"Your son's gotten to be a legend, Mrs. Calman—Oracle and a Man of Destiny and all that. Personally, I'm against him but I'm in a minority. What do you think of him? Are you impressed? Are you surprised how far he's gone?"

"No, I'm not surprised," she said calmly. "We always expected a lot from Miles."

"Well now, that's unusual," remarked Joel. "I always think all mothers are like Napoleon's mother. My mother didn't want me to have anything to do with the entertainment business. She wanted me to go to West Point and be safe."

"We always had every confidence in Miles." . . .

He stood by the built-in bar of the dining room with the good-humored, heavy-drinking, highly paid Nat Keogh.

"—I made a hundred grand during the year and lost forty grand gambling, so now I've hired a manager."

"You mean an agent," suggested Joel.

"No, I've got that too. I mean a manager. I make over everything to my wife and then he and my wife get together and hand me out the money. I pay him five thousand a year to hand me out my money."

"You mean your agent."

"No, I mean my manager, and I'm not the only one—a lot of other irresponsible people have him."

"Well, if you're irresponsible why are you responsible enough to hire a manager?"

"I'm just irresponsible about gambling. Look here——"

A singer performed; Joel and Nat went forward with the others to listen.

II

THE SINGING reached Joel vaguely; he felt happy and friendly toward all the people gathered there, people of bravery and industry, superior to a bourgeoisie that outdid them in ignorance and loose living, risen to a position of the highest prominence in a nation that for a decade had wanted only to be entertained. He liked them—he loved them. Great waves of good feeling flowed through him.

As the singer finished his number and there was a drift toward the hostess to say good-by, Joel had an idea. He would give them "Building It Up," his own composition. It was his only parlor trick, it had amused several parties and it might please Stella Walker. Possessed by the hunch, his blood throbbing with the scarlet corpuscles of exhibitionism, he sought her.

"Of course," she cried. "Please! Do you need anything?"

"Someone has to be the secretary that I'm supposed to be dictating to."

"I'll be her."

As the word spread, the guests in the hall, already putting on their coats to leave, drifted back and Joel faced the eyes of many strangers. He had a dim foreboding, realizing that the man who had just performed was a famous radio entertainer. Then someone said "Sh!" and he was alone with Stella, the center of a sinister Indian-like half-circle. Stella smiled up at him expectantly—he began.

His burlesque was based upon the cultural limitations of Mr. Dave Silverstein, an independent producer;

Silverstein was presumed to be dictating a letter outlining a treatment of a story he had bought.

"—a story of divorce, the younger generators and the Foreign Legion," he heard his voice saying, with the intonations of Mr. Silverstein. "But we got to build it up, see?"

A sharp pang of doubt struck through him. The faces surrounding him in the gently molded light were intent and curious, but there was no ghost of a smile anywhere; directly in front the Great Lover of the screen glared at him with an eye as keen as the eye of a potato. Only Stella Walker looked up at him with a radiant, never faltering smile.

"If we make him a Menjou type, then we get a sort of Michael Arlen only with a Honolulu atmosphere."

Still not a ripple in front, but in the rear a rustling, a perceptible shift toward the left, toward the front door.

"—then she says she feels this sex appil for him and he burns out and says 'Oh, go on destroy yourself——"

At some point he heard Nat Keogh snicker and here and there were a few encouraging faces, but as he finished he had the sickening realization that he had made a fool of himself in view of an important section of the picture world, upon whose favor depended his career.

For a moment he existed in the midst of a confused silence, broken by a general trek for the door. He felt the undercurrent of derision that rolled through the gossip; then—all this was in the space of ten seconds—the Great Lover, his eye hard and empty as the eye of a needle, shouted "Boo! Boo!" voicing in an overtone what he felt was the mood of the crowd. It was the resentment of the professional toward the amateur, of the community toward the stranger, the thumbs-down of the clan.

Only Stella Walker was still standing near and thanking him as if he had been an unparalleled success, as if it hadn't occurred to her that anyone hadn't liked it. As Nat Keogh helped him into his overcoat, a great wave of self-disgust swept over him and he clung desperately to his rule of never betraying an inferior emotion until he no longer felt it.

"I was a flop," he said lightly, to Stella. "Never mind, it's a good number when appreciated. Thanks for your coöperation."

The smile did not leave her face—he bowed rather drunkenly and Nat drew him toward the door. . . .

The arrival of his breakfast awakened him into a broken and ruined world. Yesterday he was himself, a point of fire against an industry, today he felt that he was pitted under an enormous disadvantage, against those faces, against individual contempt and collective sneer. Worse than that, to Miles Calman he was become one of those rummies, stripped of dignity, whom Calman regretted he was compelled to use. To Stella Walker, on whom he had forced a martyrdom to preserve the courtesy of her house—her opinion he did not dare to guess. His gastric juices ceased to flow and he set his poached eggs back on the telephone table. He wrote:

"Dear Miles: You can imagine my profound self-disgust. I confess to a taint of exhibitionism, but at six o'clock in the afternoon, in broad daylight! Good God! My apologies to your wife.

"Yours ever,

"Joel Coles."

Joel emerged from his office on the lot only to slink like a malefactor to the tobacco store. So suspicious was his manner that one of the studio police asked to see his admission card. He had decided to eat lunch outside when Nat Keogh, confident and cheerful, overtook him.

"What do you mean you're in permanent retirement? What if that Three-Piece Suit did boo you?

"Why, listen," he continued, drawing Joel into the studio restaurant. "The night of one of his premiers at Grauman's, Joe Squires kicked his tail while he was bowing to the crowd. The ham said Joe'd hear from him later but when Joe called him up at eight o'clock next day and said, 'I thought I was going to hear from you,' he hung up the phone."

The preposterous story cheered Joel, and he found a gloomy consolation in staring at the group at the next table, the sad, lovely Siamese twins, the mean dwarfs, the proud giant from the circus picture. But looking beyond at the yellow-stained faces of pretty women, their eyes all melancholy and startling with mascara, their ball gowns garish in full day, he saw a group who had been at Calmans' and winced.

"Never again," he exclaimed aloud, "absolutely my last social appearance in Hollywood!"

The following morning a telegram was waiting for him at his office:

> "You were one of the most agreeable people at our party. Expect you at my sister June's buffet supper next Sunday.
>
> "STELLA WALKER CALMAN."

The blood rushed fast through his veins for a feverish minute. Incredulously he read the telegram over.

"Well, that's the sweetest thing I ever heard of in my life!"

III

CRAZY SUNDAY again. Joel slept until eleven, then he read a newspaper to catch up with the past week. He lunched in his room on trout, avocado salad and a pint of California wine. Dressing for the tea, he selected a pin-check suit, a blue shirt, a burnt orange tie. There were dark circles of fatigue under his eyes. In his second-hand car he drove to the Riviera apartments. As he was introducing himself to Stella's sister, Miles and Stella arrived in riding clothes—they had been quarreling fiercely most of the afternoon on all the dirt roads back of Beverly Hills.

Miles Calman, tall, nervous, with a desperate humor and the unhappiest eyes Joel ever saw, was an artist from the top of his curiously shaped head to his niggerish feet. Upon these last he stood firmly—he had never made a cheap picture though he had sometimes paid heavily for the luxury of making experimental flops. In spite of his excellent company, one could not be with him long without realizing that he was not a well man.

From the moment of their entrance Joel's day bound itself up inextricably with theirs. As he joined the group around them Stella turned away from it with an impatient little tongue click—and Miles Calman said to the man who happened to be next to him:

"Go easy on Eva Goebel. There's hell to pay about her at home." Miles turned to Joel, "I'm sorry I missed you at the office yesterday. I spent the afternoon at the analyst's."

"You being psychoanalyzed?"

"I have been for months. First I went for claustrophobia, now I'm trying to get my whole life cleared up. They say it'll take over a year."

"There's nothing the matter with your life," Joel assured him.

"Oh, no? Well, Stella seems to think so. Ask anybody—they can all tell you about it," he said bitterly.

A girl perched herself on the arm of Miles' chair; Joel crossed to Stella, who stood disconsolately by the fire.

"Thank you for your telegram," he said. "It was darn sweet. I can't imagine anybody as good-looking as you are being so good-humored."

She was a little lovelier than he had ever seen her and perhaps the unstinted admiration in his eyes prompted her to unload on him—it did not take long, for she was obviously at the emotional bursting point.

"—and Miles has been carrying on this thing for two years, and I never knew. Why, she was one of my best friends, always in the house. Finally when people began to come to me, Miles had to admit it."

She sat down vehemently on the arm of Joel's chair. Her riding breeches were the color of the chair and Joel saw that the mass of her hair was made up of some strands of red gold and some of pale gold, so that it could not be dyed, and that she had on no make-up. She was that good-looking——

Still quivering with the shock of her discovery, Stella found unbearable the spectacle of a new girl hovering over Miles; she led Joel into a bedroom, and seated at either end of a big bed they went on talking. People on their way to the washroom glanced in and made wisecracks, but Stella, emptying out her story, paid no attention. After a while Miles stuck his head in the door and said, "There's no use trying to explain something to Joel in half an hour that I don't understand myself and the psychoanalyst says will take a whole year to understand."

She talked on as if Miles were not there. She loved Miles, she said—under considerable difficulties she had always been faithful to him.

"The psychoanalyst told Miles that he had a mother complex. In his first marriage he transferred his mother complex to his wife, you see—and then his sex turned to me. But when we married the thing repeated itself—

he transferred his mother complex to me and all his libido turned toward this other woman."

Joel knew that this probably wasn't gibberish—yet it sounded like gibberish. He knew Eva Goebel; she was a motherly person, older and probably wiser than Stella, who was a golden child.

Miles now suggested impatiently that Joel come back with them since Stella had so much to say, so they drove out to the mansion in Beverly Hills. Under the high ceilings the situation seemed more dignified and tragic. It was an eerie bright night with the dark very clear outside of all the windows and Stella all rose-gold raging and crying around the room. Joel did not quite believe in picture actresses' grief. They have other preoccupations—they are beautiful rose-gold figures blown full of life by writers and directors, and after hours they sit around and talk in whispers and giggle innuendoes, and the ends of many adventures flow through them.

Sometimes he pretended to listen and instead thought how well she was got up—sleek breeches with a matched set of legs in them, an Italian-colored sweater with a little high neck, and a short brown chamois coat. He couldn't decide whether she was an imitation of an English lady or an English lady was an imitation of her. She hovered somewhere between the realest of realities and the most blatant of impersonations.

"Miles is so jealous of me that he questions everything I do," she cried scornfully. "When I was in New York I wrote him that I'd been to the theater with Eddie Baker. Miles was so jealous he phoned me ten times in one day."

"I was wild," Miles snuffled sharply, a habit he had in times of stress. "The analyst couldn't get any results for a week."

Stella shook her head despairingly. "Did you expect me just to sit in the hotel for three weeks?"

"I don't expect anything. I admit that I'm jealous. I try not to be. I worked on that with Dr. Bridgebane, but it didn't do any good. I was jealous of Joel this afternoon when you sat on the arm of his chair."

"You were?" She started up. "You were! Wasn't there somebody on the arm of your chair? And did you speak to me for two hours?"

"You were telling your troubles to Joel in the bedroom."

"When I think that that woman"—she seemed to believe that to omit Eva Goebel's name would be to lessen her reality—"used to come here——"

"All right—all right," said Miles wearily. "I've admitted everything and I feel as bad about it as you do." Turning to Joel he began talking about pictures, while Stella moved restlessly along the far walls, her hands in her breeches pockets.

"They've treated Miles terribly," she said, coming suddenly back into the conversation as if they'd never discussed her personal affairs. "Dear, tell him about old Beltzer trying to change your picture."

As she stood hovering protectively over Miles, her eyes flashing with indignation in his behalf, Joel realized that he was in love with her. Stifled with excitement he got up to say good night.

With Monday the week resumed its workaday rhythm, in sharp contrast to the theoretical discussions, the gossip and scandal of Sunday; there was the endless detail of script revision—"Instead of a lousy dissolve, we can leave her voice on the sound track and cut to a medium shot of the taxi from Bell's angle or we can simply pull the camera back to include the station, hold it a minute and then pam to the row of taxis"—by Monday afternoon Joel had again forgotten that people whose business was to provide entertainment were ever privileged to be entertained. In the evening he phoned Miles' house. He asked for Miles but Stella came to the phone.

"Do things seem better?"

"Not particularly. What are you doing next Saturday evening?"

"Nothing."

"The Perrys are giving a dinner and theater party and Miles won't be here—he's flying to South Bend to see the Notre Dame-California game, I thought you might go with me in his place."

After a long moment Joel said, "Why—surely. If there's a conference I can't make dinner but I can get to the theater."

"Then I'll say we can come."

Joel walked his office. In view of the strained relations of the Calmans, would Miles be pleased, or did she intend that Miles shouldn't know of it? That would be out of the question—if Miles didn't mention it Joel would. But it was an hour or more before he could get down to work again.

Wednesday there was a four-hour wrangle in a conference room crowded with planets and nebulæ of cigarette smoke. Three men and a woman paced the carpet in turn, suggesting or condemning, speaking sharply or persuasively, confidently or despairingly. At the end Joel lingered to talk to Miles.

The man was tired—not with the exaltation of fatigue but life-tired, with his lids sagging and his beard prominent over the blue shadows near his mouth.

"I hear you're flying to the Notre Dame game."

Miles looked beyond him and shook his head.

"I've given up the idea."

"Why?"

"On account of you." Still he did not look at Joel.

"What the hell, Miles?"

"That's why I've given it up." He broke into a perfunctory laugh at himself. "I can't tell what Stella might do just out of spite—she's invited you to take her to the Perrys', hasn't she? I wouldn't enjoy the game."

The fine instinct that moved swiftly and confidently on the set, muddled so weakly and helplessly through his personal life.

"Look, Miles," Joel said frowning. "I've never made any passes whatsoever at Stella. If you're really seriously canceling your trip on account of me, I won't go to the Perrys' with her. I won't see her. You can trust me absolutely."

Miles looked at him, carefully now.

"Maybe." He shrugged his shoulders. "Anyhow there'd just be somebody else. I wouldn't have any fun."

"You don't seem to have much confidence in Stella. She told me she'd always been true to you."

"Maybe she has." In the last few minutes several more muscles had sagged around Miles' mouth, "But how can I ask anything of her after what's happened? How can I expect her—" He broke off and his face grew harder as he said, "I'll tell you one thing, right or wrong and no matter what I've done, if I ever had anything on her I'd divorce her. I can't have my pride hurt—that would be the last straw."

His tone annoyed Joel, but he said:

"Hasn't she calmed down about the Eva Goebel thing?"

"No." Miles snuffled pessimistically. "I can't get over it either."

"I thought it was finished."

"I'm trying not to see Eva again, but you know it isn't

easy just to drop something like that—it isn't some girl I kissed last night in a taxi! The psychoanalyst says——"

"I know," Joel interrupted. "Stella told me." This was depressing. "Well, as far as I'm concerned if you go to the game I won't see Stella. And I'm sure Stella has nothing on her conscience about anybody."

"Maybe not," Miles repeated listlessly. "Anyhow I'll stay and take her to the party. Say," he said suddenly, "I wish you'd come too. I've got to have somebody sympathetic to talk to. That's the trouble—I've influenced Stella in everything. Especially I've influenced her so that she likes all the men I like—it's very difficult."

"It must be," Joel agreed.

IV

JOEL could not get to the dinner. Self-conscious in his silk hat against the unemployment, he waited for the others in front of the Hollywood Theater and watched the evening parade: obscure replicas of bright, particular picture stars, spavined men in polo coats, a stomping dervish with the beard and staff of an apostle, a pair of chic Filipinos in collegiate clothes, reminder that this corner of the Republic opened to the seven seas, a long fantastic carnival of young shouts which proved to be a fraternity initiation. The line split to pass two smart limousines that stopped at the curb.

There she was, in a dress like ice-water, made in a thousand pale-blue pieces, with icicles trickling at the throat. He started forward.

"So you like my dress?"

"Where's Miles?"

"He flew to the game after all. He left yesterday

morning—at least I think—" She broke off. "I just got a telegram from South Bend saying that he's starting back. I forgot—you know all these people?"

The party of eight moved into the theater.

Miles had gone after all and Joel wondered if he should have come. But during the performance, with Stella a profile under the pure grain of light hair, he thought no more about Miles. Once he turned and looked at her and she looked back at him, smiling and meeting his eyes for as long as he wanted. Between the acts they smoked in the lobby and she whispered:

"They're all going to the opening of Jack Johnson's night club—I don't want to go, do you?"

"Do we have to?"

"I suppose not." She hesitated. "I'd like to talk to you. I suppose we could go to our house—if I were only sure——"

Again she hesitated and Joel asked:

"Sure of what?"

"Sure that—oh, I'm haywire I know, but how can I be sure Miles went to the game?"

"You mean you think he's with Eva Goebel?"

"No, not so much that—but supposing he was here watching everything I do. You know Miles does odd things sometimes. Once he wanted a man with a long beard to drink tea with him and he sent down to the casting agency for one, and drank tea with him all afternoon."

"That's different. He sent you a wire from South Bend—that proves he's at the game."

After the play they said good night to the others at the curb and were answered by looks of amusement. They slid off along the golden garish thoroughfare through the crowd that had gathered around Stella.

"You see he could arrange the telegrams," Stella said, "very easily."

That was true. And with the idea that perhaps her uneasiness was justified, Joel grew angry: if Miles had trained a camera on them he felt no obligations toward Miles. Aloud he said:

"That's nonsense."

There were Christmas trees already in the shop windows and the full moon over the boulevard was only a prop, as scenic as the giant boudoir lamps of the corners. On into the dark foliage of Beverly Hills that flamed as eucalyptus by day, Joel saw only the flash of a white face under his own, the arc of her shoulder. She pulled away suddenly and looked up at him.

"Your eyes are like your mother's," she said. "I used to have a scrap book full of pictures of her."

"Your eyes are like your own and not a bit like any other eyes," he answered.

Something made Joel look out into the grounds as they went into the house, as if Miles were lurking in the shrubbery. A telegram waited on the hall table. She read aloud:

"CHICAGO.

"Home tomorrow night. Thinking of you. Love.

"MILES."

"You see," she said, throwing the slip back on the table, "he could easily have faked that." She asked the butler for drinks and sandwiches and ran upstairs, while Joel walked into the empty reception rooms. Strolling about he wandered to the piano where he had stood in disgrace two Sundays before.

"Then we could put over," he said aloud, "a story of divorce, the younger generators and the Foreign Legion."

His thoughts jumped to another telegram.

"You were one of the most agreeable people at our party——"

An idea occurred to him. If Stella's telegram had been purely a gesture of courtesy then it was likely that Miles had inspired it, for it was Miles who had invited him. Probably Miles had said:

"Send him a wire—he's miserable—he thinks he's queered himself."

It fitted in with "I've influenced Stella in everything. Especially I've influenced her so that she likes all the men I like." A woman would do a thing like that because she felt sympathetic—only a man would do it because he felt responsible.

When Stella came back into the room he took both her hands.

"I have a strange feeling that I'm a sort of pawn in a spite game you're playing against Miles," he said.

"Help yourself to a drink."

"And the odd thing is that I'm in love with you anyhow."

The telephone rang and she freed herself to answer it.

"Another wire from Miles," she announced. "He dropped it, or it says he dropped it, from the airplane at Kansas City."

"I suppose he asked to be remembered to me."

"No, he just said he loved me. I believe he does. He's so very weak."

"Come sit beside me," Joel urged her.

It was early. And it was still a few minutes short of midnight a half-hour later, when Joel walked to the cold hearth, and said tersely:

"Meaning that you haven't any curiosity about me?"

"Not at all. You attract me a lot and you know it. The point is that I suppose I really do love Miles."

"Obviously."

"And tonight I feel uneasy about everything."

He wasn't angry—he was even faintly relieved that a possible entanglement was avoided. Still as he looked at her, the warmth and softness of her body thawing her cold blue costume, he knew she was one of the things he would always regret.

"I've got to go," he said. "I'll phone a taxi."

"Nonsense—there's a chauffeur on duty."

He winced at her readiness to have him go, and seeing this she kissed him lightly and said, "You're sweet, Joel." Then suddenly three things happened: he took down his drink at a gulp, the phone rang loud through the house and a clock in the hall struck in trumpet notes.

Nine—ten—eleven—twelve——

V

IT WAS Sunday again. Joel realized that he had come to the theater this evening with the work of the week still hanging about him like cerements. He had made love to Stella as he might attack some matter to be cleaned up hurriedly before the day's end. But this was Sunday—the lovely, lazy perspective of the next twenty-four hours unrolled before him—every minute was something to be approached with lulling indirection, every moment held the germ of innumerable possibilities. Nothing was impossible—everything was just beginning. He poured himself another drink.

With a sharp moan, Stella slipped forward inertly by the telephone. Joel picked her up and laid her on the sofa. He squirted soda-water on a handkerchief and slapped it over her face. The telephone mouthpiece was still grinding and he put it to his ear.

"—the plane fell just this side of Kansas City. The body of Miles Calman has been identified and——"

He hung up the receiver.

"Lie still," he said, stalling, as Stella opened her eyes.

"Oh, what's happened?" she whispered. "Call them back. Oh, what's happened?"

"I'll call them right away. What's your doctor's name?"

"Did they say Miles was dead?"

"Lie quiet—is there a servant still up?"

"Hold me—I'm frightened."

He put his arm around her.

"I want the name of your doctor," he said sternly. "It may be a mistake but I want someone here."

"It's Doctor—Oh, God, is Miles dead?"

Joel ran upstairs and searched through strange medicine cabinets for spirits of ammonia. When he came down Stella cried:

"He isn't dead—I know he isn't. This is part of his scheme. He's torturing me. I know he's alive. I can feel he's alive."

"I want to get hold of some close friend of yours, Stella. You can't stay here alone tonight."

"Oh, no," she cried. "I can't see anybody. You stay. I haven't got any friend." She got up, tears streaming down her face. "Oh, Miles is my only friend. He's not dead—he can't be dead. I'm going there right away and see. Get a train. You'll have to come with me."

"You can't. There's nothing to do tonight. I want you to tell me the name of some woman I can call: Lois? Joan? Carmel? Isn't there somebody?"

Stella stared at him blindly.

"Eva Goebel was my best friend," she said.

Joel thought of Miles, his sad and desperate face in

the office two days before. In the awful silence of his death all was clear about him. He was the only American-born director with both an interesting temperament and an artistic conscience. Meshed in an industry, he had paid with his ruined nerves for having no resilience, no healthy cynicism, no refuge—only a pitiful and precarious escape.

There was a sound at the outer door—it opened suddenly, and there were footsteps in the hall.

"Miles!" Stella screamed. "Is it you, Miles? Oh, it's Miles."

A telegraph boy appeared in the doorway.

"I couldn't find the bell. I heard you talking inside."

The telegram was a duplicate of the one that had been phoned. While Stella read it over and over, as though it were a black lie, Joel telephoned. It was still early and he had difficulty getting anyone; when finally he succeeded in finding some friends he made Stella take a stiff drink.

"You'll stay here, Joel," she whispered, as though she were half-asleep. "You won't go away. Miles liked you—he said you—" She shivered violently, "Oh, my God, you don't know how alone I feel." Her eyes closed, "Put your arms around me. Miles had a suit like that." She started bolt upright. "Think of what he must have felt. He was afraid of almost everything, anyhow."

She shook her head dazedly. Suddenly she seized Joel's face and held it close to hers.

"You won't go. You like me—you love me, don't you? Don't call up anybody. Tomorrow's time enough. You stay here with me tonight."

He stared at her, at first incredulously, and then with shocked understanding. In her dark groping Stella was trying to keep Miles alive by sustaining a situation in which he had figured—as if Miles' mind could not die so long as the possibilities that had worried him still existed. It was a distraught and tortured effort to stave off the realization that he was dead.

Resolutely Joel went to the phone and called a doctor.

"Don't, oh, don't call anybody!" Stella cried. "Come back here and put your arms around me."

"Is Doctor Bales in?"

"Joel," Stella cried. "I thought I could count on you. Miles liked you. He was jealous of you—Joel, come here."

Ah then—if he betrayed Miles she would be keeping him alive—for if he were really dead how could he be betrayed?

"—has just had a very severe shock. Can you come at once, and get hold of a nurse?"

"Joel!"

Now the door-bell and the telephone began to ring intermittently, and automobiles were stopping in front of the door.

"But you're not going," Stella begged him. "You're going to stay, aren't you?"

"No," he answered. "But I'll be back, if you need me."

Standing on the steps of the house which now hummed and palpitated with the life that flutters around death like protective leaves, he began to sob a little in his throat.

"Everything he touched he did something magical to," he thought. "He even brought that little gamin alive and made her a sort of masterpiece."

And then:

"What a hell of a hole he leaves in this damn wilderness—already!"

And then with a certain bitterness, "Oh, yes, I'll be back—I'll be back!"

BABYLON REVISITED

"AND where's Mr. Campbell?" Charlie asked.

"Gone to Switzerland. Mr. Campbell's a pretty sick man, Mr. Wales."

"I'm sorry to hear that. And George Hardt?" Charlie inquired.

"Back in America, gone to work."

"And where is the Snow Bird?"

"He was in here last week. Anyway, his friend, Mr. Schaeffer, is in Paris."

Two familiar names from the long list of a year and a half ago. Charlie scribbled an address in his notebook and tore out the page.

"If you see Mr. Schaeffer, give him this," he said. "It's my brother-in-law's address. I haven't settled on a hotel yet."

He was not really disappointed to find Paris was so empty. But the stillness in the Ritz bar was strange and portentous. It was not an American bar any more—he felt polite in it, and not as if he owned it. It had gone back into France. He felt the stillness from the moment he got out of the taxi and saw the doorman, usually in a frenzy of activity at this hour, gossiping with a *chasseur* by the servants' entrance.

Passing through the corridor, he heard only a single, bored voice in the once-clamorous women's room. When he turned into the bar he traveled the twenty feet of green carpet with his eyes fixed straight ahead by old habit; and then, with his foot firmly on the rail, he turned and surveyed the room, encountering only a single pair of eyes that fluttered up from a newspaper in the corner. Charlie asked for the head barman, Paul, who in the latter days of the bull market had come to work in his own custom-built car—disembarking, however, with due nicety at the nearest corner. But Paul was at his country house today and Alix giving him information.

"No, no more," Charlie said, "I'm going slow these days."

Alix congratulated him: "You were going pretty strong a couple of years ago."

"I'll stick to it all right," Charlie assured him. "I've stuck to it for over a year and a half now."

"How do you find conditions in America?"

"I haven't been to America for months. I'm in business in Prague, representing a couple of concerns there. They don't know about me down there."

Alix smiled.

"Remember the night of George Hardt's bachelor dinner here?" said Charlie. "By the way, what's become of Claude Fessenden?"

Alix lowered his voice confidentially: "He's in Paris, but he doesn't come here any more. Paul doesn't allow it. He ran up a bill of thirty thousand francs, charging all his drinks and his lunches, and usually his dinner, for more than a year. And when Paul finally told him he had to pay, he gave him a bad check."

Alix shook his head sadly.

"I don't understand it, such a dandy fellow. Now he's all bloated up—" He made a plump apple of his hands.

Charlie watched a group of strident queens installing themselves in a corner.

"Nothing affects them," he thought. "Stocks rise and

fall, people loaf or work, but they go on forever." The place oppressed him. He called for the dice and shook with Alix for the drink.

"Here for long, Mr. Wales?"

"I'm here for four or five days to see my little girl."

"Oh-h! You have a little girl?"

Outside, the fire-red, gas-blue, ghost-green signs shone smokily through the tranquil rain. It was late afternoon and the streets were in movement; the *bistros* gleamed. At the corner of the Boulevard des Capucines he took a taxi. The Place de la Concorde moved by in pink majesty; they crossed the logical Seine, and Charlie felt the sudden provincial quality of the left bank.

Charlie directed his taxi to the Avenue de l'Opera, which was out of his way. But he wanted to see the blue hour spread over the magnificent façade, and imagine that the cab horns, playing endlessly the first few bars of *Le Plus qu Lent,* were the trumpets of the Second Empire. They were closing the iron grill in front of Brentano's Book-store, and people were already at dinner behind the trim little bourgeois hedge of Duval's. He had never eaten at a really cheap restaurant in Paris. Five-course dinner, four francs fifty, eighteen cents, wine included. For some odd reason he wished that he had.

As they rolled on to the Left Bank and he felt its sudden provincialism, he thought, "I spoiled this city for myself. I didn't realize it, but the days came along one after another, and then two years were gone, and everything was gone, and I was gone."

He was thirty-five, and good to look at. The Irish mobility of his face was sobered by a deep wrinkle between his eyes. As he rang his brother-in-law's bell in the Rue Palatine, the wrinkle deepened till it pulled down his brows; he felt a cramping sensation in his belly. From behind the maid who opened the door darted a lovely little girl of nine who shrieked "Daddy!" and flew up, struggling like a fish, into his arms. She pulled his head around by one ear and set her cheek against his.

"My old pie," he said.

"Oh, daddy, daddy, daddy, daddy, dads, dads, dads!"

She drew him into the salon, where the family waited, a boy and girl his daughter's age, his sister-in-law and her husband. He greeted Marion with his voice pitched carefully to avoid either feigned enthusiasm or dislike, but her response was more frankly tepid, though she minimized her expression of unalterable distrust by directing her regard toward his child. The two men clasped hands in a friendly way and Lincoln Peters rested his for a moment on Charlie's shoulder.

The room was warm and comfortably American. The three children moved intimately about, playing through the yellow oblongs that led to other rooms; the cheer of six o'clock spoke in the eager smacks of the fire and the sounds of French activity in the kitchen. But Charlie did not relax; his heart sat up rigidly in his body and he drew confidence from his daughter, who from time to time came close to him, holding in her arms the doll he had brought.

"Really extremely well," he declared in answer to Lincoln's question. "There's a lot of business there that isn't moving at all, but we're doing even better than ever. In fact, damn well. I'm bringing my sister over from America next month to keep house for me. My income last year was bigger than it was when I had money. You see, the Czechs——"

His boasting was for a specific purpose; but after a

moment, seeing a faint restiveness in Lincoln's eye, he changed the subject:

"Those are fine children of yours, well brought up, good manners."

"We think Honoria's a great little girl too."

Marion Peters came back from the kitchen. She was a tall woman with worried eyes, who had once possessed a fresh American loveliness. Charlie had never been sensitive to it and was always surprised when people spoke of how pretty she had been. From the first there had been an instinctive antipathy between them.

"Well, how do you find Honoria?" she asked.

"Wonderful. I was astonished how much she's grown in ten months. All the children are looking well."

"We haven't had a doctor for a year. How do you like being back in Paris?"

"It seems very funny to see so few Americans around."

"I'm delighted," Marion said vehemently. "Now at least you can go into a store without their assuming you're a millionaire. We've suffered like everybody, but on the whole it's a good deal pleasanter."

"But it was nice while it lasted," Charlie said. "We were a sort of royalty, almost infallible, with a sort of magic around us. In the bar this afternoon"—he stumbled, seeing his mistake—"there wasn't a man I knew."

She looked at him keenly. "I should think you'd have had enough of bars."

"I only stayed a minute. I take one drink every afternoon, and no more."

"Don't you want a cocktail before dinner?" Lincoln asked.

"I take only one drink every afternoon, and I've had that."

"I hope you keep to it," said Marion.

Her dislike was evident in the coldness with which she spoke, but Charlie only smiled; he had larger plans. Her very aggressiveness gave him an advantage, and he knew enough to wait. He wanted them to initiate the discussion of what they knew had brought him to Paris.

At dinner he couldn't decide whether Honoria was most like him or her mother. Fortunate if she didn't combine the traits of both that had brought them to disaster. A great wave of protectiveness went over him. He thought he knew what to do for her. He believed in character; he wanted to jump back a whole generation and trust in character again as the eternally valuable element. Everything wore out.

He left soon after dinner, but not to go home. He was curious to see Paris by night with clearer and more judicious eyes than those of other days. He bought a *strapontin* for the Casino and watched Josephine Baker go through her chocolate arabesques.

After an hour he left and strolled toward Montmartre, up the Rue Pigalle into the Place Blanche. The rain had stopped and there were a few people in evening clothes disembarking from taxis in front of cabarets, and *cocottes* prowling singly or in pairs, and many Negroes. He passed a lighted door from which issued music, and stopped with the sense of familiarity; it was Bricktop's, where he had parted with so many hours and so much money. A few doors farther on he found another ancient rendezvous and incautiously put his head inside. Immediately an eager orchestra burst into sound, a pair of professional dancers leaped to their feet and a maître d'hôtel swooped toward him, crying, "Crowd just arriving, sir!" But he withdrew quickly.

"You have to be damn drunk," he thought.

Zelli's was closed, the bleak and sinister cheap hotels surrounding it were dark; up in the Rue Blanche there was more light and a local, colloquial French crowd. The Poet's Cave had disappeared, but the two great mouths of the Café of Heaven and the Café of Hell still yawned—even devoured, as he watched, the meager contents of a tourist bus—a German, a Japanese, and an American couple who glanced at him with frightened eyes.

So much for the effort and ingenuity of Montmartre. All the catering to vice and waste was on an utterly childish scale, and he suddenly realized the meaning of the word "dissipate"—to dissipate into thin air; to make nothing out of something. In the little hours of the night every move from place to place was an enormous human jump, an increase of paying for the privilege of slower and slower motion.

He remembered thousand-franc notes given to an orchestra for playing a single number, hundred-franc notes tossed to a doorman for calling a cab.

But it hadn't been given for nothing.

It had been given, even the most wildly squandered sum, as an offering to destiny that he might not remember the things most worth remembering, the things that now he would always remember—his child taken from his control, his wife escaped to a grave in Vermont.

In the glare of a *brasserie* a woman spoke to him. He bought her some eggs and coffee, and then, eluding her encouraging stare, gave her a twenty-franc note and took a taxi to his hotel.

II

HE woke upon a fine fall day—football weather. The depression of yesterday was gone and he liked the people on the streets. At noon he sat opposite Honoria at Le Grand Vatel, the only restaurant he could think of not reminiscent of champagne dinners and long luncheons that began at two and ended in a blurred and vague twilight.

"Now, how about vegetables? Oughtn't you to have some vegetables?"

"Well, yes."

"Here's *épinards* and *chou-fleur* and carrots and *haricots.*"

"I'd like *chou-fleur.*"

"Wouldn't you like to have two vegetables?"

"I usually only have one at lunch."

The waiter was pretending to be inordinately fond of children. *"Qu'elle est mignonne la petite! Elle parle exactement comme une Française."*

"How about dessert? Shall we wait and see?"

The waiter disappeared. Honoria looked at her father expectantly.

"What are we going to do?"

"First, we're going to that toy store in the Rue Saint-Honoré and buy you anything you like. And then we're going to the vaudeville at the Empire."

She hesitated. "I like it about the vaudeville, but not the toy store."

"Why not?"

"Well, you brought me this doll." She had it with her. "And I've got lots of things. And we're not rich any more, are we?"

"We never were. But today you are to have anything you want."

"All right," she agreed resignedly.

When there had been her mother and a French nurse he had been inclined to be strict; now he extended himself, reached out for a new tolerance; he must be both parents to her and not shut any of her out of communication.

"I want to get to know you," he said gravely. "First let me introduce myself. My name is Charles J. Wales, of Prague."

"Oh, daddy!" her voice cracked with laughter.

"And who are you, please?" he persisted, and she accepted a rôle immediately: "Honoria Wales, Rue Palatine, Paris."

"Married or single?"

"No, not married. Single."

He indicated the doll. "But I see you have a child, madame."

Unwilling to disinherit it, she took it to her heart and thought quickly: "Yes, I've been married, but I'm not married now. My husband is dead."

He went on quickly, "And the child's name?"

"Simone. That's after my best friend at school."

"I'm very pleased that you're doing so well at school."

"I'm third this month," she boasted. "Elsie"—that was her cousin—"is only about eighteenth, and Richard is about at the bottom."

"You like Richard and Elsie, don't you?"

"Oh, yes. I like Richard quite well and I like her all right."

Cautiously and casually he asked: "And Aunt Marion and Uncle Lincoln—which do you like best?"

"Oh, Uncle Lincoln, I guess."

He was increasingly aware of her presence. As they came in, a murmur of ". . . adorable" followed them, and now the people at the next table bent all their silences upon her, staring as if she were something no more conscious than a flower.

"Why don't I live with you?" she asked suddenly. "Because mamma's dead?"

"You must stay here and learn more French. It would have been hard for daddy to take care of you so well."

"I don't really need much taking care of any more. I do everything for myself."

Going out of the restaurant, a man and a woman unexpectedly hailed him!

"Well, the old Wales!"

"Hello there, Lorraine. . . . Dunc."

Sudden ghosts out of the past: Duncan Schaeffer, a friend from college. Lorraine Quarrles, a lovely, pale blonde of thirty; one of a crowd who had helped them make months into days in the lavish times of three years ago.

"My husband couldn't come this year," she said, in answer to his question. "We're poor as hell. So he gave me two hundred a month and told me I could do my worst on that. . . . This your little girl?"

"What about coming back and sitting down?" Duncan asked.

"Can't do it." He was glad for an excuse. As always, he felt Lorraine's passionate, provocative attraction, but his own rhythm was different now.

"Well, how about dinner?" she asked.

"I'm not free. Give me your address and let me call you."

"Charlie, I believe you're sober," she said judicially. "I honestly believe he's sober, Dunc. Pinch him and see if he's sober."

Charlie indicated Honoria with his head. They both laughed.

"What's your address?" said Duncan skeptically.

He hesitated, unwilling to give the name of his hotel.

"I'm not settled yet. I'd better call you. We're going to see the vaudeville at the Empire."

"There! That's what I want to do," Lorraine said. "I want to see some clowns and acrobats and jugglers. That's just what we'll do, Dunc."

"We've got to do an errand first," said Charlie. "Perhaps we'll see you there."

"All right, you snob. . . . Good-by, beautiful little girl."

"Good-by."

Honoria bobbed politely.

Somehow, an unwelcome encounter. They liked him because he was functioning, because he was serious; they wanted to see him, because he was stronger than they were now, because they wanted to draw a certain sustenance from his strength.

At the Empire, Honoria proudly refused to sit upon her father's folded coat. She was already an individual with a code of her own, and Charlie was more and more absorbed by the desire of putting a little of himself into her before she crystallized utterly. It was hopeless to try to know her in so short a time.

Between the acts they came upon Duncan and Lorraine in the lobby where the band was playing.

"Have a drink?"

"All right, but not up at the bar. We'll take a table."

"The perfect father."

Listening abstractedly to Lorraine, Charlie watched Honoria's eyes leave their table, and he followed them wistfully about the room, wondering what they saw. He met her glance and she smiled.

"I liked that lemonade," she said.

What had she said? What had he expected? Going home in a taxi afterward, he pulled her over until her head rested against his chest.

"Darling, do you ever think about your mother?"

"Yes, sometimes," she answered vaguely.

"I don't want you to forget her. Have you got a picture of her?"

"Yes, I think so. Anyhow, Aunt Marion has. Why don't you want me to forget her?"

"She loved you very much."

"I loved her too."

They were silent for a moment.

"Daddy, I want to come and live with you," she said suddenly.

His heart leaped; he had wanted it to come like this.

"Aren't you perfectly happy?"

"Yes, but I love you better than anybody. And you love me better than anybody, don't you, now that mummy's dead?"

"Of course I do. But you won't always like me best, honey. You'll grow up and meet somebody your own age and go marry him and forget you ever had a daddy."

"Yes, that's true," she agreed tranquilly.

He didn't go in. He was coming back at nine o'clock and he wanted to keep himself fresh and new for the thing he must say then.

"When you're safe inside, just show yourself in that window."

"All right. Good-by, dads, dads, dads, dads."

He waited in the dark street until she appeared, all warm and glowing, in the window above and kissed her fingers out into the night.

III

THEY were waiting. Marion sat behind the coffee service in a dignified black dinner dress that just faintly suggested mourning. Lincoln was walking up and down with the animation of one who had already been talking. They were as anxious as he was to get into the question. He opened it almost immediately:

"I suppose you know what I want to see you about—why I really came to Paris."

Marion played with the black stars on her necklace and frowned.

"I'm awfully anxious to have a home," he continued. "And I'm awfully anxious to have Honoria in it. I appreciate your taking in Honoria for her mother's sake, but things have changed now"—he hesitated and then continued more forcibly—"changed radically with me, and I want to ask you to reconsider the matter. It would be silly for me to deny that about three years ago I was acting badly——"

Marion looked up at him with hard eyes.

"—but all that's over. As I told you, I haven't had more than a drink a day for over a year, and I take that drink deliberately, so that the idea of alcohol won't get too big in my imagination. You see the idea?"

"No," said Marion succinctly.

"It's a sort of stunt I set myself. It keeps the matter in proportion."

"I get you," said Lincoln. "You don't want to admit it's got any attraction for you."

"Something like that. Sometimes I forget and don't take it. But I try to take it. Anyhow, I couldn't afford to drink in my position. The people I represent are more than satisfied with what I've done, and I'm bringing my sister over from Burlington to keep house for me, and I want awfully to have Honoria too. You know that even when her mother and I weren't getting along well we never let anything that happened touch Honoria. I know she's fond of me and I know I'm able to take care of her and—well, there you are. How do you feel about it?"

He knew that now he would have to take a beating. It would last an hour or two hours, and it would be difficult, but if he modulated his inevitable resentment to the chastened attitude of the reformed sinner, he might win his point in the end.

Keep your temper, he told himself. You don't want to be justified. You want Honoria.

Lincoln spoke first: "We've been talking it over ever since we got your letter last month. We're happy to have Honoria here. She's a dear little thing, and we're glad to be able to help her, but of course that isn't the question——"

Marion interrupted suddenly. "How long are you going to stay sober, Charlie?" she asked.

"Permanently, I hope."

"How can anybody count on that?"

"You know I never did drink heavily until I gave up business and came over here with nothing to do. Then Helen and I began to run around with——"

"Please leave Helen out of it. I can't bear to hear you talk about her like that."

He stared at her grimly; he had never been certain how fond of each other the sisters were in life.

"My drinking only lasted about a year and a half—from the time we came over until I—collapsed."

"It was time enough."

"It was time enough," he agreed.

"My duty is entirely to Helen," she said. "I try to think what she would have wanted me to do. Frankly, from the night you did that terrible thing you haven't really existed for me. I can't help that. She was my sister."

"Yes."

"When she was dying she asked me to look out for

Honoria. If you hadn't been in a sanitorium then, it might have helped matters."

He had no answer.

"I'll never in my life be able to forget the morning when Helen knocked at my door, soaked to the skin and shivering, and said you'd locked her out."

Charlie gripped the sides of the chair. This was more difficult than he expected; he wanted to launch out into a long expostulation and explanation, but he only said: "The night I locked her out—" and she interrupted, "I don't feel up to going over that again."

After a moment's silence Lincoln said: "We're getting off the subject. You want Marion to set aside her legal guardianship and give you Honoria. I think the main point for her is whether she has confidence in you or not."

"I don't blame Marion," Charlie said slowly, "but I think she can have entire confidence in me. I had a good record up to three years ago. Of course, it's within human possibilities I might go wrong any time. But if we wait much longer I'll lose Honoria's childhood and my chance for a home." He shook his head, "I'll simply lose her, don't you see?"

"Yes, I see," said Lincoln.

"Why didn't you think of all this before?" Marion asked.

"I suppose I did, from time to time, but Helen and I were getting along badly. When I consented to the guardianship, I was flat on my back in a sanitorium and the market had cleaned me out. I knew I'd acted badly, and I thought if it would bring any peace to Helen, I'd agree to anything. But now it's different. I'm functioning, I'm behaving damn well, so far as——"

"Please don't swear at me," Marion said.

He looked at her, startled. With each remark the force of her dislike became more and more apparent. She had built up all her fear of life into one wall and faced it toward him. This trivial reproof was possibly the result of some trouble with the cook several hours before. Charlie became increasingly alarmed at leaving Honoria in this atmosphere of hostility against himself; sooner or later it would come out, in a word here, a shake of the head there, and some of that distrust would be irrevocably implanted in Honoria. But he pulled his temper down out of his face and shut it up inside him; he had won a point, for Lincoln realized the absurdity of Marion's remark and asked her lightly since when she had objected to the word "damn."

"Another thing," Charlie said: "I'm able to give her certain advantages now. I'm going to take a French governess to Prague with me. I've got a lease on a new apartment——"

He stopped, realizing that he was blundering. They couldn't be expected to accept with equanimity the fact that his income was again twice as large as their own.

"I suppose you can give her more luxuries than we can," said Marion. "When you were throwing away money we were living along watching every ten francs. . . . I suppose you'll start doing it again."

"Oh, no," he said. "I've learned. I worked hard for ten years, you know—until I got lucky in the market, like so many people. Terribly lucky. It didn't seem any use working any more, so I quit. It won't happen again."

There was a long silence. All of them felt their nerves straining, and for the first time in a year Charlie wanted a drink. He was sure now that Lincoln Peters wanted him to have his child.

Marion shuddered suddenly; part of her saw that Charlie's feet were planted on the earth now, and her own maternal feeling recognized the naturalness of his desire; but she had lived for a long time with a prejudice—a prejudice founded on a curious disbelief in her sister's happiness, and which, in the shock of one terrible night, had turned to hatred for him. It had all happened at a point in her life where the discouragement of ill health and adverse circumstances made it necessary for her to believe in tangible villainy and a tangible villain.

"I can't help what I think!" she cried out suddenly. "How much you were responsible for Helen's death, I don't know. It's something you'll have to square with your own conscience."

An electric current of agony surged through him; for a moment he was almost on his feet, an unuttered sound echoing in his throat. He hung on to himself for a moment, another moment.

"Hold on there," said Lincoln uncomfortably. "I never thought you were responsible for that."

"Helen died of heart trouble," Charlie said dully.

"Yes, heart trouble." Marion spoke as if the phrase had another meaning for her.

Then, in the flatness that followed her outburst, she saw him plainly and she knew he had somehow arrived at control over the situation. Glancing at her husband, she found no help from him, and as abruptly as if it were a matter of no importance, she threw up the sponge.

"Do what you like!" she cried, springing up from her chair. "She's your child. I'm not the person to stand in your way. I think if it were my child I'd rather see her—" She managed to check herself. "You two decide it. I can't stand this. I'm sick. I'm going to bed."

She hurried from the room; after a moment Lincoln said:

"This has been a hard day for her. You know how strongly she feels—" His voice was almost apologetic: "When a woman gets an idea in her head."

"Of course."

"It's going to be all right. I think she sees now that you—can provide for the child, and so we can't very well stand in your way or Honoria's way."

"Thank you, Lincoln."

"I'd better go along and see how she is."

"I'm going."

He was still trembling when he reached the street, but a walk down the Rue Bonaparte to the *quais* set him up, and as he crossed the Seine, fresh and new by the *quai* lamps, he felt exultant. But back in his room he couldn't sleep. The image of Helen haunted him. Helen whom he had loved so until they had senselessly begun to abuse each other's love, tear it into shreds. On that terrible February night that Marion remembered so vividly, a slow quarrel had gone on for hours. There was a scene at the Florida, and then he attempted to take her home, and then she kissed young Webb at a table; after that there was what she had hysterically said. When he arrived home alone he turned the key in the lock in wild anger. How could he know she would arrive an hour later alone, that there would be a snowstorm in which she wandered about in slippers, too confused to find a taxi? Then the aftermath, her escaping pneumonia by a miracle, and all the attendant horror. They were "reconciled," but that was the beginning of the end, and Marion, who had seen with her own eyes and who imagined it to be one of many scenes from her sister's martyrdom, never forgot.

Going over it again brought Helen nearer, and in the

white, soft light that steals upon half sleep near morning he found himself talking to her again. She said that he was perfectly right about Honoria and that she wanted Honoria to be with him. She said she was glad he was being good and doing better. She said a lot of other things—very friendly things—but she was in a swing in a white dress, and swinging faster and faster all the time, so that at the end he could not hear clearly all that she said.

IV

HE WOKE up feeling happy. The door of the world was open again. He made plans, vistas, futures for Honoria and himself, but suddenly he grew sad, remembering all the plans he and Helen had made. She had not planned to die. The present was the thing —work to do and someone to love. But not to love too much, for he knew the injury that a father can do to a daughter or a mother to a son by attaching them too closely: afterward, out in the world, the child would seek in the marriage partner the same blind tenderness and, failing probably to find it, turn against love and life.

It was another bright, crisp day. He called Lincoln Peters at the bank where he worked and asked if he could count on taking Honoria when he left for Prague. Lincoln agreed that there was no reason for delay. One thing—the legal guardianship. Marion wanted to retain that a while longer. She was upset by the whole matter, and it would oil things if she felt that the situation was still in her control for another year. Charlie agreed, wanting only the tangible, visible child.

Then the question of a governess. Charlie sat in a gloomy agency and talked to a cross Béarnaise and to a buxom Breton peasant, neither of whom he could have endured. There were others whom he would see tomorrow.

He lunched with Lincoln Peters at Griffons, trying to keep down his exultation.

"There's nothing quite like your own child," Lincoln said. "But you understand how Marion feels too."

"She's forgotten how hard I worked for seven years there," Charlie said. "She just remembers one night."

"There's another thing." Lincoln hesitated. "While you and Helen were tearing around Europe throwing money away, we were just getting along. I didn't touch any of the prosperity because I never got ahead enough to carry anything but my insurance. I think Marion felt there was some kind of injustice in it—you not even working toward the end, and getting richer and richer."

"It went just as quick as it came," said Charlie.

"Yes, a lot of it stayed in the hands of *chasseurs* and saxophone players and maîtres d'hôtel—well, the big party's over now. I just said that to explain Marion's feeling about those crazy years. If you drop in about six o'clock tonight before Marion's too tired, we'll settle the details on the spot."

Back at his hotel, Charlie found a *pneumatique* that had been redirected from the Ritz bar where Charlie had left his address for the purpose of finding a certain man.

"DEAR CHARLIE: You were so strange when we saw you the other day that I wondered if I did something to offend you. If so, I'm not conscious of it. In fact, I have thought about you too much for the last year, and it's always been in the back of my mind that I might see you if I came over here. We *did* have such good times that crazy spring, like the night you and I stole the butcher's tricycle, and the time we tried to call on the president and you had the old derby rim and the wire cane. Everybody seems so old lately, but I don't feel old a bit. Couldn't we get together some time today for old time's sake? I've got a vile hang-over for the moment, but will be feeling better this afternoon and will look for you about five in the sweat-shop at the Ritz.

"Always devotedly,

"LORRAINE."

His first feeling was one of awe that he had actually, in his mature years, stolen a tricycle and pedaled Lorraine all over the Étoile between the small hours and dawn. In retrospect it was a nightmare. Locking out Helen didn't fit in with any other act of his life, but the tricycle incident did—it was one of many. How many weeks or months of dissipation to arrive at that condition of utter irresponsibility?

He tried to picture how Lorraine had appeared to him then—very attractive; Helen was unhappy about it, though she said nothing. Yesterday, in the restaurant, Lorraine had seemed trite, blurred, worn away. He emphatically did not want to see her, and he was glad Alix had not given away his hotel address. It was a relief to think, instead, of Honoria, to think of Sundays spent with her and of saying good morning to her and of knowing she was there in his house at night, drawing her breath in the darkness.

At five he took a taxi and bought presents for all the Peters—a piquant cloth doll, a box of Roman soldiers, flowers for Marion, big linen handkerchiefs for Lincoln.

He saw, when he arrived in the apartment, that Marion had accepted the inevitable. She greeted him now as though he were a recalcitrant member of the family, rather than a menacing outsider. Honoria had been told she was going; Charlie was glad to see that her tact made her conceal her excessive happiness. Only on his lap did she whisper her delight and the question "When?" before she slipped away with the other children.

He and Marion were alone for a minute in the room, and on an impulse he spoke out boldly:

"Family quarrels are bitter things. They don't go according to any rules. They're not like aches or wounds; they're more like splits in the skin that won't heal because there's not enough material. I wish you and I could be on better terms."

"Some things are hard to forget," she answered. "It's a question of confidence." There was no answer to this and presently she asked, "When do you propose to take her?"

"As soon as I can get a governess. I hoped the day after tomorrow."

"That's impossible. I've got to get her things in shape. Not before Saturday."

He yielded. Coming back into the room, Lincoln offered him a drink.

"I'll take my daily whisky," he said.

It was warm here, it was a home, people together by a fire. The children felt very safe and important; the mother and father were serious, watchful. They had things to do for the children more important than his visit here. A spoonful of medicine was, after all, more important than the strained relations between Marion and himself. They were not dull people, but they were very much in the grip of life and circumstances. He wondered if he couldn't do something to get Lincoln out of his rut at the bank.

A long peal at the door-bell; the *bonne à toute faire* passed through and went down the corridor. The door opened upon another long ring, and then voices, and the three in the salon looked up expectantly; Richard moved to bring the corridor within his range of vision, and Marion rose. Then the maid came back along the corridor, closely followed by the voices, which developed under the light into Duncan Schaeffer and Lorraine Quarrles.

They were gay, they were hilarious, they were roaring with laughter. For a moment Charlie was astounded; unable to understand how they ferreted out the Peters' address.

"Ah-h-h!" Duncan wagged his finger roguishly at Charlie. "Ah-h-h!"

They both slid down another cascade of laughter. Anxious and at a loss, Charlie shook hands with them quickly and presented them to Lincoln and Marion. Marion nodded, scarcely speaking. She had drawn back a step toward the fire; her little girl stood beside her, and Marion put an arm about her shoulder.

With growing annoyance at the intrusion, Charlie waited for them to explain themselves. After some concentration Duncan said:

"We came to invite you out to dinner. Lorraine and I insist that all this shishi, cagy business 'bout your address got to stop."

Charlie came closer to them, as if to force them backward down the corridor.

"Sorry, but I can't. Tell me where you'll be and I'll phone you in half an hour."

This made no impression. Lorraine sat down suddenly on the side of a chair, and focusing her eyes on Richard, cried, "Oh, what a nice little boy! Come here, little boy." Richard glanced at his mother, but did not move. With a perceptible shrug of her shoulders, Lorraine turned back to Charlie:

"Come and dine. Sure your cousins won' mine. See you so sel'om. Or solemn."

"I can't," said Charlie sharply. "You two have dinner and I'll phone you."

Her voice became suddenly unpleasant. "All right,

we'll go. But I remember once when you hammered on my door at four A.M. I was enough of a good sport to give you a drink. Come on, Dunc."

Still in slow motion, with blurred, angry faces, with uncertain feet, they retired along the corridor.

"Good night," Charlie said.

"Good night!" responded Lorraine emphatically.

When he went back into the salon Marion had not moved, only now her son was standing in the circle of her other arm. Lincoln was still swinging Honoria back and forth like a pendulum from side to side.

"What an outrage!" Charlie broke out. "What an absolute outrage!"

Neither of them answered. Charlie dropped into an armchair, picked up his drink, set it down again and said:

"People I haven't seen for two years having the colossal nerve——"

He broke off. Marion had made the sound "Oh!" in one swift, furious breath, turned her body from him with a jerk and left the room.

Lincoln set down Honoria carefully.

"You children go in and start your soup," he said, and when they obeyed, he said to Charlie:

"Marion's not well and she can't stand shocks. That kind of people make her really physically sick."

"I didn't tell them to come here. They wormed your name out of somebody. They deliberately——"

"Well, it's too bad. It doesn't help matters. Excuse me a minute."

Left alone, Charlie sat tense in his chair. In the next room he could hear the children eating, talking in monosyllables, already oblivious to the scene between their elders. He heard a murmur of conversation from a farther room and then the ticking bell of a telephone receiver picked up, and in a panic he moved to the other side of the room and out of earshot.

In a minute Lincoln came back. "Look here, Charlie. I think we'd better call off dinner for tonight. Marion's in bad shape."

"Is she angry with me?"

"Sort of," he said, almost roughly. "She's not strong and——"

"You mean she's changed her mind about Honoria?"

"She's pretty bitter right now. I don't know. You phone me at the bank tomorrow."

"I wish you'd explain to her I never dreamed these people would come here. I'm just as sore as you are."

"I couldn't explain anything to her now."

Charlie got up. He took his coat and hat and started down the corridor. Then he opened the door of the dining room and said in a strange voice, "Good night, children."

Honoria rose and ran around the table to hug him.

"Good night, sweetheart," he said vaguely, and then trying to make his voice more tender, trying to conciliate something, "Good night, dear children."

V

CHARLIE went directly to the Ritz bar with the furious idea of finding Lorraine and Duncan, but they were not there, and he realized that in any case there was nothing he could do. He had not touched his drink at the Peters', and now he ordered a whisky-and-soda. Paul came over to say hello.

"It's a great change," he said sadly. "We do about half the business we did. So many fellows I hear about back in the States lost everything, maybe not in the first crash, but then in the second. Your friend George Hardt lost every cent, I hear. Are you back in the States?"

"No, I'm in business in Prague."

"I heard that you lost a lot in the crash."

"I did," and he added grimly, "but I lost everything I wanted in the boom."

"Selling short."

"Something like that."

Again the memory of those days swept over him like a nightmare—the people they had met traveling; then people who couldn't add a row of figures or speak a coherent sentence. The little man Helen had consented to dance with at the ship's party, who had insulted her ten feet from the table; the women and girls carried screaming with drink or drugs out of public places——

—The men who locked their wives out in the snow, because the snow of twenty-nine wasn't real snow. If you didn't want it to be snow, you just paid some money.

He went to the phone and called the Peters' apartment; Lincoln answered.

"I called up because this thing is on my mind. Has Marion said anything definite?"

"Marion's sick," Lincoln answered shortly. "I know this thing isn't altogether your fault, but I can't have her go to pieces about it. I'm afraid we'll have to let it slide for six months; I can't take the chance of working her up to this state again."

"I see."

"I'm sorry, Charlie."

He went back to his table. His whisky glass was empty, but he shook his head when Alix looked at it questioningly. There wasn't much he could do now except send Honoria some things; he would send her a lot of things tomorrow. He thought rather angrily that this was just money—he had given so many people money. . . .

"No, no more," he said to another waiter. "What do I owe you?"

He would come back some day; they couldn't make him pay forever. But he wanted his child, and nothing was much good now, beside that fact. He wasn't young any more, with a lot of nice thoughts and dreams to have by himself. He was absolutely sure Helen wouldn't have wanted him to be so alone.

TITLES AND EDITORS OF
THE VIKING PORTABLE LIBRARY

(*As of Spring, 1949*)

1. AS YOU WERE: AN AMERICAN READER. *Alexander Woollcott*
2. STEINBECK. *Selected by Pascal Covici. Introduction by Lewis Gannett*
3. THE TRIUMPH OF LIFE: POEMS OF THE SPIRIT. *Horace Gregory*
4. DOROTHY PARKER. *Introduction by W. Somerset Maugham*
5. WORLD BIBLE. *Robert O. Ballou*
6. HEMINGWAY. *Malcolm Cowley*
7. SIX NOVELS OF THE SUPERNATURAL *Edward Wagenknecht*
8. SHAKESPEARE
9. READER'S COMPANION. *Louis Kronenberger*
10. CARL VAN DOREN
11. WALT WHITMAN. *Mark Van Doren*
12. POE. *Philip Van Doren Stern*
13. MURDER BOOK. *Joseph Henry Jackson*
14. F. SCOTT FITZGERALD *Chosen by Dorothy Parker. Introduction by John O'Hara*
15. NOVELS OF SCIENCE. *Donald A. Wollheim*
16. OSCAR WILDE. *Richard Aldington*
17. WOOLLCOTT. *Selected by Joseph Hennessey. Introduction by John Mason Brown*
18. FAULKNER. *Malcolm Cowley*
19. IRISH READER. *Diarmuid Russell*
20. MARK TWAIN. *Bernard DeVoto*
21. RABELAIS. *Selected, translated, and edited by Samuel Putnam*
22. THOMAS WOLFE. *Maxwell Geismar*

TITLES AND EDITORS OF THE VIKING PORTABLE LIBRARY

[illegible] OF

[illegible]

26. BLAKE. [illegible]

[illegible]

[illegible]

[illegible]

[illegible]

[illegible]

[illegible]

[illegible]

[illegible]

[illegible]

[illegible]

[illegible]

[illegible]

[illegible]

[illegible]

[illegible]

CHARLES LAMB. [illegible]

[illegible]

MATTHEW [illegible]

[illegible]

[illegible]